To Amy

Best wishe

to a former p

Wil Hulbert

the MURDER OF CROWS

William Hulbert

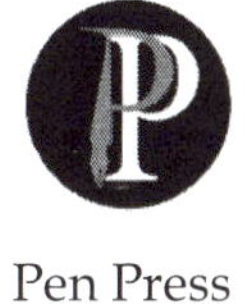

Pen Press

First published in Great Britain by Pen Press

All paper used in the printing of this book has been made from wood grown in managed, sustainable forests.

ISBN13: 978-1-78003-755-4

Printed and bound in the UK
Pen Press is an imprint of
Indepenpress Publishing Limited
25 Eastern Place
Brighton
BN2 1GJ

A catalogue record of this book is available from the British Library

Cover design by Jacqueline Abromeit

To Lin, Lee and Mark

I wish to acknowledge the assistance of the following:

Chippenham Civic Society
Chippenham Museum and Heritage Centre
Wiltshire and Swindon History Centre
Salisbury and South Wiltshire Museum
British Museum
Museum of London
Victoria and Albert Museum
The Weald and Downland Open Air Museum
The London Pageant
Stephen Hulbert

PREFACE

In the late 1960s I recall visiting the Yelde Hall, the local museum in my home town of Chippenham, Wiltshire.

An exhibition in an old-style photographic booth suggested that the Great Fire of London in 1666 had been deliberately started, and the plot was hatched in a building in Chippenham – the Lyon Inn.

John Woodman is recorded as uttering he was going to London to "light enough bonfires to make London as sad a London as ever it was since the world began."

I remember wondering how such inspiration could be the brain child of simple seventeenth-century country folk, living in a small market town a hundred miles away, and what motive their plot could have…

Today, the Lyon Inn has been replaced by a shop, although the present building complex is intriguingly called "London Buildings". Chippenham Civic Society has also erected a plaque acknowledging the episode.

In early 1666 the authorities did discover a plot by dissatisfied ex-parliamentarian soldiers to set fire to London. The plotters were executed in the spring of 1666 – yet the date they had set for their fire was only 12 hours different to the start of the actual fire in September 1666, less than six months later.

After the Fire of London a warrant was issued for the arrest of one John Woodman; he was never seen or heard of again.

The following is a blend of fact and fiction. I leave it to the reader to decide which is which.

A bouquet of pheasants…
A passel of pigeons…
A merl of blackbirds…
A wake of buzzards…
A confusion of willow warblers…
A volery of long-tailed tits…
A chattering of magpies…
A menorah of yellowhammers…
A stare of owls…
An exultation of skylarks…
A soar of kestrels…
A paddling of ducks…
A dule of doves…
A parliament of rooks…
A conspiracy of ravens…
A covey of partridges…
A plump of moorhens…
A parliament of owls…
A charm of goldfinches…
An asylum of cuckoos…
A MURDER OF CROWS.

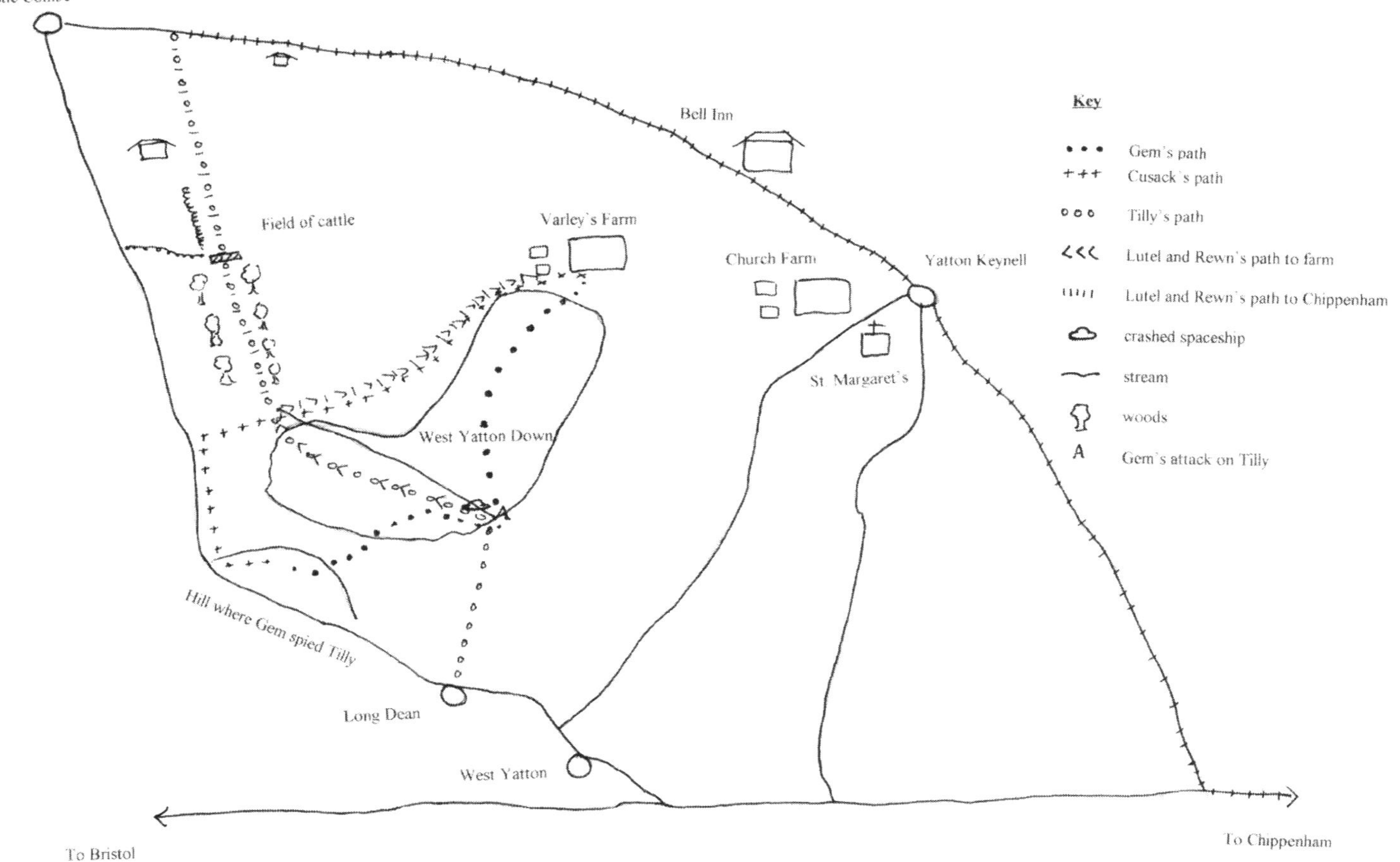

Map of West Country landing site

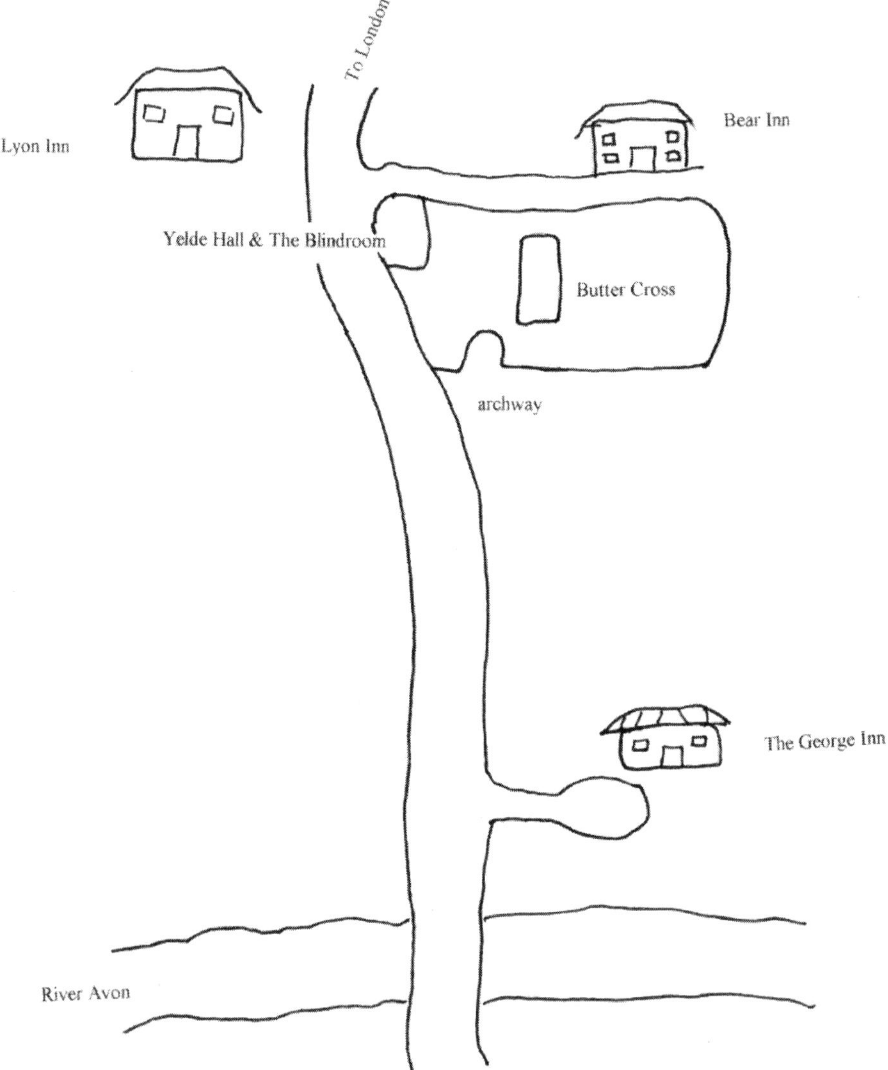

Map of Chippenham

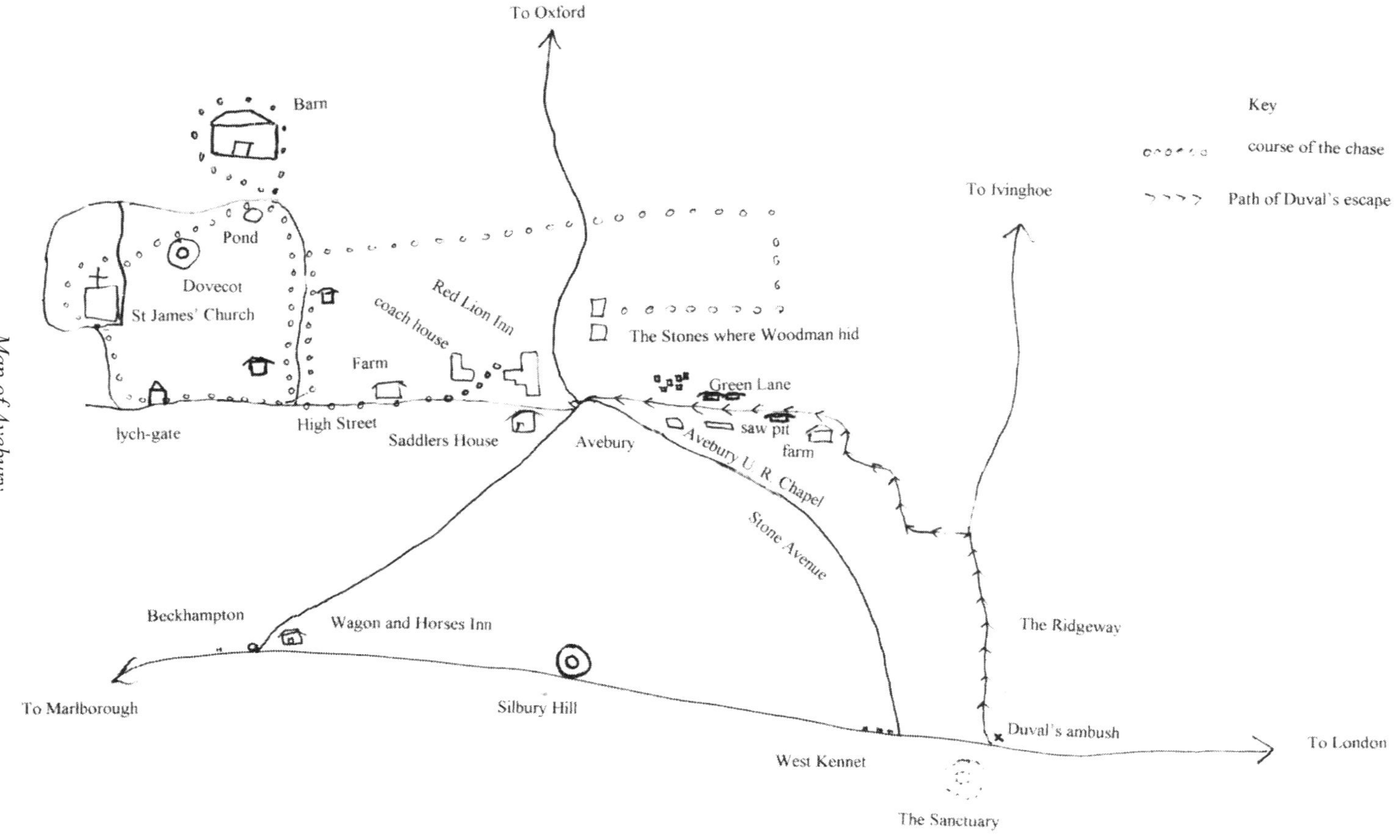

Map of Avebury

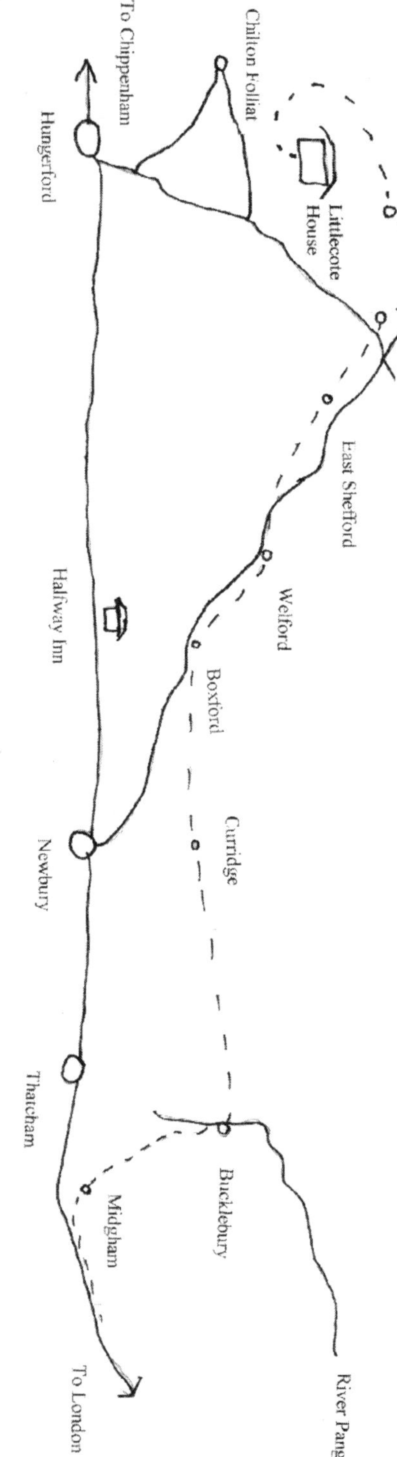

Map of Berkshire

Map of London

All maps hand drawn by the author based on a range of contemporary sources.

Part One

Visitors

CHAPTER ONE

Two Close Encounters

Summer was gently ambling towards autumn. The blazing sun had shone continually on the hills and woodland that combined to give West Yatton Down its remoteness. On the steep chalk slopes, painted ladies danced amongst the thistles, desperately seeking out the remnants of the season's nectar. The woods that bordered the down were densely populated with elm, alder and hazel. Where the two differing habitats met, speckled woods fluttered restlessly in flight, patrolling the shady outskirts of the woodland.

On a summit overlooking the down, Gem Varley took a break from harvesting. He looked over his shoulder at his day's labours. Golden stooks stood in the field, where earlier the harvesters – men, women and children from the surrounding hamlets and villages – had worked under the burning sun, until departing as evening approached to their various cottages and hovels. Most had trodden the winding track to the village of Castle Combe, which lay hidden in the wooded valley on the further edge of the field. Gem wiped the sweat from his brow and draped the yellowing neckerchief around his bronzed neck.

He had worked in these fields, on the family farm, for nearly forty harvests, starting as a young boy toiling away as a gleaner. Gem gazed around at the landscape that lay before him; away to his right the deciduous wood continued for as far as his eyes could see, stretching like a wooden frame on a painting holding the countryside in place. Far below him, in the hamlet of Long Dean, the occasional cottage roof poked through the trees. Gem's thin, sandy hair blew in the breeze. He lifted his head in order to face the wind and absorb its cool air on his burnt cheeks. Crows circled below him, cawing loudly to each other as they flew past. Before him the hill sloped sharply away over a series of ridges and came to rest on a flat plain, until it rose steeply again on the far side of the lowland.

Through the centre of this secluded valley ran a small stream, bordered on both sides by a narrow band of trees and bushes. The trees were dense enough to hide the stream from Gem's view but he smiled as his memory pierced the wooden barricade, remembering the many times he had played there as a boy, splashing bare-footed through its cool sparkling water, chasing after Cusack.

Less than twenty feet away to Gem's left stood his brother. Cusack was cleaning his sickle, wiping its curved blade with a rag. He paid little heed to the other man. The brothers scarcely spoke. The silence was only disturbed by a wood pigeon repeating its plea from its roost in the valley below.

Both men were clothed in the drab brown garb of the tillerman. Coarse, brown sack-like material clung to their bodies, glued by the sweat of the day's endeavours. The two farmers were very similar in features; each owned the strong physique of the rustic labourer. Their arms rippled with muscles hardened and honed by the vigorous effort that their employment demanded. Gem was the taller by a few inches, although he just failed to measure six feet. Their identical bronze features – dark brown eyes, long straight noses and strong mouths – often fooled strangers into thinking they were twins. Twenty years ago that had been a great source of amusement and a bonding tie between the brothers, but any filial warmth had long evaporated. They now rarely conversed, speaking only out of necessity.

The taciturn atmosphere between the brothers was not born out of any family jealousy or clash of personalities. Its origins were to be found in a long-standing difference of political viewpoint, ranging back over twenty years to the time of the Great War that tore England apart during the reign of King Charles the First. Gem had fought with the Parliamentarians, in so doing isolating himself from the rest of his family, who sided with the King and the Royalists. Neither his father Isaiah nor Cusack had actually taken up arms against Cromwell's New Model Army, but they let it be known that they strongly disapproved of the elder son's actions.

At the cessation of the Civil War Gem returned to the family farm. He had sustained an injury to the head at the battle of Lansdown and although the wound had healed over, a long scar was still visible under his hairline. The physical scar did not trouble Gem, but the blow from a pikeman had left him with mental scars so deep that even now in 1665 he was still haunted by nightmares. The injury had resulted in an easing of tension between Gem and Isaiah. There was no victory gloat on the part of the son, nor were there any recriminations on the side of the father.

Cusack had opposed his brother's return to the farm, but he was unwilling to upset his father and did not raise his voice in protest. His actions were ones of tolerance rather than acceptance; never again was there to be the same intimacy and brotherly friendship. During the war years Isaiah had grown old and weak and Gem's return was timely, as the extra pair of hands was sorely needed on the farm to support his ageing parents and two young sisters, so there was never any question of his being turned away from his birthplace.

For the past twenty years the brothers had worked for the common good of the family. It was a large farm to manage; the chalky soil of the Wiltshire countryside was rich and fertile and provided a comfortable existence for the four adults and three children who resided there. Isaiah had lived long enough to hear of the crowning of the second King Charles, whilst Cusack had married Molly Watt, a local farm girl from nearby Yatton Keynell. Molly had given him five daughters, of whom three still survived.

A startled pheasant broke cover from the woodland way over to the left; its call attracted Gem's attention. The cause of the bird's disturbance could be seen approaching along the narrow pathway that ran alongside the trees that bordered the stream.

"I'm goin' to 'ave 'er," Gem drawled in his burred Wiltshire accent. His words had broken the silence like the report of his old roundhead musket shot. Cusack looked up from his cleaning and followed his brother's gaze. He had heard these words uttered throughout the summer, and as every previous pronouncement had proved a hollow boast, he expected little difference now. Tilly Sharpe was a voluptuous and attractive farm girl. Since her fourteenth birthday at the beginning of June she had travelled daily from her home in the tiny hamlet of Little Dean to the local manor in Yatton Keynell. Her work did not require her to take up permanent residence, so at dusk each day she could be seen skipping with the exuberance of youth along the two miles to her family home.

Marriage had passed Gem by. He had endured the strict celibacy required of him in Cromwell's Model Army, and on his return home he had busied himself in the workings of the farm. After the murmurings and rumblings that had met his decision to fight for the Roundheads, he had laboured long and hard as though in compensation for his lost years away.

"I'm goin' to 'ave 'er," Gem repeated, only this time slightly louder in response to his brother's silence. The daily promise had virtually been the only source of conversation between the brothers for the preceding three months. Cusack had played his part in this daily ritual by saying nothing, only acknowledging his brother's utterances by raising his eyes towards the blonde maiden on her lonely sojourns. This evening, though, was different, perhaps through reasons of tedium or even shades of mischief-making;

Cusack broke his silence.

"You'm said that every day; you're all talk, Gem," and picking up his bundle of tools he walked away, adding to his pronouncement a dismissive, "I'm orf 'ome, supper'll be ready."

Gem stood rooted to the spot, staring at the solitary figure of Tilly. As he looked down on the maiden below, something inside him stirred. Cusack's words had unlocked twenty years of pent-up feelings. The fragile atmosphere at home, the war, Cusack's jibing, all seemed to cloud over in front of his eyes. Gem threw down his neckerchief and raced off down the steep hillside. His lumbering boots crushed the dainty flowers beneath his feet; frightened rabbits scurried away to their bolt holes in the side of the hill.

Long grasses threw out their seeds to float in the air like miniature clouds as his legs ploughed through them. Ridges gave the hillside an undulating terrain, so as Gem approached the first one Tilly disappeared from his view. Feeling cheated he bounded over the cusp of the ridge. He grinned as Tilly appeared below him, although she was still a fair distance away to his left. His heart was beating fast as he galloped down the hill. Chirruping crickets scattered in his wake but their protests fell on deaf ears as his mind was fixed solely on his prey, heedless to all around him.

Totally oblivious to his brother's intentions, Cusack was now nearing the woods where Tilly had disturbed the pheasant. He glanced down and waved to the diminutive figure that pranced along the track two hundred feet below. She returned the gesture and both continued their separate journeys.

The hillside had become steeper and Gem ran sideways to maintain his balance, oblivious to the clover and rabbit droppings crushed beneath him. Tilly had disappeared again behind a row of trees that stood between the path and Gem.

She re-emerged directly below him, still fifty yards from his clutches. Unaware of her rampant admirer she followed the path beside the stream as it curved away from Gem and headed towards Long Dean. The young girl bounded innocently along the shaded track, her back now turned towards Gem. As his quarry glided away from him Gem redoubled his efforts; thistle seeds burst high into the air around him and he spat out an offending white spore that landed in his open mouth.

In the forest the pigeons stopped calling as though in deference to some major unfolding event. Gem hugged the trees and followed the footpath made rugged by rabbit scrapings and the hoof prints left by cattle visiting the stream.

He stopped at a gap in the hedgerow. It was densely populated by mouldering brown cow parsley. Tilly was less than ten yards ahead as he put his hands on his knees and bent over panting for breath. For some unknown reason, whether from a sense of fair play or an attempt to bring himself to his senses, Gem shouted out the girl's name.

"Tilly... Tilly Sharpe."

Blissfully unaware of Gem's intentions, Tilly turned to face the voice from behind. She stared at the ruffled figure. Her first thought was that Gem had run from the manor with a summons for her to return. Tilly stood her ground, the warm breeze flicking golden locks around her face, deep blue eyes peering out from behind the strands of wispy hair. The warm weather had caused her to dress scantily, exacerbating Gem's lust. Her lightweight dress reached her ankles, but a cream blouse hung loosely around her, open at the neck, revealing a formidable cleavage that belied her youth.

Gem remained with his hands on his knees, gaping at Tilly, his head pounding from excitement and the careering run that had brought him down the hillside. Now that he had reached his prey he couldn't make the kill. The thrill had evaporated now that the girl stood there facing him.

"Wot do you want?" queried Tilly, irritated by Gem's gawking stance and continued silence. She was keen to be on her way home where she knew her mother would have prepared dinner. Three younger sisters would be excitedly peering from behind a window, vying with one another to be the first to spot her appearance along the lane. Tilly could envisage them shouting to their mother that the evening meal could now be served. The delay of reaching this welcoming scene, due to this uncouth middle-aged man who appeared dumbfounded before her, was annoying Tilly.

"Wot is it? Be it the manor? Do 'em want me back?" she demanded.

The young girl began to feel a little uncomfortable at Gem's prolonged silence. He straightened and faced her. Tilly grew uneasy as she stared into his eyes. The basket that she was carrying fell from her grasp.

An assortment of food – apples, plums and carrots, gifts from the manor to Tilly's parents – fell from the basket and rolled along the ground. As the contents spilled, a white linen cloth that had covered the fruit and vegetables floated to the ground. Gem watched the fluttering material, and as he did so something inside him stirred. The linen seemed to signal some deep primeval urge. He strode wilfully towards Tilly, with long, pronounced strides.

Although she didn't fully comprehend them Tilly read Gem's intentions and realised they purported danger. She turned and ran. Now that his quarry was moving Gem found it easy to break into a run and he raced after her, crashing through low branches and weaving his way through tussocks of grass.

Ahead of him the tantalising figure dived through a gap in the trees and into the sun-dried bed of the stream. Black-headed plantain and large green dock leaves were trampled beneath her feet.

Tilly could hear Gem thundering noisily behind, his pounding boots snapping fallen twigs. She looked over her shoulder and momentarily took her eyes from her intended pathway, and her dress became entangled in a blackberry bush. Her hands reached down in an effort to tear herself free from its detaining thorns. Blood trickled from scratches to her arms in her frantic scrabble to continue her flight.

As she reached the far side of the stream the land rose sharply up a steep incline. Tilly followed a pathway eroded by the incessant running of the rabbits from the nearby warren; behind her she could hear heavy rhythmic breathing. She scrabbled harder up the bank in response to the inevitable fate that otherwise awaited her. It proved her undoing as she caught a foot in a divot and stumbled to the ground. Gem was upon her in a flash and flipped her over on to her back. Tilly lay rigid on the hillside, her large blue eyes staring up appealingly at Gem as he straddled her. Gnarled hands tore at the flimsy blouse, revealing her plump naked breasts. Gem bent low and began to kiss them.

Tilly at last snapped out of her daze. "No, no, get orf me," she screamed. Gem's response was to fumble at her thin dress. He pushed his left hand against her shoulder whilst shoving his right hand between her legs. Tilly writhed and begged for him to stop in a desperate effort to maintain her maidenhood. But rather than dissuade Gem it further incensed his passion and he wedged a knee between her legs and ripped away mercilessly at her undergarments. Tilly's pleas turned to sobs, large tears soaked her soft cheeks as her clothes were torn away from under her. Gem towered above her, his eyes trance-like, unmindful to all around him. Beads of sweat covered his forehead and ran into his eyes but his hands were preoccupied and unable to wipe them away.

He pinned Tilly to the ground by placing one hand on her chest; with the other he fought to loosen his leather belt, attacking it angrily as though he were wrestling a snake in the grass. He whipped it free and flung it aimlessly away into the bushes and turned his attention to his breeches. Physically and emotionally his whole body was aroused and it strained in eager anticipation.

Tilly's hair was covered in dust and small plant particles as she rocked her head from side to side in disbelieving anguish. Gem's rough hand squeezed her vaginal hair as he parted her legs. Tilly could feel the full extent of Gem's arousal brushing against her thighs. As he prepared to enter her she let out a long piercing agonising scream. Her eyes opened wider and wider and her screaming became uncontrolled and frantic.

Her actions though were not solely directed at Gem's carnal attentions; her gaze shot past his left shoulder and into the evening sky at the blazing light that was descending towards them. Gem paused momentarily, disturbed by Tilly's behaviour. She stopped screaming. "The sun's falling," she cried.

"The sun's falling out of the sky!"

Gem dismissed the plaintive cry as the last-gasp efforts of a desperate young girl. He was annoyed at the puerile effort and the interruption it had caused. He turned his attention back to Tilly, who had closed her eyes. Gem took it as an act of submission, as a blazing light burst around them.

The earth moved for both of them, but not in the way Gem had intended. They were engulfed in a bright orange glow, followed by a loud crashing and splintering of trees. The two villagers were thrown apart and they tumbled and rolled to the bottom of the hill. Leaves and small twigs swirled around them and particles of dust swept into their eyes. Tilly was the first to react as she pulled herself up from among the debris of leaves and branches, and scrambled around on her hands and knees.

A short distance away from her lay a strange white object; its bright lights that had both startled and saved Tilly were now extinguished. The dust cloud that surrounded the object made a clear view impossible. Not waiting for a closer inspection and recognising but unable to comprehend her narrow escape, Tilly gathered her torn clothes around her body and scuttled away, sobbing as she crossed the stream bed. She rejoined the narrow path and, without once glancing back, ran for the safety of the family cottage.

Groggily rising to his feet, Gem put a finger in his ear and poked it, trying to stop its ringing. He looked at the figure of Tilly vanishing through the trees but showed no inclination to pursue her for a second time. Slowly he clambered up the bank and stared down at the scene below. The dust was beginning to settle and the area was now calmer, apart from the cawing of an agitated pair of crows, who protested at the disturbance of their evening roost.

Gem could now make out the white object that had been the cause of his disappointment. It was large and spherical, unlike anything he had ever seen, and encircled by flattened trees. Gem stared at the sky and back down at the object. The incident was beyond his comprehension. He turned and raced up the hillside, only pausing to look back when he reached the hedge-ringed field on the plateau of the hills. He climbed over a wooden gate and ran across two meadows towards his red-roofed farmhouse.

CHAPTER TWO

Two Strangers

As Gem disappeared up the hillside, a figure emerged on the other side of the stream, close by to where Tilly had first become aware of Gem's presence. It was dressed from head to toe in a white shiny material, culminating in a white cylindrical headpiece with a transparent violet visor. The setting sun provided a beautiful red back-cloth to the pale image.

The figure carefully reached up and released a clip on the helmet at the base of the chin. Cautiously the headpiece was removed, revealing a face that could easily belong to the English countryside of the seventeenth century, as opposed to that of a distant galaxy. The woman shook her head and chestnut tresses brushed against her shoulders. Two crystal green eyes sparkled as they looked around the countryside, narrowing as they fixed on the debris of the spacecraft. A petite nose, set above a friendly mouth, twitched as it scented the warm air. She took a deep breath and air from the alien planet filled her lungs.

She closed her eyes as she tasted the scents of the surrounding flowers. Her mind instantly flew back to Mykas. How often had she walked the purple mountains of her home planet, pausing frequently to breathe in the fragrances of the heather? The two suns on Mykas were of an even deeper red than the sun that was now falling below the horizon. The scenery in front of her could have been that of her own planet, but everything here was greener, a little fresher in appearance. Her planet was tinged with more reds, greys, blacks and purples; here the dominating colours were green, blue and yellow. From what she could tell the bird and animal life was different on this planet. The sizes seemed to be similar but the species were not familiar to her. As she looked around at the surrounding landscape she remembered one other difference that she would find.

They had warned her back on Mykas that the two planets were worlds apart in technology; just how far behind this planet was she could not yet ascertain, but there was a distinct lack of evidence in the view before her. Multitudes of thoughts criss-crossed her mind as she began to acclimatise to her new surroundings. Two insisted on pushing their way foremost: where exactly had they landed on this planet, and how far were they from the city called London?

They! She remembered that she was not alone. In the euphoria of surviving the landing she had forgotten about Rewn. She looked at the crashed spaceship. Rewn, where was Rewn? Had he survived the crash? She swiftly dived into the wreckage that lay strewn about her. Feverishly she cast aside pieces of twisted metal in her haste to delve into the mangled craft. Finally in front of her she could see a figure, slumped in front of a multi-coloured dial control panel. Coloured lights pulsed and beeped, as strange writing flashed across screens. Pieces of debris were kicked aside and the woman was able to lean over and unfasten a helmet identical to the one that she had so recently removed. The clasp proved stiff and she fumbled to undo it. Morbid thoughts raced through her head; that they should have travelled this far together, for so long, and now it could be all to no avail.

She paused, pulling herself together, stood upright and took a deep breath. Her hands once more carefully searched out the clasp and this time it sprang open. Placing her hands either side of the helmet she gently slid it off, revealing a man's face. No movement came from the black-haired occupant. He bore many features similar to the girl; his skin was fair and his ears and nose were identical, although his mouth was a little wider.

"Rewn, Rewn!" she called in an agitated voice, shaking his shoulders. Feelings of isolation began to loom in her as she was unable to extract any response. Here she was on a distant planet, miles away from their intended landing, the craft was wrecked and there was no chance of making contact with her people. She placed a hand on the man's neck. She could barely believe it; she could detect a pulse. To check, she moved her hand to try the other side; she could find nothing and her hopes fell once more. Then a groan from the man quickly dispelled these thoughts. Gently she slapped his face with the back of one hand. Rewn opened his eyes.

"Lutel? Where are we? What happened?" he asked.

"The ship malfunctioned on entry. We've been separated," she replied.

Rewn raised a hand to the back of his head and rubbed a bump. He felt little like listening to Lutel at the moment but his training and survival instincts forced him to concentrate.

"Our screen readouts last showed that we were heading for Earth in August 1665 but we are nowhere near the town of London."

Rewn shuffled uncomfortably on his backside, and Lutel placed a supporting arm below each armpit and helped him rise. He gazed around at the wreckage that surrounded him. It wasn't supposed to be like this. Back on Mykas, when the Stilax had allotted him this mission, all had seemed so straightforward and clear. In fact if the ruling council had not chosen him to take part in this mission he was all set to volunteer. Earth and its history had long been one of his interests, and the chance to visit another galaxy and a favoured planet in need of help appealed to both his sense of adventure and his philanthropic spirit.

Even more intriguingly, the planet itself didn't appear to comprehend the full potential of the danger it faced. It seemed blissfully unaware of the abyss that its future evolution was about to fall into. To play a part in the progress and development of a fledgling world: what more could a Mykasian Startraveller want?

More pleasingly, the Stilax had bowed to his request for his sister to accompany him, along with his long-standing friends Verde and Revin. A thought flashed through Rewn's mind. Had the same fate befallen them? Were Verde and Revin safe or had they too met with problems on entering the Earth's atmosphere?

A tremor of helplessness surged through his body. On Mykas life expectancy was over 150 years. Education in the first cycle lasted until you were twenty-five years old. Each adult then progressed to three work cycles. The first five years of each new cycle were dedicated to specific training related to the following twenty-year work cycle. How he would value Verde's presence now. In his first work cycle Verde had been a surgeon and during his second a geologist. Rewn suspected that these skills would be more useful than his own. His previous cycles had seen him involved in law and then architecture; not a lot of use in their present predicament, he told himself.

Revin had been a lecturer and politician, rising to just one rung below the Stilax, where many had assumed he would continue the family tradition. But a sense of adventure and wilfulness saw him fail to follow his grandfather and father's footsteps as a lawmaker of their world. Instead, he too had chosen to be a space pilot in his final work cycle and travel the stars along with Rewn and Verde.

Pigeons and rooks returned to their roosts complaining bitterly of the evening's disturbance. Momentarily they interrupted Rewn's thoughts. He looked across at his sister; she was sitting on her haunches, recovering from the scare. Poor Lutel, he thought; a glowing career in medicine and now, in the early part of her pilot's cycle with the best years of her life ahead of her, she was marooned on this faraway planet. He consoled himself with the thought that as Startravellers they were forbidden young families; at least they were only responsible to themselves.

He voiced his fears to his sister, but she was unable to allay them. Her mind focused on the practicality of the situation. Lutel had always been the pragmatist able to face a new challenge, whereas he tended to dwell on things and think what might have been.

"Rewn," she urged him, "we must move. Somebody may have seen us."

"Good," he replied whimsically. "At least they'll be able to tell us where we are."

"But they mustn't see the craft," reasoned Lutel. "The scout ships reported these people look similar to us but their technology is very backward."

"The last scout ship came here over a century ago; things will have changed."

"But not that much," argued Lutel. She was becoming exasperated at his obstinacy and lack of co-operation in facing the problem. "We know from the Stilax that the plague is still virulent."

He conceded; as always Lutel was speaking sense. After all, wasn't this level-headedness one of the reasons that he had wanted her to accompany him? Lutel could always envisage the end of the tunnel, whereas he always had trouble finding the entrance.

Lutel took a deep breath before verbalising her thoughts. They had occupied her mind ever since rescuing Rewn from the wreckage. She spoke calmly and precisely.

"We must destroy the craft. We can't risk its discovery."

"Looks to me like it's already destroyed," replied Rewn, eyeing the twisted ruins.

Lutel had expected resistance, but not defeatism. Rewn saw the disapproval in her eyes and felt a sense of guilt. After all, he was the reason for her being on this mission. He regretted his despondent attitude.

"Yes, you're right," he added.

His thoughts trailed back to the departing words from the President of the Stilax. He had warned them of the scout ships' reports, of the danger involved during entry into the planet's atmosphere. How it might even signify their possible non-return. It had been one of the principal reasons for sending two separate ships. Rewn remembered how he had accepted this decision without giving it a second thought, as he was unable to envisage the likelihood of their present situation.

As he had proudly stood on the presidium of the Stilax, the bright lights shining down on him, the crowds cheering, flanked by his smiling parents, he had paid little heed to the warnings of their present predicament. Now in the warm sunlight of Earth, he inwardly thanked the Stilax's Fathers for their foresight; a pre-arranged meeting place had crudely been decided upon to combat this eventuality.

Lutel reached for a small silver box in her left breast pocket. She bent down and paused to look up at Rewn.

"We must do it," she said. "Wiping out the plague is a vital step in the development of this country. It will have a far-reaching effect on the evolution of this whole planet. In time people will travel afar from this land, much like we are now. We must allow it to happen. Remember it's our future as well as theirs. The scant reports show it to be vital that we permanently drive the plague from London."

Then she gasped; the raison d'être for their mission was missing.

"The vaccine," she shouted, "where is it?" Lutel frantically began to search the broken body of the craft. Rewn joined her, scrabbling around on his hands and knees for the precious concentrate of vaccine that they would use to inoculate the populace of London against the plague.

Rewn suddenly stopped searching; his body froze. Lutel saw the bad news etched on his face. He had lifted a piece of panelling, and lying on its side on the woodland floor was a green plastic case containing hundreds of broken phials. The purple contents lay in a congealed pool, staining the plant life around.

"That's it, then," groaned Rewn, wringing his hands. "We were the only ones carrying the vaccine; even if we do locate Verde and Revin, what's the point?"

Lutel placed the silver hexagonal box alongside a piece of the wreckage. She placed a finger on an amber button and pressed firmly. She walked reverently backwards from the box.

"Come on," she said to Rewn.

Her brother didn't move; he stood staring at the flashing button.

"Rewn, we must go," she ordered him.

He stepped outside the circle of wreckage and stood beside his sister. The amber light stopped flashing, but remained glowing brightly. Rewn and Lutel looked away; as they did so a silver flash enveloped the debris. When they looked back all that remained were a few purple-stained leaves.

Rewn sank to his haunches, inspecting the scorched ground that was now the only evidence of their mode of arrival on this planet.

"It's over before we've even begun, then," he murmured.

"Perhaps not," mused Lutel. "If you'd studied your assignment screens you would have noticed that these people have some very quaint sayings."

Rewn's blank countenance suggested he had not researched to his sister's depth. It grieved him that she knew more than he did about one of his pet interests.

"Go on, then," he unenthusiastically replied.

"The one that comes most to mind," she said, "is that there is more than one way to skin a cat, or to be more precise in this case a rat."

Rewn looked at her; she had already turned her back on him and was walking along the path that Tilly Sharpe had earlier trodden in the opposite direction.

CHAPTER THREE

Sour Fruits, Sweet Hay

On reaching the farmhouse Gem burst through the door. A huge fire glowed from a hearth. The fireplace was built from small rectangular red bricks and stood like a tower in the centre of the ground floor, reaching up through the large timbered beams in the ceiling and beyond. It demarcated the two ground-floor rooms by its very position; on one side lay the family's sitting room and on the other the smaller kitchen.

The fire could be attended to from either side and shared its warmth equally. The uncomfortable heat it cast during this mild late August evening was compounded by a dense yellow smoke from the burning applewood. It stung Gem's eyes as he entered the room. The orange flames danced like street acrobats performing before a crowd. A pile of logs lay to the fire's left, a safe distance away from its licking flames. On the opposite side, a bundle of kindling branches stood upright in the corner in readiness for the following evening. A long and narrow highly-polished bench curved around two sides of the fireplace, affording a very warm seat to anyone who required it.

A large black pot was hanging from a hook above the fireplace. It contained the reason for the unseasonable fire: the family's supper. The contents consisted of various beef and mutton and a variety of seasonal vegetables. The umber-coloured liquid bubbled gently, vying with the smoke to fill the room with an earthy pungent smell. In the larger room a long rectangular table, stained black through its service to generations of Varleys, was attended by a mixture of wooden stools and chairs of a similar appearance.

The stoutest of the latter was occupied by Cusack, who was quenching his day's thirst with a flagon of cider. Molly Varley was nursing a small child on her lap. She was a thin woman of medium height and looks, her most striking feature being the ringlets of auburn hair that swept to her shoulders. On the opposite side of the fire in the smaller kitchen stood Hannah, their eldest daughter. She was preparing a stock of lettuce, sorrel and borage in readiness for adding to the pot. Her eight-year-old sister Mary assisted her by tearing leaves from the reddish-brown sorrel and passing them to her sister for chopping on a square wooden table.

All three daughters had inherited their mother's red hair and the two eldest shared her hazel eyes. Hannah and Mary wore similar dresses and white mop caps, as did their grandmother Nell, who from the kitchen side hovered over the large black cauldron, giving it frequent stirs with a large gnarled wooden spoon. She was a small stout woman with hunched shoulders; her thin grey hair was mostly hidden by her own mop cap. Nell looked into the pot and frequently addressed its contents with a mixture of encouragement and threats.

At Gem's appearance she dropped the spoon and Cusack choked on the swig that he was taking, causing the family's attention to briefly switch to him. Cusack recovered quickly and on regaining his self-composure reverted to his custom of the past twenty years: tolerating but largely ignoring his brother. Even if they had been on more fraternal terms, he would not have displayed any outward signs of concern at his brother's dishevelled appearance, as he attributed Gem's unkempt appearance to a skirmish with Tilly.

"The sun's fallen, the sun's fallen!" shouted Gem in an incomprehensible outburst. Grandmother Varley and Molly rushed to Gem's side and helped him into a chair. Mary began to cry, frightened by her uncle's appearance and his noisy entrance. Hannah, following her father's example, ignored the commotion and concentrated on her herbs.

Gem continued to ramble, "It's fallen, it's fallen on the down!"

Cusack, purporting to examine the contents of his flagon, stole a sly glimpse of his brother. Gem's wildly staring eyes implied more than a dalliance with a fair maiden, suggesting to Cusack that his first impression may have been misplaced.

The serenity of his womenfolk was being so disturbed that Cusack's feelings towards his brother thawed – if only out of reverence towards his wife, daughter and mother-in-law. He rose from his seat and with a diffident gait stepped towards his brother and proffered his earthenware stein. Gem took a sip of the cool, golden contents and swiftly emptied it with three large quaffs.

Gem composed himself in manner, but his speech remained uneasy, proving no more intelligible to the family.

"The stream, the sun's fallen in the stream."

Molly shook her head. "Poor lad must 'ave cracked 'is 'ead, or p'raps 'e 'as a fever coming," she suggested. Continuing her trail of thought, she deduced, "'Tis the plague. Gem 'as the distemper." Then, regretting the insensitivity of her diagnosis, clasped her hand to her mouth.

Cusack stood in front of his brother and put his large bucket-like hands on his shoulders. "Gem, 'ave 'e bin 'it on yer 'ead?" Cusack could not quite dismiss his brother's lustful intentions from his mind, and could picture Tilly striking him on the head with any solid object that came to hand. Turning to his wife, he added, "It may be 'is old wound."

Gem shook his head as if to prove that he still held full control of it. "No, 'ead's fine. Tilly's fine," he added, surmising the reason behind Cusack's question. "From the sky, a fireball in the woods."

"Oright, let's go an' 'ave a look," offered Cusack, exhibiting an unheard-of sympathy for his brother.

Gem made no effort to move.

"Come on, you'll 'ave to show me the place this 'appened," pressed Cusack. In his opinion he'd relented his feelings enough towards his brother, and he was not so benevolent as to beg him to come. If Gem did not wish to go then so be it.

Cusack made towards his chair. Gem stirred; his pride at being proved sane conquered his fear and he stood to escort his brother.

"It's just along the valley in Yatton Down," explained Gem, barely controlling his excitement. The two brothers walked through the farmhouse door with a closer bond between them than there had been for many a year.

Lutel ducked under the outstretched branch of a blackthorn tree. Her hair brushed the small silver-green leaves. Following behind, Rewn paused and picked one of its purple sloes. He tasted it and his face contracted at its sourness. He spat out the small acidic plum.

"I hope all food on this planet doesn't taste like that," he said to Lutel, who had turned around on hearing his spluttering.

"That'll teach you to be so hasty," she scolded. "We must approach all things with care."

Flies buzzed noisily around their heads. In front of them a rabbit scuttled through some thick brambles. Away to their left the sun sat like a bright red cap on the top of the hillside. They hugged the hedgerow as it curved away to their right, ducking under the low-lying branches of a hazel tree. Rewn eyed the nuts hungrily but, remembering his encounter with the sloes, left them alone.

On their immediate left stood the hillside where Gem had earlier nurtured his lusty thoughts. Rewn stared around him at the cerulean sky and his foot caught in a rabbit scraping, and he stumbled forward, just missing Lutel. She turned at the sound and a chalk-blue butterfly settled on her white boot; she twitched her foot and it flew off in search of a more promising food source. The distraction had saved Rewn from one of her remonstrations. As the path rose they could see over the treetops and beyond the stream to the hill where Gem had recently disappeared from view.

Their attention was drawn back to the track in front of them by another rabbit scuttling down the hillside, its white tail bobbing, into the bushes.

"It's a shame they can't talk," said Rewn. "This place seems full of small animals and no higher form of life whatsoever." He stood with his hands on his hips and stared around as if determined to prove his point. His eyes were drawn to a buzzard circling above them, searching for food. It was soon mobbed by a pair of crows and decided to try its luck in the next valley.

Hills now stood to the left and right of them, so they decided to go straight on, following the narrow path. Yellow coltsfoot brushed against their legs as the pathway divided into two brown trodden tracks two feet apart, one being slightly more raised than the other. Within the gap an assortment of wild flowers grew amongst the grasses. In the distance a wood pigeon called, "Take two cows, Taffy," whilst behind them the crows cawed raucously as they flapped their way over the hill towards the village of Castle Combe.

A red deer careered down the hillside and raced across the track several yards in front of them. Lutel took advantage of the interruption and paused to think. She breathed in deeply, sucking greedily on the fresh clean air. Yellow, brown and blue butterflies twinkled around the carpet of wild flowers. A willow warbler, camouflaged amongst the olive-green leaves of a hawthorn, called out its mellow musical song, before its soft liquid notes descended into a trill.

Behind them, rabbits scattered in all directions, unused to this late evening's disturbance. As they continued further along the path the trees thickened and the blackberries provided denser cover, whilst the hazel became taller. Only a single dying alder went against the grain.

The two pathways again merged before leisurely sloping down towards the stream bed. Before them the path spurred off into the woods, where earlier Tilly Sharpe had disturbed the pheasant with unfortunate consequences. Lutel chose the path that crossed the stream. They leapt over the water and began to ascend the hill in the direction of the Varleys' farmhouse. The rolling slope soon became a steep incline and their breath became shorter and faster. To their right stood the hill that Gem had earlier climbed in order to attain the plateau that they were heading towards. The ground underfoot grew stony; to their left ran a long row of alder trees that accompanied their ascent like a giant stair banister.

As they climbed the hill patches of purple clover and thistles suggested that the soil was becoming more fertile. Halfway, the alder trees gave way to hawthorns and hazels, loosely covered in white fluffy old man's beard. They bowed their heads and walked on, finally coming to rest at the top of the hill by a wide wooden gate. Beyond the gateway, two fields away, lay Gem's farmhouse. The large building was predominantly constructed of red brick complemented by a mixture of greys to give a rich and complex diaper pattern.

"What do you think?" asked Rewn.

"We tread warily," answered Lutel, scanning the buildings.

"Are we in any danger?"

"I think they will be wary of two strangers appearing from nowhere. They may even be frightened if they witnessed our landing – so yes, let's approach with care."

Stealthily they crossed the fields, utilising the various outbuildings to screen them from the farmhouse. Lutel stopped outside a small byre no more than twenty feet in length; the walls were made from stone and two partitions divided the cow shed. The building had a low red roof. Two of its sections were fronted by wooden hurdles, whilst the third was enclosed by a pair of rickety wooden doors. Rewn carefully pulled open one of the rotting doors. Light flooded in to reveal the barn was uninhabited and they slunk in, leaving the door ajar.

Rewn slumped onto a pile of sweet-smelling hay, exhausted mentally and physically by recent events. Lutel stood in the centre of the building, her eyes busily searching the gloomy interior. The grey stone walls were rugged, cold and damp; the outhouse was obviously too dilapidated to shelter animals. In one corner propped against a wall were a variety of disused or broken farm implements. In the centre of the earthen floor stood a wooden plough, one of its shafts badly splintered and awaiting repairs.

Alongside the plough was a wooden barrow, its square body attached at the front to a single wooden-spoked wheel, and at the opposite end were two crudely-carved handles. A pair of rectangular chunky legs hewn out of the same material supported the back end. Next to the barrow stood a strange-looking contraption; it looked like a cross between a chair and a sleigh. Its function, though, was clear as the seat of the chair contained a pile of logs, and the single wheel at the front indicated that this was a means of transporting firewood to the farmhouse. Lutel let forth a low whistle.

"See what I meant about their primitive technology?"

Rewn followed her gaze; he was still to be convinced.

"They may be old family heirlooms kept for their intrinsic value," he offered.

"In this neglected building and in that unkempt state?" asked Lutel incredulously.

Rewn nodded that she had a point; it was highly unlikely, he agreed, that anything of worth would be found out here. Hiding away amongst the oak beams he could just make out two small birds' nests, their occupants having flown earlier that summer. Lutel was right. This building housed nothing of value; it was merely used as a refuge for discarded equipment. It didn't offer shelter to any form of animal life; well, at least not domestic beasts, he corrected himself, as he noticed a family of field mice stealing from a sack of discarded grain.

Lutel was gingerly sifting through piles of debris.

"What are you looking for?" asked Rewn.

"Be quiet, somebody will hear us," she scolded in a hoarse whisper. "We must change clothes; our guises were destroyed in the crash. We will stick out like a purple thrarb in a snow storm."

"You'll stick out further if anyone hears you say that," admonished Rewn.

Lutel coloured, "You're right," she admitted. "It won't happen again." She cursed herself under her breath for her clumsy mistake. All that training and they had been here less than one hour and, in using a proverb from Mykas, she had made an elementary error that could have betrayed them. What made it worse was that it had taken place in Rewn's presence. No, she promised herself, that mistake would not happen a second time.

"Why bother?" continued Rewn. "Our mission has failed before we've started. We must establish our position and then look to find Verde and Revin. It was a wise decision to bring two four-seater craft. Let's hope that they have had more luck than us."

"This mission can still be a success," argued Lutel.

"Possibly," answered Rewn, "but I don't see how."

"Trust me," she said, furtively. "I'll explain later."

Rewn's furrowed brow showed he was not convinced.

"If you are right," he said, "Revin and Verde will be carrying spare Earth costumes. These suits will protect us until then."

"And how far do you think we will travel around a strange land dressed like this before we arouse suspicion?" snapped Lutel, looking down at her shiny white clothing.

Rewn did not answer. Lutel smiled thinly; the ascendancy was back with her.

It had been much the same back on Mykas. All her life she had looked up to and loved her older brother. How she admired his intelligence, sense of humour and caring attitude. She'd never dared tell him about these personal qualities, yet she'd always been quick to pounce on the little faults that annoyed her. She could excuse the bouts of pessimism that often engulfed him, but his distinct lack of common sense drove her to distraction. It manifested itself in an inability to see the obvious even when it was staring him right in the face, even when it was nose to nose with him. His razor-sharp brain was often so keen to thrust itself into the kernel of a problem that he missed the outer shell. Lutel often acted as his nut cracker and had seen him through a few awkward situations whilst they were studying together in the city of Caron for their space pilot's permits.

She stood arms akimbo with her back to the doorway. The last remnants of the setting sun danced in her hair, enhancing its chestnut sheen. Rewn looked very sheepish from his bed of hay. Lutel felt a pang of guilt; perhaps this was the wrong time to have snapped at him.

"We may well survive in these suits in the fields and countryside," she said by means of an apology, "but once we are in the throng of a town it would surely lead to our being questioned."

Rewn understood what his sister was trying to say.

"What do you think best?" he asked.

"You are right," she said; "we must travel to London to link up with Verde and Revin, but we must avoid drawing unwanted attention to ourselves, so help me look for some clothing."

Rewn pushed himself up to search the dingy interior. As he did so the shaft of light from the doorway darkened; framed in its chink stood Cusack with Gem peering over his shoulder.

CHAPTER FOUR

AN ENGLISH POTTAGE

The two yokels had returned from their hillside venture with mixed feelings. Gem had been relieved at their finding an area of scorched earth and fallen trees on the down, but both brothers were puzzled by the lack of evidence as to the cause. Having heard Lutel's scolding voice as they approached the outhouse, they had naturally followed their countryman's curiosity and crept up to the building.

"Let's be 'aven yer," ordered Cusack, with the bravado of a squire who had caught some urchins scrumping apples from his orchard.

Rewn instantly shot up whilst Lutel twisted around to face the voices. She immediately assessed that these two simple folk would be no match for the trained fighting techniques instilled into them on Mykas. Three steps, two blows and they would be through the door and on their way, but what would that achieve? Drawing attention to themselves when what they most required was information and help.

No, she mused, their best hope lay not in force but intellect, and Lutel reasoned that in this she also held the upper hand. She would need to divulge her information simply and carefully, there being little point in explaining to these humble folk that they had crash-landed in a VX Mach 2 spacecraft from the planet Mykas on a mission to rid their country of bubonic plague. Behind her Rewn moved, but she barred his way with an outstretched arm. Lutel groped for his hand and led him towards the doorway. The brothers jumped back, but on seeing that their two intruders lacked any aggressive intent they resumed their assertive manner.

"Who be 'ee, an' what yer doin' 'ere?" demanded Cusack.

Gem, inspired by his brother's confrontational approach, imitated its directness. "Where yer from?"

By now the family, alerted by the keen eyes of one of the children, had assembled outside the byre. The natural light caused Rewn and Lutel to contort their eyes, emphasising their forlorn situation. Molly had no inkling as to who these people were, nor their reason for being there, but she did recognise a fellow woman when she saw one, and, although Lutel was at pains to hide it, she could detect a woman in distress.

"Cusack, Gem, where be yer manners?" she admonished. "Can't yer zee these poor volk be in need of food an' shelter? Poor dears look exhausted; bring 'em up into the house."

The two men knew better than to argue with Molly when her mind was fixed, and for the moment they acquiesced and accompanied the strangers to the farmhouse. Rewn and Lutel were sandwiched between the two farmers, Cusack leading the way accompanied by his excited daughters, whilst Gem brought up the rear. Two agitated farm dogs ran up and down the line, barking at their visitors. They entered through the large farmhouse door. The pottage was still being attended by Grandmother Varley, who didn't look up from her stirring.

"Come, sit by the fire," offered Molly, indicating the fireside bench. Lutel and Rewn sat on the polished wood. Molly went into the kitchen and fussed around the crockery; finally locating what she was searching for, she handed two extra bowls to her mother. The old lady ladled out the boiling contents; the vegetables splashed into the liquid, spattering drops onto her clothes. Through the flames Molly spied her eldest daughters coyly hiding behind their father, who, somewhat piqued, had resumed his place in the chair. Every now and then, the girls would peek out from behind Cusack's shoulders, and emit a nervous giggle. Molly called them to serve the pottage to their guests. Lutel smiled at Mary as she accepted the bowl. Rewn's face remained emotionless as he took his meal from Hannah, but he murmured, "Thank you."

Towards the back of the room Gem grunted disapprovingly. Rewn raised his bowl to his nose and sniffed; it was an unusual aroma, new to him, but it was not an unpleasant smell. He supped from the bowl; the hot liquid burned his mouth and he spat it out. A chortle of laughter erupted from the children; a look from their mother reminded them of their manners. Gem snorted contemptuously. Molly's withering look had no effect a second time. She handed each of her visitors a hunk of bread and then attended her daughters. Rewn stared as Hannah dunked her crust into the warm broth and lifted it to her mouth. Hannah caught Rewn's eye and he swiftly mimicked her actions. Lutel looked with measured astonishment at Rewn; this was a new eating experience to them both.

"It's good, eat," he said.

Grandmother Varley had set the larger table for the family. She handed two wide-bowled spoons to the strangers.

"Blowin' it will cool it," she suggested.

This was a more familiar means of partaking of a meal and Rewn nodded his thanks, being unable to speak.

Molly smiled as they devoured their meals. Gem and Cusack stood impatiently by, glaring at the pair of intruders. They both realised it was fruitless to challenge Molly when she was in this broody mood and they waited silently, but restlessly shuffling from foot to foot, as their "guests" ate.

Molly and Nell seated themselves at the table. The broth gave off a welcoming aroma, and lured the two brothers into joining them. Throughout the duration of the meal no words were spoken. Only the slurping of the broth and the clinking of the spoons disturbed the peace, accompanied by the occasional crackle from the fire as it wafted its perfumed smoke into the muggy atmosphere. Rewn stretched his legs out as he finished the last mouthful of the pottage. Cusack, who had been waiting for the opportunity, pounced.

"Well then, what be yer doin' in our barn?"

"And what do 'ee know about the fire from the sky?" added Gem.

Lutel eyed Cusack. She reasoned that by answering his question truthfully they could avoid responding to Gem's more searching query. She seized the opportunity.

"We're on our way to London to give aid to the plague victims," she explained.

The mention of the dreaded word caused consternation throughout the room. The women stopped eating whilst the two men exchanged worrying glances. Even the children sensed that something was amiss and looked anxiously at the adults. Only the baby lay blissfully ignorant in its heavy wooden cot at the far end of the fireplace. Molly rose to remove her youngest child from the proximity of the strangers. Lutel sought to quell their anxiety.

"We do not suffer from the plague ourselves, neither have we been in contact with it," she said reassuringly.

"Quacks be 'ee?" asked Cusack perceptively.

"Quacks?" replied Lutel.

"Arr, quacks," retorted Cusack. "They do say that them Lunnon doctors do wear strange clothes in times of plague; makes 'um look like girt big ducks, so 'em do say. Though I've never 'eard tell of the strange garments you'm be wearing."

Lutel could barely follow Cusack's trail of thought, but she ascertained that he believed them to be medical people, and that he didn't seem to be displeased with the fact.

"Yes, we are off to cure the plague," she said. "Our clothing does give us protection." Though she was careful to avoid mentioning what type of protection their white shiny suits afforded.

Cusack stared at her, his wild eyes searching, trying to penetrate her deepest thought.

"I didn't know Lunnon folk had women doctors," he said.

"She's my assistant," interjected Rewn. "She helps with my preparations."

He hoped that his quick reply would satisfy this rustic curiosity, but Cusack, like one of his farm dogs with a marrow-bone, was not willing to let the subject drop so lightly.

"That may as well be," he continued, "but it don't explain what yer doin' round 'ere in our barn."

"We were looking for herbs and flowers," answered Lutel, inwardly praising herself for the thorough research that had underpinned this mission.

"Ah, that'll be the wild garlic yer wanting," said Gem knowingly.

"And the early purple orchid," added Cusack, "but that flowered weeks ago."

"We haven't met with much success," said Lutel, not untruthfully. Just how unlucky they had been she decided it best not to divulge.

"'Ave 'ee come from Lunnon, then?" enquired Molly.

"No, a lot further off than that," answered Rewn.

"Cornwall!" exclaimed Gem. "You'm come all the way from Cornwall?"

It was the furthest point known to him. Lutel realised that Gem would feel comfortable with this point of origin and nodded whilst softly murmuring, "Close by."

"You'm must be good doctors if they've sent for 'ee from Cornwall," he said mindfully.

Cusack settled back on his wooden chair; his inquisitiveness had been satisfied. Lutel inwardly sighed, and relaxed a little on her bench. The warm fire was making her tired, and her eyes began to flutter. She was ready for a sleep. She hadn't slept within walls for many a day and she was looking forward to it, however austere the surroundings. Lutel hoped that her hosts would recognise her tiredness, and offer them shelter for the night.

"The sun!" It was Gem in the background. "What about the bright light and the fire-marks?" he demanded. Cusack might be satisfied with their explanation, but he hadn't witnessed all that Gem had seen.

Lutel stirred from her daydreaming. Her mind was wide awake at this new attack. Gem, encouraged by the response his question had invoked, continued.

"A bright light came from the sky like the falling of the sun, and we've both seen the fire-marks," he said, intimating Cusack with a sideways nod.

"We needed an infusion of some herbs that we had found," said Lutel. "It needed to be made as soon as they were picked or their potency would have been weakened. We had a small fire, but I'm afraid in the dry conditions it got out of control and the mixture overheated and exploded."

Rewn looked incredulously at his sister, admiring her powers of improvisation. Gem was not convinced, but any other hypothesis was beyond his experience and imagination. Reluctantly he accepted their explanation, although he wasn't entirely persuaded that this was the cause of the interruption to his amorous encounter with Tilly Sharpe.

Lutel was relaxing for a second time, when Cusack, stirred by his brother's questioning, rejoined the conversation.

"You still 'aven't said what you were doin' in our barn."

Lutel calmly stared into his large brown eyes.

"Our clothes – our doctor's clothes – give us protection, but they are warm in the sun, and after the fire we were very hot. We hoped we could find some discarded sackcloth or farming garments in your outhouses. We would willingly pay for them," she added. Though with what she wasn't sure; like most of their belongings, the little Earth money they had been supplied with had been lost in the actual fire.

Gem snorted. "Sackcloth be no cooler than what you'm wearing. I'll do a trade wiv 'ee. I got some old clothes and boots you can 'ave, but I'll want those fancy doctors' garments in exchange."

"Very well," replied Rewn, instantly.

It was Gem's turn to be surprised; he hadn't expected a straightforward trade. He swiftly disappeared up the staircase that stood against the far wall of the house. The wooden steps were almost vertical in their ascent to the upper level and the rungs were narrow and bowed in the centre from many years of use. They could hear him rummaging fervently above them. Within a short space of time Gem reappeared and skilfully descended, his large boots clattering on the wooden steps. He was grasping a bundle of clothes under his arm, and he spread them out on the floor in front of Rewn and Lutel. The newcomers sorted through the assortment of clothes: hats, tunics, socks, breeches, boots, overgarments, everything they needed to become seventeenth-century travellers.

Lutel held up a tunic for size; Rewn laughed at the vision in front of him.

"You may try them on in one of the upstairs rooms," offered Molly, perceiving Lutel's need for privacy.

Molly led the way up the staircase. The chimney breast again dominated. It stood in the centre with four rooms radiating from it. They were shown to the largest room. A glance told them it was the master bedroom belonging to Molly and Cusack. A large Chester bed with an olive-green coverlet stood under the long narrow windows. Alongside it was a solid wooden cot identical to the one on the lower floor. Under the windows on the far side of the room was a large spinning wheel; beside it stood a wicker basket with oddments of cloth and wool protruding from its lid.

A fruit bowl adorned a small triangular wooden stool; green apples gleamed temptingly. Lutel recognised the design of the stool; the two large chairs below also bore the strange characteristic three legs and triangular seat. There were two wooden chests in the room, plain in decoration apart from a large circle carved into their front panel with a grand central "V". Upon the lid of one of the chests sat a brown vase. A jagged crack ran the length of the pot, which was still put to use holding a bunch of dried teasels. Next to it was an empty vase fashioned from a reddish-brown clay. The second chest was situated at the foot of the bed. A pair of pewter candlesticks, each containing a burned candle, had been placed at each end of the lid.

Lutel glanced above her. There was no ceiling; just the exposed underside of the red clay pantiles that formed the roof. Sturdy beams constructed from oak criss-crossed the space above them leading to the king post, which reached all the way up to the tiles, supporting the roof like Atlas holding up the sky. The walls below waist-height were covered in white mortar interspersed with black wooden beams.

Lutel and Rewn changed quickly. The fires were yet to be lit upstairs, and the rooms were a little chilly now that the sun had gone down.

"We shouldn't be leaving our clothes behind," said Lutel.

"We have little choice," argued Rewn. "They're suspicious enough without adding to their doubts. Besides, Verde and Revin should have spares."

Cautiously they descended the staircase, finding it easier to go down backwards. Rewn handed their clothes over to Gem. Gem held them up, proudly displaying them to his family as though he were holding aloft a hunting trophy.

"Now if the plague do come to these 'ere parts, I'll be as safe as 'ee," he said to Rewn and Lutel.

The exchange was complete and Gem made to show them out.

"We have ventured across many a hill and valley seeking out herbs and flowers. In truth we have travelled many a mile and are now unsure of our whereabouts," understated Lutel. "Please could you tell us how far we are from London?"

Gem laughed. "Lunnon? Why, don't yer know, 'tis over a 'undred mile from yer!"

Lutel paused; she wondered if too many questions would arouse their suspicions again, but Gem seemed too preoccupied with their ignorance to give any thought to its reason.

"In which direction should we head?" asked Lutel.

"Why, you'm need to go east," said Gem. "Head towards Chipnumb; you may get a ride from there."

"Thank you," she replied, "thank you for all your kindness," and she made towards the door.

"Stop!" said Cusack.

Lutel froze.

"You can't walk to Chipnumb tonight; 'tis five mile away. Rest 'ere 'an leave early in the mornin'. Chances are there'll be a village cart heading that way."

Lutel looked at Rewn and then at Molly.

"Of course you must stay," Molly concurred. "You can sleep down 'ere in front of the fire."

As much out of relief as tiredness, Lutel readily agreed.

CHAPTER FIVE

THE DEVIL'S GUTS

Around the time that Tilly Sharpe raced breathlessly into the family home, too stunned to ever speak of the dual shocks that her system had received, a near-perfect landing of a Mykasian VX Mach 2 took place a hundred miles or so to the east, a little to the north of London.

Verde and Revin had seen the disappearance of their comrades' ship on their radar screen. Revin, a thin man well in excess of six feet, with ginger hair and an identical beard, was the first to speak.

"They may have come out of it safely." His voice did not carry much conviction.

Revin realised that he may never again see two of his closest friends, and his angular features were even paler than usual. Seated next to him, his companion, a slightly shorter but much heavier man also sporting a matching beard and hair, but of a dark brown hue, replied in a more assured tone.

"It doesn't signify anything. They probably landed safely and there could be a hundred reasons why their craft disappeared from the screens."

"Name one," replied Revin dourly.

Verde sighed; he didn't appreciate being asked to hypothesise with so few facts, and they might as well be positive in their outlook until they knew something more definite.

"Perhaps the cloaking device was damaged and they had to destroy the ship for fear of discovery."

"Well, only ninety-nine to go," intoned Revin, whose cynicism had not been cured by the suggestion.

Verde snapped. "Look, we've been sent here by the Stilax on vitally important business. You know how imperative it is that we succeed. The screens show that Lutel and Rewn came down over one hundred miles west of here. That's a fair distance to travel given the primitive transport system. Lutel's resourceful; she'll find a way. We will give them a reasonable time to find us at the meeting place. Now throw off this despondency and activate our cloaking device before someone sees us!"

In contrast to their unfortunate colleagues, Revin and Verde had made a very accurate landing. They had alighted as planned near a forest to the north-east of Spittlefields, on the outskirts of London.

Verde pushed a button on the control console. There was a whooshing noise as a side panel opened.

He reached in to the aperture and pulled out what appeared to be no more than a bundle of rags. The pile of material unfolded to produce a set of reproduction seventeenth-century clothes. Verde handed an outfit to Revin and they changed in silence, placing their shiny suits in the vacant space. After collecting a few belongings they made their way to the ship's door. A series of further button pushes caused a second whooshing sound, accompanied by an upward movement of the door, and the two men stepped out into the green fields of south-east England.

As they climbed down a ladder of light-beams Verde turned to face Revin.

"Let's hope that they remember the vaccine," he said.

"If they come," snorted Revin as they made their way towards a small copse. The sweet-smelling country air did nothing to dissipate Revin's black mood. His temperament was more in tune with the foul air that lay behind the walls of the city – a fact that they were soon to discover.

Verde peered out from the hide, scanning the surrounding fields.

"We could not have picked a more favourable spot," he announced.

Revin looked around at the few scattered dwellings on the distant horizon; the fields appeared deserted.

"Not much use without the vaccine," he complained. "I can't see why we couldn't have split it. In fact I don't see why we didn't bring all the phials with us, considering your former cycle."

"That's Lutel's responsibility now," answered Verde. "The Stilax judged that she should have sole liability and we all agreed, so don't start."

The two travellers sat on the ground amongst the trees and bushes, contemplating their present situation. Gradually the startled birds began to return, and sing in the branches overhead. Revin had not been placated and it was he who broke their silence, though he decided to change tack.

"Where was the place we had to rendezvous if we became separated?"

Verde stared into the blue sky and fluffy white clouds for inspiration. He appeared calm and collected, but the shock of watching the other ship disappear off their screens had temporarily affected his memory. He expelled air from between his lips and the recollection burst out with it.

"A tavern," he remembered.

Revin eyed him expectantly.

"A building where they sell liquor; apparently they are very popular and well-frequented."

"How do we recognise it if there is more than one?"

"The scout ships identified one in particular; it was a long time ago and their information was sketchy, but they said there was a sign outside painted with pictures of a large black bird."

"So we are looking for a building with a picture of some birds outside and it's going to be full of people," bemoaned Revin.

"Where better to hide?" beamed Verde. "Come, our way lies to the south."

The two men made their way across scorched pastures. In the distance they spied a number of buildings, which they decided to give a wide berth.

"We are far better soaking up the atmosphere and acclimatising before meeting a native," suggested Verde, wiping the sweat from his brow. "That will come soon enough."

A wooden gate barred the way; they climbed over and walked around the perimeter of the field under the cover of the hedgerow. Wild clematis was as prevalent in the fields around London as it was in the Wiltshire countryside. A blackbird trilled its alarm call, warning all others of their presence. Verde jumped at the sound; it came as a timely reminder that they were intruders on this planet, and if a small bird could catch them off-guard then what else?

Verde and Revin pressed on, their senses heightened by their rude awakening. A short walk brought a change on the horizon. A row of small houses with red clay tiles and smoke billowing from their chimney pots was clearly visible; London was busy cooking its evening meal. So engrossed were both men in the sight that neither of them noticed a gap in the hedge.

"Evenin'," called a voice from the opening.

Leaning on a gate post was a man of advanced years, dressed in the very hue of the soil itself, his large floppy hat, waistcoat, breeches and stockings all being a variety of browns. Only his shirt differed, being of a russet tint, and then only the sleeves were visible. On his feet were large brown boots, fastened with leather strapping.

"'Tis a noice evening for a walk."

Although the travellers didn't recognise it, the old man's cockney accent confirmed that they had landed in their intended destination.

Verde and Revin had been caught unawares; the land on their side dipped away, giving the impression that the hedgerow was taller than it actually was.

The old man would have been obscured from view even if they hadn't been concentrating on the city skyline.

For a moment both men were nonplussed. It wasn't easy to find anything to say to a seventy-year-old man who had just startled you, especially when you had been on his planet for less than an hour. Verde looked away, avoiding the man's gaze, desperately searching for something valid to say. His mind was blank; he cast his eyes around vacantly and they came to rest on a particularly thick clump of the fluffy white twine.

"My friend and I were wondering what you called this plant." Verde indicated the source of his question with an outstretched arm.

The old man laughed hollowly. It was a very unnerving laugh, as though a small metal ball were swirling round in his throat.

"You town folk are all the same, don't know nuffin'. 'Spose this plague's driven you gentry folk owt now."

The old man made a rasping sound and Verde realised he was laughing at their expense. Revin looked down at his own attire. He'd assumed his was the dress of an ordinary English yeoman, but compared to the state of the old man's clothes it was easy to see why he might think more highly of them.

"Yes, it's bad," ventured Verde, hoping the old man would take his cue. He inwardly breathed a sigh of relief as the stranger continued in his inimitable style.

"Bad, bad. Ai say, thasands dyin' every day, 'ave bin since spring, still are."

Verde and Revin were finding it hard to attune to the old man's accent, but they guessed from his wild gesticulations and compliant manner that he was approving what had been said.

"It's bad, very bad. Wheelin' 'em owt in carts and chuckin' 'em in 'oles in the grand. Look there…"

The old man swivelled somewhat nimbly for one of his age, and pointed behind him with a stout ash stick that he carried in his hand. All Revin and Verde could see was a huge pile of rich brown earth several feet high, forty feet long and half as wide.

"You gowin' back there?"

"Where?" asked Verde.

"To the walls, the tawn," prompted the old man.

"Yes, we are going to see what we can do to help."

"Carn't do nofing," said the old man with an air of resignation. "Not unless you can dig, that is," and he proceeded to laugh at his own joke.

Feeling more composed, Verde decided that it was time for their meeting to finish. At least the old man had accepted their presence without suspicion or question. Better temper the excitement, he told himself; this man appeared a little senile and there were bound to be more searching examinations ahead.

"Thank you for your help," Verde said to the old man, and he and Revin continued towards the city.

They had barely taken ten paces when the old man called out, "Stop!"

Verde's blood froze; his mind raced, weighing up the options open to them. They could run, silence the old man with a bribe or force, pretend they hadn't heard him and carry on. He was still deciding when the old man spoke again.

"You thanked me for my 'elp."

Revin gave the man a long cold stare.

"But I 'aven't 'elped you yet." He picked a bunch of the wild clematis.

"I 'ave 'eard it called old man's beard," he cackled, "and some do call it traveller's joy, but us do call it devil's guts."

Verde waved an acknowledging hand.

"Thank you," he called, "thank you," but as he walked away he wasn't quite sure who he was thanking.

"Poignant," said Revin as he drew alongside Verde.

"Explain?" queried Verde.

"For us," continued Revin, "our mission – will it be traveller's joy or are we on our way to the devil's guts?"

Continuing to embrace the hedgerow, the two men headed westwards towards the setting sun that sat like a large red ball in the purpling sky. During this time neither of them spoke. Climbing through a wooden stile they changed direction, so that once again they headed in the direction of England's capital city. Dusk was beginning to fall as they circumvented several scattered dwellings near Spittlefields. They hid in a small grove waiting for the cover of darkness before proceeding towards civilisation.

As the moon shone, two figures cautiously moved in the shadows of a row of houses that bordered the outskirts of the city walls. The men bowed their heads and narrowly avoided colliding with a man pushing an empty cart. The carter swore at them as they jumped aside; the two men looked furtively around to assess the interest that the distraction had caused. In the act of peering around they bumped into a pair of men walking towards them.

"Mind yerself," said one of the men, pushing his way clear, and he hurried to catch up with the other, who was trying his best to ignore the renewed remonstrations from the cart pusher.

"Their breath reeks," said Revin softly, staring after the two shabbily-dressed characters who had jostled them, whilst wafting his hand under his nose.

Continuing their walk, they neared the end of the row and noticed that they were being stared at by the increasing number of passers-by.

"Why are they looking at us?" asked Revin tensely. "We don't look out of place; why do they gape so?"

Verde was also perplexed but he did not want to alert his already nervous companion. He cast around in his mind for a possible solution that would not increase Revin's wariness.

"Strangers; they haven't seen us before, so they are naturally inquisitive because we are strangers."

Revin briskly dismissed the explanation. "There are thousands of people in this town; they can't all know one another. How can they single us out as strangers?" His speech was becoming more agitated and his whisperings grew louder. "They've found the ship. Somebody's found the ship or saw us leaving it!" Revin's voice rose a few octaves.

Verde was convinced of the falsity of the first point, but he couldn't totally be sure on the latter; for all of their care it was possible that somebody had seen them. No, this was impossible, he told himself; the ship was cloaked before they stepped outside, and even if their sudden appearance had been witnessed, how had their descriptions been distributed?

"No," he reassured Revin, "there'd be a commotion, a hue and cry, if anyone suspected that we were not one of them."

The street came to an end, and they turned left towards a large imposing wall. Two towers straddled an impressive gateway; they had reached the city walls, and in front of them, more than thirty feet high, stood Bishopsgate. Revin took a few steps towards the portal.

"It's closed," he muttered.

"Good," replied Verde.

Revin looked askance at his friend. Verde was pleased to supply the answer the puzzled look demanded.

"Now we know why we were being stared at. The gate's obviously closed at night, and everybody we passed knew this fact, and must have wondered why we were going towards it."

There was no option but to retrace their steps.

During the planning stages on Mykas the need to acquire money at their destination had been identified as an urgent priority, as only a few coins had been gathered by the scouts. The inoculation guns would take several weeks to immunise the population, but food, lodgings and other necessities would then be forthcoming from a grateful people. These basic needs would now have to be met through their own initiatives.

Verde had further ascertained from their conversation with the old man that their medical knowledge might be too advanced for these people and they would take a lot of convincing – assuming the others arrived with the phials intact, supposing that they arrived at all, he told himself.

CHAPTER SIX

KILL OR CURE

As Revin and Verde walked back along the street, they appeared to be the only people about. The darkness was intensified by the inability of the moonlight to shine through the overhanging roofs above them. They discussed their options; Revin favoured returning to the ship, but Verde argued for sleeping rough in the fields.

As they rounded a bend in the street they came upon a violent scene; two men – the drunks they had bumped into earlier that evening – were in the process of robbing an elderly man. The victim was already face-down in the dusty street and the two rogues were systematically kicking his body, raining in blows from either side. The crack of boot against bone and the groans emanating from the casualty convinced Verde and Revin that they must act. All thoughts of discretion and prudence evaporated at the unfairness of the scene as they rushed to the aid of the old man.

The thieves were too intent on softening up their victim to hear the advancing pair. Too late the nearest cutpurse looked up at the sound of approaching feet, and the first physical contact between Mykasian and an Earthman was made as Verde's right fist entered the villain's left eye socket. The man bent double, Verde's left foot connected with his chin and he fell backwards; the plague itself could not have laid him lower.

Simultaneously, Revin had moved to attack the robber on the far side of the writhing body. This gave the second thief a fraction of a second longer than his accomplice, and he lashed out at Revin with a wild but lucky swing. In an effort to avoid harming the man on the floor, Revin made a conscious effort to leap over the body; in so doing he took his eye off his intended victim, and received a violent kick to the groin. Revin sank to his knees gasping hard for breath. The man threw himself at Revin and pinned him to the floor, striking blows with his fists to Revin's head.

Having dealt with his man Verde looked over to his comrade; three strides took him to the melee, and a scissors blow with the back of his two hands crashed into the back of the man's neck. The brute screamed out hideously, rolling off Revin, and hauled himself to his feet once more. He charged at Verde howling. As he reached the Mykasian, Verde stood his ground and thrust one hand into the villain's open mouth; at the same time he smashed the open palm of his other hand into the robber's forehead, whilst pressing down on the man's jaw. There was a loud crack and the villain lay on his back in the kennel, unable to appreciate the beauty of the stars that twinkled in the sky above him.

By now a small crowd had gathered around the scene; judging by their attire most had ventured forth from their beds. No one actually came forward to help, perhaps being too sleepy or too apprehensive to become involved. Revin was still on his hands and knees until a helping hand from Verde assisted him to his feet.

"Breathe slowly," advised Verde. "Try and touch your toes."

Revin repeatedly bent down like a chicken pecking corn, and, seeing his friend was well on the way to recovery, Verde turned his attention to the subject of their predicament. The old man lay lifeless on the floor. Verde gently rolled him over onto his back. In the darkness his first impression was that the would-be thieves had become murderers.

A woman stepped forward from the crowd, shielding a candle in a holder, and bent down alongside Verde. The flame flickered on the old man's bruised face; under his left eye, following the contour of his cheekbone, was a gash. From his swollen and blood-stained lips came the first sign of life – a splutter and feeble cough.

A second woman pushed her way forward from the back of the crowd. A dingy shawl was draped around her shoulders to protect her from the cold night air. She bent down and offered Verde a jug of water. Verde took the container and dipped his fingers in the water, gently dripping the cool liquid on the man's lips. The woman was not impressed by his caring attitude. She snatched the jug back from Verde, and promptly stood up and poured the contents over the old man's head.

"Kill or cure!" she confidently announced to Verde, giving him a disdainfully wicked grin.

Fortunately for the drenched man the latter seemed to be the case. Revin, having made a reasonable recovery, walked over to help Verde lift the old man to his feet. As they did so the two assailants, who had been largely ignored by the crowd, rose to their feet and stumbled away into the blackness. Revin relaxed his grip.

"No, leave them," advised Verde.

He could see no advantage in pursuing the ruffians, but perhaps there would be some benefit in remaining with the throng. His second notion proved to be correct as a man, who by his attentions appeared to be the husband of the water-pourer, stepped forward.

"'Tis Old John Gatleigh, Tom's father," he announced to nobody in particular, and then, turning to Verde and Revin, "Tom'll be mighty pleased with you two gents; he's fair proud of his ol' dad."

His wife interjected. "Tom's house is the last but one in the row this side; Old John do live with 'im."

By now the crowd had largely dispersed, once they had realised that their evening's entertainment was over. The man followed the water-pourer back towards the warmth of her bed, as Verde turned his attention to John Gatleigh.

The old man was barely conscious, and his feet dragged along the road, an arm draped around a shoulder of each of his Mykasian crutches. As they walked the moon appeared from behind some clouds; its light shone through a gap in the buildings opposite, casting its beam upon a passing house. Revin could just make out a red symbol daubed on the door. He thought the sign strange, but it quickly vanished from his mind as he once again concentrated on supporting the old man. Tom's house proved to be only a further five doors away.

A light flickering from a tallow candle suggested that not all the occupants had yet taken to their beds. Revin clenched the fist of his free arm and beat three times upon the sturdy oak door. A window adjacent to the door opened, and the head of Tom Gatleigh appeared, framed as if in a portrait. The face disappeared and was followed by some shouting from within the house, and a bolt cracked back on the door.

"Dad!" he cried. "What has happened?"

"He has been attacked by rogues," answered Verde.

"I feared something was wrong when he hadn't returned," said the son. "Bring him in, bring him in. Quickly, Rebecca, quickly, Father is hurt!"

Tom ushered the trio inside. His wife was descending the stairs in answer to his summons. Her partly unfastened clothes suggested that she had been in the act of preparing for bed when the disturbance had come. Rebecca let out a gasp as the limp body of her father-in-law was placed on a large wooden table that Tom had swiftly cleared of its various pewter bowls and mugs with a swipe of his arm.

The woman bent down to open a plain wooden chest. The thin metal hinges grated in protest at this late hour's opening as the lid was flung open.

A variety of cloths and a small brown bottle were swiftly removed. Rebecca hurried over to a jug of water, soaked one of the cloths and passed it to her husband. Tom cleaned his father's face, wiping away the smears of blood and dirt. From the small earthenware bottle his wife poured a few drops of a yellowish liquid onto a cloth that she had screwed into a ball. She tenderly dabbed it around John's swollen and cut lips. Either the acrid odour or the stinging sensation had the desired effect as John showed signs of life. His eyes flickered as he coughed several times. Verde pulled the old man up, cradling him in his arms.

"What happened, Dad?" asked Tom, his voice trembling.

The old man opened his mouth to speak, but only succeeded in bringing on a further coughing fit. Blood still flowed from his injured face and Rebecca renewed her nursing.

"Not now, Tom," she said; "he needs rest."

Verde read the question in the younger man's eyes. "We were returning along the road when we saw your father being set upon by two loutish types."

"They had passed us earlier," added Revin. "Their breath stank."

"What were you about at this time of night?" asked Rebecca with a hint of suspicion in her voice.

"We were hoping to find lodgings in the city," said Verde, "but we left it too late."

Tom gritted his teeth. "I've told 'im to get back before nightfall, but the stubborn old devil will go inside the walls for his drink. I've told him we live in dangerous times, there's desperate people out there that'll stop at nothing. Not even at robbin' an 'elpless old man of a few coins."

Rebecca looked up from her nursing. "Now, Tom, it's no good blaming yourself. You can't change a habit of a lifetime, I've told 'e before. Besides, I expect these two fellows could do with a drink themselves. You haven't thanked them properly in any case."

For the first time Tom turned his attention towards the two men.

"No strangers, go, go!" he shouted, and stooped to pick up a large carving knife from the floor. He waved the weapon wildly at Verde and Revin, making to escort them out of his house.

"Tom!" yelled Rebecca, alarmed at her husband's threatening behaviour.

"Plague!" he screamed. "They may be plague carriers. We could all be dead in the morning."

"Your father would be dead right now if it wasn't for the kindness of these two gents. Now put that knife down and remember your manners."

Tom gave his wife a reproachful look as she took a step towards him.

"I assure you that we are plague-free," intervened Verde, "and never likely to suffer from it." He hoped his latter comment would defuse the situation, but Tom was not to be so easily placated.

"Be 'e a devil then?" he asked acerbically.

Verde cursed his gaffe, infuriated by the situation. How could he explain to this distraught and simple fellow that he and Revin had been inoculated on a planet many miles from here?

"I swear to you that we are not infected," he reiterated, "but we will leave if you so wish."

Tom relaxed his arm so that the knife lay at his side. "They say thems that's got it don't always know, 'til it's too late, and they just drop down dead."

Rebecca again intervened. "Tom, they've risked their lives to save your father; what right have you to act in this way?"

Tom did not answer; he placed the knife on the table and helped his father into a chair by the fireside. After assuring himself that John was on the road to recovery, he sauntered through a door and closed it behind him. Verde was unsure of Tom's actions and prepared himself for a further assault.

The room was silent apart from the soft moans of the old man. Rebecca once more bathed his wounds as the door opened and Tom came in carrying a large green jug, which he put on the table. He retraced his steps and brought back four tankards, and placed them alongside the jug. He poured the contents of the jug into the tankards; the liquid splashed noisily over the wide lip, before settling in the vessels. Tom took a drink in each hand and passed them to his two visitors. He gave another to his father and kept one for himself.

No words were exchanged but the gesture was silently acknowledged. Verde looked at Revin and lifted his drink to his mouth. He sipped distrustfully at the amber liquid. His face contorted at the unusual taste, but after the initial sip his taste buds responded favourably, and he quaffed a larger mouthful. This time his gulp had been too generous and the strong liquor took his breath away. Verde involuntarily spat out the drink, and commenced a coughing fit.

"Come, stranger, can't you take your ale?" said Tom.

"Rather strong for my taste," spluttered Verde, hoping that it was an acceptable thing to say. His host eyed him quizzically, but went to relieve his wife, who was holding John's mug to his lips.

Revin had been surprised at the omission of Rebecca from the drinking, but remembering his briefing on the treatment of females on this planet, he refrained from mentioning his concern. Instead he gave his ale due respect, so as not to repeat Verde's error.

"Good?" asked Tom.

"Very," replied Revin. He wasn't as steadfast on the point as his voice sounded, but he had no intention of upsetting their host, especially one who had proved so volatile. At the very least, thought Revin, we have made a contact, a source of information, and just possibly an ally, although he couldn't be certain on the last aspect.

Inside a quarter of an hour the old man appeared to be making a reasonable recovery. As the tankards were placed on the table, Tom thanked his guests and began to make his farewells, indicating that it was time for their departure. For the third time that evening, Verde and Revin were indebted to Rebecca for interposing.

"You mentioned that you were looking for lodgings; have you travelled far?"

The two visitors answered simultaneously.

"Yes," replied Revin.

"No," answered Verde.

Tom's ears pricked up at the contradiction. Verde once again felt the discomfort of the situation.

"We used to live on the west side of the city," he explained, "but our master's family has removed to the countryside to avoid the plague. There was no cause for us to go with them to a smaller house, so we have been dismissed from his service. We have come to this side of the city to look for work; we set out several days ago, resting overnight, so we have travelled a long way, but only a short distance today."

Verde hoped that this story would satisfy Tom. He had purposely chosen the opposite side of London; then if nobody recognised them it would not appear suspicious, and by the same token it would also explain their unfamiliarity with their present locality.

"Work's the last thing on most folk's minds," said Tom. "Most are only interested in survival."

He paused and looked thoughtfully at the pair, stroking his chin.

"Are you really that desperate for money?" He glanced knowingly at Rebecca. "It's true you've done me a good turn. I'm not without contacts in this parish. You're not fussy about the type of work, I suppose?"

Verde thought over the offer that his story had induced. They had a little Earth money, but not enough to cover the cost of an extended stay.

"No, not at all," he answered.

Rebecca had read her husband's thoughts.

"No, Tom. You can't ask them to do that."

"It's all I know of," said Tom. "How desperate are you?"

"Very, aren't we, Revin?" said Verde.

"If you say so, Verde," answered his friend, less enthusiastically.

"Verde and Revin," mused Tom. "Uncommon names, but you may rest the night on the floor. I'll attend to it in the morning."

Rebecca found them two blankets, and the family took their leave, John being helped upstairs by his son and daughter-in-law.

As the noise of their hosts above abated, Revin whispered to Verde.

"Why do you think he's changed his mind? First he tries to throw us out of his house, now he's offering us shelter. He's picked up on your blunders."

"*My* blunders? What about yours? No, I don't think he suspects anything; more likely that drink mellowed him," said Verde, feeling his forehead.

Revin hoisted himself up from under his blanket onto his elbows. "Either that or he is keen for us to have those jobs. I wonder what he has in mind. His wife didn't seem very enamoured with them. I wonder what you've let us in for."

"I'm not sure, but we will find the money useful," reasoned Verde.

"I bet it's got something to do with this plague," muttered Revin as he settled down once more. His face cracked in an ironical smile, but it was lost in the darkness; the candles had long been extinguished and the fire glowed no more.

"It's fortunate we had our inoculations before we left Mykas," whispered Verde. "Who knows how long Lutel and Rewn will be before they arrive with the medical supplies?"

"If they arrive," groaned Revin.

Verde concurred with Revin's pessimism, but he kept his thoughts to himself.

CHAPTER SEVEN

THE DISCOVERERS

It was close to midnight and Verde had drifted off to sleep. The earthen floor was cold and hard, like nothing he had experienced since their days in the Discoverers, thought Revin. He brought himself back to the time when he was seventeen years old and sleeping on a floor almost as cold as this.

It was his first night away from home, and he was in a hut in the Truloes – the highest mountain range in Mykas. The room contained nine other young men and ten young women. Prior to their graduation training all young Mykasians undertook an intensive course; 'Discoverers', they called it. It consisted of several weeks in the mountains where they were tested on a range of qualities such as survival, initiative, leadership, independence and comradeship. The Discoverers was an important phase in the life of any young and ambitious Mykasian; their performance during these weeks determined their future life cycle training. Academic ability remained the crucial passport to the future, but only the successful Discoverers could progress to the upper cycles.

He'd felt very alone that first night. Before the evening meal they had played a series of games designed to stimulate group interaction, but Revin had always been a shy and self-conscious youth and being the centre of attention, something he felt the activity demanded, was not to his liking. When the Discoverer tutors had retired to their own huts, Revin had looked around; he had been the only one awake, just like now. He remembered the torment in his mind, how he had felt the sense of isolation, yet he had been surrounded by youngsters of his own age.

The following morning he had been placed in a group led by Verde. He'd admired Verde's confidence and organisational skills. Tasks were swiftly allocated and Revin found himself paired with Verde. As they headed towards a mountain stream in search of swansling fish, the two exchanged family details and personal tastes, and found they had much in common. Unfortunately for Revin as he climbed down the bank of thc stream he slipped and turned his ankle. Verde was by his side in a flash and quickly diagnosed nothing more than a sprain. However, Revin was unable to walk and Verde decided to set off for help. Revin was engrossed in a panic attack and begged him not to go. Verde waited by his side and collected brushwood for a fire to keep them warm until help eventually arrived. Revin asked to be released from the course, but his tutors declined. He was allowed to rest his twisted ankle for several days before rejoining the group.

Revin was immediately made a group leader on his return, and an hour later was looking down a steep wet precipice. Behind him sat two of his group, chatting idly and chewing pieces of fruit to restore their energy. Halfway there, he thought, as he shouted advice on handholds to the girl fifty yards below him. Revin held the rope tightly as she competently made her way upwards, smiling as she reached the top.

For the first time, Revin felt like he was enjoying himself, but he couldn't dwell on this new feeling; there was still a final climber below. Revin peered down through the mist. The girl was rather heavy and was not making very good headway. He fired down instructions in his eagerness to succeed, but they were too rapid for the timid climber and she began to panic. Revin could see failure looming large in front of him, and his response was to shout louder and give even more ambitious instructions. His concentration waned and he slackened his grip on the rope; the flustered girl missed a foothold and plunged down the rock-face. Revin felt hot and clammy as he realised his rope was lax; the girl seemed to be falling into infinity. In fact she fell less than ten feet, as the security rope of the tutor snapped tight, quivering in the wind. The girl was lowered to safety suffering from no more than minor abrasions and shock; for Revin the scars went much deeper.

For a second time he'd asked to be released from the course, preferring to face his parents' disappointment rather than the wild elements of the Truloes Mountains, but his request met with the same response. Revin failed to see the justification for the denial, as over the next few weeks he was never appointed as group leader again.

It was near the end of their time in the mountains when he found himself in a group of young men headed by Verde. Their tutors had set them a challenging task. They were to follow a course around an area of dense woodland. Each group was responsible for packaging and carrying around thirty eggs from the hoco bird – a type of domestic fowl. They would meet several challenges as they moved around the course, which included camping out overnight. The group were allowed to eat five of their eggs; the rest must arrive back the next day unbroken. Verde confidently masterminded the egg-packaging, and after consulting the group for their advice selected items of equipment for the tasks ahead.

Their map first led them to a sparkling mountain stream. It was one of many where the snowy peaks melted and flowed to the valleys below. Verde jumped the narrow water to examine the opposite bank. His feet crushed a clump of delicate white flowers that bordered the water's edge. The air was very clear in the rarefied atmosphere and the suns shone colourfully from the purple sky. There were two markers beside the stream, one where they now stood and a further one fifty yards below them. Just before the second marker the stream dipped over a mini-waterfall. The eggs had to be transported between the markers without being carried.

A tutor stood by to assess their effort; the rest of the group muttered ideas amongst themselves. Revin stood alone gazing blankly into the cool stream. He felt a tap on his shoulder; it was Verde passing him a large synthetic bag, urging him to blow it up. Without questioning he did as he was asked. Verde placed the cargo inside the bag and tied the end; he inflated two balloons and attached them to the mouth of the bag. He whispered to Revin to lower the makeshift craft into the stream, and together they cheered the eggs home, the cushion of air protecting their descent at the waterfall. As the group made their way to the next challenge the tutor took the unusual step of signalling approval, by winking at Revin as he passed her.

Smoke billowed from the campfire as the group settled down for the evening. They had collected dell berries and pent nuts from the surrounding bushes and trees, to supplement the eggs that were boiling in a pan of water suspended above the fire. As Revin stared into the glowing embers he reflected on a successful day. He'd been trusted to carry their fragile parcel across a makeshift rope bridge, and he had offered suggestions on all the other challenges of the day. More importantly, his ideas had been seriously listened to, even if they were not always acted on.

Wevern, the last of the group to return to the campfire, had picked some fungi and cheerfully distributed it. The others questioned him on its safety, but he assured them he had previously eaten the pale bluish toadstool. Revin declined his share and endured jeering and derisory comments from the group, but he remained steadfast in his convictions.

The boiled eggs had cooled, and Verde handed them round to be peeled. He reached into his travelpack and produced a pack of salt. The good-natured banter continued as the eggs were dipped into the condiment, most on the subject of Verde's prowess as a group leader. The pent nuts were filling, their soft cases being equally edible, and the dell berries were sweet to the taste; even the mountain spring water that they'd collected tasted divine. As the purple sky deepened, they fell asleep, ready to face the final challenges of the following day. Revin felt more at ease with himself than at any other time on the Truloes.

His eyes had not long been closed when he was awoken by a terrible screaming noise. At first he could not get his bearings as he stared into the glittering midnight sky; as the cool air cleared his head he remembered where he was. Wevern lay clutching his stomach and was squealing hideously; Revin threw off his covers and dashed to his side. Wevern was unable to respond to questioning, and Revin felt a pang of panic. Other members of the group were awake, but nobody came to assist him. He could tell by the soft moaning and tortured faces that they were suffering from similar symptoms.

Revin immediately suspected the fungi; he ran over to Verde to seek his opinion, but his friend was too much in the grip of pain to give a lucid answer. Revin stood up; his first instinct was to run, but what would that achieve? He knew he would never reach help in the darkness. No, he knew why he wanted to run; he would be running away from the problem. What was he to do? He was surrounded by four poisoned youths, and he couldn't even stand the sight of his younger sister being sick. The image flashed across his mind and he immediately knew what he must do. He picked up a container and ran off into the darkness.

Verde watched him disappear with pitiful eyes; even through his pain Verde managed to shout a curse at the fleeing Revin. The group lay helpless on the mountain floor and their collective wailing disturbed the silent sky. Footsteps approached but not one of the sufferers had the strength to raise themselves up to witness Revin's return. He set down a container of water and immediately rummaged through Verde's travelpack and pulled out the small package of salt. Ripping off the lid he poured the contents into the water, stirring all the time with a small twig that he had spotted near the remains of the fire.

Verde was the first to be given the crude antidote. Revin sat his friend up and poured the salt water down his throat. Within seconds Verde retched and spewed out his evening meal. Spurred on by his success, Revin attended the rest of the group in turn. His clothes were splashed with sick, and rank vomit covered the ground around them; it had been a crude and risky cure, but he had never felt so elated in his life.

Now, on Earth, Revin looked across at the snoring Verde. They had been the closest of friends ever since that evening in the mountains, and as Revin finally closed his eyes to sleep, he couldn't help wondering how much that friendship was going to be tested and relied upon now.

Part Two

Prisoners and Friends

CHAPTER EIGHT
IT'S ALL IN THE MIND

Whilst Verde and Revin were about to unexpectedly embark on a fourth career, Lutel and Rewn woke early from their fitful sleep. Embers glowed weakly in the fireplace, yet the reek of smoke still lay heavily around the room. Lutel stood up and felt her back. She raised her arms above her head and stretched as Rewn rose groggily to his feet.

"Come on," urged Lutel, "we are leaving."

"What about the ride in the cart?" yawned Rewn. "We will never find one this early."

"I'd prefer to be our own masters," came the reply, "even if it does involve a five-mile walk."

They looked around the dark room; their suits had disappeared. A chorus of soft wheezing and snoring drifted down the staircase. As they made to leave, one of the farm dogs came up to them, wagging its tail; Rewn patted it on the head. The collie took the vacant space in front of the fire and stretched out to resume its slumbers. Rewn warily opened the door and they crept outside. Dawn was breaking on the eastern horizon, silhouetting the trees in an eerie blue darkness.

Lutel constantly checked over her shoulder as they crossed the fields to the wooden gate that they had climbed less than twelve hours earlier. The hill seemed even darker in the half-light, and the ground seemed to disappear before each succeeding downward step. It was slow going, feeling their way carefully down the steep slope, searching out footholds amongst the small grassy hummocks and tussocks that littered the hillside. Ahead of them a blue line shimmered in the fading moonlight; they crossed the stream, clambered up the small bank and paused. To their left was the site of their unplanned landing.

"Which way?" asked Rewn.

"This way," said Lutel, pointing in the opposite direction, away from the reminder of their present predicament.

"How do you know?"

"Gem said London was to the east, and we need to reach a town called Chipnumb."

"I know that," said Rewn, becoming irritated, "but how do you know we must take this path?"

Lutel looked exasperatedly at her brother. "Our way lies to the east; on this planet the sun rises in the east; we go this way," she said, flinging out an arm in the direction of the path. Rewn looked beyond her arm; the first rays of light shone on a hazel coppice that straddled the pathway before them. A rickety gate barred their way. They climbed it and stepped down onto the very path that Tilly Sharpe had trodden the previous evening. The track was just wide enough to allow for the passage of a cart, and in places there were ruts that attested to its being well used. A few small rogue alders were scattered amongst the nut trees, suggesting that the coppicing had lapsed a little in recent years.

Teasels bordered the path, their prickly flower heads growing as high as eye level. Ripe hazelnuts dangled as they passed under a tree; Rewn automatically reached up and picked a cluster. He offered some to Lutel and popped one into his mouth. His teeth met with resistance and he instantly withdrew it. Rewn scoured the ground around him, eagerly bent down and seized a large stone. He placed the nut in the centre of the track and lifted up the rock to strike. His first blow failed to inflict any damage on the shell as the nut shot across the woodland floor. Rewn scrabbled around on all fours, searching in the gloom until he located the nut. Again he raised the rock high above his head and smashed it hard into the nut. Splinters of shell flew everywhere, but such was the force that the kernel was splattered beyond consumption. Rewn made to reach for another nut.

"Leave it," ordered Lutel.

"I'm hungry," he complained.

"We have no time to hang around. I would prefer to put as much distance between ourselves and this place as possible."

Rewn dropped his rock and followed Lutel along the winding path. The land to the left of them rose sharply; a single row of spindly hazel trees lined the route on this side. They were laced in the white conical threads and silky whiskers of wild clematis. The saplings were untouched and obviously not part of the coppicing cycle. Beyond the saplings was dense woodland of oak, ash and rowan. In contrast the land to the right of the pathway fell away until it reached a pasture below. The row of trees that lined this side was thicker and predominantly hazel; those closest to them showed evidence of recent coppicing, their stumps being cut just above ground level. As they walked further into the wood the size of the trees on this side successively increased.

The dawn chorus, a sweet mixture of musical notes and chords, heralded the growing daylight. Through a break in the trees, Rewn could see a colony of rabbits in the field below, scuttling around, as yet unaware of their presence. The canopy overhead thickened as they approached a mature grove and the path widened into a dirt track, doubling in size. Twigs cracked underfoot; their way was littered with white chalky stones which could also be seen mingling in the bank to their left. Rewn noticed a pile of sandy clay-coloured soil spilling onto the track in front of them. He paused; his nostrils twitched at the musky smell of foxes permeating from the earth's entrance. The smell was familiar; somewhere back on Mykas he had smelt it before, but exactly where he couldn't remember.

A loud flapping of wings startled him from his reverie as a pigeon flew from the trees above. In front of them the sun peeked through the hedgerow, shining brightly on the backs of a herd of reddish-brown bullocks grazing in a field ahead.

At the end of the wood they approached another gate. A short distance beyond, a narrow band of thicket dissected the length of the field; to the right of the brake grazed the bullocks. Lutel paused at the gate and looked around. Before the thicket lay a disused badger sett covered in nettles. There was no sign of human life, but the inquisitive cattle had started to move in their direction.

"What shall we do?" asked Lutel, eyeing the narrowing gap between themselves and the herd.

"Follow me," said Rewn. He vaulted the gate and strode purposefully towards the thicket. Lutel followed him, glancing anxiously over her shoulder. They had similar beasts on Mykas, but none quite like this, and she was not prepared to ascertain their domesticity. The blackberry bushes and mixture of small trees were too dense to allow any passage through them, so they skirted around to the far side.

"Don't look back," advised Rewn rather belatedly. "If we ignore them, they may well leave us alone."

"Too late," answered Lutel, increasing her pace to a brisk walk and drawing alongside her brother. A noise came from behind them, and without stopping to look they both broke out into a run. Lutel could almost hear her heart thumping. Her body was sweating inside her recently acquired clothes and she found the boots pinched as she ran. Rewn appeared to be suffering less and he was several strides in front of her. Lutel imagined she could hear the thumping of the hooves close behind. She couldn't be certain whether they were directly behind her or running alongside them on the other side of the thicket. All noises were muffled by the snapping of twigs as she ran and the pounding in her ears as her whole body throbbed at this cumbersome running. Bushes and trees merged into a green blur as she raced alongside them.

After running hard for over a hundred yards a gap suddenly appeared in the thicket; Rewn dived through it, confusing Lutel. She was certain the bullocks were on the opposite side and didn't fancy meeting them, yet they might be behind her. She decided wherever the cattle were she would rather face them with Rewn. Lutel glanced behind to make sure she had made the right decision and crashed into Rewn, who had stopped on the bottom path. Brother and sister lay sprawled and winded on the ground just a few yards away from the safety of another gate. Lutel pulled herself up on to her hands and knees and looked back down the line of the thicket. The bullocks were still grazing at the far end of the field; she struggled to her feet, laughing. Rewn was initially puzzled by her merriment, but when he followed her gaze, he joined in the laughter.

"The mind can still play funny tricks," said Lutel.

"Even more so on a distant planet," he answered.

Viewing the cattle in a benevolent light they looked back across the field whilst climbing over the gate. Their way now lay upon an open track bordered by wide margins of grassland that in turn made way for woodland on either side. Purple thistles and brown teasels mingled with yellow coltsfoot as they walked along the grassy path. A short walk soon brought them to another gate, and this time to a wide open field. Rewn paused and looked ironically at Lutel. The pathway followed a hedgerow directly in front of them, but to their right the land rose sharply, and on the crest of the hill was the subject of his amusement.

"It's all in the mind," said Rewn.

"I know, but once bitten, twice shy," she replied.

"Do you really want to turn back?" he offered.

Lutel mused; it had been an imagined danger, and to retrace their steps now would be a pointless exercise, fruitless in fact. She jumped over the five-barred gate.

"Come on then," she called to Rewn, but her voice carried an air of apprehension rather than confidence.

Cows grazed on the hill; their udders were heavy and awaited milking. They posed little threat to the two travellers, but Lutel's senses remained keen. She jumped as the silence was shattered by a hissing sound from the hillside above – her raw nerves stretched by a cow urinating. She eyed the stone wall to her left, gaining comfort from its height. If it became necessary she was certain that she could scale it, and it would prove too large a barrier for any charging cow. The wall was soon bordered by trees and hedgerow; long-tailed tits flitted from branch to branch, their plumage gleaming as they searched for berries.

As they quickened their pace inquisitive cows stopped grazing to stare down on them, but to Lutel's relief the cattle showed no real interest in them. Grass in the field had been cropped short; only a line of thistles at the foot of the hill had been left undisturbed, marking the boundary of the hillside and low pasture. Morning was becoming warmer and flies buzzed noisily around their heads. The sun shone on the white tail of a rabbit as it made its escape in front of them, disappearing into the hedgerow where a silver birch shimmered.

Rewn paused to look around. "It's so peaceful," he said to Lutel.

"Yes, it seems a million miles from where we are supposed to be."

"Do you mean Mykas or London?" asked Rewn.

She didn't answer; she was breathing in the sweet smells of the country filling her nostrils and lungs with perfumed fragrances, aromas that she had never before experienced, scents she could neither name nor picture.

The tearing of the grass by the grazing herd was amplified by the surrounding peace. Rewn followed her gaze. "At least they're not chewing us," he joked.

Lutel smiled back. Rewn seemed well in control now, his disposition more calm, more collected. She needed that; they were a long way from home and a fair way from London. She needed to concentrate her energies on finding a solution to their problems. A well-balanced Rewn would be a vital help, not the distraction he had threatened to be.

Climbing a further gate they left the pastures and cattle behind them. The track now narrowed, bordered on both sides by a tall hedgerow. A small brown-and-white mongrel dog came towards them, wagging its tail. A few steps more revealed a farmyard to the left of the track. The farm dog seemed unusually friendly, sniffing at Lutel's feet and accepting her patting and stroking. Lutel was puzzled by the lack of activity around the house or yard.

"Home, boy, home," ordered Rewn as the tail-wagging dog followed them across a small parcel of open land, bordered by hedgerow. The pathway ran through the centre of the land. Lutel felt exposed; she looked around for signs of trouble. A pigeon launched itself from a treetop, the beating of its wings surprised her, but it was the sole evidence of life in their vicinity.

It took them less than a minute to hurry across the exposed area. A wooden stile barred their way and when they had climbed over they found themselves standing on the deserted track that linked the villages of Castle Combe and Yatton Keynell. The dog poked its head through the bars, its pink tongue lolling from the side of its mouth.

"I said home," commanded Rewn. The mongrel cocked its head on one side, gave a small whine and scampered back down the path.

"This way?" asked Rewn, pointing to the right.

Lutel nodded. "Yes, the Varleys said Chipnumb was to the east, so we must head in this direction," she confirmed.

It had been just under an hour since they'd left the Varleys' farm. Ahead of them lay the tiny hamlet of Kent's Bottom; it contained no more than six slate-roofed cottages built of brown stone. To their left they could hear voices and swishing sounds. Rewn clambered up the verge and peered over the top of the hedgerow. A row of men were cutting corn with large sickles; some distance behind them walked a further row of gleaners, consisting entirely of women and children.

"Explains why nobody was about," he called down to Lutel. "They're all out harvesting."

The word evoked strong images in Lutel's mind. She remembered how as a child she would spend rest periods on her cousins' farm. The children would climb the orchard trees and pick the purple and golden fruits. Lutel could see the smooth velvety skin and feel the pulpy delicate fruits in her hand. The laughing and screaming as they stretched out their arms to the gatherers below, passing the fruit to be stored in large baskets. She saw in the distant mountains the large machines employed to gather in the staple crops.

Lutel closed her eyes and breathed in the fruitiness of those halcyon days. Rewn's jumping down and landing heavily beside her brought her back to the stark reality of their present position. She ran to keep up with him as he was already several feet down the road.

The first sign of the impending village of Yatton Keynell stood in the distance; towering in the skyline amongst the treetops was a tall Tudor chimney. Hazel trees still dominated the hedgerow, punctuated by the occasional mature ash tree.

A dry stone wall, covered in red and green blackberries, ran along the right-hand side as they entered the outskirts of the village. In front of them lay a farm, and partly masked by one of its larger barns stood a four-pinnacle church tower. To their left ran a series of farm buildings, their walls built flush to the road. The outhouses and barns were joined together in a long line, roofs staggered at a variety of heights. Large chalk stones were the dominating feature of the buildings, culminating in a small farmhouse set at a crossroad. A disproportionately large chimney adorned its steep-pitched roof; this was the sentinel that they had spied from afar. It had sat for years amongst the mottled, weather-beaten slates, watching passers-by trudge the roads to Grittleton or Castle Combe.

Lutel turned right, hugging the wall, into the village of Yatton Keynell. On the opposite side of the road they passed two cottages and an inn. They walked beneath the farm wall; at irregular intervals a barn or other outhouse would utilise the wall, encompassing it as a fourth side. Mosses grew from the slates of these buildings; even a small lavender bush had found the conditions between two slates acceptable for its wellbeing. Lutel stopped outside the entrance to Church Farm. Ahead of them lay the road to Chippenham; two further tracks branched off to the right, one to the village of Biddestone and the other to the hamlet of West Yatton.

They crossed the West Yatton track to sit on a grassy bank, with their backs against the ivy-clad walls that enclosed the Church of Saint Margaret whence the farm had derived its name. Warm sunshine beat down from the sky, but they were afforded some shade by a towering yew tree that grew just inside the church grounds. Behind them stood the parish church, its sloping red-tiled roof shielded from the sun by two lofty elms that also guarded a wooden gate. Four small spires reached out towards the sky, stretching for the warming sunshine.

Lutel stared ahead into the farm entrance. The yard was thick with muck, and although there was very little breeze the smell of ripe cow dung was inescapable. Low buildings to the left housed noisy squealing piglets; beyond lay the large hay barn that had earlier masked the church. It was near empty, waiting to be replenished by this harvest's endeavours.

The farmhouse stood impressively before them, its clean stone walls in stark contrast to the adjoining yard. Lutel's gaze returned to the farm entrance; straw lay in the road, blown by previous winds. She stared at the yellow dandelions that grew on her grassy-knolled seat. Her attention was drawn to the rumbling of cart wheels. She climbed onto the church wall for a better view. Peering through the trees, her eyes strained to see along the track from West Yatton. The squeaking of the cart wheels grew closer. Lutel stood on tiptoe, gripping a branch to keep her balance. An open wagon trundled into view; its driver was a youth in his late teens.

"It's only a boy on a cart," she announced to the expectant Rewn, "but we may as well be on our way; you never know."

CHAPTER NINE

YOUNG MICHAEL

Lutel led the way towards the main track which would once more put them on the road to Chippenham. They had travelled only a few yards when the cart drew alongside them. The driver reined in the dapple-grey mare in order to match their pace.

"Be you'm Rune and Lootel?" asked the youth. "Gem Varley did say you'm be wantin' a ride to Chipnumb."

Lutel and Rewn stopped walking and turned to face the driver.

"Oi'm goin' to Chipnumb to fetch our Flo 'ome. Gem said I might see 'ee on the way." The youth recognised the hesitancy in the two travellers. "Molly's sent 'ee some breakfast." He held up a bundle of food wrapped in a yellowing cloth. The pangs of hunger were gnawing at Rewn, and he put a foot onto one of the spokes of the large wooden wheels and hauled himself into the back of the cart.

"I'm young Michael, old Michael's son. We farm next to the Varleys," announced the youth by way of introduction, before handing over the food package. Rewn held out an arm to Lutel; she looked around the deserted village. Rewn gripped her hand encouragingly and pulled her up.

Lutel examined the youth. His pale scrofulous complexion contrasted awkwardly with his raven-black hair, which was parted in the middle; his tresses curled and waved naturally from the division. Young Michael did not epitomise the archetypal farm worker of the period, lacking the healthy sun-burnt complexion and glowing cheeks characteristic of the outdoor life that his occupation demanded. His spindly physique suggested that he might also find difficulty with the strenuous labours of the farm.

Rewn unwrapped the piece of cloth to reveal a hunk of carter's bread. He glanced at Lutel for guidance, but she was still studying their driver. He tore the food in half and offered her a piece; she took it and gingerly nibbled the dark brown crust. Rewn took a large bite and then, after several chews, wolfed the sparse meal down.

"There's a flagon of ale in the back," Michael called over his shoulder.

The cart began to slow down and Lutel quickly knelt up to establish the reason. In front of them was a stout yokel, whose large round bucolic face glowed bright red.

"Mornin', Young Michael. Where be 'ee goin' so broight an' early?"

"To fetch me sister," came the reply, "I'm takin' these folks to Chipnumb, as a favour to Gem Varley."

Although she couldn't be certain, Lutel thought she saw Young Michael wink as he mentioned his sister. She shuffled uncomfortably in her seat, but before she could deduce any further signals Young Michael whipped the mare, and they pulled away from the yokel. Lutel looked back at a stone set into the wall of one of the cottages. It read "97 miles to Hyde Park Corner".

Slowly the cart rumbled out of the village, the uneven track giving them an uncomfortable ride. Lutel reflected on what she thought she had just seen and looked across to Rewn, but he was too engrossed in his breakfast. The cart slowed to a sluggish pace, it was going to be a long time she thought before they met up with Verde and Revin. A magpie chattered from the top of an elm tree. Young Michael's right hand released its grip on the reins and flew up to his forehead.

"Always salute the magpie," he said. He glanced around at his passengers and noticed the puzzled look on their faces. "Why, you must know it stops the bad luck and brings the good?"

"Yes... yes, of course," mumbled Lutel unconvincingly, and she raised an arm in salute.

The grey mare plodded on, her blinkered view of the track denying her the wide observation of the countryside that was afforded to her passengers. A yellowhammer, with its golden head and beady eyes, looked down at them from a blackthorn hedge, cheeping its repetitive song.

"'Spect 'ee could do with some of that," said their driver.

"With what?" asked Lutel hesitantly.

"The 'ammer's song. *A little bit of bread and noooo cheese*," he replied, drawing out the "no", much as the bird had intoned.

"We are quite full, thank you," answered Lutel. "Molly's meal was most filling."

It wasn't true, but she was a little uneasy about the course that his conversation had taken. The youth turned around and faced the road; a thin smile broke onto his lips.

The cart drifted steadily on, their ride becoming increasingly bumpy due to the prolonged sunny spell having hardened the winter's tracks. As the wooden wheels crossed from one set of ruts to another or swerved to avoid the potholes, the passengers were jostled from side to side.

Lutel and Rewn travelled largely in silence, being unwilling to engage in any form of communication that might prove to be their undoing. Acutely aware of their ignorance of the local customs that Young Michael was employing as his only means of conversation, they limited themselves to grunts and "oh"s in an attempt to reduce any suspicions they feared he may already harbour. As a consequence, Young Michael largely conducted a monologue throughout the remainder of their journey.

"They do call this place Tiddlywinks," he explained, as they passed a handful of grey stone cottages. An old man stood in the doorway of the last cottage, and the youth raised his arm in acknowledgement. The old man reciprocated by taking his clay pipe from his mouth and pointing its stem towards the passengers. Young Michael appeared to nod. No words were spoken, only knowing exchange. Lutel fidgeted in her seat, and kicked Rewn's foot to gain his attention. She mouthed her concerns across the cart.

"It's all in your mind," he whispered. "He's just a simple lad making friendly conversation. What harm could he do to the two of us?"

As the cart turned sharp left at the junction of the London to Bristol road, Lutel tried to convince herself that her brother was right.

"That be Chipnumb in the distance," drawled Michael, pointing straight ahead. "'Tis only a mile or so away now."

Rewn and Lutel swivelled around to look over Michael's shoulders. On the horizon they could see a few wisps of smoke, two church towers and some grey slate roofs. Beyond the town, stretching into the far-off hills was the Royal Forest of Pewsham.

On the outskirts of the town more country dwellers appeared beside them. In front of an off-white, dome-shaped building stood a short rotund middle-aged man, with broad shoulders. He stared silently at the cart. The greatcoat spread across his back gave him a similar appearance to that of his dwelling. Again Lutel shifted uncomfortably in her seat, her mind racing over the last few hours.

Their arrival at the Varleys' farm may have aroused suspicion, their story of being plague doctors may not have been convincing, but surely their means of arrival and their forced landing were far beyond the parochial comprehension of these people. Besides, of what could they be accused? They had come as missionaries, not invaders. They couldn't be charged with anything, she told herself, so why was she still having these doubts? She stared at the man; he had been watching her, and he instantly looked away as she made eye contact. Rewn noticed the agitation in her face and leant forward to place his hands on hers.

"It's all right," he mouthed reassuringly.

"Be careful," she whispered.

Rewn sat back thoughtfully, musing over Lutel's worries as the cart continued its journey. At the end of his contemplation he still failed to share his sister's concerns. All in her mind, he told himself, lots of nervous energy, she'd always suffered from it. Yet Lutel possessed an intuition that he knew he lacked, so it wouldn't hurt to be on his guard; after all, he had been on this planet for less than twenty-four hours, and he wasn't used to all the quirks and customs. Whatever research and training he'd undertaken on Mykas, nothing could prepare you for the real thing. Still, he wasn't convinced of their being in any imminent danger.

In the centre of Chippenham a wooden bridge permitted its townsfolk to safely cross the Avon. Rewn stared down at the clear water below, whilst Lutel looked around warily. Rats scurried boldly through a pile of rubbish that had been thrown upon the bankside. Lutel's eyes were drawn to a beautiful wooden mill that stood beside the river. To the side of the mill stood a smart-looking maroon wagon. A man stood on its bed, receiving sacks of flour from two loaders. On the side of the cart, written in gold lettering were the words "Harcourt and Daughter – Deliverers". A nagging thought that had been lurking in the depths of Lutel's mind rose to the surface.

Michael was a delivery boy! He was taking her and Rewn somewhere to deliver them. All along he'd kept them entertained with snippets of information, teasing them, testing them, trying them out to see what they knew, looking to catch them off guard, but in a subtle, non-confrontational way. He'd been at pains not to startle or alert them but Lutel had seen the surreptitious wink and nod, besides his idle chatter also suggested he was at pains to avoid any confrontation.

Rewn noticed the change in countenance on his sister's face, the colour draining from her cheeks. He drew in his legs and placed his hands on the bed of the cart. Lutel, realising that he was preparing to jump, shook her head and cupped her hands to her mouth to shield her voice from Michael.

"We mustn't play into their hands," she said. "We've done nothing outside the law."

"What about the ship?" mouthed Rewn.

"Way beyond their comprehension," came the reply.

Young Michael turned around. "You'm oright?" he shouted.

"Fine," replied Rewn.

Michael smiled to himself, "Nearly there."

The cart rolled slowly up the slight incline of the high street; on both sides stood high buildings. Rewn, alerted by Lutel's agitation, saw danger in the face of every passer-by. Lutel too scrutinised each face that watched them from the street below or from the windows above. At the end of the High Street Michael pulled up in the Market Square.

Lutel and Rewn jumped down from the cart.

"'The Bear', serves the best ale around here," said Young Michael.

He directed them to a sandy-coloured inn.

"Thank you," answered Rewn, standing his ground.

Young Michael looked perturbed. "Take my word for it. 'The Bear's' your best bet for food and drink."

"We will return here after we have stretched our legs, they are stiff from the ride," said Rewn.

Young Michael appeared satisfied and excused himself on the pretext of meeting his sister. Rewn and Lutel looked around the square. It was an impressive mixture of fine houses, shops and taverns. On one side stood a butchers' shambles, already a hive of activity. Men scampered along with the carcasses of pigs draped over their shoulders. Poultry and game were hanging from hooks in archways, the whole area being dedicated to the meat trade. Butchers called to one another or swore at small boys who milled around the stall keepers undertaking a variety of errands or tasks.

Once Michael had left them, Rewn tackled Lutel about her fears.

"You have me worried now," he said. "Let's move on to London right now, leave this place behind us."

"They have nothing to charge us with," she said, "but I do believe they are suspicious."

"Then let's go," pleaded Rewn.

"No." She looked down at the cobblestones, and then raised her eyes to stare him straight in the face. "To run would be an admission of guilt. Besides, we need to travel by some kind of horsepower. Walking will take us far too long and Verde and Revin may not wait."

"But what about the driver?" asked Rewn.

"I'm sure that we can handle him," said Lutel. "Let's hope that we have heard the last of him in any case."

"Supposing he's talking to the authorities at this moment," argued Rewn.

"What can he tell them? It will be all supposition or superstition."

"He knows that we are unfamiliar with the lore of the country," said her brother.

"Well, that's hardly a crime."

"But it's indicative…"

Lutel ended the discussion by walking towards the sandy-coloured tavern. The frontage contained more windows than brick and on its upper floor was a balustrade on which stood a large stone bear, negating any need for a signboard. Patrons of the tavern could not fail to notice that they were entering the Bear Inn.

Rewn put a restraining hand on Lutel's arm. "Michael suggested that we come here. Let's see what else this town has to offer, just to be on the safe side," he said.

CHAPTER TEN

WOODMAN, JOHN WOODMAN

They walked out of the marketplace towards an imposing black-and-white timbered building. Across the road stood the parish church of Saint Andrew; Rewn gazed up at its tall grey spire, and in the act of staring collided with a middle-aged man. The stranger was of a lighter build than Rewn, and the swiftness of his stride had resulted in the local ending up on his backside in the middle of the dusty road.

Rewn croaked a startled, "Sorry, friend."

"No, no, my fault entirely," apologised the recumbent man.

Rewn placed his large right hand under the man's armpit and hauled him to his feet. He dusted down the stranger's tattered garb; it was threadbare and grubby, suggesting that he worked on the land. The only item of quality on him was a red kerchief that was tied loosely around his neck. The man appeared to be suffering from nothing more than a severe winding, and bent over to catch his breath.

"Perhaps you would escort me to the inn?" he asked, pointing.

Lutel shifted uncomfortably and put a restraining arm on Rewn, but he did not heed it as he felt that he had genuinely bumped into the man. Rewn supported the stranger across the road that bordered the market square. They headed towards a building in the direction of the church. Lutel followed, her eyes furtively casting around for anything out of the ordinary. Rewn and the local had already passed through the doorway when she reached their destination; she marvelled at his gullibility as she stopped outside to read the sign above the door, which informed her she was about to enter the Lyon Inn.

Rewn had sat the stranger at an empty table; as she approached them, Lutel could see the signs of embarrassment on Rewn's face. She realised that she too would be unable to offer the stranger a drink for his troubles, but her thoughts were averted from their lack of money by other matters. The inn was crowded with farmers and other local tradesman and she appeared to be the only woman. The odd glance had already been cast at her, and she was still sensitive from their time at the farmhouse and more so from their journey on the cart. Michael would soon come to hear of her presence in the inn, she thought. Lutel constantly eyed the door, half-expecting Michael, Gem or the authorities to walk through it. She was awoken from her reverie by Rewn calling her.

"Lutel, Lutel. What would you like to drink?"

Rewn had so startled her that she did not at first comprehend.

"John is offering us a drink," explained Rewn, gesturing at the man he had knocked over.

During Lutel's daydreaming the stranger had recovered his composure and had offered Rewn a drink to reward him for his assistance. The latter had gratefully accepted, as in the first place he was thirsty and in the second it relieved him of his financial embarrassment.

Before Lutel could reply two mugs of ale arrived in the hands of John. Rewn accepted both drinks, and handed one to Lutel.

"Lutel, this is my good friend John."

"Woodman, John Woodman at your service, ma'am," put in the stranger.

The three retired to a table near the window, Lutel making sure that she had a view of the marketplace and the doorway. She felt uncomfortable that her back was to the assembly inside the inn, and although Rewn sat opposite she was concerned that he seemed to be paying more attention to his drink and his newfound companion.

"Where are you from, John?" asked Rewn.

"I work on the land in Kellaways," replied Woodman, "but I come to Chippenham most market days."

"Is your town far away?" asked Rewn.

Woodman laughed. "I can tell you don't come from round these parts. Kellaways is no more than a collection of houses, about four mile away. Though it's connected to Chippenham by a lovely stone path, courtesy of the Lady Maud."

Rewn blanched at his childlike mistake; in contrast, Lutel's hue had reddened. In order to avoid her admonition Rewn supped on his ale and Woodman did likewise, and the awkward moment seemed to pass. Lutel was less than pleased when Rewn continued the conversation.

"We come from London," he lied, "and we are on our way back there now."

Woodman looked quizzically at Rewn, and Lutel braced herself in her chair.

"Why, are you mad?" asked Woodman. "London's full of plague."

"We know," said Lutel, eager to take control of the conversation. "We are going to help the sick."

"Then you are mad," chortled Woodman, "or else you are quacks, 'cause there is no cure for the pestilence."

He wiped his top lip with the back of his hand to remove some ale, and drew forward in his chair to speak with authority. "Take my word for it, most people be leavin' London, not going towards it."

He sat back in his high-backed chair to await their reply. Lutel's response was not what he had expected.

"Can you tell us how we can reach London?"

"A stagecoach leaves tomorrow morning," said Woodman, ignoring the rebuff.

Rewn's mind returned to their money problem. He drew his head towards Woodman, to speak in confidence. Woodman reciprocated.

"John," whispered Rewn, "we are temporarily without funds; we have money in London, but we have none with us now."

"Can't you sell something?" asked Woodman.

"But we have nothing of worth," replied Rewn despondently.

Lutel squirmed as Woodman looked around the room, but he merely laughed and reached out towards a ring on Rewn's finger.

"You call that nothing of worth! Why, I'll wager that would fetch several guineas," he said, reaching out and cradling the little finger on Rewn's left hand.

Rewn jealously removed the ring from his grasp, and stared at it fondly. After a few seconds' pause he transferred his gaze to Woodman.

"Can you sell it for us?" he asked.

Lutel realised the sacrifice that her brother was making; her recent hostility towards him melted. Rewn ruefully removed the bespangled ring. It had been given to him by his parents on the occasion of his hundredth birthday. Fittingly, Woodman removed his neckerchief and wrapped the precious gift inside it. He picked up his mug and swallowed the remaining ale, then slammed the empty tankard down on the table.

Lutel looked around uneasily to see if the transaction and subsequent noise had aroused any interest from the inmates of the tavern. Most seemed engrossed in their drinking or smoking and she looked back with a sense of relief.

"I'll be back as soon as I can," slurred Woodman, and he stood up to take his leave.

"Where will we meet you?" asked Lutel.

"Tell you what, I'll pay for you to have a room, or two if you prefer; you can pay me back from the sale of the ring. You can even have a bite to eat and perhaps a few drinks." This latter offer was accompanied by a wink to Rewn.

"Two rooms, please, but how do we know you will not keep the ring for your own purposes?" challenged Lutel. Rewn might not be thinking clearly, but she was not prepared to let this comparative stranger walk out with their most valuable possession.

"You have my word," Woodman assured her. Before Lutel could ask how reliable that might prove he had departed to seek out the landlord and make the necessary arrangements.

Lutel bent forward, penetrating the smog that hovered around their heads, and mouthed at Rewn, "How can we trust him?"

"We can't, but we have little choice; we need money for our journey."

At that moment a rotund, red-faced man approached their table. Lutel shifted in her chair, coiling like a spring.

"Your rooms are available, up the stairs and the second and third doors on the right. Would you like to retire now or may I fetch you more drinks?" The taverner spoke in a booming but jolly voice. Alner Brickthwaite welcomed all travellers to his inn in this manner, but especially those who had paid in advance.

"May we have something to eat?" queried Lutel.

"My wife will be more than pleased to oblige you," he said. "There is a very tasty herring pie available, though I say so myself." The landlord patted his ample stomach as if in testament to his wife's cooking.

"May we eat in our rooms?" asked Lutel.

It was an unusual request. Their host stroked his double chin; his large apple-cheeked face contorted as he considered the likely response the request would extract from his wife. Rewn and Lutel mistakenly assumed the beads of sweat were the result of a busy day. Finally after much soul searching came the reply.

"Yes, if you so wish. I am sure that will be in order," replied the landlord. He wasn't at all sure it would be with the cook, but as he had Woodman's money in his pocket, he was loath to risk returning it, preferring to risk the wrath of his wife. "What will you have to drink?" he asked, going the whole hog.

"Whatever you suggest," said Lutel with a smile.

“Very well,” replied Brickthwaite, becoming agitated once more. He had never been asked to take on the responsibility of recommending a drink at meal times.

The landlord made to depart and Rewn and Lutel made their way to the staircase.

“Have you no luggage?” enquired the landlord.

“No, we have all we need,” Rewn assured him.

“Very well,” replied their host, and he returned to his duties.

As they climbed the polished staircase, a buxom girl in her mid-teens approached them from behind.

“My father says I’m to show you to your rooms.” She spoke softly and in the dialect of the area, particularly rolling her Rs. They followed her up the remainder of the oaken staircase.

At the top of the stairs they paused; a familiar personage had just entered the Lyon Inn. The figure was accompanied by a tall man, who bore both the appearance and the posture of a body of some importance; in his hand he carried a bundle of white shiny material. Lutel and Rewn drew closer to the shadows of the wall. There was no mistaking Young Michael; he scoured the assembled gathering below before turning to the other man and shaking his head. Henry Lambert, the bailiff of Chippenham, turned on his heels and departed as swiftly as he had entered, followed by a disgruntled Young Michael.

The landlord’s daughter had continued her journey to their rooms and had missed the agitation on the faces of her guests. She opened a bedroom door, and Lutel and Rewn swept noiselessly past her.

“Anything you require, please ask. The other room is next door,” the girl said, pointing. Her composure belied her tender fourteen years, and it was difficult to see any resemblance this slim and attractive figure bore to her portly father. Her hair was clean and lustrous, and tied neatly in bunches on either side of her head. Two cerise ribbons complemented the jet-black locks.

“It’s very kind of you,” said Lutel. “What are you called?”

“Daisy,” said the girl, curtsying and taking her leave.

As the door was pulled closed Lutel confronted Rewn.

“Did you see them, Rewn?” she asked in a hoarse whisper. “They were looking for us.”

“We can’t be certain of that.”

Before Lutel could contradict him there was a knock on the door. The two of them froze; they were trapped in the room, and had only a vague idea of the geography of the building and surrounding area.

"What do we do?" said Rewn, rushing to the window.

The door slowly opened to reveal the landlord's daughter.

"I forgot to say, Ma will be up shortly, with your drinks and a bite to eat." She spoke in a meek and apologetic voice.

"That will be much appreciated, Daisy," said Lutel with a sigh of relief that was lost on the girl.

"We must leave," Rewn whispered when the door had closed, ignoring his hunger pangs in favour of those of another kind.

"No, Rewn, we must stay," said Lutel. "We must reach London as soon as possible, which means we must be on that coach tomorrow. We have all we need, and can stay in this room until Woodman returns."

Rewn wrung his hands and continued to see devils in every stranger that passed below. The shock of seeing Young Michael and his unknown companion had brought a change in mood; the signs were clear to Lutel if not to her brother. She realised it was up to her to ease his anxieties.

"Even if they are looking for us, they haven't found us yet. If they do find us, what can they do? We have done nothing wrong, and they can have no comprehension of space travel."

"We are strangers," said Rewn. "That will be good enough for some people. Look at those villagers we first met; I'm surprised they didn't accuse us of witchcraft and burn us."

The thin lines on Lutel's forehead became a fraction more pronounced.

"Rewn, you are not suggesting that we cannot outwit these simple folk?" she teased him.

The appeal to his vanity appeared to have the desired effect as Rewn sat down on one of a pair of chairs in the corner of the room.

Lutel was just congratulating herself when a second knock on the door had Rewn leaping to his feet. His uneasiness was affecting her and she found herself drawn towards the mullioned window. A measured second knock followed. Lutel discerned that such patience did not heed danger; she crossed the room and opened the door. The figure of Beth, the landlord's wife, walked in with a tray full of food and a jug of ale.

"Will you both be eatin' in this room, sir?" asked Beth, ignoring Lutel.

"We will," said Rewn, eyeing the mouth-watering pie. Beth snorted as she placed her tray on a small table, then bustled out of the room without saying another word. Rewn and Lutel sat down on the edge of the bed and tucked into the herring pie.

“It’s good,” mumbled Rewn through a mouthful of food.

“What do you think is in it?” asked Lutel less enthusiastically.

“Don’t know,” garbled Rewn, wiping a candied pastry flake from his lips.

Lutel blanched at the tangy flavour, evoked by a mixture of red wine, vinegar and cinnamon. She sat back on her bed, her pewter plate half empty. Rewn reached over for her plate and asked with his eyes. He ravenously devoured her leftovers and, whilst chewing on a tasty morsel of date, walked over to the table and poured them both a drink of the rich brown ale that was a speciality of the Lyon Inn. Rewn belched loudly as he emptied his tankard, and settled back on the bed to consider their position.

CHAPTER ELEVEN

THE BLINDROOM

Tallow light flickered on the walls, casting an uneasy shadow as Rewn paced restlessly around the room. His tranquil mood had dissipated as the effects of the ale had worn off. Lutel sat back in her chair, resigned to her brother's restiveness. She called him to sit down and reluctantly he did on the edge of the bed.

"We must stay calm," she whispered in a soothing voice. "This time tomorrow we could be midway to London."

"If Woodman doesn't return with some money, we won't be going anywhere," he muttered, frowning.

"Is that all that's bothering you?" she asked. "I thought you were worried about being discovered and captured."

Rewn looked at his sister; she painted a composed and glowing picture in the half-light, and he silently thanked her for it.

"It's not the end if friend Woodman doesn't appear," she said. "There's always another way."

"You said something similar at the farmhouse," said Rewn with a smile.

"Did I?" she said evasively.

"Yes, something about skinning a rat. What did you mean?"

Lutel had intended to keep her ideas to herself for a little longer. She needed more time to formulate her notion and to examine the consequences, but she decided it might be worth sharing her thoughts with Rewn, hoping it would relieve his fretting.

Rewn recommenced his pacing of the room. "Go on; what did you mean when you said there were alternatives to the inoculations? What else can we do?"

His voice had grown louder and more urgent. Lutel decided it would be appropriate to take his mind off the present position.

"You must see there is no way that we can educate these people. Our briefings were wrong. They relied too much on forecasting and guesswork. Even if we hadn't lost the phials, their culture wouldn't allow us to carry out an inoculation programme."

"So what do we do?" he yelled.

Lutel looked deeply into her brother's eyes. She was used to his unpredictable behaviour, his outbursts, his sulks. Rewn's moods had always oscillated like the black waters on the Cesean shore, but she'd never seen him as unnerved as this, so out of control of the situation.

"Well," shouted Rewn, "what else can we do if inoculation is out of the question?"

Lutel shot him a glance that said many things; her brother returned to her side.

"I first wondered about an education programme, but instantly dismissed the idea as the technology and communication on this planet are so primitive. Even if we could find a medium to communicate effectively, I don't think there would be a high success rate." She altered her voice to a staccato tone. "Earth people, your plague is spread by the flea of the black rat; take the following precautions." She broke off to laugh at herself, then stopped abruptly.

"What was that noise?" she asked.

"I didn't hear anything," replied Rewn, eager to hear her ideas now that she had begun to share them. "It's probably the wind blowing against the windows." He walked over to the pane and peered into the darkness. "Carry on," he said.

Lutel cocked her head to one side. From below them came the faint hubbub of the inn's clientele.

"Well?" implored Rewn.

Lutel composed herself once more, shifting on the bed to find a more comfortable position.

"We know the cause of the plague is the flea carried by the black rat."

"Yes, yes," snorted Rewn. "What are you suggesting – that we go around London catching all of its rats?"

Lutel stared up at him; Rewn dropped his shoulders.

"I'm sorry, this whole situation is driving me mad. I promise I will not interrupt again."

"Of course we will not catch the rats, but we must tackle the problem at its source. We know from our briefings, and what little we have already seen does not contradict it, that the living conditions are primitive and unhealthy. There are open sewers, a poor water supply, rubbish is thrown out onto the streets, and in the cities the houses are built too closely together. To get rid of the rats we must remove the conditions. To remove the conditions we must get rid of the houses!"

"Logically put, but how?" asked Rewn.

She turned her head to face him.

"There is only one way." She paused, before uttering in clear precise tones, "We must burn London to the ground!"

For a moment Rewn did not speak; he stood dumbfounded whilst he tried to fully comprehend what his sister was proposing.

"But how?" he asked. "And how can we be sure the mistakes will not be repeated."

"I've thought of that…" But before Lutel could expand upon her ideas the door burst open.

"Burn London, burn London? You must be mad!"

Standing on the threshold, bedecked in a large, black cloak stood the figure of a man.

Lutel leapt up and grabbed the intruder by the wrist. In one swift motion of her arm, the interloper somersaulted into the room and lay on his back on the floor. Rewn closed the door and, removing the rushlight from its holder, stood next to his sister. The flame flickered over the face of the motionless figure of John Woodman. Lutel gave Woodman a firm kick to the ribs. The man opened his eyes and made to stand up, but Rewn placed a restraining foot in the middle of his chest.

"How long have you been outside?" asked Lutel. Before Woodman could answer she followed with a further demand, "What did you hear?"

Rewn seized Woodman by the clothing around his throat and hauled him up. The trembling man staggered to his feet.

"Who are you working for?" Rewn growled.

"I don't know what you mean," pleaded their captive in a weasel-like voice.

Woodman blinked as Rewn thrust the flame closer to his face.

"Who sent you to spy on us?" barked Rewn, tightening his grip and forcing Woodman to stand on tiptoe.

"No one, honestly," whimpered the frightened man.

Rewn stared hard into Woodman's face, searching for the hint of a lie.

"I was just about to knock to give you your money, and to warn you, when I overheard you talking about strange things that I didn't understand, so I stopped to listen a little more."

"And?" said Rewn, holding the flame so close under Woodman's chin that his stubble began to singe.

Woodman answered rapidly, standing even taller in an effort to avoid the rushlight. “I do understand about burning London, but I don’t understand why.”

“Warn us of what?” asked Lutel, who had sensed danger from a source other than the one Rewn was interrogating.

“When I was about selling your ring, I couldn’t help but notice that the bailiff and some youth were very interested in two strangers.”

“How were they interested?” asked Lutel.

“They were asking after your whereabouts,” he replied.

Rewn pushed his face so close to Woodman’s that he could smell his stale breath.

“What did you tell them?” demanded Rewn.

“Nothing, nothing, honestly. If I did, don’t you think they’d be here by now?”

Lutel accepted the point, signalling to Rewn to release his grip and to look out into the hallway. Glowering at Woodman he removed his hand and walked cautiously to the doorway. He opened the door a crack; the jollification of the drinkers below could be heard more clearly. Rewn stared through the opening, and seeing no danger opened it wider. He stepped outside into the dim passageway.

“All clear,” he announced as he re-entered the room.

“All right, we believe you,” said Lutel, addressing Woodman. “I apologise for our rough treatment.”

“Think no more of it; I was wrong to pry.”

Rewn indicated a chair to Woodman, and he gratefully sat down.

“Lutel, it can only be a matter of time before these men return; we must go,” urged Rewn.

“No, you are quite safe,” said Woodman.

“Why do you say that?” asked Lutel.

“For one thing there are many strangers in town on market day, and there’s very few who will go out of their way to help the bailiff. Besides, the chap with him is not from Chippenham; there’s bad feeling between town and country folk. Believe me, the bailiff will soon tire of looking for you,” replied Woodman.

“That sounds reasonable,” replied Lutel. “But you still overheard our plans. What are we going to do with you, John Woodman?”

Woodman cowered to his knees, fearing his life was in danger.

“Please don’t kill me,” he pleaded.

“You form a wrong impression; we aim to save life, not take it. Your discovery puts our mission in jeopardy; that is why we were so rough with you. We mean you no lasting harm," Lutel assured the trembling man.

Woodman relaxed a little, and remembered the reason for his presence.

"I've brought your money. I'm afraid I could only secure two guineas," he guilefully said.

"Will it do? Is it enough to take us to London?" Rewn quizzed him.

Woodman opened his mouth to confirm that there was indeed enough money, when he stopped himself. His cunning country mind was ticking over more quickly than Rewn or Lutel would have given him credit for.

"It's not a lot," he said; "you could do with more. I have some money if you'll take me with you."

"Out of the question," said Rewn. "You would be a danger to us all."

"Please," begged Woodman. "I owe them London folks. I was swindled out of something that was rightly mine."

He elaborated no further, but Rewn denied his request for a second time. Woodman placed a small bag on the table. He loosened a tie at its neck and poured out their money. He turned and made his way to the door.

"Wait."

Both men turned their eyes to Lutel.

"You may come with us on the understanding that you do exactly as you are told. We are going to save lives, not take them."

"Thank you, thank you. I will abide by your terms," answered Woodman.

"Lutel!" protested Rewn, but he realised his sister would have her reasons and did not want her to divulge them in front of their new associate.

"Thank you," said Woodman again, glancing anxiously between brother and sister.

"Don't make me regret my decision," she said resolutely.

"You will not, ma'am," promised Woodman.

"Call us Lutel and Rewn," she said in more warming tones.

"Thank you, Lutel," he said, and turning to her brother he added "Rewn" rather grudgingly. "Most people call me Woodman, though you may use John if you prefer."

Lutel put a friendly hand on Woodman's arm. "John, perhaps you would be so kind as to step outside and see how things lie with the bailiff."

"It would be a pleasure, Lutel," said Woodman, turning to take his leave.

"Wait," she cried. She picked up a handful of coins from the table. "Will that be enough for three fares on tomorrow's coach?"

"More than enough," he said, smiling.

“What about our food and lodging and a little reward?” asked Lutel.

“Already taken account of,” said Woodman, patting his cloak, and he turned on his heel and left.

“Be discreet,” Lutel called after him.

As the door closed Rewn turned on Lutel.

“Why did you tell him he could accompany us? How can we trust him?”

“Better have him with us; at least we won’t have to worry about what he’s saying about us when we’ve left for London. Besides, he was true to his word with the money for the ring.”

Rewn looked askance at his sister. Lutel ignored the look and continued her justification.

“It might prove useful having a local who is more familiar with the customs and ways of this place. We will just have to trust him. We don’t appear to have much choice. He seems genuine; he could have led the authorities to us already.”

“He seemed a bit too keen to me,” said Rewn. “Almost unbalanced.”

“Well, you can keep a special eye on him, then,” said Lutel with a smile.

There came a further interruption at the door.

“Woodman must have forgotten something,” remarked Rewn.

He walked across to the door and opened it. Framed in the doorway stood a familiar tall figure and behind his left shoulder was Young Michael.

“My name is Henry Lambert,” said their visitor; “I am the bailiff of this town. I’m sorry to disturb you at so late an hour, but our friend here believes you are up to no good, and to humour him I’d like to ask you some questions in order to reassure him,” and after a pause he added, “and myself, if that is all right.”

Lutel stood up in order to pre-empt Rewn.

“Of course, come in,” she offered.

The bailiff walked sprightly into the room and, flicking his coat tails, sat on one of the wooden chairs. Young Michael shuffled over the threshold and leant meekly against the closed door. Lutel, wishing to appear relaxed, sat in the remaining chair, but Rewn stood in the centre of the room. The bailiff opened the conversation in a matter-of-fact and unruffled tone.

“Before we begin, are you quite sure these are the two people that you have been pestering me about all day?”

Young Michael grunted his reply. The bailiff was not amused.

“If you cannot answer in a civil manner I will leave now.”

Young Michael answered decisively. “This be definitely they. Strangers just appeared in our village from nowhere. They were found up to no good, skulking around in some farm buildings."

As Young Michael spoke, the bailiff cast his eyes around the gloomy room. He noticed the sparse furniture, the single picture on the wall and the empty floor; there was nothing here to arouse his suspicion.

"Is this true?" asked Lambert.

"We were in the area," replied Lutel.

"What were you doing there?"

"We were searching for herbs," she replied.

"To what end?"

"We are on our way to London to help with the plague. The herbs are medicinal."

"Strangest quacks I've ever seen," sneered Young Michael. "You've seen the strange garments they were wearing."

"I'll not tell you again," Lambert reproached him. "Where are these herbs?"

"We were interrupted before we could finish our search," said Rewn, casting a look at Young Michael.

"And the strange clothes that have been shown me. They are like nothing that I've ever seen."

"Have you ever been to London in times of plague?" gambled Lutel.

"No, it's not something a sane man would hanker after at any time," said Lambert, stroking his top lip with a thin finger. "Where are you from, friends?"

Lutel knew it was pointless to admit to being local, so she attempted to answer evasively. "We admit we are not from around here; is that a crime?"

"No, no. But where do you come from?" he persisted.

Lutel realised it would be difficult to avoid lying to the man. She anticipated he knew as little about the capital city as she did herself.

"We're from London, and as I said we are on our way back there now."

"That was the story you told me," said the bailiff, looking at Young Michael. "I see no crime in that."

"Ask them for their luggage," demanded Young Michael.

Lambert was reminded of the empty floor.

"Have you any luggage?" he asked.

"We travel light," said Rewn.

"Even so, London can be several days' journey from here. I must admit that it's a peculiar circumstance. What are your names?"

"I'm Rewn and this is Lutel." Rewn shifted uneasily as he spoke; Lutel sensed his unease.

"We are visiting a friend," she said. "He can vouch for us."

"What is the name of this friend?" asked the bailiff, showing a keener interest now that something more tangible had arisen.

"John Woodman; he'll vouch for us," pronounced Rewn.

"Where does this Woodman reside?" asked the bailiff

"In Kellaways," answered Rewn smartly, remembering his earlier gaffe. "But he is visiting Chippenham."

"Is he in this inn?" asked Lambert.

"He is out on business, but most likely taking of ale by now," said Lutel.

The bailiff possessed the dual characteristics that were ideally suited to his office; he was officious and suspicious. "I would like to detain you until this John Woodman can substantiate what you say. If he confirms it I will trouble *you* no more." Young Michael cringed. "Is that all right with you?" asked the bailiff.

"Yes," answered Young Michael; the bailiff ignored him and looked from Rewn to Lutel. They didn't appear to have much choice, reasoned Lutel. To refuse or to run would be seen as an admission of guilt and of no benefit to their long-term cause. Fortunately Rewn had, somewhat surprisingly, arrived at a similar conclusion.

"What if you cannot find Woodman?" he asked.

"Oh, we will find him if he is here in town," said the bailiff. "There are not that many inns or taverns to search; as long as he is not hiding from us we will find him."

They followed the bailiff out of the room and down the unlit stairway; Young Michael brought up the rear. The night air felt cold to their warm bodies, and Lutel shivered. The square was empty and the inns and houses were blurred in the darkness. Lambert led them across the road to the white-and-black timbered building that they had passed earlier that day. Six steps led them up to the Yelde Hall, and they were met within by two men dressed in solemn attire. Lutel took them to be jailers, though she could not be certain. The room they were in was poorly lit, a few tapers adorned the stone walls, but she could see that it went all the way to the roof as large wooden beams criss-crossed above their heads.

The bailiff opened an annex door; three stone steps, worn in the middle by a century of felons' feet, led down to a windowless cell. It was known by the local townsfolk as the Blindroom.

"I'm afraid I am going to have to ask you to wait in here until I have further news," said the bailiff with an air of apology in his voice. "Please make yourselves comfortable," he added with a hint of embarrassment. "We will send out for some refreshment for you, and search for your companion Woodman."

In the background Young Michael smirked triumphantly; Lutel fixed him with a cold stare as she and Rewn stepped into the room. A sturdy oak door slammed closed and three bolts were thrust into place; they were locked in. The room was well named; it was devoid of any furniture and pitch black. The walls were rough and wet whilst the floor was hard and cold. A small slit ten feet above their heads would allow a chink of daylight to shine in, but that was several hours away.

On the other side of the door Lambert issued muffled instructions to his two menials. Rewn and Lutel heard them take their leave, and the bailiff turned his attention to Young Michael.

"You've had a busy day, young man, and I thank you for your trouble, but your interest ceases here, so I suggest you find lodgings for the night or make the most of the moon's light and journey home. Your family and friends are no doubt concerned for your safe return, and keen to hear your news."

The prisoners could not see Young Michael opening his mouth to plead for an extension of his interest, or the bailiff, having guessed his intentions, taking him by the arm and gently leading him to the door.

CHAPTER TWELVE

MUD TWANGING IN THE DARK

Rewn and Lutel sat on the uncomfortable earthen floor.

"Are you all right, Lutel?" came Rewn's voice from the dark.

Their eyes were still accustoming themselves to the lack of light; even though their prison was little more than fifteen feet long, and they sat close to each other, their bodies were little more than adumbrated shapes.

"I'm fine," said Lutel, reaching out a blind hand in the darkness, and eventually placing it consolingly on one of his.

The air was musky and damp; the scent of rancid urine pervaded their nostrils.

"What do we do?" asked Rewn despairingly.

"We wait," replied Lutel calmly.

She moved her hand up to his brow; it was warm and covered in beads of sweat. Lutel brushed a strand of hair from his forehead.

"It *will* be all right," she emphasised, though inside she was beginning to have her doubts about the mission. Nothing as yet had worked out as planned; the crash landing, their discovery on the farm, the subsequent suspicions and now this incarceration. Even their release relied on a virtual stranger.

Rewn echoed this final uncertainty. "What if they can't find Woodman, or he doesn't acknowledge us? By his own admission we know that he is not a lover of officialdom. He might up and fly or deny all knowledge of us if he believes he is under suspicion."

"We wait," insisted Lutel. "Try and rest; things might look different in the morning. Let's see what John Woodman is made of."

They sat against the clammy walls of the cell. The candlelight from the outer room shone dimly underneath their door. It was the only sign of hope; at least the bailiff hadn't deserted them as he awaited the arrival of the one man who could confirm their story.

The darkness surrounding them did not ease, Lutel's legs felt stiff and her bottom was numb. No word had passed their lips for twenty minutes or more.

They both sat still reflecting upon their position. Fatigue eventually told on Rewn and he drifted into a fitful sleep. For Lutel the dark held unwelcome memories. She looked towards Rewn and drew comfort from his gentle snoring. He was handling the situation far better than she could have hoped – better than herself, in fact. Then again, he hadn't borne her experiences.

Lutel's thoughts drifted back many years, to her time as a little girl of eight, when her fear of dark enclosed spaces had first originated. She despised herself for the weakness; despite all the dangerous situations she had faced since, this fear still stood out as the one most likely to reduce her to panic.

The day had started brightly; she had waved goodbye to her mother as she skipped out of the house to join her friends Kaitli and Jorrel. A bag of food dangled at her side. "Don't venture out of the clambake site" were her mother's departing words as she closed the gate. How the others teased her when they suggested an alternative site for their alfresco meal, and she initially refused to join them. Eventually she submitted to peer pressure and went with them to a field full of deep ponds. Here they were joined by several other children from the area and Lutel soon forgot her parent's warning as the squeal and laughter of their games wiped all thoughts of disobedience away.

The area was a disused brickworks; a bygone age had mined the warm purple clay. Nature had reclaimed the land so that now most of the hollows were deep with water, but on their steep sides, traces of clay could still be found. Small blue fish shared the lakes with a wealth of insect and plant life; several species of bird, attracted by the sheltered water and the rich food source, used it as a nesting site.

The idyllic grounds were a favourite leisure spot, but over the years the lakes had claimed several victims, accidental and otherwise, and most parents forbade their offspring from playing there unsupervised.

At the edges of the lakes grew a variety of small bushes and trees. One particular species was a source of attraction to the local children. Its branches grew out from a small stool and provided the children with a whippy stick, several feet in length. It was to such a tree that Jorrel came, and he snapped off several long sticks. The branches were a bluish-grey hue, and devoid of any nodes, their prime attraction being their springiness. "Mud twangers", the children called them. Their game began with rolling a small piece of the purple clay into a ball. The sphere was poked onto the tip of a stick, then the stick, held above your head with the clay pointing towards the sky, was swung carefully backwards and then whipped forwards, propelling the ball of clay over great distances.

Lutel squealed with delight as her projectiles whistled through the air, landing in the far distance. The children targeted an island reed bed and aimed their clay bullets across the water; the wild birds squawked and scattered noisily as the balls fell short and splashed them. Next they chalked a circle on a tree trunk and shot their missiles towards it; the clay landed with a satisfying thwack as it splattered on the bark. By late afternoon a strong wind had begun to blow up, and the clay balls sailed further than any child could remember.

To more easily follow the course of the balls the children began to adorn them by poking thin reeds into the clay, so as each missile whizzed through the sky it looked as though it were wearing a green headdress. As the reeds grew at the water's edge the children had to clamber down the sides of the pit in order to pick them. The continual use of the banks was causing the clay to become slippery, and the children decided to call a halt to their mud-twanging games.

Some of the older boys made a fire, and all the children joined in by collecting wood and other combustible items to feed the flames. From an assortment of containers, bags and pockets, food was produced for a communal meal. A large amorphic vegetable called a phyrone proved a great favourite with the children; it was placed in the hot ashes of the fire and left to bake. During the cooking time the children amused themselves by building makeshift tents from brushwood and other debris. After an hour or so the cooked phyrones were removed from the fire, and their hard casing smashed with a stone. Inside lay a succulent sweet lilac flesh; the children scooped out the creamy pulp with their fingers. Often their eagerness to eat would require them to cool the food by blowing on it, the over-zealous needing to blow on their fingers.

A quick count showed that there was one fewer phyrone than children; the oldest boys decided the food should be distributed by age and that the two youngest should fight each other for the remaining vegetable. As they sat in a circle reporting their ages, Lutel just knew she would be one of the unlucky pair. Her feelings proved right; when the last child announced their age, Lutel and another girl were pronounced the youngest.

Lutel had no wish to fight and stated that she would relinquish her claim to the meal. The older boys were not to be denied their sport and a chant of "Lutel! Nathene!" began to ring out around the circle. Even her best friends, afraid that they could be drawn into the skirmish themselves, joined in the goading. With tears in her eyes Lutel reluctantly struggled to her feet, a boy next to her pushed her into the ring, and the contest began. The fight, if it could be described as such, was over before it began. Lutel raised her hands as her opponent keenly charged towards her, they briefly locked hands, during which time Nathene bit Lutel on the hand, and Lutel collapsed in a sobbing heap.

Kaitli ran forward and helped her friend to her feet. One of the older boys, alarmed at the outcome, led Lutel and Kaitli to his tent. He broke his phyrone in two and offered half to Lutel, but she was too distressed to accept it. Large tears stained her face and blurred her vision, as her whole body convulsed. Lutel remained in the tent for the remainder of the afternoon, too embarrassed to face the rest of the children; even Kaitli had given up trying to console her. By early evening all of the children had departed apart from Lutel, Kaitli and Jorrel. As the first signs of dusk formed on the horizon, Kaitli issued her final demand; she and Jorrel had to leave, and if Lutel wanted to accompany them then she must go now. Lutel did not acknowledge the ultimatum, either by look or sound, and remained seated in a tight ball.

The sky was as purple as the deepest hue of a ripe phyrone when she next looked out of the tent, and Lutel felt very alone and frightened. She began to cry again, and that was how Rewn found her. How her heart had beaten when she had first seen the bright beacon on the horizon, then as the torchlight drew nearer he was calling her name. She was so overcome that huge tears again welled up in her eyes and her jaw twitched. It was several seconds later before she could answer his cries, and then he was with her in a flash, picking her up and grasping her close to his body. That day was seared into her memory for ever, and when times grew desperate it often rose to the surface.

The church clock struck midnight and brought her back to reality. There was a disturbance in the outer room and a sound of muffled conversation. Voices grew louder as the three bolts were slid back and the heavy door protested at its late disturbance. A candle was waved in the doorway; the two prisoners blinked at the sudden intrusion of light.

"Can you identify them?"

"Yes, yes," came a slurred reply. "They're known to me; I can vouch for them."

As their eyes became acclimatised, Lutel could see the faces behind the flame.

"You are free to go," said the bailiff. "I am sorry for the inconvenience, but you can't be too careful these days." Then, as though excusing his own part in their captivity, he added, "People tend to worry about strangers, especially village folk."

The stars twinkled on their ebony backcloth as they descended the steps and walked into the street. Lutel shuddered as she strode out into the night air. Turning to the merry Woodman, she said, "Thank you, John."

Woodman was only vaguely aware of his part in their release, due to the bailiff's men having taken rather a long time in locating him. Lutel and Rewn repaid the compliment by slinging their arms around his shoulders and helping him back to their lodgings.

There were still a few late-night drinkers in the Lyon Inn; few took any notice of their entrance, bar two men who straddled the fireplace, extracting the last remaining heat from the dying embers. They ceased drinking and looked up from their tankards as the trio walked in, but resumed their imbibing as the landlord crossed in front of them to assist with the drunken Woodman.

"Your rooms are still vacant," announced their host, anticipating the likely question.

"Can he sleep on the floor?" asked Rewn, glancing at the inebriated man at his side.

"It's not usual, but as the hour is late I can see no harm," came the genial reply.

"Aye, take the drunken fool upstairs, he's going to need his sleep," came a voice from the fireplace. A tall man with a beak-like nose had addressed them. The inn filled with laughter, encouraging his companion to add to the mirth.

"Aye, take him to bed, he's going to need all his energy to burn London town!"

Raucous laughter again rang around the inn. Lutel blanched, and cursed herself for entrusting Woodman with the information. In order to conceal her true feelings she joined in the general merriment, Rewn, following her example, grinned nervously. Fortunately most of those assembled in the room were by far the worse for drink and did not appear to be taking Woodman's boast seriously.

"Reckons he's going to light enough bonfires to make London as sad a place as ever it was since the world began."

"Ever the crower," replied the woman at the fireside. She pointed at the dying embers, warming to the small gathering's attention. "Perhaps he could start here and warm us up!"

Hysterical laughter again filled the room but swiftly died away, the joke, like a dying flame, appearing to have run its course after all possible merriment had been extracted. Lutel relaxed as she realised that Woodman's pronouncement had been seen as nothing more than a drink-induced brag.

"Well, us fire-raisers must get our sleep," she quipped, and they ascended the stairs, dragging the half-asleep Woodman with them to the accompaniment of more laughter ringing in their ears.

"The coach leaves at eight o'clock sharp," shouted the landlord from the foot of the stairs. "If you're all awake to make it," he added, playing to the gallery.

"Thank you," called back Rewn, in as unruffled a voice as he could muster.

As Lutel's room was the closest, Woodman was unceremoniously bundled onto her bedroom floor, snoring before he reached the floorboards.

"What can we do?" blurted Rewn. "This fool has told them everything."

Lutel calmly reached up for the tallow, and then turned its glare towards the man on the floor. "Fortunately everybody appears to be treating it as a huge joke, or perhaps the concept is far beyond their imagination."

"But can you be sure?" asked Rewn.

"Nothing is certain," answered his sister, "apart from the fact that we must be on that coach in the morning, and we must ensure that this raving drunkard comes with us."

"You can't spend the night in his company, we know so little about him," Rewn pointed out.

"I could say the same to you," said his sister.

Woodman snored resonantly on the floorboards.

"Let's leave him here, Lutel. He's out for the count. We can both use my room and wake him in the morning."

Lutel extinguished the flame as they closed the door on Woodman and crept in the darkness of the hallway to the adjoining room.

"You have the bed," offered Rewn. "I'll be quite comfortable in a chair."

Lutel was too tired to argue. She flopped down on the bed fearing that she would pass a restless night, but nervous exhaustion took its toll, and she was soon asleep.

Rewn was the first to wake; he kicked his legs out straight and rubbed his bleary eyes. Gradually the experiences of the previous evening returned, and a sense of alarm ran through his body as he recalled Woodman's boast. He rose to his feet to check the road below, and after satisfying himself that there was no imminent danger, he gently shook his sister, who had barely stirred in the previous six hours.

"Leave me alone," she protested.

"Come on, Lutel, we must be going soon if we are to catch the coach."

Lutel swung her feet over the side of the bed, and stretched her hands above her head, encouraging her body into following her mind. The room was filled with stale sweat, and Rewn pulled down a window to allow some fresh air to circulate.

A knock on the door caused consternation. Rewn shot a troubled glance at Lutel.

"Woodman," he mouthed; was it possible that his ravings had reached the ears of the authorities?

The knock was repeated, more loudly this time.

"Who is it?" demanded Rewn.

"Just me, sir," came the reply.

Rewn recognised the burred accent of Brickthwaite, and apprehensively opened the door.

"I've brought you a jug and basin of hot water, sir, for washing the night away."

It seemed a strange expression to Rewn, but he gladly accepted the offer. He held the receptacles in his hands, waiting to close the door, but the landlord stood his ground, peering over Rewn's shoulder. Rewn coughed politely and, on attracting the landlord's attention, looked down at the water.

"May I trouble you for a towel?" asked Rewn.

"Sorry, sir, I'll right away and fetch you one. Will you be taking some breakfast, before you leave?" asked the landlord.

Rewn was slightly taken aback at having to make so simple a decision and in the end managed a nod.

Rewn placed the bowl on a cabinet and hastily poured out some water, spilling the contents onto the floor. Cupping his hands, he dipped them into the bowl and splashed himself. He shook his face in reaction to the cold water, and then pushed his sleeves up and washed his arms up to his elbows. The landlord returned with two towels and Rewn gratefully received them.

"Please do not disturb our friend," said Rewn, indicating the adjoining room.

"No need to, sir," said the landlord; "he rose and went over an hour ago."

Part Three

Plague

CHAPTER THIRTEEN

RING A RING O' ROSES

The sound of a pot being stirred woke first Revin and then Verde from their slumbers. Rebecca was bending over a large iron pan that stood on a wood-fired oven that had been crudely built into the breast of the chimney. A store of split logs was piled by the oven's side. Rebecca lifted the large heart-shaped spoon from the gravy and tasted the dark brown liquid.

"Just a little more," she mused to herself, and lifting down an orange-glazed pot from a shelf to her left, she added a small pinch of salt to the mixture. Several droplets spilled from the spoon and trickled down the outside of the vessel, congealing as they cooled. Verde screwed his face up at the unusual aroma he had never before smelled, a combination that included white port, mace, beef stock and spinach. He watched as Rebecca peeled some hard-boiled eggs and quartered them with a large kitchen knife. She added them to the simmering stock, and then turned her attentions to a shallower pan in which she placed triangles of bread. The fat sizzled as the bread was dropped into it. Verde looked over at Revin; together they decided to remain silent.

Rebecca ladled the meal into four earthenware dishes, garnishing it with the fried bread. The dishes were placed on the long table.

"Are you awake?" she called to nobody in particular.

The two visitors sat upright on the floor, their makeshift bed coverings draped around their feet.

"Your breakfast is on the table," said Rebecca kindly.

The two men folded their bedding and handed it to her.

"Please start," she said, and she climbed the stairs with the covers.

Verde was the first to sit at the table; he picked up his spoon and poked it around in his bowl, inspecting the contents. The aroma was most unlike anything they had ever experienced on Mykas.

"Try it," said Revin as he sat opposite Verde.

"You try it," answered Verde.

"You first," urged Revin. "We mustn't appear ungracious; besides, if we don't eat she might become suspicious."

Verde lifted the spoon to his mouth, expecting to spit the contents back into the bowl. Revin gave him an encouraging look, and then as the food entered Verde's mouth dared him to swallow it. Verde's countenance gradually changed.

"It's very good; it tastes far better than it looks. Try it."

Revin did not look convinced as he followed Verde's lead, but found too that the meal was quite palatable.

Verde was chewing a piece of bread that he had saved until the end of his meal when they heard footsteps descending the stairs.

"Lovely meal," shouted Verde.

"By'r Lady, who are you?" croaked the figure as it came into view. John Gatleigh had heard his daughter-in-law's call, and forced his aching and bruised body down the stairs. He had as yet been unable to recall the events of the previous evening, so it was another shock to his system to see two strangers at his breakfast table.

Revin stood as the disfigured face approached them. "I'm Revin and this is Verde."

"I don't care what people call you. What are you doing in our house?"

At that moment Rebecca returned.

"Oh, Father, you are up; how are you feeling?" she asked soothingly.

"Awful, but I'll feel a damn lot better when somebody explains to me who these two fancy-names are."

"Why, Father, these two gents came to your rescue last night; there's little doubt that without them, you wouldn't be standing here now."

"If that's what you call help, I can do without it," said the old man, tenderly feeling his jaw. "But I've yet had cause to disbelieve my daughter-in-law, so if she says I am indebted to you, then I thank 'ee."

Gatleigh senior sat next to Revin and slurped noisily on his spoon. Rebecca joined them at table and proceeded to eat her meal in silence. John was the last to finish, and he wiped his mouth with the back of his hand, removing the last traces of his meal. Rebecca rose, collected the spoons and the empty bowls and left the table.

"Strange names," said John, belching loudly.

Verde ignored the comment and quickly changed the subject. "Did you recognise the men who attacked you?"

"'Course I didn't recognise them. Do you think I'd be sat here if I knew their names? I'd be off raking that damned lazy constable out of his bed."

Verde stared around at the walls; most were bare, although the wall beside the oven displayed a variety of hanging utensils and shelves of pots containing herbs and spices.

"Is Tom not joining us for breakfast?" asked Revin as Rebecca rejoined them.

"He left at first light to see the alderman," came the reply. "He said to wait here for him and he would be back shortly."

Revin felt uneasy; why hadn't Tom taken them with him, assuming he was keeping to his word of the previous evening? Perhaps he wasn't arranging jobs for them; maybe his business with the authorities was of a different kind. Revin kicked Verde under the table.

"We must not outstay our welcome," Revin said to Rebecca. He made to depart and Verde took the hint.

"No, no," replied their hostess earnestly, "Tom said for you to stay 'til he returned. On no account was I to let you leave; he's most grateful to you."

"We will take the air inside the city walls and return later," promised Revin. "We shall only be in your way here." He looked round at the small room as if to make his point.

"Take the air!" scoffed John Gatleigh. "You must be mad. London air be nothing but foul air these days. It reeks with the stench of dead bodies; soot rains from above you and everyone do cough from that stinking yellow smoke."

John pointed over his shoulder with a protruding thumb, emphasising the whereabouts of the obnoxious substances that he was warning them about. Revin took a few paces towards the door.

"Please, please stay," implored Rebecca.

Her begging only increased Revin's resolve that they should leave.

"We will return by midday," he said. "After all, Tom may not be fortunate in gaining employment for us, and we may find as much for ourselves, so as to render unnecessary his kind attempts."

The assurance of their return placated the woman, and the two visitors once more expressed their thanks for the hospitality they had received. Rebecca reciprocated by thanking them for all they had done for Tom's father, and reminded them of their promise to return.

As they walked through the door, the church clock of All Hallows-on-the-Wall struck ten. The cold light of morning allowed for a closer inspection of their whereabouts. They were in a long narrow street outside the city walls, which were clearly visible in the distance.

Revin looked at the red cross that he had noticed on the previous evening; painted on the door below it were the words "Lord Have Mercy Upon Us". Rebecca, who had followed them into the street, called after them.

"Stay clear, the distemper's taken all of them, and 'tis worse inside the walls. I wouldn't venture there for all the gold in London."

Revin looked up from his reading. "Thank you, until later."

"Until noon," Rebecca reminded him, and she watched them walk away eastward, following the contour of the great city walls in the direction of Bishopsgate.

"What was all that about?" asked Verde, looking accusingly at Revin. He was in no hurry to secure employment and had been hopeful of a restful few hours, especially if there was a chance of being fed.

"Possibly nothing, possibly everything," said Revin.

He didn't see why he had to spell out the danger to Verde. If he could not see for himself how keen Rebecca had been to keep them in the house, then Verde had better start keeping his wits about him.

"Was something wrong?" asked Verde.

"What do you think?"

"I didn't spot anything. I was happy to stay there and wait for Tom."

Revin sighed and turned to face Verde. "And who had Tom gone to see?"

Verde ran Rebecca's speech through his mind. "You don't think they suspect anything?"

"We can't be sure whether Tom's visit to the authorities is a genuine attempt on his part to repay us."

"Then again, if it is not we have the element of surprise on our side."

"How?" asked Revin.

"We can return before the appointed hour and watch the house for any abnormal activity."

"But why bother to run the risk?" asked Revin.

"We can't wait around for Rewn and Lutel and do nothing. Besides, we will need money for food and shelter, so if Tom has secured us employment we must take it."

"But what kind of employment?" mused Revin. "You heard Rebecca's pleas."

"Don't worry, we've been inoculated."

"There may be other dangers," countered Revin.

"I don't think we are in a position to be choosy," argued Verde. "This wasn't part of the plan. We'll take anything that comes our way. We can survey the scene before Lutel arrives; that should please her."

Revin chuckled at the jibe.

"Besides," continued Verde, "we can see how widespread the plague is, and plan our strategies for inoculation."

As he spoke the sound of running feet and a loud commotion broke out behind them. The two friends prepared themselves to run. They looked over their shoulders to assess the danger; two men wielding long sticks were approaching them, pursuing a brown-and-black mongrel dog. The dog killers were swearing after the mutt and soliciting it to stop, but their intention was not clear to Revin and Verde. They fled across the road and ran in the shadows of the houses. A door opened before them, and a middle-aged crone emerged to throw a bowl of water on the road outside her house. Verde, who ran a little ahead of Revin, could not avoid the puddle and in trying he slipped over. The terrified dog raced past them; Revin braced himself for action, but the dog killers ignored them and continued to chase the hapless beast.

As Verde sat helpless in the pool of water the householder began to berate him.

"How can the likes of us poor folk keep the plague away if blithering fools like you stop me from washing the street?"

Revin reached down a hand and pulled his friend up.

"I beg your pardon, Madam. The fault is all mine," said Verde.

"Your pardon isn't going to keep the plague away," screamed the old woman. "Who is going to wash my street? That's what I want to know!"

Revin and Verde scurried away, the old woman shouting oaths behind them. At a safe distance Revin stopped and laughed ironically. He repeated a concern that, over a hundred miles away, Lutel had already expressed.

"Are you sure these people are advanced enough for our medical technology? Is it really worth our trouble?"

Verde stared at the row of houses; they were all shuttered up. Most were vacant, their occupants either dead or dying, the lucky ones having fled to the country to escape the plague. His humanitarian feelings were well known on Mykas, and were a further reason for his inclusion on the mission. He wiped his hands on his breeches to remove the water, and pinched his clothes away from his wet bottom.

"Look, Revin, we were sent here by the Stilax to do a job. I would agree that the rather feudal conditions are worse than we expected, but I would argue that their existence is an even more compelling reason for us to stay and give what help we can."

"We may never see Lutel or Rewn again; we have no medical supplies and no means of sustaining ourselves, not that there appears to be any point in doing so. I suggest we give serious thought to leaving."

Verde strained every sinew and raised himself as tall as possible to look Revin in the eye.

"The whole point is that we do stay on. You cannot have forgotten how vital it is for us to succeed. We cannot run away at the first hurdle, and let so many down. When Rewn and Lutel arrive with the medical supplies then we will decide on our course of action. In the meantime, we take any employment that we can; it will serve us best if we can learn as much as possible about these people and the plague that dwells amongst them. First-hand experience will be vital information, or have you forgotten your teaching?"

Revin was prepared to continue his argument, but Verde brushed past him, continuing his walk towards the city wall. Revin stared towards the filth-coloured sky, then followed after him.

"I'm sorry," said Revin. "You were right; I wasn't thinking straight."

Verde smiled across at his friend.

"What do you have in mind?" asked Revin.

"Like I suggested, we enter the city and survey the scene. We can start by looking for the tavern with the black bird; we could at least locate it before the others arrive. At the same time we may gain useful employment."

"Now might not be the ideal time," remarked Revin.

They had neared the towering entrance of Bishopsgate. Above the great gate a carving of a man of noble countenance straddled a rearing horse. Both men stood quite still, several yards from the entrance to the walled city. Posted either side of the gate stood two guards with large halberds, ready to challenge all who would enter. Verde realised at once that, on this occasion, Revin was absolutely right.

As they retraced their short journey from Tom Gatleigh's house, a large bird plummeted from the sky and landed dead in front of them.

"'Tis the bad air," said a single passer-by, and he kicked the pigeon as if to prove his point. Verde was visibly shocked, but Revin was uncertain whether it was from the heartless action of the man or out of pity for the bird.

Although they had left the house within the last thirty minutes, Tom had already returned, foiling their plans for a stealthy approach by spying them from an upstairs window and rushing out to greet them. Verde pondered for a moment, contemplating a mad dash away, but something in Tom's face halted his escape.

"It is arranged," Tom said, beaming. "You start tonight as official bearers to this parish, but with things being so bad at the moment, with 'undreds dying everywhere, you'll also be expected to work westwards into the parish of Saint Giles, Cripplegate, where most of your work will be."

Rebecca stood on the wooden stairs, cuddling a young child.

"Hush, Sam," she urged the little boy.

Behind her on the stairs stood two girls aged around eight. This came as a surprise to Verde and Revin. During the excitement and commotion of the previous evening, and the hastily devoured breakfast, there had been no suggestion or inkling that any children lived in the house. Revin felt a trifle apprehensive that such a secret had been hidden from them, and wondered what other surprises might be in store. He felt offended that the family had hidden the children's existence, but understood their reasons for doing so. Tom read his thoughts.

"This is Sally – we call her Sal – and Katherine, or Kate. They're twins," he explained as he ushered the two men into the house. "They stayed upstairs this morning, but how our young Sam's crying didn't wake you in the night, I'll never know."

"We thought it best to shield them," said Rebecca, "until we were a little more certain of you. And now your quick return has caught us unawares. I hope you can forgive us."

Verde could not help noticing the irony of the situation, each mistrusting the other.

"No, it is we who are at fault, returning so early," he said. "Would you like us to go?"

Rebecca opened her mouth to say something, and then closed it again. Tom looked at his wife and put a reassuring arm around her shoulder.

"You are most welcome to stay," he said, "so come and sit down and meet the family proper."

Verde and Revin slumped down in a pair of crudely fashioned wooden chairs. Odours from the children's breakfast pervaded the room; sweeter aromas than those from their own now lingered in the air.

"I've seen the church sexton," said Tom. "He's a good friend and has the ear of the parish officers – the alderman and the like – and there are always vacancies for bearers."

He looked from Verde to Revin, awaiting their thanks.

Revin continued to stare at his outstretched legs, and showed no sign of acknowledgement.

"Surely I'm not too late?" asked Tom in response to their reticence. "Collecting the dead might not appear that attractive, but at least it's a living."

"Better than a dying," answered Revin acidly, but the humour was lost on Tom.

"No, no, you have been more than kind," added Verde hastily. "We do not wish to appear rude; it's happened so quickly you have taken us by surprise." He looked over at the dispirited figure in the other chair. "Hasn't it, Revin?"

An unenthusiastic grunt emanated from his friend's lips. He might have agreed to adhere to Verde's plan, but he hadn't promised unequivocal support.

"When do we start?" asked Verde.

"At dusk tonight. I'm to take you round to the sexton, and he'll see you straight. It's fair dangerous work, mind, and not good pay: one shilling and sixpence a day."

Verde had little concept of how large or small a payment this was, but did not wish to appear ungrateful. "The money will be most welcome; isn't that so, Revin?"

A duplicate grunt followed.

Verde felt exasperated at Revin's lack of loyalty, and determined to counter it. "I'm sure we can live with the plague."

"Oh, it's not just the plague," said Tom. "There's mighty queer goings-on." He became more animated and gesticulated wildly, enthused by his subject. "What with people locked up all day in their houses, others running around the streets mad with pain, others watching loved ones screaming and dying. There's no telling the desperate acts folk will do when driven to it."

"We'll take the jobs," said Verde calmly, not wishing Tom's diatribe to give Revin further ammunition. Revin crossed his legs, suppressing his agitation, not wishing to cross Verde in public.

Whilst Tom continued to fill in details to Verde, and answer a few simple questions, Revin closed his eyes and thought. What's done is done, he told himself, and there's no going back on it, not with Verde around. Perhaps it would be best to approach this challenge positively. After all, it could prove to be an interesting historical exercise. In fact, as Revin thought about it, he began to see there was a certain amount of appeal to the work. Besides, he had been sent here to administer a cure to a people; if he was prevented from doing that for the moment, he was still fulfilling his mission in a small way, even if the physical work didn't appeal to him. Whilst musing, one thought did occur to him, and as the conversation between Tom and Verde came to an end he was able to ask a question.

"Where do we stay?"

Rebecca looked at Tom, his eyes were saying no, but his heart was willing otherwise. The two men before him had saved his father, and callousness was not part of his nature.

"You may stay here, until you can find somewhere more suitable," he uttered, and then half-regretting his outburst added, "If that is all right with Rebecca?"

"'Tis only a floor we can offer you; these are bad times and many folk believe God is punishing the wicked on this earth, but I'll not have it said that Tom Gatleigh turned two Christian men out on the street. Stay until you are fixed otherwise."

The tension in the house eased, and the twins descended the stairs and walked to the middle of the room. Kate sat on Revin's knee. Rebecca moved to reproach her and then had second thoughts. The two girls were miniature replicas of their mother, sharing her thin lips, small arched nose, and rich brown curly hair. They were slight in build and dainty on their feet.

"What's your name?" said Kate.

"Revin."

"That's a funny name. I don't know anybody with that name. Do you come from another country?"

The question was innocently asked. Verde diverted the potentially awkward answer. "It's not as strange as my name; see if you can guess it."

"Is it Sam?" asked Kate.

"No."

"I know, it's Tom," Sal chimed in.

"No, it's not," replied Verde.

The two girls then went through every name they could think of, squealing with unfounded certainty at each new guess.

"I know, I know, it's Ben," shrieked Sal. "Ben Shuke's her boyfriend."

Kate coloured.

"No he's not, he's your boyfriend," she retorted.

"It's Verde," said Revin, anxious about the path down which the conversation was heading.

The twins stopped their bickering and giggled; Kate climbed down from Revin's knee and walked over to her sister. Kate grabbed Sal's hands and the two girls danced wildly in a small circle, chanting.

"Ring a ring o' roses, a pocket full of posies, atishoo, atishoo, we all fall down!"

On the final word both girls threw themselves to the floor, giggling hysterically. Rebecca scolded her daughters for their irreverent and boisterous behaviour. The dance brought Tom's mind back to the seriousness of the situation.

"You'll be wanting a sleep; it's a long night ahead. Nod off in the chairs if you can. I'll wake you in good time."

Verde looked over to Revin to seek his opinion, but his eyes were already closed; the long flight was still taking its toll.

"Thank you," said Verde, and he bowed his head.

CHAPTER FOURTEEN

THE HOLE IN THE WALL

Around nine o'clock that evening Verde felt a tugging at his arm. Upon opening his eyes he immediately closed them against the smoke wafting from the fireplace. His nostrils sensed the smell of cooking. Rebecca, flanked by the twins, stood at the oven over a large black saucepan. Tom repeated his tugging on Revin.

"Wake," he urged. "Rebecca has provided a spicy caudle to protect you against the bad air."

"They'll want more than this," said Rebecca, looking up from the pot and passing the spoon to Sal to take her turn in stirring. She touched an amulet that was hanging around her neck.

"Powdered toad," explained Tom, waving a hand towards the amulet. "For protection."

Verde yet again smiled at the simplicity of the people, inwardly sighing at the daunting task that lay before them.

"How is your father?" asked Revin.

"Much better; he's asleep upstairs," replied Tom. "He's a tough old bird, but the other night fair took it out of him, and Rebecca insists that he rests for a few days."

Rebecca threw more wood onto the fire, and the flames crackled and spat as they enveloped the logs; within minutes a sweet sickly smell pervaded the room. Revin's eyes watered with the smoke and Rebecca apologised for the discomfort.

"The physicians say strong smells keep the plague away. We did use gunpowder but that got too dear; besides, it made Father's chest bad."

"Some folk do swear by leather, and throw old shoes and scraps of it on the fire. Wasteful that is, I say," commented Tom.

He looked mischievously at his lodgers and drew forward, lowering his voice like a naughty schoolboy about to share a closely guarded secret.

"Vicar has fled the parish like so many of his kind, and his orchard is just standing there unattended, so several of his trees are no longer standing."

"Hush, Tom Gatleigh, or the devil himself will come and take you for such wickedness." Rebecca was embarrassed by her husband's admission and the unfavourable impression it might make on their lodgers. But Tom was not to be silenced on the issue and let his feelings be known.

"All the rich folk, merchants, clergy and even some doctors have left the city for the country. The poor man has been deserted and left to fend as best he may. If the vicar's no use for his trees then there are others that have."

By now Tom was standing up and shouting; the twins were weeping sorrowfully.

"Be quiet, Tom, you're frightening the children."

"Will the devil really come and take Father?" sobbed Kate.

"No," said Tom. "Don't say such things, Rebecca. You're doing a far better job of scaring our daughters than I am."

Rebecca decided the only way to silence her husband was to fill his mouth, and she hastily ladled him a huge helping of the brown, sickly-smelling gruel. Tom greedily devoured his meal as Revin and Verde were handed a bowl of the wine-laced caudle. They were again pleasantly surprised by the appetising taste; it proved more appealing than the smell and appearance suggested, and warmed their stomachs for the evening's enterprise.

As darkness grabbed the last few rays of daylight, three men emerged from the doorway and slunk quietly along in the shadows. The evening was balmy and the atmosphere oppressive, made worse by the acrid sulphurous smoke that lingered around ground level, there being no wind or breeze to disperse it. Although it was late August, many superstitious Londoners still burnt coal fires, even when there was little need for them apart from for cooking an evening meal. Disinfectants were added to the fires in the belief that they would purge houses of the bad air.

Verde and Revin both felt breathless in the stifling conditions. Tom paused, took out a whitish object from a legging pocket and, dipping into his large coat pocket, pulled out a wooden box. He carefully lifted the lid of the box and took out a small leather pouch. Verde's brow furrowed as Tom proceeded to fill the object with the contents from the pouch and press his left forefinger into the little clay bowl, gently applying pressure to the tobacco. Tom returned to the box and poured a small pile of tinder onto a wall. He then gripped a flat piece of metal that wrapped around his clenched fist, and holding the strike-a-light over the pile he struck down with a flint until a spark ignited the tinder. Tom poked a sulphur-ended taper into the glow and transferred the flames to the bowl of his pipe whilst sucking on its stem. He mistook their amazement for a desire to indulge.

"Smoke?" he said, tendering them a pipe each.

The habit was unknown to the Mykasians and they respectfully declined his offer, judging that they were already surrounded by enough smoke.

"Put it in your pockets for later," he said, thrusting the tinder box towards them. The two men, failing to appreciate the generous gesture, obediently did as they were instructed.

Having turned left outside Gatleigh's house, the trio headed westwards, keeping the city wall on their inner side as they made their way to the sexton of All Hallows-on-the-Wall. As they neared the churchyard their nostrils were filled with a putrefying and pungent smell. Verde felt as though his lungs were filling with a poisonous gas; he spluttered and choked several times, fighting to compose himself.

"Now you see the reason for this," laughed Tom, waving his pipe at Verde.

The sweet-smelling tobacco now seemed a very attractive alternative to the stench that inflicted itself upon them. There followed a rather comical lesson from Tom on how to fill, draw and light a pipe. After several futile attempts Revin was all for giving up, but Verde's persistence eventually paid off, and not to be outdone Revin soon followed his friend as a bona fide pipe-smoker.

After several large puffs, Verde was in a position to continue speaking.

"What is it?"

"A laystall," replied Tom. "Didn't you gents have them out west?"

Verde again felt the vulnerability of their position.

"Nothing as potent as that," he improvised.

Fortunately, Tom did not develop the conversation, as they were approaching their destination. He stopped just outside the church wall of All Hallows. In the fading light Verde and Revin could just make out an expanse of green land leading away from the city wall. They were the first fields that they had seen since the night of their arrival, and although that had only been a short while ago, the sight was a comfort to them after their stay under Tom's roof.

Neither of them realised they were staring at Moorfields – land procured by Londoners from the marshy fens that had once covered the spot where they now stood. The area was still full of pockmarks and craters, and crossed by a series of foul-smelling streams, full of decomposing rubbish and discarded debris that had been either carelessly tossed away or washed down from one of the nearby parishes. In the far corner of the field stood a mountain of refuse, a stinking monument to the area's nightsoil, waste, rotting foodstuffs, faecal material and all things putrid. Here stood the reason for Tom Gatleigh's pipe. As the balance between daylight and dusk tilted in the latter's favour, the last of the flies that surrounded the laystall, like an unstable crown on a decaying head, partook of their last mouthful of food or laid their final eggs, before giving way to the forager of the night – the black rat.

The church tower stood erect and unmoving in the greying night. Its steadfastness contrasted starkly with the bleak uncertainty of its parishioners, several of whom could now be made out alongside the length of its easterly wall. Tom made his way towards this group, and Revin and Verde followed behind, excited by the eeriness that surrounded them.

A barn owl hooted from a distant tree as a tall man dressed in a long black cloak with matching breeches stepped forward from the group. He wore an air of self-importance and looked disdainfully at Tom's companions. In his hand he carried a long thin stick with a silver knob at its thickest end.

Tom turned to Verde and Revin. "Gentlemen, may I introduce you to Mister Solomon Whyte, sexton to this church," then pausing for thought he added, "Mister Verde and Mister Revin."

Whyte proffered his hand and then withdrew it, acknowledging their presence with a stiff bow of the head. His complexion was pale, even more so in the moonlight, and his features were gaunt; there was not an ounce of spare fat on his body. His most distinguishing features were a large hooked nose and piercing eyes that gave him the look of a bird of prey.

"Good evening," he said, adding after an impolite pause, "gentlemen."

Verde and Revin greeted him with a far greater respect and manner than was justified.

"Gatleigh has explained our terms, no doubt. You will be paid daily, as you may not live long enough to collect a weekly wage."

At the other side of the little circle that the group had formed, Tom coughed in order to avoid Revin's gaze.

"We have four carts," said Whyte, indicating with his arm, "to cover the parishes of Bishopsgate, Aldgate, Cripplegate and Moorgate. You will work from dusk until dawn, taking your orders first from Mister Priddy."

At this point he turned and a wizened old man with a gnarled face stepped forward. The man swore under his breath, but his comments were inaudible to all who stood near him. Joe Priddy gave the impression that he had seen most of life, and that what he had seen he didn't much care for. He was uncouth in appearance and vulgar in manner, yet somehow, somewhat surprisingly, he commanded the respect of the sexton.

"We go out in teams of three," said Whyte.

"We go out in teams of three," corrected Priddy.

"That's what I said," said Whyte.

"No, *we* go out in teams of three; you hurry home to sit on your bony arse," growled Priddy.

Whyte acknowledged the interruption and continued with his instructions to Verde and Revin.

"As I was saying, you go out in teams of three," and he stopped and looked at Priddy, and seemed almost disappointed when his words had no effect. "The carter and two bearers, one who will carry the bell and the other the lantern. As I said, Mister Priddy knows the score. He also knows where to reach me in the unlikelihood of there being any problem that he cannot deal with."

With that the sexton put a scented cloth to his nose and bidding them goodnight disappeared abruptly into the darkness.

Tom sidled up to them.

"Good luck," he wished them. "I'll see you at morn." He dropped something into Verde's hand, and then scurried away in the opposite direction to the sexton. Verde opened his hand to examine Tom's present.

"What is it?" asked Revin.

"Looks like the feet from an animal," said Verde. "Here, have one."

Priddy walked over to his two new associates and looked them up and down as though he were inspecting goods before a purchase.

"Name's Joe," he said, and he proceeded to make the apparently difficult manoeuvre of moving his clay pipe to one side of his mouth and spitting out of the other, all this being accomplished without the use of his hands. "You can put them bloody things away; they'll be no good to you."

Verde slid Tom's parting gift into his pocket; he wanted to say that he agreed with Priddy's assessment of their usefulness, but he felt little warmth towards the man, unlike his feelings towards Tom.

Verde looked at the weasel-like features of their overseer; his mouth was thin and cruel yet the eyes twinkled mischievously, their sparkle masking a sinister nature. Long, lank, straggly brown hair that hadn't been washed for weeks, draped over an unfortunate combination of rounded but hunched shoulders, all supported by a squat but muscular body. Priddy was dressed entirely in black; he wore a compass cloak that was several sizes too large for him, torn knee breeches and long stockings. On his head sat a large battered felt hat, consisting of a broad brim and a tapering sugar-loaf crown.

"Well," said Priddy.

"Yes, thank you," replied Verde.

Although of small build Priddy drew himself up menacingly.

"Not bloody well; what's your bloody names?"

Verde corrected his mistake. "This is Revin and I am Verde," he answered.

"I bloody know that, you stupid sods; what do they call you?"

Verde reiterated, "Verde and Revin."

"By Christ's wounds, what have they sent me this time?" exploded Priddy.

It dawned on Verde that the raving carter was seeking their first names. He was just in the act of christening Revin and himself when the impatient Priddy interjected.

"Well, Mister Bloody Revin and Mister Bloody Verde, if you'll just be so kind as to follow me to the bloody cart perhaps we can make a bloody start."

Priddy strode away and the two men stared after him.

"A colourful character, isn't he?" observed Revin.

"Too bloody sarcastic for me," laughed Verde. "Come on, we'd better follow. We don't want to be accused of being bloody late on our first night!"

Priddy led the way back to a group of men who had gathered beside the churchyard wall. In their midst stood several horse-drawn carts, each attended by their bearers. The gathering ceased their conversation and made an opening for Priddy to join them. The men were dressed even more raggedly than Priddy and came from the low life of London's streets. They had a choice of taking such jobs or losing their parish relief, and most had chosen to chance their luck with the dead cart.

Priddy reached down to a loose stone in the wall; his gnarled hands wiggled it from side to side, and the stone slid gently from its place, exposing a small cavity.

"The usual?" he asked the crowd.

A muttering of replies in the affirmative came from the throng of vagabonds.

"Let's be 'aving it then," shouted Priddy.

Verde watched in amazement as the men delved into various orifices in their clothing and emerged with a collection of coins. Priddy cupped his hands, and the coins were carefully counted out by him with all the fiscal acumen of a merchant banker. Priddy placed the coins in the vacant hole in the wall and sneered at the two newest recruits.

"And you, if you want to be counted as one of us. A groat each."

"Why?" asked Revin.

"'Cause I bloody said so," snapped Priddy.

"My friend meant to say that we will willingly oblige, but we would like to know to what we are contributing." Verde held out a coin in his hand as a gesture of his certitude.

Priddy was becoming impatient as the other carters were making ready to leave; reluctantly and swiftly he explained the position.

"It's a little kitty, a wager on the side – to make the night's work a little more interesting. Whoever tips the most bodies into the plague pit between now and first light keeps the money. Now pay up as we're bloody late already."

Verde released his groat into the clutching hands. Revin fished around in his clothing and eventually handed over his coin.

"It's a shilling, a bloody shilling," screamed Priddy, examining the coin. "Are you poxy bastards trying to take the piss out of me?"

"It's a good will gesture, first night and all that; keep it," interrupted Verde.

Priddy was not so easily appeased.

"Oh, charity, is it now, bloody charity? Well, Mister Bloody Revin and Mister Bloody Verde, let me tell you, we don't need your bloody charity."

"Yes we do," said a voice from a departing cart.

Priddy looked up and shouted after the driver. "Well, I say we bloody don't."

He put his large callused hand into the tiny hole and withdrawing a handful of pennies tossed them at Revin; the coins scattered on the ground.

"Right, let's bloody go," he said. "Those bastards have already got a head start."

Priddy swung himself up into the front of his cart, which was pulled by a large grey mare, and threw down a long-handled bell to Verde. Then twisting around he reached for a link lantern behind his seat and handed it to Revin, who stared vacantly at the torch, unsure as to what was expected from him. He did not have to wait long.

“Well, light the bloody thing,” shrieked Priddy. “Where have you come from, Bedlam?”

Revin remembered Tom’s gifts. He pulled out his tinder box and methodically attempted to fashion a flame by gently striking the flint across the strike-a-light.

“Christ, you strike like a bleedin’ whore. Give it here,” screamed Priddy, snatching the objects from Revin. His first brutal attempt produced a spark.

Priddy swore at the grey mare and lashed the reins across her back; the cart rolled off into the night, its large wooden wheels clattering against the irregular cobblestones. Revin yanked Verde’s sleeve.

“It’s only until Lutel and Rewn arrive,” said Verde, reading his friend’s thoughts. “Come on, let’s see how the land lies.”

“I know how the land lies, and I’d like to put him in it.”

Verde stopped walking.

“Revin, remember our mission is a peaceful and humanitarian one. I admit things appear different to what we were led to expect, but it still holds good that we are here to help.”

“I’ve seen your idea of help, giving him most of my money,” said Revin.

“You got it back, didn’t you?”

“No thanks to you.”

A mouthful of oaths emerged from ahead, encouraging them to catch up. Revin and Verde broke into a trot.

CHAPTER FIFTEEN
THE TALLY MAN

Priddy's collection area lay westwards towards Cripplegate. Revin looked up at the full moon. The cloudless sky twinkled with many a bright star, reminding him of his own planet far beyond the reaches of the dark and sparkling patchwork above. Revin pictured the cherub face and red curly hair of Mosa, his great-granddaughter. As he stared harder into the depths of the sky the faces of her black-haired brothers Cast and Nyvig formed in Revin's mind; their flawless florid complexions and ebony eyes shone out from above him.

The last day of his holiday before his mission to Earth had been spent with his great-grandchildren. He had taken them to visit their great-great-great-grandparents on their island farmstead in the north of Mykas. Most of the journey had been undertaken by air, but as there was no landing base on his grandparents' farm they had left the space hopper on the mainland and taken a leisurely row across to the island.

Gee 4s had been at the embarking bridge to welcome them. Four-year-old Mosa, Cast, aged five and seven-year-old Nyvig leapt out of the boat to hug them.

"My, how you've grown, Mosa," said Poppa Gee 4.

"So have I," insisted Cast.

"You both… all have," corrected Momma Gee 4.

Mosa and Cast held their elders' hands and dragged them up the grey sandy beach.

"Hey, what about Gee 2?" said Poppa Gee 4.

The party paused and waited for Revin to tether the boat before rejoining the group.

"Good to see you Gee 1s. How are things on the farm?" asked Revin, as he kissed his grandmother.

"Fine, it's been a kind year."

Mosa began to cry; Revin picked the little girl up and hugged her.

"What's the matter, Mosa?"

"They're Gee 4s, my Gee 4s; you called them Gee 1s. That's not their proper names."

Revin explained to Mosa how all Mykasian grandparents were numbered Gees, depending on how many generations removed they were. The nomenclature had been shortened due to the longevity of Mykasians. It was therefore not uncommon to have great-grandchildren, to whom you were a Gee 2, and at the same time be a great-grandchild yourself.

"So that's how your Gee 4s are my Gee 1s, and I'm your Gee 2," explained Revin. "Do you understand, Mosa?"

Mosa put her arms around Revin and kissed his cheek.

"A little bit," she said.

"Don't worry, you'll understand as you grow older."

Revin threw her into the air and Mosa screamed with delight; as he caught her he twisted round so that she landed on his shoulders.

"Hold tight," he said, and he chased after the others with Mosa riding on his back.

Crinaught had retired to the island with Delva at the end of his final work cycle. Crinaught had always led an active life and rather than vegetate idly away, they had brought in a variety of livestock to supplement their fresh food and to keep Crinaught busy. The farmhouse was built on three levels and had been designed by Revin's father. Although it was predominantly of black brick, it contained much glass and gave panoramic views of the whole island and the sea beyond.

"What would you like to drink, boys?" asked Delva.

"Gee 4's special," shouted Nyvig and Cast in unison.

"And how about my little Mosa?"

"The same please, Gee 4, and I'm not little."

"Of course not, I'm sorry. You can come and help me mix the specials as you are such a big girl."

Delva and Mosa disappeared into the kitchen, soon to return with a variety of drinks. The children's specials were in tall tumblers containing several distinct bands of colour, each with its own flavour. Floating in the glasses were tiny silvery particles that shimmered in the liquid. Nyvig took his drink and held it up to the light for a better view; the two children copied their older brother.

"Mine've vanished," said Nyvig.

"I can still see mine," said Cast.

"And me."

As the silver particles dissolved, the children concentrated on drinking their Gee 4 specials.

"Which is your favourite, Nyvig?" asked Mosa.

Nyvig stopped sucking on his tube and examined his drink.

"I like the green. I always save it for last."

"Mine's yellow… no, blue," added Cast.

"I like all of them," giggled Mosa.

They returned to dipping their tubes into the tumblers, choosing the flavoured band that they wished to taste first. When one colour had been finished they moved on to another.

As Mosa slurped to a finish she turned to Crinaught. "Poppa Gee 4, please may we feed the sparklies?"

Nyvig and Cast joined in the appeal.

"Later, later, children. We have several other chores to do first."

"I want to feed the sparklies," continued Mosa.

"And so you will, but we must go to the hills and pick their food before you can feed them. Besides, we have to feed the other animals first. Is anybody able to help me?"

Crinaught was greeted with a chorus of "me"s.

"Let's go," shrieked Mosa.

Crinaught led the way to an outdoor storehouse. He opened the door to reveal a variety of large red tubes containing different foodstuffs. The tubes were stacked upright and each bore a white number painted on its side.

"Who is going to feed the biljou?" he asked.

"Me, me," screamed Mosa.

"Can you remember the numbers that you need?"

"Four, seven and nine," rattled off Mosa.

Crinaught handed her a square container and the young girl placed it at the foot of the tube. Mosa pressed the number four button on a control panel that was situated on one of the walls, and a slot opened at the bottom of the requisite tube and dispensed a measured amount of food. She repeated the process at the other two tubes, and her Gee 4 lifted the heavy mixture up.

Nyvig sidled up to his elder. "May I feed the deluu?

"You may," came the kindly reply.

"Let me remember," said the boy. "One, two, three, six and nine."

"You missed seven," said Crinaught. "Don't forget, all birds require a supplement of seven."

"It's not fair. Nyvig has more buttons to push than me."

"His container will be too heavy for you to carry."

"Why can't I press more buttons?"

"I've told you before, Mosa, all animals have a different balanced diet."

"Come on, Mosa," called a voice from the doorway. "Let's go and feed the biljou, and leave the boys to Gee 4."

Mosa left the boys to finish their tasks, and led Revin to an enclosure at the rear of the farm. The biljou were cropping the grass, their soft lips tearing at the blades. As Mosa shook the container the biljou lifted their heads and, making a whistling sound, ran towards her. Biljou had been domesticated by Mykasians for centuries; they were the size of deer, but their features – long creamy shaggy coats and curved horns – were more characteristic of goats. Biljou were now mainly kept for their dairy produce, but in times past their flesh and coats had been highly valued for food and clothing. Mosa stood on the wooden rails and offered a handful of feed to the bravest biljou. She chortled as the rough tongue licked her hand clean. Scooping up another handful from the bucket Mosa tried to feed a different biljou, but the master of the herd would have none of it.

"It's no good, Mosa, you'll have to tip it out," said Revin.

"But I want to feed that one," cried the anguished girl, pointing at the smallest biljou.

"Give me the container, then."

Revin tipped the feed into a long furrow at the bottom of the fence and the herd quickly spread out along the channel of food.

"Here," said Revin, handing Mosa a handful of the mixture.

The yearling had been relegated to the end of the line. Mosa had no trouble singling him out for special attention and his pink tongue greedily gathered up her offering.

Behind the biljou enclosure stood a range of purple hills, rolling away into the distance before merging with the skyline. At times it was difficult to see where the land ended and the sky began, such could be the propinquity of their hues. Lying between the enclosure and the foot of the hills was a small lake; it was here that Mosa next insisted on dragging Revin. She stood disappointed at the water's edge, scouring the black surface.

"I can't see any sparklies," she wailed.

"Sparklies are very shy; they'll come out when we have something for them."

"But where are they?"

"Hiding, I expect, between the reeds and rushes."

Mosa scanned the lake once more as they were joined by Crinaught and the boys.

"All finished," announced Crinaught.

"Have you seen any?" asked Cast, standing alongside his sister and following her gaze.

"No. Gee 2 said they are all hiding. Make them come out, Gee 4."

Crinaught chuckled at the young girl's demand. "It will take more than an urging from me, young lady."

Mosa's face oozed disappointment at the denial of her request.

"Best we start our walk to the hills soon," said Crinaught. "Let's go and see if our picnic's ready."

The children raced away in the direction of the farmhouse, leaving the two men to saunter back. By the time Revin and Crinaught arrived, Delva had been coerced into packing their lunch and was just coming out of the building. Revin relieved her of a heavy covered box she was carrying over her shoulder and strapped it to his back. Crinaught made the same gesture towards Nyvig, who was struggling to come to terms with his load, and the party set out for the hills.

It was one of the most relaxing days that Revin could remember. The leaves on the trees were just changing from their reds and purples to shades of black and grey; the last flowers of the season strained to put out a final burst of colour. Small birds darted from bush to bush, gorging on the berries.

After their picnic, Revin sat and discussed his coming mission with Crinaught whilst Delva supervised the children as they scampered around picking the bright red rallips from the small bushes. As always, Crinaught was full of encouragement and sound advice. He was very proud of his grandson and Revin had always been a particular favourite of his. It was not only his adventurous spirit but also his looks that reminded Crinaught of his younger self. Those same keen features were still visible, but the hair had greyed and his face bore the lines of old age. Revin had much more to ask but the children, having filled the empty boxes with large round rallip berries, were impatient to return to the farm and badgered their elders into leaving.

The sparklies were what the children called the vyanies – small round silvery creatures that lived on the surface of the lake. A fully-grown vyany was no larger than a child's fist, although their size appeared greater due to the silver fronds that grew out of their upper bodies, giving rise to their nickname. Vyanies were a form of animated sponge and scurried around the lake, cleaning its surface of purple algae and any debris that would otherwise choke the water and reduce the oxygen content for the fish that dwelled below. Cast took a handful of berries from a box and threw them into the water; the red balls bobbed up and down.

"Keep still," whispered Delva.

The children did as they were told and their patience was rewarded by a rustle from the far side of the lake. Two small silvery objects emerged from a weed bed; they whizzed across the pond towards the rallip berries. As they fed on the red berries the two sparklies whipped the water with their silver fronds. In response to the call vyanies emerged from seclusion from all directions of the lake. The black water was covered in silver blobs waving their fronds as they fed. Revin looked at the contented faces of his great-grandchildren and felt a glowing sensation inside.

Priddy was several yards in front, driving his cart in the middle of the lane, the cobbled street having turned to little more than a dusty track. Verde walked to the right and just behind the cart. The number of red crosses on the doors was increasing, each accompanied by their poignant messages. Revin was dawdling, still dreaming of home as they turned right into a narrow alleyway. His reminiscences came to an abrupt end as he fell flat on his face. The lantern fell from his grasp and his first thought was that he had stumbled over a pile of rubbish. Verde dropped the bell and it rolled away, clattering and ringing resoundingly; he stooped to pick up the flame to examine Revin's injuries.

Priddy stopped the cart and swore. "Not so much bloody noise, you'll wake the dead," and he proceeded to laugh himself into a coughing fit.

Revin was only winded and was soon up on his feet, bending over to touch his toes. Verde waved the flame over the cause of Revin's fall, and gasped at the unexpected sight below them. It was the body of a young girl, no more than sixteen or seventeen years of age, her ashen face and long blonde hair being the only exposed parts as she was wrapped in a white linen cloth and propped against the corner wall of a house. Revin felt a sickness in the pit of his stomach as he dusted himself off. The solemnity of the moment was broken by Priddy's voice.

"Well, come on, you dozy buggers, lift her up. At least you've made a good start; I missed her!"

Verde leant the link against a wall and took the young woman under the arms, whilst Revin mindfully picked up her feet. Priddy fidgeted in his seat as they carefully laid the girl on the cart; even so the linen shroud draped open. Moonlight shone on her white throat and pert breasts; there wasn't a mark on her. Verde fetched the lantern in order to cover the exposed flesh.

"Bloody hell," said Priddy, "we're not laying her out. From now on just dump 'em in or you'll owe me tonight's wager."

Revin opened his mouth to say something, but before he could articulate his feelings, Verde spoke.

"She hasn't any signs of death."

"Well, she ain't bloody breathing," sneered Priddy.

Verde ignored the jest and continued in a more serious tone. "There are no blotches or buboes on her body."

"Where have you come from?" asked Priddy.

Verde fell silent, but Priddy was in no mood for cross-examination.

"That's bloody normal. Some don't have any tokens until hours after they've passed on, others have huge sores days 'aforehand. Plague's no respecter of bodies, dead or alive."

For an instant Priddy almost showed a speck of remorse, a glimpse of a man not hardened by his environment or the nature of his work, but the fleeting moment passed.

"Now bloody come on; we're late starting up. I bet Zeb Drolling's got half a bloody cartful already."

Not wishing to displease their mentor any further, Revin and Verde marched keenly off, leaving Priddy behind them.

"Where the pox are you going?" screamed a voice behind them.

The two men stopped, and turned around to face Priddy.

"You said to get a move on," said Verde through gritted teeth.

"Haven't you forgotten something?" Priddy jerked his thumb over his shoulder. The bell lay where Verde had dropped it. He ran back and retrieved it, narrowly avoiding the rearing horse as Priddy whipped it into action. As Verde drew alongside the cart Priddy called down to him. "Right, let's get started."

Verde strode off once more to catch up with Revin. Several expletives rapidly emerged from Priddy's mouth; most were unintelligible to the two men, although they did manage to grasp the words "fools, bastards and pricks".

Verde tramped back to Priddy.

"Look, you've told us to get started and we have; what's your problem?"

Priddy looked down from his cart; his lips twisted into a snarl and his eyes twitched in fury.

"Not all the dead bastards are so considerate as to lie about the streets waiting for you to fall over them. When I say get started, I mean ring the bloody bell and yell out to the people so they know we are outside and can give us their bloody dead to take away."

Verde and Revin inwardly chastised themselves for appearing so foolish in the eyes of this hard-hearted lowlife, and determined to sharpen up. Verde made a start by placidly ringing the bell, and almost apologetically announcing, "Dead cart, dead cart."

Priddy leapt up in his cart. "Are you friends of Zeb Drolling?"

"No," said Verde.

"Then why are you trying to lose me this bet?"

"We're not," said Revin, who had walked back to the cart. "We're working, aren't we?"

"Not bloody much," screamed Priddy. "Give us it here."

Verde offered him the bell, and Priddy snatched it from him, wrapping both of his hands around the long handle.

"Now, as you seem to know so very little, let me give a small demonstration of what you are supposed to be doing every time we move into a new street."

Priddy swung the bell furiously about his body whilst roaring, "Bring out your dead; bring out your bloody dead!"

The startled mare sprang several paces forward, and Verde grabbed her bridle to halt her progress; unfortunately his actions were not swift enough to stop Priddy from falling backwards in the cart. Verde resisted all temptation to laugh and with as straight a face as possible handed Priddy the reins and received his bell in exchange.

The horse was not the only one to be moved by the pealing of the bell; several doorways along the street opened up, casting faint shafts of light on the road ahead. For a short while the deserted street filled with people and as their doors opened a cacophony of screaming, wailing and crying washed into the road, as mothers, fathers, sons, daughters, grandparents and all manner of loved ones were placed outside.

Revin felt the hair standing up on the back of his neck as the harrowing scene unfolded before him. In all his years he had never witnessed such a pitiful and moving sight. In one doorway a man dragged a wailing mother from the body of a small child. Verde too looked around at the hollow soulless faces and was deeply moved. He wiped a tear from his eye but was woken from his quiescence by a now-familiar voice.

"Well, bloody hurry up."

As the despair and despondency of the street had increased, Priddy's joy and pleasure had risen. Their misery and death was his comfort and livelihood. He seemed to be devoid of any sympathy towards the victims or their families.

Verde and Revin systematically worked their way along the lane. All of the doors were now closed, but still the muffled sounds of wailing and crying could be heard. They didn't count the bodies, but Priddy could have told them that there were nine. As they meandered through the twisting alleyways the cart steadily filled. At each new street Verde would ring the bell and the sad spectacle would be repeated.

Apart from the occasional rummaging dog or scurrying rat, the streets were virtually deserted as soon as the departed relatives had been placed outside the houses. The only other sign of human life walking those dark alleyways was a small army of men dressed in half-length tunics, baggy breeches and stockings with leather boots. These were the parish watchmen, who were paid to ensure that nobody broke out of the plague-stricken houses. Passers-by were warned to stay clear, and the watchmen carried a long halberd as a reminder of the serious nature of the plague within and to discourage any attempts from those inside to escape. Priddy seemed to be on speaking terms with many of these men, but in most cases he offered no more than a grunt of acknowledgement of the other's right to be there. He had no time to dwell on pleasantries or conversation.

Priddy had smoked his way through several pipes of tobacco and the stench emanating from the cart persuaded Verde and Revin that they should follow his example. Their journey had brought them to an open grassed area bordered on two sides by houses. In the field Verde could just make out several large circular objects, their purpose being unclear to him in the half-light.

"What are they?" he enquired.

For once Priddy answered in a civil tongue.

"That's the artillery ground, where bowmen practised firing their arrows before..."

He broke off, unable to finish; the memory was too real. As things stood, he could pretend there was no time before; no time when there was laughter and merriment and comradeship.

"Before the plague," finished Revin.

"Before the plague," echoed Priddy, sadly. "Yes, they learned to shoot dead straight; now most of them are just dead." He had almost dropped his guard to reveal another self, but the harshness of the times was now too deep, and in Joe Priddy's case it was unlikely ever to surface.

His cart was now full and the bodies piled high, casting a ghoulish sight against the moonlit sky; a white mountain of corpses, unceremoniously trundling to their final resting place. At the end of the artillery ground they turned right into Bun Hill. Here the ground was very rutted and the old mare struggled to pull her load. Priddy climbed down from his seat and led the horse by its harness, encouraging it in his own inimitable style.

"Keep bloody going, you soddin' 'oss."

Verde contemplated how much more difficult their journey would have been if the fenland had not been baked hard by the summer's drought, and what methods Priddy would have resorted to if the ground had been covered in mud. Eleven o'clock chimed from the distant church clock of Saint Giles as they continued along the length of the artillery ground towards Finsbury Fields.

Beyond Bun Hill they could see a flickering of lights hovering just above ground level. Verde and Revin were at first puzzled as to what they could be and their purpose. As they drew closer they saw a mountain of earth and before it lay a large hole in the ground, some forty feet in length. The plague pit was surrounded by lanterns, their burning candles flickering mockingly at the departed.

"Where are we?" asked Verde.

Priddy looked at him scornfully. "Deadman's Place."

Several men were standing around the perimeter of the pit, taking orders from a stout man with a large and unusually square head that was covered by a long black curly periwig, although in the darkness none would have seen the balding pate that it hid. Henry Southwold was a churchwarden, and every night he could be found overseeing the burial of the dead in the plague pits. His overcoat and breeches were dark but their exact hue could not be discerned in the moonlight.

Southwold's visits were spread throughout the night, as his duties would not allow him to remain throughout the hours of darkness. When he was present there was a notable improvement by the bearers and buriers in the respect they showed towards the corpses. As they approached he was talking to a little band of roughly-dressed men who were leaning on shovels.

"This pit will not hold many more; tomorrow you must start another over to the east." Southwold waved his arm, vaguely pointing out the direction he was referring to. "The constable will be here at first light to advise you."

Picking up his lantern, the churchwarden made to depart, passing Priddy as he left. "Evening, Joe; good night's work?"

"It's all right for them that can get to warm beds," answered Priddy. "Some of us have another few hours to go."

The churchwarden stopped as though to give answer, then thinking better of it he walked away southwards in the direction of Moorfields.

"Stupid bastard," mouthed Priddy, as soon as the man was out of earshot. "Come on, you two lazy sods; the sooner we empty this lot the sooner we can go again."

Priddy skilfully backed the cart up to the edge of the pit; his horse whinnied nervously and trampled the ground.

"Hold her," he barked to Verde.

Verde scrambled across the loose soil and soothingly patted the mare's head and whispered softly in her ear. She grew quieter and Verde stroked her matted mane.

Priddy climbed over the bodies to the back of the cart and let down its tailboard. He then proceeded to push and kick the bodies off so that they rolled into the abyss below. Revin looked over the side; the pit must have been all of fifteen feet deep, but it already contained several layers of bodies and the night's work was likely to fill it. He was stunned and offended by this callous regard for life but felt helpless to intervene. Priddy continued to unload, rolling the bodies with his hands and then heaving them off with his feet. One victim became wedged at the top of the pit.

"Well, move the bloody thing, you idle bastard," he shouted at Revin.

All the sinews in his body tightened but Revin fought his anger and tried to blank out his mind. A tear in the shroud revealed the body to be that of an old woman – her face covered by hideous red sores. Revin looked away from the task he had to perform and feeling with his foot gently rolled her over the edge of the pit. The fall pushed the last air from her lungs and a sighing noise rose up from the pit. Revin leapt backward, believing the old lady to be still alive. Priddy collapsed on his hands and knees and howled with laughter and the cart moved a little closer to the edge of the pit.

"Hold that bloody horse still," he shouted, regaining his composure.

He had come to the body of the young girl that Revin had earlier fallen over; he cradled her in her arms and for a moment Revin thought he was going to show some remorse towards the girl. Instead, Priddy ripped back her shroud and lecherously looked over her naked body. Revin stepped forward to end the macabre sight.

"Stay back," snarled Priddy.

"Do as he says," called Verde; although unsighted he could guess the gruesome behaviour of which Priddy was capable, but he was concerned that they should avoid the attention of the authorities should any fracas develop.

Priddy leered down at the retreating figure of Revin. "That's right, do as your friend says."

He began caressing the girl's breasts and running his filthy hands along the contours of her body, stroking her milky white thighs. He played with her vaginal hair, twisting the blonde strands around his fingers. Revin was sickened by the defilement and refused to remain silent.

"Stop it now!" he yelled.

Priddy looked up with a lascivious grin on his face. He was enjoying teasing Revin almost as much as the torturing of the body. Licking his lips he bent forward to kiss the torso and then alighted on the girl's nipples and sucked them. Revin jumped on the wagon and grabbed Priddy by the hair, yanking his head upwards.

"All right, all right," said Priddy, realising his night's debauchery would have to end, and he gave the body a hefty kick into its final resting place. "Bastarding sod," he mouthed under his breath.

"What did you say?" challenged Revin.

Priddy shied away from a confrontation with a living body, and satisfied himself with a prediction. "You won't be so bloody coy after a few nights. When you've buried as many as me you'll see things differently."

Revin glared. "Never in the way you do."

Their conversation was interrupted by a man who had been lurking in the shadows, who until now had gone unnoticed. He was dressed in the rags of the time and in his hand he carried a long stick.

"I make that sixteen for you, Joe. Zeb had fourteen but he's already out again."

"What about Abe and Luke?" asked Priddy.

"They haven't come yet."

The man held up his stick; it was about four feet in length and had three rings carved at equal distances, dividing the stick into four parts. Two of the quarters were as yet unmarked, one contained fourteen notches and the old man was completing the sixteenth notch in the final segment.

Priddy put his face close to the teller's. "You just make sure you count the other bastards right. Let's go," he called to Revin and Verde. "Climb on board. I've got a sodding wager to win."

Verde looked across at the disgruntled figure of Revin; he felt sympathy and rapport for his friend. They were standing beside a pit of death, in the middle of a field, in the midst of the night, on a strange planet, waiting for medical supplies to save a race whose members contained debauched and deranged characters. Remember Tom and Rebecca and their family, he told himself; they're not all like this, some deserve to be saved. Besides, we have little money and no food and, at the moment, no choice.

"Let's see it through," he said to Revin, who, not having been party to Verde's reasoning, shrugged his shoulders and followed him onto the cart.

CHAPTER SIXTEEN

This Damn Plague

Before they reached the artillery ground the plague cart turned left, and they soon found themselves once more amongst the rotting stinking smells of the back alleys. A watchman lifted his halberd as they approached the house that he guarded.

"Evening, Joe."

"Evening, Nathan; have you anything for me?" asked Priddy, with an expectant grin.

"Not heard or seen a thing all day according to Edward Ridley. I took over from him at ten this evening and I've not heard a word either; strange, really, because they usually want some fetching or carrying of medicine or food supplies. Though I do admit that late last night, after you'd gone, all I could hear was screaming and moaning. They do say this plague do drive many a folk mad, and I reckon 'tis happened here."

"Or the sad fools have been put out of their misery," suggested Priddy, climbing down from the cart and examining the padlocked door.

"Oh," said Nathan. "I do 'ave the key; do you really think it bad, Joe?"

"What do you bloody think? They are hardly having a carousal inside."

The watchman produced a long iron key and fitted it into the padlock, the key turned and Priddy snapped the bolt back. The carter tried the door, anxious to claim the effects inside, but to no avail.

"Must be barred," said Nathan.

"'Ave to break it in, then," snapped Priddy.

The door shook as Priddy put his shoulder to it, but it refused to open. He eyed Nathan for help but the old watchman cut a pathetic figure. He was over sixty and very frail; his coat and breeches were much too large for him, having probably been stolen. There was a thriving trade in second-hand clothes at the time, much of it acquired for free, due to the lack of resistance from its owners.

Priddy signalled to Verde and Revin for their assistance. They slowly climbed down from the cart.

“’Tis part of my job,” explained Priddy, expecting a lack of co-operation. “We’re not allowed to leave folk dead in their houses; we must give ’em a decent burial.”

Revin snorted, but together with Verde he shoulder-charged the door. Under their combined effort, its hasps and hinges splintered from the wood, and Priddy roughly completed the removal of the door.

A pungent smell drifted out into the night air; a sickly aroma of brimstone, saltpetre and amber filled their nostrils. The doorway led straight into the sitting room and in the gloom they could just make out the silhouettes of a sparse collection of furniture.

Several chairs surrounded a wooden table, in the centre of which stood a smouldering chafing dish, the poor man’s plague purger. It proved to be the source of the fusion of smells that had greeted their entrance.

“Look in the bedrooms,” ordered Priddy.

Revin led Verde up the bare creaking steps, using the flickering flame from his link to light the way. It cast their two shadows on the rough plastered wall, the grotesque silhouettes adding to the gloomy atmosphere. Only the sound of Priddy and Nathan, stumbling around in the dark ransacking the drawers and searching any likely hiding place, disturbed the eerie silence.

An even stronger graveolence greeted them as they reached the top of the stairs. The new smell was very different from the purifying scent of the disinfectant downstairs; this was an acrid smell. It reminded Revin of meat that had been left too long, something he had encountered once or twice on his grandparents’ island. Before them stood two doors, one open, the other not; they entered the former where the smell appeared to be strongest. The small room was dark; its heavy curtains were drawn; below them in the far corner of the room was a bed, its sheets apparently rolled up on top of it. Revin waved his flare to light up the nook; a scuttling and squeaking of black rats protested at the intrusion.

Both men wished that Tom’s pipes were still alight, but the tobacco had long been smoked. Verde moved closer to the bed and saw that the rolled sheets were in fact the body of a middle-aged man. His face was contorted, and as Revin held the flame directly above the bed they could see that his entire body was covered in sores and rat bites. One or two rats lay dead on the bed beside the body. Verde felt himself heaving and rushed out of the room. Revin moved the flare closer to the man’s face; one eye was missing. From the decomposition and general state of the body Revin guessed it had lain there for several days. Returning to the landing Revin noticed Verde's pale face, and put a supporting arm around his shoulder.

"Are you all right? Not quite what we came for, is it?"

"Quiet," said Verde, "they'll hear you."

But Priddy and Nathan were far too absorbed in arguing over a pewter plate that one of them had found to notice any of the activities above them.

"Are you all right to continue?"

"Yes."

"Are you sure? Because I'll finish this if you like, and you can wait outside."

"I'm all right."

Revin led the way to the closed door; he put his hand on the handle and pushed. The door refused to budge.

"Help me," he said to Verde.

For the second time that evening the two men shoulder-charged a door, but this time the resistance was much greater. They managed to move the door slightly, but something was obstructing it.

"Try pushing," suggested Verde.

He altered his position of attack and proceeded to push the door face-on with outstretched arms. Revin copied him and under their combined effort the door gradually gave in. A small gap wide enough to squeeze through opened up. Revin poked his head around the door; all was darkness. He turned sideways and eased his body partly into the room and waved his flare around. Light from his lantern danced around the four walls; the room was smaller than the other bedroom but its contents were greater. As his eyes became more accustomed to the darkness he let out a horrified gasp. Several bodies were strewn around the room, one laid against the door being the cause of the obstruction. Revin passed the torch back to Verde and pushed his full weight against the door, moving the body a few inches. Verde followed him into the airless room.

The atmosphere was stifling and they held their hands to their mouths, attempting to block the rancid fumes. Lying against the door was the body of an old hag; she was dressed in rags and a wound to her head showed that she had cheated the plague. Verde handed the torch back to Revin and stepping over the old woman crossed the room to the bed. At first sight it appeared empty; he reached down and pulled its covers back and discovered the lifeless bodies of two small children dressed in their night attire. He lifted the pillows to reveal the angelic faces of two small boys, perhaps six or seven years of age. If he hadn't known better Verde would have assumed them to be asleep, there being no plague marks upon them.

"Revin!"

As the lantern was held above their faces, the two men noticed a discolouring around the lips.

"Suffocated?" mused Verde.

"But why, and by whom?"

Revin's eyes moved to the far side of the bed; slumped against the wall he could now see the body of a young woman. She was sitting in a pool of blood, staring blankly in front of her. Revin bent down and examined the body; her wrists were slashed and beside her lay a small bone-handled knife.

Revin looked at Verde.

"Murder and suicide?" he asked quizzically.

"But why... how could anybody...?" Verde's anguish checked his speech.

Revin moved to the open doorway. "Priddy, Priddy!" he shouted.

"I'm bloody coming, you tossers," came the infuriated reply.

Priddy swore all the way up the stairs; he didn't much care for leaving Nathan on his own. But his fears were ungrounded as the watchman felt much the same about Priddy, and followed him into the room. The carter surveyed the scene with an air of normality; neither shock nor horror etched itself on his face.

"There's another body next door," said Verde.

"Sad, very sad," said Nathan. "Edward reckoned she was going mad. Many's the mother who has killed her own childer through grief rather than let the plague be a taking of them."

"What of the old lady?" Revin pointed to the bundle of rags near the door.

"She be... was the nursekeeper, sent by the parish to heal the sick." He laughed at the irony of what he had just said. "More likely to hinder them and help them on their way than to do any good; no doubt she deserved it."

For the moment Verde could not see how anyone deserved such an inauspicious and untimely end. As an act of reverence he bent down to the young mother and put his hands over her eyes to close them, then tenderly brushed her long black hair from her cheeks.

"Do you mean she was driven to this?" he asked Nathan.

"This damn plague has a lot to answer for," replied Nathan scornfully. "If you were locked in a house for forty days with only the plague to look forward to, and your loved ones dying all around you, how would you feel?"

Verde looked at Nathan in disbelief.

"Do you mean to say that the healthy are locked in with the sick? That cannot be right."

"Quite so," said Nathan.

"On whose orders?"

"Well, they say the King and the Privy Council be gone to Salisbury, and left orders for the Mayor to do as he thinks proper."

"The Mayor?" queried Verde.

"Aye, Sir John Lawrence, him and the Duke of Albemarle are the only ones left running the city. Rest of the rich folk, clergy and doctors have mostly gone." Having delivered his explanation, Nathan spat contemptuously on the floor, giving vent to his feelings on the whole judicial matter.

A grating sound of a drawer being opened came from the next room. It made them jump and they looked nervously at each other.

"Where's Priddy?" asked Nathan.

Revin led the way to the next room. Priddy was busy searching it for anything of value. As Revin opened his mouth to protest, the would-be thief forestalled him.

"If I don't have it, then it all goes to the parish to pay for the dying, so I'm having my share now, so who is going to stop me?"

Revin felt that he should meet the challenge, but realised the futility of the situation. Priddy was probably telling the truth, and had no doubt repeated the trick many times before. He reasoned that any authority that so ill-treated its people had no more right to their valuables than Priddy, so decided against responding.

Revin and Verde each carried a small child as the five bodies were loaded onto the cart. The children were carefully laid in the open wagon, whilst Priddy and the watchman slung the nursekeeper on board and returned for the father. Verde looked on in anger as the carter and Nathan repeated their disrespectful action, but realised there was little scope to educate at this late stage. Somewhere in the distance, as Revin and Verde reverently laid the poor deranged mother on the cart, a church clock struck one.

"May as well be getting back," intoned Priddy. "Not many folks are willing to stir after the small hour."

With that he whipped the horse with the reins, and after weaving through a succession of alleyways they were soon travelling along the artillery ground towards the plague pits.

Revin and Verde volunteered to lay the bodies in their final resting place, and did so with care and compassion. Priddy had not objected as his evening's work was over, and he eagerly sought out the teller to learn the result of the night's wager. He found the man leaning against one of the other carts.

"You're the last back," said the teller with a wicked smile on his face. He held up the tally stick and baited Priddy by waving it under his nose. "Zeb's packed in thirty tonight. The money's his."

The champion of the evening emerged from behind his cart.

"You want a faster 'oss," he goaded. "Either that or fresh bearers. Not that pair of tosspots that they've landed you with."

Priddy swore under his breath; he refused to be drawn into a show of anger because he knew that would give his rival even more satisfaction than pocketing the purse. He reached inside his large coat, and fumbled around in a pocket. He knew what he touched there was worth far more than the sum of their wager; the delay had been worth it.

Failing to excite any emotion in Priddy, Zeb tried a new tack.

"Churchwarden's gone; said he couldn't wait around all night, he'll pay you double tomorrow."

This time Zeb's tormenting did have its desired effect. Priddy kicked the stones around his feet and the silence of the night was broken by his loud screaming.

"Sodding bloody bastard. By Jesus, I'll see him in that pit, you just see if I don't. Christ, I'll—"

Exactly what Priddy was promising to do to the unfortunate churchwarden was never heard as his blaspheming was curtailed by the screaming of a naked figure that was racing up the fields towards them. It proved to be a young man barely out of his teens, wearing neither clothes nor footwear. Blood trickled from cuts to his feet where he had trodden on the stony ground. As he approached, his screams became distinguishable, if not altogether decipherable.

"Piggygogger, piggygogger, piggygogger!" he repeated over and over again.

The poor lad had been driven mad by the pain of his swelling buboes and had become totally deranged by the time he drew alongside the night's assembly. Verde noticed a look of complete horror and fear in the youth's eyes as he sped passed him towards Priddy and Zeb.

"Stop him, another bloody pit jumper," yelled Priddy.

"What?" shouted Verde.

"Bloody pit jumper. They're always at it. Bloody mad – it saves us the bother, but they don't bloody count."

The distraught youngster had now reached the precipice of the pit and stopped, standing on a bank of recently dug soil, teetering on the brink. For a moment his eyes ceased blazing as though a fleeting glimpse of sanity had returned.

Verde moved towards the young man, who looking over his right shoulder realised he had an audience.

"I've been punished, I've been punished," he screeched. "The Lord God knows I took my neighbour's daughter and lusted her. He knows, he knows. 'Tis God's punishment to the wicked!"

Before Verde could move closer, the youth hurled himself into the pit. Revin raced around the far side of the hole, where Priddy and Zeb remained unmoved. A ladder used by the diggers to climb in and out of the pit lay on the top of the bank. Revin lifted the ladder and started to lower it into the pit.

"What the bloody hell are you doing?" barked Priddy.

Revin paused; his foot was on the uppermost rung and the last thing he wanted now was one of Priddy's pearls of wisdom. He started to descend the ladder.

Priddy put a restraining hand on Revin's shoulder. "A pox you will. He wants to die; if you bring him out he'll only harm himself some more. He might even hurt an innocent."

Revin's mind flashed back to the scene he had witnessed earlier that evening. It seemed an age ago, but he reminded himself that it was less than an hour past. He pulled himself up the ladder.

"We can't just leave him there," said Revin.

"Let me," said Priddy.

He seemed sincere, so Revin gave way and allowed the carter to descend the ladder.

Priddy reached the bottom of the pit and stooped to pick up a discarded shovel. He walked over the shrouded bodies, using them as a bridge to reach the tormented boy. The lad moaned and groaned as he rolled amongst the dead. Priddy lifted the shovel skywards and brought it down like an axe on the writhing youth's head. There was a sickening smashing sound, and the groaning ceased.

"There," said Priddy, climbing up the ladder, "now we are all happy." He pointed towards the pit. "He has met his maker and cast off his sins. You don't have to worry about looking after a demented soul, and I can get home to bed."

Verde and Revin stood rooted to the spot, frozen by the shock of witnessing the act. Revin moved towards Priddy, his disgust for the man superseding all other feelings. Verde put out a restraining arm.

"There's nothing we can do; our path is a different one from this."

"But he's just committed cold-blooded murder!"

Revin backed down from his confrontation. Priddy laughed as he climbed up onto his cart.

"Same time tomorrow, gents. Don't be late." He turned to face Revin before driving away into the darkness. "And make sure you bring the right bloody money."

Revin and Verde surveyed the scene of decay that lay below them.

"There was nothing we could do," soothed Verde.

"How…" began Revin, but he couldn't articulate his thoughts.

Verde spoke for him.

"We will no doubt witness many such sights that we would wish otherwise. Some we may prevent, but many we will not be able to. We have no jurisdiction here, and to risk interference may impede or even nullify our cause. Desperate times breed desperate people. We will help them all soon."

"All?" replied Revin. "Some not, surely?"

"Then you would be little better than they," remarked Verde.

"Have you nowhere to go?"

They had forgotten the tally man, who had appeared out of the darkness.

"We are new to the area and just discussing the best way home," Verde answered.

"Where do you live?"

"We are lodging near Bishopsgate."

"Then you must go due south," he replied. "Follow in the line of that tree," and he pointed to a tall elm in the distance. "Travel along the alleys until you reach the great wall; then your way leads west."

"Thank you," said Verde.

"I bid you good evening, gentlemen."

As the three men drew apart, Revin turned to the tally man.

"Where did you find those sticks?" he asked.

The tally man looked down at his wooden rods, amused that they could cause such interest.

"Why," he chortled, sweeping his arm in a panoramic motion, "the trees are plenty in these fields. Why, there are nearly as many trees as there are souls of the dead."

"May I have one?" asked Revin.

The tally man again examined his bundle as though he had missed some important point.

"Please."

He failed to find any unusual feature and, with a slight frown at such an odd request, threw one to Revin.

"Have one, yet they are free to all men."

With that he turned his back on them and walked away, scrutinising his bundle of sticks as he went.

It was past two o'clock when Verde and Revin reached Tom Gatleigh's house. They crept silently through the unlocked door.

"Rebecca," whispered Verde, acknowledging her thoughtfulness.

Snores and wheezes floated down from the rooms above. The candles had long burned out and they fumbled in the darkness for their bedcovers.

"Verde," Revin called as he snuggled down under his blankets, but there was no answer. Verde had fallen asleep almost immediately, the cold, hard floor proving no impediment to his rest.

Although they had gone to their beds several hours after the rest of the household, Verde and Revin still woke first. A chink of light shining through the curtain told them it was morning. The embers in the fireplace were sad and brown; Verde bent down and raked the ashes, then set about building up the fire.

"Don't you think it warm enough?" queried Revin.

"These people keep their fires going constantly to fend off the plague."

"But you know that's a futile action. They need lessons in hygiene; they could start by reducing the rubbish in the streets and culling the rat population. Have you seen the streets? They're open sewers."

"Tom and Rebecca have shown us a kindness; we can at least respect their views and appear helpful. Besides, keep your voice down," urged Verde.

"So what are you suggesting?"

"We stay here another day, collect our wages, then find our way into the city. We must search out the sign of the black bird."

"What if Lutel and Rewn aren't there?" asked Revin.

"Then we seek out the authorities. We can start by finding the Mayor."

"Do you really think he'll understand, let alone sanction a mass vaccination programme? We're talking about widespread ignorance here. Look at the superstitions and beliefs that we've encountered so far."

"We can try," said Verde. "So far we have only dealt with the lower classes; perhaps the authorities will be more enlightened and open to suggestion. The least we can do is advise them on the cause of all their suffering."

"You've heard these people," said Revin. "They believe it's the work of their god. How do you think they are going to react when you tell them the plague is caused by a tiny flea no bigger than a pin head? Oh, and by the way, you've got to kill all the black rats because the fleas hitch a ride and move amongst the populace!"

"Perhaps we will leave that to Lutel," suggested Verde. "She is our medical expert. But it's wrong to lock up the healthy with the sick. They need quarantine areas; at least let's try and make them understand that. I have had enough of Priddy and his sadistic cronies."

"We still need the money," argued Revin. "In any case, I think you are going to enjoy our next encounter with Joe Priddy."

He had a mischievous twinkle in his eye, but try as Verde might he would not expand upon his suggestive remark.

Within an hour the whole household had woken, Rebecca had been the first to greet them and immediately set about preparing breakfast. She refused an offer of help, insisting that they needed to catch up on their sleep after a night's work, although the clattering of pots and pans and the crackling of the fire ensured that would not happen.

"May I borrow this?" Revin asked Rebecca, pointing to a sharp kitchen knife.

"Help yourself."

Revin mysteriously disappeared into a corner of the room, and began whittling away at the tally man's stick.

By the time the children, who were the last to appear, arrived for their meal, Verde and Revin were at the table hungrily devouring cold pork and ale. As Sal and Kate took their place at table, they squealed with delight at the present that lay in front of them. Rebecca smiled at their excitement, but Tom admonished them for making so much noise.

"Leave 'em be, Tom, they've had little pleasure these last few months."

Tom could see his wife's point, and returned to tearing a piece of meat.

"Me first, me first," said Sal.

She took the whittled whistle in her mouth, and blowing into the narrower end made a futile attempt to play it.

"Let me, let me," screamed Kate, seizing the instrument from her sister.

She too was unsuccessful in producing any noise. Revin took it back.

"Watch," he said, "you have to move this piece up and down and blow at the same time. The note you make depends on how far you move the lower piece up or down."

He skilfully plied his fingers on the whistle and played a melodious tune. The girls screamed with delight, and both demanded a second try.

"Pass it here."

It was the voice of Old John, who had sat quietly finishing his breakfast. His injuries were healing fast and he was now more like his old self, according to their hosts. Revin passed his handiwork to the old man. John examined the whistle. It consisted of two cylindrical tubes, one being slightly smaller so that it would fit inside the other. The larger tube had three small round holes cut into its lower end. John placed the narrower end in his mouth and blew whilst moving the larger tube up and down. A noise emanated from the whistle; it could hardly be described as tuneful, but it was musical.

"Move your fingers," suggested Revin.

John followed the advice, and the notes changed in pitch. John stopped for breath and the children burst into applause, and the adults joined them.

"Well done, Grandfather," said Kate.

"Damn funniest instrument I've ever seen," said John, handing the whistle to his granddaughter. "Where did you learn to make those?"

Revin realised that even the most unwitting of deeds could lead them into dangerous waters.

"My great-grandfather showed me," he answered truthfully.

"Then he must have been a very old and wise man," remarked John.

"He is… was," said Revin, and the moment passed as the twins once more argued over ownership. "There's enough wood left to make you one each," he said to them.

"You are too kind," said Rebecca, and she smiled at her husband. The expression was missed by most, but Tom knew he had been forgiven for inviting the strangers into his house.

The two recently-appointed bearers remained in the house for the rest of the day. A second whistle was produced before Revin and Verde spent several hours asleep in the wooden chairs. Rebecca had banked the fire up, so it was no hardship to snooze in front of its snug glow. Even the piercing notes of the wooden whistles failed to stir them from their much-needed slumbers.

Whilst they dozed, the dependable Rebecca once more worked to provide the table with a feast. On the oven a scum boiled away in a pot filled with left-over pork bones. Rebecca busied herself chopping onions and shallots, and added them to the pot. She then sprinkled in some salt and pepper and, after replacing their jars on the shelf, brought down a third container. It contained a fine brown powder, and Rebecca added a pinch of the mace.

After a while she spooned out a sample to taste; she pulled a face and responded by pulling down the blue salt jar. Eventually, the cook was satisfied with her concoction and strained the liquid through a muslin cloth before leaving it to cool. Next she turned her attention to a plate that contained minced pork, which she seasoned with salt and pepper and more of her favourite mace. Disappearing into a side room, she swiftly returned carrying a green vegetable and two eggs. Rebecca shredded the spinach and cracked the eggs for their yolks, and added the two ingredients to the meat. Several more herbs found their way into the mixture before the cooling pork broth was also added. Finally she rolled the minced meat in brown bread crumbs, and fried the pieces in a pan.

An hour or so before dusk saw Verde and Revin stirring from their chairs. On the table were several plates filled with piping hot sausages. It was yet another new experience for the travellers' taste buds. The spicy sausages were much to their liking. Revin devoured his first mouthful and held his hand to his mouth. Tom responded by pouring him a glass of red sack. Revin gulped the liquid down, soothing his burnt tongue.

"Not too much at once," said Tom, holding up the jug of sack.

"It's delicious, what is it?"

"Raspberry sack; I make it myself. Here, try some," he said to Verde.

Verde held up his tankard, and the vermilion liquid flowed invitingly into it. Several measures of sack were needed to wash the sausages down, so by the time dusk arrived both men were quite merry.

"May I borrow a whistle?" asked Revin as he prepared to leave for work.

Both of the twins were reluctant to let their prized possessions go, but eventually Kate felt she could not deny their kind benefactor and offered Revin her instrument.

"I'll bring it back. I promise."

With farewells all around, the two men set out on their short walk to meet Priddy. The route was firmly etched in their memories so there was no need for Tom to accompany them. Their unaccompanied sojourn also gave them confidence as they successfully negotiated the alleyways to the church.

A group of men stood around the walls; their voices were strangely hushed. Revin approached the edge of the solemn circle.

"No wager tonight?" he asked Priddy.

"Not tonight, mark of respect," answered the scoundrel. "Plague's done for Zeb."

Revin felt a pang of remorse; nobody deserved to perish by such a painful disease, though the irreverent treatment handed out by Priddy and his cronies towards the dead meant the news did not evoke as much sympathy as it may otherwise have done. Revin felt guilty at having such little compassion. After all, perhaps the dire nature of their work dictated the circumstances that prevailed. No, he thought, the humour and the banter were acceptable, but the lack of dignity extended to the dead was inexcusable. At least they'd shown some honour among thieves by cancelling the wager.

Verde looked at Priddy. "Sorry about Zeb, but surely he was only with us last night?"

"Told 'ee before, 'tis the way of the distemper; some knows it's coming, some see it there for several days, some don't know and never do 'til it's too late. One minute they're fine, the next they're dropping dead in the street, just like poor Zeb. Stupid sod."

For a moment Verde had thought that Priddy was going to finish a speech containing no profanities. His last pronouncement was true to character, and Verde could rest assured that all was well with the world; well, at least Joe Priddy's world, he told himself.

"Manny was with him." Priddy indicated a member of their group with his eyes.

Manny was delighted to be the centre of attention, as it was a position he rarely aspired to, and proceeded to relate to the newcomers what had previously been repeated several times to the circle that evening.

"'Twas just outside the Spotted Cow," said the little wizened old man. "Fancy a drink, I says to Zeb. Yes, he replies, and follows me into the inn. Sit there, I says," and Manny pointed to an imaginary seat. "I'll get 'ee a tankard, I says. And Zeb sits himself down, and I fetches him a drink of ale and puts it down in front of 'im. That should put 'ee to rights, I says. I've never known a warmer spell, I says. Can't remember a drier spring or a warmer summer, I says. Then I notice Zeb 'asn't touched his ale. Something wrong with your drink, I says, and I turns to Zeb and he's just staring in front of himself. Dead."

"This plague's a right bastard," said Priddy, "no respecter of honest folk." After a moment, he was drawn back to the present time. "No bets tonight but there's still work to do. Come on, you tossers."

CHAPTER SEVENTEEN

MIDNIGHT'S TUNE

Verde and Revin followed the cart as it trundled through the alleyways of Moorfields and Cripplegate. As Verde tolled the bell the same sorry spectacle would be regularly repeated.

Priddy halted the cart for a chat with Nathan, who had been allocated a new watch. "What's the score?"

"Nothing much yet, but I've high hopes, Joe. I couldn't help noticing a very pretty necklace when the lady of the house asked me to fetch her some water."

"She pay you?"

"Of course she did, wouldn't have handed over the bucket otherwise."

Revin and Verde chatted idly at the back of the cart whilst the conversation continued.

Priddy finally bade Nathan farewell, and noticed he only had one bearer.

"Where's he bloody gone?" he snapped.

"Gone for a piss," replied Revin, pleased with his mastery of the vernacular.

"Stupid prick!"

Revin could not think of a suitable reply as they continued down the alley. At the far end lay another body wrapped in a shroud. Revin called to Priddy for assistance. The carter reluctantly descended, swearing profusely, declaring to all who had ears what he would do to Verde when he reappeared. Revin carefully took the body by the arms whilst Priddy grabbed the feet.

"That stupid poxy pisser better hurry up or they'll be no money for him," warned Priddy as the body was dumped in the cart. He took the reins and turned left into the next alleyway. The cart rumbled along the dusty track, bumping over the deep ruts and stones that littered the way.

"Bring out your dead," yelled Revin, ringing the bell with gusto. Priddy looked down approvingly on his reluctant protégé.

A door opened and a small child silently beckoned them. Priddy and Revin walked over to the house and followed the child who had summoned them. As they entered the room, the familiar mixture of death and sulphur hit them. Several children lay moaning and groaning on the floor, surrounded by loose faeces and vomit. Revin attended each in turn; he did what little he could to make them comfortable, his sense of frustration growing with each successive case.

There was no sign of any parents or other adults, apart from the parish nursekeeper. Revin restrained himself from attacking her either physically or verbally; to do so, he reasoned, would not improve the lot of the remaining children. She pointed Priddy towards the body of a child that lay in a corner of the room. In turn, Priddy signalled to Revin to remove the body.

As Revin carried the child to the cart the whole ghastly scene was etched in his memory. For the entire time that he had been in the house, he felt as though he had taken part in some macabre mime, a gruesome tableau where no words had been spoken. Death had been personified in the shape of those tiny defenceless children. As the door closed behind him, it felt as though death itself were being locked away in that despairing household. If only it were so, he thought. How many more harrowing scenes would he be required to witness before they were in a position to help?

"Give us a hand," said Revin.

"It's only a poxy child," said Priddy. "Throw him up yourself."

"I've twinged my back."

"Useless bloody tosspot, give him here."

Priddy climbed onto the wheel of his cart as Revin handed the lifeless form to him. As he threw the child into the cart a body sat bolt upright.

"This calls for a tune," it said, and it proceeded to play a ghostly air on a wooden whistle.

For all his debased ways Priddy was still a superstitious and God-fearing fellow.

"The Devil!" he screamed. "Lucifer has come for me!"

Priddy gave vent to a bloodcurdling yell that convinced many a death-hardened household that the devil did indeed walk their streets that night. Losing his grip on the side of the cart Priddy fell backwards to the ground; he picked himself up and, without once glancing at Revin, raced into the night, continually screaming as he fled.

The body on the cart laughed aloud; Revin held out a hand to help it down from the cart.

"I never thought you'd make it in time," he said.

"Neither did I," chortled Verde. "I became lost round the back alleys.

Worked rather well, though, didn't it? You make a good whistle!"

"Let's hope he's learned his lesson, and perhaps he'll think twice in the future."

Verde unwrapped himself from the blanket, folded it and placed it on the cart. "Let's finish the round," he said, picking up the reins. "Then we can go and collect our wages and leave this job behind."

"Perhaps we could collect Priddy's as well," said Revin, grinning.

The two men laughed as the cart moved forward. It had been an irreverent trick to pull, but they felt fully justified; it had also helped them cope with the immense pressure that had been building inside them.

Revin woke early the next morning and reaching over he shook Verde.

"I'm going for a walk," he announced. "I'm feeling a bit stiff and the exercise will do me good. Besides, if we are leaving I thought I would go and see how things lie between here and the gate."

"Do you want me to come?"

"No, stay here; it might arouse suspicion if we both went."

Verde closed his eyes and rolled back under the covers. Inwardly he was content, as he was not used to manual work, and he preferred to rest his aches.

"Be careful," he said to the departing Revin.

Revin tiptoed stealthily to the door, whilst Verde pulled his blanket up even higher. Brilliant sunshine continued to pour from the sky, putting Revin in an optimistic mood as he retraced their steps of the first morning towards Bishopsgate. Secretly he hoped he could report back to Verde that a way into the city was open to them, and they could begin the search for their friends.

A raker was at work clearing away the rotting rubbish from the streets. The man whistled tunelessly to himself as he loaded the refuse into his wooden barrow. He stopped his whistling to wish Revin a good morning before continuing with his tune.

Revin held his breath as he passed the street's waste, then turned to reply.

"Where do you take all this?"

"To the laystall, just over yonder," the man said, pointing.

All the more reason for the rats to stay, thought Revin, and he opened his mouth to tell the raker so and then thought better of it.

A mature fetid smell followed Revin as he moved away; it arose from the kennel that ran down the middle of the street. This channel was supposed to improve the local hygiene, but left to rot under the burning sun its concoction of waste had ripened to disgusting proportions. Red crosses now appeared the norm on the doors; very few had escaped the deadly daub. As he hurried past one door a man was chalking a white cross. Revin was interested in the change and stopped to question the spindly youth.

"Why no red cross, friend?"

Startled at his interruption the nervous lad dropped his chalk; as he retrieved it from the ground he stood up to face Revin. His clothes were dirty and torn and covered in red and white blotches; a thatch of blond hair straggled from underneath his battered hat. In appearance, the "artist" would not have been out of place standing in a field scaring away crows; his eyes lacked sparkle, as though all of the fight had long left his body.

"D-d-death has l-l-left h-here," he stammered.

"I don't understand," said Revin, indicating the white mark.

The scarecrow pointed at the house with his piece of chalk.

"If th-there is n-n-n-no m-more p-p-plague for tw… tw… twenty-eight d-days, th-then all m-m-may walk f-free."

Revin thanked the youth for his explanation, and hurried away.

To begin with, Revin's sojourn was largely a lonely one, as few people walked the streets at this early hour. Many did not risk them at any hour, unless their journey was absolutely necessary.

As most of the wealthy had quit the city, the traders and merchants had followed them. Those who had remained behind had little custom, most people being either too poor or too frightened to venture forth. Occasionally, discarded servants could still be found roaming the streets, escaping the vile lodgings of the back alleys. Their choice was a stark one; they could either seek shelter in a foul airless cellar, along with twenty or more of their kind, or join the tented throng that lived rough off the land on the outskirts of the city.

A band of noisy wandering vagrants approached. Revin sensed trouble as the group drew closer and prepared himself for flight. Six or seven youths headed towards him; their manner was aggressive and belligerent. For the moment the bellicose youths had not noticed him; they were too intent on throwing stones at the rooftops, aiming to hit the birds that perched there.

As they drew closer the leading youth pointed at Revin, who prepared himself for the inevitable. But en masse the group crossed the road to the other side, purposely avoiding him. Revin's relief was tempered by the thought that his identity had been discovered, but as he looked behind he saw that the gang were corkscrewing across the street, avoiding contact with any traveller they encountered. This peculiar behaviour was repeated by most people who came towards him; some, he noticed, even held their noses or put posies to their mouths as they passed a red-crossed door. These strange practices were given credence as he approached the end of the row; from behind an open window a head suddenly poked through the curtains. A woman with tangled hair and crazed eyes thrust herself forward and breathed over him.

"Got you, got you!" crowed the hag, withdrawing whilst cackling perversely.

Revin was shaken at such callousness, but nothing was beginning to surprise him, and he quickened his step and dived into an alleyway.

A tortoiseshell cat mewed at his feet as he paused to find his bearings, Revin bent down to stroke the animal and it submissively toppled over onto its back. His long fingers tickled the exposed tummy, ruffling the chocolate and cream fur.

"At least somebody's glad to see me," he said to the cat as it purred in delight.

A barking noise came from an adjacent alley and his newfound friend raced away. Revin continued towards the barking, and as he drew nearer a second sound could be clearly heard, a rhythmic throbbing noise as if someone were beating a drum.

As he reached the top of a side alley, both noises were explained together. A small black-and-white terrier snapped around the heels of a man who was smashing his head against a door and screaming in pain. Another victim, surmised Revin, either directly or indirectly affected by the plague. He wanted to offer the man solace but he knew a cure was out of his hands at the moment, and mere words seemed totally inadequate.

Rotten smells once more filled the air as he drew nearer to the great gate. Armed guards were still on duty, and as Revin watched from the shelter of a doorway most people were refused entry, halted by the thrusting halberds.

As he mused, the guards drew aside for a most strange-looking creature. It was dressed in a large leather helmet that covered the best part of the shoulders. The face was hidden by a mask with a sinister glass eye at each side, and protruding from the front was a huge beak. The apparition was topped by a large distinguished-looking hat, and the whole effect was completed by a sweeping full-length gown made of a waxed material over a pair of black breeches. Revin was at first taken aback by the garb of the physician, and watched in amazement as the plague doctor met with no resistance from the sentinels. As he passed through the gate the man waved a red stick, no more than three feet in length, and all gave way before him. Smiling to himself, Revin turned around and pondered on the scene that he had just witnessed as he sauntered back.

Still reflecting on the sight, as he approached Gatleigh's house he did not immediately notice a crowd had gathered outside. An old crone stood on the step dressed in the rags of a pauper, the grey shawl on her shoulders stained and threadbare; her dress was too long for her and the hem was soiled and ragged. In her hand she carried a white wand. Revin cogitated on the significance that sticks seemed to be having today, and wondered on their symbolism. His anxiety was justified as this woman was a searcher, employed by the parish to establish the cause of death amongst its inhabitants.

A man appeared from behind the old woman, just as Revin had summoned up the courage to approach her. He whispered something in the searcher's ear and she responded by beckoning to a person in the crowd. There were mutterings of sympathy and fear as a man walked forward. Revin recognised him as the youth with the white chalk, to whom he had spoken earlier. This time he was to daub the dreaded red cross on Gatleigh's door.

Revin ran up to the man who had recently emerged from the house, the man who had spoken to the searcher. "You must let me in."

"In?" said the man. "It's my duty as the constable of this parish to see *they* stay in," and he pointed at the house with his thumb, "and *you*," jabbing Revin in the chest, "stay out!"

Part Four

Delays

CHAPTER EIGHTEEN

A Date with Destiny

Lutel stopped washing and dried her face as quickly as possible, readied herself and dashed out of the bedroom door in pursuit of her brother. On hearing of Woodman's departure Rewn had brushed past the landlord and raced down the stairs.

Lutel cursed the time they had met Woodman; the man seemed to be a jinx, and appeared to be at the centre of their every action whether they liked it or not. Lutel skipped down the stairs, missing every alternate step; reaching the bottom she juddered to a halt. In the far corner two men sat at a table; one had his back to her, but the other had watched her descent and, at her appearance, motioned to his companion. Rewn turned around and beckoned his sister to join him and Woodman for breakfast.

A third bowl of porridge had been ordered in anticipation of her arrival. Lutel stared at the food in front of her; it was still steaming and she stirred it with a spoon, examining the peas and beans that were mixed with it.

"How?" said Lutel, unable to comprehend the scene.

"I was just telling your brother, miss, I had a last-minute piece of business to attend, then I thought I should check on the coach, and no sooner was I back than Master Rewn comes charging down the stairs, and all but flies past I. In fact, if I hadn't spoken to him I do believe he would have gone right out the door without stopping."

Woodman paused to wipe away a dollop of porridge that had dripped onto his chin.

"Then I thought, breakfast – must have something warm before we start our journey, so I took the liberty of ordering for all three of us. Landlady was most obliging, kept yours back until you was ready; your brother said you were on the way, so we bade her fetch out yours with his."

Woodman turned his attention back to the bowl in front of him. Lutel took a mouthful and sat back in her chair with a disparaging look. She pushed the bowl away from her.

"And is all set with the coach?" she ventured.

“Leaves shortly,” replied Rewn.

Woodman reached over for the discarded bowl. “Still plenty of time,” he said.

Stale smoky air in their lungs was replaced by a fresher variety as they followed Woodman across the road from the Lyon Inn, towards the large building that had been their prison. Rewn breathed in deeply, savouring the sweetness of freedom. A glint from the ground caught his eye; he stooped and picked up a small disc.

“What is it?” asked Lutel.

Rewn was examining the object. “I do believe it’s some of their money.”

“Well, put it away for now; it may prove useful.”

Woodman had turned left around the side of the building, disappearing from view down a small dark alleyway that was bordered by the high stone walls of several buildings. Lutel tugged at Rewn to keep pace with Woodman. A small brilliant blue rectangle was their only view of the azure sky that shone above them. They caught sight of Woodman passing through a narrow tunnel and bounded after him, passing underneath one of the flint-coloured buildings that enclosed the shambles.

Rewn and Lutel stepped out of the darkness and into the light of the high street, and almost bumped into the frame of their guide who had stopped to wait for them. Together they walked down the dusty road towards the River Avon. On their right-hand side a row of smart red-brick dwellings continued all the way to the waterside. On their near side, the buildings were a sprawling contrast of medieval and more recent Tudor. A black-and-white timbered construction stood next to a pink lathe and plaster house offset with natural oak timbers. Many of the buildings doubled as shops, fronting on to the high street, the living quarters housed towards the rear or on the upper levels. Lutel looked askance at the various merchants, who were already in the act of plying their wares or starting the business of the day.

Woodman halted just above the bridge, in front of a pale stone-faced building. A central archway, large enough to allow for the comfortable passage of a coach, led to a courtyard beyond. Woodman strode over the cobblestones, and headed for a group of ostlers and stable lads who were attending to teams of horses. Lutel drew in her cheeks; the air reeked with the sweat of horses, fresh manure and fetid straw.

Beyond the cobblestones stood the majestic Bull Inn, its walls constructed of the same rich Bath stone as the imposing archway. In front of the building stood a team of four horses, harnessed to a coach.

"Wait here," said Woodman.

He brushed through the crowd of stable-lads, and on to the groom who stood at the head of the harnessed team. On Woodman's approach the groom put down the foreleg of a bay that he had been examining. As Woodman sidled up to him, Lutel and Rewn strained to overhear their conversation, but the whinnying of the horses and the clatter of metal on the cobblestones drowned their speech. The groom accepted something that the other offered to him, and Woodman beckoned his companions forward with a wave of his arm.

A fresh-faced lad of tender years opened the coach door. Rewn placed a foot on its step and hauled his body up. Pausing at the opening, and balancing on one foot, he thrust his head forward to satisfy himself that no danger lurked within. Lutel clambered up after him, and sat opposite with her back to the driver. She looked around at the carriage; the seats were upholstered in black, and smelled of leather, but they were hard and uncomfortable to sit on. Windows on either side were curtained in a similar colour, and the floor was wooden and plain, giving the coach a severity that Lutel felt it did not deserve.

The coach lurched to one side as someone entered and Lutel turned to speak with him.

"How long before we..."

Her face reddened as she realised the new passenger was not Woodman, but the tall, thin, aquiline-nosed man with whom they had briefly been acquainted the previous evening: one of the laughing drinkers from the inn. The coach lurched for a second time as he was quickly followed by his female companion, also of their previous night's acquaintance.

"We leave within the next ten minutes," said their fellow passenger, correctly guessing her question and sitting down next to Rewn. The woman dusted the seat next to the stranger with the back of her gloved hand, and plumped herself down. Although her mistake had been of no consequence, Lutel burned inside at her carelessness, knowing that the error could have been more costly.

Silence reigned in the coach for the next few minutes; not even the genial newcomer made any attempt to instigate conversation. Rewn and Lutel stared down at the coach floor, whilst outside last-minute orders were being shouted from driver to groom and then on to the stable lads. Lutel was relieved when at last Woodman entered and sat himself next to her, removing a new wide-brimmed hat and placing it at his side on the remaining vacant seat.

Above them the driver, a burly man in his late forties, indicated to all who were prepared to listen that he was ready to leave. Tugging the collar on his large brown coat, he pulled his matching sugar-loaf hat tighter to keep any possible breeze from his balding pate. Horses neighed as he whipped the team and reined them round to the left in a half-circle. Once more the sound of iron shoes clanging on the cobblestones masked the surrounding voices and their farewell wishes. The clattering intensified as the coach drove through the archway and turned right, heading for London. As they drove up the incline away from the river, they saw that activity in the high street had intensified as the townsfolk of Chippenham went about their daily business.

Their coach rumbled past the teeming butchers' shambles; the yellow buttercross was packed with hanging game-birds and the carcasses of pigs and sheep. Lutel looked away from the sight, trying to avoid eye contact at all times, but the townspeople were so busy that they paid little attention to the local stage. Rounding a bend, Lutel could see the lock-up, which was now literally and metaphorically behind them.

As they drew alongside the Lyon Inn, Woodman looked over at Rewn. "This stage goes as far as Hounslow. The driver will venture no further for fear of the plague in London."

Lutel's mind focused sharply on the purpose of their journey. She closed her eyes and imagined Revin cursing impatiently as a new day dawned and they had failed to arrive. And what of Verde? she thought. Dear Verde would be as phlegmatic as ever, and taking practical measures towards solving their problems.

The coach swayed on its leather straps as it headed eastwards out of the market town. The rhythmic clatter of iron rim on stone softened to wheel on earth as the travellers passed through Pewsham Woods, a large deciduous royal forest on the edge of Chippenham. Shrivelling leaves on the oak trees showed early signs of autumnal colours, evidence of the long drought. As they climbed the hill out of town, their nostrils twitched at the scent of wild garlic that wafted into their carriage. The coach slowed down as the horses felt the pull of the hill, causing the garlic to linger and outstay its welcome.

"How long before we reach Hounslow?" asked Rewn.

"Depends on the conditions; two to three days or possibly more," replied Woodman. "We should make Newbury by nightfall, given no hitches."

Rewn blanched at the length of time. He sat back in his seat and closed his eyes.

He was travelling along a beam of violet light. There was no sensation of movement; the corridor of colour remained unaltered, giving no clues as to the speed of his journey. Rewn had been standing in the same position for less than a minute, and would soon reach his destination. Four other Mykasians shared his journey; all stood silently, staring into the beam. The four had joined Rewn in one of the many beam bowls that were situated throughout all the major residential areas of Mykas. Every large dish was bedded below the surface; only the rims were at ground level. Travel dishes were accessed by underground shafts that led to the centre of each dish, where there was room for five people to stand. Every few seconds a beam of light flashed on, and the passengers began their journey along the light tunnel to one of the four space confines in the sky.

The space confines were situated on the outer edges of the planet's atmosphere, so that between them they could transmit light tunnels to or receive them from all parts of Mykas. Travellers could reach any major city of Mykas within minutes, either by beaming directly from a space station to a dish below or, if their intended destination was in a different hemisphere, by travelling along a light tunnel to one or more of the three sister confines, before beaming back down again. Rewn had decided to start his holiday by winding down at the thrarb races at his favourite resort.

Palladin was a popular resort, and drew Mykasians from all walks of life. Many wealthy Mykasians owned their own thrarb farms, and appointed thrarb masters to tend and train their animals, visiting only during the racing festivals. A less desirable element of Mykasian society was also attracted by the betting and associated practices, and all manner of shady characters swarmed around the area. Rewn found his hotel and after a relaxing meal retired for the night, determined to wake early the next morning.

Palladin's wealth and popularity had been founded on the thrarb markets and subsequent racing. Rewn strolled around the pens searching for a thrarb of his own. They were housed in small corrals, separated by low walls of snow. It was still early in the day and many holidaymakers had yet to rouse from their warm hotels; Rewn intended his discomfort to provide him with a prize specimen. Pausing in front of a pen, he stared at its inmate; the thrarb looked back at him.

Rewn was attracted to the unusual markings of the thrarb below him. It was principally a light grey, but its flippers were a lighter shade of purple. The friendly egg-shaped creature waddled on its two tiny flippers towards Rewn, across its snowy enclose, and stared at him with its two round eyes.

Leaning over the wall he tickled the short, tight curls on the thrarb's ears. He was rewarded by a contented cooing sound from its circular mouth.

"Is he for sale?" Rewn asked the thrarb master.

The burly man slowly stroked his long black beard. "Will be, later on today."

"Will you take an offer for him now?"

"That depends on your offer. It's more than my job's worth to accept anything below a hundred."

Rewn brushed aside the price with a laugh. "That's more than a seasoned champion would fetch; his tag shows this thrarb is an unraced yearling."

The master pointed to the sign on the snowy wall. "Read further and you'll see his champion lineage."

"That may be so, but he's unproved."

"We'll see after the trials. Then watch the bidding go."

Rewn was keen to avoid the bidding, as his pride often triumphed over his self-control, but a hundred trusts for a novice was unheard of. As he walked away the thrarb cooed softly behind his back. Rewn turned around. He remembered the frenetic pace of the thrarb auctions, and how difficult it sometimes proved to make your bid known.

"I'll give you seventy."

The thrarb master wiped a hand across his moustache. "I'm tempted."

"I should think so; fifty would be a fair price."

"If he were mine I'd let him go – but as I said I answer to another."

"Seventy-five."

The seller hesitated, looking from the thrarb to Rewn. The tiny animal once more cooed pitifully, encouraging Rewn.

"Eighty," offered Rewn.

"Ninety."

Rewn looked behind him at the rival bidder. A slender young girl had crept up unnoticed; only her green eyes and forehead were visible from the warm, cream clothes that protected her.

"Ninety-five," countered Rewn.

"A hundred," retaliated the woman.

"A hundred, a hundred…" The figure ran along the walls and soon a small crowd had gathered at the pen. All eyes were on Rewn, awaiting his reaction, but his bid did not come; instead he turned to his rival and, pulling her hood aside, whispered in her ear.

"You promise," she said.

"Everything, straight down the middle, costs and rewards."

"Agreed."

"A hundred and twenty," announced Rewn. "It's our final offer."

A gasp of disbelief burst from the crowd. The perplexed master looked from Rewn to the girl, unsure as to whose bid he was accepting.

"He's yours, yours," he said eagerly, turning from Rewn to the girl.

"Sixty from each of us," explained Rewn.

"As long as I receive the full one hundred and twenty trusts, I care not who or how many pay me," gasped the excited man.

Rewn removed his gloves and placed his hand on a circular metal disc that had been pushed towards him. The thrarb master pressed several buttons on the rim of the disc, and there followed a buzzing and beeping noise, culminating in the disc flashing green.

"Your turn," said Rewn, turning to the girl. "I realise we are partners, yet I don't even know your name."

"Shai," she said, smiling, as she removed the wrap from around her mouth. Shai repeated the transaction with the disc.

"You can pick him up this evening, in time for the first race; all enquiries will be complete by then."

"Where are you staying?" Rewn asked, as he and Shai walked away.

"Nowhere at present; I've only just arrived."

"You mean you haven't reserved accommodation? All vacancies are booked far in advance of the races."

"I like to do things on impulse," said Shai, daring Rewn with her eyes.

He woke several hours later; the sky outside was vermilion, and the room was in darkness. Rewn sat bolt upright.

"No!" he shouted out loud, and leapt out of bed in search of his clothes.

The disturbance woke Shai; she pulled herself up. "Don't tell me we've overslept."

"We've just time for the first race."

"Apart from one thing."

"What's that?"

"We need to register, and we haven't thought of a name," she gasped, whilst dressing rapidly.

Rewn threw Shai her slacks.

"I hope they will be warm enough," she said with a hint of admonishment.

Rewn laughed. "Shai, why don't we call him Ecstasy?"

"Don't you think that's a little exalted for the tiny guy to live up to?"

"What do you suggest then?"

"I don't know. How about something that reflects our meeting? Partner, for example."

"Now you've gone to the other extreme; that's far too indifferent."

"Well, I still think we need something to reflect our chance meeting," said Shai. "What about Lucky?"

"Yes, but rather common, not very imaginative. How about Chancer?"

"No," they said together.

"Something reflecting our unforeseen meeting," murmured Rewn.

"Got it," shouted Shai. "Destiny."

"Right, let's go and register our Destiny, before it's too late."

Racing took place on the outskirts of the town; crowds were already flocking into the streets, and they were jostled continually. At one point Rewn thought they would never register in time, but the flow of the crowd was heading towards the race track and they made the registration office in plenty of time.

"Let's have a bet," said Shai.

"Why not?" replied Rewn, who would willingly have walked to both of Mykas's suns and back, if only Shai had asked him.

They approached a man who was standing inside a round hole in the middle of a large disc; the console was divided into coloured segments. Shai searched the sections and on locating Destiny's segment, she placed her hand on the orange portion.

"How much?" asked the sprightly man, from the centre.

"Twenty," said Shai confidently.

The orange portion flashed several times, and the bet was made. Rewn led Shai away to the banked seating, and they sat high up in the stand. A piercing wind cut them to the quick, and Rewn put a warming arm around Shai, who responded by snuggling into his shoulder.

A man-made mountain of snow towered above them, conical in shape and glistening in the evening moon. A spiral track had been cut into the sides of the mountain; this was the thrarbs' racetrack. The tiny creatures were taken to the peak and released, their small shiny flippers being ideal for sliding down the icy circuit. They were encouraged to go faster by an overhead device that worked on a cable system. A small container was suspended a little way in front of the thrarbs, containing a fishy concoction that proved irresistible to a hungry thrarb. Descents were made individually, and were relayed to the crowds by several large screens so that the entire run could be seen. At the finish a computerised time was instantly flashed up on the screens.

A gantry of lights was switched on behind them, and a loud cheer greeted the impending races. A dazzling array of lights encircled the arena, giving a feeling of warmth against the chilling wind. Expectation reached fever pitch as the first tiny creature began its descent down the snowy spiral. Rewn hailed a snack seller, and bought two warm drinks and a variety of food. Shai queried the amount he purchased.

"I need to replace the energy I used this afternoon," he joked.

Shai coloured and released his hand. At the time Rewn thought nothing of the gesture, assuming her to be embarrassed, or freeing her hand for eating. It was only later that he was to regret his public declaration, and to understand another side to Shai's character. Her action here, if he had read it correctly, might have saved him many years of sadness and regret. But that was all in the future; another form of destiny was now occupying his mind, in the shape of their tiny thrarb.

Rewn stood and cheered Destiny from the moment the buzzer sounded, standing on his chair to procure a better view. As the speed of the descent became apparent many in the crowd followed his example, and by the end of the run few remained in their seats. Rewn looked at one of the giant screens and yelled with delight; he glanced across to hug Shai, but her seat was empty.

CHAPTER NINETEEN
DUVAL

In just under half an hour's travelling they had reached the outskirts of Calne. Descending suddenly into a dip, they glimpsed a hunting lodge away to their right, but their view was restricted by the surrounding woods. On the opposite side, at the foot of the hill, stood a farmhouse – a large building constructed from the local flint. Several dogs barked as the coach rattled past; a brown-and-white collie snapped around the wheels until they had rounded the next hill, when a combination of oaths and flaying whip persuaded the animal that it might be best to retreat. From the brow of the hill, the small hamlet of Calne came into view. A scattering of buildings gradually thickened as they drove along its main rutted highway.

In the centre of Calne they passed a large sandy-coloured house, decorated in ornate Tudor roses; Lutel noted that it appeared to be the only building of substance, apart from the occasional inn.

As they left the sleepy hamlet behind, the road deteriorated and the shaking caused Rewn to open his eyes. The first thing he saw was a pair of magnificent white horses, standing proudly on a hillside under the canopy of a giant elm. The green stable was enveloped by lush hills that folded around it, giving protection from the elements. The beautiful beasts stood with dignity in the centre of the grassy stage. From their hillside vantage, Rewn could imagine them intently scrutinising every ant-sized passer-by. In stark contrast, a few spindly storm-swept trees stood guard at the base of the escarpment. The man they did not know, who had remained silent since his opening pronouncement, leant across his companion and spoke to the animals through the open window.

"White horse, white horse, bring me good luck. Good luck to you, good luck to me, good luck to everyone I see!"

Woodman answered the puzzled expression on Rewn's face.

"It's a superstition about these parts; brings good luck if you do say it to any white horse you see."

Lutel again wondered at the simplicity of these country folk; here was further proof, as though she needed it, that Mykasian technology and medical knowledge would be too advanced and unacceptable to the inhabitants of this country. She felt inside her clothing. Next to her body was a long thin metal object; Lutel sighed at its presence. In the excitement of the last few days she had almost forgotten its existence; it was now the only object that linked her to her home planet. The clothes she wore, even the boots on her feet, all came from England.

Lutel looked out on the landscape; the Wiltshire Downs stretched away into the far distance. Fields on her near side were bleak, the rolling hills dotted with sheep; as far as her eye could see the vista was chalk downland, interspersed with the occasional copse and large rocks.

Within a few yards the coach reached the village of Beckhampton and was pulling in to the Wagon and Horses Inn. The inn was a popular resting post on the route, and their driver had acquired a taste for the landlord's ale. In the humid conditions the horses also appreciated the stop for water. Rewn climbed down first, admiring the newly thatched roof that sat grandly above the weathered red brick of the walls; he then turned to help the two ladies disembark.

Standing in the porchway with welcoming arms was the expectant landlord, greeting the travellers with a jug of ale. Rewn could not help observing that a characteristic feature of the few landlords that he had so far encountered was a large rosy face and a jovial personality; he wondered if it were so with all such taverners. Their host called to his son to fetch a bucket of water. A small frail boy limped from the side of the inn carrying a wooden pail; each horse was visited in turn and allowed to slake its thirst.

Rewn felt the cool drink trickle down his throat; he could grow to like this ale he thought. The landlord, who had been engrossed in conversation with the driver, walked over and collected the pewter tankards. Woodman produced a coin from his jacket, as did the long-nosed passenger. Rewn remembered his lucky find and reached inside his coat to feel for the coin. He pulled it out and handed it to the landlord. The host of the Wagon and Horses eyed the gold sovereign.

"You jest, sir. We are only a small establishment; I cannot possibly find change for this, especially at such an early hour."

"I have nothing smaller; keep it." He smiled at the landlord, not willing to divulge his ignorance or purse, but little realising the consternation his generous action was causing.

Having quenched his thirst, their driver had resumed his position at the front of the stagecoach. One by one the passengers filtered aboard and reconvened in their previous seats. As Lutel made herself comfortable, the landlord was joined on the inn steps by a swarthy-looking man. They watched intently as the coach pulled away and continued its journey towards Marlborough.

Once again the fields took on a bleak aspect as they left the small hamlet behind them. To their right, the plains rolled on endlessly as far as the eye could see; to their left the horizon was broken by the distant downs that lay some two or three miles away. Immediately before them deep, rich-brown open fields were a testimony to their recent ploughing. Interspersed with fallow green pastures, they gave the impression of a giant chessboard sweeping across the landscape.

The lead horse missed its footing and stumbled; halting the coach, the driver climbed down to assess the damage. Rewn took the opportunity to lean out of the window; sweet warm air caressed his face and he closed his eyes and let the fragrances wash over him. A skylark hovered above their coach, its pleasant song disturbing the serenity of the morning. Rewn stared hard into the blue sky to catch a glimpse of the bird, but the sun's strong rays rendered his attempt useless; as his gaze returned groundwards he caught sight of a large green knoll in the distance. Puzzled by its nature, he was about to question Woodman when the driver, satisfied that there was no permanent injury, patted the horse on its rump and climbed aboard. The passengers shot forward with a jolt as the coach descended into West Kennet, a few red-brick cottages, set back from the main road, being the sole dwellings.

Rewn was intrigued as they drew alongside the large green hill. Sheep grazed around its base and were also dotted across its peak, nimbly traversing the paths that weaved their way around the steep slopes of the mound that was Silbury Hill. It stood like a huge green molehill, towering above their coach for some two hundred feet.

"What is it?" asked Rewn.

"Gert 'ill," said Woodman. "Built years ago, they do say."

"Who by?"

"Dunno; been here before the Romans, they say."

Before Rewn could glean any further information from Woodman, a figure emerged from the far side of the hill, galloping on horseback in their direction. One glance at the masked rider, wearing a tricorn hat, convinced the coach driver to lash the horses in an attempt to outrun their pursuer.

Unfortunately the rider had chosen his spot well as they had reached a steep incline in the road, and the cloaked figure was soon upon them. A pistol pointing in his direction convinced the driver to rein his horses in, and the coach ground to a halt amongst whinnying from the horses and a general commotion from some of its passengers.

They had halted alongside a double circle of small stones, the outer ring being no more than forty yards in diameter. It was known locally as the Sanctuary, and legend claimed it to be the site of a prehistoric charnel house. An avenue of stones linked the circles to the village of Avebury a mile or so away on the other side of the road. On their left, The Ridgeway, a centuries-old beaten track, ran along the crest of the downs towards the Thames Valley.

The highwayman could not have chosen a more bleak and desolate spot to carry out his robbery. He had ridden hard since leaving the landlord of the Wagon and Horses, taking a course in juxtaposition to the road as soon as the coach had departed. Now he had emerged from the far side of Silbury Hill to take the stagecoach by surprise in a vulnerable spot. Lowering his head into the coach, he pointed his pistol at its occupants.

"'And over your monee!" he demanded, in an accent that was unfamiliar to Rewn and Lutel.

A voice from above shouted down advice.

"Better do as 'e says. 'Tis the Frenchie!"

The angular passenger produced a ring and his companion unfastened a brooch; both were eagerly grasped by the highwayman.

"Tout le monde, s'il vous plait… everybody please."

"We ain't got nothin'," growled Woodman.

The Frenchman's eyes narrowed from behind a red-and-white spotted neckerchief; they were his only visible features.

"Step outside," the highwayman invited him, with a wave of his pistol. His grey steed snorted as Woodman jumped down, causing the team to become restless and stamp their feet. "Hold zem still," he snapped, pointing his pistol to reinforce his demand.

"Et toi aussi," he demanded. Although they could not grasp his language, the two Mykasians surmised from his mannerisms that they too were being ordered to disembark. Lutel stepped down, followed by Rewn. The Frenchman held his weapon at Rewn's head, and searched his clothing. Rewn impulsively snatched at the bag of coins that his ring had procured; a pistol butt swiped him across the head, and he crumpled to the ground. Lutel made to go to her brother's side.

"Leave 'eem."

Lutel stood still, looking on helplessly as the highwayman relieved the unconscious Rewn of his money.

"Do not disappoint me," advised the thief, turning his pistol on Woodman.

A few loose coins and a white handkerchief were swiftly emptied on to the floor.

"Pick zem up."

Woodman handed over his property.

The robber turned his attention to Lutel.

"I have nothing of value," she protested.

The thief was not so easily satisfied; he manoeuvred his horse closer to Lutel.

"I theenk I weel be the judge of that. Excusez-moi, mademoiselle, forgeeve the intrusion."

His hand felt her clothes, skilfully rifling through her pockets, but still came out empty. He thrust it inside her coat, and alighted on the metal object around her neck. The highwayman paused in his searching.

"Well, what 'ave we 'ere?"

There was a long tearing sound as Lutel's shirt was ripped at the front, and several buttons fell to the ground as it opened to reveal a shiny silver tube no larger than a finger, dangling from her neck. Gasps flew from her fellow passengers as the sun's rays fell on several crystals that were encrusted in the tube; a spectrum of colours glinted from the tiny jewels. The highwayman climbed down from his horse; he had never before seen such an object.

"Zis is far too precious to be carrying around on zee neck; somebody may steal it!" he joked. "It will be far safer with me."

His gloved hand grasped the pendant, and with a sharp flick of his wrist, the chain that had been holding it in place snapped. Lutel winced with the pain. Her body bent forward and she felt the back of her neck. By the time she had straightened, the horseman had mounted and was disappearing from view along The Ridgeway.

Woodman helped the semi-conscious Rewn to his feet; his left eye was swollen and closed, whilst above it was an ugly gash.

"Here, take this."

Rewn accepted Woodman's handkerchief, and attempted to stem the flow of blood.

"'Twas the Frenchie, most dangerous highwayman this side of Hounslow Heath," observed the driver knowingly.

"Who is he?" asked Lutel.

"It's Duval," came a woman's voice from within the carriage. "His name is Claude Duval. They say things became too hot for him in France, so he's crossed the channel to make easy pickings from us English."

Another time Lutel might have been flattered at being mistaken for a native, but now she stared down the track after Duval. The highwayman was no longer visible; only a cloud of dust betrayed his whereabouts.

"We must go after him," she said.

"Leave it, my pride hurts more than my head."

Lutel turned and faced Rewn, staring him straight in the face.

"He's taken the key," she explained.

"The key!" echoed Rewn.

Woodman looked from Lutel to Rewn, unable to comprehend the consternation at the loss of so small a trinket.

"I thought we were going to London to b—"

A withering glance from Lutel, who was not in the mood for any of Woodman's bungling, cut short his sentence.

"At the moment the key is more important," explained Rewn.

"Didn't look like no key; didn't look like nothing I've seen on this earth."

CHAPTER TWENTY

ROADSIDE FRIENDS

Rewn looked towards the path that the highwayman had taken. Their hopes of a safe return seemed to be disappearing along the ancient track. The key was vital to the return journey, being one of a pair that was needed to engage the booster system of either spacecraft. Many centuries earlier, an expedition to a parallel galaxy had ended in disaster when the captain of a ship had refused to wait for the crew of a sister ship that had been damaged in landing. On the sole ship's return, the Stilax had decreed that on any future mission involving more than one craft, a safety system should be included, to avoid one crew being stranded. The episode had now blurred into Mykasian mythology, but all captains now carried a key around their necks, which had to be exchanged between ships before departure was possible.

"Where does it lead?" asked Rewn.

"Why, all the way to Ivinghoe, near Lunnon," answered the driver. "But more likely he'll turn off back towards Avebury, or just carry on 'cross the downs. Most of his robberies be along the Lunnon Road; they do say his roadside friends do protect him – for a price."

"Roadside friends?" queried Lutel.

"People that do hide and protect him," explained the driver. "Farmers, cottagers, landlords and the like. Everyone's got their price."

"I guess they have," mused Lutel. "Let's go and find out how dear they are."

Dust clouds puffed around her feet as Lutel marched along The Ridgeway, following in Duval's path. Rewn hurried to keep pace, then after a few steps he turned to Woodman, who was standing on the step of the coach.

"Come on, then."

Woodman looked at the driver, then at the coach. Common sense was telling him to climb aboard; his inquisitive nature, which had brought him to this predicament, urged him otherwise. He looked inside the coach at the beckoning, comfortable seat.

"Wait," he called, and he jumped down after Rewn.

The coach driver sat open-mouthed as his three passengers took off in pursuit of the French highwayman.

"Close the door," he yelled to the remaining passengers, and on the completion of his order he whipped the horses up and continued his journey.

Woodman ceased running as he drew alongside Lutel and Rewn. Three large round barrows lay to the right of them in the adjoining field. Wiltshire Horn sheep, their spiral horns glistening in the early morning light, cropped the grass, keeping the conical mounds well-shorn like three balding green pates.

"What's so important about a key?" he asked. "I've paid good money for the coach to London and now it's gone, and we're chasing a bloody Frenchman around the countryside, because he's pinched some key!"

"It's very important to me," explained Lutel.

"But what does it open? A door, a box? It didn't look like any key I've ever seen."

"It's the key to my future."

Woodman didn't possess great intelligence, but he could tell from Lutel's tone and manner that the subject was closed.

"So what now?" he asked.

"We retrieve the key, and then continue our journey," said Rewn.

"Oh, that simple," said Woodman, with an uncharacteristic hint of sarcasm.

All signs of Duval had disappeared; the way was baked hard and they were unable to discern any fresh hoofprints amongst the small chalk and flint stones that littered the track. Ahead of them the landscape was austere, punctuated by the odd copse or isolated tree. Deep ruts along the length of the route made walking arduous and Lutel balanced upon the raised ground between two channels. Long grasses bordered the margins of The Ridgeway, frequently interspersed by yellow vetches and the taller cow parsley. Although the day was sunny a stiff breeze cut across the track set high in the bleak downs, causing Lutel to pull her open collar tighter around her neck. Far away to their left, two farmhouses and their accompanying buildings were the only signs of life. Duval was nowhere in sight.

Lutel became more competent with her balancing act, and quickened her pace, zigzagging from rut to rut in an effort to traverse the easiest path. A variety of plants joined the thickening hedgerow; purple thistles and yellow coltsfoot mingled with stinging nettles along the borders of the track. After several hundred yards they passed another barrow. Lutel paused to admire it, and realised the two men were lagging behind; she urged them on. Behind them, in the distance she caught sight of the nestling church tower at Manton poking through the treetops.

Lutel felt a pain in her foot and sat down on a large flat stone at the side of the path; she pulled her boot off, and tipped out a small pebble amongst the grasses and bright red poppies that grew upon the side of the fallen lichen-covered sarsen stone. Tiny black-and-white snails were climbing the plants, and Lutel thought how much she would like to study the flora and fauna of this planet. Behind her a singing skylark rose vertically from the ground; it startled her back to reality and the task of regaining the key.

Woodman and Rewn had caught up with her and the three of them walked on together, pausing shortly at a track that veered left off The Ridgeway, back towards the village of Avebury.

"Straight on is Lunnon, must be eighty-odd miles away," reasoned Woodman.

"It's a long walk," said Rewn.

Lutel frowned at his defeatist tone.

"Our immediate problem is the path taken by Duval," she responded.

Rewn cupped his chin in a hand and was silent for a moment. His black hair glistened in the sun, and his eyes sparkled like the surrounding grasses that shimmered in the wind. His burnt complexion tightened as he strained in concentration. Lutel knew better than to interrupt his musing.

"We go this way," he said, pointing with a sweep of the hand along the track that led westwards.

"How do you know he went this way?" asked Woodman.

"I don't, but if Duval seeks help from the country folk, then the only signs of life are in this direction," he answered, indicating the distant farm buildings. "If I am wrong then we may still gain information, or purchase horses to pursue him."

"It may have escaped your attention, but we have just been robbed," Woodman pointed out. "We've nothing to buy horses with."

"Not quite."

Both men looked at Lutel.

"When Duval was assaulting me, I relieved him of these."

She pulled off her left boot and held it upside down; several gold coins fell into her hand.

Woodman laughed. "Well, you're a sly one, I must say. I'm going to enjoy your company, I can see that."

A rabbit scurried across the track in front of them and disappeared into a field of corn. It certainly seemed less bleak in this direction and the episode lifted their spirits slightly. The path sloped gently downhill as they passed another barrow on their left-hand side. It was covered in a grove of beech trees, the green mast revealing that they were still in late summer. Corn fields now bordered them on both sides, and as they continued their descent they came upon a group of farm labourers busily toiling away cutting the sheaves. The group worked in a long diagonal line; the swish of blades carried on the strong wind that now blew directly into their faces, ruffling their hair. A woman and two children were closest to the track; they stopped their gleaning as the trio approached.

"Good day to you," called Woodman. "Has a horseman recently passed this way?"

The woman felt her back and straightened; she scowled at her children before turning towards the track.

"We know of no rider, sir," she answered, and once again she fixed her offspring with a look.

"Thank you," called Rewn as they continued on their way.

"She's lying," said Lutel.

"How do you know?" asked Woodman.

"Female intuition," said Rewn with a smile.

"No," replied Lutel, and she raised her eyes along the track. Several yards away lay a pile of steaming horse droppings.

Spurred by the encouragement of the fresh dung they hurried on, convinced that Rewn's hunch had proved correct. Green dominated the skyline in the shape of the hills of Cherhill, darkening in hue as the treetops of Avebury came into view. Half a mile away twenty large stones faced each other in two lines, standing several yards apart, daring each other to take the first step forward from their centuries-old footings. The downs now swept gently away in a wide undulating panoramic scene, and the chalk stones underfoot became smaller, giving way to a softer carpet of plantain and clover. Small chalkhill blue butterflies danced on the path, blissfully unaware of the travellers' presence until they were right on top of them, when the insects would flick away to settle on a neighbouring flower. Crickets chirped in the fields beside them, hiding amongst the moon daisies and grasses.

At this point the track sloped steeply downhill. The wind cut even more cruelly, blowing the poppies in the cornfield so that their petals billowed like hoods clinging to the stalks, making them look like old maids wrestling with their bonnets.

They reached the bottom of the slope, and had now been walking for half an hour. The track flattened and then rose again. To their left stood a farm; a herd of brown cattle grazed in the field closest to the buildings. Clouded yellow butterflies fluttered amongst the mixed vegetation that grew on the boundary of the farm. In front of the farmhouse stood a large pond; the sun danced on the choppy water. A variety of ducks bobbed up and down, their feathers ruffled by the blustery conditions. Shading the main farmhouse was a large beech tree, its branches spread in a protective awning over the slated roof; here the track reached a grassy junction.

"We go left," said Rewn; "the other way would take us back towards The Ridgeway."

"What about the farm?" suggested Lutel. "Duval could be hiding there."

Remembering her previous encounter with such buildings, Lutel stealthily led them down the farm track towards a barn. There was no sign of any horse, and they continued towards the next building. Berkshire pigs squealed as they walked against their sties, their sandy red bristles complementing the low sun. A kestrel silently glided away from its perch on the sty roof.

"Where is everybody?"

"They're out harvesting, Rewn," answered Woodman.

An old woman had been drawn to the door, attracted by the noise of the animals. She wore a white mop cap and was dressed in a dark green dress made from a very heavy material totally unsuitable to the present climate.

"What be you wantin'?" she croaked.

"We're looking for a friend," tried Lutel.

"Oh, ah," came the non-committal reply, "they're all out in the fields."

"No," said Woodman, "we're looking for Claude Duval. Has he passed by here?"

The old hag's eyes narrowed.

"He's no friend of mine. Be off before I set the dog on 'ee. Toby, Toby," she yelled over her shoulder. "Toby, you lazy hound! Where are you?"

"We're going, we're going," stammered Rewn, and they hastily retraced their footsteps to the track.

"And don't come back," yelled the old woman after them. "You can tell Duval I'll have no truck with him, whatever my stupid son says. He doesn't frighten me!"

"What do you make of that?" asked Lutel when they had covered a comfortable distance.

"I think even if I was Duval, I'd probably keep on riding," answered Rewn.

CHAPTER TWENTY-ONE

The Saw Pit

The track had changed again to a fine powdery dust. They walked along the side of the farm towards Overton Hill and on towards Avebury. Horse chestnut and sycamore thickened the hedgerow, providing a tunnel of shade. A distant rasping noise reached their ears, disturbing the erstwhile peace. Underfoot the grass was soft and lush, giving the track its name: Green Lane. Lutel paused at a grassy hillock that marked the end of the track, having walked for nearly three miles. She brushed the dust from her legs and moved on towards the village.

A thatched cottage greeted their arrival; its dark timbers, newly painted black, contrasted starkly with the white walls. Two men covered in sawdust were emerging from a hole in the ground. Rewn and Lutel stood intently watching the workmen.

"Haven't you ever seen a sawing pit?" asked Woodman.

He didn't wait for their reply, but walked over to the pit. The men, having finished their sawing, were stacking the oak planks over the entrance to the pit. Sharp teeth from a two-handled saw gleamed in the midday sunshine; there must have been a distance of ten feet between the two wooden handles.

"Has anyone passed here recently on horseback?" asked Woodman.

One of the sawyers ruffled his hair and woody specks floated to the ground. He was covered from head to toe in sawdust and chippings.

"We 'aven't seen anyone," came the terse reply.

"No, we 'aven't seen a soul," echoed the other.

Woodman realised the futility of pursuing this line of enquiry; the two bumpkins were obviously too involved in their carpentry to be of any help. Lutel gazed around for other signs of life. Opposite stood a small pair of flint-stoned cottages, their slate roofs covered in orange lichen; at either end of the roofs stood an unusually wide red-bricked chimney. Behind the cottages lay six large sarsen stones, brought by an ancient people for religious ceremonies. The land between the saw pit and the next cottage was being worked by a small band of rustics; a sign displayed that they were digging the foundations for, appropriately enough, the Avebury United Reformed Chapel.

"Have you seen a horseman?" shouted Woodman.

All three men continued with their work, and Woodman repeated his question. The eldest of the workmen leant on his shovel as though glad of the rest.

"Sorry, friend, I did not realise that you were addressing us."

"Has anybody ridden by on horseback within the last hour?" interjected Lutel.

The yokel shifted his weight to lean on his other leg.

"Boys, 'ave 'ee seen an 'orseman pass by?"

"No, Father," came the united reply.

"No horseman has ridden by here today," announced the grey-haired man, and he returned to his trench.

A few paces on and the track met the road north to Oxford; beyond them stood the Red Lion Inn. They crossed the road and entered. The inn was surprisingly busy. Travellers were stopping over, or resting on their journeys; next door the coaching house provided a change of horses. A sprinkling of locals mingled with the visitors, and few eyes were raised at the entrance of three more strangers. Rewn ordered a jug of ale, which was eventually served at table with three tankards by the landlord, a solemn-faced man with a pointed chin. His greying hair fell lankly from a parting through the centre of his head, and his cloudy eyes added to his featureless attraction. As he bent forward to place the drink in the middle of the table, Rewn placed a restraining hand on his wrist.

"We're looking for a man named Duval. Has he happened this way today?"

Removing his arm from Rewn's grip, the man answered in an uninterested tone. "I know of no such man." He looked around the room. "We have many travellers. I know few of their names, just as I don't know yours."

The landlord made to leave them.

"He's a Frenchie," Woodman chimed in. "You'd recognise a foreign tongue, wouldn't you?"

"I'm sure I would. But I know of no such person. If you'll excuse me, I have much to do today."

Wiping his hands on a yellowing cloth that was tucked into his breeches, he shuffled back towards the large barrels of ale that lay in the shade of the far wall. Before serving his next guest, he spoke briefly into the ear of a young girl, who hurried away and hastily climbed the wooden stairs to the upper floor.

Rewn had followed the action with interest, and alerted Lutel to the little charade that their questioning had induced. Having waited so long they thirstily quaffed their drinks and then Rewn led them outside.

"The landlord knows of the man we seek."

"How can you be sure?"

"Did you see him send that girl upstairs? She's probably a messenger. I think our man is in the inn itself."

"Why aren't we waiting inside?" asked Woodman.

"He won't show himself whilst we are still in the building."

"Let's go and flush him out, then."

"Hardly a practical suggestion, Woodman; I can't see the landlord standing idly by whilst we search his inn. Besides, these old inns will have too many hiding places for the three of us to discover."

"What are you suggesting, Rewn?" said Lutel.

"We must place ourselves in strategic vantage points and watch the inn. He'll come out sooner or later, and if we are not around I suspect it will be sooner."

Woodman was despatched along the road towards Oxford; he climbed a large grassy bank and strode over to one of two large stones. They must have been twice his height and several feet wide. Positioning himself behind the stone nearest to the road, he peered out around it, keeping his eyes sharply focused on the east wing of the inn. As the hot sun beat down on his head he asked himself whether it was all really worth it. Lutel had crossed the road outside the inn and crouched down alongside a saddler's house, a position that offered an uninterrupted view of the front of the inn and its westward side. Rewn had allocated himself the task of covering the back of the Red Lion. He walked around the white-walled building and peered up at its thatch, satisfying himself that there was no way out across the rooftop. If Duval, as he suspected, was inside, he would have to leave the inn by the front or side doors or from a window.

At the back of the Red Lion, Rewn could see an L-shaped wooden building; from the smell and stamping noises he surmised that this was the stables. He signalled to Lutel and walked the short distance down the narrow high street that led into the main body of the village, then he crept behind the stable.

The musky smell of damp straw filled his nostrils as he closed the door. It was still the middle of the day, but Rewn could not see his hand in front of him. Neither lamp nor window allowed artificial or natural light to brighten the gloom. A horse whinnied as he took a step forward, and Rewn felt the hairs on his neck stand on end. He ran his hands down one wall and touched something leaning against the side. He felt rough bark in his hand and picked the piece of wood up to prop the stable door open.

More stamping and snorting came from the nervous beasts; Rewn walked along the line of horses. In the light from the doorway he counted six in all, five of a brownish hue and one the colour he was looking for. The horse nearest to the door let out a piercing neigh, causing Rewn to start. It reminded him of his vulnerability and of how little he could gain from his present position. Patting the horse on the mane by way of thanks, he removed the prop and walked once more into the fresh air. The bright light dazzled his eyes, and he rubbed them with his hand; in the act of his doing so a particle of dust lodged in his eye. As the pain receded he gradually recovered his vision, and inspected his hand. It was covered in small specks.

Lutel watched him stare at the Red Lion and then wave across to her; she was at a loss to explain the broad grin that lit up his features.

Throughout the day they waited, enduring hunger and thirst pangs; occasionally they would be disturbed by a passing villager and extract a questioning look. Dusk descended, and Rewn ruminated on the possibility that he might be mistaken, and wondered if, after all, he should instigate a search of the tavern. The thought was still nagging away when a silhouetted figure, dressed in black, emerged from a lower-floor window at the rear of the inn and scuttled between the Red Lion and the coach-house, heading in the direction of the high street.

The figure had climbed out of a window at the far side of the building to Rewn's observation point. On seeing the direction it was taking, Rewn raced behind the other side of the stables, intending to cut the figure off. He emerged from the far side and on to the high street, but his quarry was several yards in front of him. Lutel had witnessed the activity from her vantage point and immediately set off in the direction of the high street, but due to her being stationed further up the road, she trailed Rewn by twenty or thirty yards.

A large black cloak swept behind the figure as it raced in front of them. Ruts and potholes made the surface difficult to run on. In the distance the village church clock struck; Rewn counted the chimes in his head: one, two, three, four, five, six, seven, eight, nine o'clock. His lapse in concentration caused him to stumble in a wheel rut, and he tumbled head-first onto the dusty road. Lutel was immediately helping him to his feet.

"It's Duval," he wheezed.

"I saw."

A dog began barking as they stood talking below the steep-pitched roof of Manor Farm. Ahead of them the fugitive had made the most of their delay and had turned right at the farm and into a side lane. The pursuers chased it along the path under the shadow of a high stone wall. To their left stood a barn; a man was standing in the entrance to its hayloft. They stopped, but instantly realised their mistake and redoubled their efforts. More farm buildings stood on their right-hand side and they were further delayed as they peered intently into each one.

Close to the pathway a flight of steps led to a further hayloft. Yet again they paused, scrutinising the large wooden door at the top of the steps, weighing the risk of ignoring the possibility. Lutel had just put one foot on the first step, when a loud quacking sound further along the path disturbed the silence of the night. A pair of roosting mallards rose into the air, protesting at the disturbance to their sleep. Guessing the reason for the ducks' displeasure they headed towards the commotion just in time to see their game-bird disappearing around the corner of a huge barn. Rewn followed in its wake, whilst Lutel took off in the opposite direction with a view to ensnaring their victim in a pincer movement. The barn consisted of more than ten sides and thirty or so seconds had elapsed before Rewn and Lutel met again outside the pond, but the figure had given them the slip.

"Where's he gone?" asked Rewn incredulously.

As they circled about themselves, searching the darkness, the moon appeared from behind a cloud as if to mock the futility of their chase. Rewn held out his hands in mystification, at a loss to explain their failure. At that moment a noisome fluttering of wings came from the far side of the pond, in the direction of the church. It was not the protest of flapping wildfowl, but a gentler, softer fluttering of feathers, accompanied by a gentle cooing. Rewn dashed off in the direction of the disturbance, and was so intent on its source that he ran straight into the pond. For a second time the inhabitants quacked their protest, as Lutel held out an arm to Rewn.

"It's not funny," he said.

"I know," she replied seriously, and then she burst forth into mirth.

Rewn circumnavigated the water and before the moon deserted them once more he could just make out the outline of a very large turret-shaped building, at least thirty feet in height. He ran his hands over the large rough flint stones of which it was constructed; they diminished in size the higher he reached. As though accepting defeat the moon once more illuminated the red-slated conical roof, and Rewn was able to see to its very apex, which was crowned by a small temple capped by a stone ball. One or two white birds emerged from small holes towards the top of the dovecote that supplied the local manor with eggs and meat. As Rewn searched for an entrance a winged shadow flew out of the birdhouse, sending him sprawling to the ground.

"Don't make a habit of this," said Lutel dryly, as she picked him up once more.

"I don't intend to," replied Rewn, and he headed towards the wall behind the turret-shaped building. He cleared the wall and jumped a second one, landing in the yard of Saint James' Church. Eerie gravestones, presided over by the tall grey tower of the church, compounded the blindness of the night.

Rewn turned to Lutel as she arrived at his shoulder. "It's hopeless; he could be anywhere."

"We must keep searching," said Lutel. "We must retrieve the key. You nearly had him back there."

"Wasn't the best place to choose, was it? Perhaps he's getting careless."

"It would help if Woodman was here; we could fan out."

"Probably couldn't see from where he was watching," explained Rewn. "Actually, he's probably asleep."

"If he's still there!"

Rewn recognised the significance of Lutel's statement; the last thing they wanted was a further search. The one in hand and Revin and Verde's were enough, without having to instigate a third.

Rewn cast around for inspiration, and at that moment a dark figure, silhouetted against the grey sky, mocked them from the top of the church wall near a gateway. Fired by the cheekiness, Rewn called Lutel to follow him as he raced diagonally across the churchyard towards the spot. Clearing the wall with effortless leaps they found themselves once more back on the tiny high street. Ahead of them their prey darted down the lane at the side of Manor Farm.

"Here we go again," said Rewn.

This time they were close enough behind to see the flapping cloak race away to the right up a bank that led directly into a field. Rewn and Lutel scrambled up; a track about a hundred yards long curved away towards the Oxford road. Dotted along the track were a number of large sarsen stones;

below them was a deep gully which followed the contour of the track. On the far side of the gully stood another ridge, with a second parallel track. It was here that the figure again stopped to taunt them.

"You've got to admire his nerve," said Rewn.

"He'll want more than nerve when I catch him."

Again they gave chase, diving into the chasm below and running up the steep side to the second track. As they emerged at the summit the figure was already crossing the road ahead and racing off into the field beyond.

A steep grassy hillock hampered their progress as they once again found themselves facing a green gully bordered by two ridge paths. Not to be outfoxed a second time, Rewn shouted to Lutel to take the lower course whilst he remained on the high ground. Lutel scrambled down the bank whilst he raced off along the top path. After running the curve of the wind-swept outer bend Rewn could see a runner ahead of him in the gully. He glanced back at Lutel and saw that she was thirty or forty yards behind. In the distance Rewn could just make out that the ridge tapered away to the right before sloping to ground level and the gully.

Spurred on, he summoned every last ounce of strength in his body; his lungs protested as he gained on the gully-runner below. As he flew down the slope he fully expected to catch the elusive black-cloaked figure. Out of the corner of his eye he noticed that their course was leading them towards the saw pit. Rewn had every confidence that he could overhaul the figure before it could reach Green Lane.

Using the impetus of the slope Rewn flung himself forward with his arms outstretched. At the last second the figure sheered away to the right and Rewn was left grasping thin air. Staggering up he bent double, his hands on his knees, winded by the fall. Lutel was soon at his side, having had the benefit of running in the sheltered gully, and the advantage of the shorter inside route.

"He's doubling back towards the road," gasped Rewn. "D… don't wait for me."

But Lutel was already out of earshot.

Their quarry was indeed leading them a merry dance; the route since crossing the road had been in the shape of a horseshoe, and now ran down the far side of the field back towards the road. Lutel had wasted little time attending Rewn, but the few valuable seconds she had paused to check his safety had allowed the shadowy figure to once more disappear into the darkness.

She rested at an isolated sarsen stone, leaning against its smooth face. Her heart leapt as she once more caught sight of the fleeing character fifty yards ahead and spurted after it. Her heavy and cumbersome clothes were less than ideal to run in, and for the first time she felt a twinge of doubt as she felt a stitch in her side, but the thought of losing her key impelled her to an increased effort. Every part of her body ached. The muscles in her legs felt heavy and her breath was now coming in great pants; worse still, the elusive toying figure was pulling away from her again. Shafts of yellow light dimly flickered from the distant Red Lion; the figure was heading for a gap in the hedgerow in the direction of the inn. Once more it stopped and waved a taunting arm at the chasing Lutel, then turning it raced on between a pair of tall sarsen stones.

A man emerged from behind one of the stones and wielded a branch into the face of the oncoming runner. Pole-axed, the cloaked figure slumped backwards to the ground, and the assailant sat on the body, ensuring there would be no escape.

"Well done, Woodman, we are much in your debt," said a breathless Rewn as he arrived at the scene. Lutel bent double, gasping for air.

"I doubt it," came the less-than-enthusiastic reply.

Woodman tore away the mask that covered the face of his captive. The pale moonlight sparkled in the blue eyes of a beautiful blonde girl as she stared up at them.

"See what I mean? Duval came galloping out of the stable and shot down the road." Woodman pointed towards Devizes. "I ran after 'im shouting, but you must have been too busy chasing missy 'ere. Fancy falling for that old trick!"

Woodman had climbed to his feet whilst delivering his rebuke. He released his grip on the girl and she raced off into the night. Woodman made to follow.

"Leave her," called Rewn.

Woodman turned around.

"She'll tell us nothing that we can't guess. You're right, we have been outfoxed by this Frenchman, but the hunt is not over yet."

Rewn looked thoughtfully at the swirling clouds as they sped once more over the moon.

"No, this fox may have run out of lairs," he said mysteriously, but he didn't elaborate on his musings.

Part Five

Of Medics and Mayors

CHAPTER TWENTY-TWO

MEG DADFORD

For a moment Revin pondered the use of force against the parish constable, but the appearance of a watchman, complete with his halberd, caused him to refrain. The sound of a padlock being hammered into place echoed in his ears as he trudged sadly away from Gatleigh's house with a bowed head. He glanced around and raised his eyes to the upper floor and saw the bemused and sad faces of Kate and Sal, their noses squashed against the glass.

Revin had no idea of the direction that he was taking; he was too numbed by the news. A thousand thoughts whirled in his mind. Who in the house had the plague? Was Verde all right? Of course he was, he told himself. Verde had been inoculated on Mykas, but perhaps this was a different strain of the plague, a more virulent strain… was there more than one strain? No, there was only one bubonic plague, their medical specialists on Mykas had been certain on that point … but how did they know? Earth was light years away.

His thoughts were rudely interrupted as he crashed into a palliard. Revin's pace knocked the old man to the ground, and he stooped to help him to his feet and then swiftly recoiled at the boils and sores that covered the beggar's face. Doubts filled his mind, although he would have still lurched backwards even if he had realised the extent of self-infliction.

"Spare us a groat, sir," entreated the man, sensing he had chanced on a likely victim.

Revin searched in his pocket and threw the beggar a coin, then, neatly side-stepping, he brusquely walked on.

"Thank you, thank you," a feeble voice croaked from behind, but Revin had no ears.

He found himself at a patch of green and, casting his eye around, realised he was at the artillery ground. A broken rush target lay on its side, and putting his head in his hands he sank down onto it.

The scene at Gatleigh's door played over in his mind time and time again. Fear and despair were etched onto the faces around, whether they were inmates or jailers. Revin tried to think how he could rescue Verde, but each time a plan formulated his mind wandered back to the pitiful faces of the twins. How he wished Lutel or Rewn were there – then the sole responsibility would not fall on him. Loneliness surrounded him as his thoughts turned from Gatleigh's front door to a large green door back on Mykas.

It was the very early part of his Gee 4s' retirement cycle, and as a means of celebrating, Revin and his cousin Kol were being treated to a holiday. They had come to the far west of Mykas – an area that was popular with vacationing Mykasians. Warm grey sands filled miles of small coves, each with its own secluded bay, with a sheltering cliff backdrop that gave protection from both sun and wind. A warm sun and pleasant breeze had decided the small party to walk the relatively short distance from their travel dish.

The family resemblance was easy to see as two carrot tops raced ahead of the adults. The walk along the purple cliff top had been fun to the two boys, who found entertainment in racing ahead and jumping out from behind the small blue-flowered bushes in an attempt to startle their Gee 4s. Kol, who was two years younger than Revin, had started the game and the older boy had joined in. The presence of any other holidaymakers in the area would have dissuaded Revin through reasons of embarrassment, but as they played in solitude, he kept his cousin company until they neared their destination.

The pathway led into a large clearing at the top of the cliff face. Holidaymakers converged on them from all sides, most having taken the local hover rail that linked directly between the travel dish and the beach. Silver doors hissed open and upwards on the carriages, and expectant trippers stepped down onto the sandy floor. A few arrived by private space hopper: bottle-shaped craft that hovered just above the ground, the transparent sides allowing its two passengers a panoramic view.

"Stay close," warned Momma Gee 4. Revin had ceased the childish game and mooched just behind the party. Kol held his Momma Gee 4's hand and pointed excitedly as the sea appeared between a large fissure in the cliff face. Only three hundred holidaymakers were admitted to the area; they were divided into small groups so that no more than twenty shared a bay. Poppa Gee 4 marched them to a wall at the cliff's edge towards a series of different-coloured doors. A gargoyle of a mythical Mykasian beast had been carved into the rock above each door.

"That is our door," said Poppa Gee 4, pointing towards the wall.

Revin had bent down to tie his shoe.

"I'll catch you up," he promised.

Momma Gee 4 wanted to wait, but an excited Kol was dragging her onwards, so the group carried on. Revin tied the offending lace and was about to stand up when something landed beside him. He stared up into the face of an elderly couple, and held out the purse.

"You are careless, Sanglica. Thank you, boy," said the husband.

"I was only looking for our entrance colour. If your memory was any better there would be no need for me to go searching around in my bag," remonstrated Sanglica as she accepted the purse from Revin. "Be a dear and tell us the colour on this card."

"It's dark green, anyone can see it's dark green," said her husband peevishly.

"How am I to tell the exact shade in these?" asked Sanglica, pointing to the dark glasses that adorned her face.

"Thank you, boy; you had better be off."

Revin had stood mesmerised by the old couple, and as he ran towards the wall there was no longer any sign of his Gee 4s amongst the growing crowd that was filtering towards the doors. Panic swept over him as he realised that he had not been listening properly to Poppa Gee 4, and he did not know the colour of their door. Poppa Gee 4 had pointed somewhere in this direction; he narrowed his options down to four doors: bright red, pale yellow, dark green or light blue. Revin still stood below the high wall, unable to make any firm decision. Most of the crowd had brushed by him when he was overtaken by the old couple.

"Everything all right?"

"I've forgotten my door colour."

"Don't worry," said Sanglica. She paused. "Most are going through the dark green door. I'm sure your family will be waiting for you at the end of the tunnel. He can come through with us, can't he, Bir?"

"Of course he can."

Bir pushed the dark green door open and they walked into a tunnel. A pinpoint of light from the far end revealed the long distance that they still needed to travel to reach the beach. The roof of the tunnel was smooth and cream, with a continuous strip of lighting along its apex. Even so, the way ahead was murky, and Revin felt very uncomfortable in the gloomy surroundings. The tunnel sloped gently downward and the pinpoint of light was no longer visible as they were overtaken by an expectant party of day-trippers. Revin reached out to the tunnel wall, expecting to feel the sleek texture of the ceiling; instead his hand touched a rough sludge and he instantly withdrew it.

Dark thoughts began to fill his mind; what if he'd come through the wrong door? What if his Gee 4s went back to look for him and found him gone? Then he began to harbour misgivings about the old couple who temporarily appeared to have adopted him. Revin knew nothing about them. Had the purse been dropped by accident? How often had his family warned him of the danger that he now experienced?

"I must go back," he announced.

"Go back, why?" said the old man.

"I'm in the wrong colour."

"You don't know that."

"I want my Gee 4s."

"They are probably waiting for you at the end of the tunnel," said the elderly woman, smiling. "Aren't they, Bir? Besides, I don't like to think of you wandering around on your own."

Revin did not like the tone the conversation had taken.

"I must go," he said, and he raced off down the tunnel.

"Careful," said a voice as he pushed through the group in front. The pinpoint of light was growing as Revin slowed down, mindful of the slippery slope beneath his feet.

At last he burst out onto the grey sands. As he emerged he glanced around; he spied two groups of trippers but neither belonged to him. He rushed around the cliff face, searching between the small fissures and hidden coves, but to no avail. Revin stared out at the empty sea with tears welling in his eyes. Behind, the blue-heathered rock face sheered above him; none but the nimblest of animals could traverse its vertical slopes that curved around the bay.

Revin sat down on a rock and began to cry; he hated himself for it, but he felt so miserable. Disappointed that at a time when he should be feeling so happy, he was experiencing the opposite emotion, and frustrated at his inability to solve his problem.

He sat there unmoving for several minutes, kicking his heels into the grey sand. Crashing waves and squawking seabirds were the only sounds that reached his ears, as tears rolled down his face.

"I thought you were in a hurry to get here when you pushed past us, Revin, even more so when you went on ahead of us in the tunnel, so why so sad?"

Revin looked up; everything was going to be all right.

In Gatleigh's house, the air was already full of choking sulphurous smoke and distressed wailing. John lay dead in his bed, having succumbed in the night. On being informed the parish authorities had responded instantly. Verde, from feelings of pity, had stayed to comfort the family and now paid for his humanitarianism by being incarcerated in a plague house. Following hard after the red cross and the arrival of the watchman, another creature had appeared. This woman was even more haggish than the searcher woman, having been spawned from the lowest classes of the London streets.

Meg Dadford had never risen beyond the profession of prostitute, and now that her looks and youth had deserted her, she relied upon the charity of the parish to keep her. In return, at such desperate times, the parish now requested Meg and her kind to repay their debt to society. The offer was stark: attend the sick or lose all parish relief and starve. Needless to say many chose the path that Meg now trod.

As the padlock was released and the door opened, Meg set foot inside the house. Rebecca came screaming down the stairs.

"Out, out, I'll not have the likes of you in my house!"

She ran to Meg and beat with her fists against the nurse's shoulders. Verde put a restraining arm around the distressed woman and she collapsed sobbing into his arms.

"The door is barred, and this lady is here to help." He beckoned Meg to step further into the house.

Rebecca tried to push herself away from Verde. "No, no, no," she screamed, and again broke down into a fit of sobs.

Meg introduced herself to Verde, assuming him to be the master of the house, or at the very least its only sane member.

"The name's Meg Dadford. I'm here to give succour to the ill," she wheezed, "but I'll not be treated like that."

"She's very distraught," explained Verde.

"So are many folk just now, but there's no need for your wife to act as she did."

"She's not my wife."

Verde objected to the knowing look that Meg gave him, but not wishing to antagonise her further he ignored the slight.

"Please do what you are able," he said.

"Very well, as you asked me civil."

Meg sneered at the semi-conscious woman and made her way up the stairs, whilst Verde sat Rebecca in a chair and made her a drink of warm posset.

The heat of the room was oppressive; in her saner moments Rebecca had lit chafing dishes in every room. Downstairs a huge stink pot puffed out clouds of brown smoke and the fire roared. Verde felt the sweat on him as he walked upstairs. Meg had taken a cloth and soaked it in water; she was pressing it against Tom's brow. Laboured breathing came from the far side of the room, where the twins had rapidly yielded, whilst Sam screamed from his cot. Verde lifted the tear-stained baby.

"Come on," he said, "you can help me."

Verde knew the help he could offer at the moment would be little more than tendering comfort. Any medicines, potions or unctions that were stored in the house would be useless, but he couldn't walk away from a family that had befriended him, and in truth, albeit in a short time, one of which he had grown fond.

Sometimes the plague would move slowly through a house, like a snail scaling a large wall; progress would be gradual but steadfastly achieved. At others, it raced at a cruel speed, like an eagle swooping from the skies, the prey not sensing the danger until all too late. By midday, Tom's fever had worsened and the twins had joined their grandfather. Once more the parish authorities were informed. Rebecca was inconsolable at the death of her girls, and vented her feelings on Verde.

"It's your fault, if you hadn't brought the plague into my house…" She flew at Verde and pounded him with her fists. It was a mark of Verde's character and understanding that he stood there unflinching, until her rage gave way to exhaustion. Rebecca slumped to the floor. Verde scooped her in his arms and carried her up the stairs and laid her on a bed. He opened a window to let in some fresh air.

"Close it," yelled the crone, "you'll let in the bad air." She gripped the window in two hands and slammed it shut. Verde opened it again using only one hand.

"Seems to me it's already here."

Meg muttered an oath under her breath and went back to her nursing.

By early evening Verde lay slumped in a chair, recovering from the day's exhaustions. A figure stole towards him, checking his breathing. Satisfied that he was asleep, the woman crept upstairs and into John's bedroom. His body lay on the floor awaiting collection. Bending down she unwrapped the shroud, and produced a small spoon from her apron. A noise from an adjoining room caused her to pause and look around. Satisfied of her solitude, with meticulous care she wiped the spoon on her apron, and dipped it into one of John's sores, collecting a sample of pus. Then she retreated back down the stairs and once more approached the sleeping Verde. His mouth lay open and she raised the spoon, ready to pour in the putrefying liquid. Verde shook his head and muttered incoherently as though a sixth sense were warning him of the imminent danger; the woman paused expectantly, but Verde settled again, and the spoon hovered around his lips, waiting for his mouth to open. As the spoon touched his lips, a pewter plate smashed down on the-would be murderess's head. Verde shot bolt upright, awakened by the crashing and spinning of the pewter plate; his first sight was Rebecca holding the spoon.

"She was going to infect thee with this," said Rebecca, pointing first at Meg and then at the spoon.

"How, why?" asked Verde, in dumb amazement.

"'Tis an old trick," said Rebecca, kicking the senseless body of Meg. "They take the poison from an infected body, and place it in a healthy one."

Verde comprehended the method but not the motive, and his blank look said as much to his saviour.

"Reason's simple: as soon as they kill everyone off in a house, they can rob it and move on to fresh pickings."

A look of incredulous disbelief crossed Verde's face. "Can somebody really be that evil?"

"Look," said Rebecca, and she bent down and felt inside Meg's apron; she pulled out several pieces of cutlery that he recognised, and his strike-a-light. His attention was momentarily distracted as he pondered his loss; too late he realised Rebecca was no longer taking from Meg, but giving. The spoon and its festering contents were thrust into her mouth in an act of revenge, and Rebecca twisted and lifted the spoon to ensure its contents were deposited.

"There, that's the last time she'll play that trick."

CHAPTER TWENTY-THREE

Resignation

A succession of church clocks argued over the timing of the approaching hour; they all agreed on the hour of ten, but some arrived at the decision a little earlier than others. During this apparent expansion of time, the watchmen of the parish ended or began their shifts.

"Any sign of trouble?" asked the new incumbent at Gatleigh's house.

"Quiet as church mice," replied his counterpart, and handing over his halberd and other effects, he strolled off into the night.

Barely had the relief settled into place when he was disturbed by the approach of the dead cart. The driver checked the horse as it drew alongside Gatleigh's door and, climbing down from the cart, sauntered over to the watchman.

"Special orders from the constable; we've bodies to collect," said the driver, his large hat tilted forward at an angle shadowing his features.

"Coffins? Must be special, but don't expect me to help you."

"I've brought assistance," said the driver, indicating a passenger on his cart.

"Can't you ring the bell, then?"

"Constable says the family's distraught, might even all be dead."

"Well, it's no odds to me if you want to enter a plague house; just leave me out of it."

Ralph Hawkley was uncommon amongst watchmen; he was little more than twenty years of age, although his thinning hair suggested he was much older. He was officious and unbending in his duties as a watchman, and had never accepted a bribe from within or without a plague house, seeing it as his devout responsibility to remain within the framework of the law at all times. Hawkley asked for nothing and gave nothing in the service of his duties, and remained upstanding to his principles throughout his nightly shifts.

The two bearers lifted down four empty coffins from the cart, whilst the watchman fumbled in his coat pocket for the key. In order to procure a clearer view of the padlock the guard tilted it towards the moonlight. Soft yellow rays danced on the shiny restraint and the key clicked as it threw the bolt. Wasting no time the driver and his associate pushed past the watchman, who had to take evasive action in order to avoid being pinned by the coffin that they carried.

Once they were inside the house the door shut fast behind them. Verde had come to the top of the stairs at the unlocking of the door. He held a candlestick in his hands, which he dropped as the driver pushed back his hat.

"Revin!" he shouted, and raced down the stairs to greet his friend.

Revin laid down his end of the coffin; Verde clasped him by the shoulders, and in so doing caught sight of Revin's accomplice.

"Nathan?" he asked in an incredulous tone.

"Yes," said Revin. "I *persuaded* him to be a coffin bearer for the evening."

Nathan said nothing, but not for the first time that evening, his hand checked the contents of his pocket.

"How are things?" asked Revin, with genuine concern.

"John and the twins are dead and Tom's in a bad way. Rebecca's state of mind is in the balance, but at least young Sam shows no signs as yet. But if he stays locked up in this hell hole, it will only be a matter of time."

Revin felt a lump in his throat; he had been very fond of the twins. Besides, they were only innocent children and had played no part in their sad demise.

Rebecca joined them at the bottom of the stairs, but stared vacantly into space as Revin outlined his plan.

"We've brought coffins," he said. "We can carry the living out in them."

"What about the dead?" whispered Verde.

"We can come back for them later, if all goes well. Have you anywhere that you can stay?"

"I'll not leave my twins," said Rebecca, in a moment of lucidity and resignation.

Revin faced the distraught mother. "It's your only chance, don't you see? If you stay here you'll all die!"

"That it may be, but I'll not introduce plague to another's house, and I won't leave my Tom alone."

"So there is somewhere that you can go?"

Rebecca did not answer. Revin shook her in frustration.

"Stop," ordered Verde. "Can't you see she's in shock?"

"And we'll be adding to it unless we leave here soon. He'll become suspicious out there if we fail to show."

Verde put a comforting arm around Rebecca. “Rebecca, you know what’s likely to happen to you if you stay here?”

“I don’t want to die, but I’m not afraid to. I will not leave Tom.”

“Let us take Sam, then; there is no cause for him to stay.”

Rebecca tussled with her responsibilities as a mother. She was steadfast over her duties as a wife, but there was no need to increase Sam’s risk, and she was sure that her sister would take good care of the lad, if she failed to survive.

“Very well,” she said. “My sister lives at Spittlefields; take Sam there.” She walked in a daze upstairs to prepare the infant, and to say her last goodbye.

Revin, Verde and Nathan fetched the twins and John, and placed each of them in a coffin. Verde wiped a tear from his eye as he gently laid Kate into the crude wooden box. He brushed a strand of hair from her cheek, even though he realised the futility of his action.

Rebecca returned with Sam as the lids were being hammered into place. Revin opened the fourth coffin lid and Verde prepared to climb in. He kissed Rebecca tenderly on the cheek.

“We will be back for you,” he promised.

“Only if God wills it,” she replied.

Her eyes displayed a searing loyalty to her husband, and Verde knew it would be impossible to persuade her to change her mind. He was about to take his place in the coffin when a thought suddenly struck him.

“I must say farewell to Tom.”

“He sleeps; I’ll say your farewells for you.”

Verde lay back in the coffin, and Revin sensitively removed the babe from his mother’s bosom.

“My sister lives but three doors down from the Cock and Bottle,” she said calmly. “Her name is Verity, Verity Cannling. Tell her I will come for Sam as soon as I am able.”

She planted a kiss on the sleeping babe’s forehead, a tender kiss as only a mother could impart. Revin handed Sam to Verde, and with Nathan’s help the lid was put in place. As the nails were quietly knocked into the last coffin the finality of the situation hit Rebecca; she threw herself across the coffins and sobbed hysterically,

Revin wished Verde to be on the other side of the lid; this was a situation Revin was not equipped to cope with. If Sam awoke there would be a danger of discovery. Revin did the only thing that came to mind. He raised his hand

and slapped Rebecca across the face. The instant the blow was struck, he regretted his action, and he inwardly swore that he would never again strike in such a way. He was helped by Rebecca recovering her composure.

"I'm sorry. I don't know what came over me."

"No, it's me who should apologise; my action was inexcusable."

"Your action has probably saved that child's life."

Nathan had remained silent for so long that it came as a timely reminder to hear his voice.

"We'd best be having these aboard," he said, pointing at the four coffins. Together, the two men began the sad task of loading the coffins, leaving the special one until last. Inside the coffin Verde held his breath; Rebecca's outburst had disturbed the slumbering infant. As they lifted the final coffin, Rebecca sidled up to Revin.

"You'll see him again soon," Revin said. But they both realised the unlikelihood of his statement.

The mother placed a hand in her apron pocket, and pulled out a small leather pouch. She untied the bag and tipped the contents into the palm of one hand.

"We won't be needing much of this," she said, and she pressed several coins into Revin's hand. "Please give some of this to my sister – for Sam, but some is for your kindness.

Revin tried to resist, but Rebecca put a restraining finger across his lips. He planted a kiss on her forehead and continued with his final load. As he did so, the forgotten figure of Meg Dadford emerged from the shadow of the stairs.

"I see your game," she screamed.

"Go quickly," said Rebecca. The coffin carriers heeded the danger and moved towards the door.

Rebecca launched herself at the old nursekeeper and pinned her to the floor. Meg swore every oath possible, fighting and scratching like a wild cat. Rebecca summoned strength from hidden depths, motivated by the knowledge that her child's life was at stake. The two antagonists rolled on the floor; clothes ripped and furniture crashed around them as Rebecca managed to manoeuvre herself around so that she straddled Meg's head, and sat on the crone's mouth, ignoring the bites to her thighs, such was the mother's desperation.

Revin and Nathan lifted the final coffin, with its double load, onto the cart. The struggle from within the house was clearly audible to Hawkley.

"What's the problem?" he asked Revin.

"How would you feel, if these were your children?" asked Revin, pointing at the coffins.

Detecting no movement, Verde was beginning to suspect all was not well, and his uneasiness grew as Sam started to show signs of waking. Revin was tempted to leap aboard the dead cart and drive away, but Hawkley, suspecting all was not as it should be, had climbed aboard.

Too late Revin realised that they should have replaced the padlock on the door. Meg suddenly appeared screaming incoherently, shortly followed by Rebecca, who threw herself on to the hag's back and wrapped her arms around Meg's neck so that they both fell to the ground. By now the grappling of the demented women had convinced the watchman that his suspicions were not groundless. Revin was torn between aiding Rebecca and thus risking declaring their hand, or brazening the disturbance out and hoping that Hawkley would see the altercation as nothing more than a mother's grief.

"Escape, escape," cried Meg.

The watchman bent over one of the coffins; he gripped his halberd at its pointed end and knocked on a coffin lid. Meeting with no response he repeated the action on a second lid, only to receive the same reply. The ghoulishness of the situation caused him to doubt Meg's word and he prepared to climb down from the cart.

Meg broke free from Rebecca's grip and ran to the cart. "I tell 'ee there's live bodies in there," she said, pointing at the two remaining coffins.

The commotion had finally woken Sam, who cried out at his strange surroundings. Verde gently put his hand over the infant's mouth, praying that Revin would start their journey.

"There!" screamed Meg.

Hawkley walked towards the two remaining coffins and paused, listening for further clues as to the impropriety of the situation. Inside Verde fought for calm.

Convinced that he would be neglecting his parish duties if he did not respond in a positive manner, Hawkley gripped his weapon halfway down its handle, forcing its point into one of the coffin lids, and using it as a wedge levered open the coffin. Staring up at him he saw the ghastly figure of John Gatleigh, and recoiling from the grisly sight and his mistake he stumbled into Verde's coffin. The frightened infant lashed out with his feet at the coffin lid, whilst the watchman stood transfixed at the rear of the cart.

Apart from his officiousness, Hawkley was a superstitious man, and having once broken protocol and disturbed the dead, he wasn't over-keen to transgress again. Besides, he couldn't be sure that the old hag was telling the truth; something supernatural might be lurking in the coffin.

"Go on then," urged Meg. "What be 'ee waiting for?"

Hesitantly, Hawkley took one pace towards the offending coffin. As all eyes turned to the watchman, Revin leapt aboard the cart and whipped the horse up; the sudden jolt forward caused Hawkley to lose his balance and he shot off the back of the cart. Nathan jumped aboard, and Hawkley, sitting on his backside, could only watch as the wagon rattled away into the distance.

"I told 'ee so," gloated Meg.

Rebecca, who stood behind her, kicked the old crone on the backside, and she fell forward face-first into the dust. Rebecca missed her expletives as she turned on her heels and marched back into her house, slamming the door on the world and her dying husband. As the cart sped away, Verde kicked off the lid and hauled himself and the distressed Sam into the cool refreshing night's air.

Before the night was out, the persuasive tongue of Verde had explained the position to Sam's Aunt Verity. Miss Cannling was at first reluctant to allow a potential plague sufferer into her domain, but she lived alone and the production of the coins softened her heart, as did the strong family bond that existed amongst London's poorer classes. Revin handed over the slumbering babe and the woman lifted his clothing, found nothing, smiled, and carried her new family into the house.

"Do you reckon 'e'll be oright?" asked Nathan.

"He stands a far better chance there than imprisoned in that germ-infested house," said Verde.

Nathan comprehended little of Verde's statement, but he nodded his head, not willing to admit otherwise.

"Besides," added Verde, "Sam's better off than us; at least he will have a roof over his head."

They climbed into the bed of the cart and Revin signalled to the horse, and the journey back to All Hallows began. Solomon Whyte was waiting for them as they rolled into the churchyard.

"What time do you call this?" asked the sexton.

"We've been busy," answered Revin.

Using a wheel spoke as a ladder the official peered into the near-empty dead cart.

"If that's what you call busy, I'd hate to see a slack night's return. And what are you doing taking coffins with you?"

"Like I said, Mister Whyte, we've been busy."

"Well, I can do without that kind of busy. If you ask me you've been up to no good, and if it was up to me I would release you on the spot."

"It is up to you," said Nathan.

Solomon Whyte looked flummoxed at Nathan's simplicity, but quickly recovered his composure.

"As I was saying, if it was up to me I would release you on the spot – but for the fact that healthy bearers are at a premium right now."

"You're right," agreed Revin.

"I know I'm right," said the sexton, accepting the reins from Revin. "Hold on; where do you think you are going?"

Revin and Verde had begun to saunter away, leaving Whyte with the task of stabling the horse.

"We will not be returning. Good night, Mister Whyte. We resign."

Solomon blustered several incomprehensible words at their departure, but the two men merely turned their backs and walked away.

CHAPTER TWENTY-FOUR

A New Image

The moon had disappeared as they walked aimlessly along. Revin slipped Verde a handful of Rebecca's bequest. The sound of running footsteps approached from behind, and they turned to face the expected attack.

"'Tis only me. I been thinkin' about what you said."

"Which bit exactly, Nathan?" asked Verde.

"About you not having a roof over your head. I think I can help."

Nathan lodged in Cripplegate. Their walk took them along filthy alleys, where deep layers of rubbish and excrement lay as rotten partners, the rakers never daring to venture close to these most dilapidated of slums. Putrefying smells from the decaying matter under their feet rose to choke them. In their short stay Verde and Revin had witnessed scenes of squalor, but none to match those of Mouse Lane. Nathan led them down a short series of steps and tapped on the door at the bottom. As the hinges creaked a filthy face appeared.

"Two more, Marlip?"

Marlip widened the crack to look beyond Nathan. A torn cape was draped around his shoulders, from which he extended a grubby hand.

"Usual agreement."

Nathan turned to the two men standing behind him. It had not occurred to either of them that payment would be required.

"How much?" Verde asked.

"Two groats for the week," grunted Marlip.

"How much for a night?" asked Revin, who was already beginning to regret Nathan's offer.

"Don't deal in days," came the blunt reply.

The astute landlord had calculated that many of his lodgers would not be around to take the full benefit of their weekly tenement, and therefore he could increase his clientele and pockets. Revin thrust the coins forward and Nathan passed them to Marlip, who produced a candle to ensure he was not being cheated.

Marlip's lodgings proved to be no more than a dark, dank airless cellar, tucked away amongst the maze of rat-infested back alleys. A stench of unwashed bodies, foul warm air, rancid urine and reeking tobacco smoke greeted the travellers as they descended four further steps. A room no larger than twenty foot square, lit only by the single inspection candle, greeted them for the night.

"Just for one night," whispered Verde in answer to Revin's protesting tug on his sleeve.

The floor was solid earth, but very little of it could be seen in the candlelight, as most of it appeared to be covered in bundles of rags, which on closer inspection were revealed to be twenty or so sleeping bodies. A symphony of snoring, groaning and whistling reverberated around the vault. Nathan pointed out a small space in one corner, and the two men weaved through a maze of legs and arms to the chosen spot.

Verde lowered himself to the floor, and running his hand down the wall he discovered the reason for the availability of this nook. He wiped his slimy palm on his clothing and settled down, where he could more fully appreciate their surroundings. The ceiling was low and covered in a tapestry of spider webs, dust and green mould. What little light the candle could muster sparkled on rivulets of damp that meandered above their heads and across the walls. A woman stumbled over their bodies, swearing at them for their troubles. In the dark she was featureless but her voice suggested she was no longer in her prime. From the far wall came a tinkling sound of urine spitting against a solid surface.

"What did you wanna do that for, Nellie? Now you've started me off," groaned a voice in the darkness. The complainant soldiered over to the row of buckets that stood along the wall; from his grunting it was soon evident that he was defecating, a fact soon to be confirmed by the choking aroma that wafted around searching unsuccessfully for a crevice by which it could escape into the night air. Once the bucket visits had started there appeared to be a constant stream of visitors throughout the night. Revin and Verde managed only fitful periods of sleep, punctuated by long periods of insomnia.

Morning seemed an age in arriving and most of the buckets were now full; some had even overflowed in the dark, producing yellow rivers on the floor. Verde poked Revin, who had just managed to snatch a brief sleep due to his exhaustion.

"I'm all for skipping breakfast," he joked. "Let's depart."

Revin could see nothing remotely humorous about their predicament. The atmosphere was oppressive and stifling, and he needed little encouragement to leave the living cesspit behind and climb the stairs to the relatively fresher air of the London streets. Nathan followed them to the great outdoors; the three dishevelled figures were a comical sight as they stood in dawn's early light, rapaciously breathing in deep breaths of air. Verde turned to the pitiable figure of Nathan.

"We must leave you… thank you for the shelter, but we must reach the city."

"Not dressed like that," said Nathan. "They don't let beggars through the gates."

Revin and Verde eyed each other and then in turn looked at themselves. Nathan was right. The hostile environment had taken its toll on them. Their clothes were torn and filthy, their hair was unkempt, and both their beards were straggly and untidy.

"Where can we buy new clothes?" asked Verde.

Nathan chortled at the question. "You'll find no tailor on this side of town, or on any other, come to that."

Revin beat his fist into his hand, and his eyes blazed with anger. He grabbed Nathan by the clothes around his throat.

"You mean to tell me that I have to stay dressed like this for—"

Verde released the arms of his distressed friend. "It's not his fault," he admonished him. "Besides, I think the look quite suits you."

Revin snorted, but slowly recomposed himself.

"I'm sorry, Nathan," he said. "I'm rather tired."

"I didn't say I couldn't help you," stammered the startled man.

Nathan looked up and down the alley and beckoned the two men towards him. Verde and Revin lowered their heads to meet with Nathan, who jumped back a pace as the latter came a little too close.

"How desperate are you gents?"

"We must enter the city; we have business to attend to," replied Verde.

"What I told you was true; there are no tailors…"

Revin sighed and stood up.

"Take no notice," said Verde encouragingly to Nathan, managing to keep a calm demeanour, although he inwardly fumed at Revin's tantrums and the risk they were posing.

Nathan paused, again checking the street.

"There's a fair trade in used clothes." He looked at Verde's disappointment, and hastily added, "It is good quality. Well, most is."

Revin had joined the circle again, attracted by this latest revelation.

"Much of it is good quality," repeated Nathan, reassuringly. "It comes from them that don't be wantin' it."

"Can't be much use if others have discarded it," sneered Revin.

"Wouldn't say they actually discarded it," said Nathan.

"I understand," said Verde. "Can you take us there?"

Nathan glanced at Revin; he was anxious to avoid another contretemps.

"No," he said, and quickly facing his tormentor he added, "No need. Just walk to the end of this alley and knock on the door next to the wizard. Ask for Flo."

"Wizard?" scoffed Revin.

"Y-y-yes," stuttered Nathan.

"How will we know this house," boomed Revin.

Nathan had started to back away. "You will," he said anxiously, and he turned to go.

"Wait!" demanded Verde.

Nathan froze in his tracks, like startled prey not knowing which way to turn. Verde strode over to the rigid watchman, and put one arm around his shoulder.

"You have been more than kind and very helpful to us."

"Thank you, any time," shouted Nathan, examining an assortment of coins in his hand, and he cracked a thin smile as both men walked away.

At the end of the alley they stopped. Diagonally opposite to them stood a house; its windows were covered in an assortment of posters, advertising all manner of medicinal cures for the plague. Bright red lettering offered "Doctor Hayle's Cordial", which sat above a more sombre and faded "Wondrous anti-pestilential pills", and written in sharp black print below was "Capital Treacle".

Revin stared at a wooden sign that was hanging crookedly above the door. It read, "Here lives a wizard. Plague cures and fortunes told".

"I'd like to go and tell his fortune right now," hissed Revin.

"We haven't the time," reasoned Verde. "Besides, there's plenty more to take his place, London will be full of such quacks."

"But these people pay hard-earned money, probably their last few desperate coins – for nothing more than a sham."

"I agree it's scandalous to trick the ignorant, and to take advantage of them, but our future – their future lies here."

Verde knocked on the door of the adjacent house; above them a window creaked open. A spindly thin face with a large hooked nose spoke down to them. "What do you want?"

"We are looking for some clothes," shouted Revin.

"Then you've come to the wrong place," bawled the woman from under her cloth cap.

"I'm sorry, we were told to ask for Flo," said Verde soothingly.

"Who told you?"

"Nathan, the watchman."

"Why didn't you say?"

"You didn't ask?"

Verde stood in front of Revin, and pushed him backwards. "We would be much in your debt if you could direct us to this good woman."

"Stay there."

Dust fell from the window ledge as the window slammed shut. The two men waited outside the door; a key turned from within, and the thick wooden door was pulled back, its hinges protesting bitterly against this early start to the morning.

Before them stood a woman in her late twenties, dressed in her night attire of a flowing white gown and matching cap. Verde thought it was rather too grand for the woman's calling, but the situation promised well.

"Can't be too careful; come in," she invited them, wiping a dewdrop from her nose.

Verde and Revin followed the woman indoors, and stepped immediately into a room full of garments, blankets, bedding and various other items of clutter.

"So you're friends of Nathan?"

"Yes," replied Verde quickly. "Our work has thrown us together, but circumstances now dictate that we should improve our clothing."

Flo sniffed, and looked them up and down. "Can't fall much lower," she deduced. "Anything in particular you be fancying? I've plenty here; just look around you."

Revin and Verde tiptoed silently around the room to the accompaniment of Flo's nasal interruptions. She was true to her word; clothes took up every conceivable space in the room, draped over chairs, piled on the table, scattered over cupboard surfaces, and stacked in huge piles around the floor.

"Business must be good," said Revin with a smile.

"It's all paid for," sniffed Flo, still harbouring doubts.

"I'm sure it is," Verde reassured her.

"I buy lots of my stuff from the nursekeepers. Relatives of the dead don't be wanting any plague things."

Verde wondered what say the relatives had in the relief of their loved ones' best clothes and bedding, but wasn't prepared to argue the point with Flo.

"This is all aired," said Flo. "Nothing wrong with it."

"I suppose it stops the family members squabbling over the belongings," mused Revin dryly.

"Ignore my friend," urged Verde. "He's suffering from a lack of sleep."

"I can recommend the good doctor next door," said Flo.

"How about this?" said Revin hastily, thrusting a long black cloak at Verde.

"A good choice, sir; that used to belong to a churchwarden, hardly worn as you can see."

Verde was fingering a pair of breeches; he rubbed the clothing between his hands.

"You have good taste too, sir; those belonged to a parish officer, God rest his soul."

Verde's countenance showed that he wasn't impressed. Revin lightened the moment by holding up a gaudy pink dress against his body.

"Is it me?" he asked Verde.

"Most fetching," laughed his friend. But the whimsical interlude had its desired effect, and both men settled down to a serious search of the clothing. Within a few minutes, Revin had found an olive-green coat to go with the parish officer's breeches. Flo rummaged through a pile of clothes and threw him a matching pair of black stockings.

"Don't mind me," said Flo as Revin hesitated. "Many a body has undressed in here. I've seen it all before."

Revin slowly removed his rags, and as he pulled his shirt over his head he felt a cold hand cup his testes and gently squeeze them. He whipped the shirt over his head and jumped backwards in one motion, falling over a pile of clothing. Verde, who was sporting a coat, breeches and stockings in a variety of dark browns, chuckled at the incident.

"That'll be two guineas, sirs," demanded Flo, who seemed unmoved by her failure to excite Revin.

"Have you anything that might tidy this?" asked Revin, stroking his straggly beard.

Flo crossed the room to a chest and pulled out a cut-throat razor and soap.

"Should just about cope," she sniffed, running her fingers through Revin's beard.

He again backed away from the over-familiar gesture.

"A florin for the pair?" said Flo in a wounded tone.

Revin counted the money from Rebecca; it was more than enough, but it seemed wrong not to haggle with the woman, who appeared to be expecting such action.

"We'll give you a guinea for the lot," said Revin.

"Huh," sniffed Flo, who would have been more amenable had Revin not rebuffed her attentions.

"One pound and ten shillings, take it or leave it," offered Revin.

"Leave it, then," grunted Flo.

Verde could see not only their new wardrobe disappearing, but with it their immediate chances of entering the city.

"Two pounds," he offered, not wishing to upset either side.

Flo mellowed a little, weighing up her chances of extracting maximum profit. As she pondered, Revin cast his eyes around the room in exasperation, and they fell on some items of clothing in a dark recess that until now had eluded his vision.

"Three pounds and those," he said, pointing to an assortment of leather equipment.

"The quacks' uniforms?" scoffed Flo. "Why, be you wantin' to scare folks half to death?"

"No," said Revin, fondling his beard, "but we might if we don't tidy ourselves up."

"Tell you what, for three pounds I'll throw in some hot water." Having not lost face, at least in the bargaining stakes, Flo was now prepared to forget Revin's rebuff. Besides, the morning was turning out to be very profitable and her avarice overshadowed all other vices.

They stripped to the waist as Flo placed a large bowl of steaming hot water in front of them. In turn they shaved each other and then took advantage of the situation and washed their bodies. Flo threw them a towel to dry themselves, and then they stood back and admired each other. Verde felt his smooth chin.

"How long is it?" asked Revin.

"Some time during the second work cycle. How about you?"

"I'm not sure, but I hope I've lost as many years as you."

Flo could not follow their banter, but her mind stayed focused. "Three pounds," she reminded them. Revin passed the money to Verde to give to the grinning Flo, who still wore her smile as she showed them to the door and watched them walk down the alley.

They struggled along, each weighed down by a leather hat, a pair of leather gloves, a full-length waxed coat, leather breeches and a red stick. Pausing in a doorway, Verde demanded to know why he was carrying such a heavy bundle.

"I didn't like to embarrass you in front of your admirer, but why have you squandered our money on these?"

"These are our key to the city," replied Revin. "They are worn by the plague doctors. I saw one walk straight through the city gates when you were locked in Tom's house. You heard Flo; nobody comes near them. Not even the guards will challenge us."

"What about this?" asked Verde, holding out his red stick.

"All part of the apparel; at least we will look authentic."

"The joke is we know more about medicine than all their doctors put together."

"But who are you going to tell? And who will believe you?"

Verde held up the helmet that he was carrying. It was like a huge bird mask; at each side was a large glass eye, and from the front protruded a long beak.

"We will look like a pair of giant ducks," he said.

"Perhaps that is why they call them quacks," quipped Revin.

Both of them broke into laughter. The camaraderie between them was still very strong; if anything the bond between them had grown stronger due to the dire circumstances that they had found themselves in.

"To the city," announced Revin triumphantly.

"Yes," concurred Verde, "to the city, the tavern of the black bird, and Lutel and Rewn."

CHAPTER TWENTY-FIVE
BUGGERLUGS

A host of flies buzzed around the heads of the two duty guards at Bishopsgate. The wall behind their backs was warm from the late summer sunshine. As yet the towering city wall offered little or no shade as the sun shone brightly from the east.

Revin had anticipated no resistance to their entering the city garbed in plague doctors' clothing, but he had not calculated on the prickliness of the sun-drenched guards. Their halberds crossed as he and Verde made their attempt to pass through the gate.

"What business have you?" asked the taller sentry, whose manner and poise bore all the hallmarks of an ex-soldier. His upright posture and clipped speech suggested he may well have seen service in the great wars of the 1640s, but had now fallen somewhat from grace. Revin was not prepared for any challenge and stood dumbfounded, looking at his dusty feet. Verde removed his helmet.

"We are called to see the Lord Mayor, to report the conditions in the outer parishes," he said authoritatively. He replaced his helmet, tapping it firmly into place with one hand to indicate that his speech and their conversation was at an end.

It was the guards' turn to be nonplussed; they looked at each other and the taller opened his mouth to speak, but nothing came to mind. His attention was distracted by a shot and commotion behind him; a yelping and whining mongrel dog had been wounded by the dog killers. A fat hunchbacked man pursued the limping animal through the gate, passing between the guards and out into the dusty road. A sadistic sneer crossed the hunter's lips as he raised his musket at the frightened dog.

Not wishing to risk detection, Verde and Revin felt a surge of helpless frustration as they watched the man finish the job. The lifeless body of the tan-and-black mongrel was left in a heap on the road to await the arrival of a raker. Flies were already swarming around the red pool of blood as the assailant stalked off in search of another half a groat's worth of glory. The ex-soldier had not been impressed by the fairness of the competition, and allowed his mind to drift back to the carnage of the battle of Roundway Down. Verde took a pace forward; the ex-soldier made no effort to stop him, and nor did the second guard, who seemed to be looking to his companion for guidance. Revin followed his fellow doctor into the great capital city of England.

They threaded their way between the towering walls and continued at a brisk pace for fear of a change of heart by the guards. As they walked along Bishopsgate Street the imposing Gresham College loomed into view; the grounds were void of scholars and the biscuit-coloured building seemed deserted. Very few Londoners were walking the streets; those who did gave them a wide berth out of respect or fear, the red sticks acting like magic wands and opening up a pathway in front of them.

Branching right into Threadneedle Street, they paused in a side alley. Revin placed his hands on either side of his helmet and lifted it. He shook his head to loosen his tresses. The herbs in the beaks had long diffused their scents, and the stale air they had been forced to breathe was now replaced by pungent sulphur fumes that mixed with the fresher variety. Verde took a deep breath, and then wished he hadn't. He coughed several times and then sat down on his haunches, his back resting against the wall of one of the alleyway houses. Revin slumped down beside him.

"Well?" Revin eyed Verde.

"Well," answered Verde, "somewhere in this city is an inn, with the sign of a black bird. It's rather a tenuous meeting place, but at least a building is fairly constant; the elders did not foresee us landing so far apart. Let's hope Lutel and Rewn have the presence of mind to find it."

"Or the patience to wait," snorted Revin.

Verde smiled at his friend. "Given the means of transport, I very much doubt that they've been there long, or even yet reached it."

A young boy approached them chasing a small puppy.

"Stop, Buggerlugs, stop!" yelled the youngster in pursuit of the animal. Verde lurched to his left and grabbed the terrier by its neck; the dog put up little resistance as Verde cradled it in his arms. Its rough tongue licked his face, and he rather regretted taking his helmet off.

"Must be a day for dogs," exclaimed Verde.

"Thanks, mister," cried the boy, as he took the tail-wagging puppy. Under his curly mop of golden hair his face was red with exertion, and tears mingled with the sweat on his cheeks. The lad had a fresh-looking freckled face; most unusual given the present plight, thought Verde. His build was slight but athletic; his clothes, faded and torn, looked like they had belonged to an older brother, the breeches having been cut off at the knee.

"He escaped when me ma was sweeping the street," he explained. "Naughty boy, Buggerlugs."

"He's lucky to have a master who cares for him," said Revin. But if the boy heard the compliment, he ignored it, as he was too wrapped up in the safety of his beloved pet.

"If the shooters see him, they'll kill him," he continued, as he held the puppy tighter at the thought of what might have happened to him. Buggerlugs, who was oblivious to the concern he had caused, was obviously not averse to salt water as he cleaned the boy's face.

"What's your name?" asked Verde.

"Charles, sir, but everyone calls me Charlie."

"Well, Charlie, perhaps you could do us a favour in return. Do you know of an inn or tavern that is named after a black bird?"

"Can't think of one, sir, but then I couldn't read the sign if it was right above me head."

Verde considered this obvious but unforeseen difficulty. "Have you ever seen a picture of a large black bird outside one of these buildings?"

Charlie paused; taverns were something he was yet to frequent, but the far-away look in his eye revealed that he very much wanted to help Buggerlugs' saviours. He searched his young mind's eight years' experience, but drew a blank.

"I'm sorry, sirs, there's no such place around here; I can't think of any…"

For a second time Charlie racked his mind, the sun glistening on his curls; he was so preoccupied that even Buggerlugs' attentions failed to distract him.

"Yes," said Verde encouragingly, "any information might be useful."

"Well, before the plague, me dad used to take me to the Tower to see the executions. I didn't much care for them, but it was a day out. Me dad said that's how I'd end up if I didn't behave. He used to stop for a drink, to toast the dead, he said."

"Is this getting us anywhere?" interrupted Revin.

"Patience," entreated Verde. "Carry on, Charlie, take no notice of him."

"Well, that's it: I'm sure the inn had a sign of a bird outside."

"How far was the inn from the Tower?" asked Verde.

"Fairly close," said Charlie hesitantly.

"How far away is it from here?" demanded Revin.

"Not far, about a mile."

"Can you take us there?" asked Verde.

Revin drew Verde aside. "Can we really trust the word of a small boy? He doesn't seem that sure of himself."

"We have no other leads at the moment; what harm can following this one do?"

"He might not want to take us."

Charlie watched the two men as they whispered.

"We will pay you for your troubles," offered Verde.

The boy's eyes opened wide, Buggerlugs was payment enough, but he wasn't going to turn down the opportunity to line his pockets.

"How much?" he asked boldly.

"A florin," offered Verde.

"Blimey, I ain't ever had that much money. Follow me."

"What about your parents?" asked Verde.

"Oh, they'll think I'm still chasing Buggerlugs. They won't mind, doubt if they'll notice. Besides, I'll be back in an hour."

They made an amusing trio as Charlie, carrying Buggerlugs, led a bedecked Verde and Revin in a south-easterly direction towards the Tower of London. Charlie took them past the Royal Exchange where only the ghosts of merchants stayed to trade business, the living having sought refuge in the countryside, along with the rest of London's wealthy classes. He led them across Cornhill, by the wooden conduit water supply, and continued east along Leadenhall Street. Revin smiled to himself as the sight of his clothing gave them unquestioned access at various guard points along the way.

Turning south, they left Fenchurch Street behind them and passed into Mark Lane. Here the houses grew denser, but were of a far better quality than anything they had encountered outside the city walls. On the skyline between the houses the huge grey walls of the Tower could now be clearly seen. Charlie turned left into Tower Street and just past the junction with Seething Lane he stopped. Tower Hill lay impressively before them. Revin and Verde's attention was drawn towards the neighbouring Tower. There had never been a building like this on Mykas, and even allowing for its purpose, they could still admire its architectural beauty.

Charlie let out a yell and pointed to a building less than twenty yards away from him. A raucous noise of singing and talking drifted from its open windows. Plague was a way of life or death for some Londoners, and nothing came between them and their merriment. Others saw the local taverns as a source of solace, and unscrupulous landlords flouted what little law existed to stop the spreading of the pestilence in public places. A wooden board hung outside the inn, too heavy for the light breeze to swing its rusty hinges. As they moved closer, a black bird with a large bill and long wedge-shaped tail fixed them with a beady eye. Above the image, written in red, was the name that the bird gave to the tavern: The Raven.

"I told you, I told you," screamed Charlie.

Verde put his hand inside his clothing and pulled out a coin, which he handed to Charlie. The boy stared at the golden disc in his hand.

"This ain't what you said."

Verde glared at the ungrateful comment.

"No, no, I mean it's more, you don't owe me all this!"

Verde resumed his previous countenance. "You've done a good job; now be off, and stay clear of those guards."

"Thanks, mister, and don't worry about the guards; they won't catch me. I'll set Buggerlugs on them," laughed the mischievous urchin. Verde was about to thank him again, but Charlie was already running down the road.

Verde stared at the sign of The Raven; paint was flaking around its wings, giving the impression that they had been clipped.

"Best put your helmet on," said Revin. "We don't want to risk refusal."

"I can imagine the look on Lutel's face if she sees us dressed like this."

"I somehow think that's unlikely."

A plume of smoke met them as they entered the tavern. All laughing and singing stopped, from all sides of the room. Eyes turned towards them. A large, heavily-built man, almost as tall as themselves, spoke to them.

"What is your business, gentlemen? We have no need of your services here."

They removed their helmets, and a gasp of disappointment reverberated around The Raven.

"Take no notice," said the landlord. "It's rare for folk to see who is underneath; they expected a two-headed monster." The landlord laughed at his own joke, and those of his patrons that were in earshot humoured him by joining in. "So if you are not here to frighten my customers, what do you want?"

"We would like a drink, friend, if it is all right with you," responded Verde.

"We don't like strangers," answered the landlord. Verde could see the truth in his statement, as many of the drinkers were still neglecting their ale and observing the proceedings. A cursory look at the customers had shown them that they were indeed first at the rendezvous point, and there seemed little point in antagonising their intended host.

Verde looked at the landlord's balding head; it shone with sweat, his apron was beer-stained, and his large hairy forearms looked more suited to the village smithery than to serving drinks. Brawn was definitely not an option; guile or some other means would need to be employed if they were to gain lodgings.

"We are curers, not carriers of the pestilence," tried Verde.

"You're frightening my customers," answered the landlord bluntly, aware of the continuing unease. "Take off your quacks' garbs, if you want a drink."

They removed their physicians' outfits, and the landlord at least seemed to relax a little. Verde lifted his shirt to the wider audience. "There, no sign of plague," he cried.

"Proves nothing, some die unmarked," said a voice from the crowd. But others appeared satisfied and returned to their libation.

"Hersa's right," said the landlord; "it proves little. Many an inn wouldn't let you through the door; you'd be lucky to be served on the doorstep even if you were the richest man in all England."

Revin glimpsed the opening for which Verde had been searching. He slipped a coin into the landlord's hand.

"That's for a drink, and a room," he offered.

The innkeeper gave a sly downward glance at his hand; his manner instantly changed. "Why, gentlemen, you may stay for a week, and drink yourself giddy if you wish."

"Don't trust them, Knox," advised a regular from one of the far tables.

"I say they stay," said the landlord firmly, backing his judgement with what lay in his hands. "Their money is as good as yours, Peter Hersa; leave if you wish."

The disgruntled customer rose, making to call the landlord's bluff, but his half-finished drink and the lack of support from around the tables caused him to think again.

Knox again turned his attention to his new lodgers. "What will it be, doctors? A glass of sack, a cider, ale…"

He never managed to finish listing The Raven's fare as Revin interrupted. "We'd like to put our things in our room first."

"Certainly," replied Knox. He was unwilling to lose this potential pot of money by asking what or where the things actually were, the quacks' uniforms being the only surplus baggage on view. "Please follow me up the stairs."

Knox called to an equally large woman who was sitting around a table with three other drinkers. She folded her playing cards and knocked out her pipe before taking over her husband's serving duties.

"What brings you gentlemen to my inn?" asked Knox, as they climbed the spiralling oak staircase.

"Oh, just searching, Mister Knox," answered Verde rather carelessly.

"I didn't know it was the role of the physician to search out the plague."

"We're not," barked Revin.

"Then what are you searching for?" asked Knox, beginning to glower.

"Searching for a cure," interposed Verde.

"You'll be rich men if you find it. There's many that's tried but none have succeeded. All quacks are the same if you ask me." He looked at them hard, emphasising his feelings for their kind. "I'll have no plague bodies here, or I'll set the dogs on you. Otherwise, if you pay good money and don't go out of your way to upset my customers, you are welcome to stay as long as you like. I dare say if you find a cure the Mayor will be mighty pleased with you. Poor Sir John has had his work cut out now that Parliament has moved to Oxford. He's governing this side of the city, whilst Lord Craven has the west. Yes, I dare say he'd pay you gentlemen your weight in gold if you could rid him of this pestilence. Though personally, I think you've more chance of flying to the moon than beating this foul distemper."

The landlord paused to gather breath. It was not his custom to make such long speeches, and the exertion of climbing the stairs was no help.

"Is it something I said?" he asked Verde, who was biting his lip in an attempt to control a chortle.

Fortunately he did not pursue the reason for Verde's mirth but looked around the hallway at the several doors that led from it.

"At least you have joined us at a good time; we have no other guests at present, so you may have your pick of the rooms."

Verde smiled thinly at Knox, trying to mask his disappointment.

"Thank you," he said, "this will do fine." He led Revin in through a door and was about to close it when Knox crossed the threshold.

"Anything you want, just ask. Meals are served at seven."

Knox closed the door, put the gold coin to his lips and bit it. His wide smile returned as he put the coin into a little leather purse that he kept tied to his waist, underneath his apron.

Verde's mask and gown crashed to the floor as he slumped into a crudely-fashioned wooden chair and looked around the plain room. Revin lay down on the only bed. It was large but hard, its straw mattress offering little comfort. At least it would be good for the back, he thought, where he still felt the odd twinge from his time as a bearer.

Midday was still several minutes away, yet the two men fell asleep, exhausted by their recent exertions and tired through a lack of sleep from the previous evening. Verde was the first to wake; darkness shone through the unshuttered window. He guessed it would be too late for dinner, even though the pangs inside told him he was wrong. Revin still lay on the bed, snoring contentedly. Verde stood up and looked out on the cloudless night; the stars sparkled like beads of metal burning in the sky. He remembered his science lessons in the academy at home.

He was fourteen years of age and standing beside Maran at the perimeter of a colourless worksurface shaped like a large ring. Their lecturers moved around the inner circle, pausing frequently to offer advice and tuition. The laboratory was several storeys high, and they were working on the uppermost level. The panoramic view of the purple mountains made an idyllic setting. Verde nervously offered Maran a sharp instrument.

"Thanks, Verde," she said, and he blushed.

"Where are you going to cut?" asked a voice from within the circle.

"Here," came the confident reply.

"What do you think, Verde?"

Verde was less certain; he wanted to suggest another part of the organ, but he did not wish to contradict Maran.

"I agree," he lied.

"Try it."

Maran cut into the animal's organ and blood gushed from the opening, spurting all over Verde. Maran screamed and her tutor took the instrument from her.

"Where do you think you went wrong?"

"I'm not sure."

"How about you, Verde? Verde?"

Verde wobbled slightly, then, rocking backwards, slumped to the floor.

That day with Maran he'd learned two important lessons: never to let love rule your head and that he couldn't stand the sight of blood, thus being a surgeon was out of the question. Ironic, he thought, that six years later he had enrolled for the Medical Academy. Fortunately their science was far more advanced than anything on planet Earth and Mykasians benefited from a concoction of preventative measures in their water supply, which took care of the more common ailments. These were supplemented by prescribed medicines to meet individual needs and also stop their immune systems from becoming accustomed to all of the available antidotes. Personal diagnosis was still required and most ailments could be determined and treated by ionic discs, but if these failed there still remained a case for specialist surgeons.

After a two-year general course Verde was able to specialise. Initial diagnosis was given by a leading practitioner, who neither prescribed nor operated, but directed the patient to the next stratum. In the majority of cases, the next level was sufficient; it was here that Verde had found his niche. Specialist doctors like him were peripatetic, and they covered a large area of Mykas. Verde travelled around the south-east medical centres of Mykas as the consulting allergy specialist. He was never required to take blood or patch wounds. When a patient was referred to him, he attached a small cylindrical disc to their wrist, and ionic pulses were beamed backwards and forwards between the wrist and the disc. The disc was removed and inserted in a computer port, where a screen readout would enable Verde to determine the exact allergy. The majority of allergies proved to be food-related and his task then was to compile a healthy diet that would avoid the allergy, whilst providing a nutritional balance.

Every four years the doctors were expected to take a year's sabbatical for research purposes. During his second sabbatical Verde had undertaken research on the allergic reaction to insect bites. His studies had met with notable success, and at the request of the Stilax he had continued with his research for another two years. At the end of this time he had produced a definitive paper that was widely acclaimed throughout Mykas. His work from over forty years ago had not been forgotten when the selections for the mission were being discussed, but his squeamishness was still on his record, and as Lutel had only recently retired as a surgeon, it had been decided she was to be chief medic.

Verde woke from his reverie. The moon still shone; he wondered if Lutel and Rewn could see its yellow face. Were they still alive to gaze at its beauty? Revin was still snoring, and whilst he slept, Verde thought deeply about their plight.

CHAPTER TWENTY-SIX

BEWARE OF PASSING RATS

Just before midnight Revin stirred; he opened his eyes to see Verde sitting on the edge of the bed, the back of his hands resting on his cheeks. He was still buried in thought.

"Well?" queried Revin.

Verde stirred, pleased that at last he could utter his thoughts.

"We have only been here for a few days. There's still time for Lutel and Rewn to arrive, but whether they or the antidote have survived we can't say."

"We could go looking for them," suggested Revin.

"No, we don't have a good enough fix. Besides, all our equipment is in the ship."

"We could fetch it."

"But to what purpose? Rewn and Lutel will have moved by now – if they were able. If we go looking for them our paths may cross and we could end up missing them. They could be here waiting for us and we could be out in the country looking for them."

"So, what are you suggesting?" asked Revin.

Verde sighed and stood up from the bed. He clasped his hands in front of him as though he were preparing to give a public speech.

"Even with the antidote, I can't see our chances of success will be very high. You've seen these people. They're incapable of understanding or accepting our technology or medical thinking. We must concentrate on prevention, not cure. I suggest we go to someone in authority, and explain about the squalid conditions and the rats."

Verde waited for Revin's response; it was much as he anticipated.

"Do you really think they'll believe us? Your pestilence is caused by a little flea! They'll throw us in their Tower, or worse, burn us for being heretics or witches."

"Wizards."

"Don't be bloody facetious, Verde."

"My, you are becoming a native."

"At least I can think like one."

"What do you mean by that?"

"You understand."

"Understand what?"

"Understand this!" roared Revin, and he launched himself at the bed. The two men fell onto the floor locked in each other's arms; they rolled around, each looking to pin the other to the floor. As they parted Verde was first to his feet and punched Revin before he found his bearings. Revin fell backwards against the single chest that ordained the room; a blue jug crashed to the floor. Revin stood up and felt the blood around his lips; he wiped them clean with the back of his arm, then lowering his head he charged at Verde. His head made contact with Verde's midriff and the momentum sent the pair of them crashing into the door. Verde raised his knee and it jutted into Revin's jaw; he rocked backwards but quickly recovered and retaliated by whipping Verde's legs from under him. Verde's head crashed against the wall, and Revin grabbed the clothes around his throat and hauled him to his feet. Revin landed a punch of his own to Verde's eye, and the two men again clasped each other and fell once more to the floor. Frustration and stress poured from both men as they continued to grapple around the room; so intense was their struggle that they failed to hear the knocking at their door. Eventually it opened and the comical figure of Knox in his night-dress stood before them.

"Is everything all right, doctors?"

The two men stopped fighting. "Just a difference of medical opinion," answered Revin.

"I dare say," said Knox. "May I presume that the matter is closed?"

"Yes," said Verde shamefacedly. He dug in his clothing and pulled out a coin. "This is for any damage."

Knox checked that the coin was indeed a true sister to its predecessor.

"Goodnight… uh… gentlemen."

As he closed the door, Revin and Verde roared with laughter. They felt like naughty schoolboys discovered in the dorm in the middle of a midnight prank.

"Sorry," apologised Verde.

"No, it was my fault, I wasn't prepared to listen. I apologise."

"No, it was unprofessional of me. I should have handled the uncertainty and frustration."

"Friends?" offered Revin.

"Of course."

"Explain your ideas again; this time I will hear you out."

Verde sat next to Revin on the bed.

"Say we go to the Lord Mayor; he's a figure in authority. We could explain about the rats. You're right, they probably would not understand about the fleas, but that wouldn't matter if we concentrated on their hosts. The point is they are killing the wrong animals; the more dogs and cats they kill, the fewer natural predators are left to help control the rats. We can explain about the fresh air and the dangers of infected clothes and bed linen. We could even try and persuade them about the cruelty of locking people in – we could suggest the building of camps to take the infected people."

Verde tailed off; he began to see Revin's point.

"No, you are right," Revin encouraged him, reading his friend's thoughts. "The least we can do is try and put forward some of the more pertinent points; things that are within the compass of their understanding. First thing in the morning we will seek out this Sir John."

Tiredness prevailed over hunger, and soon both men were again sleeping soundly.

Several hours later they were woken by a noise outside their door. Revin was the first to react and sprang to his feet, whilst Verde perched on the edge of the bed. Revin pressed his ear to the door, straining for any sound, but all they could hear was the gentle cooing of a pigeon from a ledge outside. Revin relaxed and started to make his way back to the bed when Verde pointed to the twitching door handle. Revin crept back to the door, his tense body mirroring the now-still handle.

Verde joined Revin's side. "Somebody must have noticed something," he whispered almost inaudibly. His heart raced as the door slowly opened. Revin, who had perched behind the door, signalled that he was ready to move; Verde posted himself on the opposite side.

"Now," said Revin, and he flung open the door. Unable to keep his grip on the handle, the large frame of Simon Knox was sent sprawling onto the floor. Crockery, utensils and a variety of food fell around him, porridge dripped down his front, and ale rippled across the floor, making a chestnut stream on the polished floorboards.

Fearing this could lead to their eviction, Revin rushed forward and helped the startled landlord to his feet. Verde began to pile the spillages onto the wooden tray that had fallen from Knox's grasp.

"I'm sorry, we thought you were a thief," gasped Revin, realising the landlord must have formed a very unfavourable view of them. Knox looked from one to another, his lips tightly pursed. Verde looked at the mess on the floor, the comical clutter on the tray and the dishevelled landlord. He expected the worst.

"Thief! Thief!" bellowed the innkeeper, and he cast back his head and roared with laughter. A relieved Verde tried to wipe the food from Knox's hair, but to little avail as the man convulsed. "I've been called it by my customers many times, but I've never actually been mistaken for one. I'm too slow to be a cutpurse, and too large for climbing in and out of windows." He launched into another barrage of laughter, and only composed himself after several minutes had passed.

"We were worried about you after last night." Verde and Revin felt the barb of shame. "When you didn't arrive for breakfast as well as missing last evening's dinner, Mrs Knox says to me, 'Knox, you go and see if those fighting doctors are all right; they might be in need of a physician themselves. You can take them up some breakfast while you are at it.'"

The good lady arrived on the scene with a large jug of hot water; the sight of her husband and his obvious enjoyment of the early morning jollifications did not impress her.

"I thought you might like to wash before breakfast, but I see there are more than two of you in need of this." She placed a white jug and a shaving dish on a small dressing table. "I'll make some more porridge," she said curtly.

They offered to share the water, but Knox was eager to put matters straight with his wife, and they could still hear him talking to himself as he disappeared down the hallway and descended the stairs. "Thief, me a thief," followed by a cackle of laughter.

Revin and Verde burst out into tension-easing guffaws of laughter themselves. The simple episode had improved the atmosphere. Revin picked up the shaving dish and examined the decorative pictures for a clue, but gained nothing from the central figures of a yeoman Stuart and his goodwife, nor did the pictures of a comb or razor around the edging elicit any clues to its actual usage. Finally, through trial and error, he solved the puzzle and placed the cut-away semi-circle of the round dish under his chin to protect his clothing. Then, picking up the ball of soap Mrs Knox had also left them, he washed and shaved cheerfully.

Shortly afterwards, sitting opposite Verde at a small rectangular table, Revin traced with his finger the scars of many knocks that the surface bore;

the stains of many a jar of ale vouched for its age. Mrs Knox arrived with a huge trencher of bread, two large bowls of porridge, some cold beef, and a jug of ale.

"Try to keep these on the table," she said with a hint of sarcasm.

Verde threw back his chair, stood up, seized her plump and wrinkled hand and, lifting it towards his mouth, kissed it. "Thank you, fair lady, and please excuse our earlier misdemeanours; they were much out of character and the result of cumulative stress."

The "fair lady" blushed. Such courtesy was unheard of in The Raven. For a moment she was dumbfounded and unsure of a response; she understood the physical compliment, but Verde's eloquent speech was nothing more than mere ramblings to her. She wondered if her original impression had been right and they were sheltering two mad doctors. Still, it was a special moment, and her basking in the gallantry was only dashed by the arrival of her spouse.

"Thief!" he exclaimed, beaming. "Me a thief!"

The smile on his wife's face disappeared instantly. Knox brought an additional flagon of ale and sat down at the head of the table.

"Maybe I could be one of the Four Thieves," he said enthusiastically, as though a romantic notion had entered his head. His wife had heard enough, and sighing deeply she flounced away to the sanctuary of her kitchen.

"Four thieves?" queried Revin, who thought he'd better take the bait that was being dangled even if he wasn't that interested in the landlord's ravings.

Knox sat upright in his chair, and poured them all a drink. "The Four Thieves," he echoed. "Don't tell me you haven't heard about the Four Thieves?"

"We have travelled much these last few days," answered Revin truthfully.

If there was suspicion there, Knox passed over it, eager to relate his story. Drawing his chair closer he bent forward towards his two guests.

"'Tis a local story; dare say you could have missed it. Ever since this pestilence has been among us, four thieves have been going around the city, searching out houses that carried the dreaded cross. They'd break into the houses and rob the dead and dying." He paused to ensure that his listeners had grasped the unique folly of such an action. "Not content with that, they robbed dead bodies in the street; they even scavenged the plague pits in search of belongings. Yet," and he drew in his breath to a whisper, "those men didn't have a mark of the plague on them! When they were eventually caught the constable asked them how they never became infected themselves."

Knox looked around the otherwise empty room, as though jealously protecting his little anecdote. Revin took a large bite from his bread. "Go on," he mumbled.

Knox took a swig of his ale, and composed himself.

"Well, the thieves claimed that before they went out robbing a body they washed themselves in vinegar, as a preventative against catching the plague." Knox sat back in his chair with the grin of a sage who had just imparted the secret of the universe. "Of course the apothecaries were not slow to spot some business, and you can buy Four Thieves vinegar from most of their shops around here."

At the end of the tale, Revin realised the necessity of implementing Verde's plan. Knox finished his ale and walked off in the direction of the kitchen, intent on irritating his wife with a further retelling of "The Four Thieves". By the look on her face when she came over to clear Verde and Revin's table, he had succeeded.

"Where exactly does Sir John live?" asked Verde.

Mrs Knox gave him a sharp look. "You're asking me where the Lord Mayor's house is?"

Verde cringed; try as they might, even the simplest of actions and questions were fraught with danger.

"We are unsure of the direction that we should take from here," covered Revin.

"What be you wantin' with Sir John Lawrence?"

"We are aiding him," explained Revin in a half-truth.

"Lord have mercy upon us," pronounced the woman. "Well, they say he works in mysterious ways. Bishopsgate is north of here. Though what the Lord Mayor can see in a pair of—"

"Thank you," cut in Verde, and again he kissed her hand. "We are unsure when we will return; if anyone should come looking for us, please ask them to wait. This should cover their expenses, and keep our room free."

Mrs Knox made certain that her avaricious husband was otherwise occupied, and placed the coins amongst her clothing. "What names will they use?"

"Our friends are called Lutel and Rewn," stated Revin.

The landlady shook her head, further convinced as to the instability of her guests. "Who will they be asking for? You haven't told us your names."

After all the suspicion and confusion, Revin realised, their hostess was right.

"Revin and Verde," he said, pointing at his friend as he spoke his name.

"Doctor Revin and Doctor Verde," said the landlady, making sure she could tell one from the other.

"Correct," confirmed Revin.

The two doctors retraced their steps of the previous day. In order to walk unhindered they had donned their physicians' uniforms. By ten o'clock they had come again to the Royal Exchange and as they walked along Threadneedle Street they approached a watchman on duty. The sentinel looked like a spectral apparition, being dressed in a grey woollen hat, with hair and clothes to match. Verde lifted his helmet and asked the frightened man for directions, which were nervously despatched. In less than a quarter of an hour, the two men were standing a short distance from Bishopsgate, outside the house of Sir John Lawrence in Great Saint Helens.

"We could have saved ourselves a journey," complained Revin.

"But you wouldn't have met the delectable Mrs Knox."

"I could have foregone that pleasure."

"But our locating The Raven was vital."

"True, true," mused Revin.

Before them stood an impressive four-storey timber-framed building with ornate carvings of cherubs and heraldic shields decorating the window surrounds of its middle two floors, giving the ground and top floors the appearance of the plain outer layers in a garnished sandwich. Carved into the centre of one shield was the date 1662, declaring the house to be no more than three years old.

A small queue had formed outside the left-hand door; Verde and Revin joined it. An assortment of people stood in front of them, each suspiciously eyeing the others. Most appeared to be of the lower merchant classes but one or two were obviously close to destitution. After half an hour of standing around in the hot sun, a smartly-dressed servant showed Verde and Revin into a room. The floor was highly polished, matching the oak-panelled walls.

"Please sit down, gentlemen."

They swivelled around to face the speaker; there was nobody there. For a moment they stood transfixed and confused.

"How can I help you?"

The voice came from above them; perched in a low gallery was the fine figure of Sir John Lawrence, Lord Mayor of London.

Verde and Revin seated themselves in a fine pair of elbow chairs, the tall backs embroidered in a deep maroon and gold tapestry. Verde recognised a similar motif to one of the shields at the front of the house.

The Mayor rested his hands on the gallery rail. He had a kindly but worried disposition, and freely despatched advice with tireless patience to all who sought it. Verde's attention was drawn to the lyres hanging on the wall behind him.

The Mayor coughed politely. "Your names, gentlemen?"

"Doctors Verde and Revin, Mister Lawrence… Sir John…"

"Your Worship or Lord Mayor will suffice."

"Our names are Verde and Revin, Your Worship."

"Very well, Verde and Revin, how may I assist you?" Due to his position the Mayor had no difficulty with the lack of Christian names and did not fall into the trap that had ensnared others before him.

The Mayor's lofty position was unexpected and Verde felt the difficulty of speaking as an equal to a man so physically far above him. He bit his lip and falteringly commenced.

"I, that is we, Revin and I …"

The Mayor's silent tolerance loosened his tongue.

"We believe that we know the cause of the plague!"

"Do you, by Jove? Well, you won't be the first to give me such counsel. I am all ears, gentlemen." Lawrence folded his hands on the balcony rail and rested his chin upon them. His back bent in a casual but attentive manner.

Verde was again uncertain of how he should proceed. The Mayor unfolded his hands in a welcoming gesture.

"We believe the cause of the plague is the rat," Verde blurted out.

Sir John burst out in guffaws of laughter; for a moment he seemed in danger of toppling over the balcony. Revin and Verde stared at one another in amazement as he staggered around above them.

"Very good, very good, gentlemen," he cried, wiping the tears from his eyes. "It makes an amusing change from the comets, the poors' wickedness and the bad air. But pray, what leads you to this conclusion." He laughed again before calling out, "Why say you this? Have you any proof?" And once more the senior citizen of London convulsed into laughter. It was so infectious that Verde and Revin found themselves unwillingly joining in the amusement.

"Yes, we have – well, not exactly, you see," replied Verde.

"No, gentlemen, I do not see," said the Mayor, adopting a more serious mood. "I've not met you before; where do you practise?"

"Oh, west of here, Sir John," said Revin.

The Mayor gave him a rebuking look.

Revin continued, "You see, the rat carries bacillus and if the rat dies the fleas find another host, and—"

"Stop!" yelled the Mayor. "You speak in riddles. If I follow you correctly you are telling me the plague, this death and destruction, is caused by a louse, a flea?"

Verde was beginning to wish they had not come, and Revin was becoming very uneasy with the situation. He shouldn't have listened to Verde; he sensed they were in a very vulnerable position.

But Sir John Lawrence had not risen through the ranks by accident. He had a keen brain and although he did not believe or fully comprehend what they were telling him, he could see they were educated men and that they were sincere. For these reasons he judged it best not to completely dismiss their ramblings.

"You have proof?" he asked.

Verde decided a half-truth would be most in their interests. "None that we can show you."

"In that case, gentlemen, the best you can do is to bring me something tangible. Why don't you visit Hodges? He seems to be very interested in this sort of thing."

"Hodges?" enquired Verde.

"Ah… yes… not from these parts. Still, Hodges is very successful; surprised you haven't heard of him. Doctor Nathaniel Hodges, down at Walbrook. Take your ideas to him."

"Oh yes, Doctor Hodges; why didn't we think of him before?"

"Don't push your luck," said Verde through gritted teeth.

The Mayor gave a dismissive wave and rang a small handbell. The servant reappeared and showed them to the door.

"Gentlemen," boomed the Mayor from above.

Verde cursed Revin's cheekiness. "He suspects something," he whispered.

They faced the Mayor.

"Beware of passing rats!"

They left him laughing at his own joke.

"What do you think?" asked Revin, once they were back on the street.

"I think we should be careful about what we say. Let's go and find this Doctor Hodges, but leave the talking to me."

CHAPTER TWENTY-SEVEN
THE POOR'S PLAGUE

As they sought shelter from the burning sun, there followed some discussion as to whether they should return to The Raven or make straight for the doctor recommended to them by the Mayor. Revin felt it better to return to the inn for refreshment and to plan their next move, whilst Verde favoured immediate action.

For the third time in two days they found themselves outside the Royal Exchange, having discovered from a further member of the watchman's army that it lay on their path to Walbrook. A brief sojourn along Cornhill and across Poultry Square, and Verde's wish was fulfilled. The houses were widespread and their general appearance was cleaner and far more impressive than the alleyways of Nathan and Tom. A plaque on a doorway announced that the good doctor indeed resided here.

"That's something," observed Verde.

"What?"

"At least the Mayor must have taken us seriously, not to send us on a wild goose chase."

"Let's reserve judgement on that," replied Revin, climbing the steps.

A knock brought a young girl to the door. Her dress and demeanour suggested that she belonged to the servant classes, and indeed Margaret Travers was the housekeeper to the good doctor.

"Is Doctor Hodges within?" enquired Revin.

"I'm afraid he is still out on his rounds," answered the young girl, her flaxen hair glistening in the early September sunshine.

"Have you any idea when he will return?"

The servant turned to face Verde, her eyes squinting in the bright light.

"He's usually home by one o'clock; he doesn't like to miss a meal. The doctor believes a healthy diet aids the fight against the plague."

The girl misinterpreted the exchange of glances between the two men.

"If you are ill, you may wait in his consulting room at the side of the house." Margaret pointed in the requisite direction, and as she spoke a nervous-looking youth made his way down the side of the house, heading for the very room.

"We are not ill," announced Verde firmly. "We are Doctors Revin and Verde and wish to consult the doctor on a medical matter."

Margaret eyed the helmets under their arms and reddened. She played with a ring on one of her hands, twisting it round and round.

"It's most important," urged Revin. "We must speak with Doctor Hodges."

The servant looked up and down the street, but found no answer there.

"Please may we come in and wait?" pleaded Verde.

Margaret had not been placed in such a position before, having only been in Hodges' service a few weeks. Her instructions had not covered the present situation, but the import of the visitors' garb was not lost on her and she meekly stood aside.

"Please could you wait in the library?" she said falteringly.

Verde and Revin were shown into a room that led from the main hallway. It was small but the space had been cleverly utilised. Three of the walls contained bookcases, and the fourth had a large window set into it that gave a panoramic view of the street. A large leather-topped desk was set beneath the window, accompanied by an elegant upholstered chair.

"Obviously a learned man," remarked Verde, as he looked through a beautiful calf-bound book with fine gold lettering.

"Yes, but how learned?" said Revin.

Verde reached for one of the many light-coloured volumes and began to thumb through it. He scanned the first few pages, snorted and replaced the book.

"Not my taste," he said in reply to Revin's questioning look. "Another example of this planet's fixation with the undead. Some character called Hamlet, looking for the ghost of his father."

"Who wrote it?"

Verde examined the spine of the book. "A William Shakespeare…"

A loud knocking on the front door disturbed their literary discussions. Verde went over to the window to espy the caller. It was a stout man in a long navy blue coat with matching breeches and a black cravat. The loud noise had been caused by his knocking a large gold-headed cane against the door.

Within the minute the caller was shaking their hands and welcoming them to his home, apologising for not having been there to greet them. Doctor

Nathaniel Hodges had a florid complexion and multiple chins. He looked as though the life of a medical man suited him; although he was only in his mid-thirties, his corpulent figure suggested a man of middle age. His hands were plump and red and still grasped his cane, which he now laid on the desk.

"To what do I owe this pleasure, gentlemen?" he boomed in a rich, resonant voice. "I ascertain from my somewhat flustered housekeeper that you are medical men, but your faces and names are unknown to me."

"We have come from Sir John Lawrence. We have news concerning the plague."

The large squat figure of the doctor stiffened at the mention of the word.

"Pray sit down and continue, ah…?"

"Call me Verde," he replied, "and this is my colleague Revin."

"Obliged, I'm sure," said their host with a smile.

Verde faced the stolid figure of the medic, wondering where best to begin and how much should he try to explain.

"We have a theory concerning the plague," he said calmly.

A larger smile creased the doctor's mouth, but his mellowed gaze implied interest.

"The city is full of idle quacks, alchemists, fortune tellers and charm sellers, all with similar claims, all false of course. Tell me, what makes yours any different?"

Verde stood up and took an anxious step forward. "We are not in the business of making money. Our aim is to rid this planet of the plague."

"Noble sentiments and interestingly humanitarian ideals. It is a wide and difficult task you set yourself."

Verde realised that he may have overstepped the mark in his efforts to kindle Hodges' enthusiasm, but his ebullient manner appeared to succeed. Hodges rang a small handbell, and a further servant arrived to take an order for tea.

"Please continue," Hodges urged as the servant departed.

Verde stood with his hands linked in front of him. "We, that is my colleague and I, believe that the plague is caused by the black rat carrying deadly fleas."

Hodges sat unmoved, his chin resting on the back of one hand. He sat so long that Verde was uncertain if he had heard his explanation. The maid returned with the tea, and as Hodges poured he spoke.

"You shared this theory with the Mayor?"

"Yes," said Verde.

"And he sent you to me?"

"Yes."

"Did he say anything else?"

Verde hesitated. "He laughed, he was very dismissive."

Hodges snorted a laugh. "Yes, I can imagine he was. Gentlemen, this is one cause that I have not heard propounded and I must say sounds extremely unlikely, but you must tell me more over dinner. I am fascinated to hear your ideas and how you came by them. Will you join me?"

Explaining the source of their ideas would need careful handling, thought Verde, but if their cause was to advance at all, accepting the offer seemed a logical and necessary step to take.

"We would be delighted," replied Verde, smiling at Revin, who was still working his way through to a similar conclusion.

"Yes, thank you, Doctor Hodges, dinner would be most welcome," seconded Revin.

"Finish your tea; I find it a most refreshing drink for this weather."

The maid appeared, summoned by the bell.

"Sarah, please inform Margaret that there will be two extra for dinner," the doctor instructed her. Sarah curtsied, then collected the empty cups and pot, before scurrying away to make the necessary arrangements. Hodges walked over to his desk and reached for a crystal decanter.

"This, on the other hand," he said, pouring out three glasses, "is one of my preventatives against infection: a glass of sack before each meal."

Verde and Revin accepted their glasses in turn and watched as Hodges raised his own glass to his lips, savouring the drink. Verde took a large swig and immediately began coughing and choking.

"It's good, very good," he assured the doctor and Revin, "but rather hot."

"My own additions," boasted the doctor. "I always spice my sack with a few ingredients of my own choosing. This one contains several herbs, but you may have noticed that the dominant flavouring is walnut."

Revin raised his glass to eye level and inspected it against the light; finding nothing untoward, he sniffed its contents and then sipped carefully. He raised his eyebrows and toasted the doctor before draining his glass. Verde followed suit, but this time in a less cavalier manner.

"Another glass, Revin?"

"Very much so."

"Verde?"

"No, thank you; one's quite enough for me."

Just after one o'clock the three men were seated at a grand oval dining table. Rich tapestries adorned the oak-panelled walls, but the room was far smaller and much less ostentatious than the one they had visited earlier that day. It was by far the most sumptuous and enjoyable meal that they had experienced since they had left Mykas. Hodges was a generous and jocular host, and the drink and conversation flowed. Verde was careful to stick to general discussion, and the doctor was happy to dominate the meal with his lively and amusing medical anecdotes. The medic's table largely comprised a variety of meats. Neither Revin nor Verde had ever experienced the likes of roast fillet of beef cooked in a fresh green peppercorn sauce, or a roasted suckling pig with its accompanying sauce of redcurrants.

Revin noted how most of the doctor's courses seemed to consist mainly of meat, with few or no fresh vegetables, although he seemed to have a penchant for pickles and sharp relishes, mostly of the fruit variety. By the time Revin had eaten two larded woodcocks, he was beginning to feel uncomfortable, and regretting his lack of self-control, especially as he had matched the doctor in washing down the food with large quantities of sack and wine. It was one of the longest meals that they had ever partaken in, and Verde feared it was never going to end.

Finally, Hodges called for some apple and orange tart, and a fine red wine. Verde swallowed his final bite, swished the last of his drink around his mouth, swallowed and belched vociferously.

"Now, gentleman, a flea," said Hodges, rubbing his hands and gazing at them through a warm glow.

Verde having imbibed to a much lesser extent than Revin, and having long anticipated this moment, cautiously approached the subject.

"We believe that we can greatly improve the lot of the poor, who seem the most affected by the plague."

The doctor leant back on his chair, and folded his arms as though in consultation with a patient who was outlining his symptoms.

"It is barbaric to lock the healthy in with the sick," said Verde. "It is little short of a death sentence. Surely it would be far better to clear a wide area, such as a remote village, and use it as a refugee camp, where people who develop the plague could be taken. Resources could be centralised and concentrated on such a site."

Hodges nodded in agreement. "I have indeed argued as much myself, but I am a lone voice, powerless to do anything. The authorities say that the healthy family members will still develop the plague, and to allow them to roam free would increase the spread. This is not news to me, gentlemen. But tell me about our little black rat and its fleas; it amuses me greatly. Please expand."

Verde was unsure if the doctor was merely amused and coveting another anecdote to add to his repertoire, or if there was a genuine interest in what they had to say. But he felt suitably encouraged to continue. He could feed the information piecemeal, and stop at any time.

"You cannot have failed to notice how this plague afflicts the poor."

"True, very true, but it is not solely their burden; many a wealthy man has been stricken."

"All right, but you agree the plague has hit hardest in the poorer parishes?"

"I can concur with that statement, but others would argue that the poor are more plentiful, and most of the wealthy folk have left town to avoid the affliction. Therefore it's only the poor that are left to succumb."

"But would you agree that the plague is more likely to first appear in the poorer quarters? Spreading throughout the city from those parts, I agree it then pays no attention to a man's position."

"I haven't exactly thought of it in those terms, but there is logic in what you say."

"Right. Given that the plague emanates from the poorer quarters, look to isolate the factors that distinguish the poor."

"You mean their lack of money for food and medicine, their filthy living conditions?"

"I mean exactly their atrocious living conditions; inside and outside the houses there is absolute squalor and filth. These conditions attract the rat population, and it is these very rats that carry the plague in the form of a tiny flea. Once bitten by the flea a person develops the plague!"

Hodges looked up over his spectacles. "You are asking me to believe that a bug that can barely be seen by the naked eye is causing this destruction?" He shook his head and poured himself another glass of sack. "The loss of hundreds of lives daily, you would have me believe, is due to a rodent, or the flea that lives upon it. No, gentlemen, this I find hard to digest; after all, the black rat is always amongst us, so why does the plague come and go? I agree the abominable living conditions that the poor endure could well be a factor, but this plague is of the poors' making. It is them it hits above all others. Where's your proof that a thing so tiny could cause so much destruction?"

Verde felt the frustration of the situation. How could he confront Hodges with the full medical facts, and the part played by ships' rats? If he explained to the good doctor the answers he so longed to give, they would not be believed and the possible consequences could be dire, even jeopardising their return to Mykas.

"Perhaps we could accompany you on one of your rounds," suggested Verde. "It may be to our mutual benefit."

Hodges slapped his thick thighs. He had not risen to the top of his profession without a little open-mindedness; after all, advancement in medicine was all about questioning. "Yes, that I would be happy to do." He rose and looked at his pocket watch. "The time is coming up to three o'clock. I am a punctilious man, gentlemen, and I have patients awaiting my arrival in my consulting rooms."

He slipped a green, coffin-shaped lozenge into his mouth. As he walked to the doorway he stopped to address them.

"Perhaps you would care to join me, sirs, see a little of my methods. Though I'm afraid I cannot promise you any fleas." He winked, and chortling inoffensively he led the way out. Then, turning in the doorway, his face took on a graver countenance. "Pray, mention nothing of your ideas. These are simple folk; many have spent their last penny on a cure or preventative. Do not alarm them with talk of fleas and rats."

"Of course we will respect your wishes, doctor," promised Verde.

Nathaniel Hodges' consulting room was full of thirty or more patients. They sat on wooden benches around the perimeter of the room. In the wall opposite to the side that Revin and Verde entered was the outside door by which the sufferers showed themselves in. The hubbub of noise fell as Hodges entered the room and then, as if a switch had been turned on, it rose again to a crescendo. Overtures from all sides were directed at the doctor. Hodges remained calm and unflustered, motioned with his arms for quiet, and the noise rescinded.

"All will be seen," he announced with stern authority, and he signalled to an elderly woman to follow him through an alcove that had been curtained off.

Verde and Revin did not follow the doctor; they looked around the room. Fresh air burst through the four large windows that straddled the exit. The breeze was strong enough to billow the cubicle's curtain, yet even with all the windows open the stench of sweat and urine was overpowering. A sea of helpless faces, united in their impotence and belief, stared at the two strangers. Young and old mingled alike, their features wizened and grime-ridden. Had it not been for the manner of dress, their sex would have proved indistinguishable. Plague was a great leveller, and personal pride and hygiene were as far away to these people as the planet Mykas.

Hodges reappeared from behind the curtain; he signalled a second patient and beckoned Verde and Revin to join him. Verde pulled the orange dividing curtain aside; it was the sole ray of brightness in the sombre room, shining as a beacon of hope to the forlorn patients. Behind the drape were two wooden chairs, one each for doctor and patient, although the former spent most of the time on his feet. Against one wall stood an examining couch covered in an olive-green cloth, and next to it a table with a collection of jars containing medicines, ointment and pills, as well as an assortment of medical equipment, including a variety of saws and knives.

"Most of these people come to me through reasons of misguided fear or in search of a preventative," explained Hodges, refraining from looking up from his examination of a young woman. "Those already afflicted are too ill to come, or, as you've mentioned, are more likely to be locked in." The young woman unfastened her clothing and Hodges examined her sweaty armpit; he prodded and probed amongst the hairs. "Nothing here. Any pain in the groin?"

"No, doctor," replied the girl, "but I've bin sneezin'."

Hodges examined her throat, and reached into a drawer in his table. He gave the girl a small blue bottle.

"Take a small dose in water, every morning," he instructed her.

"I've got the plague, an' I?" screamed the agitated girl.

Hodges placed a hand on one of the girl's shoulders. "No, Mary, you do not have the plague?"

"Then what's in that?" she asked, staring at the little blue bottle.

Hodges smiled. "Don't worry, I take it myself. It's an anti-pestilential electuary."

Verde whispered to Revin, "Do you think he's another quack, out to make his fortune?"

Mary put the bottle back on the table, and his question was answered.

"It's all right, child, you haven't got the plague, and you can take the medicine with my compliments."

Mary seized the bottle and, holding her open blouse together, scuttled from the room.

"How do you afford to give your cures away?" asked Revin.

The doctor looked puzzled. "The same as all true physicians," he answered: "treating the poor for free, but charging those that can afford it high enough prices to compensate. But surely that is what you do with your own rich patients?"

Hodges' look showed more surprise than suspicion, and they were relieved when the next patient, uninvited, pulled back the curtain.

Over the next three hours a succession of patients came and went. Hodges treated all with the same benevolent approach in manner and gift. Most, in their ignorance, were simply frightened and sought only comfort and reassurance in their time of need. At the end of the surgery not one patient's fears had been confirmed. Hodges picked up his coat, which had been dangling from a hook during the latter hours of the consultation.

"Well, gentlemen, I hope you weren't too disappointed. Prevention is better than cure, I say."

"We'd agree with you on that point, doctor," concurred Revin.

"I think we'd agree to differ over the cause," he said rather curtly. "If you are really interested in this pestilence, join me on my evening rounds. Then you will experience some genuine sad cases. See if you still think your little friends could wreak so much havoc as I am able to show you."

Verde thought the offer over; it sounded genuine, but at the back of his mind he harboured a fear that Hodges was suspicious of them. Did the doctor smell a rat, and wish to detain them? Verde smiled at the image. If they were to have any chance of success, they would first need to convince intelligent men like Hodges.

"What time do you leave?"

"Oh, my dear fellows, not yet, not for another two hours; we must first have food and drink to fortify us."

If Revin was a little peeved at not being consulted on their accepting Hodges' original offer, it didn't show the second time.

For the second time within six hours, Verde and Revin found themselves as honoured guests around the doctor's dining table. When he saw the extent of crockery, cutlery and sweetmeats that already adorned the table, Verde wondered how many guests were coming to dine.

"I apologise for the pitiful selection of food, gentlemen, but most of the countryside has stopped sending foodstuffs to the city. Fortunately I have a reliable source out Enfield way; otherwise I might even have to consider joining the exodus."

Revin was not sure whether to believe him on either count as he tasted a mouthful of stewed broth of mutton.

The doctor took his food very seriously and initiated little conversation.

His taciturn manner also meant that he could keep to his busy time schedule. When he did speak it was usually on some aspect of the meal in front of them.

"I find this cheese tart is much improved by the addition of a little rosewater," he said through a mouthful of food.

"It's most agreeable, sir," answered Revin.

Verde was already beginning to fall behind when the doctor called for the next course.

"Hope you don't mind, but time is of the essence," he said as a sausage of mutton in an anchovy sauce was placed before them.

Verde had barely started when the fish dish arrived. The fillets had been rolled in breadcrumbs and secured with a wooden toothpick. Hodges served himself, and passed the dish to Revin; he then removed the toothpick and set about dislodging a piece of meat from between his teeth. By now several tankards of ale had accompanied a large quantity of wine, and Verde was more than relieved when the doctor accepted his offer of the remaining fish.

"That was most acceptable," said Revin, as Hodges belched loudly on the completion of the course.

"I'm glad you think so," said Hodges. "Time for the main course of the day."

On cue a huge dish was placed on the table.

"Verde, Revin. May I introduce you to my favourite dish, Barthelmas beef? I'm sure you will appreciate its succulence, cooked as it is in a sweet white wine with a mixture of herbs. I would be interested to hear your opinion on the nutmeg, ginger and cinnamon. I personally find them a delightful combination of companions."

Huge helpings were doled onto three plates. Revin was pleased to see the late addition of some root vegetables, but this was offset by the prospect of some filling dumplings.

"Mustard, gentlemen?" And that was Hodges' final word for the next twenty minutes or more.

Verde now felt extremely uncomfortable. He did not wish to give offence to his host by refusing the food, but it was all rather different to what he would have chosen back on Mykas. Just when he thought he had completed the ordeal, a final pudding was placed before him. He sipped at the thick frothy cherry syllabub; once again he could taste one of the strong spices from earlier dishes.

"Nutmeg?" he asked in a vain attempt to seem enthusiastic.

"Surely it's ginger."

Verde looked at Revin; he seemed ready to eat it all again, almost matching the hearty appetite of Hodges. How they would ever undertake the promised evening rounds was a source of concern to Verde.

Eventually, Hodges pushed his platter away and wiped his lips on a red-and-white chequered napkin. He stood up and patted his stomach and walked to the hallway, indicating to his guests to follow him. The doctor put on his large overcoat, picked up his gold-headed cane and brown leather medical bag, and set foot out of his house.

They turned into Watling Street and headed for the Cathedral of Saint Paul. The church clock ahead of them struck eight times. As they walked along the street Verde and Revin noticed bundles scattered outside some of the houses. As he approached one, Revin stopped to inspect it. The piles contained wood and faggots, and beside each pile of timber was a barrel. Revin placed a hand inside one and found to his cost that they were filled with tar. Further along the street a watchman was filling a barrel with tinder and using a strike-a-light to set fire to the contents. Hodges read the bemused look on Revin's face.

"Haven't you heard?" he asked. "Fires are to be lit in the streets to purify the air! Stuff and nonsense if you ask me, but no more ridiculous than soldiers in Hyde Park firing their muskets skywards to stop the bad air! Now light them indoors, by all means; that's where you'll find the infection. But there again, I'm only a humble physician; who wants my opinion?" he added sarcastically.

Almost a case of the blind leading the blind, thought Revin, but not quite. He was beginning to warm to this doctor; his intentions were honourable even if his methods were not quite what Revin would have hoped for.

Revin counted the fires as they proceeded down the street; there was one outside every sixth door. By the time they had reached the entrance to Friday Street the area was alive with flames licking the warm night air. Faggots crackled and plumes of choking black smoke leapt skywards, forsaking the plague-ridden city and escaping into the night sky.

They walked halfway along the street before stopping outside a small house on their left-hand side. A watchman unlocked the padlock when the doctor loudly rapped the door three times with the knob of his cane. Hodges reached into his pocket and pulled out a battered tin; he extracted a lozenge and placed it in his mouth.

"Go on, it will fight the infection," he urged Verde and Revin, and noticing their reticence added good-humouredly, "It will keep your rats at bay."

Verde haltingly accepted the offer; it had been made in good faith and he saw no harm in indulging Hodges. Revin refused, and the tin was tucked safely away.

A pallid youth, in his early teens, opened the door. His long tangled mass of brown hair stood in stark contrast to his lacklustre face; dark rings around his eyes accentuated his ashen complexion.

"Are the coals alight, Matthew?" demanded Hodges.

"As you ordered, doctor."

"Another sound piece of advice I would offer you gentlemen. Never enter infected premises without the safety of a good fire."

Having thus been reassured they followed Hodges into the house. Inside the air was even staler and smokier than that which they had just left. An old woman stood over the hearth fire, ladling disinfectant from a bucket onto the glowing coals. They sizzled as each fresh ladle-load landed on the fire, filling the room with a sickly sweet smell. Verde loosened the clothing around his neck.

"How is he?" asked Hodges.

"Worse," replied the ladler.

Hodges addressed his companions, lifting his eyes towards the ceiling. "Isaac Tolnath is a remarkable case. To my knowledge this is his sixth visitation. He has made a full recovery from the previous five."

"He's badder this time," croaked the woman, and she emphasised her opinion by throwing an extra-large measure of disinfectant onto the fire. The flames shrank in submission and then leapt back, spitting defiantly. "He's had the blains for two or three days, but he's been screaming with pain and says he's on fire. This afternoon his eyes were like saucers and we could barely hold him down on the bed, but he's sapped out now and sleeping."

"Well, Sukie, let's see for ourselves, shall we?"

Hodges led the way up the stairs, followed by the other two visitors. Matthew and Sukie remained below.

CHAPTER TWENTY-EIGHT

DEATH BY MOONLIGHT

The bedchamber was dark, the atmosphere even more repugnant as the purifying air of a stink pot added to the blanket of smoke. Hodges drew back the curtain to allow for some light; the bedridden man stirred and screamed.

"Just for a minute," soothed Hodges. "Close your eyes, Isaac."

Revin wiped his foot on the floor; it was covered in refuse, dirt and dust. He could feel his body sweating up in a panic attack; the effect of the wine and sack compounded by the smoke and the unpleasant conditions.

"Are you all right?" asked Verde.

"I'll be fine in a minute."

"Would you like me to ask Hodges for one of his lozenges?"

Revin laughed at the jibe and his breathing became easier.

Hodges pulled open Isaac's night-shirt. Even in the half-light they could plainly see small red and purple spots on his stomach. The physician felt under the man's armpits.

"It's bad this time," he said, showing no consideration towards his patient. "These buboes must be made to break."

From his bag he pulled a long shiny instrument. Hodges tested the sharpness of his scalpel on the hairs on the back of his hand and called to Sukie to fetch some hot water. Within a few minutes the old woman's laboured gait could be heard on the stairs. Hodges delved into his bag again, fetching forth a collection of jars containing herbs, medicines and flour. Within a few minutes a hot poultice had been prepared.

"Lift him into the chair and take an arm each," instructed Hodges. Revin and Verde lifted the old man into a chair at the side of the bed, and Hodges applied his poultice to the buboes. Isaac screamed and writhed in pain.

"Hold him," demanded Hodges.

Revin was amazed at the strength of the sick man. He tightened his grip on the arm, whilst Hodges removed the poultice and cut into the bubo. A putrid-smelling yellow substance oozed from the cut, mingling with the red blood. Hodges waited for the bubo to drain, then applied a plaister and tied pieces of linen around the arm and shoulder. He repeated the process for the other arm, and still Isaac had the power to lash out. He cursed and swore oaths, but Hodges remained calm throughout and never wavered from his intentions.

As he finished the second dressing Hodges broke his silence, which had virtually lasted throughout the treatment.

"That's the way to cure the plague, gentlemen. Would you know that some scandalous quacks actually lance the buboes with the tail of a live chicken, then cut a live pigeon in half and apply it to the sores? Can you imagine such barbarism?"

Verde and Revin remained speechless, still coming to terms with the practice they had just witnessed. Hodges interpreted their silence as a sign of approval.

"And you mean to tell me, gentlemen, that you believe this hideous distemper is caused by a flea!"

At that moment Hodges felt something run across his foot; he looked down to catch a glimpse of a black rat scurrying into a hole in the rough-plastered wall. Verde smiled at the doctor.

They took their leave of the Tolnaths with Hodges promising to return the following evening. Revin sighed on feeling the cooler air as it engulfed his body. After turning left into Cheapside and left again into Old Change they walked across Carter Lane and down Lambeth Hill, turning right into Knightrider Street. As they strolled through the dust-baked street several watchmen were still attending the purifying fires, their orange flames still dancing skywards in a vain attempt to accomplish their purpose. Hodges pointed towards their next appointment. As they approached, the watchman fumbled with the lock.

"There's a terrible commotion a-goin' on," spluttered the watchman.

"Open the door," ordered the doctor.

All four of them burst into the house. The entrance led directly into a dimly lit room, a tallow hanging on the wall being the only source of light. At first the room appeared empty. They moved stealthily forward. Two figures appeared to be asleep on the floor; as Verde approached them he felt something slippery under his foot. He knelt down and put his fingers to the ground; in the half-light he could not make out what he was standing in. Revin brushed by him, and stooped down beside the forms of two small children. He tried to shake the closest one awake; as he did so the child rolled from its side to its back, displaying a huge red wound in its chest.

Verde examined the second child; like his brother, he too had been stabbed in the heart. Verde felt the pit of his stomach welling up.

"How, who?" stuttered Revin, standing up.

"Nance," cried Hodges. "Nancy, where are you?" he called into the darkness.

They searched around the room; the only sounds Revin could hear were his own heavy breathing and heartbeat.

"Nancy," cried Hodges, "I know you are in pain. I can help."

Still there was silence. A rat scurried across the room, startling all four of the men.

"What's going on?" hissed Verde.

"The pain can drive men and women to desperate things… even attacking their loved ones."

"Their parent killed these children?" asked Revin incredulously.

Before Hodges could answer a blood-curdling scream came from the doorway that led to the kitchen. Verde just caught the glint of a flashing blade as he put out an arm for protection. His wrist felt hot as he fell to his knees clutching the searing pain. The naked figure of Nance Carnes rushed past them and raced up the stairs. Revin and the watchman raced after her as she disappeared through a door at the top of the stairs.

Revin paused at the doorway, fearful of an attack in the dark.

"Nance," he cried, "Nance, we can help you."

"You can't take away my pain," she screamed.

"We can help." Revin slowly entered the room, shuffling sideways and keeping to the contour of the walls. Nance stood in the middle of the room; her naked body, glistening with sweat, was surrounded by an aura of moonlight. She pointed the knife between her breasts.

"Stay back!" she screeched.

"Let me help you," he said in a soothing voice, though inwardly he felt anything but calm. Nance let forth an agonised screaming wail. Revin felt the hairs stand on the back of his neck; falteringly he took a pace forward into the dark depths of the room.

"Let me take away your pain; give me the knife."

Nance raised the knife above her head; all reason had deserted her wild eyes. Her left breast and right arm were covered in blood, but Revin was unable to judge if the gore came from self-inflicted wounds or from her children. The sight of such carnage caused him to waver and he stood facing the demented woman.

"Please let me help you."

"You can't take away my pain," she howled.

"I can, I can."

"No, no, no," she screamed and whirled her head in a wild circular movement, her long black hair tumbling wildly around.

Revin took a measured step forward, and Nance stopped. Her eyes were now blazing and wide.

"Let me take away your pain; give me the knife," he begged, holding out a hand.

"Don't come any closer," cried the woman, and she twirled the knife around menacingly.

Revin remained rooted to the spot, deciding against any sudden movement. He reasoned that the darkness favoured neither of them; he couldn't risk a sudden rush at the woman even though he would be a blurred target. Words were still his strongest weapon.

"I can heal your body, Nance."

"But not my pain," she screamed. "The pain is in my head – I've murdered my children!" Nance began to sob, and the killing hand fell to her side and the knife dropped to the floor. On hearing the thud Revin inched towards her, still wary of any sudden movement.

Revin was no more than a few feet from her when Nance raised her head and shot him a withering look. Revin felt an enduring pain shoot through his body; the untold suffering and grief in her eyes momentarily mellowed his feelings towards her. He reached out a comforting hand and placed it on her arm. Nance brushed it away, and ran towards the far window. Revin could only watch, helpless to intervene as the tormented woman leapt headlong through the glass.

At the splintering and shattering the watchman rushed in from the landing. Revin stood dumbfounded.

"You all right?"

"I think so."

The two men rushed over to the window and peered out onto the road below, at the motionless figure. Nance's raven hair framed her once-beautiful face and her dark eyes stared up at the moonlight that she would never again see.

Hodges and Verde raced out through the door and into the street. Hodges bent over the body whilst Verde waved with relief at the window, his makeshift bandage catching in the moonlight. A group of neighbours had gathered around the scene. Hodges despatched a bystander to fetch the parish constable.

"I think that's enough excitement for one evening, gentlemen."

"Yes," agreed Revin. "We must return to our lodgings; we are expecting friends."

"Where are you staying?"

"Near the Tower, at an inn called The Raven."

"The Tower? That's a fair walk. Come spend the evening with me; your friends can surely wait. Besides," he added, "I need to take a proper look at that wrist."

"It's nothing; we can take care of it," answered Verde.

"That may be, but I've my reputation to think of. I dressed the injury; that makes you my patient, whatever your skill."

As they sauntered along Old Fish Street, Revin took the opportunity to whisper to Verde. "How's your wrist?"

"Fine."

"Best let him look at it."

"But we're more than qualified to deal with this."

"Still, don't want him to suspect anything."

"He knows we are medical men."

"Humour me," murmured Revin.

"It's not your wrist. You've seen their archaic measures."

"He's not likely to saw it off," laughed Revin. "We might arouse suspicion if we hurry back to The Raven. He's right; if Lutel and Rewn have arrived they will wait another day or two for us."

Verde was about to protest, but his wrist really was sore and the sooner it received attention the happier he would be. The longer he argued with Revin the greater the delay. As they reached Dowgate, Hodges was informed that they would accept his kind invitation.

CHAPTER TWENTY-NINE

RAIN

Verde was woken by the drumming of raindrops on glass. He lay on his back, opened his eyes and examined the white plastered ceiling. It was not instantly recognisable. Perhaps he was at The Raven; he twisted his head to the side and the pale blue walls belied that possibility. He couldn't be bothered to think any more as the dull ache from his wrist occupied his attention. A red spot, like a bloodshot eye, stared at him from the yellowing bandage. Events of the previous evening came flooding back to him; he turned to speak to Revin, but his friend was snoring gently beside him. Verde refrained from waking him; instead he crawled out of bed and pulled back the curtain.

Outside, the street had changed in appearance; the dusty brown track was now a glistening rich tan. Puddles had formed in potholes and long stretches of water sparkled in the ruts left by the carts. The rain had doused the fires from the previous evening. Verde looked along the street and could see several smouldering piles of wood, emitting their last few belches of smoke before finally succumbing. He opened a window. It was rather stiff and made a grating sound as he forced it open with a jolt. Verde peeked around to see if the noise had disturbed Revin, but a look of cosy contentment remained on the sleeper's face. The cooling breeze played upon Verde's cheeks, and he leant out and took a deep breath.

It was early September and this was the first rain that he had experienced since their landing. The showers had purified far more than any watchman's bonfires could ever hope to achieve. His lungs filled with air; it was fresher and far pleasanter than the humid, stale atmosphere that had so far typified their stay. Scents of summer flowers – sweet roses and honeysuckle – filled the bedroom as the change in ambience succeeded where the jarring of the window had failed. Revin stirred and screwed up his eyes at the bright daylight. Verde withdrew his head; his hair was wet and rainwater trickled down his cheeks.

"We are at Nathaniel Hodges'. We are going to accompany him on his morning round."

"You remembered all that with a sore arm. By the way, how is it?"

"You took yourself off to bed whilst my wrist was being seen to; thanks all the same… It's a little sore but I'm sure it will be fine. The wound was superficial, but still painful."

As Revin threw back the grey blanket, a firm knock came on the door.

"I'll get it," offered Verde.

"Master would like to know if you would care to join him for breakfast?" enquired Sarah. She lifted a large jug of water that she had placed at her feet and handed it over to Verde, along with some towels that were draped over her arm.

"Thank you, Sarah. Please inform your master that we will be down shortly," answered Verde.

The girl curtsied and scurried away to continue her duties. Revin playfully snatched the jug from Verde.

"Hey, she gave it to me."

"You are already wet," laughed Revin, who proceeded to splash his face with the warm water.

Verde had just started his ablutions when they were interrupted by a further knock at the door. Revin's face was still buried in a towel, so Verde opened the door for a second time to Sarah.

"Master asked if these would be of any use."

"Thank you, indeed they will," said Verde. He closed the door on the maid and threw a ball of soap at Revin. "Will you give me a shave?" he pleaded, holding out a cut-throat razor.

The two clean-shaven travellers descended the stairs. Hodges was already seated at his breakfast table.

"Good morning gentlemen; come and join me," he offered as they stood in the doorway. In front of their host lay a plate of hot rolls and as the two men sat down, Sarah entered with some steaming coffee.

"I believe in a light breakfast," announced Hodges, almost apologetically. "It's work that sharpens and develops the appetite."

Verde and Revin still ate heartily and more rolls were called for; the warm butter dribbled down Revin's jaw. As they ate, Hodges produced a piece of crumpled paper. Unfolding it, he pushed it towards Verde.

"Now, do you still say your rat flea can cause that much harm?"

Verde flattened the paper out and placed it between himself and Revin. It was a Bill of Mortality. The two men scanned the piece of paper.

The Diseases and Casualties this Week

Abortive	*4*	*Livergrown*	*1*
Aged	*45*	*Meagrome*	*1*
Bleeding	*1*	*Palsie*	*1*
Broken legge	*1*	*Plague*	*4237*
Broke her scull by a fall	*1*	*Purples*	*2*
Childbed	*28*	*Quinsie*	*5*
Chrisomes	*9*	*Rickets*	*23*
Consumption	*126*	*Riling of the Lights*	*18*
Convusion	*89*	*Rupture*	*1*
Cough	*1*	*Scurvy*	*3*
Drophie	*53*	*Shingles*	*1*
Feaver	*348*	*Spotted Feaver*	*166*
Flox and Small-pox	*11*	*Stilborn*	*4*
Flux	*1*	*Stone*	*2*
Frighted	*2*	*Stopping of the stomach*	*17*
Gowt	*1*	*Strangury*	*3*
Grief	*3*	*Suddenly*	*2*
Griping in the Guts	*79*	*Surfeit*	*74*
Head-mould-foot	*1*	*Teeth*	*111*
Jaundices	*7*	*Thrush*	*6*
Imposthume	*8*	*Vomiting*	*10*
Infants	*22*	*Winde*	*4*
Kingsevil	*4*	*Wormes*	*20*
Lethargy	*1*		

Christened: Males 90, Females 81, In all 171
Buried: Males 2777, Females 2791, In all 5568 (Plague 4237)
Increases in the Burials this Week: 249
Parishes clear of the Plague: 27
Parishes Infected: 103

The Assize of Bread set forth by Order of the Lord Mayor and Court of Aldermen,

A penny Wheaton Loaf to contain Nine Ounces and a half, and three half-penny White loaves the like weight.

Verde and Revin scrutinised the list, growing more and more incredulous at the recorded statements of death. Hodges misinterpreted their bewilderment as a justification for his argument.

"Who records these deaths?" asked Verde.

"They are produced by the parish clerks, but their information comes from a variety of sources."

"Such as?"

"Oh, the physicians, family members, the searchers, nursekeepers…"

Verde's countenance changed slightly, but Hodges missed the knowing look. He was far too engrossed in winning his argument to notice or understand any nuance in facial expression.

"Turn over, turn over," he urged them.

Revin turned the paper over and noted the date: from the 15th of August to the 22nd, 1665, not long before they had arrived on the planet. It listed the recorded deaths for each individual parish. A lump came to Verde's throat as he noticed the greatest number of plague deaths were in the parish of St Giles Cripplegate, and his mind was drawn back to Rebecca and Tom. He wondered how long it would be before they were mere numbers on a page.

"Now you would still have me believe that over four thousand people have died in one week because of a rat? And these are old figures; the latest Bill shows over six thousand are dying weekly, and no doubt this week's total will be more, judging by the scenes in the streets.

Verde felt the frustration at being unable to present Hodges with the full facts and contented himself with a discretionary reply. "I agree such numbers are staggering and of the greatest concern."

"Indeed, indeed. I wholeheartedly concur," agreed Hodges with an air of triumph in his voice. "And these are not the true figures."

"No?" queried Revin.

"I should say not, sir. The parish clerks and the searchers are both open to bribery: the former for reasons of propriety and the latter through causes of want and ignorance."

Breakfast was washed down with even more glasses of the doctor's favourite sack, and by nine o'clock they were threading their way through the muddy puddles in the direction of Lombard Street. Hodges explained that his morning rounds encompassed patients to the north and east of his abode, whilst patients at the two other compass points received his attention in the evening. They stopped outside a plague-ridden house in Gracious Street; although by no means grand, the house was elegant with beautiful wood carvings adorning its front. Above the door was carved a wooden anchor, suggesting its owner had made his fortune from the sea. Below the anchor, painted on the stout oak door was a bright red cross.

"A sad case: a well-to-do family by the name of Silke. The husband made his fortune from the wool trade. Yet he stubbornly refused to leave the city, more worried about his chattels than his life. He's paid for his avarice. It's his family I feel sorry for."

A watchman lay dozing in the doorway. Hodges gave him a hefty kick. The sleeper awoke, and from his speech it was apparent that he had been in more of a stupor than a slumber.

"Whaat dy'wan?" he slurred.

"To enter," boomed Hodges crisply.

The bedraggled watchman staggered to his feet and fumbled with the padlock. The iron key clanked on the cobblestones. Revin stooped and picked the key up from between his feet and opened the door. Hodges shoved the drunken guard from behind and the man stumbled forward, landing on his hands and knees in the kennel.

Inside, the house was dark and gloomy, the walls were clammy to the touch and a dismal atmosphere pervaded. An old hag warily approached them.

"Put this on the fire," barked Hodges.

The old nursekeeper took the parcel of disinfectant and followed the doctor's instructions. Hodges sucked on one of his lozenges as the acrid smoke began to fill the room.

"This will aid us, gentlemen."

"What's in it?" queried Verde.

"The usual: a mixture of saltpetre, amber and brimstone; a trusted purifier."

"More likely to drive all the rats away," jibed Verde.

Hodges stiffened his posture, ascended the stairs, and entered a large bedroom. A small chink in the curtains allowed Verde to examine the room. It was tastefully furnished with wall hangings and several chairs and dressers. His eye followed a series of small paintings around the walls, before alighting on the opulent bed where a man lay in a reclining position.

Several blankets were drawn up around the man; his face was gaunt and covered in sweat; his breathing came in short gasps. On his head a night cap added to his discomfort; small wisps of soaked greying hair protruded around its edges. On a small dresser at the side of the bed was a multitude of medicines purchased from quacks in a desperate and vain attempt to find a cure.

Hodges picked up one of the jars and disdainfully examined it. "What is it today, Jemima? Powdered unicorn horn, plague-water, Doctor Setchell's anti-distemper elixir?"

The attentive wife, sitting at her husband's bedside, lifted her head. Her eyes revealed that she had lost her faith, and all fight had left her. Evidence of her desperation – a final appeal to some higher order – adorned her neck: a pendant spelled out the magical incantation "abracadabra". Jemima was a frail woman, with short black hair and teeth that protruded sufficiently to give her a small speech impediment. Her face was emaciated, and her black pupils dwelt in even darker circles around the sockets of her eyes. Her figure was trim through worry rather than any specific attention to diet or looks.

"I don't know," she lisped, in answer to Hodges. "I give good money to Denchworth for medithnes, and he bringths me very little in return. I'm thure he'th spending it elthwhere."

Hodges mellowed slightly. "I've told you to keep Henry warm; his buboes have been lanced and the sores will soon rise. Then we must trust in the Lord to do his will."

The physician lifted the blanket and pulled off the man's plaisters, reaching into his bag for replacements. He then turned his attention to the doting wife. "You'll be no good to Henry if you don't sleep."

"I hath no care for mythelf," answered Jemima. "My plathe ith at my huthbanth's thide, but I fear for our thweet Jayne."

"Let me see her."

Hodges led the way to a smaller, less ornate bedroom. Inside a child of nine or ten years lay asleep in a small bed. The physician leaned over the girl and brushed her long, brown, ringleted hair from her face. She had the look of a cherub, and as they stood gazing down on her, she opened her misty green eyes.

"Hello, Doctor Hodges," she said meekly.

"Good morning, Jayne," replied Hodges. "How are you feeling today?"

"I feel hot and my throat's rather dry," croaked the girl.

Hodges twisted around and called to the nursekeeper for fresh water. The old crone arrived, carrying a goblet and jug, cursing at having to climb the stairs.

"This is all there is," she snapped, pounding the water down on a nearby dresser.

Hodges poured the contents of the jug into the goblet, held it up to the unshuttered window and sniffed it.

"It will do," he announced, and he cradled the small girl in his arms so that she could more easily slake her thirst. Verde noted the sharp contrast between the little waif and the powerful arms of the imposing doctor.

"Am I going to die?" asked the girl weakly.

For a moment Revin thought he caught the trace of a tear in the man's eye. If he had glanced at Verde he would have seen another; instead he looked skywards, cursing Lutel and Rewn for not being there with the antidote, cursing the fact that he and Verde had travelled in the smaller scout craft. Although the scout's seating capacity was twice that of the other ship there was still not enough room for the medical supplies, hence Lutel and Rewn's journey in the two-man but much larger cargo ship. Even if mass inoculation of the city should prove impossible because of their archaic beliefs and knowledge, he could surely make an exception for the odd individual, like the young girl that lay before him.

"You are not going to die!" Hodges reassured her firmly. "I will come and see you again tomorrow."

The child leant forward and kissed him on the forehead. Hodges squeezed her hand, and walked silently from the room. Revin followed the doctor out, but Verde noticed that Hodges had forgotten his medical bag. It was still open, and he furtively slipped his hand inside and removed several phials. He read the labels in turn and then replaced them in the bag as he finally alighted on the one he was searching for. Carefully he hid it in his clothing and made to leave the room, when he realised Jayne had been observing his actions. Verde placed a finger to his lips.

"Shh," he whispered. "It's our little secret. I will see you soon."

The girl fell back on her pillows and Verde left the room in a more contented state of mind.

Out on the street Hodges had noticed his loss. Revin had offered to return to fetch the bag and also hasten Verde's departure. When he was halfway up the stairs Verde emerged from the master bedroom.

"What are you doing?"

"Just fetching the bag."

"Come along, then; Hodges is becoming impatient."

Verde led the way out of the house, carrying the beaten leather case.

"Yours, I believe."

"Thank you," said the grateful but oblivious owner.

"What are the young girl's chances?"

"Not good; once plague strikes a house it's usually empty within a week or so."

Verde placed a restraining hand on Revin's sleeve.

"Doctor Hodges, you have been very kind, but we must return to our lodgings." Verde indicated their dishevelled appearance, to illustrate the necessity of their departure. "Please may we visit you again?"

"Any time, gentlemen; my door is always open to men of a scientific mind. But please don't bring any of those," said Hodges with a grin, pointing in the kennel at a scuttling rat. He laughed at his own joke and continued on his round. Verde was not sure how serious the parting comment had been.

"Why…?" began Revin.

"Not now," said Verde. "Let's seek out The Raven."

Part Six

Ups and Downs and Inns

CHAPTER THIRTY

A MATTER OF TRUST

Rewn led the way back to the Red Lion and ordered three rooms for the night. The landlord gave him a knowing look, but neither guest nor host laid forth their thoughts. A hearty meal of boiled mutton with lemons was placed before them. Woodman reached for a slice of dry bread from a side bowl, but before he could dip it into his stock, Rewn gripped the landlord's wrist and invited him to join them.

The landlord's hair dangled limply over his eyes; at all costs he avoided meeting their gaze. "Very kind of you, sir, but I've already eaten tonight."

"Nonsense, there's plenty here for four," said Rewn, emphasising the quantity of the broth by ladling it over with a spoon.

"I'd rather not, sir."

Rewn picked up a soldier of bread, and dipped it in the bowl. "I would welcome your comments on the salt content. Neither my friends nor I relish an over-salty dish; perhaps you would be as kind as to give us your opinion, and spare us the discomfort… should it prove so."

"I can assure you that nobody has ever found fault with Truster Selwayne's food," spouted the landlord, at last plucking up the courage to face Rewn. He wiped a strand of hair from his face, as if to declare he had nothing to hide.

"Then you can have no objection to my request," argued Rewn, proffering the dipped morsel. Selwayne snatched the food from Rewn's hand and stuffed it in his face, before storming away.

"Wait," called Rewn.

The man stood still, and slowly turned around. "What?"

"How is the salt content?"

"Judge for yourself," he snarled, and strode away.

"Yes, I think we shall," said Rewn, and he triumphantly placed the soggy crust in his mouth. "Much to my liking. But a little too much pepper for my taste," he mischievously added.

Lutel kicked Rewn under the table; he had become carried away and was savouring the moment in more ways than one. She wished to preserve their anonymity, and Rewn had proved his point and was now endangering their position. Rewn accepted the admonishment, and the three of them safely tucked into their meal and washed it down with generous quantities of warm ale.

A villager sidled up to them as they devoured their meal. His hair was grizzled and his face roughly hewn, like the stones of his village. Lutel eyed the man suspiciously and cursed Rewn's bravado.

"You bent stayin' the noight?" ventured the interloper, as he sidled between the two men.

"Bent we?" mimicked Rewn, scarcely looking up from his meal.

Lutel fumed at Rewn's short memory and prepared to make an exit.

"You bent scared, then?" continued the man.

"Of what?" asked Rewn, slightly more dignified.

"Ghosts!" replied the man, as though he expected them to already know the answer.

Lutel stared at the square-jawed interloper and relaxed a little, now that he had declared his hand.

"What ghosts?" piped up Woodman, who had ceased his chewing.

The old man settled himself more comfortably in the chair, and drawing himself forward sucked on an empty clay pipe.

"Any baccy?" he asked hopefully.

"No," said Woodman.

"Story's worth some baccy."

"Let's hear it first," growled Woodman.

The man paused and looked at his audience. He'd witnessed their strength of character and decided to risk his telling.

"The ghost of Lizzy Hancock walks this inn at night."

He looked round the table; their silence encouraged him.

"Doors do bang, objects move and eerie footsteps pace the halls!"

The teller leant back on his chair, tantalising his listeners.

"Go on," Woodman encouraged him.

"That's it," pronounced the old man.

"There must be more."

"Baccy?"

"At the end," promised Rewn.

This seemed to satisfy the man, and he resumed his position of confidentiality. "Lizzy's husband was landlord here twenty years or so ago – in the time of the great war that set England's brother against brother. At its end, he wended his way home expecting to find all ready; instead he found Lizzy in bed with her lover. Her admirer fled, and Lizzy was never seen again. A few years later, her husband couldn't live with the guilt, admitted he'd thrown Lizzy down the garden well. Quite a shock really; most had assumed she had followed her lover, but a few whispered otherwise. They hanged him on the gibbet over at Morgan's Hill."

He pointed at a window to his side, and the three followed his finger.

"Now they say that Lizzy do walk the inn."

The villager sat back in his chair and looked at his empty pipe.

"Have a smoke on us," said Lutel, and she placed a coin on the table. The man snatched it up and hurried off to seek out the landlord.

They finished their meal and went upstairs. The rooms on the upper floor were stark and bare. Both Rewn and Lutel spent a restless night, one physical and one mental; the former because of his uncomfortable bed, and the latter because of her concerns over how the fates seemed to be conspiring against them. Woodman, suffering no such unpleasantries, had to be woken for breakfast.

Cold meat washed down with ale was a regular occurrence for the early meal of the patrons of the Red Lion, and today was no exception. Woodman devoured his breakfast and leant back belching whilst his companions finished theirs. Rewn chewed his breakfast thoughtfully; an idea had formulated in his head and he was waiting for an opportunity to speak to Truster Selwayne in confidence. Near the end of his meal the moment arose and he seized the chance to confront their host.

"I know some people who would pay well to be informed of Duval's hiding place."

"I don't know what you mean," snapped the landlord fiercely.

Rewn knew his hunch had been right.

"Perhaps I'd better have this conversation elsewhere," he said, smiling.

"Yes, do that."

Selwayne turned his back and left him. Rewn was annoyed that his bluff had not paid off and called tersely to his companions to leave. The three walked outside, and Rewn stood staring up at the building.

"Leave it, Rewn. You're like a dog with a bone," said Lutel.

"You want your key back, don't you? I know Duval is around here somewhere, or at least he was."

Rewn moved around the back of the inn and gazed up at the windows, expecting to see a mocking face appear behind any one of the mullioned panes. He heard a voice call to him; he stared along the row of windows but could see no substance to the sound. Again the voice called and he realised it was coming from behind him in the direction of the stables. Woodman and Lutel, who had been watching his movements, joined him in the shadows as Rewn furtively pushed the door open. Lutel pushed past him and the others followed her inside.

Cobwebs clung to their faces in the darkness; Rewn felt around for his prop, but it was no longer there. The stable was deserted apart from a few remaining horses.

"I definitely heard a voice," muttered Rewn.

"You wanted to, you mean."

"No, Lutel, it was calling me, I swear."

"Well, there's nobody here now," observed Woodman. "P'raps 'twere the horses."

"Don't be stupid."

"Rewn, calm down, there's no need to be rude."

"Sorry," whispered Rewn, though the darkness hid his expression.

"Now there's no one here, so let's go."

Lutel was moving towards the door when a sudden creaking noise from the floor startled all three. From under the straw a trap door had been opened.

"Follow me," called a voice from the depths.

Rewn recognised the landlord's nasal tones and set foot on the steps that led from the trap door. Woodman followed him to the opening.

"Wait," cried Lutel, "it may be a trap."

Rewn paused; his head and shoulders were still above ground level.

"Wait here, then," he said, impatient to descend. "Woodman can accompany me."

Before Lutel could protest further the two men had disappeared into the tunnel of darkness. They felt their way down several slimy steps and were able to stand upright at the bottom, allowing their eyes to become accustomed to the even darker surroundings. Several yards away, at the end of the passage, a light flickered. A voice hailed them from behind the torch.

"This way."

"What do you want?" shouted Rewn.

"Follow me."

Rewn and Woodman were impulsively drawn towards the source of the command. As they moved forward, the light moved away from them. The passageway proved to be very straight and narrow, though in parts the roof was uneven, and several times the taller figure of Rewn cracked his head on the stones above. Tantalisingly, the flickering flame maintained a constant distance from them, and it was not until they had walked for forty or fifty paces that the distance between them decreased. It did so as they reached a flight of stairs to a second trap door, and the torch bearer turned at their head to better light their ascent. Rewn and Woodman hauled themselves through the small exit, and out into a cold damp room surrounded by wooden casks.

The cellar of the Red Lion afforded greater height and Rewn was relieved to stand upright without hindrance. Orange flames danced on the slimy green walls; a damp musty smell filled the tiny vault.

"You mean what you say? You'd let it be known that I shelter Duval?" asked Selwayne.

Rewn cast his eyes over the wooden casks; he tried to alert Woodman to their potential danger, but in the semi-darkness any signal would prove futile. A non-committal approach seemed the best way forward, reasoned Rewn. "What if I did?"

The torch was thrust towards Rewn's face; he stood his ground but jerked his head back to avoid being singed.

"Can I trust you?"

Rewn relaxed a little; the situation was feeling less like a trap, but he remained wary. "What are you suggesting?"

With a sweep of his arm the landlord withdrew the flare in a flamboyant arc and transferred its heat to Woodman.

"The Frenchie's becoming too bold and daring. He'll be caught sooner rather than later, and I'll be damned if I'll hang with him."

"What do you propose?" asked Rewn.

"I can't be seen to turn him in. Duval has many friends about these parts, and my life would be snuffed out like that." He thrust the flame at a fluttering moth and there was a sizzling noise as the insect flopped to the ground. "Now, if *you* were to hand him over, then no suspicion would befall me."

"What would you gain, apart from your life?"

"Why, that's enough for most men, isn't it?"

Rewn grabbed Selwayne's wrist and turned the flare to illuminate the landlord's features.

"Half the reward! You accept the full thousand guineas and then pass five hundred to me."

The man's greedy eyes did not blink under the flames as Rewn deliberated on his suggestion. Money, even such a large total, meant little to Rewn in the present circumstances, but the return of the key was paramount. It seemed to Rewn that the two were intertwined to such an extent that for the present there was little possibility of extricating one from the other. If he declined the offer the trail could go cold for a long time, perhaps for ever.

"I… we agree."

The landlord looked furtively around; Rewn braced himself, but the action was merely a precaution.

"Duval has a camp in the middle of Savernake Forest, over Marlborough way," the landlord said, lowering his voice. "He has many bolt holes – like my own – but he always retreats to the great forest; he doesn't feel comfortable in enclosed spaces."

"Can you hire us some horses?" asked Rewn.

His new partner laughed. "Take the two horses nearest the stable door; they belong to Duval."

"We need three," requested Woodman.

"Two," corrected the landlord. "The lady can wait with me. Let's call it a matter of trust."

The two men retraced their steps along the underground passage, blindly feeling their way without the aid of light. As they pushed open the trap door Lutel stood above them with a raised pitchfork. She put it down as she realised that there was no danger. But as Rewn outlined the plan to her, she was close to picking it up again as the extent of the bargain with the landlord became clear.

"I'm not staying," she protested.

"We've only two horses," argued Rewn.

"Then you stay, or better still, Woodman can be his hostage."

"He'd be on his own," said Rewn.

Woodman failed to see the harm in his remaining behind, but Rewn was adamant that they should keep to his word, and reluctantly Lutel saw the sense of it.

After receiving directions and provisions, Rewn and Woodman saddled up and galloped away in the warmth of the afternoon sunshine towards the town of Marlborough. On Selwayne's suggestion they avoided the main road and skirted the town to the north, riding through the dark deciduous forest.

Selwayne's directions had been vague, as he was unable to pinpoint the exact spot of Duval's hideaway and, as he pointed out in his defence, in a forest one tree looks much like another. "You will have to use your wits, trust your ears and your eyes," he had told them. Inside the dense forest of oak, elm and beech, such advice seemed totally inadequate. They searched around until dusk but apart from the occasional rabbit or red squirrel, they found little sign of life.

As the first chill of nightfall approached, they reached a sheltered glade and stopped to tie the reins to the branches of a giant elm tree. After they had unsaddled the horses they slumped against the trunk to savour their evening's meal. Stars glistened through the swaying branches, giving the impression that they were flitting around the sky. In the protection of the gathering gloom the forest began to stir with life. A dog fox barked in the distance and was answered in a far-off hollow. An owl glided silently overhead, tracking a field mouse. It skilfully descended on its prey and fixed it in vice-like talons. As it tore at the small creature with its razor beak, Woodman stretched a stiff leg and snapped a twig. The owl departed noiselessly into the night, carrying its furry treasure.

"It's fine for Selwayne to say use our eyes and ears," protested Woodman. "We might stand a chance if we could fly like that barn owl."

A prolonged sigh came from deep within Rewn, as he recognised the validity of Woodman's observation. He was right; they could spend hours, days even, searching the great expanse of woodland and still not find any trace of Duval.

"The Frenchie's too clever to be caught," stated Woodman. "That's why the price on his head is so high."

Rewn finished his mouthful of tart and wiped his lips with the back of his hand. "But he doesn't know *we* are after him, and that we have inside knowledge and help."

"Help!" snorted Woodman, gesturing at the wide open spaces around them. He suddenly broke off his gesture and stood up. Rewn watched as his companion sniffed the air.

"Perhaps you are right; perhaps our Frenchie is too cocky."

"What do you mean?" asked Rewn, joining him. Woodman had captured his interest.

"Smell the air."

Rewn breathed in several times. "I don't smell anything."

"Take a deep breath."

Rewn did as he was instructed, and the faint smell of smoke that Woodman had detected gently pervaded his nostrils.

"Where's it coming from?" asked Rewn.

"A fire," said Woodman.

"I know it's a fire, but where?" said Rewn. At times he found Woodman's literal interpretations infuriating, and now was one of those times.

Woodman circled about himself, pausing at each compass direction and violently sucking in the air.

"This way," he said, pointing eastwards. "Leave it; he'll hear us approaching."

Rewn retied the reins of his horse and followed Woodman into the night. Silently they crept forward on a carpet of humus; every so often Woodman stopped and checked the air for directions. Progress was slow as they stealthily avoided sudden noises, meandering and weaving their way around small bushes and crouching to avoid overhanging branches. As they looked up from ducking under a series of boughs, they found themselves at the edge of a clearing. Across the glade was a faint pinpoint of orange light. Woodman grabbed Rewn's arm and silently pointed in the direction of the campfire; Rewn nodded.

The fire was still a fair distance away, its smoke having been carried to them on the light breeze. Woodman now argued that they should return for the horses and ride part of the way. Having been earlier rebuffed, Rewn was unwilling to let the fire out of his sight and persuaded Woodman that they should continue. Cautiously they loped across the clearing and into the trees beyond. Occasionally the fire disappeared from view, their sight of it masked by the trunks of gnarled trees as they rambled through the undergrowth. Blackberry bushes ripped at their clothing; a clear pathway became of secondary importance as their eyes concentrated on the fire in the distance. After a quarter of an hour's toil, and many scratches, they were less than a hundred yards from the fire.

Rewn cupped his hands to Woodman's ear. "You circle in from the left, and I'll go to the right."

"What do we do when we get there?"

"We'll jump on him," said Rewn.

Woodman was about to ask what they should do if Duval was not alone or how Rewn recognised the refugee of the forest to be the French highwayman, but Rewn had disappeared behind a thicket.

Due to the easier traversability of his route, Rewn arrived first at the outer edges of the campfire. Flames crackled noisily as the fat of a freshly caught rabbit dripped from an impromptu wooden spit and onto the fire. A man sat at the campfire, and although his back was turned towards Rewn there was no mistaking the figure of Duval encapsulated in the orange glow. If further proof were needed, a white horse was tethered to a bush on the far side of the encampment – the side from which Woodman would approach. In his mind's eye, Rewn could only see the key; it had clouded his thinking, and now that he was actually at Duval's side he realised the hastiness of his plan.

He looked around the leafy floor for a branch or piece of wood to use as a weapon, but none came to view. Rewn had just decided to review his plan more carefully when the horse whinnied and reared with fright. Duval and Rewn guessed the source of the scare, although the Frenchman was at a disadvantage.

"Now!" shouted Rewn, and he rushed into the circle of light heading straight for Duval. Rewn's intention had been to bowl the highwayman over and between himself and Woodman to overpower him. Woodman had just entered the edge of the bushes that encircled Duval's camp as Rewn was rushing towards the fire. On hearing his horse's cry, the Frenchman had reached into the fire and pulled out a large glowing ember. He whirled around to face the direction of the shout. The advancing Rewn protected his face by covering it with his outstretched arms. Duval side-stepped his attacker and lashed out with his fiery weapon; Rewn plunged by and stumbled to the ground, his right arm stinging with pain. In a twinkling Duval had raced to his horse, untied the reins and was astride his mount and crashing through the trees to safety. Woodman hesitated between attacking the Frenchman and going to Rewn's aid, and in the end did neither. As Duval made his escape, Woodman walked over to attend Rewn, who was lying on the ground and clutching his arm.

"I'm all right," he said as Woodman helped him up. His arm was burned but not seriously wounded; the same could not be said about his pride. "Where were you?" he demanded.

"You didn't give me…"

But Rewn was not listening; he was already heading back towards their horses.

"Run!" he yelled. "We don't have to keep quiet this time; we'll be after him before he knows it."

"He's still had too big a start on us," said Woodman, "and besides, there's another problem."

"Yes?"

"What's going to be said when it's known that we've let Duval escape?"

"Duval can have no proof that anybody, let alone Master Selwayne, has informed on him."

"I was thinking of Lutel."

"Ah. That's quite another problem," said Rewn, "so it's probably a good thing that I know where our friend is heading."

During the time that it took them to retrace their steps to the horses, Woodman continually probed Rewn for an explanation, but on all attempts remained unsuccessful. As they untied the reins Woodman made one last effort.

"What happens if we become separated? How am I supposed to meet you?"

"All right, back to the Red Lion," said Rewn with a grin, and he rode off in the direction of Avebury, with a puzzled Woodman close behind.

CHAPTER THIRTY-ONE

FIND THE LADY

The journey out of Savernake was proving arduous; apart from the occasional clearing or glade they seldom reached a canter or a gallop. On the main road between Devizes and Marlborough they increased their speed, but the moon provided insufficient light to illuminate the ruts and potholes and they frequently had to adjust their pace.

For once Rewn seemed unhurried; it was Woodman who pressed to quicken their horses.

"We know where he is heading," said Rewn, by way of explaining his unhurried bearing.

"But he'd be simple to go back to Avebury, knowing we're after him."

"He doesn't know it's us. In the dark and quickness of the moment, he couldn't have recognised us."

"But he may have seen our faces; he's clever is that Frenchie."

"Oh, he's clever," agreed Rewn, "but he was away too fast to take stock of us. We'll soon see how clever he is." The last few words were spoken under his breath, and out of Woodman's earshot.

It was a good half an hour after midnight before they arrived at Avebury. At the sight of the Red Lion Inn, Woodman spurred his horse and galloped ahead. He leapt from his saddle and without waiting to tether his horse crashed through the door of the inn. The startled landlord and Lutel shot up from their wooden stools as he rushed in.

"Where is he? Where's the Frenchie? Quick," he shouted. They watched agog as the agitated man raced up the stairs, halted before reaching the top, raced back down again and headed for the cellar door.

"Quickly, no time to waste," he yelled.

"What's happened?" demanded Selwayne. "There's no one here."

"Yes there is," exploded Woodman. "We followed that French highwayman here."

"No one has walked through that door for over an hour," said Lutel.

Woodman slumped into a chair, nervous exhaustion having drained him of all energy. The landlord poured a drink, but before Woodman could take a sip, the loud cracking sound of an exploding firearm reached their ears.

"Rewn," shouted Lutel, and she careered outside into the road. In front of her at the carpenter's cottage in Green Lane a figure was standing above the saw pit. As Lutel drew closer she could hear voices raised in anger. Several of the boards that had covered the pit lay strewn upon the ground.

Several minutes earlier Rewn had approached the saw pit armed only with the stable pitchfork. He had bravely thrown back the covering planks and as Duval aimed his pistol, Rewn had raised his pitchfork and brought it down in a huge wielding arc, knocking the weapon from Duval's arm just at the moment of fire. The twin prongs of the same pitchfork now lay embedded in the timber walls of the saw pit, straddling the neck of Claude Duval. His horse snorted and reared in its underground stable whilst Rewn crowed triumphantly.

"Rewn! Are you all right?"

"I'm fine, Lutel; only a small burn for my troubles."

"We heard a shot," she called down as Woodman arrived breathlessly at her side, accompanied by a smattering of villagers.

"Useful weapon," said Rewn, gripping the long handle of the farming implement.

Woodman walked down the timbered ramp that had been Duval's mode of entrance into the pit. He stood in front of the restrained highwayman and spat in his face. Duval snarled and muttered an oath, but it was not in the language of the simple countryman, and the insult failed to barb.

"Leave it," Rewn ordered Woodman. "Take the horse up."

Once Duval's mount was at ground level Rewn asked for the saddle-bag to be opened. Woodman duly obliged and searching its contents pulled out a clutch of gold coins, rings, brooches and an array of other trinkets. A ripple of gasps and mutterings emanated from the small crowd.

"Bloody hell," said the more direct Woodman.

"Anything else?" asked Lutel expectantly.

"What else do you want?" asked Woodman, incredulous.

"Just check, please."

Woodman felt to the recesses of the bag, but apart from a few dry leaves and blades of grass there was nothing else.

"Come and hold this," ordered Rewn.

Woodman climbed down into the pit, gripped the handle of the pitchfork and pushed against it. Rewn faced Duval. He ripped the Frenchman's shirt at the neck, revealing a long cylinder tied with a red ribbon. Rewn took hold of the object and yanked hard. The highwayman flinched as the ribbon snapped, yielding its treasure to Rewn. Momentarily, Woodman was distracted from his task, and Duval took advantage of the relaxed grip. His right foot was raised swiftly and kicked Woodman in the groin. At the same time he placed his hands on each prong and forced the pitchfork out of the wood, knocking Woodman backwards with the thrust of his action. The Frenchman swiped the handle into Rewn's stomach, causing him to double over, then raced up the ramp, pushing Lutel to the ground. He vaulted onto his horse from behind and galloped off into the night. Woodman made to give chase.

"No, let him go," gasped Rewn, climbing out of the pit. "We have what we want." Helping Lutel to her feet, he tenderly tied the key around her neck. Lutel smiled at her brother, and stroked the key. Its safe return was a great relief.

Still puzzled by the key's importance, Woodman tackled Lutel. "You've still never said what that so-called key opens."

"Nothing that would interest you, John, but to me it holds great value." How could she explain to this simple rustic of the planet Earth that the key would fire a spaceship back to her home planet of Mykas?

Woodman shrugged his shoulders and seemed content with the explanation.

Still the crowd of villagers stood around, some gaping; a few women and children cried whilst some men shouted after the villain. The trio brushed their way through the rustics and made their way back to the Red Lion. Truster Selwayne hovered in the doorway, having hedged his bets.

"He has many bad friends," he said, excusing his absence from the fray.

"Don't worry," said Rewn. "He knows nothing of your part in this."

"How did you know of his hiding place?" asked Woodman.

"A speck of sawdust in my eye," answered Rewn cryptically.

"From the saw pit," guessed Woodman. "But how—"

"I didn't think Duval would go there," interrupted the landlord. "But of course, now I think of it, if he was being chased it was the obvious choice."

"You mean hide in the saw pit until the hue and cry had died down?" asked Lutel.

"Yes, then he would leisurely make his way to a place of safety."

"Like the inn," barked Woodman harshly.

"It's over," said Rewn. "I doubt if he will try that little trick again in a hurry."

Rewn held out his hand to Woodman, who reluctantly emptied his hands of the collection of coins and jewels. Rewn took the gold coins and placed them in a leather pouch, then proffered the remaining items to Selwayne.

"These should compensate for the loss of the reward. We'll keep Duval's horses," he said. Then he placed several coins in the landlord's hands, adding, "This should be enough for a further evening's board, plus a further horse from your stable."

"More than enough," answered Selwayne, his greedy eyes failing to disguise his extreme delight. "I own the bay mare, a very gentle animal; consider her yours."

The following morning three figures rode quietly out of the village, unobserved, apart from by the odd farm dog and Truster Selwayne. They rode beside the stolid sarsen stones, through the quaint town of Marlborough, and crossed the county boundary into Berkshire and on into Hungerford. Travel was restricted to a steady gallop so as not to overstretch the horses, but after several hours in the sun, both man and beast were parched. On the outskirts of Newbury they approached the Halfway Inn. Rewn pulled up his horse as the others drew alongside him.

"We should stop here for refreshment; besides, the horses need rest and watering."

The services of an ostler were expeditiously engaged and the horses were led away to a stable behind the tavern, where they could recover with feed and water. The three riders entered the Halfway Inn. The tavern was surprisingly full, and there was a buzz of excitement amongst its occupants, many of whom seemed strangely garbed. Two men conversed in a corner, one with a large dragon's head at his feet, the other dressed as a knight sporting a white tabard with a red cross emblazoned upon it. Men in white shirts, with garlands of flowers in their hats and small bells tied around their knees, laughed alongside men with painted faces and dwarves. A theatrical group were rehearsing lines in an inglenook; judging by their raucous behaviour and rich language Rewn guessed that they had been drinking since early morning.

"A touch too much, my gentle love," protested a young man in a falsetto voice.

"Thou shalst know my true touch shortly," barked an older actor, lunging at the boy.

The troupe broke out into guffaws of laughter as the younger man stepped swiftly aside and his pursuer landed in a heap in the empty hearth. The actor stood up and made a vain attempt to brush the soot from his costume. He rubbed his hands down the cheeks of the young boy, leaving a black smudge in his wake.

"Let that be lesson to all shrew wenches," he laughed.

Their entertainment continued at a boisterous pace. Unless you were an insider it was impossible to discriminate between conversation and dialogue.

On receiving their ale Rewn asked the landlord the reason for such a bohemian gathering.

"Best you're a stranger," came the answer.

"We're riding to London."

The landlord was very tall and sported copper curly hair and bushy side whiskers. He looked at Rewn down his crooked long nose, the result of a tavern dispute. "Why, 'tis the fayre at Newbury today; 'twill be hoss racing, sideshows and the like you'd never seen."

"A fayre with the plague?" queried Rewn.

"That's miles away in London. Let 'em pass what laws they like, they ain't stoppin' our fun. Why, they say King and Parliament's only up the road at Oxford; what's sauce for the goose is sauce for the gander. There's no plague around here, and if you take my meaning you won't go searching for it. Stay here awhile and enjoy the fayre."

"How far away is it?" asked Rewn.

"A tidy step, more than a short walk," came the unhelpful reply. If the landlord was drumming up custom, he didn't appear to be going out of his way to do so.

"Is there anything to eat?" asked Rewn, casting his eye around at the various sweetmeats and plates of food.

"There's plenty if you're stopping. But you'll be waiting a while; the world and his wife are 'afore 'ee."

"We can wait."

"What'll you have?"

"Food for three. Anything will do; just heap the plates up."

A look of doubt crossed the landlord's face.

"Hurry up, Eziekel, some of us are dying of thirst," called a voice.

"Money up front," demanded Eziekel bluntly.

Rewn took out his purse and removed a gold coin. The landlord continued to look at him distrustfully. He put the money in his mouth and bit it.

"Stolen?" he said.

Rewn reached for the coin.

"Just askin'. Fair do's," he said, and handed Rewn several small silver and brown coins as change.

Such was the popularity of the inn that there were no seats to be had, and Lutel and Woodman had placed themselves near the doorway. The ale was eagerly swilled and the three of them slaked their thirst with no thought of conversation.

Rewn let out a satisfied gasp as he wiped the froth from his mouth. He could easily acquire a liking for this drink, he thought.

"There's a fayre," he pronounced.

"We know," replied Woodman, nodding in the direction of a midget by way of explanation. "Our friend here has been acquainting us with the event."

The small man touched his cap and bowed his head to Rewn. His hair was mousy with a striking fleck of blond across his forehead. As he smiled, his irregular teeth matched the long thin strands. "English Chitterne at your service, sir."

"This is Rewn," announced Woodman by way of introduction.

"Find the lady?" asked English of Rewn.

For a moment Rewn assumed that somebody, most likely Woodman, had been talking out of turn, and that the lady in question was Lutel. As his look grew blanker the midget beckoned the uncomprehending Rewn to his table. Not wishing to risk drawing unnecessary attention to himself by refusing the hospitable offer, Rewn moved several paces sideways. English produced two playing cards: the two and three of clubs, and then added the queen of hearts. Rewn marvelled at the pristine condition of the playing cards when compared to their dealer. English turned the first two cards over and placed them face down on the table; he then placed the queen in a similar position between the two cards. With a confident thud, English set down a groat on the table alongside the three cards.

"Find the lady, and the groat is yours. Fail to find her and you buy me a drink."

Several interested bystanders gathered around the table, and Rewn wondered if it might be more politic to refuse the invitation and risk a moment's embarrassment.

"Come, sir, come make your choice," crowed English.

Rewn suspected all was not what it seemed but realised the crowd was eagerly waiting for him to make a decision. Confidently he placed his index finger on the middle card.

"Ha!" shouted English, and he turned over the card to the right of centre to reveal the queen. Rewn grinned, and took a large gulp from a tankard of ale that Woodman had thrust in front of him.

"Again?" said English.

Lutel moved to dissuade her brother, but the drink had played a trick of its own and inflated his confidence.

"Again," he roared.

Once more the three cards were placed face upwards. English gathered them up and slowly replaced them on the table, leaving the queen to last, and placing the final card to the left of centre. The crowd had increased in size with a dozen or more spectators now watching the action. English stared up from the table, his face beaming and eyes shining. "Find the lady!"

Rewn took another swig of ale and studied the cards.

"Here!" he said assuredly, indicating the card to the left of centre with his finger.

English's mouth dipped into a frown, and a baleful look filled his sorrowful saucer-shaped eyes. Rewn puffed his chest out expectantly and a chain of murmurings passed around the crowd. Rewn nudged Woodman and stretched his hand out for the coin. Another hand arrested its progress and English flipped the card over and let forth a stream of uncontrolled laughter.

Rewn stared disbelievingly at the two of clubs and shrugged his shoulders. A ripple grew to a crescendo as the experienced crowd burst out laughing at Rewn's ill luck. He drained his second tankard in an effort to disguise his annoyance.

"Very good," slurred Rewn begrudgingly, and he delved into his pouch to produce a gold sovereign. The crowd around gasped, encouraging more than half the customers to turn their attention to the table; even the landlord had temporarily ceased plying his trade.

Lutel recognised the urgency of the situation. Two tankards of ale with no food had robbed Rewn of his senses, and she pushed her way through to the table.

"We must go," she hissed in his ear.

"No, no," slurred Rewn, palming her away. "I'm just beginning to enjoy myself."

Cheers from the crowd egged on Rewn's defiance.

"My sovereign against the two drinks I owe you," burbled Rewn, hiccoughing.

English hesitated. "It wouldn't be fair of me."

"Go on, English, rook 'im!" encouraged a voice in the crowd.

Rewn thumped his fist down on the table. "Deal!" he demanded.

"Very well," said English, "but I'll match your sovereign," and he reached inside his coat to produce a similar coin.

"As you wish," boomed Rewn.

English repeated the rigmarole of slowly laying the cards out, carefully ensuring that the queen was apparently laid to the extreme right. The gambler, who had been resting his hands on the table with his legs set wide, straightened and wobbled slightly from side to side. Rewn alternated his glance between English and the cards; the crowd had hushed and watched with intense silence. Rewn stared hard for several seconds, as though his eyes were trying to burn away the very backing of the blue and white playing cards.

"Make haste," shouted a voice, and the crowd erupted into a cacophony of noise.

Rewn held his hand over the cards and wavered between the three choices.

"Silence," yelled the landlord. "Let there be no doubting his choice."

Rewn took a pace backward from the table and almost fell; several hands pushed him forward, and the combined effort sent him lurching towards the table. He put his left hand out to steady himself, but his other hand shot forward and he flicked over the centre card.

"This one," he shouted, and collapsed onto his knees.

The gasps and cheers from the crowd told the onlookers at the back, whose view had been hindered, that Rewn had found his lady.

English looked up with total disbelief painted on his face. "Again, sir?"

"No," said a voice firmly. Lutel picked up the sovereigns and, linking an arm through one of Rewn's, shepherded him away to the safety of a vacant table. As the crowd muttered their disappointment it was a timely relief to see the landlord's daughter approaching with trenchers of food.

"Eat this, and keep quiet," growled Lutel tersely.

The large bread plate was covered in sliced meats and a selection of sweet pickles. All three of them ate heartily, although Rewn managed to drop several pieces of his topping onto the floor, where they were eagerly accepted by the resident grey Irish wolfhound.

At the completion of the meal, Lutel and Woodman dragged Rewn outside into the fresh air.

"You're angry," said Rewn. "I can tell. You go all quiet when you are angry."

Lutel transfixed Rewn with a cold stare.

"You're right, I'm angry," she replied through clenched teeth.

Lutel pulled him further away from the inn, and looked around before continuing with her admonishment.

"You risk everything – our capture, the mission, our lives, even Revin and Verde's lives – by drawing attention to yourself in a public place."

"I won."

Lutel's top lip tightened and her cheeks flushed.

"It suits you when you are angry," garbled Rewn.

Lutel considered walking out on Rewn there and then, but her dedication to the cause stopped her. A sobering clout around the ear to wipe the silly grin from his face was more in order, she decided; at least it would make her feel better.

An intrusion by Woodman unintentionally defused the situation and probably saved Rewn from physical harm.

"That was a brilliant guess," he said as he approached the pair.

"It wasn't a guess."

Woodman waited patiently. "Go on," he implored.

"My great-grandfather taught me that trick, whilst I could still sit on his knee."

"Could he teach me?" asked Woodman innocently.

Lutel burst out laughing at the simplicity and impossibility of the request and, guessing that he had been forgiven, Rewn joined in the gaiety. Woodman was amazed at the change; one minute the two were at each other's throats, and now they were being frivolous over a matter that was totally lost on him. He preferred the latter situation and roared heartily, even though he didn't know why he was laughing.

Woodman decided to take advantage of the improved relationship. "Can we go to the fayre?" he asked.

Lutel stopped laughing; her look became more serious, but Woodman's thirst for entertainment was not to be so easily extinguished.

"The horses will need two or three hours' rest. If we travel later in the day it will be cooler, so we could spend our time watching the races instead of waiting around here drinking."

He calculated that the barb might sway the argument his way. Although she did not find it compelling, Lutel could see some logic in his suggestion.

"All right, let's go," she said, "but there's to be no drinking or ganderflanking"

Rewn bowed his head like a naughty schoolboy as a stream of people made their way out of the tavern. Most were walking, others on horseback, whilst a few rode in coaches or wagons. A youth, who had obviously spent too long in the inn, staggered past them.

"Hurry," he gushed, "the firs' race starts at midday."

They made to follow the hobbledehoy along the road, but before they had left the shadow of the inn, a wagon pulled up alongside them.

"Care for a ride?" said the passenger up front.

Lutel hesitated, but Woodman and Rewn clambered into the open wagon, using its large wooden spokes.

"We'd like that very much, English," she said as she heaved herself into the back.

CHAPTER THIRTY-TWO

WINNERS AND LOSERS

The wagon trundled along at a gentle easy pace, making their journey far smoother than any they had recently experienced. The wooden wheels met the uneven ground with a lenitive calm, so their bodies were not jostled by any sudden movement.

The few miles to the fayre were filled with English giving an account of his life. He had been born, he told them, in Hereford on the border of England and Wales. His father had been an itinerant blacksmith and his mother was the daughter of a farm labourer. His father's work had resulted in them crossing the border into Wales many a time, his mother always accompanying her husband on his travels.

It transpired that during one visit to Llanvapley, a small village between Abergavenny and Monmouth, she had been heavily pregnant, although several weeks away from the expected birth. During the visit she had slipped on a cowpat whilst carrying out a menial farm task. The fall, or the shock of it, had caused her to go into premature labour. The poor woman, against advice, had insisted on travelling back to her parental home in Hereford, and a farm cart was suitably prepared with blankets and sheets for the journey, along with a girl for company. Before the cart had reached Monmouth she had safely delivered a healthy baby boy. To her own and her husband's amazement, she continued to have contractions. Within twenty minutes, the farm girl was holding a very tiny child. It was so small and weak that nobody on the wagon, including the mother, expected it to live. Due to the fact that they had now crossed into England the husband hastily decided to name this arrival English and, in an inspired burst of imagination brought on by the ecstasy of the births, called the first-born Welsh. English had not been expected to survive the journey, let alone the night – but confounded everyone by doing both.

His formative years were spent accompanying the family around the counties that bordered the two countries. Welsh was perfectly formed, but as English grew older it was obvious that he would never rise to any great stature; in fact he was destined from birth to become a midget. As though in compensation the small boy had a resilient character, and survived many health scares. His physical strength was matched by a mental toughness which was tempered by cruel jibes and taunts wherever he travelled – the worst offenders being children of his own age.

To English's credit he survived intact, but by his early teens he had accepted that he would never be able to follow in his father's footsteps. Welsh was physically built in their father's image, and it was no surprise that he became the apprentice with a view to eventually taking over the business. English decided that his future lay away from agriculture and the country.

One summer, a travelling band of players descended upon Abergavenny and English was captivated by their outlandish lifestyle. He watched their performances and visited them at every opportunity – talking, laughing and helping out wherever possible – and it came as no surprise that when the time came for the players to move on, he left with his parents' blessing. English had worked with the troupe ever since, and as an additional source of income he had developed a little batch of sideshow tricks, by which customers of inns and taverns were often entertained.

The cart had reached a large expanse of open ground on the outskirts of Newbury. A large crowd continued on its way along their route. English's driver stopped the cart.

"You jump off here," said English, his friendly tones bearing no malice towards Rewn. "Come and watch us later on."

"We will," promised Lutel.

They were standing outside a purple tent with large yellow stars on it; a sign at the entrance showed its inhabitant to be Madame Rosa, fortune teller. On Lutel's suggestion they decided to separate and meet again outside the tent before the first race. Woodman and Rewn decided to "study the form" and run their eyes over the runners of the first race. Lutel announced that she would try her luck around the side-stalls. The historian in her secretly hankered after the chance to observe the various aspects of country entertainment that were on display.

Whilst Rewn and Woodman sauntered around the roped-off paddock area, where the day's first runners could be inspected, Lutel began her tour of the fayre, passing through a small crowd that was being entertained by a magician. As she broke through the circle a voice from above her warned her to keep clear. Lutel followed the direction of the voice and trailed it to a radiant face at the top of a pair of stilts.

"Wouldn't want you coming to any harm," said the beaming performer, as he touched his hat.

A young woman stood outside a row of tents occupied by even more fortune tellers. Lutel watched as she vainly attempted to persuade her young man to undertake a reading. Behind the tents a large greasy pole stood vertically out of the ground. An assortment of youths queued up to try and climb to the top – a suckling pig being the tantalising prize for the first one to achieve the feat. Most of the competitors failed to reach further than halfway up the pole before sliding back down; some, the worse for drink, lost their grip and plummeted to the ground, much to the amusement of all who partook.

Lutel watched for several minutes, amused by the antics of the young men, before moving on to view a slightly more sedate game. Children and adults alike were throwing horseshoes at an iron pole that had been pushed into the ground several paces away. Lutel asked the stall-keeper for a throw. The wizened old man looked up from his stool; several of his teeth were missing as he gave her a gummy smile.

"Fancy playing Hurlbat do you? That'll be a Harrington to you, missy; you get three throws for that."

Lutel was caught off her guard; she had no coin at the ready and had to search her person for the correct money. No obvious coin came to view. The old man misinterpreted her predicament and, fearful of losing a customer, unwittingly came to her aid.

"I've change for a penny."

Lutel handed the coin over and the old man produced three farthings from his grubby sunburned hand.

Lutel tested the weight of the horseshoe by swinging it to and fro; the watching crowd were impressed by her seriousness. The first shoe fell well short of its mark and Lutel repeated her preparation. A clang of metal promised much, but Lutel had overcompensated and the horseshoe ricocheted away from its target and came to rest in a heap of straw behind the pole. Lutel pursed her lips and narrowed her eyes in a picture of concentration. It might only be a sideshow, but her character was so honed and tuned that even something as insignificant as this game became a personal task to overcome. She focused on the iron pole and flicked her final throw; again it struck the pole, repeating the metallic clanking sound as the horseshoe rebounded into the turf.

"A good try, missy. Will you be having another go?"

Lutel never walked away from a challenge, but a crowd had gathered and she had the discretion to decline even though the defeat rankled. During the next half an hour she witnessed entertainment as diverse as a Punch and Judy show to cock-fighting, but wherever she went the shock of the horseshoe game caused her to keep a low profile. As the crowds around the sideshows began to thin and make their way towards the centre of the field she guessed that the first race would soon be starting.

She retraced her steps and found a restless Rewn and Woodman waiting outside Madame Rosa's. An old woman dressed in black, with a face like a shrivelled prune, was attempting to entice the two men into a palm reading. Madame Rosa had persistently refused to be discouraged by Woodman's less-than-polite rejections, and Lutel's timely arrival was of great relief. The old woman cursed them and disappeared into the depths of her tent, yanking the tent flap behind her.

Woodman led the way to a grassy knoll that offered an unobstructed view of the race although it was a fair way down from the starting line. A crowd of several hundred had gathered at the track-side, held back by impromptu fencing mainly consisting of wooden posts hammered into the ground, linked together by strands of fraying rope.

The field had already made their way to the starting line by a diversity of routes and the crowd around them jostled to improve their position.

"Ramrod," asserted Rewn.

"I told you – no chance," argued Woodman. "Hunters Moon by a distance."

Lutel was flanked by the two gamblers and looked suspiciously from one to the other. Rewn caught the look and sensed disapproval.

"It's only a small wager," he said apologetically.

"Explain," demanded Lutel.

"We've had a bet on the race," Woodman blurted out.

Lutel sighed; she deliberated over her admonishment, but before she could reach a decision the crowd surged forward as the starter dropped his flag. Five furlongs away the jockeys kicked their mounts into action amidst a flurry of whips. As the field drew ever closer, the gentle ripple of encouragement grew to a deafening cheer. Lutel was carried forward by the momentum of the crowd, her feet barely touching the ground. She had started to count the horses but stopped to concentrate on her own safety – several of the people in front of her had already tumbled down the hillside, unable to repel the enthusiasm of the crowd. Behind her Rewn was staring into the distance and screaming.

"Go, Ramrod! Go, go… run!"

Woodman was similarly transfixed and neither of them was aware of her plight.

"Come on boy, come on boy!" he shouted.

It was only as the horses raced by that Woodman realised that something was wrong; he ceased his cheering and pushed his way forward. Lutel was being edged further and further away. He pushed his way through the crowd with his arms as though he were swimming through the air. Lutel had not noticed his approach and it was a pleasant relief to feel his strong arms haul her back to safety. As they climbed the bank the race was reaching its climax. Woodman stopped to see the finish, but their view was blighted by the many bodies that were leaping up and down. Rewn was one of them, but he ceased as the others approached him.

"I've won, I've won!" he cried joyously. He was at a loss to explain Lutel's reaction.

"The rank outsider?" said an amazed Woodman, showing more interest. "How did you do it?"

Rewn plunged down the hillside in search of his winnings. The crowd were milling around in all directions, sporting a variety of expressions. Woodman grabbed Lutel's hand and pulled her through the throng on the trail of her brother, pausing every few seconds to crane his neck and check Rewn's whereabouts. They caught up with him beside a well-dressed gentleman who wore the fashionable overcoat of the day with matching black breeches and shoes, set off by bright yellow stockings. The man was counting a large sum of money into Rewn's outstretched hand. Rewn was filling his purse with sovereigns.

"You were the only one to pick that nag," growled the man. "Rank outsider – who would ever believe it?" He begrudgingly placed the last of the coins in Rewn's hand, still unable to believe his bad luck. "Are you certain you have no connections with that horse?"

"None," replied Rewn. "It was just a lucky guess."

A crowd of people applauded Rewn as he pocketed his winnings.

"About time that miser got done," growled a voice.

"Well done, lad."

"Fifty pounds – he won't dine tonight."

"I hope he does – and chokes," were just some of the appreciative comments that greeted Rewn's success.

Woodman laughed as Rewn came over to them.

"Why, there's as much cheering for thee as there was for the winning hoss," he observed.

"That's because I was the only one to back it," said Rewn, smiling.

Woodman nodded. "Smart guess."

"No," said Rewn. "I noticed at the start how it was sweating up; my grandfather told me that could mean one of two things in a race – though it was usually the other…"

He tailed off as Lutel's silence dawned on him. What a fool, he thought, as he realised that for the second time that day he had inadvertently attracted undue attention to himself.

"Rewn, let's look at the runners for the next race," suggested Woodman. "Perhaps you could pass on some of your tips."

"No," replied Rewn, looking at Lutel. "I feel all my luck has been used up for today."

The threesome were immersed in a throng of people and soon melted into the crowd. Lutel kept on walking, eager to put as much distance as possible between Rewn and the scene of his triumph. The numbers quickly thinned to a trickle, but almost immediately grew again as they came upon a circle of people standing three or four deep. They had been attracted by a group of Morris men putting on a mummers' play. Saint George was dressed in the white and red-crossed flag of England; the dragon's head from the Halfway Inn was now perched on the head of its owner. A hobby-horse waltzed around, and a Turkish knight drew jeers from the crowd. On the periphery of the circle a small man introduced himself as Malkin the clown; it was the rather sad figure of English.

Woodman begged to watch the performance, so they settled at the edge. At the end of the play the crowd cheered and English took off his hat and walked amongst the crowd. When he reached the trio Rewn hesitated, unwilling to incur Lutel's wrath. English looked up at the tall handsome Mykasian.

"I hear you've been lucky," said English.

"How do you know?"

"You can't keep a win like that quiet."

Rewn placed a sovereign in the hat, and slipped another one into English's hand.

English did not speak, but his warm look said it all.

"We must be going now," urged Lutel. "We have important business in

London and our horses will be well-rested."

"God's speed," said English, and he continued his journey around the dispersing crowd.

"Can't we stay a little longer?" pleaded Woodman. "It's still too hot for the hosses."

"I fear the horses will be too hot for you if we stay," joked Lutel, but her humour was lost on Woodman. Rewn, however, understood the taunt and supported his sister.

"It's a fair walk back and we must eat before we ride again. The sun will be low in a few hours and we will be able to ride in comfort until dusk."

Walking against the general direction of the crowd they made their way to a gap in the hedge where they had first entered. It was mid-afternoon before they arrived back at the Halfway Inn.

CHAPTER THIRTY-THREE

SPY MASTER PURSUIVANT

"Queer name," observed Rewn.

Woodman followed his gaze. "For a clever chap you do have some strange misunderstandings. The inn be halfway between Bristle and Lunnon." Woodman puffed his chest out in recognition of being able to impart a piece of knowledge to Rewn – a man who had risen inestimably in his esteem since his two gambling coups of the day.

The inn was now much quieter, its patrons having mostly departed to the fayre. Woodman offered to check the horses and made his way to the stables where he found all three fully recovered and in fine fettle, having been groomed and fed. A hefty piebald horse was sweating in one of the bays; Woodman patted it on the side of the neck and the horse nuzzled his shoulder. He felt for a handful of hay from a feeder and held it out to the restless horse, but it declined his offer. The morsel was gratefully received by one of the other horses and he repeated the gesture twice more.

He felt hungry himself, and remembering Rewn's promise he set off towards the inn. As he entered, Woodman was surprised to see Lutel and Rewn seated at a table with two strangers. As he crossed the threshold he felt the cold prick of a rapier against the back of his neck. He stopped abruptly.

"Welcome," drawled a voice from behind him. "Allow me to introduce myself. I am Sir Edward Laungechamp, Spy Master Pursuivant to His Royal Majesty, King Charles the Second. Please come and join us." The rapier was removed from Woodman's neck and pressed into his back. A hand shoved him towards the other captives and he stumbled forward towards a vacant seat.

Laungechamp remained standing. He presented a commanding figure; his pale complexion was offset by a striking black beard and bushy moustache. As Woodman sat down he noticed a cocked pistol pointing at Rewn's ribs. The table obscured his view of Lutel's side but he surmised from her stiff posture and the drooping of the other stranger's hand that she too was sitting at pistol point.

Laungechamp called to a doorway at the back of the room. "Come in, Master Fennor."

A man of medium height with an aquiline nose emerged from the shadows accompanied by a woman. Woodman, who was facing the doorway, thought they looked familiar.

"Come closer," ordered Laungechamp.

The pair shuffled forward; the man held his hat in front of him, fingering it with both hands. They stopped at the side of the table. Rewn and Lutel recognised them as the couple who had overheard Woodman's boasting in the Lyon Inn, and had later been their travelling companions on the stage from Chippenham.

"Are these the ones?" asked Laungechamp curtly.

Nicholas Fennor needed only a brief glance. "They are, my lord," he mumbled.

"Does your wife confirm this?"

"She does, Sir Edward."

"Let her speak for herself," demanded the interrogator.

"I do, sir," said the woman timidly.

Reaching into his clothing Laungechamp produced a small leather pouch. He loosened the tie, removed a handful of coins and threw them down on to the table. For a moment the scene froze; nobody spoke or moved. Laungechamp was not a man to be trifled with.

"Take them and be gone," he snapped.

A nervous hand reached out and scooped up the coins. Fennor clutched them to his chest and scurried out of the inn, closely followed by his wife. Laungechamp, ensuring the couple had departed, turned his attention to the table.

"I understand that you are going to London," he said, addressing Woodman, "to create a huge conflagration!"

The accused shuffled uncomfortably in his chair. After all, it wasn't his idea, so why should he be the one to be picked on? He began to regret the looseness of his tongue. At that precise moment he was ready to swear that never again would a drop of liquor pass his lips, but as things stood it seemed that such an oath might prove to be unnecessary.

"Not at all, sir," came a slightly nervous reply.

"Madam, I was not speaking to you," replied the King's spymaster, in a cold but measured voice.

The interruption had given Woodman time to compose himself and collect his thoughts. "'Twas nothing more than the drink, sir. I talk too much when I've supped the ale."

"Possibly, possibly so," mused Laungechamp, as he fingered the point of a dagger that he had drawn from his side. "I have made enquiries. You are known as a man of singular opinions, John Woodman." Laungechamp placed the blade under Woodman's chin, forcing him to raise his head. "Yet… you have not the wit to plan such an episode. However, *you* are not known to us," he said, switching his attention to Lutel and Rewn and in so doing plunging his dagger into the table.

The sentries remained unmoved but the three prisoners all flinched as the blade splintered into the wood. Woodman knew the possibilities of torture that lay before them, whilst Rewn and Lutel were unaccustomed to the barbarous action.

Laungechamp recovered control of his faculties, apart from his voice rising a notch. "Your names, sir, madam?" he intoned.

"Rewn, and this is my sister Lutel."

"Good," replied Laungechamp, spreading his hands widely apart on the table and leaning towards the pair. "A good start. What is your family name?"

Rewn wondered how he could answer the question without displaying the lie, as the truth would only tell further against them.

"Bird," Lutel blurted out – it was the first thing that came into her head; she'd been worrying over Verde and Revin and could imagine them waiting impatiently at the sign of the bird for their meeting. A meeting that was now under threat of even greater delay.

"Well, Master and Mistress Bird, where do you reside? We've made enquiries around Chippenham and the surrounding villages, and you seem to have appeared from nowhere in the middle of the Wiltshire countryside."

Laungechamp little realised how close to reality he actually was, although it would have been beyond his comprehension if Rewn and Lutel had admitted the truth. They made no answer as they could think of none that would suffice; both avoided eye contact with their interrogator as they each racked their brain for a plausible explanation.

"As I thought. Let me tell you what I think, Mistress and Master Bird – or should I say Monsieur and Mademoiselle Oiseau?"

The accused pair raised their eyes.

"Yes, I thought that might prick home," said Laungechamp with a triumphant swagger. "Rather a stupid mistake keeping your French names;

you surely couldn't have expected to remain undetected using such foreign names as Rewn and Lutel."

Woodman seized the chance to extricate himself from the situation.

"They never told me they was Frenchies," he muttered, squirming. "Why, they even chased a Frenchie, getting off the stage to do so."

"Exactly," said Laungechamp, folding his arms in satisfaction at Woodman's evidence. "It's my belief that you are in contact with a network of French spies, intent on causing destabilisation of his Majesty's Kingdom."

Rewn did not know whether to laugh or cry; any explanation or denial seemed totally pointless.

"Consider yourselves under arrest," Laungechamp commanded them. "You will be taken to Oxford for further…" and he paused before adding with a sinister glint in his eye, "…questioning!" The word was delivered with the semblance of a snarl.

The seriousness of the situation dawned fresh on Woodman, who believed he had justified his own innocence. "I bent French," he protested.

"My dear fellow," crooned Laungechamp smoothly, "nobody is suggesting that you are."

"Can I go, then?" asked Woodman expectantly.

The Spy Master Pursuivant threw back his dark mane and laughed. The two attendants followed his lead. Laungechamp eventually stopped and delivered his words slowly and precisely.

"No… you… can't! Have you never heard of aiding and abetting?"

"N-n-no," stammered the confused Woodman, thinking back to his flutter at the races. "Since when's betting been a crime?"

"Simpleton," snapped Laungechamp, his tolerance exhausted. "You will accompany your French friends to Littlecote House. There you will be held prisoner until arrangements to transport you safely to Oxford can be made."

The two guards ushered the prisoners to their feet; the taller pointed his pistol at the trio, his bare skinny arm locked tight. His accomplice produced three lengths of rope and proceeded to tie their hands together in front of their bodies. Lutel blanched as the guard breathed over her. A length of rope was left trailing from the hands of each prisoner; at the completion of the tying the taller guard replaced his pistol in his breeches and grasped the ropes of Woodman and Rewn. The other continued to hold Lutel's rope, and under the watchful eye of Sir Edward Laungechamp they were dragged outside.

Waiting for them at the front of the inn was the landlord and one of his stable lads. Between them they held three horses. Laungechamp and the two sentinels mounted and each prisoner's rope was tied around the neck of a horse. Two further youths appeared from the direction of the stables leading three horses. One of the lads mounted Lutel's horse and the other two horses were tethered to it. The small band started off back towards Hungerford, retracing the route that they had so recently ridden with more joyous feelings.

Lutel had never felt so depressed since their arrival; even the shock of the crashed ship had been surmountable. Now her fate was in other hands and she desperately thought to make it not so, but her scheming was suspended as she broke into a run to keep pace with Laungechamp's horse. Behind her she could hear Rewn's feet tripping lightly over the ground, whilst Woodman spluttered as the dust flew up in his face and pleaded in vain to his captor to slacken the pace. Lutel wished she had taken her mother's advice and remained at home, but her father had been so proud when her name was listed for the mission.

She thought back to that day on Mykas. It had started brightly as she travelled in one of the family space hoppers to an outback in the Mykasian Hills. Varna, her friend since childhood, had accompanied her. They had squealed like a pair of young girls as they hovered over the mocornel. Below them, small mocorns scampered around their pens.

"Aren't they cute?" screamed Varna.

"Look at that skewbald one," shouted Lutel in reply.

Grey dust showered the hopper as they came to rest in the landing zone. The two friends unbuckled and ran over to a wooden shack that nestled comfortably in the hillside. An old man in a floppy grey hat stood amongst a variety of tall bins.

"What can I do for you ladies?" he asked as they brushed through the sliding door.

"I'd like a mocorn," said Lutel, smiling and nudging the giggling Varna.

"I'd rather guessed that might be your reason. What type do you have in mind?"

Lutel was keen that the breeder should take them seriously. "Be quiet, Varna," she ordered. "I would like a finderling, please."

"Follow me, the finders are this way. Are you sure you want a young 'un?" added the old man in a resigned tone.

"Quite sure; I aim to train it myself."

They squeezed through a side door that led to a large enclosure. High wire pens with enclosed mesh roofs stood on either side of their pathway. The pens were full of mocorns, the older animals being housed closest to the shack.

Lutel examined the small furry animals as they followed the old man. They were a little larger in size than the cats she was later to see on Earth, and their coats were shaggy, reaching to the ground. Their heads were also a little larger, and differed from those of Earth cats by having a much wider nose that included a third nostril. Here lay the secret of their popularity with Mykasians, because the mocorns possessed an extraordinary sense of smell. If trained from an early age the mo-nostril could be sensitised to search out any specific smell. Mocorns had a wide range of uses; the authorities used them to track missing people or a range of contraband, geologists to search out minerals, diviners to locate water and everyday Mykasians for pleasure. Once tamed, they became loyal family pets, having the additional qualities of being clean, easy to feed and hardy.

As they searched, the varying natures of the creatures became apparent. Some stole away to hide behind the dense undergrowth that filled their pens, others stared out from the sanctuary of their sleeping boxes, whilst the bravest and most inquisitive came right up to the wire and poked their noses through to gain a better scent of their visitors.

Varna paused at every pen to admire one or more of its inhabitants, but Lutel's mind was already made up and she led the farmer to the furthest pen in the right-hand row.

"That one, please." She pointed.

"A wise choice," he chuckled.

The farmer took a small box that dangled from a chain around his waist, and pointed it at the pen lock. A small bleep was emitted from the door, and a silver light continued to flash until the farmer slid the door open. A chorus of yowls met the farmer's entrance, some in protest, others in greeting. Amongst those that snuffled around his boots was a purple and silver mocorn. The man slipped a lead around the animal's neck and led it from the pen.

Lutel held her hand in front of the mocorn's nose. "Hello, Rithes," she said, scratching the small animal's ears.

Varna arrived to admire the acquisition and the farmer led the way back to his shack.

"You'll need some of this," advised the man, indicating his feeding bins.

"What do you suggest?"

"She's only a youngster; anything specific in mind?"

"No, just a general companion. Thought I might take her huxhling with me."

"A huxhler, are you?"

"For pleasure, nothing serious."

The farmer handed Lutel a bag of foodstuff. She tucked it under her arm and placed her hand in the middle of the payment disc; on completion the disc flashed green and the excited girls made to leave.

"You'll also need this," called the old man, and he handed Varna a small octagonal token. "It contains all of her records," he explained.

"Thank you," called Lutel, and she picked up Rithes to carry her back to the space hopper.

Some time later, Lutel hovered over the blue roof tiles. The stream that meandered around five sides of her family home reflected the hopper, until the landing disturbed its calm waters. She carefully came to rest next to an identical space hopper. Lutel was surprised though pleased to see her brother Rewn was visiting.

Lutel and Varna hurried to the house, eager to show Rithes to Rewn. Five sides of the building were built with the traditional local grey stone so beloved by Mykasians. The sixth side was principally a clear material, similar in its properties to glass, but it could be cut and shaped without splintering. In this instance the window protruded from the side of the house, splaying outwards to increase the vista. It had a further property of magnifying everything from inside, so that the wooded hills, in reality several miles away, appeared very close when viewed from inside the house. It provided Lutel's father with an excellent view of the forest's wildlife, enabling him to carry out his hobby from the comfort of his own lounge.

Lutel peered through the large embrasure. She could see Rewn talking to her father; they both looked very serious, although her father's countenance suggested pleasure. Rithes was momentarily forgotten. As Lutel entered the room her mother was sitting in a chair sobbing.

CHAPTER THIRTY-FOUR

THE FACE AT THE WINDOW

The intermittent traveller stared as they made their way through the Berkshire countryside. Occasionally, something was shouted – condemnation from those who knew nothing or cared little for their situation, just relieved that it was not they who were treading the bleak trail. Once a vegetable was thrown at them, splattering on Rewn's back.

The journey was close to ten miles. The road from Newbury to Hungerford was virtually deserted, and it wasn't until they reached the outskirts of the small market town that they again encountered any significant signs of life.

As they passed a few scattered cottages, a pack of three dogs barked around their feet, nipping at their ankles. Laungechamp reached down with his whip and lashed one of the mongrels across the back. The brown-and-white animal yelped and raced away with its tail between its legs. Laungechamp attempted to repeat his assault on the other two dogs, but missed his target on every occasion; eventually the animals, tiring of the fray, ran off to rejoin the unlucky mutt.

Several patrons of the Bear Inn leant out of the window and shouted derisive and lewd comments as they trudged by. Laungechamp stared straight ahead and spurred his horse onward; Lutel stumbled as the speed increased. Taking their lead from the Master, the two guards whipped their mounts. Rewn could not keep his footing and fell forward on to his face. He was dragged along the dusty road for several yards, only recovering as his rider slowed down to take a right turning towards the village of Chilton Foliat.

"Are you all right, Rewn?" shouted Woodman.

"Yes, John. I am bruised but not hurt."

"Quiet, dogs," ordered Rewn's rider, raising his whip threateningly.

In silence they crossed the bridge over the River Kennet and the road into the village narrowed considerably, so that the horses had no choice but to go in single file. The track was bordered by hedgerow on one side, and wide open meadows on the other. Many of the fields had been ploughed, the rich reddish-brown soil showing signs of having recently been tilled. In the corner of one field a man laboured away with a single horse, the iron coulter of the plough slicing through the dry fertile soil. At a bend in the road they disturbed a covey of partridges, the family group bursting into flight with noisy exploding wing beats as the band of horses flushed them out. Several cries of *chirrick, chirrick* filled the air as the birds flew low over the open fields, their brown and grey plumage blending into the rich soil as they swooped low over a distant hedgerow, before deeming it safe to settle once more. If only escape could be so easy, mused Lutel as she watched the birds disappearing.

A short distance onward Laungechamp turned left into a long driveway. The way was bordered with tall, dense trees and the foliage afforded no view on either side. They trotted in the dim light until towards the end of the drive the trees thinned out, and away to their right, between the branches, Lutel spied some tall and impressive Tudor chimneys. A full view of the impressive Elizabethan mansion was soon afforded them as the trees gave way to open pastures. Despite her present predicament, Lutel could not help but admire the architectural beauty as they approached Littlecote House. Tall chimneys sat proudly on the lichen-covered slate roof. The red brickwork was interspersed with a generous array of windows, causing the house to be warm in the summer but very cold in the winter. Both the west and east wings contained arched windows that curved gently, similar to the windows found in many country churches of the time. The body of the house contained an even greater number of windows; in places glass almost stretched from the ground to the roof. An impressive porch with a wide wooden door jutted forward from the centre of the house, beckoning the visitors welcome, as they approached across the lawns.

Two soldiers came out of the door and ran over to receive Laungechamp. One held the bridle of his horse whilst the Spy Master dismounted. The other accompanied him inside. Laungechamp strutted purposefully along a series of corridors. Beeswax candles, spaced evenly apart in iron holders along the walls, lit the murky passages.

The Spy Master halted outside a room near the centre of the house. Pushing open the door he confidently strode in. A man dressed only in riding boots lay on top of a voluptuous naked girl. The pair were entwined on a chaise-longue – the man's rear end was like a full moon thrusting up and down. The girl's legs encircled the man's body as she whipped his back with a riding crop in time to his strokes. She screamed as Laungechamp entered the room, but her lover seemed unconcerned and continued to pump away at the girl who now screamed with pleasure. Laungechamp raised his hand to his mouth and coughed politely. The man noisily reached his climax and climbed off the girl. She picked up her clothes that lay strewn around the floor and attempted to hide her nakedness.

"Back to your work," ordered the man disingenuously.

The girl bent down to gather up the few remaining garments and rushed from the room.

"Can't you knock next time, Laungechamp?" said the man irritably.

"I didn't realise, Florrent, that you entertained the servants at such an hour," came the brusque reply.

Florrent was a small, well-built man of around forty years of age; his rounded stomach bore evidence to the good life that he had surrounded himself with. Nonchalantly he began to dress, as Laungechamp addressed him.

"I have need of accommodation for the evening. I have three prisoners, and I am accompanied by two men."

"Two men? That's unlike you, Laungechamp. It must be something important."

"It may prove so; there again, it may come to nothing."

"Where are you heading?"

"We leave for Oxford in the morning."

"I can spare you two of my own men to watch your prisoners; they can be held in Daryl's room. It is three floors up and only has one door."

"The King will hear of your hospitality," promised Laungechamp.

"The King hears only what he wants."

A servant was summoned and despatched to fetch the prisoners.

Lutel and Rewn marvelled at the beautiful oak panelling and polished stairs as they were escorted at a keen pace through the house. Woodman, never having witnessed such finery, marched in a daze as they passed along corridors adorned with exquisite furniture and with beautifully framed family portraits that graced the walls. Lutel appreciated the style of the more recent Stuart paintings; they seemed more real. The subjects' poses suggested some action, unlike their Tudor predecessors with their bland lifeless features.

The artistic interlude was all too soon ended as they were bundled through a door. A bare four-poster bed stood prominently in the centre of the room. The prisoners were seated on the bed, each next to one of the corner poles. Their ropes were loosened and retied behind their backs with the ends lashed to a pole. Rewn and Lutel sat at the foot of the bed, whilst Woodman occupied the opposite end. The air was musty, as though the bedroom had not been used for some while.

Laungechamp entered the room and inspected the knots. Having satisfied himself of their proficiency he stood at the end of the bed and addressed his captives.

"Guards will be placed outside the room. The windows are locked. In any case there is a drop in excess of thirty feet. In short, there is no escape. We leave early tomorrow for Oxford. Make yourselves comfortable; morning will come all too soon." Laungechamp took a step towards Lutel and pinched her cheek. "I suggest you obtain as much beauty sleep as possible."

Lutel drew in her features and fired a withering look.

"Yes, I shall enjoy interrogating you, madame," he said in a tone that both teased and threatened.

The Spy Master made to leave but whirled around on reaching the door.

"Bonne nuit," he said, and he blew a kiss with his hand in Lutel's direction. His eyes twinkled mischievously as he pulled the door shut with a heavy thud. A large iron key snapped in the lock as if mocking their fate.

Lutel and Rewn immediately began to sway vigorously around the bed in a vain attempt to loosen their bonds. After several minutes of futile writhing they both collapsed in exhaustion.

"You do not think with your strength," gasped Lutel, quoting an old Mykasian proverb.

"So what do you suggest?" replied Rewn, his wrists bleeding from the effort.

"Nothing as yet, but we must think our way out of this problem."

"Slightly more than a problem," suggested Woodman.

Outside the night closed in. Lutel sat in solemn frustration, racking her brain for a suitable solution to their predicament.

"Whatever it is, we haven't that much time left," muttered Rewn, as the burnished moon drifted across the windows, framing itself through one of the small panes.

"'Tis a hunter's moon tonight," joked Woodman, who had resigned himself to his fate, and faced it with an air of jocularity. His effort to relieve the tension failed as neither Rewn nor Lutel laughed.

Around midnight the key rattled in the lock; Lutel was still awake and instantly her body went rigid. The two men had been dozing and were only coming to their senses as a figure entered. It was the young servant who had been on the receiving end of Florrent's amorous encounter. She carried a tray that contained a jug of water and half a loaf of bread. A small tallow candle burned from its holder on the tray; it threw a warm half-light into the room. Lutel thought of bribery or some means whereby they could overpower the girl.

"What's your name?" she asked.

"Marie," answered the girl.

"Could you brush a strand of hair from my face? I'll make it worth your while."

Before Marie could reply one of the guards stepped into the room, and the door was locked from the outside. Sir Edward Laungechamp had not become the King's Spy Master Pursuivant by chance or fortune. Even his enemies begrudgingly acknowledged his resilience and methodical manner, meticulous to the finest detail.

Marie visited each of the prisoners in turn, tearing off a hunk of bread which she held to their mouths. At the swallowing of each mouthful she made an offer of water by holding up the jug to their lips. Eating was not an easy matter; Woodman choked on a piece of crust that caught in his throat and received a hefty thump between his shoulder blades. He continued to wheeze for several seconds thereafter. Marie assured herself of Woodman's recovery and moved on.

Lutel spilled the water so that it dribbled from either side of her mouth, the two streams joining under her chin and running down her neck. The servant girl bent down and wiped Lutel dry with her apron; she opened her mouth to speak, but before she could articulate the guard barked out orders.

"That's enough, time to leave." He banged on the door and the key once more jangled. Marie placed the remaining bread and water on the tray, and cast a sorrowful look at Lutel before she was ushered out of the room. The guard in the room stared at the prisoners, then moved over to Rewn and spat in his face.

"There's for you, Frenchman," he said bitingly. He seemed about to continue his bullying, but his companion called out to him.

"Come on, Jack, I've to lock the door."

Jack sneered at Rewn, and punched him in the stomach before noisily treading his way across the floorboards and out of the door. This time the turning of the key in the lock had a sickening finality.

"Are you all right?" asked Lutel.

Rewn was doubling over and breathing heavily.

“Just winded,” he sighed, and as if to prove the point he threw himself into a wild lurching, but the wooden pole was too thick to snap and the rope too strong to break. Blood oozed from his sore wrists as he sank forward in despair.

“Sleep,” suggested Lutel. “Don’t waste energy; we’ll need our strength and wits about us tomorrow. John, how far away is Oxford?”

“In miles, I’ve no idea. But from Chippenham, ’tis over half a day’s ride.”

“In that case it must be at least two hours away,” analysed Lutel. “Plenty of time.”

“Not if we are placed inside a prison cart, it won’t be,” muttered Woodman.

With the cynical comment ringing in their ears they fell into a fitful sleep, punctuated by wild dreams. Woodman called out often in his sleep, keeping the others awake. Lutel eventually lost count of the number of times that she had been disturbed. At each new waking she had lulled herself to sleep with a new and more successful escape plan. Now, several hours into the new day, a face appeared at the bedroom window. It signalled to her but she ignored it; her mind had plummeted to desperate measures, she thought to herself.

A hand appeared beside the face and firmly tapped the window. For a moment Lutel’s mind was numb. She turned her head. The face seemed to be staring right at her; she sat up straighter to shake the dream away, but still the face beckoned her.

“Rewn,” she hissed. “Rewn, are you awake?”

No reply was forthcoming, and Lutel began to doubt herself. In the darkness a gentle snoring noise confirmed Rewn’s state. I must be awake to hear the snoring, she reasoned.

“Rewn,” she called a little louder, not wanting to risk the guards overhearing. Her brother began to stir.

“Wake up,” she urged. An eye fluttered open. “Wake up, Rewn,” she repeated through gritted teeth. “There’s somebody at the window.”

“You’re dreaming,” replied Rewn. “We are several floors up. Go back to sleep.”

At that moment the moon broke from behind the clouds, and the ghastly distorted face pressed itself against the pane, like a hideous spectre. Its nose was squashed against the glass, and the eyes were wild and excited.

“Do you see it?” asked Lutel.

“I see it,” came a shaky reply. “It’s a ghost!”

Disturbed by the noise, Woodman had woken and followed their conversation to the window.

"It's a…"

"*Quiet*," ordered Lutel, in an almost-shouted whisper.

The reprimand came too late, and a key turned in the lock. A guard waved a candle around the room; its hot wax dripped onto the floor, and in the silence landed with a resounding splash. As each prisoner was illuminated the guard satisfied himself that all was well before leaving the room, but this time the click of the key was met with relief and expectation.

Several minutes dragged by before they deemed it safe to move. All three strained to look through the window, but only the blackness of night greeted their gaze.

"It must have been a trick of the light," suggested Rewn.

"There was no light until the moon shone."

"I tell you 'twas a ghost."

"Be quiet," snapped Rewn.

As they spoke the apparition reappeared.

"Do you see it?" pressed Lutel.

"Yes," answered Rewn.

Woodman stared blankly ahead and his teeth began to chatter.

The figure clutched something in its hand and held it against the glass. A faint grating noise drifted across the room and Lutel swivelled her head towards the door.

Outside, a man perched in the vines that grew above the porch. He was athletically built, although slight of figure, with salt-and-pepper hair and a matching beard. From a coat pocket he had produced a ball of wet clay, which he squashed against the small pane of the mullioned window. Skilfully balancing in the vine, he leant inwards towards the wall. Holding the flattened ball in one hand, he proceeded to cut a circle in the glass with the other. The ring of glass came silently away with the clay, and a long arm reached through the small hole in the pane and unfastened the catch. The window opened outwards; the intruder skilfully ducked below it and hauled himself into the room, landing silently on the hard floor, before walking lightly towards the captives. Partway over a floorboard creaked; to those gathered in the room it was an ear-splitting intrusion. The intruder froze and waited a good thirty seconds whilst the others held their breath. No sound came from without and the man continued his tiptoeing.

"Who are you?" whispered Rewn as his knots were untied.

"Later," answered the man, holding a finger to his lips. The stranger motioned to Rewn to untie Lutel's ropes, whilst he freed Woodman. They greeted their release by stretching their limbs, but were immediately ushered to the open window.

“Don’t look down; just feel your way slowly along the ivy. We have time on our side, but do not make a sound. Make for the bushes,” he ordered in a hushed tone, pointing into the darkness. His expression was grave and no further advice on the solemnity of the situation was needed.

Gallantly he took Lutel’s hand as she lowered herself through the window. Rewn managed to stifle a chuckle as she felt for a footing and slowly started her descent. Woodman was the next to climb down, the stranger again offering a helping hand; the offer was repeated a third time but rejected.

By the start of Rewn’s descent, Lutel was nearing halfway; she had reached a spot just above a window when a light suddenly appeared from within. A lantern had been placed on a sill. She stopped and gripped the plant tightly, holding closely to the wall. She looked down to calculate the possibility of jumping. The light illuminated the trail of ivy below; it had been hacked away to increase the amount of natural light entering the house. As quickly as it had appeared the glow faded away, and Lutel deemed the room to have been vacated. At least she had been alerted to the thinning trail of ivy, and she carefully negotiated her way down it. Above her Woodman had watched her descent and had learned from her experience. Last to leave, the mysterious stranger pushed the window shut and again reached through the small hole, but this time he locked the clasp to prevent any intervention from the breeze.

Lutel reached the bottom and stared into the night.

“This way,” called a voice from the darkness a little to her right. Woodman joined her as she headed in the direction of the call.

Rewn had noticed the temporary halt and believed it to be due to the lighted window; on reaching the slender ladder he was quite unprepared. Lutel reached the bushes just as a crashing noise came from behind her; it was directly followed by a groan.

“No, no, this way,” said a familiar voice, as she made to return. “Mount up. I will see to it.”

From within the house came the sounds of dogs barking, soon to be joined by a variety of voices shouting orders. Uncharacteristically, whether through shock or surprise, Lutel obeyed and took the reins from English. All three of their horses were saddled, and two more were tethered to a branch.

“Hold these,” she said, recovering her poise. Woodman grasped the two sets of reins, whilst Lutel swung into the saddle and grabbed back Rewn’s horse.

Voices were growing louder and more agitated; candlelight bathed the room that had been their prison. A guard flung open the window and waved his light on the scene beneath him.

"They're down below," he yelled.

Rewn was supported on either side by English and the stranger as he hobbled in the direction of Lutel. They bundled him onto his horse as Woodman arrived with the remaining mounts.

"Follow me," said English as he hauled himself up into his saddle. The five riders galloped into the dark fields as the commotion from the house became more frenetic.

They rode hard for several miles, their journey made dangerous by the uneven track, the moon failing to reveal the roughness of the ground they covered. The risk was outweighed by the knowledge of the fate that awaited them all if they were recaptured. English had been thorough in his preparations. They headed towards Hungerford, but circled back in a northerly direction to the village of Woodlands St Mary and onto the Lambourn Downs. English brought them to a halt as they approached the hamlet of East Garston.

"Thank you," said Rewn, "but—"

"Wait," commanded English, and he turned his horse around and cocked his ear in the direction of possible danger. "It's safe... for the present, but you must not stay in these parts. You would be in great danger."

"That suits us fine," declared Lutel. "Which way is London?"

"East," said English, pointing. He kicked his horse forward. "We must keep moving, but we are not being followed as yet, so a steadier pace is in order. How's your ankle?"

"Sore," came the reply, "but I think it is only sprained." Rewn looked sheepishly at Lutel. "Why...?" he asked English, keen to steer the conversation in another direction.

"Because you showed me great kindness," explained English, anticipating the question, and he reached into his coat and pulled out a gold sovereign. "All my life, I've been treated with disdain and cruelty, but you showed me a warmth and understanding that few friends, let alone strangers, have displayed."

"How did you find us?" asked Woodman.

"We must not linger," came the reply. "I'll explain as we ride." He kicked his horse and set off across the Downs, following the River Lambourn towards the sleepy villages of Great and East Shefford.

English told them how he had returned to the Halfway Inn to hear tales from the landlord of the taking of three Frenchies by the King's men. After hearing the story several times, he realised that when all the embellishment had been torn away, the prisoners were clearly the very people he had befriended that afternoon. A stable lad was plied with drink and encouraged to divulge his version of events, which included letting slip that the prisoners were being taken to Littlecote House. English foresaw that the company of his friend Tasker Dove might prove beneficial, Tasker having spent a good many years as part of an acrobatic troupe before taking to the more rewarding occupation of cutpurse and thief.

English told them that he had been at Littlecote for over an hour, but could not locate where they were being held. Tasker had climbed all around the house, pressing his face against the windows in an effort to discover their whereabouts. Once or twice he had peered into a lighted room and narrowly avoided detection by its occupants. The arrival of the guard with his candle had provided the clue to their position, and they had given him time to settle before commencing with the glass cutting.

Dawn rose on the horizon; Lutel looked at her reflection as they followed the stream through the sleepy villages of Welford and Boxford. Even allowing for the murky and rippled water, she barely recognised the dishevelled image that stared back at her.

From the corner of her eye she caught sight of a red flash as a moorhen splashed noisily away from its dabbling in a reed bed. Clouds of dandelion seeds floated on the gentle breeze, dispersed by the heavy hooves of the horses. Crows cawing an early-morning alarm to one another from the treetops warned of the possible danger that approached. High in the saddle, Lutel surveyed the idyllic landscape; how she would love to explore the sights and scents of this country. Yes, she thought, it was the fragrances and aromas that excited her; they were clean, fresh, new. Then her mind drifted back to the reality and harshness of her situation and although the sweet odours still pervaded, she no longer noticed them.

English cut eastward towards Curridge; they should avoid Newbury at all lengths, he advised, as Laungechamp would no doubt be concentrating his search attempts on the towns. A blood-red sun rose above the hills as they crossed the River Pang at Bucklebury; turning south they passed through Midgham before meeting up with the road to London east of Thatcham.

"We must leave you now," stated English. He offered his hand to Rewn, who released his grip on the reins and extended his own hand towards

English. Rewn had never shaken a hand before and was amused by this quintessential piece of English etiquette. English repeated the action with Woodman and then rode over to Lutel.

She kissed him on the cheek. "Thank you."

"The pleasure was all mine," he said, blushing. "Your way lies east; just follow the rising sun."

He turned his horse about and cantered away to catch up with Tasker, who had already commenced his journey back to Newbury. Lutel continued to look back over her shoulder until English disappeared from view around a bend in the lane. She wiped away a tear at the thought of never seeing him again.

CHAPTER THIRTY-FIVE

The Bodies in the Barn

Fenchurch Street was unusually busy, so Revin's ignorance was extended a little longer as Verde refused to divulge the nature of his secret assignation. Diverse palliards approached them, begging for money as they scurried along the road, exposing hideous open sores. Verde dropped his shoulder, grabbed Revin's arm and jostled his way through, barging them aside. He hated himself for doing it, but there was a greater good, he told himself.

A raker was removing filth from the front of the houses. He whistled tunelessly but surprisingly cheerfully as his pile of rotting food and excrement, made slimy through the previous evening's storm, was mashed into submission by his wooden rake, before loading an oozing pile onto his rickety barrow, its wheel so exceedingly warped that it remained a wonder how it could be pushed in anything like its intended direction.

As they approached the corner of Mark Lane an old woman, bearing a white wand, was bent over a body that lay slumped against the wall of a house. She was wearing a full-length dress and a matching black conical felt hat. Around her shoulders was draped a faded ragged shawl. As the two men advanced the crone turned to face them and warned them away with a wave of her wand, and a mumbling of expletives that were impossible to discern as they were garbled through a mouth containing only one tooth. Verde looked back as they hastened by; the old pauper woman had ripped away the victim's shirt.

"Searching for signs of death," he remarked, once they were out of earshot of the old woman.

"More likely to be searching for anything of value," replied his friend cynically.

Verde stopped and yanked Revin's arm. "Are you all right?"

"Yes, fine."

Verde, jerking his head quizzically, stood his ground. Revin's gaze met Verde's and he recognised the sympathetic outlet.

"It's all becoming too much for me. I feel so helpless, so frustrated. We came here to help, yet I feel powerless… inept."

"I know, I know," agreed Verde supportively, "but we must keep going. The Stilax chose us amongst other things for our fortitude; we can't give up now. Besides, Lutel and Rewn will be here soon. In fact they might already be here, waiting for us now at The Raven."

"No, they won't," said Revin.

"If not today then soon. Lutel's pretty resourceful; she'll think of something when she comes. You must know that."

Revin perked up a little. He wasn't feeling as disconsolate as he made out; he had just needed to get a few things off his chest, and the affable figure of Verde had instantly obliged.

"I already have," said Verde, "in a small way, thought of something."

A change in countenance came over Revin; the prospect of a plan to alleviate the pain of the masses rekindled some hope.

"We'll rescue that child in Gracious Street tonight."

Revin walked briskly on. He should have known better than to suspect Verde of having egalitarian thoughts at this moment in time. Verde chased him into Seething Lane and finally drew alongside him.

"I've thought it all out." he explained. "I've taken some laudanum from Hodges' bag. We'll give some to the watchman, and Jemima will pass Jayne through a side window away from that nosy hag of a nursekeeper."

Revin began to wonder about Verde's sanity; he seemed quite fixed upon this little escapade. He searched his friend for signs of madness. "And what do you intend to do with the child once you've rescued her?"

"They've relations north of Spittlefields, near to where we landed."

"You didn't…?"

"No, of course not; do you think I'm mad?" retorted Verde, hurt at such a thought.

"No, I don't," replied Revin, relieved at only finding single-minded enthusiasm. "So that's what you were plotting when I came for Hodges' case."

"Yes. Say you'll help; I've given the mother my word."

Although somewhat reluctant to undertake such a perilous venture, Revin considered that taking such risks were preferable to doing nothing, despite their minimal impact.

"If Lutel and Rewn are not at The Raven, I'll help," he answered.

They turned left into Tower Street and walked into The Raven.

"Welcome back," Knox greeted them, reaching for a tankard. "You are the first customers I've had all day." He winked. "This plague will be the death of me."

The empty inn drew mixed emotions from the travellers. Verde appeared more than happy, whilst Revin rather sombrely refused the landlord's offer of a drink and asked for a meal to be sent up to their room. The intermediate hours were spent talking over Verde's plan for the evening. Revin had grown rather tired of hearing it, and was relieved when the landlord arrived with their meal. A tray was set down containing a large mutton pie, pieces of cold beef and a flagon of sack. Verde inhaled the aroma of the food.

"This will do fine," he said with a smile. "Please excuse our lack of socialising; we are somewhat weary."

Their host appeared not to mind; only too glad of their custom, he explained as he made his exit. Verde tore at the meat and attempted to go through his rescue plan again.

"Not now; finish your meal," sighed Revin. He poured a large measure of sack and handed it to Verde, who swiftly washed down his mouthful of food.

By the time the mutton pie had been consumed, a large quantity of drink had passed Verde's lips. He no longer spoke of his "grand plan", but now insisted on reminiscing over the "good old times" back on Mykas. Revin was beginning to think that the evening arrangements were far preferable and perhaps he had been wrong in being so liberal with the sack, now that he was forced to continually interrupt Verde, imploring him to keep his voice down lest they be overheard.

Slowly the crisp sunny shadows of the day made way for the penumbra of the moon. Revin reached for the last of the sack. Verde snatched it from him.

"No, we're going to need this."

"I know. I was merely removing it to a safer place."

Revin looked through the mullioned window at the dark blue sky; night was nearly upon them.

"It's time," he announced. "Do you still want to go through with this?"

"Try stopping me." Verde stood up and fell over his own feet.

Revin helped him up. "Perhaps I should have said 'are you still up for this?'"

"I'm fine, just fine. I just need some fresh air."

Verde leant on Revin's shoulder as the pair made their way to the door.

"Wait here," instructed Revin as he propped Verde against the door frame, and walked back to collect the near-empty flagon of sack.

Revin directed his friend along the short corridor, and as they reached the top of the staircase Verde grasped the banister and tentatively swung one foot forward.

"Quietly," Revin urged him. "We mustn't wake the landlord."

"Or his good lady," slurred Verde. "It's all right; you can let me go. I'll be quiet."

Verde's foot dangled in mid-air, and he confidently aimed it at the next stair. Revin winced as his partner completely missed his footing and fell on to his backside before sliding all the way down the stairs, finally crumpling in a heap at the bottom. Revin rushed to his aid and checked him for any sign of injury, whilst nervously glancing around for the potential arrival of the landlord and his wife. Fortunately the pair had great confidence in their wares, and the crashing down the stairs had been no more than a minor impediment to their evening slumbers.

Relieved at their solitude, Revin smiled at Verde. "If that's what you call quiet, I should hate to hear the noisy version!"

"It's all right," said Verde, "the fall's sobered me up. I'll be fine now."

Indeed such was the shock that Verde now showed no apparent sign of his imbibing, and as if to prove his point he took the flagon from Revin and marched out of the inn.

Once more they made their way to Gracious Street. Under the cover of darkness the emptiness of the roads took on a bleak eeriness. Only the occasional watchman broke their nocturnal isolation, offering any form of companionship. Verde noted that many doors were now painted with red crosses, but very few were guarded; there was no longer the need. Several church clocks announced that the hour of ten fell short by a quarter, and more importantly the watchman of the morning would soon be relieved of his post. Verde emptied a few drops into the flagon of sack and shook it. He left Revin standing in the shadows and walked towards a doorway.

"Evening, friend," offered Verde.

The startled watchman fixed his halberd.

"You're no pissin' friend of mine," he snarled. "Piss off, or I'll run you through."

"If that's how you want it," replied Verde, backtracking. "I only came to share a night-cap with you. I thought you might be thirsty on guard here all through the hot day and into the warm night. Besides, I was here this morning and I didn't like the way you were treated."

Verde's tone was now very conciliatory, and had the desired effect. The watchman lowered his weapon.

"But I'll be on my way then," Verde added, "if that's what you wish."

"That fat bastard better watch who he's pushing around. If the sod comes near me again he'll be short of a prick. I'll hang it on my halberd like a sausage."

Verde, laughing at the image, held out the flagon of sack. The watchman snatched it from him and took a large swig.

"Do you meet with much violence?" asked Verde.

"Most bloody dangerous job in England… what's yer name?"

"Verde."

"Most bloody dangerous job in England, Verde." The watchman belched loudly and offered the flagon back.

"No, no, your need is greater than mine, ah…?"

"Matthew, Matthew Denchworth."

"Drink, Matthew, drink," Verde encouraged him.

Denchworth looked suspiciously at Verde and then at the flagon, but his thirst was stronger than any doubts that he harboured. He sat down with his back against a wall and Verde joined him. Denchworth took another large quaff and the contents dribbled down the sides of his mouth. Verde prayed the wastage would not be significant.

"There was a watch down Newgate, name of Neeld. Bastards blew him up with gunpowder. I'd have run the bastards through, or better still tied their pricks to a barrel-load of the stuff."

Verde winced and fervently hoped that he not only had guessed the correct dosage, but would never experience the delights that the watchman envisaged.

Denchworth paused for another few swigs. "I should say ten, maybe twenty watchmen have been killed this plague, and for what? Seven lousy bloody shillings a week. I'd rather let the poor sods inside go."

"Would you?" enquired Verde, somewhat taken aback.

"Would I piss; no bastard in their right mind would come anywhere near me and my weapon." At this Denchworth whirled his halberd in a circular motion above his head, then returned his attention to the sack. "Sorry, friend, it seems to have all gone."

"No matter," answered Verde. "Have you ever been attacked, Matthew?"

"No, not me. I'd stick any bastard who tried it on me. A watch down the road from me was shot last month."

"Did you see it?"

"'Course I pissin' seen it."

"What happened?"

"Bastards got clean away, all three of 'em."

"Didn't you give chase?"

"No, no, not me; I'm paid to stick at me post. If I do leave to do an errand for the house this here key goes with me." Denchworth proudly showed Verde the key hanging around his neck, as though he were displaying a medal of war.

"Don't they ever offer you money?" asked Verde with a wink.

"Bribes? Me take bribes? Never," said Matthew in an unconvincing astonished tone.

"Go on," said Verde, and he nudged the watchman in the side with his elbow.

Denchworth reciprocated the nudge. "Let's say I do the poxy bastards the occasional favour, like relieve them of some gift. But" – he paused to laugh – "they don't always get what they're paying for, stupid sods."

Denchworth, contorting with laughter, threw his head back so far that it cracked against the wall as he pictured the mean tricks that he had pulled on his innocent frightened plague victims.

"Desperate people know no bounds; they'll believe and sacrifice anything," he said, grinning.

Revin began to grow impatient in the shadows and shuffled in his doorway.

Denchworth sprang bolt upright.

"Who's there?" he cried, fixing his halberd. "You got somebody with you?"

"No, what makes you think that?"

The watchman pointed his halberd as if to charge the invisible Revin, then turned threateningly on Verde. "You have, you lying…"

Verde never found out what colourful noun Denchworth was about to label him as the laudanum finally took effect on the watchman, and he collapsed to the ground, his halberd falling harmlessly at his side.

Verde put his arms around Denchworth's body and dragged him towards the seclusion of the doorway. "Gather up some small pebbles," he ordered the approaching Revin.

"Why?"

"Just do it."

By the time the unconscious man was propped against the door, Revin had collected a handful of small stones, and handed them over. Walking around to the side of the house, Verde threw a cluster at an upper window. They made a noise like the spattering of hailstones against the glass. Inside Jemima had been eagerly anticipating their arrival. Shortly a window several feet above the ground opened and Jayne appeared, wearing a long white night-shirt, with a heavy dark grey blanket wrapped around her shoulders.

The small trembling waif looked like a tortured spirit, as her mother held her close to her body and tenderly kissed her forehead for the final time. Jayne clung to her mother, but a remonstrating word in her ear saw the grip released. Jemima summoned up her failing strength, and the frail figure lifted her daughter and delivered her out of the window to the waiting arms of Verde below. His arms were held aloft, but he managed to cradle the child and support her weight until Revin was able to take her legs and lift her down to the ground. He rearranged the blanket that had become loose in the manoeuvre.

"Shoes," hissed Verde.

Jemima was well-prepared; she bent down, momentarily disappearing from sight, then threw down a pair of child's boots.

"Will you come?" Verde urged her.

The woman looked torn, but instantly replied, "No, it is as we agreed; I must look to Isaac."

For the second time Revin and Verde witnessed complete devotion to a partner – a love that would almost certainly result in the ultimate sacrifice.

Verde cradled the small girl in his arms and tears filled her eyes as she gazed at her mother for the last time. Jemima threw her daughter a kiss as the church clock of Saint Bennet struck ten, and from around the corner the relief watch arrived. As fate would deem it, Sol Speke was accompanied by one of the parish constables, returning from a meeting of the parish officials. The sleeping figure of Denchworth and the disturbance at the side of the house instantly seized their attention. Speke rushed at Revin with his halberd. Revin nimbly skipped aside and grabbed the weapon, pushing the horizontal halberd along with Speke back into the path of the parish constable. Verde had already taken flight with the girl, and he carried her through the now-familiar territory towards the Royal Exchange.

At the junction of Cornhill and Gracious Street stood a water conduit supply. It was damp and covered in green slime and also the home of several rats, but from behind the wooden construction Verde and Jayne watched Revin race off towards Threadneedle Street, pursued by the two men.

Verde lifted one of Jayne's feet and rested it on his lap. "Are you all right to walk?" he asked kindly, whilst easing her feet into her boots.

The girl didn't answer.

"It will help me. It will help your mother."

In answer the frightened girl stood up. Verde took her hand and led her swiftly along Bishopsgate Street.

The chilly night air was a welcome relief, cooling Revin's sweaty brow as he raced blindly into the night through a series of alleys. Finding himself in Broad Street, he stopped to listen for footsteps and dived into the nearest alleyway. His pursuers came to a halt at the entrance of the alley; he placed a hand over his mouth in fear that they would hear his heavy breathing.

"I can't run any further, Banyon," wheezed Speke.

The constable, although not young, was several years younger and not so keen to give up the chase. "You go on back to Silke's. I'll search a little longer; they're out here somewhere. That child will slow them down."

The watchman trailed off to resume his post. Banyon made to go in the opposite direction, when a cat raced past Revin and shot out at the head of the alley, drawing the constable's attention. Such was the blackness that Revin remained invisible. Unheedful of this fact, Revin decided to take no chances and hared off in the opposite direction, only to stumble into a rut. He grimaced as a pain shot through his right ankle, but hauling himself up limped speedily across Broad Street and into Lothbury.

Like many of his breed, the constable proved tenacious, and even though he was in middle age, he kept Revin firmly in his sights as he followed at a distance.

Revin made his way to the Guildhall and crouched on the steps, sitting at the base of a pillar which had seen many things in its time, but never before a Mykasian examining his foot. Although it wasn't broken the ankle had ballooned badly, and Revin felt sick with the throbbing pain. He looked up for inspiration and stared straight into the eyes of the parish constable.

Banyon bent over Revin as a cat might toy with a bird before making the telling swipe.

"Up you get, you pisspot, it's the magistrate for you. Helping plaguers escape – a whipping at least, or probably worse. It would go for you if you told me the whereabouts of your accomplice."

Revin did not answer, but stared into the twinkling sky.

"They say if you go into Newgate you don't walk out."

Banyon stood back waiting for his threats to take effect. He interpreted Revin's silence as an act of submission and continued his taunting.

"Never see the light of day again, or the black of night come to that. Now that little missy can't be worth all that, surely." He leered.

Banyon bent down in order to make his arrest; as he did so, Revin felt the plinth of the pillar below him. He placed his hands behind his back and pushed up with all his strength, grunting at the pressure that he put on his weak ankle. As he shot skywards the top of his head smashed into Banyon's face and an ominous crack boomed out as the parish constable's nose split wide open down its bridge. The man fell backwards as if pole-axed, his head hitting the ground with a sickening thud. Blood gushed from his nose and for a brief moment Revin was stricken with guilt, and stooped to attend to the man's injuries, but a cry from along the road persuaded him otherwise.

Limping badly, he hobbled around the Guildhall; in the distance he could see the towering shape of the London wall, and he tottered towards it. He leant against the towering structure and paused for breath, then staggered along its base, taking great pains to avoid the guards at Moorgate, and moved on towards Bishopsgate.

Verde was the first to see the shuffling figure skulking along in the shadows. Still holding Jayne's timid hand he moved towards it. "What happened to you?"

"Just twisted my ankle, it's nothing," muttered Revin, wincing, "but I've a rather nasty headache." He rubbed the top of his head and felt a tell-tale lump, then looked towards the huge wooden gate and the two guards below it. "What do you suggest now, Verde?"

"No problem. Their task is to stop people from entering."

Revin did not look at all convinced; he had allowed himself to be talked in to the evening's escapade and so far he had good cause to regret it. Verde saw the wave of doubt roll across his friend's face.

"Just to make sure, I've offered them a little something to hasten our departure." Verde patted his waist and a jingle of coins revealed his confidence. "And if we are back at the same hour tomorrow night, they'll let us back in."

"But that makes you no better…" Revin did not continue; he felt his head, and his ankle was far worse than he had at first imagined. "You have been busy," he acknowledged.

A guard pulled back two large bolts that fastened the gate; his companion gave Verde a knowing look as they sauntered through.

"Tomorrow night," Verde reminded him.

"Don't be late," growled the guard.

The hunter's moon beamed brightly from the sky. They made their way north-eastward towards Spittlefields. Jemima had given Verde directions but in the dark, landmarks were hard to distinguish.

"We should pass two farms on this road," commented Verde, running through the instructions out loud to convince himself of their accuracy. "At the second we turn right in front of it, and follow a track for half a mile until we come to a thatched cottage. Jemima's brother is a labourer on the second farm," he added by way of explanation.

Jayne was shivering and trembling, through a combination of the cool night air and the traumatic change in her circumstances. Verde lifted her up and carried her over his shoulder, several times stumbling on rocks or potholes, but never losing his grip on the tiny girl. As they left the city walls behind them the land became more and more open, and signs of the changing environment started to emerge. A barn owl flew overhead, its white chest ghosting silently past them. In the distance a dog fox barked to its mate, startling Jayne, and she began to cry. Verde put her down and placed a comforting hand on her shoulders.

"I want my mother," she cried.

"We're taking you somewhere safe," Verde soothed her. "Your mother will join you there as soon as she is able." But he couldn't look the young girl in the face as he spoke the final words. He clasped Jayne to his chest and she sobbed uncontrollably.

"We must rest," he muttered to Revin. "How's your foot?"

"I seem to have walked it off," then, looking at Jayne, "but I dare say a rest would be most welcome. Besides, we cannot call on her family at this late hour. If they are farming folk they will probably set the dogs on us." Revin strained his eyes and peered into the distance; moths flitted in the moonbeams searching for evening nectar, but in the distance a range of small triangular shapes puzzled him. Unusual trees, he mused. "How far are we from the ship?"

Verde shrugged his shoulders. "It's further north than here, but we will never find it in this light. I think there is an outbuilding in the corner of this field," he observed, pointing along the hedgerow.

Dry twigs snapped under their feet as they stumbled along a track that followed the course of the hedge. Within a few minutes they had reached a cow byre, the inside smelling of stale hay mixed with the unmistakable odour of cow dung. Revin felt inside his clothing and pulled out his strike-a-light. After several attempts he was able to light a small pile of hay, which in turn briefly illuminated a clean pile in the far corner of the otherwise filthy farm hovel. Revin had begun to make his way towards their intended bed when it suddenly moved. Jayne let out a piercing scream as two heads poked through the hay.

"We're doin' no 'arm, masters, please let us stay," begged a voice.

Two round ruddy faces with half-closed eyes and dust-filled hair looked up from their rough bed. The flames flickered and died, but by now Revin and Verde's eyes had become more accustomed to the darkness of the byre.

"Who are you?" asked Verde authoritatively, realising that he held the upper hand.

"I'm Swallow and this is my brother Robin," answered one of the men. "We've nowhere to sleep since our master didn't have need of us."

"Up and left us," added Robin, hoping to add some substance to their argument.

"Soon as the distemper came they fled for the country," added his brother. "Had no further need for the likes of us."

Verde, deciding that the brothers offered them no danger, dropped his officious manner.

"We mean you no harm; like yourselves we only seek shelter for the night. This is Revin," and he pointed at his friend. "This young lady is Jayne, and I am called Verde."

"Well, join us," offered Swallow. "We thought you were that miserable devil of a farmer come to throw us out. His cows have no need of this byre in the summer, yet 'e sets 'is dogs on us whenever 'e catches us 'ere."

Swallow and Robin rearranged the hay; they shook it around and tossed it over, scattering it across a wider area. Verde placed Jayne beside him and Revin settled the other side of the girl. He buried himself deeper, trying to find a comfortable position; the hay irritated his exposed face and the dust made his nose itch. It's not quite the same as Hodges' bed, he thought, and he turned to say as much to Verde but found that he was the only one left awake. Dust from the hay caused him to sneeze and his mind wandered back to the time of his youth.

For four summers in succession he had worked on his uncle's farm helping out with the harvest. On balmy nights as a special treat, Revin and his cousins were allowed to sleep out in the large storehouses before the buildings bulged with the season's gatherings. The day would start early with his aunt waking them from their slumbers.

"What's for breakfast, AT 1?" he would ask eagerly.

After washing they would throw on their old clothes and devour a huge breakfast before racing down to the lake carrying a cumbersome bundle under their arms. At the lakeside they would find a convenient bush and presently emerge in a glinting gold suit. The skin-tight clothing would cover them from neck to toe, completed by a matching helmet and visor. Around the waist they wore a sparkling silver belt, held by a silver clasp. When this was pressed small pulses were emitted, and as the boys swam through the water the small silver particles shed by the vyanies were attracted to the golden suits.

When Revin felt that he could swim no further he hauled himself from the lake and staggered to one of the large drying rooms. Standing in a square container that came up to his knees, he pressed the clasp for a second time and the sparklies fell from their golden backdrop. Revin scooped them up in his hands and placed them on a circular conveyor belt where a continual current of warm air blew them dry. Within a few hours the sparklies were ready for storing in open pots almost as tall as Revin himself. Some were sold, others kept for use in the family's own drinks. Revin recalled another favourite pastime – collecting rallip berries for the vyanies. The red berries contained a wide variety of vitamins and minerals and were not only fed to some of the livestock but also used in a health drink, believed by their elders to cure a range of aches and pains.

Revin remembered the long hard work of picking the rallip berries by hand and placing them in baskets, before they were loaded on to small trailers and taken back to the largest store barns. Rallip berries were a viable cash crop, being in wide demand from farmers as a staple diet for their vyanies over the winter. The rallip barns were full of fruity smells and Revin loved sleeping rough in one of the lofts after a tiring day in the fields. How they would scare one another with tales of giant vyanies in the lake or the ghosts of old farm workers haunting the barns, until everyone in the barn had fallen asleep – apart from Revin; things hadn't changed much, he consoled himself.

Part Seven

The Murder of Crows

CHAPTER THIRTY-SIX

A MURDER OF CROWS

Shafts of sunlight seared into the barn as the dawn chorus sang sweetly outside. Stretching his stiff body Revin rose from his makeshift bed. Verde held a protective arm around Jayne whilst the two brothers whistled and snored from under the hay.

Walking to the edge of the building Revin peered out across the horizon; a large black bird was perched on the roof and it cawed wickedly before flapping away over the fields. Revin followed its flight, and as it skimmed the hedgerows his eyes were drawn to his bewilderment of the previous evening. He could now see clearly in the strong sunlight that which the soft light of the moon had failed to reveal. In the distance stood a tented city – a variety of temporary homes spread across the field as far as the eye could see. Some were little more than sheets or blankets fixed crudely over branches of wood. Already a few people were wandering around aimlessly in his view.

Revin felt a presence behind him and turned to face Swallow. "Who are those people?"

Swallow peered out from under his mane of red hair, his eyes squinting in the bright light, his freckled complexion revealing that he had spent many hours in the sun. "Them?" He scoffed. "Them's like us. Folk that have nowhere to stay in the city."

"Why don't they go elsewhere?" enquired Revin innocently.

Swallow snorted and raked his fingers through his tousled locks. "Same reason as you and me; they ain't welcome in any other town or village, so some do live in tents, those that are lucky that is. Others sleep in the hedges or trees, or take a risk like us and spend a night in a farm dwelling hoping they won't be caught."

Revin noticed that before Swallow started to speak he swallowed deeply. He had not noticed it in the dark, but now he clearly saw Swallow's protruding Adam's apple sliding up and down before each sentence commenced. It had earned him his nickname as an adolescent, now so familiar that he had even taken to calling himself by the sobriquet.

Revin walked back inside the byre. Squatting down on his haunches he gently shook his friend awake. Verde slowly opened his eyes, carefully extricating himself from the sleeping child. His effort proved fruitless as the young girl began to wake. Swallow had not shown the same compassionate qualities, and had firmly kicked his brother in order to achieve a similar effect. Whilst the three late risers stretched their aching bodies, Swallow was able to confirm the whereabouts of Jayne's relations.

"Can you take us there?" asked Revin.

Swallow looked a little sheepish, and stared away over the fields. "'Tis easy to find; as I said, just over this hedge, across the field and on through the wood. It will bring you out on the track that you want."

"Couldn't you show us the way?" pleaded Revin, conscious of the time that the hastily-made offer was now costing them.

Swallow peered at Revin with his large brown eyes. The stranger looked trusting but his own survival instincts had heightened of late, and he wasn't prepared to take unnecessary risks.

"I'll take you as far as the track," he offered.

"Thank you," replied Revin, clapping his guide on the back.

Swallow peered over his shoulder, watched Revin disappear into the byre, and then gazed out once more on to the tented field as he was joined by his brother. Robin was a smaller version of his elder brother; although he lacked the idiosyncratic throat movement he didn't remain totally unblemished, as any strong light caused him to flutter his eyes even to the extent of constantly squinting. This mannerism had not been seized upon by any kin, kith or peer and, unlike his brother, Robin kept the name that he had been given at birth.

Swallow led the small bedraggled party along the hedgerow; hips and haw berries shone brightly in the morning sun and goldfinches twittered and flew around them, scolding their disturbance. A wooden stile covered in orange lichen led them into the adjoining field. Verde wiped his hand on his clothes to remove the mossy particles before helping Jayne. The field was full of meadow flowers; yellow buttercups, red poppies, brilliant blue cornflowers, white moon daisies all vying with each other to create a patchwork of bright colours as far as the eye could see.

Excited by the long grasses and plants Jayne forgot her present troubles and skipped ahead of them, sending seeds scattering and a myriad of butterflies to seek calmer shelter. The flowers tickled her legs and she shrieked with delight as she raced across the field. Robin allowed his childish nature to become enveloped by Jayne's frolics and chased after her, whooping loudly. Jayne quickened her pace, screaming even more excitedly as Robin closed in, trampling over the late summer flowers in his boyish pursuit.

Jayne had reached the middle of the field when in front of her a flock of large black birds took to the air, raucously cawing their annoyance at her intrusion. Halting abruptly she let out a piercing scream. The birds flapped noisily away to seek protection in the direction of the adjoining wood, where, from lofty boughs, they could stand guard waiting for the trespassers to vacate their field. Robin was first to reach the distraught girl's side but she continued to howl.

"Come on," he said, "no need to be frightened by those old crows."

His attempts to placate the distressed Jayne all failed and he stood uncertain at her side. Verde arrived running, alarmed by the girl's behaviour and concerned that it might attract unwanted attention. He picked Jayne up and lifted her so that her face was level with his. Jayne ceased screaming and instead sobbed uncontrollably on his shoulder.

"'Tis only birds," said Robin, pointing at the sentinels in the treetops.

"It wasn't the birds that startled her," said Revin.

Robin turned and followed Revin's reasoning. Lying in the grass, half-hidden by the wild flowers, was the body of a youth. He was dressed in the clothes of a servant and could not have been much older than Jayne. He lay on his back staring skywards, but the beauty of the azure sky was lost for ever on him. In the middle of his unrecognisable face were two bloody hollows. The birds had pecked out his eyes. In several places his clothes were torn where his body had been eaten by various visitors, the birds being only the most recent to take advantage of the free meal. A large number of bluebottles buzzed around the open wounds, settling more comfortably since the birds' departure.

"Poor sod," said Swallow.

Revin moved closer to inspect the body.

"No, stay back!" shouted Swallow. "Many as die of the distemper are left in the fields, country folk won't touch 'em – nor for that matter will I, so they lie unburied. Dogs and foxes ain't that fussy, they'll take a meal wherever they can find one."

A squeamish Robin looked over Revin's shoulder. "Sometimes they ain't quite dead when the birds do come, so I bin told. Peck out their eyes whilst they're still alive, so I've heard."

Robin turned to see if his words were having their desired effect on Revin.

"That's enough," said Verde. "The girl's been through more than many of older years could stomach."

"Even so," continued Robin, "'tis a terrible way to die – murdered by crows."

Revin stepped forward so that Robin's head fell from its perch on his shoulder.

"Funny, though," added Swallow. "Reminds me of the old inn on the hill. Many a happy hour I've spent drinking there. What I wouldn't give now to be downing a flagon of ale at The Murder of Crows."

Revin and Verde looked at each other.

"What hill?" asked Verde urgently.

Swallow, excited by the unexpected concern his statement had caused, gave an extra-long swallow, testing the listeners' patience, before answering.

"The hill up from London Bridge."

Revin and Verde spoke as one. "We've been waiting at the wrong inn!"

"Where exactly is this inn?" asked Verde.

Swallow stared at him.

"You come from the city, yet you've never heard of The Murder of Crows?" He snorted.

Verde felt the all-too-familiar feeling of discomfort creeping up his back, but such was Swallow's excitement at being able to impart his knowledge that he did not follow up his perceptive observation.

"Just up from the bridge," he replied, "on the north side of the Thames, you know, up Fish Street Hill."

Verde managed to communicate a silent signal to Revin, warning him to conceal his excitement at this revealing piece of information. Jayne, meanwhile, had recovered her composure and they walked on towards the woods and the ever-impatient crows, which Revin now viewed in a fresh light.

Revin's head was still swimming with thoughts as they approached the fringes of the wood. How good it would be to see Lutel and Rewn again and hear their tale. Would they have the antidote with them? Even if they didn't, they would soon be off on their return journey to Mykas. Such thoughts engrossed Revin that he was oblivious to the speckled wood butterflies skimming past the hazel trees as they entered the wood. Their chocolate-brown wings were as invisible to his far-off eyes as his ears were deaf to the "cuck" of the parting cuckoo indicating its imminent departure from this plague-ridden land. The fragrant scent of the white dog rose never registered with his nose. The wrong inn, he kept telling himself over and over again. How could they have been so stupid? He should have guessed there could have been more than one inn associated with black birds. They had been so excited and sure of themselves once they had stumbled across The Raven that no other possibility had ever entered their heads.

No, he told himself, how could they have known? It wasn't their fault the scout ships had provided insufficient information. He cheered himself up with this latest line of thought and turned to imagining happier times. What would Lutel and Rewn say when they turned up after all this time? Rewn would feign displeasure, then laugh, keeping up a constant barrage of jokes and teasing at their expense. Lutel would be more practical. She would be displeased at the mix-up, but delighted that they were all united safely and able to proceed. But perhaps they weren't waiting for them; maybe he and Verde would still be the first to arrive. His thoughts again turned darker. What if Lutel and Rewn had arrived at the meeting place days ago? They may have grown impatient and left, assuming something untoward had happened to him and Verde. These agonising thoughts continued to circle around Revin's head until they at last stumbled out into a clearing that formed part of an old drover's track. Swallow and Robin stopped.

"To your right is the farm," said Swallow, pointing, "and that way is the cottage I believe you are seeking."

"Will you not accompany us?" asked Revin, snapping back to reality.

"Our way lies yonder," said Robin, gesturing towards the farm. "We must find our breakfast," he added with a wink.

Swallow blushed, his red face matching his hair.

"I'm sure Jayne's aunt would provide you with some eggs or even a breakfast," said Verde.

"You think so?" asked Swallow.

Jayne looked at Verde. Her wide eyes began to water.

"Revin and I must urgently return to the city," Verde explained.

"To tell my parents that I am arrived safely?"

Verde felt awkward; lying had never come naturally to him, especially to children. He paused and knelt down to face Jayne; he stared into her trusting eyes. "The next time I see your mother, the very first thing I will say to her is that you are safe with your aunt and uncle."

"And Papa?" Jayne peered into Verde's kind eyes and saw nothing beyond honesty. "Please tell them I love them, and will they come and collect me as soon as Papa is better? I should like that very much."

Verde could make no answer. He stood up and spoke to Swallow.

"Promise me you'll see her safely to her aunt's."

Swallow looked at Robin; previous indiscretions were coming to the surface.

"We will," replied the younger brother, "but it's only a short walk from here."

Verde walked up to Swallow and taking him to one side addressed him out of earshot of the others.

"We have urgent business in the city," he whispered. "This is for your troubles, and if you can see that that poor soul in the field has a decent burial I would be more than grateful." He pressed a coin into the other's hand.

Swallow furtively examined his spoils.

"Both will be done," he promised. "I give you my word."

Revin and Verde made ready to depart, Jayne ran up to them and threw her arms around Verde. He picked her up and she kissed him on the left cheek.

"That's for my mother," she said, and then repeated the action on his other cheek, "and that's for Papa." Then she kissed Verde tenderly on the forehead. "And that's for you."

Verde kissed her forehead. "Take care," he whispered.

He placed her back on the ground; Swallow and Robin took a hand each and they set off down the track, Jayne continually glancing over her shoulder. Revin and Verde stood and watched as the trio rounded a bend. Jayne released her grip from Swallow and waved farewell. Verde returned the gesture and wiped his cheek. He had grown very fond of the young girl in the short time that he had known her; she reminded him of someone back on Mykas.

"Do you think she'll be all right?" asked Revin.

Verde sighed. "She'd have had little or no chance if we hadn't rescued her. Out here things do seem a little better."

"Let's go and increase her odds, then," said Revin.

"What do you mean?"

Revin gave Verde an exasperated look. "Find Lutel and Rewn, of course!"

As they retraced their steps of the morning and previous evening they fervently discussed the upcoming meeting with Lutel and Rewn. Verde was relieved to be able to articulate his thoughts and soon their conversation turned to arguing the reasons for inoculation and the case against mass vaccination; their plan of action seemed to change as many times as there were species of trees around them.

Revin had even planned a celebratory meal and mapped out a rousing speech culminating in a congratulatory toast, before settling in for a relaxing evening's drink, during which they could swap tales of their time on Earth. For their part there would be much to tell – their time at the noble and warm-hearted Gatleigh's, the unscrupulous Priddy, a meeting with the Lord Mayor, the redoubtable Doctor Hodges and now this most recent adventure with Jayne. Revin suggested that they pass the time surmising what tales Lutel and Rewn would have to tell, always supposing that Rewn was bound to have a more exciting and unbelievable episode to relate. They laughed heartily at Rewn's expense but there was a renewed spring in their stride, and before they realised it they were once more on the outskirts of the city, and the scorching sun had yet to reach its highest point of the day.

As they sauntered past Bedlam Hospital their thoughts returned to the present.

"Your friendly guard will not be on duty until tonight," said Revin.

"Let's move closer and see."

Keeping to the cover of the overhanging houses where even the glaring low September sun could not penetrate, they reached within fifty yards of the great wall. Verde stopped and grabbed Revin's arm.

"We're in luck," he chortled. "He must have changed his shift."

Revin followed the line of Verde's nod; to the left of the gate stood a tall man. "I don't recognise him."

"But you never spoke to him face to face."

"Are you positive?"

"Of course; besides, if I am wrong and they refuse us entry, we can come back this evening."

Verde led the way across to the gate; as he approached the guard moved forward in recognition.

"We were quicker than we expected," explained Verde. Revin felt uncomfortable as he caught the guard staring at him, but the gaze was withdrawn the instant their eyes met.

"Another sweltering day," added Verde. "Those rains didn't last long; you must find it difficult standing in the heat for so long."

The guard grunted a reply and Revin's uneasiness grew. He was about to suggest to Verde that he must be mistaken, and that they come back later in the day, when the guard flourished a signal to his accomplice at the gate and the large heavy door was opened. Verde strode through the portal, followed by a relieved Revin. Once inside the city walls Bishopsgate closed behind them with a noisy thud. Revin quickened his pace in order to catch up with Verde, but before he could do so a voice came from the wall behind him.

"That's the man, arrest him!"

From both sides of Revin armed guards appeared as if from nowhere. His arms were grasped and he was held firmly in the grip of two men, whilst a third confronted him with a halberd under his nose. A tall thin man approached from under the foot of the wall, and circled around to face Revin.

"Yes, this is the man," said the parish constable, and he signalled to a wagon. "Take him away."

Verde looked back helplessly as Revin was bundled into a cart, flanked either side by two armed soldiers. Apart from being outnumbered, the action had taken place so quickly and unexpectedly that his friend was in no position to come to his aid. The constable climbed up alongside the driver, a whip was cracked over two black horses and the cart rapidly disappeared down Bevis Marks.

Bishopsgate creaked open and the guard walked in; his duty over, he sidled up to Verde.

"Sorry," he said. "They threatened to cut out my tongue if I didn't help."

A soldier appeared to one side of the guard. "We still might," he said, and he made to march the guard away.

"Where will they take…" Verde paused and carefully concluded, "that man?"

"Do you know him?" quizzed the soldier.

"No," lied Verde.

It didn't sound convincing, and Verde knew it, but the soldier had his prisoner and, although he suspected Verde's involvement, he was not going to risk losing the one prisoner in the attempt to arrest a second.

"Then it shouldn't bother you. He's taken where we are going: the Tower."

The soldier turned smartly around and escorted his prisoner along the road that had recently witnessed the disappearance of Revin.

CHAPTER THIRTY-SEVEN

THE MURDER OF CROWS

Verde decided not to follow. He knew the whereabouts of the Tower in any case. Instead he walked along Bishopsgate Street and down through Gracious Street – the cause of their present predicament. Remembering his promise, he wondered whether to call on Jayne's family, but decided that there was little to gain from so doing, and it was possible he would be walking into trouble. He carried on, crossing Canning Street and down Fish Street Hill. Here he cursed their luck; they had passed so closely to this spot several times whilst out with Hodges on his rounds. He walked down the hill towards London Bridge, stopping a third of the way down the street. Set a little way back from the road, so that it was slightly obscured from view, was a large timber-framed building. A sign hung above the door depicting a stook of corn, above which flew seven black birds. Painted in bold red letters at the bottom of the sign was the inn's name: The Murder of Crows.

Verde walked through the doorway with mixed feelings, entering a room that was thick with acrid tobacco smoke. Discoloured pale green walls were interspersed with burnished wooden beams, generating an ambience of faded elegance. Several locals sat around scattered tables supping ale whilst talking and laughing noisily, as though oblivious to the peril that lurked outside. The haze of smoke made his eyes water and added to the difficulty of perceiving anything or anybody in the room. He was about to go outside when a voice shouted from a corner table.

"Verde! Verde! How are you? Where's Revin?"

There was no mistaking Lutel, welcoming and to the point. As the fug momentarily cleared from above the table a man stood up.

"Hello, Rewn," said Verde. "Revin's in the Tower," and he collapsed on to the floor.

A spider was dangling from a silken thread, as Verde opened his eyes and stared at the high-beamed ceiling. The roof reached its apex directly above him, and the spider was hanging just above his nose. He blew gently to test that he was awake; the spider swung gently, oscillating on its long swing like a miniature pendulum. A cool sensation soothed his burning forehead, and he reached up and touched a wet cloth that was lying across his aching brow. From the shadows a figure drew closer to the bed.

"How are you feeling?" enquired Lutel.

"Don't ask," he replied groggily. Apart from his throbbing head, a searing pain shot down either side of his nose.

"You'll live," continued Lutel, paying little attention to her patient's complaints. "Here, drink this," and she offered him a spoonful of posset from a round clay pot, consisting of a tangy mixture of wine, milk and herbs.

"Ugh," complained Verde as he tasted the spicy concoction.

"Swallow it," ordered Lutel. "It's the best Rewn could find in the circumstances."

"Yes, they are rather primitive," observed Verde, lifting himself up by placing his arms behind him and pushing against the bed.

"Lie down," Lutel commanded him; "you need the rest. I've examined you as thoroughly as I was able and all you are suffering from is mental exhaustion – though I can't think what you can have been doing to cause it. We're the ones who should be suffering, not you."

"What happened to you?" asked Verde. "We saw your ship disappear from the screen and didn't know what to think."

"We crash-landed about a hundred miles west from here; the ship's finished. We made our way across country, but we were detained a few times on the way." Her eyes clouded as her thoughts drifted back to English. "Eventually we acquired some horses and rode to the outskirts of the city; there we sold the horses and made our way here on foot."

"How long have you been here?"

"Three days."

Verde laughed ironically. "We are… were no more than two streets away, just around the corner," he sighed, as he thought of Revin.

A knock came at the door.

"Who's that?" cried Verde anxiously.

"One of the reasons for our delay."

Woodman poked his head around the door.

"Come in, John."

Woodman stepped forward and grunted. "Good to see you're olright, sir."

"Thank you…"

"Woodman, John Woodman at your service. Come to help with the fires."

"Woodman!" hissed Lutel.

"Sorry, sorry," he said. "Your friend don't know?"

"I'm more concerned that anyone behind that door will," she scolded him, glancing towards the passage. "It's surprising who you find listening at doors."

Woodman coloured, but the interplay was lost on Verde, though not the talk on fires.

"What does he mean, fires?"

"Later, you need to rest. Don't go upsetting yourself again." Lutel placed a hand on either side of his shoulders and gently pushed him downward into the pillow, like a mother placing her newborn babe to sleep.

A board creaked outside the room. Lutel froze; surely her little analogy was not going to prove true. Verde again sat upright in his bed. Woodman picked up the medicinal jug and held it above his head, waiting expectantly behind the door. He just managed to restrain himself from crashing it down on the arrival's head.

"Mind you don't spill that," said Rewn, mock-oblivious. "I went to a lot of time and trouble, not to mention the expense."

Woodman replaced the jug and the tension eased, whilst Rewn closed the door and walked over to his two compatriots.

"I've paid for another room," he announced, "and I've made a few discreet enquiries about the Tower. If Revin is in there it's going to take a fair amount of planning to release him. Longfellow says prisoners that are taken there are either hanged or forgotten about."

"Let's hope Revin falls into the latter category or we will have to work fast," said Lutel.

Now that he had awoken, Lutel took the opportunity to further examine Verde. She examined his eyes, and probed various parts of her patient's anatomy.

"As I suspected, a good rest will soon put you to rights; nothing more serious than a severe case of exhaustion."

Much to his indignation, Woodman was delegated the task of nursing Verde. His excitement about torching London would ensure his loyalty and continued presence, argued Lutel. A plentiful supply of food and a sensible amount of ale were brought up to the room, in order to ensure Woodman stayed put and his utterances would be free from all ears apart from Verde's.

Lutel and Rewn made their way down Fish Street Hill and turned left at the water that gave Thames Street its name. When they reached the Tower they stared up at its forbidding grey walls, surrounded by its imposing moat.

"Gives you a stiff neck just looking at it," observed Rewn.

Lutel played with her hair as she pondered the problem that confronted them.

"There's no way we can breach those defences by brute force; it will have to be guile. There's nothing more we can do here; let's move before anyone becomes suspicious."

They retraced their steps but when they reached Fish Hill Street, they headed in the opposite direction towards London Bridge, preferring to talk over their ideas away from the confines of the inn and the possibility of being spied on. Besides, suggested Rewn, they didn't want to excite Verde any further, and it would be wisest to present their plans as a fait accompli as soon as he was strong enough.

The bridge was home to a multitude of houses and shops, there being no uniformity to the size of the buildings. The silhouetted rooftops unevenly meandered the length of the bridge, apart from a gap at the northern end – the result of a previous fire. Tall chimneys reached their sooty fingers skywards in an attempt to defile the clouds. Rewn looked over the parapet at the murky water below swirling its way to the sea through an avenue of tiny archways that supported the grand structure.

Pensively they strolled silently over the bridge; as they approached the Southwark end a gruesome sight crystallised their thoughts. On top of the Great Stone Gate the heads and limbs of two criminals were displayed on spikes as a savage reminder to all its citizens. Lutel took one look at the bulging eyes of one "traitor" and screamed. The demi-pupils gazed skyward in an expression of agony. The spike skewered the protruding windpipe and dried blood was splashed around the neck as a swarm of flies buzzed noisily around, feeding mercilessly from the soup. Blood dripped from the nose, ears and eyes and the ripped lips gave evidence of the torture the poor felon must have endured. She buried her head in Rewn's shoulder.

"It's horrible," she said. "And we want to help these people?"

Rewn pushed her gently away, stroking her cheek comfortingly.

"What if they do that to…?"

Rewn put a restraining finger on his sister's lips.

"They won't," he promised.

But as they walked back along the bridge, he contemplated the urgency of rescuing Revin.

Neither of them spoke again until they had reached The Murder of Crows. The climb up the wooden stairs to the first floor seemed an inordinately long one. Verde was fast asleep, whilst Woodman dozed serenely in a chair, his breath filling the air with alcoholic fumes. The countryman startled awake as the door opened.

"Oh, 'tis you; bin no trouble," he said, but his remark was ignored.

"Verde had best stay in here tonight; Lutel, you can have his room," suggested Rewn. Walking over to a wooden chest he picked up the jug of ale. To his surprise it was half-full and he took a hearty swig; the cool liquid soothed his parched throat, and he offered some to his sister. She emptied the jug, whilst Rewn tore a hunk of bread and handed it to her with a slab of hard cheese. Lutel hungrily devoured the unappetising supper, and rubbed her eyes.

"Get some rest," said Rewn. "We'll talk in the morning."

Lutel made to protest.

"We can't help Revin tonight," argued Rewn. "Sleep; you will need your wits about you tomorrow."

Lutel was too tired to disagree and bade them goodnight as she exited. Rewn had hired a room a little way along the corridor; turning a corner in the passageway, she opened the door, shuffled in and flopped onto the bed. Before Rewn and Woodman had entered the room next to the snoring Verde, she was fast asleep.

CHAPTER THIRTY-EIGHT
A SECRET ADMIRER

Verde let out a huge belch; Lutel gave him a reprimanding look. She couldn't really be cross, she told herself. It had been three days since Verde's abrupt arrival, and he had slept for most of that time. Verde licked his greasy lips, then wiping his mouth with the back of his hand he brushed away any stubborn crumbs or morsels from his sausage and bread breakfast – all satisfyingly washed down with a drink of sack.

"What's to be done?" asked Verde.

"About what in particular?" she queried.

"Everything; it's all gone wrong. Revin's in prison, we've lost a ship, the people here will never understand inoculation."

"Ah, that's another problem."

"How?"

"I'm afraid the antidote was destroyed in the crash."

Verde let out a long groan.

"Don't fret; there are signs that the plague is abating. Rewn saw a poster for the weekly death totals and they are coming down."

"But the conditions haven't gone away, there will be more plagues," he whined.

"Not necessarily," Lutel hinted. She eyed Verde, wondering if now would be an appropriate moment.

"Go on, tell me," he pleaded at her silence.

Lutel sat down on the edge of the bed and faced him. Verde seemed stronger, but she didn't wish to risk triggering a relapse through any undue excitement. Lutel pressed the back of her hand against his brow. The fever appeared to have abated.

"Rewn is out now with Woodman. We befriended a Tower guard in The Raven."

Verde pricked up at the mention of his old haunt.

"We plied him with drinks," she continued. "Revin is apparently being held in a place called the Bloody Tower. Rewn and Woodman are hoping to meet him again; you may have noticed money is a major driving force here, and Rewn is judging the moment to see if Revin's escape can be procured. As for the ship, well, at least we are left with the craft that seats four, so although we have lost our cargo, look on the bright side; we can all go home again once we've sorted out everything here."

Verde nodded at Lutel's reassurance. "What do you mean by 'everything'? Surely we secure Revin's release and then depart?"

Lutel sighed deeply, placing her chin on a hand, and gazed deeply into Verde's eyes.

"We must cleanse this city before we leave."

"What do you mean? It's surely too dangerous to stay now."

"Not necessarily. Revin's release may take time; we don't have to sit idly by. You were right, what you said a moment ago. The conditions are a major contributor to the plague. The buildings are too close together, the streets are airless, rats breed in the filthy rubbish that lies on street corners; they probably even breed between the wooden walls of the houses."

Verde showed signs of restlessness, but Lutel was determined he should hear her out now that she had suggested as much.

"We must destroy these abominable conditions; they are a scourge on humanity."

"How do you plan to do this?" he contended.

Lutel's eyes narrowed to tiny slits, as though to protect them from the angry outburst she anticipated.

"By burning it to the ground!"

The tankard saved Lutel. Verde spluttered and put it down before emitting an incredulous laugh.

"That's rather drastic. Wouldn't we be causing a great loss of life? I thought our mission was to save, not destroy."

"Our mission is to eradicate this terrible disease for ever, and nothing purges like fire. Rewn calculates that a fire starting in the east of the city would be difficult to stop, because of the proximity of the buildings. Given a favourable wind it should spread over a great area in a gentle arc. It will give people plenty of time to escape."

"But they will be homeless," argued Verde.

"Homeless but alive," responded Lutel defiantly. "Which would you prefer?"

"But is there no other way?"

"None that will be so effective," stated Lutel. "Then this city can be built again, stone and brick will replace the rotten rat-infested wood, wide streets will alleviate the cramped diseased alleyways, adequate draining can replace the open sewers, and space between the houses will allow the air to circulate and remove the stale atmosphere."

"Sounds rather grand, but we can't build a city," intoned Verde.

"No, but we could leave a few ideas and pointers behind us."

"Well, put like that, I suppose we've no other option."

The door opened and Woodman walked in, followed by Rewn.

"Well?" asked Lutel expectantly.

"It's good and bad news," Woodman sighed.

"Master Honeyball must be the most honest yeoman of the Tower," muttered Rewn, frowning.

"Have you divulged our purpose?" asked Verde.

"No, what do you take me for?" answered Rewn.

Verde wiped a finger around his plate and popped it into his mouth. It seemed an ideal way of holding his tongue.

"Honeyball let it be known in our conversation that he frowns upon such activity. He recently betrayed a fellow warder who had taken a bribe."

"What's the good news?" asked Lutel.

Rewn laughed and his eyes sparkled mischievously as he poured a drink and offered it to Woodman.

"Friend Honeyball very much..." Rewn stopped and laughed again. Before continuing he swigged the remnants of the sack from its jug. Lutel placed a hand on the container and gently forced it from Rewn's lips.

"What of 'Friend Honeyball'?"

"He wants to see y..." slurred Rewn incomprehensibly, and he roared with laughter, accompanied by Woodman who had no need to understand Rewn's speech.

Lutel sat on Verde's bed whilst the two men continued to shake with mirth; just as one would come to his senses the other started a further fit of giggling, and it was a good minute before both had regained their composure. Rewn cleared his throat and faced Lutel.

"He very much wants to see you again," he said clearly and concisely, before once more falling into a bout of uncontrollable laughter.

Lutel shot off the bed and attempted to stand face to face with her convulsing brother. "That is not funny!" she said tersely through clenched teeth.

"Well, it's not my sweet breath that he wishes to kiss," replied Rewn in a mocking romantic tone. Tears were running down Woodman's cheeks. Even Verde cracked a smile from his bedside.

"I hope your warped sense of humour has not arranged anything that your brain cannot account for."

"He'll hang for sure." It was Woodman who had brought sanity back to the conversation. Lutel resented his interjection, and she wanted to tell him that he was only there as their minion, and not as a decision maker, but the statement permeated her to the bone because in truth she knew Woodman was right.

Jollifications ceased with Woodman's observation, and a serious determined atmosphere fell upon the room as the implication of their failure dawned upon all present.

"All right, suppose – just suppose – I go along with this idea. Honeyball's no more likely to take a bribe from a lover if he is as high-principled as you've discerned."

"True," said Rewn, "but he does hold responsibility for the prison keys."

Lutel stared out of the window at the blue sky, seeking inspiration. Mares'-tail clouds flecked the horizon. It was going to be another warm day.

"Can't you 'remove' the keys from Honeyball?"

"I shouldn't think so; they never leave his quarters in the Tower apart from to be used for their purpose."

"Are you suggesting I go *inside* the Tower?" asked Lutel, incredulous.

"As his guest," said Rewn reassuringly.

CHAPTER THIRTY-NINE

WATERGATE

During the October and November of 1665 they continued to keep a low profile in The Murder of Crows. Their landlord, Jeremiah Longfellow, was untypical of his profession, being both taciturn and discreet. He, his wife and their two daughters kept themselves very much to themselves. The Crows, as they affectionately referred to the inn, became a second home to the guests. They were left to their own devices in their rooms and were free to come and go as they pleased.

Longfellow was content with a regular income at such an uncertain time and rarely bothered his guests except around meal times. Unless they took themselves into the body of the inn to drink, the foursome seldom encountered their host, apart from every Friday evening when Rewn sought out the sandy-haired landlord and handed over the money for their lodging and food. Longfellow lived up to his name, being close to six feet tall; he was portly, but fell short of being stout. Never looking Rewn in the eye when the weekly transaction took place, instead he blinked as though embarrassed at taking their money. He was always immaculately dressed in a fresh white shirt with a colourful neckerchief. His black breeches and boots never bore any sign of a stain or scuff, which considering the nature of his work was no mean achievement.

Something resembling normal life had begun to return to London, to such an extent that Rewn and Verde were on the verge of going out into the city to seek employment. During the autumn many plans had been suggested, discussed and rejected; finally they had agreed to infiltrate various companies that dealt in a flammable trade, such as spirits, tallow, coal, hay, wool and timber. They intended to co-ordinate the information gathered and plan the intended conflagration accordingly, starting their fire when as large a number of warehouses as possible were full.

Both men had virtually decided on their list of targets when all their planning was put on hold as the plague reared its ugly head again. The returning merchants and well-to-do classes came back to houses where no airing of bed linen had taken place. In numerous cases the plague flea was still prevalent, and many returnees were cut down by the invisible hand of death that they had sought so hard to avoid. This delayed the expected upturn in commerce and caused the plotters to spend several more frustrating weeks, especially so for Woodman, around the tavern area of The Murder of Crows.

The season did not prove so inactive for Lutel. She often walked out with Gaymor Honeyball, visiting the taverns around the Tower. More than once Lutel had to rebuff the amorous attempts of the yeoman of the guard, and at each successive venture Lutel premeditated a fresh favour that Revin would owe her. Appeasement was going to be a long and painful process, she promised herself as she once more shrank away from Honeyball's foul breath.

The yeoman would not have been considered a good catch even by women from the lower ranks of London society. For a well-educated and civilised Mykasian the pretence was almost above the call of duty. Her suitor took little pride in his appearance, which was not helped by an unfortunate plethora of warts on his face that even grew on his tongue. His hair was lank and greasy and a permanent residence for headlice, several days' growth of whiskers adorned his chin, and his body odour often caused Lutel to feel sick. Honeyball drank heavily and belched and farted continually once he was in drinking mode. His belly gave testament to his heavy drinking, being very fat and round, a feature shared with his face and limbs. Thick matted black hair bedecked his chest, back, arms and legs and sprouted from every orifice; his unattractive appearance was matched only by his uncouth manners and low level of conversation.

Finally, in late December, to Lutel's intense relief, he agreed to show her the inside of the Tower. In an exceptional moment of intoxication, even by Honeyball's standards, he promised to smuggle her in through the aptly named Traitor's Gate the following evening.

Early the next morning Rewn was despatched to a local alchemist in search of a sleeping draught. A large painted sign outside a building in Lime Street showed him his journey was at an end. Inside the shop a wild-eyed balding man was busy with a mortar and pestle, pummelling a yellow and purple mix of herbs and dried flowers. He carried on with his work as Rewn approached him and still continued as his customer hovered over him.

"Good day, sir," offered Rewn, but still the alchemist ignored his visitor. When he was at last content with his efforts the man raised his eyes in expectation of being addressed.

"I am finding difficulty sleeping these warm nights," explained Rewn. "Have you anything to help?"

"I have many excellent draughts that will suit your purpose; how severe is your malady?"

"Oh! bad, very bad indeed. I twist and turn so that my bedding becomes tangled and far too uncomfortable to lie in. Have you a really strong powder?"

The alchemist took a step backwards and spread his arms wide; his shop was filled with a mixture of smells, too many for Rewn to isolate and identify. Behind the man was a series of shelves filled with assorted jars and bowls. He pushed his sleeves back, reached up to the top shelf and brought down a dark blue jar; lifting the lid he poured a whitish mixture into a phial.

"Dissolve this in a liquid; milk or water will suffice, and you will be asleep before the blanket is creased," promised the alchemist.

Rewn took the phial and sniffed the contents; it proved to be virtually odourless.

"Is it kind to the palate? I have a weak stomach," he checked.

"The taste is not unpleasant, sir, almost undetectable; a little bitter, but with a spoonful of honey is most acceptable."

"Are you sure it is fast-working?"

The alchemist sighed; to him the creation of his potions was his raison d'etre. The selling of his concoctions was an inconvenience that he accepted with little grace, even though it allowed him to indulge and continue his pastime.

"Sir," he said emphatically, and his eyes bulged as he leant over the counter to face Rewn. "I normally advise purchasers to avoid mixing this particular potion with alcohol, as I am told it is likely to leave you with a severe headache. But if you are so desperate for sleep, then may I suggest in your own case that you do exactly that? I would further advise you to take the draught whilst in bed, as the effect is very immediate!"

"How much?" asked Rewn.

"A crown," came the snappy reply.

And cheap at the price, thought Rewn as he handed over the money. Placing the phial carefully inside his clothing, he made his way swiftly back to the inn, avoiding the gaze of all he met, lest they should guess his intent.

On the south side of London Bridge the church clock of Saint Olave struck ten of the evening. Lutel walked on the northern side of the Thames, the unmistakeable aroma of fish filling her nostrils as she neared the marketplace at Billingsgate. She turned right into an alley just before the Custom House and there at the water's edge waited Honeyball, in a small lighter. A wherryman sat in the centre of the boat, gripping two wooden oars tightly as though expecting them to be ripped from his grasp at any moment by some unforeseen force. Honeyball stood up as Lutel approached the river; the gentle bobbing of the boat somehow made his disagreeable appearance even more unpleasant, even lending a comical mode, as he smirked towards her. Still leering like a besotted youth in the infancy of some whirlwind romance, he held out his hand. Lutel contented herself in contemplating a further series of fiendish compensations that she would extract from Revin once this unfortunate charade had secured his release. The small figure of the wherryman held the boat fast to the steps as Lutel came aboard and settled safely in her seat. Honeyball signalled and the wherryman removed his hooded cloak and threw it to him.

"Wear this," growled Honeyball.

"I'm not cold."

"It's not to protect your face, it's to hide it. All are on their mettle at the Tower; the Lieutenant has doubled the guard."

"Oh!" shrieked Lutel involuntarily, an uncomfortable knot appearing in the pit of her stomach.

"Fear not," said Honeyball, oblivious to the reason for her startled outburst. He gently stroked her cheek with the back of his podgy fingers whilst holding a lantern to her face. Lutel felt sick as she noticed the thick black dirt that sat in his fingernails. "We have aristocratic company tonight; the Duke of Buckingham and the Marquis of Dorchester have traded blows in the House and both are committed to the Tower."

Lutel relaxed into her seat, but her action was premature.

"Well, pick up the oars," Honeyball ordered her. "I can't be seen to row into the Tower."

Fortunately their way lay only a short distance downstream, and after catching several crabs, a combination of Honeyball's mirth and sheer determination on her part saw Lutel rowing with acceptable aplomb. By the time she steered the boat to the very shadows of the Tower any watching eyes would not have suspected that anything was amiss. She rowed past the Queen's Stair and Honeyball instructed her to row to the left, under Saint Thomas's Tower, through Watergate and on to a darker opening.

"Traitor's Gate," said Honeyball with a nod, hoping to impress Lutel.

His statement had a far more alarming effect than he could ever had imagined or intended. Lutel looked at the bottom of the lighter, hiding her feelings. Honeyball exchanged passwords with a guard at the Gate and the way was open for them to pass through.

Honeyball made Lutel climb out of the boat unaided, and they made their way between Wakefield and Bloody Tower. Before them stood the foreboding White Tower, its pale walls shimmering eerily in the gloom of the night. Her suitor led the way around the perimeter of the ghostly building to the far side, where they crossed a courtyard and entered the Constable's Tower. Lutel followed Honeyball up several stone staircases to a small square room at the top. A warder stood guard outside a barred door.

"Who is this?" growled the man from under a string of rats' tails that passed for hair.

"None of your business, Smythson."

"You're late; been fetching your fancy woman, 'av yer?"

Honeyball's hairy arm gripped the man around the throat and lifted him from the floor. Smythson trembled as he realised he'd overreached the mark; his spindly legs shook as they dangled helplessly.

"I'm here now, and if you want to be here tomorrow, you'll button your lip."

The fingers tightened, and Smythson made a queer gurgling sound; his eyes said what his mouth could not, and Honeyball threw him with such force he crashed into the wall behind with a sickening thud. A large bunch of keys spilled from his grasp and fell onto the flagstones. The frightened man picked himself up and scurried away down the stairs, glancing over his shoulder in case Honeyball had a further lesson for him.

The smitten jailer singled out a key from the ring and unlocked the iron door. Beyond was a room with rough-hewn walls embedded with flintstone. A low ceiling gave the impression of standing inside an empty box, there being a dearth of furniture; two dusty wooden chests that served as chairs were its only concession to comfort. Torches cast their precious light from three of the walls in a vain attempt to cheer the room. Honeyball wiped his arm across the top of the chests in order to remove the less stubborn grime. As they sat down, Lutel produced a parcel of food.

"Well, aren't you the fair one?" said her host, reaching out for a mutton tart, in the process transferring his seated position to become closer to his intended. Lutel cringed at his foul-smelling breath, and shuffled away to the edge of her chest.

"A kiss for my maid?" asked the unperturbed Romeo.

"Later," replied Lutel. "We have all night."

The burly yeoman's eyes gleamed lecherously at the promise, and he removed his arm from around her shoulder in order to concentrate on another vice. Flakes of pastry fell from his mouth as he tore at his supper.

"Good, very good," he mumbled through a mouthful of food, returning part of Lutel's offering to her. She nonchalantly wiped the crumbs away.

"Gaymor, tell me about this place."

Honeyball sparked like a firebrand as Lutel called him by name.

"Your voice is so pure, so unblemished, my love; you don't want to know about this hell hole. The only reason I agreed to bring you was so we could spend an undisturbed night together."

"But I love to hear of your work, the dangers you face and the desperate men whose confinement you are entrusted with."

"You're a strange one, you are, missy; you'll make a good wife."

"Tell me, were there prisoners in that large building that we passed?"

"The White Tower? No, not at this moment." He took several more bites of his tart and bent forward. "That's full of the Navy's gunpowder at the moment," he confided in the quietest whisper he could manage. "Just waiting to be delivered to the French or Dutch." He winked. Lutel tucked the information away; it could prove very promising to their future plans.

"I'm responsible for the Bloody Tower," boasted Honeyball. "That's what most of these keys are for," and he tantalisingly jangled the bunch in front of Lutel's eyes.

"May we go and see the prisoners, Gaymor?" asked Lutel in mock innocence.

"My dearest Lutel, your interest in my work is most flattering and augers well for our future, but you do not need to take your devotion so far, I assure you."

"Please?" asked Lutel resolutely, cursing the one small trait of humanity that Honeyball had so far shown.

"Why, I'll be thinking you have some business down there, if I didn't know you better." Honeyball gave her a perspicacious look, and Lutel decided to probe no further.

"Brr," she said. "It is cold in here."

The lovesick Honeyball fell into the trap and instantly removed his coat, tenderly draping it around Lutel's shoulders.

"You go too far," she protested.

"Nonsense; it was remiss of me not to think of it earlier. This place was not built with the likes of fair roses in mind. I fear you will take a chill."

Lutel seized the opportunity and delved deep inside her clothing, and produced a small leather flask. She removed the cap and offered the container to Honeyball.

"After you," he said, showing annoying gallantry.

"No, your need is greater than mine; you have no coat."

Lutel felt the warmth rising inside her; she damned this isolated stubborn streak that ran like a band of silver through a worthless rock.

"I insist," she said, "…my love." She almost choked on the words, but she had calculated correctly and it was Honeyball who now choked on the brandy as he took a deep quaff, not suspecting its strong contents.

Lutel slapped him on the back, fearful he would drink no more.

"My, one surprise follows another with you. I presumed so fair a maid would carry nothing more than a good honest sack. It's certainly warming," he said as he recovered his composure and pride. Honeyball offered the flask to Lutel; she held out a restraining hand.

"Please, Gaymor, take your fill; I can wait."

Honeyball examined the flask and, holding the neck to his nose, sniffed its contents. Lutel could think of no distraction, but fortunately Honeyball's greed resurfaced and he took another large swig.

"Here, my love," offered Honeyball.

Lutel just managed to take the flask from his outstretched hand before he keeled forward in a deep sleep. The keys jangled for a second time and Lutel lifted one of Honeyball's eyelids. The dilation of his pupils showed that he was well under the influence of Rewn's draught. It was very tempting to take the keys and release Revin, but it had been agreed beforehand that such action was likely to prove fruitless. Locating Revin may not prove easy; if she did find him, a number of guards would have to be evaded, and even if they did succeed then suspicion would fall on Lutel, and they would be hunted down and forced to leave their corner of London, which did not suit their future planning.

Lutel rolled back her sleeves and untied the wool that bound several beeswax candles to her arms. Wax spattered as she took a light from one of the wall torches, and a small blob splattered and solidified around her feet. Finally the wick of one candle caught and she picked up a second candle and warmed its base over the flickering flame. Melted wax dripped rapidly on to the wooden box seat; she placed the unlit candle in its own pool of wax and stood it upright – her own yeoman of the guard, she thought. Lutel glanced at Honeyball to check the alchemist's boast; he was snoring loudly from his uncomfortable bed. For a moment she worried that his snorting would attract attention, but she could hear no undue sound from without.

Lutel lit the standing candle and proceeded to melt the remaining tallows using the flame from her "Honeyball". As each successive candle melted, she collected the wax and quickly rolled it into a sphere. She then pressed the ball on to the box in order to flatten it, and carefully placed the end of a key into the soft wax. A sweet smell of honeyed beeswax filled the room, and Lutel's eyes stung as the smoke lingered unable to find an escape through the thick walls. Lutel worked tirelessly without a break until she had an imprint of all ten keys. After the final mould had been taken she picked up all her wax tablets and wrapped them in a cloth. She stuffed the cloth inside her blouse and scraped the box clean before lying on it. Lutel closed her eyes and yawned, hoping that the effects of the sleeping draught would soon wear off.

She awoke with a start to a clamour of noise: a roaring, chattering and squeaking. In the dark she was disorientated and panicked, unsure of her whereabouts. A snoozing sound from the corner helped bring her to her senses, and she fumbled her way towards Honeyball, guided by his snoring.

"Wake up, wake up," she urged as she vigorously shook the sleeping guard. Honeyball stirred.

"Oh, my head," he said, raising his hands to either side of his temple.

"What's that terrible noise?" asked Lutel.

"The inside of my head," replied Honeyball.

"No, listen," she persisted.

The cacophony of sound reached his ears.

"Oh, that's just the animals," said Honeyball, unperturbed.

"Animals?"

"Yes, the King's menagerie – lions, monkeys, ostriches – they're all down there."

Lutel, thankful that she had not deviated from their plan not to search for Revin, pulled Honeyball up. "Come, I must go," she said.

"What hour is it?"

"I don't know."

"Have I slept long?"

"I'm pleased to find you are such a sober man; you are obviously not used to drinking strong liquor."

The praise was not merited by the confused Honeyball, but he did not deny it. He felt for his keys and smiled at Lutel before taking her hand and leading her out of the room. They meandered their way through a series of dimly lit passageways and stairs.

Lutel blinked as her eyes took time to adjust to the dazzling daylight even though it was a dull morning, the natural light being in stark contrast to the gloom that she had left behind. Honeyball led the way back through Watergate and along the river. As Lutel stepped from the boat at the landing stage, Honeyball made her an offer.

"Spend Christmas with me?"

"What?" she gasped.

"Christmas. It's only three days away. Come and spend it at my house. They're good times, so enjoyable since the King's return."

The reference to the puritanical days of the Commonwealth was lost on Lutel, but she did understand the problem of the invite.

"I can't," she excused herself. "I'm spending it at my mother's."

"Does she live far?" asked Honeyball hopefully.

"Quite a distance."

"When do you return?"

"Not until well into the New Year," she said knowledgeably.

"I don't know where you live," bemoaned Honeyball.

Good, thought Lutel. "I'll come and find you," she shouted.

Honeyball was left with only her promise as she disappeared from view, running back to Rewn and Verde, her heart beating with excitement.

CHAPTER FORTY

BIG J

Early next morning the four conspirators met in Lutel's room. It had been decided to send Woodman out in search of a blacksmith, and then Verde and Rewn would approach the smith for signs of sympathy or dishonesty. By these means Lutel could avoid suspicion and recognition if the counterfeit keys were ever traced back to their source.

Woodman was absent for several hours, having travelled westward in his quest towards the tall spire of Saint Paul's Cathedral, which he had decided upon as a landmark. He left the city through Ludgate and searched the alleys outside the city walls. In a small alleyway off Shoe Lane he finally came upon a smithy. The smith wore a pair of breeches and a leather apron, whilst a stout pair of shoes protected his feet. His upper body was bare, though his muscular shoulders and chest were covered in a dark mixture of hair and dust. Sweat from the heat of the forge glistened on his body. A small boy, whom Woodman judged to be his son due to the likeness of fair curls and facial similarity, pumped the bellows to order. Woodman, noting the blacksmith's evident upper body strength, approached him with trepidation. The man did not stop in his work and the red-hot metal twisted on his anvil as the hammer repeatedly rained down blows.

"Again," he ordered his young assistant, and the bellows sent a swirl of air into the forge. A circle of coals radiated brightly where the oxygen entered, and the blacksmith plunged a length of metal into the centre of the glow, holding it there for several seconds. Woodman, forced by the heat to keep his distance from the forge, admired the smith's tenacity. He was intrigued by the blacksmith's metalwork, but at first could not determine what was being created. Sparks flew around the craftsman's bare wrists as he toiled away, but he did not flinch or deviate from his task for a moment. Finally, Woodman realised the metal was being fashioned into a hook. For an instant he was disappointed that the final product should turn out to be something so mundane, but as the blacksmith dipped the object into a bucket of water, the loud hissing sound recaptured his awe and interest.

“That’s nice, very nice,” said Woodman in a sycophantic voice.

For the first time the blacksmith took notice of his visitor.

“It pays,” he grunted.

Woodman was encouraged by the thought that the blacksmith held money so dear. “What’s it for?”

“A fire hook.” Like most craftsmen and artists, the blacksmith was only too pleased to talk about his work at the appropriate time. He despised the rude interruptions that tested his concentration. “An order for the local alderman,” he continued, “though I’d fair pull his house down with it, along with many others I could name.”

Woodman could not believe his continuing luck, as the blacksmith straightened his aching back whilst flexing his shoulders back.

“What do you require of me, friend?”

This direct approach rather put Woodman on the spot, and he immediately regretted staying so long. His brief was to find a smith who might prove bribable; the tricky negotiations were strictly to be left to others.

“A friend of mine is, um… looking for a small job,” stuttered Woodman.

“I have all the help I need,” replied the other, pointing with his tongs at the small boy. “There’s plenty of work to be found in the city now that plague’s over. Many a countryman’s taking to the town to fill dead men’s boots.”

“No, I meant that she would like you to do a job for her,” explained Woodman meekly.

The blacksmith threw back his mane and roared with laughter at his own misunderstanding. He slapped Woodman on the back, sending him stumbling forward. Heartily Woodman joined in the mirth, hoping to humour the blacksmith.

“So ’tis a woman who sends you?”

Woodman’s laughing finished as abruptly as it had started. The other noticed the change in countenance and puzzled at the transformation.

“Is something wrong, friend?”

“No, no,” said Woodman timidly.

“Come,” said the blacksmith, and he clapped a large hairy arm around Woodman, “It’s time for a drink.”

He led Woodman to the back of his forge, and brushing some coal dust from a sawn-off stump indicated to Woodman to sit down. The blacksmith introduced himself as Jack Jaycock. “My friends, what are left of them, call me Big J,” he said, beaming, “and you are?”

After a short pause Woodman could only murmur, "John Woodman." He flinched as he spoke his name, having promised Rewn faithfully that he would not divulge it. Hastily he accepted the flagon from Jaycock's outstretched hand, and nervously gulped its contents. Woodman spluttered and spat a golden fountain into his lap.

"Why, steady, John Woodman; that's good cider, not to be quaffed like a dog at his drinking bowl."

Woodman squirmed at the mention of his name, and sought solace in a further drink, but this time sipping the cider. Courage began to return to him and an idea formed in his mind. What did Verde and Rewn know? Who were they to tell him what to do? What if he returned having completed the business himself? Then let them shout at him.

"My friend has a valuable key," he said, testing the water.

Jaycock pulled in his outstretched legs and put down his drink.

"Keys themselves, I find, are often valueless. It's what they lead to that's of value."

"This key don't open anythin' of worth," continued Woodman. "It's the key to another friend's door. His friend's worried lest he might lose his key, and seeks a duplicate to guard against such a loss."

Jaycock rocked on his stump, pulling his feet up on to his seat, and entwined his legs with his arms. Woodman thought that he would fall off at any minute, but the art was well perfected, and the blacksmith remained seated.

"You speak in riddles, John; you ask for your friend's friend. Why can't he… or she ask me direct? Speak plainly."

Woodman realised that he had dug a hole for himself. He had not calculated the blacksmith's perceptive powers, and he at least had the common sense to stand up to go.

"You're right," he said. "I'll ask *him* to come and see you."

"Who?

"My friend."

"Is this your friend, or your friend's friend?" teased Big J.

The wit was too much for Woodman and he stood transfixed, uncertain which way to turn. The blacksmith looked around his forge; it was enclosed on three sides and, apart from his son, no person lay in view.

"Would your friend prefer this key to remain a secret?"

The openness caught Woodman off-guard, and before realising he again blurted out his answer.

“Yes, in fact it’s not an actual key, it’s an impression.”

Jaycock stood up and sidled closer to his tense visitor.

“Tell your friend’s friend to bring it to me this evening. I’ll have some molten metal waiting.”

Jaycock gripped Woodman’s hand and shook it, staring hard into his eyes; Woodman felt uncomfortable, as though it were he who was being inspected when it was supposed to be the other way around.

“Tell your friend to bring two sovereigns with her,” said the blacksmith, smiling.

“Actually there are several keys.”

Jaycock gave a repeat performance of his manic laugh, quite alarming Woodman for fear it should draw attention.

“In that case tell your friend to bring a bag of gold!”

“I will, J, thank you, thank you,” stammered Woodman, and he scurried away. The blacksmith’s eyes burned into Woodman’s back like glowing coals from his forge until his visitor disappeared from view.

“Come, Toby,” he said, as he tidied up his tools. “We’ve work to do.”

CHAPTER FORTY-ONE

AN UNLIKELY RESCUE

Verde drummed his fingers with increasing ferocity as Woodman related his day's excursion. They were huddled around a table in a corner of the public room at The Murder of Crows. Only two other travellers were enjoying the inn's hospitality; both patrons were far too engrossed in their meal to notice the minor consternation that Woodman was wreaking as he whispered his tale.

"I knew we shouldn't have let him go," complained Verde, with the confidence of one with hindsight even though he had been party to the final decision.

Lutel took a more practical approach. "No harm has been done; *our* names and whereabouts have not been divulged," she said, letting Woodman know that she did not condone his actions.

"How do we know for sure?" asked Verde.

"God's truth, he only knows you as my friends," Woodman assured them, shaking his head. "He's very keen to help, told me so."

Verde snorted. "I say we don't go. There must be other blacksmiths."

"You try finding 'em, then."

"We'll still encounter the same uncertainty," argued Rewn.

"Exactly my point; we don't go."

"Fine. We'll just leave Revin to fester and die," said Lutel coldly.

Verde coloured, realising he had allowed his prejudices to stand in the way of reason. He had totally forgotten their ultimate aim. Revin was a good friend and Verde had every intention of standing by him. He cursed himself for letting this outsider rile him.

"I'll go with Woodman," he volunteered, "and Rewn can watch from a distance. Can't you, Rewn, in case anything goes wrong?"

"I'll go with Woodman and you watch. You are too blinkered," retorted Rewn.

Lutel stepped in to stop the argument from developing.

"I know that we are all tired and missing home, and this business with the plague is taking far longer than expected, but the last thing that Revin or we need is for us to fall out."

Silence descended, as the two men recognised the pragmatism of Lutel's statement. Rewn had thrown his sister a warning glance at the mention of home, but Woodman remained oblivious to any consternation.

The moment passed and thoughts returned to Revin's rescue, which was of paramount importance to them both, and they sat mealy-mouthed, awaiting further instruction.

"You all three go," Lutel surprisingly announced, "and I'll watch from a distance."

An immediate consensus greeted the suggestion. In any case, Rewn and Verde would not have dared to argue with Lutel when she held that determined look in her eye.

"But we will not go this evening; the dark is a friend to entrapment. We will go tomorrow morning, when we shall all feel better for a rest."

The meeting dispersed and they all went to their separate rooms. Lutel was the last to climb the stairs, following behind Verde. She touched his sleeve and he turned around to face her.

"We're in this together," she said with a smile.

"I'll see you at breakfast," replied Verde, grasping her meaning.

As they made their way along Cheapside, shop boys stood outside the buildings calling their wares. London was gradually returning to normality, after the severest ravages of the plague.

"Fine hats, fine hats," cried a small fresh-faced boy, sporting two prominent front teeth.

"Best gloves in London," chirped another from across the road.

Every day new signs of commerce were breathing fresh life into the city, although the air was made pungent with acrid smells from the returning industries that accompanied the increasing hustle and bustle. Most noticeable were the rank soap boilers, whose emissions were greeted by the locals with the return of a variety of posies and perfumes that had so recently faced a more serious antagonist.

"Their industries certainly are primitive," remarked Verde, as he stared around the skyline. Lutel elbowed him in the ribs and nodded towards Woodman, who walked a few feet in front of them. Embarrassing mistakes were all too frequent of late, and she was as guilty as anybody, but it did concern her that all of them had relaxed somewhat, and the next one might have telling consequences. Fortunately, Woodman missed this most recent blunder; he had spent all of his thirty years in the country, and the timber-framed houses with their jutting storeys and ground-floor shops so intrigued him that he was deaf to the conversation behind him.

They passed through the wall at Ludgate, and Woodman led them to the top of the alley that led to Jaycock's forge. Slowly, they wended their way down the dark narrow path.

Lutel stopped at a conduit water supply, and beckoned the others to proceed, before hiding herself behind a large wooden structure that marked the outlet. From her concealment she saw a burly figure, smoking a long clay pipe, emerge from the forge. The man looked furtively around and Lutel was preparing to break cover when Woodman introduced Verde and Rewn to Jaycock.

After the welcoming the blacksmith continued to peer around, his eyes searching for things unseen. Lutel scanned the area, her heart pounding for the men as the small group disappeared from sight into the smithy. Lutel shifted her position and strained for an improved view, but the angle did not allow for any greater insight. Torn between letting her friends know her suspicions and staying clear of trouble herself, Lutel stood her ground, reasoning that she could be of little use if she fell into a trap.

There was no sign of the four men, and as one minute gave way to two, and two stretched to five, she began to feel most uneasy. After what seemed an eternity the three men reappeared, with a smiling and waving Jaycock following some way behind them. Lutel finally allowed herself to relax, and made to move from her hiding place. As the trio headed towards her she noticed a figure out of the corner of her eye; it was emerging from the shadows of the building that stood alongside the smithy. The individual was joined by two others and Lutel drew further back behind the conduit.

"Keep walking; you are being followed," she hissed from her cover, "and don't look behind."

Without giving Lutel so much as a glance the three men continued their journey towards the nearby city walls. Lutel edged around her hiding place as the three newcomers went by. From behind she could see that they were poorly dressed and so intent on the three men in front of them that they failed to notice her presence. Lutel allowed them a reasonable distance and then followed behind, keeping close to the cover of the ramshackle buildings.

As Rewn, Verde and Woodman turned down a side alley three further men stepped out to block their way. Their obstructers were similarly garbed to their pursuers, and even Woodman realised that a sinister plan was afoot. Pretence was no longer required, and they spun around to face the men behind. All the vagabonds carried wooden clubs. One of them stepped forward and he opened his mouth to speak, revealing the loss of two front teeth, victims of his trade.

"You have something we want," he whistled.

By now the men in front had closed in on their intended victims, sandwiching them between the six assailants. Verde noticed that the fronts of the houses on both sides of them afforded no escape, and braced himself for the imminent assault.

"I have nothing of value, let me free," pleaded Woodman, as the six men tightened the vice.

Lutel stood unnoticed behind the back three men; one instinct was telling her to run and live to fight another day, but a strong bond of loyalty submerged any thought of self-survival. Besides, six against four were not bad odds, considering three of them were highly trained, but she harboured a nagging doubt about Woodman. He couldn't be relied upon or expected to face up to such desperate villains. Lutel had just pinpointed her first victim when a further disturbance approached from her rear and barged past her.

"Be gone, you soddin' bastards, before I have every one of you!"

The thundering frame of Jaycock waded into the gang of thieves, wielding around his head a large iron pole that still faintly glowed from its tempering in the forge. On hearing his voice one of the assailants made to attack the blacksmith. Hot metal dashed against his cheek, emitting a sizzling sound, and he screamed in pain as his flesh seared. The wounded man dropped his weapon and clasped his face where a gaping disfigurement would serve as a permanent reminder. A second robber bent double as the red-hot pole was thrust into his stomach, burning through cloth and skin alike, giving forth a scorching stench. Rewn and Verde snatched up the discarded clubs and stood ready to fight, but they had no need, as a combination of the gyrating Jaycock and the pain-ridden screams of his two victims convinced the other members of the gang to turn tail and flee.

"Thank you," acknowledged Rewn as they all gathered their composure.

"I thought I spied Dick Peters when you first came. I said to myself, here's trouble. But I couldn't be sure if they were after my gold or yours. I thought you might be handing over the gold with one hand and taking it back with the other. I had to be sure."

"That's why we have to come back for the keys," said Verde.

"Partly," answered Jaycock; "'tis quite a skilled job and a long one."

A groan came from the ground; they had almost forgotten the remaining attackers. Jaycock walked up to the man with the burning cheek; he was crouching on one knee, whimpering and cradling his face. Jaycock defiantly raised his iron pole above his head like a valiant knight waving his lance.

"Begone, and never dare bother folks around these parts again," he snarled, "or I'll be burning your eyes next time, you see if I don't."

The miscreant rose to his feet and staggered away to the safety of the side alleys. Stretched out on the cobblestones the second casualty remained lifeless as Jaycock aimed a kick in his ribs. The blacksmith repeated the dose several times, and the longer the miserable wretch lay in the road, the more Jaycock kicked him.

"Get up, you snivelling sod," he yelled, as another blow struck its victim.

"Please leave him," said Lutel, who now deemed it safe to intrude upon the scene.

"And who might you be?"

"Lutel, a friend," interposed Woodman.

"My, my, you do know a lot of people," replied the blacksmith, staring at her.

Verde sneered at Woodman for his divulgence, but Jaycock made light of the situation.

"Bring all of your friends ten days hence at the same time. Your keys will be ready."

Without looking back or awaiting their reply, he strode away in the direction of his forge, whilst the four companions silently made their way to the gate and back towards The Murder of Crows.

Days passed by very slowly. Verde, Rewn and Lutel spent most of their time around The Crows. Lutel had deemed it wiser to remain in the vicinity of the inn, so as not to jeopardise their mission with any other unfortunate confrontations. Woodman, in contrast, became more of a free spirit and acted as their ears and eyes on the outside world. He roamed the London streets during the day, but was under a strict curfew to return by dark. His activities were curtailed by giving him a small daily allowance – enough to purchase adequate food but not a plentiful supply of liquor. The attraction of an evening's drinking at The Crows was enough to ensure his prompt arrival at the inn before dusk, much like a tomcat returning from a daily inspection of his territory. Lutel had devised this arrangement as it gave the three of them time to plan and discuss in private, it also served to distance Woodman from Verde, who, uncharacteristically, found him a great source of irritation.

The night preceding the handing over of the keys was marked by Woodman's late arrival. Verde revelled in the blackguard's failings.

"I said all along not to trust this man. You've only got to look at him or hear him talk; he's uneducated, crude and a drunkard. Right now he's probably laid out on some tavern table, telling the whole inn our history and intentions."

Lutel had grown used to these outbursts, and found them easy to ignore as they usually promised more than they actually delivered. But Rewn had become increasingly agitated, as a hint of nervousness crept into the gap made vacant by Woodman's non-appearance.

"Verde's right; perhaps we should go and search for Woodman before it is too late. We should at least vacate The Crows before they come. Better still, we leave this planet."

"Exactly." Verde paced impatiently round Lutel's room.

"You're happy to explain why we deserted Revin? Face his family and friends?" asked Lutel.

"Don't get high and mighty with me!" barked Verde. "It's your fault we are in this mess; now you are trying to tell me what I can and can't do. Well, madam, I suggest you just shut it before—"

Rewn might agree with Verde's sentiments but he was not prepared to see his sister bullied. He dived on Verde and knocked him to the ground. Lutel screamed for them to part as they rolled around the floor knocking the furniture flying. Months of frustration poured out of the two men; no longer able to store them up inside, both gave vent to their feelings. Verde held his hands tightly around Rewn's neck as he sat astride his victim, but Lutel pushed him off in a vain attempt to halt their skirmish.

"Stop, stop," she cried. "Somebody will hear us."

But still the tussle showed no signs of abating as the two men rallied to their feet and began to trade punches. Rewn threw himself at Verde and the pair of them fell back towards the wall. As they crashed into the door a loud knocking came from the other side. The pugilists froze as though struck by an unseen force, and still the rapping came. Lutel pushed the men aside and opened the door. A ghastly white face fell into her arms.

"John, whatever's happened?" she gasped.

"I told you," crowed Verde as they helped Woodman into a chair. "No good would come of it, having him out there talking to the world."

"Be quiet," ordered Lutel. "This bickering stops now."

Rewn had poured a drink of ale and handed it to Lutel. She held it to Woodman's lips and he sipped it silently.

"I've some bad news."

Verde snorted, but Lutel forestalled any reoccurrence with a withering glance. She took the tankard from Woodman and passed it back to Rewn, then bent down beside the shaken man and lowered her face to be in line with his own. Looking into his eyes, she spoke kindly but forcefully.

"What's your news, John?"

Woodman stared straight ahead, as though Lutel did not exist.

"Honeyball is dead."

Lutel was taken aback, but had feared worse. She could handle this news.

"From the plague," continued Woodman. "It still lingers in some quarters."

"I'm sure we will all be safe," Lutel said gently, guessing what was in Woodman's mind.

"There's more."

Lutel felt a sinking feeling in her stomach.

"The prisoners he was in charge of have been moved to isolation."

"I'm sure our keys will open many doors. We fetch them tomorrow. We'll find a way even without Honeyball."

"You don't understand," blurted Woodman. "Revin's in Newgate prison."

CHAPTER FORTY-TWO

NEWGATE

A figure with a bowed back and sloping shoulders shuffled over to a pile of canvas and rope. His movement was inhibited by the leg fetters that bit sharply into his skin, causing a huge weal and sore to erupt on one of his legs. He was joined by thirty or so others, all scrabbling at the heap, jostling and pushing each other for the best pickings. A fight broke out between two men as they both emerged from the pile with opposite ends of the same piece of material. The larger man, his face caked in dirt, his hair long, knotted and wild, snarled at the smaller. The lesser man gave way, and diverted his attention towards the bowed man. The latter gathered his cloth together and, holding it tightly to his chest, stepped backward into the dim light. Frustrated, the would-be attacker fell into the pile of canvas and flailed about wildly until he finally emerged, clutching his very own piece as though he held in his hands some long-lost treasure.

The man with the drooping shoulders picked his way over several bodies that lay scattered around the floor. Moving carefully in the poor light to avoid unnecessary injury, he tied one end of his hammock to the central pillar that stood in the middle of the prison cell. The last throes of daylight shone weakly from a single grating high above him as he weaved his way back to the outer wall, where he looped the other end of his rope. Around the circular room, men were repeating the evening ritual of preparing their nightly resting place. Their hammocks were tied between a central post and the outer wall at three different heights. The end result was like the spokes of three wheels circling the prison cell. Even amongst these unfortunates or dregs of society a pecking order existed, with the topmost berths reserved for the stronger men. In this den of iniquity rank paid scarce regard to power, privilege or wealth, not that many of its inhabitants would lay claim to any of those attributes; quite simply, those willing and able to fight their way literally to the top succeeded, whilst the rest made do, with the least able filling the bottom row. If your strength placed you at neither extreme then you took your place in the middle row.

The top hammocks bore several privileges. Not only were you closer to the fresh air vent, but you could safely pass the night without anyone being sick or urinating over you, or in some cases even worse.

In most societies an underclass existed, and the prison was no exception. Those prisoners who were too ill, too old or too weak to fight for a hammock slept on the floor on straw pallets. Thus, those that were in most need of the best conditions were relegated to the very worst. The cold floor, bodily fluids and the scurrying rats were all their bedfellows.

Virtually all of the guests flopped, collapsed or sprightly climbed into their assortment of stained and torn hammocks. Only the man with the sloping shoulders differed; by contrast, instead of climbing into his hammock on the lowest tier, he returned to the last body that he had stepped over and helped it to stand. The frail man leaned heavily on the caring inmate, and with an effort slumped into the vacant hammock. The ropes went taut as the body crashed into the canvas, but the knots were well-tied and held firm.

"Thank you," he wheezed. "The Lord will remember you."

"Sleep, David," soothed the other.

The man looked around and noticed that there was one berth still not taken, there being no prisoner left with the strength or will to fix the remaining hammock. He picked it up and put his hand through a large hole in its centre. It was very threadbare and yellow; the man held it to his nose and gagged. Even so he thought it worth the bother, and with some difficulty, as its eyeholes were broken, he tied its two ends to their respective hooks. Eventually he slumped into the spot next to his ailing friend, who was already snoring loudly; in that respect David was no different from many of the other prisoners.

Revin lay on his back and crossed his hands over his body, staring upwards through the hammocks, watching the purple light change to grey, and then into blackness. How long had he been in this prison? Had it been for six or seven nights? In the semi-darkness, day blurred into night, and he found the daily meal of bread and water a far more reliable indicator of time. Mealtime roused even baser instincts than the nightly squabbling over hammocks, and once – or was it twice? – he had gone without food.

David cried out in his sleep. Revin remembered how he had befriended him when they had been thrown in the same dungeon in the Tower. In those early days it had been David who had been the strong one. David had shown him the ropes, how to survive the day. It was David who had protected him from the bullying and intimidating environment, and shown him all sorts of kindness. They'd shared food, and talked together at great length. Though even in his darkest moments, Revin had resisted the temptation to inform David of his true circumstances. Each day he fully expected to be rescued, but the days were growing in number and Revin had begun to wonder. The other prisoners assumed him to be a thief, and he found it convenient not to deny it.

In the early days David had been fit and healthy, but under the austerity of prison he had grown weak. Since their move to Newgate, David seemed to have deteriorated rapidly, and with each successive decline Revin's apprehension increased. Revin, too, had not remained unscathed by his incarceration. Apart from his weeping leg, nights of sleeping on the floor in the Tower had given him a permanent ache in the back, causing his shoulders to droop in compensation for the pain.

As he stared at the darkness, he wondered how long he had been held captive. All track of time had been lost in the harsh regime at the Tower, but he reasoned that his confinement must have extended to two or possibly three months. Revin was puzzled by the non-appearance of his colleagues, and their failure to contact him, but he guessed they would have their reasons. He made to scratch his chin, but found his way barred by a tangled mass of hair. His fingers ruffled through the beard; it was long, very long. His anxiety increased. Surely the product of at least six months, he found himself thinking.

In these moments of melancholy he found he missed his companions most of all; there was nobody amongst the prisoners, not even David, whom he felt confident of sharing his problems with. Revin silently cursed the others for not being there; they must know where he had been all this time. Every day he'd been expecting to be released, either through peaceful or other means. He was certain that Lutel would think of some plausible story or explanation. She would convince the authorities that it had all been a terrible mistake. If not, she had the brains to outwit the crude confinement to which he had been subjected. He pictured Verde mounting a rescue with Rewn at his side. Then, in darker moments, he morosely went over possibilities for their non-arrival.

Perhaps Verde had never met up with Rewn and Lutel, maybe Verde was dead, perhaps they were all dead – their antidote may not have been the answer after all. No, no, he discounted that possibility; he had not lost that much faith in Mykas. Far more likely that they had all been captured. Perhaps they were here in Newgate all along, or maybe the Tower. Had they forgotten about him, or not bothered with him? They might all be back on Mykas now, their mission completed. Revin lifted his hands to his face and pinched his cheek. Yes, it really was happening. He scratched his long louse-filled beard. At least things couldn't get any worse, he told himself. As he lay there trying to sleep, his worst nightmare came to mind.

"Worst nightmare," he said out loud.

"Quiet!" shouted a voice from the dark.

Funny, thought Revin, he had not experienced his recurring bad dream since landing on Earth. Usually he could count on being woken at least once during a month, dripping with sweat and panting heavily.

The nightmares had started the inaugural night that he had left home at the age of twenty to commence his first life cycle studies. As he left the academy and hurried down the steep tree-lined track on his way to his lodgings, he felt somebody's presence. He glanced behind, thinking that it would be a friendly gesture to share his walk with a fellow student. To his surprise the path behind was empty.

Revin carried on walking, his first day's lectures running through his mind. As he marched through the gateway he was certain he heard footsteps running down the slope. This time he stopped and turned around, but again the path was clear. Revin looked beyond the track and on to the adjoining grass but still he could not see anyone. He crossed a stretch of open grassland bordered by some housing. In the middle of the square, he again had the feeling that he was being followed – he whisked around, but to no avail. He was pleased to reach a higher density of buildings. Perhaps my mind will stop playing these tricks, he thought, as he sped alongside the houses with their welcoming lights. A hot flush came over him as once again hollow footsteps beat the path behind. Revin called out this time. "I know you are there. What do you want?" No answer came from the gathering gloom. Revin wondered if he might seek help from one of the nearby households. "I know the people that live here," he shouted at the night. Still no answer came as he quickened his pace.

A cold tingle ran down his back as he tightened his fists. Purposefully, head bowed, he strode on. He came to a recreational park; the gate rattled as he pushed against it. Revin panicked as he saw the dull box. An alleyway ran in juxtaposition with the park – it was narrow and dark but the only alternative to retracing his steps. Footsteps echoed behind him as he loped along. Still the noise persisted and he ran down the alley, only stopping when he reached the bottom. As he emerged into a road bordered by more buildings, he caught sight of a man out of the corner of his eye.

“Evening,” offered Revin to the stranger. The man continued as if he hadn’t heard.

Revin’s mouth was dry as he scuttled along the road, his head bowed into the stinging wind. He reached a second alley, shorter but darker due to the high stone walls on either side. As he ran down its steep slope his feet clattered on the hard surface. Behind him steps echoed loudly, and as he reached the exit Revin spun round. Halfway up the alley a shadow darted from the passageway and into a side turning. Revin contemplated giving chase, but his feeling of relief was so great that he had no wish to disturb the peace; on the other hand his inquisitiveness urged him to walk back up the alleyway. As he deliberated over a decision Revin woke up in a cold sweat.

The dream repeated itself regularly; each time he walked the same route, and each time the mysterious figure lurked in the background. Every time that Revin reached the second alleyway he spun round with a mixture of fear and anger, and each time the stranger dodged into the side turning, but Revin had taken to swivelling further up the slope and at each successive dream he glimpsed a little more of his pursuer – a foot, a leg, the tail of a coat but never anything more. Finally, on the point of nervous exhaustion a plan had struck him. Next time *he* would dive into the side turning.

Revin was breathing heavily; as he ran down the slope every sinew tingled with excitement. As he reached the side turning he darted to his left – and waited with short sharp breaths. Sure enough footsteps were ringing out from the alleyway, coming closer and closer, running in desperation. Revin judged the moment the footsteps would reach the side turning. He jumped out, preparing to confront the stalker with a loud scream, but stood open-mouthed confronting himself. When the dream reached this point Revin would awake. He had endured the nightmare many times, but it never continued beyond this point.

Revin drifted in and out of sleep in the prison; sometimes he would wake and wonder where he was. At other times he imagined that he was home on Mykas, and for a brief moment his spirits would rise, until the whistling and snoring and shadowy outlines of the hammocks would cruelly bring him back to reality. His longest spell of sleep was broken by the inmate directly above retching and spewing all over him. In the middle of the night, at Newgate prison, there was no means of mopping up the vomit that lay in a pool around his head. Revin merely stepped out of the hammock and changed ends, but his mind was active once more, and sleep was a long time coming. His thoughts again sank to his present circumstances; would they ever end? The dirt, the pain, the squalor, the darkness, the ghastly smell of sweat and all the accompanying odours, and perhaps worst of all, the never-ending boredom.

Prison rules forbade any form of entertainment; there was no card playing, no gambling with dice, no drink, and the routine was only interrupted when the prison chaplain visited, sometimes twice a day, to lead the singing of psalms. Revin almost smiled; it made a comical sight. These grown men were rapists, thieves, probably several undetected murderers, others like himself guilty of minor offences; some were no doubt innocent – their only crime being in the wrong place at the wrong time. Yet in the presence of this humble chaplain they all became meek and mild, and sat quietly on the floor, participating without a single protest, their gruff tuneless voices barking out the words of the psalms.

CHAPTER FORTY-THREE

KILL TWO BIRDS WITH ONE STONE

On Lutel's suggestion they had accepted the futility of returning to Jaycock's for the duplicate keys. Woodman suggested that they employ similar tactics in an attempt to gain a set of keys to Newgate.

"That approach seems rather doomed," retorted Lutel.

"How are we to free Revin, then?" asked Rewn.

Verde nodded. "We can't leave him to rot."

"We will visit the area tomorrow," she replied. "We can look to see if there are any weaknesses that we can exploit."

Rewn crossed the room and sat down at a small table opposite his sister. Woodman fiddled with a pack of playing cards that had been loaned to him by the landlord. An unlikely truce now existed between him and Verde, and the rustic had been teaching Verde the intricacies of Costly Colours. The game itself held little more than a passing curiosity for the Mykasian, but he was appreciative of its ability to fill idle hours. The two of them sat at the table, presided over by Lutel, just to ensure fair play was observed; even though she was ignorant of the rules, her mere presence was sufficient.

"Newgate's almost as bad as the Tower, they reckon," Woodman said, pausing in his dealing. "Best we move as soon as possible."

"On that point, I'm with Woodman," agreed his newfound ally.

"It's mid-winter," said Rewn. "It can't be very pleasant for Revin. We've been here seven months and the sooner we leave this planet, the better."

Woodman looked askance at Rewn; not for the first time he had uttered something that didn't make sense, but the meaning was beyond his comprehension, and as on the previous occasions he let the matter pass unchallenged. Lutel was not so benevolent, and she kicked her brother under the table.

"Rewn is right," admitted Verde. "We have wasted valuable time planning Revin's escape. Who is to say that we will be any more fortunate next time?"

"Good planning is the secret of success; luck is avoidable. We should have anticipated the eventualities," snapped Lutel.

She put her elbows upon the tavern table and clasped her hands in front of her. It was late in the evening; all the patrons of The Crows had departed. Even Longfellow had retired to bed. He had grown used to these midnight meetings and raised no objections, as long as all was tidy by the morning and any ale was paid for. The group had become accustomed to their own company and had grown bolder in their discussions, safe in the knowledge that any words spoken went no further.

Several hands of cards had been dealt and Rewn had replaced two candles before Lutel leant back in her chair, and the game stopped.

"You are right, time has been wasted. We must look to the fire; we are forgetting our purpose."

"What about Revin?" responded Woodman.

"We will not forget him."

"What are we going to do?" asked Woodman eagerly. His sense of adventure had been blunted for too long, and he sensed that it was about to be ignited, like the inferno that he envisaged in his mind's eye; however, his involvement was not quite what he had in mind.

"You are going to get a job, John," Lutel announced. She rarely referred to him by that name, and it had the effect of mellowing the shock.

"How can that help?" scoffed the incredulous Woodman.

"There are many warehouses along the street at the bottom of this hill."

"Thames Street," chipped in Verde.

Lutel ignored the interruption. She found correction difficult; it was a fault that she had often tried to address and eradicate, but somehow it was one that she couldn't deal with.

"These warehouses must contain many inflammable goods – oil, tallow, spirits," she explained. "See if you can find out exactly what they hold, or how much. It will determine the time that we strike."

The pun was lost on Woodman. "You want me to get a job in the warehouses, and tally the goods!"

Lutel sensed his unease.

"It's important," she assured him. "The more goods, the larger the fire. Who knows; you may be able to get a job that exerts some influence. You could make certain the warehouses stay crammed full of combustible materials."

Woodman wasn't too sure of the "combustible materials" part, but Lutel had made it sound important.

"I'll be up at dawn," he vowed. "You can count on me." He rose from the table. “Early night if I’m to have an early start,” he explained, and promptly took himself off to bed.

“Well, that’s galvanised him,” observed Rewn.

“But how far can we trust him?” whispered Verde.

“Leave it, Verde,” said Lutel. “What harm can he do in a warehouse?”

“If there’s trouble, Woodman will find it,” stated Verde prophetically. “He could ruin the whole plan; isn’t it a risk relying on him?”

“Not really,” replied Lutel with a grin. “After our trip to Newgate, you two are going to look to the city for jobs.”

“Doing what?” asked Rewn.

“Finding employment at the various companies’ halls; similar to Woodman, really, but more of an executive role. Try and influence the amount and type of goods they store. Treat it as a test of your persuasive powers.”

Verde did not look convinced; his brow was tightly knitted.

“Come on,” Lutel urged them. “You must see that if we are to set this town ablaze, it will need a chain of key tinder sources to ensure that it burns and spreads. Look to guilds like the leather, wood and wool companies – the list is endless.”

“I’m ready to give it a try,” acquiesced Rewn.

“All right, as long as we don’t forget Revin,” grunted Verde.

“Revin will not be forgotten, and to those ends I suggest that we follow Woodman’s lead.”

Slowly they made their way to their rooms, where each reflected on the task ahead, but none of their contemplations lasted far into the night and stillness soon descended on The Crows.

It was the last day of February 1666 and they breakfasted on very hot porridge and warm sack, before going their separate ways.

“We’ll see you this evening if all goes well,” cried Lutel, as Woodman headed off down the slippery hill.

A sharp frost had fallen overnight and the leaden sky looked like it would expel its snowy contents at any minute. Woodman gingerly made his way down the slope. Even at this early hour small children had been abroad making a slide on an area of the hill that was not covered in cobblestones. Their boisterous behaviour, laughing and screaming, was in sharp contrast to the serious mood of the attentive woman. Lutel watched Woodman for a short while. As he slipped and slithered, a small doubt nagged away at the back of her mind, but she felt helpless to tackle it. Dismissing it from her thoughts, she turned away and was soon crossing the road at the corner of Canning Street and Gracious Street.

Rewn and Verde were waiting impatiently, flapping their arms in an effort to defy the bitter cold.

"Do you think he'll be all right?" asked Rewn.

"I honestly don't know."

"My mother always says it's better to have an opinion and be wrong than to have no opinion at all," complained Verde.

"I don't know," she restated, her crisp reply matching the weather.

Silently they trudged along Gracious Street; their spirits too reflected the sudden change in the climate. Winter had been late in coming, but now it had arrived with a vengeance. Verde opened his mouth to speak, then chose not to mention the memories that this street held for him; the only thing to pour forth from his mouth was his breath, which was clearly visible in the bitingly cold air.

No word was spoken as they reached Cornhill and came upon the Royal Exchange. Here they were greeted with a hive of activity and aromatic smells. They paused to watch spices, pepper and other exotic goods being wheeled in on sack trucks or rolled in barrels. A makeshift carpet of empty sacking had been placed over the icy ground in an effort to facilitate the movement of the goods, but as the wheels regularly rucked up the covering it appeared to hinder the transfer of the commodities more than it helped.

"This would make an ideal spot," mused Lutel, breaking the silence.

"For a job?" asked Rewn.

"For a fire," she murmured.

Flakes of snow began to tickle the exposed areas of their faces as they headed westward along Cheapside. The flakes turned heavier, and by the time they had reached Newgate prison the swirling snow fell thick and fast. It settled on their hats and shoulders, eventually clinging to their clothing like powdered glue.

"They really are sugared loaves now," joked Rewn, pointing at Verde's hat.

Verde saw the funny side and chortled out loud. The tension was broken and all three broke out into relief-filled laughter.

"Better a sugar hat than sugar brains," retaliated Verde, tipping the snow that had settled on his hat over Rewn's head. The two men scuffled along in mock battle, until they became aware of Lutel's indifference. She was staring at the impressive wooden fortress that was Newgate prison. A huge wooden door stood as the dominant feature, like a giant guard warning all who dared approach. Its height was at least twice that of a man – a very tall man, thought Lutel – and it was reinforced with decorative ironwork, which rather belied its purpose.

Verde pursed his lips and whistled, scattering a surprised snowflake that was about to make a landing on his nose.

"That's pretty impressive," he said. "Almost as awesome as the Tower!"

"Not quite," Lutel corrected him. "There's a lot of wood in that structure. It's just a question of setting the right fuse."

"You mean you intend to torch the prison?" blurted out Rewn.

Fortunately, all those on foot outside the prison had bowed heads as they battled against the snow, and no ears had lingered long enough to catch the outburst.

"Let's discuss it elsewhere," suggested Lutel calmly. "But yes. This time we rely on nobody else; we will use the fire to our advantage, use it as a diversion to rescue Revin. I believe the local saying is 'to kill two birds with one stone'."

CHAPTER FORTY-FOUR

Winds of Change

Trudging back to The Crows was a slow business as the ground was now covered in a carpet of crisp white dust. They decided to postpone their plans until the following morning, when hopefully the weather would be more favourable to the task of securing work. The rest of the day was spent warming themselves in The Crows. Longfellow proved a considerate host; warm log fires blazed in all of the rooms, and their sodden clothing was soon steaming dry.

The landlord recommended a mixture of rum, lemon, spices and ale. He mischievously referred to this potent mix as his very own "Murder of Crows". Before serving the concoction he placed several iron pokers in the hottest part of the coals. After several minutes he withdrew a poker, its tapered end glowing red-hot, and he plunged it into a tankard that contained the drink. The cold dark liquid hissed and spluttered in protest, and a sweet fragrance filled the room. Longfellow repeated the action until all three of his guests had been handed their very own Murder of Crows.

Rewn examined his tankard and sniffed its contents; encouraged by the inviting aroma he took a sip, and was pleasantly surprised at the taste. His hands and body were swiftly warmed by the warm tankard and powerful drink, and he eagerly asked for a refill. Cupping his drink between his hands he stared into the dancing flames.

In his mind the weak flames flickered and the fire died.

"Make the most of it, Rewn," said the man tending the fire.

"Thank you, Tag."

Rewn accepted the warm bowl of broth from Tag. His leg throbbed and his head was light.

"Drink," insisted Tag. "It will fight the cold."

Rewn lay in the snow, his back propped against a desert boulder. The snow had stopped falling, but it lay deep on the ground. Tag had managed to save the survival bag from the accident and a blanket covered Rewn's legs and body. He had pulled Rewn from the wreckage before the space hopper had exploded in flames. Rewn had barely had time to shout "there's snow blocking the furmoil" before they had plummeted to the ground.

The next thing that Rewn remembered was being dragged through the snow by Tag. The pain in his leg was unbearable and blood trickled from a cut above his nose. Tag had packed a ball of snow and placed it on Rewn's wound.

"How long have we been here?" asked Rewn groggily.

"Two hours; help will come soon."

"Did you alert base?"

"No time, but they must have seen us disappear from the screen."

"But we were flying low."

"They'll have missed us by now." Tag put the bowl to his mouth and slurped the spicy red liquid.

"Good," Rewn said.

Rewn continued to lapse in and out of consciousness.

"Rewn, Rewn," prodded Tag. "Come on, we've made it this far, don't give up on me now."

Tag slapped Rewn around the face, and lay down beside him, pulling the blanket over the two of them.

"Remember the star chart reading challenge? You bailed us out of that one, Rewn. I never saw the catch."

"No," said Rewn hazily.

"Yes, you do," replied Tag. "The map, remember the map."

Rewn closed his eyes, Tag couldn't tell if it was the pain or if he was thinking.

"Oh, yes," groaned Rewn.

"That was brilliant. Fifteen items – list them in order of usefulness for an expedition to the desert pole," mimicked Tag. "Remember, Rewn… Rewn?"

Tag nudged his friend with his elbow.

"Yes, yes," mumbled Rewn, coughing a laugh.

"A gun for shooting flectra! What use would that be? Flectra birds are harmless. Though I suppose you could eat them," mused Tag.

"Would you fancy a flectra?"

"The snow suit and the visors – they were obvious," said Tag.

Rewn smiled. "Everybody placed those correctly."

"Yes, but only we put the map at fifteen. Totally useless – and only you noticed."

"Yes," said Rewn. "Cunning man, that Professor Swyld."

“But not cunning enough for you,” commented Tag. “Wrong desert – a map of the west side… totally useless, and only you spotted it.”

“One desert’s much like another,” replied Rewn modestly.

“Don’t do yourself down, Rewn. Our group, the lowest score ever recorded – brilliant!”

Rewn smiled at the memory, but he couldn’t muster the strength to answer.

“They’ll be here soon,” Tag reassured him. “Twenty-eight points, even Swyld said that will take some beating – record score, eh? Rewn?”

Rewn did not answer. Tag put his arm around his unconscious colleague.

As night began to drift over the horizon Tag began to doubt his optimism, fearing that Rewn would not last the night. Tag eased himself free from Rewn’s body and reached over for the survival bag. As the temperature plunged his frozen fingers fumbled in the gloom, locating the signal flares. He wondered if he would ever have the opportunity to use them. Tag fought to stay awake, his eyelids increasingly blinking. As his eyes screwed into narrow slits, the stars elongated in long silver threads and the creamy moon blurred. Eventually he was unable to focus, and lost track of whether he was awake or dreaming. The moon seemed to be shining even brighter and Tag lifted his right arm into the cold night sky.

When Rewn first regained consciousness the bed felt so soft that he imagined he was still lying in deep snow. On opening his eyes, the whiteness did nothing to contradict him. Rewn eventually became aware that he was lying in a room with a high white ceiling; it was warm and cosy, smelling of sweet scents.

“Ah, doctor, he’s just coming round,” said the watching nurse.

“Good, good.”

Rewn recognised the voice, but he couldn’t place it. The mystery encouraged him to force his eyes open and he turned his head sideways. A doctor with long black hair and two familiar eyes was staring at him.

“Shai,” gasped Rewn.

Whilst they enjoyed the cosy comforts of a fireside chat, Woodman had proved remarkably industrious. At the bottom of Fish Street Hill he had come to the aid of a well-dressed gent who had slipped over in the wintry conditions. The philanthropic influence of Lutel and Rewn had not been lost on him; back home in Wiltshire he may well have mocked or at best ignored the unfortunate victim of the weather. Now he found himself stretching out an arm to the well-groomed man, who had risen ungainly on the cobblestones as far as his knees, but seemed unable to make any further progress.

"God bless you, stranger," thanked a voice from under a sleek head of jet-black hair, as the man accepted Woodman's gesture. "I am indeed fortunate that you ventured forth today. Indeed, were it not for a particularly important item of work, the day would have found me at home."

Particles of ice and dust fell from the thin-faced man's breeches, as he brushed them away with the back of his gloved hand.

"'Tis a similar reason that brings me out-of-doors," ventured Woodman, eyeing the tall straight-backed stranger. Woodman's rustic cunning told him that here was an opportunity that might prove worth pursuing, and he was in no mood to hurry away.

"Your work is in Thames Street?" barked the other in a military tone.

"No, I seek work amongst the warehouses here."

The man studied Woodman, eyeing him up and down as though he were carrying out an inspection of a company of soldiers.

"You must be desperate – or keen – to seek work on a day such as this."

"My mother always said there was no time like the present," said Woodman, hoping the man would be as impressed by his mendacity as he himself was.

"This distemper has created a huge void; a man might have his pick of occupation. What line of work do you seek?"

"I am no man of letters," replied Woodman shamefully, "but I am strong, and have never shirked from heavy work."

"Apologise not; 'tis no dishonour to work with your hands. I may well be able to put something your way."

The man placed his cane over one shoulder and pensively stared at Woodman, who, growing uneasy at the scrutiny, stared around at the whitening rooftops. He was about to make his apologies and leave when the cane slapped the side of the man's leg; a decision had been reached.

"Your name, sir?"

"John Woodman."

"Pleased to make your acquaintance, Master Woodman; allow me to introduce myself. My name is John Rathbone, retired colonel of the Parliamentarian Army, and owner of the company Winds of Change – an importer of the very finest eastern spices."

"Pleased to meet you, sir," replied Woodman, extending his hand for a second time.

Rathbone accepted the friendly gesture and took Woodman's hand in a vice-like grip. "I am not without influence, Woodman. If you care to accompany me there will be something for you; as I said, this sad plague has opened up fresh opportunities to its survivors."

Side by side, the contrasting pair made their way along Thames Street. The road itself ran parallel with the great river whose murky surface was being refreshed by the dancing of tiny snowflakes. Around London Bridge the area was popular with wharfingers, as were all the adjacent lanes in the close vicinity. The warehouses themselves were large wooden structures towering into the sky, whose presence from the ground they tended to obscure as they were packed closely together. Woodman was grateful for this density as it afforded good shelter from the increasing intensity of the wind-driven snow.

Rathbone led the way beside several tall buildings and then stopped outside a wooden door. After rummaging around in his pocket he produced a bronze key and proceeded to unlock the door. The two men stepped out of the snow. Woodman's eyes took several seconds to adjust to the darkness of the building. When they did he stared at the large open space in front of him and the high roof above where several pigeons fluttered on the supporting beams.

"Let me show you around," offered Rathbone, and he picked up a horn lantern that had been resting on a beam in a shadowy corner. He blew away a layer of dust before lighting it, and the tour commenced.

Rathbone led the way to the back of the building. Under their feet rats squeaked and scurried away into the safety of dark recesses.

"Down here we store the heavier goods," Rathbone pointed out, raising his lantern so that the dim light shone on a stack of wooden barrels. "That's oil," he said. "Above us we have hemp, and on the top floor there are spices. We tend to store the lighter goods on the top storey."

He led the way up some rickety wooden stairs to the first floor.

"Mind your step, there's a broken one here," called Rathbone over his shoulder. He swiped a cobweb from his path with his free hand before continuing. Jute sacks covered most of the floor space, and the musty smell grew stronger as they crossed the room to a further flight of stairs that led them to the final floor.

"There's nothing here," said Woodman, casting his eyes around forlornly.

"I know. There would be little work I could offer you if the place were full. Now things are resuming an even keel, the coastal vessels and traders from foreign parts are docking in increasing number. You said you weren't afraid of manual work; do you hold to that? There's a job for you unloading goods at the wharfside and accompanying the wagons back here to unload a second time."

As they descended the lower flight of stairs Woodman obligingly accepted the position. Several men were now making their way into the warehouse.

"When do I start?"

"Right now," came the equally laconic reply.

Rathbone hailed a labourer, who was about to go down a flight of stairs to a cellar.

"Bill, Bill, come here!"

Bill paused on the steps and made his way towards the two men, favouring his right leg as he walked.

"Old war wound," he explained, in response to Woodman's steady look.

"I didn't mean to stare," apologised Woodman.

"John Woodman, this is William Saunders," barked Rathbone, brushing the episode aside.

"Morning, Colonel." Saunders saluted. "Please to meet you, John," he added, showing there were no hard feelings.

As Woodman shook hands, he noticed several other men behind Saunders disappearing down the steps and through a door, beyond which he could not see, although he strained every muscle in an effort to do so.

"Good day, Henry, Thomas," Rathbone greeted two men about to make their way down. They answered the Colonel by addressing him by his rank, much in the manner of Saunders.

"Use to serve with me in '43," explained Rathbone by way of clarification. "Good soldiers, all of them; now look at them, reduced to this."

He appeared as though he were about to add more, but Saunders asked for instructions and Woodman was denied further explanation as to Rathbone's sudden change in manner.

"Take John to the wharfside – set him to work with Berryman," ordered the Colonel.

Saunders started for the exit but Woodman remained rooted to the spot, his eyes fixed on the cellar stairs.

"Don't bother yourself with that room; this area's a warren of vaults, pits and cellars."

Woodman shook himself free from his daydreaming.

A passing thought crossed Rathbone's mind and he quickly added, "Very useful for storing wine, brandy and other liquor in cool temperatures, but prone to flooding if the tide's high." He pointed to the group descending the steps. "They're carrying out repairs just to be on the safe side. We should be all right this far above the river – rather dangerous work, though, so stay away from those stairs, John Woodman; we don't want any walls falling on you."

Rathbone finished speaking with something of a glower – rather harsh, thought Woodman, as he'd no intention of exposing himself to injury. Still, he was the new boy and Rathbone was probably being over-protective, although Woodman couldn't help noticing the men carried no tools with them.

"You coming or what?" bellowed Saunders from the doorway.

Startled into action, Woodman followed his guide through a door in the rear of the building, and down some wide well-worn steps that led to a passageway. Smaller wooden buildings stood on either side of them; most were ramshackle and deserted, having fallen into disrepair. Their owners had either prospered and moved to the larger warehouses on higher ground or, having been ruined by successive flooding, left the buildings to rot. Now the principal tenants were the sleek black rats, and even they found the pickings too poor to warrant a permanent settlement. Woodman noticed that a few of the less damaged buildings were actually inhabited; now and then a pale drawn face appeared at a window, or a ragged child dashed screaming inside a doorway, chased by two or three other ragamuffins.

Saunders led Woodman to a wharf where he was introduced to Berryman. His immediate impression was one of astonishment, as the docker proved to have only one good leg, the other being a mere wooden stump.

"Lost it at the Bloody Battle on Roundway Down," said Berryman, with time-tested presupposition. Woodman again coloured at his own lack of sensitivity.

"I hadn't, I wasn't…" he stumbled.

"Most ask, or are at least wondering," observed Berryman, "so I put them out of their misery by telling them mine." He grinned broadly to show there were no hard feelings, displaying a set of black decaying teeth, the result of having regular access to an uninterrupted supply of sugar – a perk of the job as he saw it.

Before departing Saunders issued some instructions into Berryman's ear.

"A boat is due on this morning's tide. When it berths send Woodman to the warehouse for more men."

As he left them an afterthought struck him, and he called back to the two men who were about to make themselves comfortable on some large coils of rope.

“No need to be idle, you can tidy the cordage – it goes tomorrow.”

Berryman grunted and Saunders turned on his heel and set off along the passageway he had recently trodden.

“Can’t stand the bastard,” said Berryman. “Back in the army I was his senior; now he gives me the orders and the bastard enjoys every minute of it.”

“You served with Rathbone?”

“Colonel Rathbone,” corrected Berryman. “I’ll not hear a word against the Colonel. He sought me out after the war and has given me food in my mouth these last twenty years or more. Colonel Rathbone is a good man with sound ideas – pity there aren’t more like him these days.”

Woodman looked over his new workmate. He had an oval face that was finished by a small jutting chin. He was balding on top, but hair aplenty – a curious mixture of sand and gravel – covered his ears and almost reached his shoulders. Berryman wore an olive-green neckerchief, brown shirt and breeches, and heavy leather boots with red stockings. He looked more suited to a pirate ship than a city dockyard.

The two men began toiling away on the coils of rope. Woodman took an instant liking to Berryman, whom he found easygoing and friendly, with a colourful vocabulary that appealed to Woodman’s baser instincts. Although Berryman was his senior, he exhibited no signs of pulling rank and was more than happy for both of them to work at a comfortable pace, keeping up a regular flow of conversation centred on his military experience.

He’d joined the Parliamentarian Army at the commencement of the Civil War and soon found himself under the command of Colonel Rathbone. Within six months he had risen to the rank of sergeant, enjoying the trust, friendship and patronage of his colonel. In 1643 at the Battle of Roundway Down, just outside Devizes, the Parliamentarians had fallen into a Cavalier ambush. The battle was bloody and fierce and by the end of the day the rolling green hills were strewn with bodies, and a long ditch, surrounding the base of one of the hills, ran red with blood, to be known for evermore as the Bloody Ditch.

Berryman came to a natural break in his life story, and he moved towards a pile of timber for a rest. The snow had stopped falling and, clearing a space, he beckoned Woodman to join him. As his companion sat down, Berryman reached into a small gap in the wood pile and pulled out a flagon of ale. The plug popped as he withdrew it, and the old soldier threw his head back and took a long cool swig of its contents. Staring thoughtfully at the slow-moving river in front of him, he passed the flagon to a thirsty Woodman.

Late in the afternoon the tide came in, but no vessel accompanied it. A dash of late winter's sunshine had made a welcome appearance, and the two men basked on the log pile as the last of the snow melted around them. Long shadows were cast to their side by the low milky sun.

"By the time my head reaches there," said Berryman, pointing to a spot on the ground, "it'll be too late."

Woodman stared at him blankly and Berryman gestured to his shadow.

"If the boat doesn't come soon the tide will have turned," he explained.

Within half an hour the designated mark had been reached and, as if to prove that there was as much sailor as trooper in Berryman, the tide had virtually reached its peak.

"You may as well go," offered Berryman. "I'll let the Colonel know."

"I pass that way; I can tell him."

"Very kind, but I've other business with the Colonel."

"But the boat still might come."

"Very unlikely; if it does we won't be unloading it this evening."

Berryman made his way up the passageway that led to the warehouse. Woodman reckoned his own way would be shorter if he followed the river to London Bridge, and turned up Fish Street Hill. He watched Berryman limp off and then began walking along the wharfside, pausing to watch some ducks on the water. Several mallard drakes were making amorous advances towards a lone female, in the process submerging her until the duck was close to drowning, water spraying all around as the quacking became intense. For a moment the competing birds disappeared from view as they splashed around in sun-dappled ripples. Spring was coming, he told himself, and with it the fire drew ever nearer. Woodman glanced up from the courting birds and blinked as a large trading vessel sailed into view. He watched it head towards the wharf that he had just vacated. Retracing his steps he ran along the passageway and turned into the alley that led to Rathbone's warehouse. Pausing for breath, he bent over on the steep hill, resting his hands upon his knees. Recovering, he ran on up the hill and climbed the steps to the warehouse. The door was unlocked and he burst in – the room was deserted.

CHAPTER FORTY-FIVE

Dust

"It's only me," called Woodman as he peered into the dimly lit storeroom. Surely Berryman must still be here, he reasoned. He'd only parted from him a few minutes ago, and besides, Woodman told himself, Berryman couldn't run as fast as him. Stepping further into the building, he paused at the stairs that led to the forbidden cellar. No sound came from below but a light shone dimly under the base of the door. Curiosity decided Woodman against calling out, and he descended slowly, feeling each step carefully before trusting his weight upon it. The repairs that Rathbone's men were supposedly carrying out were not very evident.

Woodman paused at the cellar door; he could now hear the sound of faint voices, not exactly whispers, more like low-hushed tones. Putting his ear to the door, Woodman listened intently; he held his breath in an effort to diminish all distracting noise. Eventually he was able to attune to the discussion, and he recognised the voice that was speaking.

"So, Thomas, you and Henry will be responsible for Aldgate, and William and John will look to Bishopsgate."

Woodman continued to listen in earnest; he caught snatches of conversation, recognising some familiar landmarks, but he could not decide what they were discussing. It was definitely Rathbone's voice doing the majority of the talking. Perhaps it was trade, he thought, but why conducted in such a clandestine manner?

"What about the bridge?" asked a voice that he didn't recognise.

"Taken care of," said Rathbone. "Berryman has seen to it."

"Have no fear, Colonel." Woodman recognised the voice. "I've a select little band, sorted and primed to go."

It began to dawn on the eavesdropper that more was being discussed than mere commerce, but as yet Woodman could make neither head nor tail of the subject of their furtiveness. Mindfully he transferred his weight to his other foot, pressing even closer to the door so that his ear was squashed flat against the panelling. A rustling sound came from beyond the door.

"Now, gentlemen, this sketch of the Tower: I have marked the points where the fire will cause most confusion, and we can attack here, here, and here."

Whispered murmurs of agreement accompanied three poundings on the table. At the mention of the word "fire", Woodman's whole body tingled with excitement – they were planning to burn London. For what reason he didn't know or care but he found himself in a predicament, torn between running back to The Crows to inform the others of this rival plan and standing his ground to glean more information.

Before he could decide, a third possibility occurred to him: perhaps he should knock on the door and offer his help. For several seconds he stood wondering, and then put his foot on the first step and instantly withdrew it. He raised his arm to knock, and then pulled back with his fist a short distance from the door. Woodman had finally decided to press his ear to the door again, when fate decided for him. Apart from being very dark, his hiding place was also very dirty. His agitated movements had disturbed some dust, and a few specks landed on his nose and caused him to sneeze. Immediately the soft droning on the other side of the door ceased, freeing Woodman from his vacillations. He spun around, intent on making a rapid exit; as he did so the door flew open and in his haste he missed the first step and fell flat on his face. Before he could recover a pair of large hands seized his shoulders.

"Not so fast," snarled his captor.

"Well done, Flint; bring him in," ordered Rathbone.

Woodman struggled but to no avail; held in a vice-like grip, he was thrown into the cellar where he lay sprawled on the floor. Staring up he saw the underside of a large rectangular table. As he was hauled to his feet between two men, the only things he could see were candles burning on the table top. Their flickering flames illuminated several papers and maps, but before he could study them a figure emerged from the shadows and rolled them up. A skinny man with a weather-beaten face took a torch from the wall, and held it so close to Woodman's head that some of his hair became scorched and a singeing smell began to permeate the room.

"Let's have a closer look at our spy," said the torch-bearer.

"Careful, Myles, no harm yet," said Rathbone. "Why, it's friend Woodman." He pulled a chair from the table. "Come and sit down, John."

The Colonel's voice was warm and friendly; Woodman was again bewildered as he was placed in a chair beside Rathbone. Two burly men stood behind him on either side; they did him no harm physically but their presence was menacing, and Woodman realised that he was a prisoner in all but name.

"Tell me, John, why are you here?" asked Rathbone, with characteristic forthrightness.

Woodman realised he would be no match for the interrogations of the army officer, and chose to rely on a mixture of honesty and innocence.

"I came to tell you the boat came in, sir. Just after you left," he meekly said, glancing over at Berryman who skulked in the shadows.

"And how long have you been outside?"

"Long enough," said Woodman, intending to explain that it was long enough to hear of their plans, and how similar they were to his own. By such means he was sure he could ingratiate himself with Rathbone and his followers. But before he could expand upon his reply the Colonel's countenance changed alarmingly, and the mood of the group became ugly.

"We must kill him," proclaimed Berryman, stepping into the light. "He's a government spy."

A murmur of consensus ran around the room, bouncing off the enclosed walls; such was its intensity that Woodman broke out into a cold sweat.

"No, no, it's not true," he stammered.

"Not true you're a spy, or not true you were listening?"

"No, Colonel, I mean yes… I'm not a spy, but I was listening?"

A noisy clamour again filled the room on this latest admission and Woodman swallowed hard. Rathbone produced a long thin dagger from inside his clothing and purposely walked around the table, taking sideways steps, never once removing his eyes from the prisoner. Woodman made to move, but he was heavily pinned down and his attempted action merely compounded his guilt in the minds of his captors. A queasy sensation filled the captive's stomach as the sharp point pricked his chin, and beads of sweat trickled rapidly down the contours of his cheeks like gushing streams rising after a flash flood.

How he wished that Rewn or one of the others were here, or better still that he were back on the family farm in Kellaways, but neither scenario was possible. Rathbone was towering over him, his menacing black cape giving him a sinister appearance.

"What did you hear?" he demanded in a tone now harsh and purposeful, any hint of conviviality having disappeared from his voice.

"I h-h-heard," stammered the terrified man, "I heard y-y-you say y-y-you're going to attack the Tower."

There, he'd said it, and Woodman relaxed a fraction, awaiting the consequences.

"Yes," said Rathbone, drawing out the word, "go on."

Encouraged by Rathbone's less hostile manner and the fact that he hadn't plunged the knife into him after his admission, Woodman found an ounce of confidence.

"You're going to use fire."

"He knows too much," screamed Berryman. "Kill him!"

The prisoner bit his lip. If he told the truth he was incurring the wrath of his friends; if he held back he invited suspicion from his captors. His position seemed both helpless and intolerable. Woodman keenly felt the frustration of his situation, and realised betrayal might be his only course of action, though even in these wretched circumstances he still felt a bond of loyalty to the others. Glancing around the room he recognised how sombre the mood had turned as the gathering waited expectantly.

Rathbone drew back his arm.

"Wait, wait," cried Woodman.

"Well?" said the Colonel.

"I've friends, friends in London near here. They're planning the same thing."

Berryman sneered. "You can't expect us to believe that. Don't believe it, Colonel; he's lying."

"Be quiet, Berryman," snapped Rathbone. He had not reached the rank of colonel without acquiring and employing a wide range of talents and skills, and hastiness was not one of them. It was just possible that this was more than a plea of desperation; a few minutes more was not going to endanger their plans. "You are going to attack the Tower?"

"Yes, no, yes, not quite." Woodman faltered. He couldn't think where to begin. He knew that once he had started it would all come out, but the thoughts were all jumbled up inside his head, and in his excitement and anxiety to save his life they were all screaming to come out at the same time, and subsequently blocking each other's exit.

"Lies; kill him, let's be rid of him, or it will be our necks."

"Hold your tongue, Myles. We have nothing to lose in hearing him out; we can wait. Release your grip."

The two henchmen took their hands away from Woodman's shoulders, and he sighed deeply. Rathbone reached for a jug and poured its contents into a tankard.

"A drink, John." He offered the tankard to Woodman, who nervously accepted.

"Go on, drink it," Rathbone urged him, calmly sitting down. "Then tell us your story."

"'Story' is about it."

The Colonel spun round to glare at Berryman, and the latter melted back into the shadows. The cellar fell silent as the ale was guzzled down. Woodman wiped his mouth and chin with the back of his hand, and leaned back in his hard chair.

"Some friends of mine are going to burn London," he said, "and I am going to help them."

"Why are they doing that?" asked his inquisitor.

"I'm not quite sure," answered Woodman, the truth dawning on him.

Berryman snorted, with renewed confidence. "'I'm not quite sure'," he mimicked. "Surely you can see that he is lying, Colonel? I say we kill him now."

There were a few murmurs of approval, but most had known the Colonel for too long to dismiss his procrastination.

"I'm not telling you again, soldier: be quiet, or trade positions."

"Sorry, sir." Berryman saluted and once more stepped backwards into obscurity.

Rathbone spoke calmly and firmly, and Woodman was reassured by his composed tone and manner. "Now, John, in your own time. When are your friends going to burn London?"

"Soon, but one of them has been arrested. He was in the Tower and we had planned to rescue him; we even acquired some keys." Woodman felt a tinge of guilt as he divulged the secrets, but his instincts for survival were no less than could be expected from many in his predicament, and thoughts of loyalty were gradually being dispelled.

Rathbone stiffened in his chair; this story interested him. His soldier's instinct told him that there was some truth behind these words, and he was determined to extract as much information as possible. "You stole some keys? Very impressive."

"No," corrected Woodman, "we made some copies."

Rathbone's interest increased; he felt vindicated for his decision to hear Woodman out. "Did you use the keys?"

"No, Revin was moved to Newgate."

"Revin?" Rathbone seized on the slip.

Woodman cursed his mistake; well, it was his life in the balance, he excused himself, and he decided to disclose as much information as would be necessary.

"We're going to burn London to get him out."

To the majority of the men in the room Woodman's story remained unconvincing. Rathbone's was still the only dissenting voice.

"I'll believe you," he said, "and spare your life, if you can tell me where to find your friends."

It was a fair offer, and Woodman saw it as such, yet before him arose a vision of Verde's smug countenance, his arms folded. "I told you so," he was saying. Lutel and Rewn had been good to him since their chance meeting in Wiltshire. He balanced these thoughts with the near-certainty that his throat would be cut if he didn't divulge their whereabouts.

"What do you want of them?"

"We may be able to work together. If you are telling the truth, I'm sure they would welcome the chance to join forces for the common aim."

Just what Rathbone's aim was still wasn't clear to Woodman, but he didn't feel in a position to refuse.

"Come, Woodman, you have nothing to fear if you are telling the truth."

"Let me go to them, alone," pleaded Woodman.

"I'm your only ally in this room," Rathbone pointed out. "If you alienate me, there is only one alternative."

"Would you betray your friends, if you were in my position?"

Rathbone breathed in through his nose, and looked at the ceiling.

"Admirable sentiments; I warm to you, Woodman. But your friends are in no danger if you speak the truth; besides, your course of action is rather limited."

"Let me go to them, to prepare the ground, as it were; you can come with me."

Rathbone had a gut feeling about Woodman's story; his experience told him there was some truth to it, and he was interested to meet and possibly join forces with these resourceful people, but he did not wish to risk personal danger. Neither was he prepared to be dictated to and lose face in front of his group. He walked around his chair and rested his hands on its back.

"You may go to your friends," he said, "but Berryman and Flint will accompany you."

Realising any protest would be futile, Woodman readily agreed to Rathbone's terms.

The Colonel whispered something into Berryman's ear before Woodman was led from the room. Berryman hobbled and jumped his way up the stairs, as Flint followed behind Woodman. At the top of the flight Berryman turned to face them.

"Don't try to escape," he growled, "or you will be sorry," and he patted something hard inside his shirt.

CHAPTER FORTY-SIX

THE BORNHATE

Thames Street witnessed little snow underfoot, most having been trampled by passers-by. An iron-grey sky suggested that a fresh fall was imminent and the three men pulled their clothes around them in protection from the biting north wind. Woodman stopped outside The Murder of Crows.

"This is the place."

"You wait outside, Flint; I will accompany friend Woodman in. Await my signal."

A few drinkers raised their heads to stare at the one-legged man as they entered the inn. Woodman cast his eyes around for a familiar face but drew a blank. Berryman sidled up closer and patted his chest. Woodman nodded to show he understood the silent threat.

"They are probably in their rooms," he reasoned.

"Then why are we waiting?"

With a minimum of disturbance Woodman led the way up the familiar wooden staircase, stopping outside Lutel's room. A thought flashed through his mind as he raised his arm to knock on her door. He opened his mouth, but all thoughts of crying out loud to raise the alarm disappeared as he felt something push into his back.

"Are you there, Verde?" called Woodman.

Inside the room Lutel was alerted to the possible danger. Woodman might mistake the room, but he would never call for Verde. She glanced around for a weapon, but before anything came to mind the door flew open and Woodman was bundled in at knife-point.

"Take it easy, missy," said Berryman, pushing the door closed, "and perhaps nobody will be hurt."

"He's a friend," said Woodman. "Don't alarm yourself."

Lutel calmly sat down.

"Do you know this man?" Berryman asked.

Lutel sized up the situation and read the answer in Woodman's face.

"Woodman? Yes, of course; what have you done now, John?"

Berryman pushed Woodman further into the room, circling his hostage around to the window, so that Flint could see them from below. It also gave him the advantage of facing the door, which at that moment again flew open. Verde and Rewn, having heard Woodman's call and the commotion that followed it, had immediately decided to investigate.

Berryman pushed Woodman forward into his would-be rescuers and, moving remarkably deftly for a man with one leg, was too quick for Lutel; she found herself in Woodman's place, with a knife pricking at her throat.

"He's a friend, he's a friend!" screamed Woodman. "Don't do anything!"

"We're hardly likely to," snapped Verde, staring at the glistening blade. "What's all this about, Woodman?"

"They're going to burn London and kill me, and I said that you were doing the same thing and could help. They didn't believe I was telling the truth, so they've sent Berryman and Flint to check," he blathered.

"Slow down, slow down," said Rewn placatingly, recognising the situation called for some composure, and realising the knife would slit Lutel's throat before he or Verde could reach Berryman. "We mean you no harm, friend; let the lady go."

"I told you I was telling the truth, Berryman," uttered Woodman in a state of agitation.

Rewn addressed him. "I don't quite understand your garbled story, Woodman, but am I to gather this is not a robbery or any other violent crime?"

Before Woodman could answer, Berryman spoke.

"Are you to burn London?"

Verde calculated the chances of successfully overpowering Berryman, as he was loath to part with such damning information. He too was doubtful that either Rewn or he could reach the miscreant before Lutel's throat was ripped. Safer to do as Berryman asked, he decided, and then once Lutel was free they could deal with this reprobate. Verde viewed Berryman as an enemy, being still unclear as to his motive for being there, and Woodman was falling further into a similar category, as he appeared to be the agent behind the present circumstances.

"What if we are?"

"Why?"

"Why, what?" asked Verde, being deliberately obtuse.

Berryman tightened his grip on Lutel, and she winced as the blade pricked harder against her skin.

“Don’t play games with me. I served Cromwell in the cause, and spilt more Royalist blood than missy’s body holds.”

Verde glanced at Rewn for approval. It was his sister with the knife point at her throat, and the burden of responsibility lay heavy with him.

“We aim to burn this pestilent city to the ground, and rebuild it after a more befitting fashion,” said her brother.

Berryman only partly understood Rewn’s meaning, but he grasped the words “burn to the ground” and briefly removed the knife to signal approval to Flint, who still waited impatiently below. Before anyone could respond, the blade flashed back into place and once more rested against Lutel’s fair skin. Rewn noted the motion and decided on a less confrontational approach.

“If we are to work together, we must show trust.”

He prayed his tactics were correct; after all, his sister’s life was at stake. Rewn reasoned Berryman must have some purpose in not murdering her instantly, and the one point he seemed obsessive on was the fire.

“If I let her go, what’s to stop you jumping me?”

“Trust,” answered Rewn simply.

“Open the door,” barked Berryman.

Verde stepped across the room to comply.

“In here, Flint!” shouted Berryman.

A shady figure cautiously entered the room. Thomas Flint looked shiftily around like a weasel not quite able to believe its luck at stumbling over a nest of fledglings.

“Come here, Tommy.”

Flint shambled across to Berryman’s side.

“These folk are going to burn London. What say you?”

Flint raised his eyes but avoided any eye contact. “Can’t burn much if you’re holding a knife to her throat, Jim boy.”

Rewn was as much surprised by the answer as Berryman, the look on whose face showed that he too had not expected such a perceptive response.

“We’re unarmed,” bargained Rewn, making the most of this surprising turn of events. “What…” – he hesitated and waved his hand towards the newcomer – “…Flint suggested makes sense. Put the knife down and we can talk.”

Flint puffed his chest out, unused to having his opinions taken so seriously. “Come on, Berryman, don’t be so bloody stupid; the Colonel didn’t ask for this.”

Rathbone was held in such deep respect by Berryman that his very image almost materialised before his eyes. Berryman blinked as a shaft of sunlight caught a pane of glass, and the knife dropped to the floor with a light clank as he released his grip on Lutel. She ran over to Rewn and he put a protective arm around her, as she uncharacteristically buried her head in his shoulder. Lutel had faced many dangers in her life, but she could never recall having been as petrified as she had been by this coarse and crude creature.

"Now how about a drink?" suggested Verde. "I'll go and fetch some wine."

Flint silently restrained Berryman, whilst Lutel made to object and then thought better of it.

"You do that, sir," agreed Flint.

When Verde returned he found Woodman and his two visitors sitting upon the edge of Lutel's bed, whilst brother and sister were perched on two high stools. An uneasy calm had descended on the room, and nobody was prepared to risk breaking it. Woodman had fetched out his foul-smelling tobacco pipe and offered Flint and Berryman a smoke, but both had declined, preferring to savour the ale that Verde now offered to them. A formal introduction had been conducted in his absence, and was completed by Berryman and Flint grunting on making Verde's acquaintance.

During the drinking, Woodman's story was repeated at a more comprehensible pace. Verde spilled his drink at the recounting of the uncertainty of listening at the door, but only the teller read its significance.

After some minor questioning of detail and straightening of facts, Berryman watched for signs of disclosure on their faces. "So what say you to joining forces?"

"How many of you are there?"

The question came from one of the wooden stools. Berryman seemed unwilling to answer, but the silence decided him to reply.

"There's the Colonel… and eight more of us in the Bornhate."

"The what?" asked Lutel.

Berryman frowned; he did not feel comfortable with the situation.

"'Tis a play on the Colonel's name – we use it privately amongst ourselves," explained Flint. "We do the planning, but there are many sympathisers who are ready to act."

Flint explained how the Bornhate consisted of officers and soldiers of the old Parliamentarian Army who still remained loyal to the Commonwealth. They had grown increasingly disenchanted with the second Charles Stuart, and intended to burn key areas of London, attack the Tower, and restore

Britain once more to a republic – in a blaze of glory.

"Literally and metaphorically," observed Rewn.

"Similar method, different reason," concluded Lutel, "but I think we could work together for the common good."

Lutel saw the advantages of working with Rathbone and his men. The increase in manpower could prove expedient and bring forward the timing of the fire. It would also seem advisable to keep a watchful eye on these fellow plotters, for fear they might jeopardise their own operation.

Berryman continued to look strangely at Lutel; he had never experienced a woman in a position of power, and looked between Verde and Rewn for confirmation.

Verde obligingly responded. "Ask your Colonel Rathbone for a meeting."

"Where?" replied Berryman.

"Not here, it would be too conspicuous," remarked Lutel.

"You must come to the cellar," said Flint.

"Tomorrow at noon," suggested Berryman.

"How do we know that it won't be a trap?"

"Trust," said Berryman with a smile, shuffling to the door, then pausing in the doorway to address Woodman. "You don't need to show for work tomorrow, John; just make certain that you deliver these good men on time." He bowed to Lutel as Flint left the room. "Good day to you, ma'am," he said, compounding the slight.

As soon as Berryman closed the door Woodman threw his arms in the air, sensing and anticipating trouble.

"I had no choice," he wailed. "They were going to kill me!"

"You could have left as soon as you'd caught wind of what they were planning," snapped Verde.

"I was going to, but the dust…"

"What's done is done," interjected Lutel. "We must look to make the most of this and turn it to our advantage."

"How?" demanded Verde.

"There are but four of us, excluding Revin. If we can convince them to extend the number of fires, to include areas pinpointed by ourselves, we are more certain of success."

"You mean ask them to seek employment in the halls and yards?" asked Rewn.

"I doubt if they'll go for that," groaned Verde.

"We do not know their exact plans, or how far they are from executing them. That is why it is important that we make contact; we don't want them usurping us and doing only half a job."

"But Lutel, their reasons are treasonable," argued Rewn. "Can we justify interfering in such a way?"

"I would say that we are going to interfere in quite a consequential way by razing the city. But you are right; though our actions are humanitarian, theirs are political. All the more reason for keeping them under observation, and keeping tomorrow's appointment. Well done, Woodman, you've possibly saved this mission."

Woodman didn't quite see how or why he was in Lutel's good books, but he smiled with relief, and on seeing the exasperated look in Verde's eyes, his smile widened to a grin.

CHAPTER FORTY-SEVEN

A SALUTATION

The resonant and melodic sound of the church bells of Saint Olave chimed out the midday hour as Woodman led the way along Thames Street, to the riverside warehouse. A sentry observed their coming and signalled to a second, who scurried away. As they reached the shadows of the building Berryman stepped forward from the shade.

"Follow me," he grunted, and he led them through the door and down the steps. As the five of them entered the cellar, an imposing figure stood up to greet them and offered his hand across the table.

"Welcome, gentlemen. Rathbone, Colonel John Rathbone at your service. Please be seated." He waved his arm in an indicative sweep. In turn they gripped the hand of peace. Verde and Rewn introduced themselves, followed by Lutel. At the sound of her voice Rathbone raised his eyes to look in Lutel's face.

"Madame, my apologies, you are especially welcome. Where are your manners, Tucker? A seat for our fair guest."

A scar-faced man at the end of the table slowly stood up and picked up a vacant stool, which he placed noisily in front of Lutel. Two more seats quickly appeared from behind the group.

The Colonel introduced the other men present; John Cole, Thomas Evans, Thomas Flint, John Myles, William Saunders, Henry Tucker, William Wescot and finally James Berryman all bowed their heads in turn.

Lutel sat down on the stool, flanked by her compatriots, whilst Woodman stood a little behind Rewn. Lutel studied the man opposite; Rathbone cut an impressive figure even though he was over sixty years of age. A florid complexion confirmed the outdoor life that he had undertaken, including many years' service as a soldier. A large curvilinear scar rode the contours of his left cheek, a permanent reminder of the Civil War. His figure had just started to lean towards the portly, but due to the ravages of time rather than any weakness in diet. She admired the large strong hands, the size of small buckets and very hairy.

Rathbone appeared polite and softly-spoken as he reached for a tiny ornate box from the table between them. "Snuff?"

All three visitors who were made the offer declined; only Woodman would have accepted.

"Please forgive the vice; it has lain around me for too many years for me to stop now."

Rathbone slid back the miniature lid and tapped the box, emptying a small amount of white powder onto the back of his free hand. Raising the powder to his nose he sniffed an equal measure through each nostril, and then sat back and waited for the inevitable sneeze that he knew would ensue. At its approach he twisted around, in deference to his guests.

"That's cleared the head; now to business," he said, shaking his shoulders, as if to alert the rest of his body to the activity that was about to be required. "It appears we have a common aim." His military background had taught him no other way but directness.

"This may be so," responded Lutel, "but not a common purpose."

A slight tremor of an eyebrow betrayed the Colonel's displeasure. "I am not used to dealing with… how can I put this without appearing offensive?"

"A woman, Colonel Rathbone?"

"Precisely," he said, and reached for the comfort of his snuff box.

"She speaks for us all," pronounced Rewn.

Rathbone paused, fingering the box on the table; he could feel several pairs of eyes burning into his back, expecting a firm resolve.

"Very well, pray continue."

A movement came from behind; the Colonel whirled around. His action was sufficient to quell any thoughts of revolt.

"Perhaps I should speak first. We wish to burn London," announced Rathbone candidly.

"Our intentions follow a similar vein," replied Lutel.

A murmur of approval echoed around the cellar.

"What are your reasons?" asked Verde.

The Colonel faced him, and relaxed into his chair. "We are all ex-soldiers of the Parliamentarian Army," he said, gesturing around the room.

The group nodded and muttered their approval.

"Times are very hard in this country. Plague has touched all common men deeply; we all know someone who has been visited by the distemper."

Louder mutterings resonated around the cold brickwork as Rathbone embraced the broader opinion.

"The moral foundation of our society has collapsed; ever since the return of Charles Stuart there has been a growing increase and acceptance of fornication, degradation, whoring and thieving."

As he pronounced each vice, Rathbone banged the snuff box loudly on the table, emphasising his feelings and drawing forth cheers of approval from his cronies.

"In short, gentlemen and lady, England has once more become a godless country."

"True, true," shouted John Myles, amongst a general chorus of accord.

Rathbone continued his tirade; although he kept a check on his emotions, his speech became more rapid.

"God has punished England's wickedness; the sending of the pestilence is a clear sign of His disapproval. We are going to raze the corrupt corners of this once-great country, and re-establish the penitent days of the Commonwealth."

A cheer broke out amongst all the members of the Bornhate, continuing for several seconds with back-slapping and stamping of feet, until their leader raised his hand.

"To these ends we have formed the Bornhate – dedicated to the restoration of moral values and the destruction of this devil lust."

Lutel waited for calm before responding to Rathbone's heartfelt diatribe. She looked straight ahead, requiring no ratification, as she knew that Verde and Rewn's views would replicate her own.

"We hold no views on your politics," she said. "If you can gain your ends with no blood spilled, then we have no objection."

Rathbone again shuffled uncomfortably in his seat.

"What are your aims?" he asked, bending forward with his head resting on his elbows. "I've heard scraps from Berryman, but please expand on them for us."

Lutel composed herself; her words would have to show sympathy towards the Bornhate, but at the same time commit to nothing that would prove unacceptable to the Stilax. An expectant silence descended on the cellar; only the sound of her own quick breathing reached Lutel's ears.

"We believe the fabric of London's buildings is in need of as much attention as the moral fibre of its inhabitants. Our aim is to purge the city of the filth and disease that corrupt the body, as you would cleanse its soul."

A large grin spread across Rathbone's face, and mutterings of approval increased, as those who were unable to follow Lutel's statement read the accord in their leader's countenance. Rathbone raised his arm, and the conversation dropped to a whisper, until he politely cleared his throat.

"It sounds like we have a mutual cause; perhaps we should think of a pact?"

For the first time since negotiations had opened, Lutel consulted Verde and Rewn. Rewn nodded his agreement and Verde, after a slight pause, followed suit.

"What are your plans?" asked Rathbone, eager to cement the new partnership, but wise to the necessity that the newcomers should not upstage his own designs.

Lutel again received permission before outlining their intentions to the Colonel.

"When we are convinced that conditions are favourable, such as the storage of combustibles, dry weather and prevalent winds…" Lutel stopped, pausing to reconsider. The effect, however, was dramatic; every ear strained in undivided attention so that she felt compelled to continue, and did so in a restrained tone. "We will start fires throughout the city."

Such they all knew from Woodman, but Lutel's imperious position within the group brought forward gasps of approval, as though those present in the room were hearing the idea for the very first time.

Rathbone clapped his hands together twice; it was a slow and deliberate act of approval. "Very commendable," he said, then stopped and mused as a thought struck him. His pensive action was not lost on the remainder of the Bornhate, and a hush again descended on the room. Lutel swallowed hard and tried to remain composed.

"I hope you weren't intending to… the admirable Woodman, of course," and he dismissed his musings with a chuckle. "How much of the city do you intend to destroy?"

"As much as possible."

"You aim high," observed Rathbone, "but how will being homeless help the common man?"

"London will be rebuilt on a grand scale," claimed Rewn. "Not buildings of wood, but beautiful stone houses. No overcrowded conditions, but wide streets fit for any man to live in."

"These are indeed grand designs," enthused Rathbone. "Although they do not exactly mirror our moral crusade, they dovetail agreeably. We have targeted more specific areas such as the Tower and Horse Guards, but perhaps we should reconsider in light of what we have heard today."

"Be you sure we can trust them, Colonel?"

The lone dissenting voice crackled from the back of the room. All eyes stared at Berryman.

"We know so little of these people."

"We know little of you," returned Lutel, concerned that their pact would be broken before it had emerged from the embryonic stage. However uncomfortable it might prove to work with Rathbone and his band, she would much prefer it to having them plan their separate ways.

"Both points are valid," said Rathbone. "But we each know rather too much about the other; it's a reciprocal guarantee."

There were no further objections and the Colonel called for a toast. Tankards were filled with sack and keenly accepted by all in the room. Rathbone pushed his chair back and stood with his drink in hand, preparing to deliver a salutation.

"Gentlemen and lady, I give you the Commonwealth, the memory of our Lord Protector, and the success of this alliance – may our combined fires purge the city of all its festering sores, and confine them to eternal damnation and everlasting flames!"

To cries of the Bornhate, the tankards were instantly emptied, and Lutel, Verde, Rewn and Woodman saw no reason to antagonise their hosts.

"Have you considered thwarting the meddling authorities?" asked Rathbone, regaining his seat.

"What are you proposing?" asked Verde, throwing the question straight back.

"Answer me this," said Rathbone. "What puts fires out?"

Verde and Rewn stared at each other.

"Rain," offered Lutel.

The Colonel shook his head playfully.

"Water," shouted Woodman from a corner.

Rathbone looked disdainfully in the direction of the voice that had stolen his thunder, but it was a fleeting irritation, and he was keen to impress Lutel with his knowledge. "Water, yes, what else?"

Lutel was at a loss for an answer, and Rathbone gave no time to ponder.

"Pulling down houses," he said. Much to his joy, Lutel still failed to grasp the significance. "Stops fires spreading. I can see you haven't properly thought this through."

"We are indebted to you, Colonel Rathbone. How will you counteract these issues?"

"Stop the authorities bringing help in. There are few soldiers inside the city walls, fewer still since the plague."

"Surely there are not enough of us to fight soldiers," said Lutel, surveying the room. A thought struck her that maybe there were more members of the Bornhate than were present, and she abhorred the prospect of violence.

"No need," chortled the Colonel, and he unfurled a map that lay in front of him. "These crosses mark the city gates," he explained, running a gnarled finger over the map. "We will have men posted at these sites to lower the portcullises and stop the King's men from entering the city!"

"What about inside, Colonel Rathbone?" asked Lutel.

"To what do you refer?"

"Do you not envisage any resistance from within the walls?"

"Most people will be with us, once we begin our campaign for freedom, but you have struck an important point. The city has a water supply, driven by five water wheels at London Bridge."

"We could put them out of action," interrupted Verde.

"A commendable proposition," enthused Rathbone.

"There's also the new river system to the north," pointed out a further member of the Bornhate.

"You are right, William Wescot," said Rathbone. "Now if we could obtain the keys to the stopcocks, we would be in a position to stem the supply."

The meeting continued to late in the afternoon; Rathbone was in his element. Duties were assigned and tentative friendships began to develop. Verde, Woodman and Flint were selected to investigate the possibility of procuring the stopcock keys, whilst Rewn and Myles were to concentrate on the prospects concerning London Bridge. It was agreed to meet again in three days' time, in order to report on progress and plan future operations.

CHAPTER FORTY-EIGHT

CREAM TOAST AND GRAVY SOUP

The following evening Lutel lay on her bed, having spent the bulk of the day pondering Revin's plight. She had twice walked to Newgate, but each visit had proved fruitless. A sweet smell of cinnamon from some slices of cream toast filled the room. The landlady had provided them over an hour ago, but due to her lack of appetite the sprinkling of dark brown sugar had soaked completely into the brown bread. As she picked at the food, waiting for the others to return, Lutel could see no alternatives to the plan that they had already formulated.

Rewn was the first to arrive.

"Any luck?" she asked.

"Should be easy," replied her brother, "or at least the idea is simple. It may prove a little more difficult in its execution."

"Well?" asked Lutel, breaking off from her meal.

"Myles and I managed to climb down the side of the bridge. There are quite a few gaps between the buildings on the bridge, and it's not hard to reach the river."

Lutel resumed her chewing and offered up the plate. Rewn took a piece of the cream toast, examined it, and then took a huge bite. Crumbs dropped down his front, and he brushed them away before wiping his mouth with the back of one hand.

"This is good," he mumbled, and his speech became less clear as he attempted to satisfy not only his hunger, but also Lutel's inquisitiveness. Further fragments shot from his mouth as he continued to explain. "It's true the water system is served by five wooden wheels. If we can find some way of putting them out of action, there will be no water to douse the fires."

Rewn popped the last piece of cream toast in his mouth, and licked his lips approvingly.

"Have you given any serious thought to how this can be achieved?"

"Yes. Why do you think I've been so long? I realised straight away that the obvious solution was to do to the wheels what we intend to do to the city.

A local conflagration will render them totally useless; ironically, one of the very troubles they are intended to combat will be their own downfall. I suggested as much to Myles, and we agree that a dousing in oil will cause a rare old blaze once the fire reaches them."

"How will this be accomplished?"

"That's the tricky bit," sighed Rewn. "We will need to store some barrels on the bridge, or below the arches themselves. Well, at least that was our first thought, but further investigation proved it to be impractical."

Lutel paused in lifting a piece of food to her mouth.

"The houses on the bridge obviously have no cellars, so renting a storeroom is out of the question," continued Rewn, "and even if we could lower the oil over the side of the bridge, it would still leave us with the problem of storage."

"An interesting problem."

"Exactly. We thought of tying some ballast to the barrels, or tethering them to the arches, but both ideas are open to discovery."

"So what are you going to do?" asked Lutel in exasperation. She had witnessed this preparatory rambling in her brother before. She knew it preceded a solution that he was preparing to spring on her as the inspired answer. First he would paint a picture of near-impossibility, and then, when all seemed lost, trot out the explanation as if none but a fool could have failed to see it. Only this time Lutel did not feel in the mood to play his game, so she merely took another bite of toast.

Rewn sat on the end of her bed, and waited silently. Lutel recognised the signs of an imminent sulk. Why did she allow herself to fall into these traps? she asked herself. She finished her meal and then allowed an acceptable lapse in time.

"So it's impossible, then?"

Rewn leapt from the bed and faced her.

"No," he said. "We can acquire a wherry, and row down the river."

"So have you done this?"

"No," replied Rewn, in mild surprise. "We must show the utmost care and cunning. We will deliver the oil a few hours before the fire is to be started."

Lutel did not feel her charitable climb down to be worth this information, so she rather coldly remarked, "It took you all day to hire a boat?"

"No. That will be simple. The river is full of craft; they are as common as the flies around the dung hills. No, Flint and I have visited the Tallow Chandlers' Hall, and all the necessary arrangements have been made; the boat and oil are safely stored in the warehouse."

Lutel snorted. Her response was not quite what Rewn had anticipated.

"Well, at least I've done something," he grunted. "I've not sat around on my backside all day."

Lutel rolled over and reached under the bed for a jug of sack. In one deft action she threw the contents over her brother.

"What did you do that for?" he cried angrily.

Lutel did not reply; she was convulsed with laughter. The sight of him dripping wet was just the antidote she had needed to release her from the frustration of the day.

"I've done it again, haven't I?" asked Rewn, smiling, and he joined in his sister's amusement.

Rewn had dried out, and he and Lutel had retired downstairs, before a weary Verde and Woodman returned to The Crows. The latecomers witnessed a scene of merriment, as Lutel and Rewn drank and talked with a small party of locals.

"…And then she said four," croaked a robust man, bedecked in the garb of a fisherman. Laughter rippled around the circle until the joke was understood, and then large guffaws burst forth.

"You're 'aving us on, George Bulyon," screeched a woman, who appeared the worse for the sack that she held in her hand.

"'Tis as true as I stand here, Ver Jacob, you mark my words. Ain't it so, Will Mencham?"

"I thought she said five," replied Will. The circle howled with laughter, as Verde and Woodman accepted their drinks from Rewn and joined the ring. After the telling of a few more anecdotes and jokes, the landlady brought Verde and Woodman their evening meal. Lutel and Rewn accompanied them to a peaceful corner of the room that afforded a large degree of privacy.

"It was a fair trek," said Verde, and he paused to tuck into his tansy of spinach; it had become a particular favourite, and barely a week went by when he failed to pay their host at least one early-morning visit to especially order the rich omelette. Nutmeg was a novel taste to him, and he had acquired a distinct liking for the dish since he had first tasted it around Christmas time, even though Lutel frequently pointed out the likely effect of so much whipped cream on his waistline.

"It took us the best part of two hours," explained Verde, as he chewed another large mouthful.

"And you found?" enquired Lutel.

Verde reached inside his shirt, and pulled out a small package of brown cloth. Unfolding it carefully he laid three small keys upon the table; their gleaming metal glistened in the candlelight.

"We must return them within two days."

"How did you come by them?" asked Rewn.

"Flint can be very persuasive," said Woodman.

"You didn't involve yourselves in violence?" demanded Lutel. "We've enough problems with Revin in prison without you being arrested!"

Verde cut himself another piece of the tansy, and small morsels shot forth from his mouth like miniature cannonballs as he endeavoured to continue the story of his day.

"There was no violence," he assured her. "Money opens many doors."

"Not to mention stopcocks," guessed Rewn.

"Or closes them," said Woodman, smiling.

"We must make copies and return them by the day after the morrow," said Verde. "Failure to do so will result in their disappearance being discovered."

"Jaycock?" suggested Rewn.

Lutel frowned. "Again?"

"My thoughts exactly, Rewn," agreed Verde. "I wonder if he still has our other keys?"

Verde stared skywards at the intimidating portcullis above him, and wondered if Jaycock would be so accommodating this time. No reason he shouldn't be, he thought; after all, he had been paid for his work, even though they had failed to collect it. His hand moved upwards to his chest, checking that the package was still in place. Verde's eyes focused on the backs of Lutel and Rewn's heads, as they led the way along Shoe Lane. Woodman let out a shriek of delight as he spotted some smoke billowing from the forge ahead.

"Well," said Jaycock, "you were the last people I would have expected to see around here today." He stopped his hammering, and placed his tongs on the anvil.

"Fret not, you may keep your money, even though we have no need of the keys," said Verde, beaming.

"All the same if you did," answered Jaycock.

"What do you mean?" asked Lutel, glancing around the area.

"I no longer hold them. A few days after your visit a man came asking questions. He claimed your acquaintance and asked for the keys. I presumed he was a friend and he took them with him. Mind you, he called back several times to see if you had called. I began to suspect, and questioned him; he never returned after that. But he did leave an address to contact him, should you return yourselves – said it would be to my advantage if I were to let him know instantly.

"Where are you to contact him?" probed Lutel.

"I think he was jesting with me."

"The address," barked Verde brusquely. "Have you noted it down?"

"By the Lord, no," said the blacksmith; "no need to. What man could forget the Tower of London?"

"What manner of man approached you?"

"You might ask, madam. A strange-looking cove if ever I've seen one, and believe me I've seen plenty. Tall, very thin, with a remarkably long nose."

"Laungechamp!" cried Rewn.

Lutel exchanged glances with her brother and Woodman, but Verde stood in ignorance.

"Are you telling me this man is not a friend?" asked Jaycock.

"We know of him," said Lutel.

Verde frowned. "Do we?"

"You have not met him."

"I'm sorry about the keys. I still have the moulds," said the blacksmith with a wink.

"It no longer matters," Lutel assured him.

"Then what have you come for?"

"It's no longer important."

"Will you stop for a drink? This wind freezes the very marrow; east winds are not common, but when they blow they do so with a vengeance."

"Yes," said Rewn.

"No," Lutel contradicted him. "We must leave."

"Are you sure there is nothing I can do to assist you?"

"Yes," said Lutel. "Should this man come asking for us again, tell him you have not seen or heard from us."

Jaycock looked disappointed. "Is that all?"

"That's plenty."

Lutel turned and walked briskly away; Rewn and even Woodman followed her trail of thought and followed close upon her heels. Still in the dark, Verde sensed the danger signals and, after nodding to Jaycock, pursued the departing trio.

Scurrying to catch them, he soon arrived at Lutel's side.

"What is it? Who is the man asking after us? Do you know this Longnose or whatever his name is?"

During their return journey, Lutel explained the circumstances behind their fears.

"Has this man followed you to London?"

"It appears to be the case," replied Lutel.

Verde peered back over his shoulder. "Shouldn't we check that we are not being followed now?"

"We would not be walking freely if he had traced us."

"What about the keys?" persisted Verde.

"We return them," she said. "We had best lie low again for a while, and rethink our ideas. At the moment we don't know who we can trust."

"What about Revin?" asked Verde.

"We will be of no use to him if we keep him company; a small delay is inevitable, given the situation."

"What about the Bornhate?"

"We move cautiously on that front," advised Lutel. "Woodman can take a message and say that we are indisposed – a fever has taken us, and we will be unable to attend the next meeting. You can also return the keys to Flint, John."

Woodman made to object, and then thought better of it.

Upon reaching The Crows they asked for the evening meal to be served upstairs. Once again they crowded Lutel's room to eat communally. The gravy soup was their most sombre meal for some time. No attempt was made at humour, and the soup was as cold as the atmosphere that pervaded the bedroom. There was a realisation that they were no longer fully in control of the situation – events were now dictating to them; destiny had slipped slightly from their grip. Laungechamp's shadow seemed to linger over the room and every noise from without took on a sinister significance.

"Well, he can't know our whereabouts," reasoned Rewn in an attempt to cheer, "or he would have been here by now."

"How do we know that he has not been?" snapped Verde. "He may be spying on us, watching and waiting to see what we are up to. He can't know that much."

"Laungechamp is clever," admitted Lutel, "but not that subtle. If he knew that we were here, he would have made a move to arrest us; he answers to the King."

“So we just sit around and do nothing,” snarled Verde, spilling his soup and storming around the room.

“No, we sit around and think. We evaluate and appraise,” said Lutel. “If we use our brains then we will hold the upper hand. If we trust to the violence of Rathbone, or rush in without planning, then we lose the advantage.”

“What advantage?” sneered Verde. “Revin is in prison and we are doing nothing to help him. We are stuck here and no closer to home.”

“Where is your home?” asked Woodman, homing in on the blunder.

“Quite a way from here,” answered Lutel honestly.

Woodman had not ventured as far in all his days as he had since meeting Rewn and Lutel, and his concept of “quite a way” satisfied his curiosity. He imagined a home in excess of one hundred miles; several hundred light years was beyond both his experience and his comprehension, and he let the potentially awkward subject drop.

“You go to the meeting tomorrow, John. Make our apologies, and return the keys to Rathbone.” Lutel congratulated herself on her swift response, and the evening drew to a close with no further discomfiture, nor any subsequent decisions.

Woodman awoke early the following morning, and breakfasted in the company of the landlord. The two men were of a similar ilk and they had grown very friendly towards each other, finding they shared much in common in ideology, trade and background. After devouring his cold meat and ale, Woodman returned to his room and removed a package from under his pillow. The keys were still wrapped in their material and he stole quietly from the room.

Halfway down a stair complained as he trusted his weight on it, and the noise reverberated throughout the quiet inn. Woodman stopped and listened, then crept briskly down the remaining stairs and out of the door. A few street hawkers were preparing to go about their business; otherwise very few people were abroad. Woodman planned to find Berryman at the wharfside as he did not anticipate that Rathbone or any other member of the Bornhate would be in the cellar until far later in the day.

Fish Street Hill was deserted as he made his way towards the riverside and along to the wharf, where there was no sign of the peg-legged soldier. Woodman waited around for a few minutes, blowing into his hands to warm them; as his feet increased their protestations he decided the walk to the warehouse would at least keep him warm. As he approached the building he detected a movement from the corner of his eye. Pulling out a rag, he stopped in pretence of blowing his nose. Peering over his hands he noticed that somebody was creeping around in the shadows. Woodman, assuming it to be Berryman, was about to call out his name, when a second body appeared, soon to be joined by several others.

Pressing himself close to the wall beside him, Woodman kept very still; the shadowy figures wore the unmistakable uniform of the King's guard. He was certain that he had not been observed himself as the focus of their attention was Rathbone's warehouse. The soldiers were encircling the doorway, and Woodman edged away, walking sideways in order that he could keep his eyes glued to the men. He had no intention of witnessing the unfolding drama, and as soon as he was out of sight he turned his back and made a hasty retreat. He made his way back to Fish Street Hill, but there he found that he had recovered sufficiently and, instead of returning to The Crows, decided the scene warranted a closer inspection.

Driven by curiosity he walked along Thames Street towards Rathbone's warehouse. He judged a safe distance in the canopy of a doorway from which prying eyes would not be suspected and watched in fear and trepidation as twenty or so soldiers poured out of the warehouse. In the midst of the melee Woodman recognised the members of the Bornhate. He placed a bent finger in his mouth to suppress a shriek, and rapidly made his way back to The Murder of Crows.

On hearing the news, Verde's first instinct was one of panic, and he insisted that they should leave their rooms. Lutel argued that Laungechamp would already have come for them if he knew their location.

"But Berryman and Flint have been here – Woodman brought them," Verde said, looking accusingly at the latter.

"There is nothing to link them with us," Lutel assured him.

"But they will be interrogated!"

"Verde has a point," said Rewn.

"Woodman, were all of the Bornhate arrested?" asked Lutel.

"I didn't hang around to find out, but I recognised Rathbone, Berryman, Flint, Myles—"

"There you are," Verde butted in. "Berryman and Flint are taken and they are bound to talk."

"If they have all of the Bornhate, they will be seeking no others. There will be a swift trial and that will be the end of it," said Lutel.

"How can you be sure? Dare we take the risk?"

"I can't be that certain, Verde, but we have nowhere to go, and nobody is likely to shelter us from the law. It's a setback, I'll admit. We must delay our plans even more, but we've waited for several months; a few more weeks will not make any difference."

"It might to Revin."

CHAPTER FORTY-NINE

SCANDAL AND BLOOD

In April the trial of the Bornhate aroused great public interest. The authorities used it as an excuse to enforce an even crueller and stricter regime. Lutel's decision to remain at The Crows had proved to be correct, as they were safely ensconced in their lodgings; no suspicions had been raised or questions asked. Verde attended the Old Bailey, disguised in a black wig and even bushier beard, in order to gain first-hand knowledge should there be any unfortunate revelations. A noisy crowd gathered daily, thirsting for scandal and blood. Rathbone and his men looked a sorry sight, chained in a long row, their bodies bruised and bent. The Colonel sported a matching scar on the other side of his face, and one of his eyes was bruised and closed. Most of the other members of the plot were visibly shaken and displayed signs of distress and torture; their clothing was ragged, dirty and torn.

The prosecution spoke of revolution and the wave of rumours that was sweeping the city. Rumours that suggested the possibility of other traitors still being at large. A collective gasp burst forth from the gallery. After the judge had restored order, Rathbone surveyed the courtroom. Verde attempted to melt into the background as the Colonel's gaze paused at the man in the bushy beard.

"We are the sole members of the Bornhate," he announced in all truthfulness.

The prosecution attempted to make more of the claim, but the judge was under orders, from on high, to reach a swift and satisfactory conclusion and to banish all suggestions of further mischief. Verde had little trouble in remaining undetected, and he was able to report daily to the others on the latest developments. Nobody spoke in defence of the Bornhate – not even the Colonel himself. The trial was swiftly completed and by summer the rumours began to subside, finally dying out with the execution of the Bornhate themselves in June.

As the middle of August passed with no further unnerving incidents Lutel decided they could again become active. Verde, Rewn and Woodman were sent forth to inspect the ever-bulging companies' halls, and as they toured the area, all the signs pointed to London once more becoming a vibrant and prosperous city. Trade had obviously been resumed with many, if not all parts of the globe. Few merchants had been directly touched by the plague, due to their desertion of the city, and the businesses of those who could no longer trade were swiftly filled by their surviving contemporaries who possessed a quick eye.

Their base having been established in the east end of the city, it followed that most of their planning was concentrated around that area. An easterly wind would be required to fan the fires across London, and much anxiety and concern was caused by the prevalent winds blowing from the opposite direction. The date of the torching could not be planned. It remained in the hands of fate. Verde argued that they should remove themselves to the west of the city, but Lutel remained steadfast. She argued that the logistics of the move, in addition to setting up in new accommodation, might well cause questions to be asked. England was at war with the Dutch, and rumours and scaremongering were still rife; besides, the shadow of Laungechamp was always lurking in the background.

"Furthermore, Verde," pronounced Lutel, when they had gathered in her room for a late-night rendezvous, "the steelyard is full of cordage, and its proximity to the timbered buildings on the river is ideal. And this morning I found the perfect place for the fire's inception."

Lutel rocked back in her chair and took a further bite of her herring pie. Its sharp tang caused her to wince as she bit into the glazed pastry, but the fish was fresh, and they had learned to appreciate any wholesome food that came their way.

"Where?" asked Verde.

"By chance in the adjoining street, I am to be housemaid to Thomas Farynor of Pudding Lane – the King's own baker, no less!"

"But why there?"

"Because a bakery has large ovens and a fire there will be less suspicious. No one will ever believe that it was started deliberately, and its location is precisely what we require."

"Won't working for a man of the King be dangerous?"

"I don't see it as a problem, Verde."

"Fine," said Rewn.

"There is one problem."

"What?"

"I have to live in, and I start tomorrow."

Lutel began to tidy their meal away in an attempt to hinder any further discussion. She relieved Woodman of his utensils and crockery, and reached for her brother's.

Rewn put a restraining arm on her wrist, and Lutel faced the inevitable objections.

"It's far too dangerous to separate; we will not be able to communicate, let alone plan efficiently. Besides, we know nothing about this Farynor. You could be there for months."

"I think not," said Lutel. "Tomorrow is the last day of August, and autumn will surely bring a change in the weather."

Woodman had been listening intently to the conversation. Here was the culmination of his expectations, yet he wore a despondent frown.

"Why so sad, John?" asked Rewn.

"Well, if the fire is to start in the next lane, and is to be blown westward, won't we be in its path here?"

"A small sacrifice, surely," answered Lutel. "We are forever ridding this city of pestilence. A whole new future awaits it!"

"Might as be," said Woodman in a melancholic tone. He looked around for a sympathetic face.

"Go on," said Rewn.

"It's just that I have been really happy here; these last few months have been… well, you know. Where do I go when this place is gone?"

"You can go back to the country," suggested Verde.

"Hardly," intoned Rewn. "He announced his pyromania in Chippenham. Nobody believed him at the time, or so we thought. But they'll certainly sit up and take notice after the fire."

"Can I stay with you?" asked Woodman. "Where *do* you live?"

"You would not want to come with us," answered Lutel evasively.

"How do you know I wouldn't?" pleaded Woodman in a hurt voice. "You don't want me."

"We'll see," said Lutel, eager to avoid a scene and its possible repercussions.

Verde opened his mouth.

"Let's start the fire first," said Rewn abruptly. "Right now we need to do a little planning; it might be our last chance for quite a while."

Lutel was grateful for the support, but the sting in the tail did not go unnoticed.

A large pool of wax had melted on the table by the time their discussions were finalised. In the gathering gloom it had been accepted that Lutel could sneak away to contact them, and if she was unable to leave her new master, Woodman would act as their go-between. Rewn was the last to leave her room.

"Take care, no heroics."

"Don't worry," she sighed.

"Are you worried?"

"No. A touch of Woodman's romanticism; this will be my last night under this roof."

Rewn hugged his sister closer to him, then helped her to her bed.

"You'll soon be home," he said, and blew out the candle as he left the room.

Part Eight

Fire

CHAPTER FIFTY

IN NEED OF A FIRE

Thomas Farynor sat back in his chair, and pushed his thumbs into the top of his breeches in a futile attempt to loosen their pull on his girth. He was a heavy man, pale-complexioned with black swept-back hair, flecked with grey. Around the table sat his petite wife and their daughter Lydia. The young woman, for she had recently reached her eighteenth birthday, had inherited few of her parents' features; her faultless complexion was florid but not burned by crude and excessive exposure to the sun, as characterised many of the peasants who spent their working days in the fields. Midnight tresses cascaded over her shoulders, and deep blue eyes sparkled in a beautiful face that was accentuated by the glow of candlelight. Lydia was in the transitional period when girls mature into young ladies, and many a young blood's head had already been turned by the baker's daughter.

Farynor surveyed his cosy sitting room. It was bathed in soft light from the moon, and the tallow candles flicked shadows onto the walls.

"That will be all," he said to his serving girl. "You may retire to your room as soon as the table has been cleared, and the plates cleaned."

"Thank you, sir," replied the girl politely.

"Tell me, have you enjoyed your first two days, Lutel?"

"Very much, sir." She curtsied. "The situation is very much to my liking."

The baker beamed at the presumed compliment.

"It's nothing special," he said. "A baker's hours are long and unworldly, and if this abode is my reward, then so be it."

Lutel curtsied again, and started to remove the dirty tableware. John, the baker's manservant, handed Farynor a glass of brandy; it had become a regular custom over the years. Sipping his night-cap, the baker took out his pocket watch.

"Nearly ten of the clock; time to draw the ovens and dampen the fire." Farynor stood up and leant over to kiss his daughter goodnight. He began to make his way out of the room, but stopped in the doorway and circled around to address his new servant.

“Be certain that all of the windows are closed. We do not want any air fanning the ashes.”

Mother and daughter bade the servants well, and descended the stairs to their respective bedrooms. Lutel cleared the remaining cutlery and tankards, and carried them to the kitchen.

“Is there anything you need?” enquired John.

“No, I am fine, thank you.”

“Then I will see you in the morning, just after five o’clock.”

Lutel remained in the kitchen, cleaning and tidying away. She stared out of the window across the silhouetted skyline. Wrapped in a cloak of black, the buildings were an engaging spectacle. Lutel felt a twinge of guilt as she contemplated the fate that she was about to bestow upon them.

Within an hour the whole house was still; only the rhythmic snoring of the King’s baker and the occasional rattle from a window frame disturbed the peace. Lutel put down the knife she was holding; a small flutter ran through her heart. Gripping the window in both hands, she pushed it open; a gentle breeze cooled her warm face, and the quiver was replaced by a shaft of excitement that surged through her whole body. Did it dare to come so soon? She was almost annoyed at its premature arrival. She hadn’t had time to complete her preparations, and consider her actions.

Lutel stealthily made her way to the front door; a floorboard squeaked in the hallway, and she stood rooted to the spot. The snoring stopped and she held her breath, praying it would continue. After all these weeks of waiting it seemed unbearable to be undone by so trivial a matter. All the real dangers that they had faced – the blindroom, Duval, Laungechamp and most recently the Bornhate – and now to be denied by a mere piece of wood seemed too absurd to be fair. Lutel’s body ached with the effort of standing still, and just as her hopes were ebbing away the soft droning from above resumed.

Reaching the door on tiptoe, she stretched for the strong bolt at the top of the door frame. It proved very stiff, and she resorted to wiggling it backwards and forwards very gently, in order to release it from its catch. The large iron key was cold to her hand, and Lutel felt its resistance as she tried turning it. She gripped it with both hands, but still it failed to budge. In desperation, she wrapped her skirt around the key, to gain more purchase, and the lock opened with a crack. The noise was like a bullet ricocheting around the hallway. Once more she turned to stone. To leave now would mean a difficult return if her absence was noticed. A full ten minutes elapsed before she deemed it safe to open the stout oak door and step outside into Pudding Lane.

Lutel pulled the door behind her to stop any breeze from entering the house; she placed one hand on the ironwork that laced the door in order to prevent a sudden gust of wind from forcing it open or slamming it shut. As her eyes became accustomed to the dark, she peered up and down the road, scanning the darkness. Around ten houses away, on the corner of Thomas Street, a man emerged from the shadows carrying a dimly lit horn lantern, and started to walk purposefully towards her. Lutel tightened her grasp on the door as the figure loomed closer, his identity obscured by the glowing light. Her hand became moist, diminishing her grip. Her shoulders dropped as she greeted the prowler.

"I didn't recognise you, John."

"There's a cold wind blowing. I wasn't for waiting around much longer."

"But it's an east wind," whispered Lutel, excitedly. "Tell Rewn it's tonight!"

"That soon?"

"I know. But we may have to wait a long time for a second chance."

"Tonight, really?"

"Yes!"

"The fire!" said Woodman in an exhilarated voice.

Lutel clapped her free hand over his mouth.

"Do you want the whole city to know?" she hissed.

"They're going to find out soon enough."

Woodman recognised the withering look; it would sober an inn of drunkards, he told himself, so there's no shame in complying.

"Tell Rewn to meet me here three hours from now."

"Three?"

"Yes, that should allow enough time to oil the water wheels at the bridge."

Woodman swivelled on his heel.

"John," she called. Woodman glanced over his shoulder. "Good luck!"

Lutel felt guilty at her treatment of him, and worried that such a responsibility was falling on a man that she didn't really know that well. As Woodman's broad back disappeared into the inky night, she wondered just how much her trust was warranted.

Woodman entered The Crows and, ignoring an invitation from the assembled company, bounced up the stairs to Rewn's room. Verde stood up as Woodman entered the room.

"She's for tonight," babbled Woodman.

Rewn let out a long low whistle. "That's much quicker than I was expecting. What's she up to?"

"We're to take the oil to the bridge, and then you are to meet Lutel, at Farynor's, in just under three hours."

"Then we must move," entreated Verde.

Several heads turned as the three men made their way out of the inn door. An owl hooted in Fish Street Hill as it glided above their heads. Rewn glanced skywards and caught a glimpse of tawny plumage in the moonlight. Beyond the bird, the clock face of Saint Magnus was also illuminated. Its hands showed it was twenty minutes to midnight. Less than two and a half hours to go, thought Rewn.

Their footsteps echoed uncomfortably as they finally stopped outside Rathbone's warehouse. Woodman furtively perused the area, before setting foot in the building. The warehouse was much as Woodman remembered it from some six months earlier; for reasons known only to the authorities it had been left untouched. Rewn lit a horn lantern and stealthily rummaged amongst the goods. In one corner lay a wooden barrel; Woodman tipped it over and, together with Verde, rolled it to the back exit. Rewn pulled back the bolts, and they pushed the barrel down the steps. It made an ominous clatter as it bowled over the uneven alleyways, but they made their way to the quayside without any voice being raised in objection and, as far as they could discern, unseen by prying eyes.

Woodman sat on the barrel as the other two men returned to the warehouse and promptly reappeared carrying a boat. Small ripples gently lapped its bow as they lowered the wherry into the river. Their reflections shimmered at them from the moonlit Thames; what a sight they made, thought Rewn as he spied his Stuart costume. He had paid little attention to his appearance in recent times, and his unkempt state momentarily shocked him. Verde leapt into the craft and it tilted alarmingly, the sudden surge causing an angry disturbance of the water, shattering their dishevelled images like a hammer smashing into a mirror. Verde struggled to regain an even keel, and floundered once more as Rewn and Woodman lowered the barrel into the boat, causing it to rock violently.

"Not much of a sailor, are you?" observed Woodman.

Verde's energy was channelled towards keeping afloat, and the barb missed its mark. Rewn gripped the sides in an effort to stop his friend from falling into the river, and once calm was restored he and Woodman joined

Verde. A pair of oars lay stashed in the hull of the boat, and Woodman sat with the barrel as the other two made to row. It was a new experience for Verde and Rewn, and they frequently missed their stroke and soaked the unamused Woodman.

"Here, let me!" he said, making to take both oars.

"Sit down, you'll have us all in," shouted Verde nervously.

"Quiet," Rewn urged them. "Someone may hear us!"

"Can I say one thing?" asked Woodman.

"No!" exclaimed Verde tersely, still grappling with his oar.

"But..."

"Quiet, Woodman, I have the mastery of this now," crowed Verde, as his oar pulled sweetly through the water and the wherry began to move serenely along.

"I just wanted..."

"What?" said Rewn, who was also showing a deft touch and sympathised with Verde's irritation at Woodman's interjections.

"I just wanted to say, we are going the wrong way!"

Rewn and Verde stopped rowing. Indeed Woodman was right; they had sat facing the bridge, but, having been so wrapped up in their endeavours, they had failed to realise that they would be travelling in the opposite direction.

"Wheel around," instructed Woodman. "No, not you, Verde – just Rewn."

Rewn continued to row, and the small craft circled around, much to the consternation of a group of ducks that had been bobbing in their wake.

"Now we can start," proclaimed Woodman, rather tetchily.

Verde and Rewn gripped the oars and vented their embarrassment on the water. As they reached the arches at London Bridge, and drew alongside the waterwheel system, a church clock struck half past midnight.

"Now what are you going to do?" shouted Woodman over the noise of rushing water, as he clutched a wheel with both hands in order to moor the boat.

"Be quiet," ordered Rewn.

Rewn looked at Verde; neither of them had brought any tools or vessels to assist in oiling the wheels, and they understood Woodman's disbelief.

"There's a knife in my belt."

Rewn crawled along the boat on his hands and knees, and reached up to withdraw the weapon from Woodman's sheath. He decided that now was not the time to ask its owner why he was carrying it. Verde steadied the barrel, whilst Rewn knelt beside it, prised the knife into its top and slowly levered up the lid.

"Hurry," said Woodman, fighting against the tide of water as it funnelled into the arches with increasing speed.

Rewn could make little headway from his position, so he stood up to increase his purchase on the lid. Still the barrel refused to yield, and he braced himself for one final assault. Standing on tiptoe he concentrated all his strength into one huge effort. He grunted as the lid flew into the air and into the water, instantly to be followed by Rewn lurching backwards and over the side of the boat. Rewn disappeared under the water, rising to the surface well out of reach from the boat, and was swiftly washed away by the current. In the shadow of the bridge and the dark sky, he was soon lost from view.

"Rewn!" screamed Verde.

"Bloody brilliant," commented Woodman, who had not been at all impressed by the night's events.

Rewn swam furiously against the tide, but could make little headway and was carried away towards the far end of the waterwheel system. As he swirled by the construction he made a desperate grab – his hand fastening around something solid. Spray drenched his face, and he was unable to see that he had made contact with the apparatus until he had hauled himself closer to it. The river rushed over his shoulders and his head bobbed up and down in the icy water like an apple that had fallen from a bankside tree. Gradually he inched himself back towards the boat, using the wooden construction to propel himself along. Through all the noise and confusion he was encouraged by voices from the boat and they acted as a spurring guide. Rewn could feel his strength sapping away; the cold, the shock and the effort were all taking their toll, and he was swallowing increasing amounts of water.

Suddenly he felt himself rising, as a pair of hands hauled him into the boat. He fell headlong into the hull, coughing and spluttering.

"Is that what you mean by 'quiet'?" said Woodman, and he wrapped his dry coat around the rescued man.

"Now what?" said Verde to Woodman, somewhat resentfully. "You seem to have all the answers."

Woodman picked up an oar. "Use these; we can ladle it on."

"But that will take ages."

"Have you any better ideas?"

"Can you hold the boat still, Rewn?" asked Verde.

"He's better off keeping active," suggested Woodman, handing Rewn the other oar.

Verde made to take the oar.

"It's all right, I feel better, and Woodman's right; I'm best keeping warm."

They began to ladle the oil over the water system. Although slow, the oars proved useful because of the length to which they reached. After an hour the barrel was near-empty, though a fair part of the oil seemed to lie in the bottom of the boat, or covered their bodies – especially Verde's, whose role had resulted in a generous share, much to his distaste and Woodman's amusement. Verde swore that Woodman was deliberately soaking him, a claim that was hotly denied.

"Come on," said Rewn, "we can lift it now."

Woodman helped Rewn lift the barrel and Verde relaxed his grip to allow the boat to move forward. He held it firmly in its new position as the barrel was turned sideways and its contents splashed over the woodwork – though a fair spillage found its way directly into the river.

"Time to go," muttered Rewn through chattering teeth. "I will be late for Lutel, and I am freezing."

"You need a good fire," laughed Woodman.

Fortuitously, all of The Crows' inhabitants were snugly tucked up in their beds, yet Rewn still insisted on their removing their boots before entering the inn. Once in his room they threw off their oil-soaked, sodden clothes, and Rewn vigorously rubbed himself with a sheet. Verde poured out three cups of sack and handed them around. Rewn gulped his down, spluttering and coughing as the drink took his breath away.

"Thank you, John. I was a little snappy out there; I don't know what came over me. You did well. I apologise."

"Forget it, you must be going soon," urged Woodman, but his humility masked the pleasure that he was feeling.

CHAPTER FIFTY-ONE

A Dream Come True

The sky glowed a radiant red, sparks showered like flaming fountains, and timbers cracked; rooftops as far as the eye could see were burning fiercely. The London skyline was covered with an incandescent light. Noise from the townsfolk could scarcely be heard above the blaze of the fire as they ran around shouting and screaming, saving first their souls and if possible their belongings.

A gentle breeze wafted against Lutel's cheeks as she leant out of the open window, picturing the scene in her mind's eye. The cool wind woke her with a start from her daydreaming and she drew back inside the bakery. She strolled across the room to a faggot pile, bent down on her knees and carefully searched the wood. Eventually she withdrew a long tapering stick and walked across to a large oven. Opening the door she flinched as the hot air enveloped her, then recovered and thrust the stick into the glowing embers, wiggling it around amongst the hot coals. Lutel blew on its point. Her first effort was unsuccessful, then after a few more tries the kindling stick ignited. Shielding the flame with a cupped hand, she returned to the faggot pile and inserted the stick into its centre.

Lutel stood back to await developments. At first little happened and then a small pop announced that the flame had caught its neighbours alight. The dry kindling crackled as the fire greedily ate its way from the centre, searching for more fuel. Lutel crossed the room to a pile of brushwood that she had secured from the bavin in Farynor's backyard, and neatly placed some larger logs around the small fire, standing them upright to form a conical enclosure around the flames inside.

An easterly wind rushed through the open window and fanned the flames. The fire blazed and belched noisily and smoke began to fill the room. Lutel opened the door that led from the bakery to the remainder of the house, and the smoke raced along the passageway and up the stairs. Stout oak framed the walls of the bakery, and Lutel felt a thrill of excitement as the flames began to lick at the very structure of the room.

Lutel had planned meticulously. The fire was to be a slow, thorough affair; she had reasoned that it needed a firm base, and from these beginnings it would travel slowly down Thames Street. Here it would encounter the warehouses that they knew would be full of brandy, hay, tallow, oil, spirits, hemp and many other forms of combustibles. Then along the open wharves where hay and timber would quickly ignite, followed by the slower but longer-burning coal.

Their plans had been scrupulously thought through. The fire would run along the riverside for hours, driven by an easterly wind, before it moved inland to the city. Verde had argued that the fire should be a more flamboyant and spectacular affair, but Lutel had pointed out that a slow-burning fire would best serve their purpose. It would not at first raise suspicion or undue alarm, and moreover the citizens would have time to leave their dwellings and move to safety. Their mission was to save lives, she had reminded Verde, and few or hopefully no Londoners should perish in the fire.

"Fire, fire!" shouted Lutel.

Upstairs the household were awaking to choking smoke and the sound of popping wood. The dry timbers of the bakery had caught more rapidly than she had anticipated and already the ground floor was well alight. The stairway would soon be unusable as an escape route, and Lutel ran up the stairs, coughing her way through the dense smoke. John had roused Lydia, and the baker and his wife met them on the landing.

"How, how?" cried Farynor. "I checked everything."

His wife sobbed at his side, and Lydia began to scream as the flames lashed up the stairs.

"This way," shouted John, and he shepherded them up a second flight of stairs that led from the landing. John ushered them through the attic door and closed it behind them, then rushed over to a garret window and tried to open it. The wood had warped from the recent long hot summer, and the window refused to budge. He grabbed a stool and threw it at the pane – glass shattered and splintered to the floor. The servant picked up the stool and stood on it in order to haul himself up through the opening.

"This way," he implored, as he reached down from the roof, thrusting his arms through the gap. The baker helped his daughter onto the stool, and John hauled her from the room. Farynor repeated the action for his wife, and then turned to Lutel.

"Come, girl, don't be afraid," he said as she backed away.

"No, you go next," Lutel urged him.

"Don't be foolish, the smoke is coming under the door!"

"I have a fear of heights," lied Lutel.

"You'll perish for such foolishness," shouted Farynor above the growing inferno.

"I will be all right – you go," she yelled back.

"Be it on your own head," said the baker, and he climbed on to the stool and into John's waiting hands.

The Farynor household clung to the guttering as John leant through the hole. Smoke now filled the room, making it impossible to see. He pulled himself up, his face wet with sweat and black with soot.

"It's no use," he said to his master. "We must look to ourselves."

The four gingerly fingered the guttering to steady themselves as they made the short distance across the rooftops and into the waiting arms of a neighbour.

"Don't look down – keep coming," shouted Seb Greer, as he passed the survivors to a second man, who showed each in turn to the doorway and safety. John was the last to be hauled in, and he bent double through his heroic efforts.

"Where's Lutel?" asked the second man.

"Who?" asked John, confused at hearing the name.

"The maid!"

John sadly shook his head. "We couldn't save her."

Rewn plunged through the window and made his way through the burning house. Thin orange flames now danced through the garret window, and smoke billowed into the night air.

"Lutel, Lutel!" he blindly shouted through the smoke and flames. A beam snapped with a horrible crack, and crashed straight through the burning floorboards, bouncing noisily away. Rewn felt a dreadful sinking in the pit of his stomach.

"Lutel!" he screamed even louder, but still there was no reply. Rewn leaned into the room as far as he could, but the heat drove him back, and the smoke compounded the tears in his eyes as he reluctantly made his way back to safety.

Outside the bakery, Farynor and his family stared helplessly at the conflagration.

"I've lost everything," cried the baker.

"Not as much as I have," gasped Rewn.

The baker stared in bewilderment, and then put a consoling arm around his wife and daughter; as he did so Lydia fainted from a combination of the heat and nervous exhaustion. Rewn was standing behind the girl, so he was able to instinctively break her fall. He cradled her in his arms, until an onlooker indicated for him to carry her inside her own house, a few doors away. The woman led the way to a bedroom, and Rewn carefully laid Lydia down on a bed.

"Water, bring me water."

The woman disappeared and soon returned with a bowl. Rewn dipped a cloth from his pocket into the water, and squeezed it out, before gently bathing Lydia's forehead, brushing aside her flowing black locks with the back of his fingers.

Perhaps due to his recent sense of loss, Rewn felt an overwhelming desire for the girl that lay before him. He placed his hand in the bowl, and ran his wet fingers over her red lips. Lydia's eyes fluttered as her doting mother arrived in the room, shrieking joyfully at her daughter's recovery. Lydia placed a soft white hand on Rewn.

"Thank you," she whispered.

"You're welcome," he answered kindly, as he gazed into her eyes. They reminded him of the seas back in Mykas, crystal clear and warm.

"Have we met before?"

"I think not."

"Then you remind me of somebody, but I can't think who."

Subconsciously, her mind returned to Lutel.

"The girl, is she safe?" Lydia pulled herself up on the bed. The room fell silent; nobody was prepared to answer. Rewn was reminded of his true sadness by the two references, and he pulled his hand from Lydia's.

"We must help her," she cried.

Her mother came over and sat in Rewn's place, and Lydia cried into her shoulder.

"Don't upset yourself, Lyddy. You are safe, we are all safe now."

Rewn knew the falsehood of the statement, and it reminded him of his true purpose. As he took his leave, he glanced at the girl. She had raised her head, and he left the room with the blue eyes emblazoned on his heart.

Rewn rushed outside and slouched down with his back against the wall. He reflected on how he'd lost the other most important woman in his life.

When he had opened his eyes in the hospital and seen Shai a surge of positive energy had rushed through his body. He had known immediately that he would make a full recovery. He'd remained in hospital longer than was necessary as he felt no urgency to leave the protection and care of Shai. On their first meeting she had been warm and optimistically attentive. From the first, Rewn tried to engage her in conversation, desperate to find out where she had disappeared to during the thrarb racing in Palladin. Shai had advised him to rest and compassionately side-stepped the contentious issue. In the first few days Shai had visited him during her morning rounds, and then found time to pay him a social visit during the afternoons. That much she felt she owed Rewn, but she would never allow herself to be drawn on any matters regarding their previous encounter.

On the morning of his discharge Shai did not attend his bedside, and Rewn dressed and set off to confront her. A nurse pointed him in the direction of her office and Rewn soon found himself standing outside Shai's door. He hesitated and then knocked boldly.

"Come in."

Rewn entered; Shai had her back to him, as she examined a large computer readout that covered the wall. Rewn stared at the images and writing, but although he recognised the parts of the body he had no idea what she could be searching for.

"Just leave them there," said Shai.

On being confronted with her back Rewn's courage had deserted him.

"Shai." He spoke falteringly.

Shai removed the medical visor that she had been using.

"Rewn, I thought you were somebody else… you shouldn't be here."

"Why, why?" demanded Rewn.

Shai walked towards him. "Rewn, you must leave!"

"I will leave, but please, please, for my sanity, tell me why you left."

Shai sighed. "Remember that little thrarb we raced?"

"How could I forget Destiny?"

"Exactly… Destiny. As he raced down that slope I knew if I stayed another minute my destiny would have been decided."

"What do you mean?"

Shai looked up, her green eyes opened wider than even Rewn in his daydreams had imagined they were capable of.

"I knew if I stayed that I would love you for ever. That we would marry, have children and so on and so on," said Shai.

"But… but… I wanted that too."

Shai stroked his cheek. "I know – that's why I had to leave."

She paused, waiting for Rewn to speak, but he remained silent, inviting her to explain.

"Ever since I was a little girl, I dreamt of being a surgeon, not just a surgeon but the very best. If I had stayed with you that wouldn't have been possible."

"You could still have been a doctor, even a surgeon," said Rewn.

"But my loyalties would have been divided – my time split."

"You're a respected surgeon now. Marry me."

For a moment, Shai's mouth formed into a "yes".

"No," she said emphatically.

"Why?" he said, becoming agitated.

"You'd better go."

"You can marry me and still keep your career. I won't interfere."

"It's too much to ask and it wouldn't work."

"Tell me you don't love me and I'll walk out of here and you'll never see me again."

"Rewn!"

"Tell me!"

She called his bluff. "I don't love you."

"I don't believe you."

"Ah!" she exploded in frustration. "Rewn, I am on my way to becoming a top, no, the top surgeon in Mykas. You are not part of my plans."

Rewn looked crestfallen. He turned to go.

"Wait."

Rewn spun around, his heart beating fast. Shai placed her hands on either side of his face and kissed him long and lovingly. As she pulled herself away, Rewn made to grab her.

"No!" she said.

"Goodbye, Shai."

"Goodbye, Rewn. Take care on your travels. I don't want to see you again."

Rewn decided to walk back to The Murder of Crows to break the sad news to the others. An array of Londoners, standing in their varied night attire, had gathered outside the bakery. The small crowd were warmed by the heat from the fire, and appeared to be more fascinated by the scene than they were disposed to extinguishing it. Only a few of the closest neighbours had attempted to fetch leather buckets and an assortment of improvised but crude and totally inadequate modes of fire fighting. The occupant of the house next to the bakery had fetched a cart and was busy with his family, loading all their worldly goods on board. As he broke through the small circle of spectators, Rewn caught sight of a figure in the shadows.

"Lutel," he said to himself, and he ran towards the spot. The flickering shadows danced around him, mocking the emptiness that he found – no figure emerged from the darkness, and he trudged disconsolately back towards the inn.

As he climbed Fish Street Hill, he gazed at the fire in the distance, and images of his sister flashed through his mind. He saw her as a young woman on Mykas, her piloting of the ship, their journey from the West Country, and her planning today's sad event. She had been so right in everything: the best time was with an easterly wind, and at the weekend. "Why?" he had clumsily asked her. Because the mechanism of government would not be in place on a Saturday or Sunday, she had reasoned. Sunday would be better still. "Why?" he'd asked again. He could see her face as she looked at him pityingly; because Saturday was the busiest working day, she had pointed out, all the city folk would be tired and asleep in bed. Rewn thought of the disorganised, apathetic scene that he had recently witnessed in Pudding Lane. "You were right, you were bloody right," he said under his breath.

CHAPTER FIFTY-TWO

A SMALL CONFLAGRATION

Rewn forlornly entered The Murder of Crows, wondering how he was going to break the news. Although it was early morning, a small crowd had gathered at the inn to discuss the fire. From what Rewn could see, it was merely an excuse for more drinking as there appeared to be little consternation on the subject. Verde and Woodman stood with someone he didn't recognise; they were drinking and laughing. Their companion, who had their back to Rewn, particularly found their company amusing. Rewn was in the mood to explode, and he pushed his way through the throng, never once taking his eyes off Woodman and Verde. As he reached the group, he opened his mouth to give the revellers a piece of his mind. The amused stranger turned around.

"What kept you?" asked Lutel.

Rewn's mouth dropped open even further, and he sank to his knees.

"You're dead," he said, reaching out a hand to touch Lutel's arm.

Lutel examined herself; her clothes were dirty and sooty. "A little charred, perhaps, but not dead."

"How? Why?" spluttered Rewn.

"Sit down," ordered Lutel, "and have a drink."

Verde picked up the flagon from the middle of the table, and poured Rewn a long cool ale. Lutel checked that she could not be overheard; all of the occupants were deep in conversation, mostly joking about the fire. The four of them bent forward to reduce the conversation to a whisper.

"If they think I'm dead, they won't search for me."

"Why would they want to look for you?"

"If they decide the fire was started deliberately I will figure fairly high on the list of suspects," she said softly.

"Ah," said Woodman, the dawn of truth etched upon his face. "If they think you did it, and they think you are dead, they won't come looking for you."

"Precisely," said Lutel.

"But how did you escape?" asked Rewn. "I came back for you but you were not there."

"A woman is entitled to her secrets," said his sister, with a mysterious smile. "We must all have our secrets, mustn't we, Rewn?" she added knowingly.

Rewn blushed at the insinuation, but the allusion was lost on Verde and Woodman and the moment passed.

"I think a little reconnaissance of the area might be in order," suggested Lutel. "But we may well not be coming back here, so collect any personal belongings before we go."

They went separately to their rooms in order to avoid suspicion, arranging to meet outside The Crows. Lutel took one final fond look at the inside of the inn, and made her way towards the door. Verde followed soon after, but Woodman waited for Rewn, who had walked over to the landlord. Woodman watched as his friend pulled off a ring from his little finger, and dropped it in the surprised host's palm.

"What was all that about?" asked Woodman as they exited the inn.

"Longfellow has been a friend for many weeks. Look at those flames – the wind is gathering pace and they'll soon be coming this way. The Crows will be no more."

Woodman nodded in silent recognition of the generous act as they joined the others.

The wind had indeed increased in strength, and there was an eerie feeling in the air. Several houses in Pudding Lane were now ablaze; even from a distance they creaked noisily as the wind fanned the flames around their timbers. Sparks began to fly in the wind and were carried to the adjacent houses in Fish Street Hill. The yard and outbuildings at The Crows were stored with all manner of flammable materials like hay and firewood. The landlord and his clientele raced out into the street as cries of "Fire!" began to ring out around the inn.

As the foursome stood watching their home of several months catch fire, a man fell sprawling to the ground and the crowd parted to make way for an elegantly dressed man. Sir Thomas Bludworth, Lord Mayor of London, was not in the best of moods, having been woken from his bed in the middle of the night, whilst others in authority lay undisturbed. Stopping next to Rewn, he placed his hands on his hips and surveyed the scene.

"What say you, cousin, to this fire?"

Rewn glanced around, only to discover that it was he whom the Mayor was addressing.

“A small conflagration, Your Worship.”

“My thoughts entirely.” Bludworth signalled to one of his accompanying officials. “Damned inconsiderate,” he snarled. “Pish, a woman might piss it out. Fetch buckets from the church, and use water from the river. Go to it, man!” he ordered. “And don’t wake me again!”

As the Mayor rode away, the wind gathered in strength, as if to mock his indifference, and the flames of Pudding Lane and Fish Street Hill appeared to race one another, vying to be the first to reach the riverside quays and warehouses that lined Thames Street.

“Come on, you heard His Worship,” shouted the berated official. “There will be leathern buckets under the Tower of Saint Margaret’s.” He hurried away, followed by a small crowd, in the direction of the church. The mob reached Saint Margaret’s just in time to see the spire catch alight.

“Quickly, men,” yelled the Mayor’s official.

The crowd stopped at the church door.

“Come on, you cowards!” he screamed.

“You go and fetch them,” shouted a voice from the crowd. It was Rewn. The official hesitated and stared at the flaming spire; the fire had taken hold and was lapping its way swiftly around the pinnacle of the church.

“Where’s the nearest church?” shouted the official.

“Here,” yelled Rewn.

“You’ll need more than a prayer,” shouted Woodman.

“Saint Magnus the Martyr at the foot of London Bridge,” cried a voice of reason.

The official set off down the hill, pursued by the howling mob. Rewn started moving in the direction of the bridge.

“No,” said Lutel. “We have had enough excitement for tonight. The fire has a firm hold; this unruly crowd will not dampen it. The Lord Mayor epitomises the blasé attitude of those who count. Let’s find somewhere to sleep. The situation may require our attention in the morning.”

Verde led the search for a bed as the mob emerged from Saint Magnus’ Church waving and fighting over the fire buckets, as though they were some prized token to behold. Bright orange flames swept down Fish Street Hill and like a giant pair of fire tongs engulfed the spire, setting up a beacon of flame that could be seen across a wide area of the city. The hour proved too late to secure lodgings, so they slept rough in a churchyard, and subsequently woke early the next morning. A huge plume of black smoke billowed away in the east, and the sound of the crackling fire proved Lutel’s prediction to be correct. London had not yet taken the fire seriously, it being supposed to be similar in threat and nature to various predecessors.

Very few people were on the streets as they made their way to the seat of the fire. Near London Bridge, the occasional cart was transporting household goods to safety, but considering several hundred houses were now engulfed in the fire, there was little evidence of panic or concern. Even the bridge itself was now alight, and at the northern end the flames rose especially high as they fed on the oil from below. Try as it might, the fire could not leap the gaps between the houses on the bridge, and the buildings on the south side of the river were thus spared. But as Lutel pointed out, the plague had caused little trouble here, and it had never been their intention to inflict damage on this area. The wind had veered around towards the north, and the fire showed it was no respecter of large or important buildings as it burnt Fishmongers' Hall in its wake. Even more significantly, the decaying timbered houses at Red Cross Alley, situated on land below Thames Street, were consumed by the gigantic orange wave.

Shortly after they had arrived at the spectacle, the irritable figure of the Mayor again appeared on the scene. The crowd, which was growing in number by the minute, suggested to him that the blowing up of houses to stop the fire spreading was the only solution open to him. For a moment, Lutel became anxious, but several people in the crowd, who stood to lose their homes by this strategy, wanted to know who would pay them compensation. Bludworth was unwilling to accept the responsibility or the cost, and he sadly trudged away.

A smile returned to Lutel's face. "This wind is most favourable; it blows the fire towards the north-west of the city. It could not be more co-operative if we held the power to control it ourselves. When it reaches Newgate, we must be ready."

"Ready for what?" asked Rewn.

"To free Revin, of course!"

Revin, thought Rewn. He'd been so wrapped up in recent events that he had almost forgotten his friend, and under his breath he cursed his selfishness.

"Should we not be leaving for the prison now?" asked Woodman.

"No, we must stay close to the action; forewarned is forearmed. Let's make certain there are no more bright ideas that could thwart us."

Just before midday, Lutel's strategy paid off as word spread amongst the crowd that the King had personally intervened. The berated official from the previous evening appeared, surrounded by a group of men.

“His Majesty has given orders to pull down any house that lies in the path of the fire,” he announced. “I am in need of assistance.”

“Come,” said Lutel, on hearing the news, “we can be of service here.”

“Help fight the fire! Are you mad?” queried Woodman.

“Trust me.” She smiled, and ran after the volunteers.

Lutel led the way to a crowd of people who had gathered in an alley abutting Fish Street Hill. In their midst stood an officious-looking man sporting a long black periwig – a peculiar thing to be wearing at such a time, thought Lutel. Samuel Pepys was barking out orders, and overseeing the handing out of long-poled firehooks. Still the fire raged hungrily; its fearsome roar could now be heard many yards away.

“Sir, sir, save my house,” pleaded a distressed young woman in the crowd. She was cradling a baby and two other small children hid their faces in her long skirt.

“We will do our best, madam – I am somewhat overstretched.”

Lutel could feel the intense heat from the fire; it was less than fifty yards away. She grabbed a firehook from the unsuspecting man standing next to her.

“Oi!” he shouted.

“Madam!” protested the periwig.

“This way,” she shouted, and the baying mob, frantic for action, left Pepys standing on his own, calling vainly for them to return to him. Lutel led the rabble to within a distance of twenty yards of the fire. The heat was intense, but the hysteria of the mob and the bravado of being so close to the fire dulled all semblance of common sense, and very few of the volunteers withdrew. Lutel thrust her firehook upwards, to about twenty feet above the ground. A small iron loop had been built into the wall. Lutel hooked the curved end of her firehook into the ring and called to Rewn, Verde and Woodman to join her. Several of the crowd assisted and they heaved as one, straining every sinew in their bodies. Sweat from the sheer effort and fierce heat poured from their brows, but the building stood firm.

“Again,” demanded Lutel, as the smoke belched into their faces and sparks showered them from overhead. “Pull,” she urged. The wall began to rock, giving just the encouragement they needed, and after one more concerted effort the side of the house collapsed. At this success the baying mob became demented, and very soon six or seven houses in the row were being attacked. Rewn took a break from his exertions and stared at the giant ball of crackling flames.

“We are too close to the fire, it will overtake us,” he shouted in Lutel’s ear.

“Exactly,” she replied.

As Rewn deduced and Lutel had predicted, the fire was soon upon them. As they stood in the debris of the flattened houses sparks sailed over their heads like golden arrows, and underfoot the very floorboards of the houses that they had pulled down in an attempt to stem the red tide burned in the scorching heat. Within minutes the houses behind them began to crackle, and the crowd were forced to retreat. Many were so convinced of the fire’s invincibility that they rushed away in all directions, to save their own belongings.

“Stay, stay,” yelled the forlorn figure in the periwig.

“Too late, Mister Pepys,” said a man at his side. “They’d rather save their own goods than save their neighbour’s house.”

“The short-sighted fools,” he oathed, and he remained staring at the flames until the heat forced him to retreat.

CHAPER FIFTY-THREE

THE KING'S MEN

The streets emanating from Fish Street Hill were beginning to fill with carts and people, and by early afternoon a vast crowd had flocked into the open to view the free spectacle. Many had taken up vantage points on rooftops or surrounding hills, in order to gaze down on the blazing orange ball with its sinister black halo that surrounded the area north of London Bridge.

Lutel and the three men roamed the streets, watching the results of their handiwork unfold, with mixed feelings. At present the fire was no more than a colourful sideshow to the vast majority of Londoners.

"Have we done the right thing?" Rewn asked her.

"We're banishing pestilence and plague from this city, for ever," she assured him. "There's plenty of time to save your soul, if not your belongings."

"But think of all the homeless," said Rewn.

"Think of all the lives that we will have saved," she countered. "Think of the opportunity that lies ahead to rebuild this city."

Rewn did not answer. He stared thoughtfully at the cloud of smoke that rose over the fire. Its hue was changing to a deep yellow, and at that moment, Lutel's dream seemed a long way off – but yes, he could share her ideals.

As the fire continued to burn, showing no signs of abating, they patrolled its periphery, ever watchful to its development. Even in such times of adversity there were those who sought and found opportunity; the carters were taking a good trade, running backwards and forwards between the area of Thames Street and the higher ground of Canning Street where people imagined they would be safe from the ravages of the fire, on the ridge of its hill. Carts were loaded with all manner of goods – clothing, bedding, pottery, crockery, furniture were all piled high on the small hand carts. It was amusement itself to view a neighbour's goods, and the objects that people considered of value. Many a husband and wife argued on the exact nature of the load, and what could or could not travel on the cart, quite often for so long the fire would intervene and nullify their dispute. As the fire grew in size, it was matched by the carters' greed, and by mid-afternoon there was not a cart to be had for less than two guineas.

As the four walked along Canning Street they came upon a mob brutally beating a carter, who had obviously pushed his price too high. Rewn made to intervene, but Lutel called him back.

"We cannot intervene in every injustice that we witness; our task lies towards the greater good."

The man lay cowering in the kennel as he was repeatedly kicked and punched. Blood streamed from his nose and he sported an ugly gash above his eye. He pulled himself to his knees in time to see his attackers gleefully making off with his empty cart.

London continued to be full of rumour and counter-rumour during the early hours of the fire. It gave rise to bands of youths roaming the streets intent on searching out trouble. Inevitably the four stumbled on such a mob during the late afternoon. The long-haired dishevelled youth at their head confronted them.

"What manner of men are you?" he demanded.

"What's it to you?" retorted Verde.

"What manner of man be 'ee?" repeated the youth in a threatening tone, unaccustomed to such resistance.

"I'm afraid we don't understand," answered Verde.

Behind the boy, the mob stirred; their blood was up and they needed little excuse for action.

"They don't understand," bayed their leader. "They must be bloody Frenchies."

The crowd jeered and surged forward, preparing to attack. Lutel noticed that they were being encircled, and for once she had no solution. Woodman pushed in front of Verde and stood nose to nose with the leader.

"'Course we're not Frenchies, you stupid bastards; now piss off and leave us alone."

Woodman's language was instantly discernible to the uncouth and ill-educated mob, but they still stood their ground.

"What about them?" said the youth, pointing at the trio behind Woodman. He was eager to keep face with the crowd, and was not yet prepared to back down.

"I speak for us all, you little tosser," growled Woodman. He looked down at the fireballs in the youth's hand, and hoped he hadn't overstepped the mark. "Ply your trade elsewhere."

The mob were becoming restless for action, and started to break away to continue their search for French or Dutch nationals elsewhere. The youth, seeing his grip as leader slipping away, spat in Woodman's face and raced back to the head of the mob.

"Let's fire the bastard French," he yelled, and the howling rabble followed him down a back alley.

"You prove your worth once more, John," said Rewn.

"People like that deserve to be burned," said Verde.

Lutel sighed. "The fault's not entirely theirs."

"You're condoning these people?" asked Verde.

"No," answered Lutel. "But look at the conditions that they live in – it's easy to understand why they act as they do."

Verde was about to contradict her when a young woman came hurtling towards them.

"The King is on the river," she shouted, as she raced past them.

"Perhaps we should make our way to the Thames," observed Lutel.

Woodman led them northwards away from the fire and along Canning Street; from there they headed south at Dowgate, and made their way along part of Thames Street that had yet to succumb to the fire. Emerging through an alleyway, they found themselves at Queenhythe. As they approached the river, the crowd became more animated, some through the excitement of the King's proximity, whilst those with more worldly minds grew fearful of the long orange stream that rivalled the waterway for nearly half a mile in length. Disappointment greeted them as they reached the river's edge as the Royal Barge, in all its red and gold splendour, was disappearing from view back towards Whitehall.

The Thames was now seething with small craft; wherries and lighters were packed tight with people and their belongings.

"It's about time we took a closer look at the fire," reasoned Lutel. "We should ensure that it still makes progress, especially towards the direction of Newgate," and she headed along Thames Street towards the fire. Frantic householders were flinging goods into boats, and the Thames was becoming full of floating belongings, as panic overtook reason. Amongst the more unusual objects, a harp floated by below them. Rewn watched this desecration of culture, and sighed.

Lutel noticed his anguish. "We really are helping these people," she reassured him, putting an arm on his shoulder.

"Yes, but is it enough?" mused Rewn, as he watched the river bubbling from the heat of the fire. For some reason that he was at a loss to explain, an image of Lydia Farynor flashed before his eyes – where was she at this moment? What had happened to her chattels and goods? He shook himself free from his reverie and chased after the others.

As they approached the centre of the fire, the noise of crackling wood and the dense yellow smoke became unbearable. Again they trekked northwards, breathing hard as they climbed a steep alleyway. A rattling and crashing sound approached them through the smoke; visibility was so poor that they were unable to detect the source of the disturbance. As they rounded a corner, a pair of urchins emerged from the smog banging saucepans. A group of people followed behind, carrying a bed shoulder-high. Verde and Lutel, who were closest to its path, just managed to pin themselves against the side of a house, to avoid being run over. The slope had made it impossible to stop, and the warning urchins had prevented a serious injury. The bed's occupant – an aged woman in night cap and gown, with a blanket round her shoulders – was sitting bolt upright in her bed, issuing orders to her porters. Woodman and Rewn found the incident particularly amusing, and burst out laughing. Lutel, through reasons of solemnity, and Verde, through personal design, initially failed to see the humorous side of the affair, but eventually both relented and joined in the mirth.

Many people wore makeshift headgear, protecting themselves from the firebrands that flew persistently around the sky. A youth with a chamber pot on his head walked past them, bumping into Verde.

"Piss off," shouted the youth, as he rolled off the man, and Woodman alone found the episode funny, as the others' minds had now crystallised on the release of Revin.

Canning Street was heaving with people as they once more skirted the fire. The sad figure of the Lord Mayor rode through the crowd on horseback, looking very tired as he spoke to an official.

"I've been pulling down houses all day," protested the Mayor, "and the people take no notice of me."

"Go home and rest," said the other. "The King shows his concern. He sends forty of his horse guards – they will soon have this fire under control."

As they pushed by, the official stared at Lutel. He'd seen that face before, but so busy had his day been that he could not remember where or in what context.

"Have we met before?" he hailed her.

Lutel felt a little uneasy, remembering her actions of the morning.

"I know not your name, sir," she answered truthfully.

"Pepys, my name is Pepys."

"I do not believe we have met before today, sir," and she continued on her way.

It was late evening, and they had been on their feet for several hours. All four of them were covered in soot from head to toe, and if any one of them had now come across one of the others for the first time that day, they would probably have walked straight by.

"This news disturbs me," said Lutel.

"The King's men?" guessed Rewn.

"Yes. Let's find something to eat and appraise the situation."

"We can't fight soldiers," said Rewn incredulously.

"No, but we may be able to hinder them."

An inn on Watling Street proved willing to serve them with food and drink, and, after persuasive negotiation, agreed to put them up for the night. Most Londoners were now making for the river, but the landlord remained confident that the fire would not reach his inn. A hasty preparation of poached meat balls was served with hunks of bread. Verde poked through his meal.

"Haven't these people heard of fresh vegetables?" he complained.

Lutel stood on his foot. "I think we should be most grateful for their hospitality, given the trying situation," she said.

Several tankards of sack were needed to slake their dry throats, and Woodman wobbled precariously as they set forth for an evening inspection of their work. The fire still raged, the flames making no distinction as they swept through the timber-fronted houses of the nobility, with their projecting plaster fronts, or engulfed the rotten weather-boarded shacks of London's poor.

As predicted, the King's guard had arrived on horseback, and the fire-fighting was becoming more organised. Many of the guard had dismounted, and offered their reins to people in the crowd to hold whilst they immersed themselves in issuing orders. Lutel questioned herself on the judiciousness of taking the meal as she watched chains of men and women systematically passing buckets of water from the river, to be poured hissing on to the flames. Teams of men shouted encouragement as they used gleaming brass hand squirts to douse the roofs. The long cylindrical nozzles were dipped in water; whilst two men held handles on each side, a third manoeuvred a piston. The amount of water the device delivered was insubstantial, but the signs of organisation that it embodied were a worry to Lutel. Houses were now being pulled down in a sensible pattern, and there was a distinct atmosphere of control.

"Let's see if we can tip the balance," said Lutel as she led the way to the fire line.

Rewn seized an axe from a youth, who was coughing from smoke inhalation. He wielded it above his head, and brought it crashing down on one of the wooden water conduits that laced the city.

"Water, more water," he bawled to the crowd as he hacked, and water rushed from the pipe and soaked his legs and feet. A few people left the chain of buckets in order to tap this immediate but exhaustible supply, and soon enough links had left the chain to ensure its demise. Although the fresh source initially increased the amount of water that found its way onto the fire, the fountain soon dried up, and the organisation of the bucket chain proved impossible to resurrect as many of its members had drifted away.

Verde picked up the axe, and smiled at Lutel. "I'll see you back at Watling Street. This ruse of Rewn's is worth repeating," and he plunged into the crowd.

People still rallied around the horse guards, and more of the riders dismounted to assist directly with the fire-fighting; the likelihood remained that the fire would be quelled in this quarter of the city.

"We must act," Lutel confided to Rewn. "Success breeds success, and who can imagine what new endeavours these people can be rallied to?"

"What else can we do?"

Lutel looked on helplessly as signs of regrouping began to take shape all around them. The flames continued to fizz under a renewed deluge of water as a horseman galloped into the ranks of the crowd.

"Look to your weapons, arm," he yelled, and he sped away before any of the soldiers could recognise or question him.

"I'm beginning to think that our encounter with friend Woodman is proving more and more invaluable," said Lutel, smiling.

"He's certainly displaying hidden talents," agreed Rewn.

"Let's make sure it works."

They took up the cry. "Arm, arm!"

The fire-fighters, recognising the invasion cry, stopped their work and dispersed in various directions in search of French or Dutch invaders. Lutel and Rewn joined in the hue and cry, and confusion filled the air. The soldiers were unsure as to where their duty lay – some were for fighting the fire, others the perceived enemy. Lutel and Rewn did not await the outcome; they led the baying masses through the streets in search of the invisible foe.

CHAPTER FIFTY-FOUR

THE TRAINED BAND

Whilst they slept in their Watling Street beds, the fire continued to rage. The river was a hive of activity throughout the night, with small boats using torches to light the way. A smoke-covered moon silhouetted the buildings, straining to cast its reflection on the river. From a distance, the Thames looked as though it were covered in small fireflies, flitting around within its banks.

On the morning of Monday the third of September, the four arsonists of the Great Fire of London watched the inferno unveil itself before them. The previous day's fire had covered only a small area of the city, all within a quarter-mile radius of London Bridge. Now, as Lutel had planned, the fire secured a firmer hold, burning westward and northwards – devouring whole streets in quick time. Londoners who had thought that their goods were safe in their friends' or acquaintances' homes were soon moving them again in their efforts to outpace the fire. The first of many refugees now started to head towards the fields that surrounded the city walls.

Standing outside the Royal Exchange, Lutel and her co-conspirators watched as the fire swept down upon the elegant building. The air was filled with the scent of warm spices that cooked under the arc of the fire. The square stone tower of the Exchange conducted the heat from below, so even its grasshopper weather vane melted, and molten metal trickled down the tower, before the whole structure eventually caved in. Within a short space of time the ornate and beautiful building had been reduced to a charcoal ruin.

Lutel looked down on the wide circle of fire that lay before them.

"They'll never put that out," she predicted. "It's too wide to encircle; they'll never have the organisation or manpower to pull down enough buildings."

Threadneedle Street was relatively empty as they skirted between the firebrands; the reason was soon apparent as they were confronted by a group of the Trained Bands, sent in to deter looters.

"Where are you at?" challenged their officer.

"Sir, we are escaping the fire," pleaded Lutel.

The leader poked a musket at Lutel and moved her clothing.

"Search them," he ordered.

Three men appeared from behind, and frisked them in turn. One of them found Lutel's key.

"What is this for?" asked the searcher.

"It's my door key."

The man made to keep his find; Lutel stood firm, and he thought better of it and shoved the key back into her hand. The three searchers glanced at one another in disappointment.

"Nothing to report, sir," announced one of the men.

"You may go," said the officer, and he stood aside to let them pass.

Wicked flames raged all around them, snapping and crackling hideously from the core of the fire. No building was safe, whatever its height, shape or condition – the fire made no exceptions. Fire stations had been set up, fanning out like a peacock's tail around the advancing fire. Each fire post was attended by the parish constable with upwards of one hundred men. Beer, cheese and bread had been supplied by the King, with a promise of a shilling per man if they remained true to their post during the hours of darkness.

Still the fire raced on; buildings were pulled down in Thames Street, yet the fire jumped as many as twenty houses at a time, as it inevitably crept ever closer to the west of the city. Northwards it progressed beyond Gracechurch Street, Lombard Street and Cornhill, devastating the houses of the merchants and bankers who resided there. Many conduits had been destroyed, either by Verde or by others who had imitated his attempts to release an instant supply of water. The lack of water had been compounded by the long dry summer, which had caused the levels of the city wells to fall. Throughout the day the sun shone and the wind picked up speed, burning churches, company halls, houses, whole rows of shops, taverns and any other building that stood in the fire's path.

Fear finally gripped the city, as they patrolled around mid-morning.

"'Twas foretold in the comet," cried one man, to anyone who had the time to stop and listen.

An intrepid youth, who had ventured too close to the fire, ran around with his clothes ablaze. Verde responded to the boy's screaming by jumping on him and rolling him over to douse the flames. Two friends carried the lad away to seek medical attention, deaf to Verde's calls as he offered further help.

Verde noticed as they crossed Poultry Square that they happened to be heading in the direction of Walbrook. His gaze extended to a row of fine houses; there, blazing in the middle, stood the house of Nathaniel Hodges. The street was full of people, racing around in all directions with no sense of purpose. Not surprisingly, the good doctor was nowhere to be seen amongst the melee.

A man came from a house on the other side of the street; the fire was yet to consume it. He hailed a passing carter.

"How much for your cart?"

"Twenty pounds."

"Twenty pounds!" exclaimed the merchant incredulously.

"Suit yourself; there's plenty who'll pay, if you won't," said the carter, making to leave.

"No, no, twenty pounds it shall be."

"Money first," demanded the carter.

The merchant walked down his steps, produced a small pouch, and counted out the requisite number of gold coins. Verde watched as the man, his family and his servants raced in and out of the house carrying armfuls of valuables. Fine chairs, silverware, books and clothing soon filled every conceivable space in the cart. The household all returned inside to make one final scrutinisation, and the carter, seizing his chance, ran along the road pushing the loaded cart. The merchant arrived on the doorstep to witness all his valuables disappearing into the distance.

"Stop, stop," he yelled, "I haven't instructed you where to take the goods!"

"He ain't interested, he's robbin' yer," advised a bystander.

A look of absolute horror crossed the merchant's face, and his astonished family arrived in the doorway to see him chasing after the carter.

"Thief, stop, thief!" he hollered. But such was the noise from the fire, and so desperate was the situation, that nobody paid him any attention.

Roads and alleyways that provided escape routes from the fire soon became congested with huge numbers of evacuees and carts, which thwarted the authorities' most recent attempt at extinguishing the blaze. They endeavoured to move huge portable cisterns, but their progress was so hampered by the fleeing citizens that by the time they had reached their destination, the fire had beaten them to it and moved on in search of fresh fuel.

"I think we are winning," announced Lutel to the others. "It will not be long before the fire leads us to Revin."

"Can we go there now?" asked Woodman.

"Let's not get ahead of ourselves," advised Lutel cautiously. "We do not want to tempt fate."

"We don't want to miss it either," replied Verde.

Lutel had just drawn breath to explain her hesitancy to Verde and Woodman, when a runaway horse, frightened by the fire, galloped towards them. Its eyes were wild with terror, and the crowd parted before it as the snorting animal raced uncontrollably through the street. Rewn, who lingered behind his friends, was slow to see the horse's approach, and just managed to fling himself behind a massy post as the beast brushed past him. The crowd once more surged forward to fill the void left by the careering runaway. Two carts vied for the same ground and neither owner was prepared to make way.

"Move over."

"I was here first; you give way."

"Back down or be made to."

"I'd like to see you try, you fat fart."

"Don't you call me a fart, you great tosser."

The inevitable scuffle broke out and very soon fists were flying all across the road. Tempers had been frayed by the worry of the fire, and fanned by the intense heat, so very soon the scuffle developed into a near-riot as the crowd took sides. Woodman and Verde somehow became embroiled in the conflict, and a large woman brought a frying pan crashing down on Verde's head. The blow knocked him to the ground, and he was in danger of being trampled underfoot. Woodman hauled Verde to his feet and dragged him away from the action, but before he could reach the perimeter of the fight, the large lady, who appeared to have taken a distinct dislike to Verde, again loomed with her frying pan.

"Madam, we have no quarrel with you," Verde assured her.

"Take this, you prick," answered the woman, lifting her weapon in readiness to strike another blow. Verde raised his arms to deflect it, but only succeeded in further antagonising the woman. Successive blows rained down on all parts of Verde's body.

"Hit her, Verde," shouted Woodman.

"She's a woman," replied Verde, as he ducked and dived.

Woodman, who held none of Verde's scruples, punched the assailant in the face. The woman stood her ground, and held her hand to her nose in disbelief. Blood poured down her fingers, but instead of backing down she let out a bloodthirsty scream, and rushed at Woodman. From his position on the floor, Verde reassessed his values, and as the woman sped by he stuck out a foot, sending her sprawling to the floor. Woodman delivered a huge kick to her backside, and she went tumbling into the crowd. Before she could reappear, the Trained Band arrived, and men with cut faces and broken teeth emerged from the fracas to avoid their clutches. Lutel grabbed Verde and, with support from Woodman, they led him to the shelter of a side alley. Lutel inspected Verde's wounds, which appeared to be nothing more than superficial cuts and bruises.

"I enjoyed that," said Woodman, grinning.

"Don't let me stop you," said Verde groggily.

"Verde!" exclaimed Lutel.

"Thanks, Woodman."

By midday, the yellow smoke plumed over the city like a giant mushroom. People coughed and spluttered, and children screamed and cried from stinging eyes and fright. Walking under the cloud of smoke was no better than walking blindfold, and where the fire had burned great care had to be employed in order to avoid bumping into the towering brick stacks that protruded from the ground like rectangular stalagmites.

Once more they found themselves at the Thames, south of Knightrider Street. The area teemed with people bustling towards the river. Rewn stared at the water; even in the middle of the river people in small boats shielded themselves from the heat and sparks, improvising fireguards from anything that they could lay their hands on. He raised his eyes along the bank to his colleagues; their faces were bathed in a warm glow from the unwavering heat of the fire.

That night they did not return to Watling Street but again slept rough, under the shadow of the wall just south of Ludgate. Across the rooftops of Blackfriars they could still see the orange flames, with their head-dress of yellow smoke, wreaking havoc across the city.

CHAPTER FIFTY-FIVE
AN OLD FRIEND

Rewn had enjoyed little sleep; the hard ground and raging fire had physically kept him awake. Mentally he was suffering emotional torment at the thought of the destruction and homelessness that he had been party to causing. It weighed heavily on his mind, and contributed largely to his wakefulness. He still bore a sense of guilt, however convincing Lutel's argument had been and despite the knowledge that his actions had been philanthropic. He wondered if Lydia Farynor would consider them so, and excuse his behaviour. During his fretful night, it was very hard to see beyond the orange curtain and dense smoke and into a plague-free future.

As the sky lightened behind the thick fumes, they sauntered along Blackfriars. At Ludgate Hill, they were pleasantly surprised to be able to purchase some bread from an itinerant baker. Rewn's mind was drawn back to his thoughts of the previous night, as he hungrily tore at the loaves. Why couldn't he stop thinking of the baker's daughter? he asked himself.

The fire still raged to the south-east, over a quarter of a mile away. Lutel looked at the crackling distant flames, and then poked a finger into her mouth and held it to the wind.

"Today," she uttered as she continued to stare at the fire. The freshening wind blew smoke over their faces and in the distance came the noise of a church bell tolling its own demise as it plunged to the ground.

"Yes, definitely today," she confirmed.

Three blank faces turned towards her.

"The fire will reach this spot today," she said excitedly in answer to their enquiring looks.

The significance was lost on Woodman.

"We'd best be going, then," he suggested in a matter-of-fact tone.

Lutel pointed northward; they followed the line of her finger to the Old Bailey.

"Today the fire will reach the prison," she confidently forecast. "We must watch and wait. Today we free Revin."

They followed her gaze. Under the city wall stood the depressing prison of Newgate – Revin's abode for the last few months. After all the waiting, planning and disappointments both Rewn and Verde were lost for words.

Standing outside the prison, they found its tall drab walls encapsulated the misery that they felt for Revin.

"How do we know that he's still alive?" asked Woodman.

"Oh, he is. I just know he is," replied Lutel.

Already men were coming through Newgate with their empty carts in search of easy money. Rewn noted that a few Londoners were moving in the opposite direction, escaping from the fire that relentlessly moved towards them.

"How can you be certain that the fire will reach here?" asked Rewn dubiously.

Lutel sighed. "Look at these people," she said, indicating the growing exodus that rushed through the city gate. "They are only concerned for their own safety – not one in a thousand is staying to fight the fire."

Indeed the refugees were growing by the minute, leaving the city of their birth by foot, on horseback, or by cart. Some brought with them nothing, having lost all to the fire. Others led horses pulling wagons piled high with their belongings. Small children perched excitedly on the top of the goods, whilst mothers cradled screaming infants. An unpleasant thought came to Lutel – to fail at this late hour would be a disaster; the fire had yet to purge a half of the city. They were on the brink of successfully achieving their mission, albeit by drastic measures, yet what if her confidence was misplaced? Rewn was right to express doubt. They must do all in their power to ensure that nothing stemmed the path of the fire, or interfered with the release of Revin.

"Let's check on the fire's progress, just in case things are becoming organised," suggested Lutel.

In places where the flames raged, the ground was so hot that it glowed red. Along Paternoster Row a pigeon circled around the ground; eventually, exhausted by the heat and its efforts to find a safe landing, the singed bird fell at their feet. Rewn picked the pigeon up and stroked the back of its head; the wing feathers were scorched brown. He placed it on a wall just outside Saint Paul's Cathedral, so that it might safely recover. Thick black smoke now dared to surround the building. An assortment of ashes, predominantly timber, had been whipped up by the bracing wind, and peppered their faces. Grey dust sprinkled their hair and lodged in their eyes, whilst cinders covered their clothing. Lutel grinned as she noticed their smutty faces and the very ground they walked on, which resembled a black sandy beach.

The road widened as they walked eastwards into Cheapside, towards the heart of the fire. Rewn admired the houses. They were in stark contrast to the hovels that he had experienced in the far east of the city. Here were examples of the finest Tudor and Stuart architecture, some reaching up to four storeys high. Each succeeding level projected further into the street, covering the cobblestone alley below until in the centre of the street the buildings almost touched like flirtatious lovers. It seemed blasphemous that these beautiful buildings would soon be sacrificed on an altar of flames. Around a dozen men prepared to fight the fire at this point; a ladder rested against a beam that extended horizontally from a house. A sign hanging from the timber informed passers-by that the building belonged to a goldsmith. Further evidence, if any was needed, was suspended next to the board in the shape of a golden gryphon. A chain of men passed buckets up the ladder to two men who threw the contents onto any cascading spark that dared to alight on the roof.

A further team of men were using ropes, firehooks, axes and pickaxes to pull buildings down. Into the midst of this overworked band rode a posse of noblemen. At their head, sitting proudly on a white charger, was the royal figure of King Charles, accompanied by his brother the Duke of York, complete with an escort of guards. His Majesty produced a velvet pouch from his shoulder, and addressed the elite band.

"A golden guinea to each of you if the fire stops at this point," he regally announced.

Momentarily the fire-fighting came to a halt as they listened in awe to the words of their King. They quickly redoubled their efforts as the royal party dismounted to assist with the fire buckets.

Lutel, Rewn, Verde and Woodman unwittingly found themselves coerced into the chain, urged by His Majesty. Rewn found himself next to the King.

"If we save Cheapside we will save the north-west corner of my city," the King shouted.

Lutel appreciated his appraisal of the situation.

"I'll move the horses further from the fire, sire," she offered.

The horses had been tied to several massy posts that lined Cheapside and the crackling flames and drifting ashes were clearly distressing the beasts.

"Of course, of course, lead them to safety," came the hasty royal reply.

Within a few minutes Lutel had untethered the horses, beckoning Woodman to assist. She fought to control the uneasy steeds as they reared in response to the flying embers. Woodman grabbed a bridle to check a bucking stallion and together they led the team away to the relative safety of Foster Lane. Charles Stuart with his helpers, both zealous and unwilling, continued to fight the fire, and Lutel and Woodman's non-appearance was only noted by Verde and Rewn.

"What's she up to?" mouthed Verde.

"I've no idea, but she must have some plan. She clearly intended us to stay here."

"Did she?"

A young woman approached the group, accompanied by three younger girls. Each carried a jug of ale and the fire-fighters stopped to refresh themselves.

"I quite enjoy fighting fires with His Royal Highness," joked Verde, as he quenched his thirst during the third interval.

The King was ordering the pulling down of houses at the far end of the row. He was overseeing the work when Woodman rode furiously into their midst.

"Your Majesty," he boldly addressed the King.

The King refrained from giving orders and faced the intruder. Although Woodman sat several feet higher than the monarch he still felt uncomfortably small. The King appeared to be looking down his nose at him and Woodman's nerve began to fail. Impatiently the royal made to turn away to continue with his work. It was the spur that Woodman needed.

"Your Majesty…" Woodman tried again.

The King once more gave him his undivided attention, facing the horseman full on. Woodman hesitated once more. Rewn stared at Verde.

"Tell us your news, friend," Verde encouraged him.

Woodman glanced towards Verde and, no longer transfixed by the King's gaze, he was able to blurt out his information.

"Fire breaks out beyond the city walls!"

"Where?" shouted Verde.

"At the Temple," replied Woodman, and he collapsed forward on to the neck of his horse.

The King interpreted this final act as one of nervous exhaustion and hailed his brother and several guards to accompany him. As they galloped away in search of the second fire a guard reclaimed his horse.

"Time to go," said Woodman, deftly dismounting. The three of them made hasty tracks along Wood Street.

"Brilliant," Verde praised him. "Is there really a fire at the Temple?"

"Not yet," said Woodman, "but there will be."

"How do you know?" asked Verde.

"Lutel!" surmised Rewn.

She was waiting for them on the corner of Warwick Lane and Paternoster Row. Their plan had worked as the fire had broken through Cheapside and was raging helplessly out of control towards Newgate. Behind them stood the sad sight of Saint Paul's Cathedral. They had watched the fire start in the great tower and then melt the lead, causing molten tear drops to ignite the structure below. A ring of flames imprisoned the great building, ensuring there would be no escape. Rewn wiped a tear from his eye as the roof cascaded in with a sickening crash – it saddened him to witness a work of such beauty razed to the ground.

As they contemplated the ruins before them, they were woken from their daydreaming by the thunder of gunpowder blowing up rows of houses over at Cheapside. It reminded them that the fire was fast approaching Newgate.

As they approached the prison, smoke was drifting across its walls and roof.

"What should we do?" asked Rewn of Lutel. "We cannot stand by and do nothing as Revin fries."

"We must attack," said Woodman.

Lutel ignored the suggestion, as her eyes seared into the prison walls as though she were attempting to pierce the very stones, and see beyond into its dark recesses with their terrible secrets. She knew the others expected a solution from her.

Easy solutions… her mind drifted back to her mother crying in the family home.

"It's all right, Lutel," her father had assured her as she walked in.

Lutel handed Rithes to Varna and placed a comforting arm around her mother.

"Tell me," she urged.

Rewn opened his mouth to explain, but their father pre-empted him.

"Rewn has given us some news that has upset your mother."

Lutel pulled her mother closer and awaited developments. Redolent fragrances from a bunch of discarded flowers drifted towards Lutel; she made to pick them up, but her mother put a restraining arm on her daughter's knee.

"It's not what you are thinking, Lutel," said Rewn. "You've been listed for the Earth mission! You're to accompany Verde, Revin and myself."

Lutel jumped up shrieking, disregarding all other thoughts.

"You're not serious. Don't tease me, Rewn, you know how much it means to me."

"I wouldn't lie to you about something like this." Rewn nodded towards their mother.

Lutel felt awful as she comprehended the situation. She subdued her excitement and returned to her mother's side.

"Mother, you know how much this means to me. I never dreamt that I would have any chance…"

"It's a wonderful opportunity and fully deserved. Take no notice, she'll come round," said her father benevolently, pulling his daughter towards him.

Lutel felt like a piece of meat being fought over by two ravenous mocorns.

"You are being unfair," said Rewn to his mother.

"The thought of never seeing your brother again was bad enough, but losing both of you would be unbearable."

Rewn paced impatiently around the room; many times in his youth had he felt the frustration of maternal protection. "We'll be perfectly all right; the scouts have given us invaluable information."

"Out-of-date information," she retorted.

"It might be rather sketchy but it's adequate," argued Rewn, standing over his mother.

"The Stilax have bestowed a great honour on our family," said their father. "Rewn and Lutel are just as likely to have a space hopper accident here on Mykas."

"That's not my point."

"What is, then?"

"If they are injured I won't be able to see them. From your own mouth I've heard you say how backward their science and technology is."

"Verde and Lutel are trained medics."

"Verde! What use will an allergy specialist be?"

"His medical knowledge will still be more advanced than Earth's," argued Rewn.

"Exactly," shouted his mother, and she commenced her sobbing again.

"Don't you think we should let Lutel decide?" reasoned her father.

All eyes turned towards Lutel, but she had left the room.

A search of the house and grounds failed to locate her. Rewn sat down with a warm drink of gylsit in his hand.

"Look," he said, pointing through the vista. In the far woodlands a woman was moving stealthily through the trees with a mocorn at her side.

"She's taken her huxhler," said her father, making for the door.

"Leave her," said his wife. "You are right. Lutel is her own woman now."

Rithes ran around Lutel's feet, then scurried away into the undergrowth to absorb the countless smells. Lutel delved further into the wood, paying little attention to the direction that she was taking. After a while she removed a small floppy object from a sack around her waist, and calling Rithes to her held it under the mocorn's nose. Two twisted flanges encircled the red ball.

"A huxh," she said three times to Rithes, then she threw the huxh into some nearby bushes and encouraged the mocorn to find it. Rithes needed little inducement and duly led Lutel to the hidden huxh.

"Good girl," said Lutel, tickling the mocorn's ears. Rithes let out a low growl of appreciation. Lutel repeated the game several times; each time Rithes led her to the resting place and Lutel continued to reward her.

Over her shoulder Lutel carried a rectangular metal box with folded legs. She unfolded the tripod and placed it firmly into the soft ground. Lutel placed the huxh inside the sights and other digital aids, and pressed a red button. There was a whistling sound and the huxh shot out of an aperture at the side of the box and disappeared into the distance. Rithes surprised her mistress by racing into the undergrowth. She's a natural, thought Lutel as she brushed through wild brambles in pursuit of her pet. After several hundred yards Lutel found Rithes jealously guarding the huxh.

"Good girl, Rithes," she said, making an extra-long fuss of the mocorn. "You will be competition standard in no time."

Lutel's thoughts turned to the huxhler competitions that were such a popular pastime with Mykasians. A course covered several square miles of woodland, hills and meadows. Around the course there would be several green targets that the huxh had to hit. The distance between each target was often several miles, requiring many shots before the red ball reached its destination, and hence the need for an accomplished mocorn to search out the hidden projectile.

Each time Rithes located the huxh Lutel increased the range. Rithes never once waited for encouragement from Lutel to pursue the whizzing red blur. As Rithes once more charged off in the direction of the missile Lutel came to a decision.

"You certainly are a single-minded mocorn and know what you want from life; I'm impressed," she murmured.

Lutel could find no easy answer, and her thoughts became less distinct as the smoke shrouded the prison. She continued to search the smog for inspiration and as she squinted, her eyes stinging, the wind blew an extra-strong gust and for an instant the smoke billowed skywards. The clearing lasted for less than a second and for a moment she did not know whether to trust her watering eyes. In that twinkling of visibility Lutel thought she had seen some activity around the large wooden door. Several of the inmates were being led from the prison by their guards.

"Over there," she shouted to Verde, pointing at the blanket of smoke. "Keep looking. Rewn and Woodman, follow me."

Lutel ran towards the gate in the wall that gave the prison its name, pursued by the two men. Confusion reigned throughout the area, as panic-stricken city dwellers were still arriving in their thousands to escape the flames whilst the country folk with their carts fought to enter the city. Newgate became a bottleneck and tempers flared as town met country. Carts overturned, their contents strewn about the road, and sobbing housewives and swearing husbands scrabbled around on their hands and knees, trying to rescue their belongings from beneath the feet of the crowd. A fire cistern arriving from the liberties jammed the gate as it met a large wagon from the opposite direction. Sporadic bouts of fighting were springing up all around as nerves were stretched to the limit. Lutel rushed into the centre of the throng.

"The French, the French are attacking the prison," she shouted.

Rewn blanched at the absurdity of the statement; it might have worked in the city centre, but here was a different proposition. Who would defend a prison when they were seeking their own freedom? He had not reasoned on the mentality of the crowd – the frenzy of their hysteria knew no bounds and all semblance of calm and logic had vanished. Lutel's cry was taken up; at first lone voices repeated the alarm, soon rising to a tumultuous crescendo.

"This way," screamed Lutel, leading the mindless masses.

Within minutes several hundred people were racing towards the prison, running through Newgate marketplace and back again. Total confusion had broken out as the whole street erupted in turmoil. Those who reached the end of the street first stopped, believing that they had missed the action, then raced off to retrace their steps. Bodies were trampled underfoot as the unruly mob continued to charge from one end of the street to the other. Fighting broke out as false accusations of nationality were freely uttered by the mob.

Verde tried to stand his ground as he was jostled by the rabble. Several prisoners had now left the prison but he had so far failed to recognise Revin.

The crowd swept him along in their frenzied wave of excitement, and he attempted to regain his position in front of the prison door, but the sheer number of bodies pressing against him was too great. He shouted at the mob but all ears were deaf, and he was soon unable to command a view of the exit.

It was a full half an hour before the crowd began to realise that they had been mistaken. Verde found himself a short distance from Aldersgate, where the fire was close to the city walls. Jostling his way with the other refugees, he barged through the gate and, turning left, kept close to the contour of the wall. On reaching Newgate he searched for the others; it proved an impossible task amongst such a surging crowd. It felt like he was the only one travelling westward. After pushing against the flow for several minutes Verde decided to change direction. He travelled with the masses back towards Aldersgate and then on to Cripplegate. At each gateway, more and more screaming and shouting people poured out from the city, but their combined crying paled into insignificance compared to the bellowing roar that issued forth from the fire. Lapping flames now licked the city walls and in places had begun to breach them.

As he approached Moorgate Verde recognised familiar landmarks; he realised that he was walking his old haunts. He smiled to himself as he remembered the times with Joe Priddy, and how he and Revin had played their trick on the old devil. Sad though the reminiscence was, it had the effect of cheering him up.

Trapped by the crowd, Verde had never felt so alone in his life. Ironic, he told himself; here I am surrounded by thousands of people and I don't know a soul. Then a voice inside him said, "I do." Bishopsgate, the scene of their entry over a year ago, lay before him. Gatleigh's, Tom Gatleigh's: did he dare go there? Verde remembered the sad departure. Was Tom still alive? Would they remember him? He might no longer be welcome as a friend; after all, he'd made no effort at contact. In any case he doubted if he could find the house again. Doubt after doubt nagged him, but right now he sought company and he was willing to clutch at the thinnest chances of finding it. His desire grew stronger and stronger until it grew warm enough to melt his uncertainty. Tom could help him find the others; he would have friends that could assist with their location. He just needed to find his bearings.

A church loomed in front of him. A wide grin broke out over his face as he recognised the tower of All Hallows-on-the-Wall. Tom's house was close, very close; of that he was adamant. As he came to a row of familiar houses, Verde ran his fingers in a relieved greeting along their walls. Several of the crowd gave him a peculiar stare; others gave him a wide berth – convinced that they were witnessing the actions of a madman. His heart sank as he noticed the fading red crosses that still bedecked many of the doors. Verde ran along the row, hesitating only to check for the desired house. At last he came to a door that appeared very familiar. With difficulty he stepped back amongst the flow of people to take a better look. A man bumped into him and knocked him to the ground; with some effort he rose to his feet. Verde delayed no further; he banged his fists on the door.

"Tom, Tom!" he yelled. The depths of all emotion burst forth from his voice as he called the name.

Slowly the door began to open. A tall grey-haired man with a distinguished beard stood before him. His back was bent slightly, as though life had paid him no favours.

"Sorry," apologised Verde. "I was hoping to see somebody else."

In that fleeting moment all hope seemed to ebb away. He had lived on his nerves on a strange planet, survived bubonic plague and fire, and now the fact that a fleeting friendship was not to be renewed took a heavy toll. His despair was absolute; his head became light and, overcome by dizziness, he staggered forward. The grey-haired man opened his arms and caught him.

"You'd better come in, Verde," said Revin.

CHAPTER FIFTY-SIX

DECISIONS

It took several swigs of brandy before Verde was able to fully comprehend his surroundings. The room was largely as he remembered, but not the people. He believed he was hallucinating; as he stared around the room he could see all of his friends. It was not until he reached out and touched the tangible greying beard in front of him that he believed his eyes. It was indeed Revin. Verde could see that now; his face was gaunt, the lines more etched, but the handsome features remained.

Verde listened in silence as first Revin, then Lutel and finally Rewn explained how Revin had literally fallen over them during the melee outside Newgate prison. Swiftly, they had whisked him away through Newgate before anyone was apprised of his disappearance. For similar reasons to Verde, Revin had felt the pull of Tom Gatleigh's, and as the house lay between them and the spaceship it seemed a natural resting place before embarking on their return journey. This last explanation was delivered by Rewn, mindful of those who should not be listening. Here they now all sat amidst Tom's family, complete with Rebecca and Sam.

"How did you know I would come here?"

"Call it a woman's intuition," said Lutel, smiling.

A knock on the door caused Verde to leap from his chair.

"Stay," said Lutel.

Verde trembled as Tom opened the door; would all their good fortune dissolve so soon?

"You had better come in," said Tom.

Verde stood up. "Revin, may I introduce you to an old friend, John Woodman?"

"We have already briefly met outside the prison," said Revin.

"You gave him this address," said Verde, with a nod.

"A valued, old friend," added Lutel.

"Not so much of the 'old'," retorted Woodman. "No wonder I couldn't find you," he said to Verde.

"Thanks for trying," said Verde, his head now clear enough to grasp the thoughtful gesture.

Revin delved into a second bowl of Rebecca's nourishing broth. "This takes me back," he said between slurps as he spooned up another mouthful.

Lutel smiled and glanced over at Woodman. She would miss his gruff, blunt manner. For all his surly ways, he possessed a true heart. There was hope for this planet whilst it produced men like John Woodman, she reasoned. Then her gaze rested on Revin. It had been a shock when they had first seen him; he'd been the one to recognise them, and a good job he did, she thought. She should have guessed the toll that a year in prison would have taken on him. She castigated herself for not freeing him earlier, but she had been so engrossed in the plague and then planning the fire that time had just swept by. After all, "the mission was the important thing", she could hear the Stilax saying, but was it? Was it really more important? she asked herself.

Verde and Rewn were chatting happily to Tom and his wife. Nobody would think that there were light years between them, she told herself. Here were four people from two very different cultures, and they were talking like old family friends. She eavesdropped on their conversation; naturally it centred on the fire.

"Frenchies, I've heard them say the Frenchies were responsible," said Tom.

"Even the King himself has been out," added Rebecca.

"Do you think it will reach here?" asked Woodman.

"Of course not," said Tom. "His Majesty will not allow it."

As evening approached the wind dropped, and the blowing up of houses around Cripplegate proved Tom's prediction correct.

"Perhaps some good will come of it," said Rebecca, as she stared out of an upstairs bedroom across the ruined city.

"I'm sure you are right," answered Revin as he looked wistfully out of the window.

He kissed Sam goodnight, and joined the others downstairs. Lutel was relaxing in a chair, a contented observer; then her thoughts turned once more to Woodman.

He was the only living soul, outside their quartet, who knew the truth behind the fire. Lutel feared for his safety once he was left to fend for himself. Nobody would listen to his story if he did talk, surely – a drunken boast, nothing more, people would say. No, Woodman would not betray them; he would be putting a noose around his own neck.

Then her mind returned to Chippenham and the Lyon Inn. Woodman had boasted to the assembled drinkers how he was off to London to fire the houses. Her mind became uneasy as she remembered Laungechamp. Back on Mykas they would be safe, but even if the authorities dismissed Woodman's account as the ravings of a lunatic, they were still likely to punish him. A thought came to mind – no, it would be impossible, she decided, but still the question lingered. What if Woodman travelled back with them? Would he agree to it? What would Verde say? Would the Stilax approve? Admittedly it was outside normal procedure, but it had been an abnormal mission; interfering with the history of a planet was a measure only taken after long and serious consideration. Whatever the case, they would leave tomorrow, she decided, and before then she would broach the others for their opinion.

Then she remembered the crash landing back in the woods of the Wiltshire countryside. The plan fizzled out. Had they still had two ships, she was certain, all would have worked out perfectly. Now, as the house fell quiet, the thought continued to bother her until she too drifted into sleep.

The next morning Rewn had risen early and left the house. Tom had been the only one to see him go.

"Said he wanted some fresh air and needed a walk," explained Tom.

"He won't get much fresh air around here," sighed Rebecca as she laid the table for breakfast.

Lutel was vexed as she particularly wanted to discuss her worries with her brother. She immersed herself in helping Rebecca, until such time as Rewn should return.

The fire had been brought under control by early morning. Sporadic outbursts occurred here and there, and cellars were destined to burn for many months. But the Great Fire of London had by all accounts burned itself out, and all that remained for the fire-fighters was to stamp out its subdued embers.

On the fields that encircled the city, rich and poor slept alongside each other. The hard ground made no allowances for class, and tanner lay beside goldsmith, as a doctor might lie beside a dyer. In places, improvised tents had been set up by the more pragmatic members of the camp, but largely the masses lay out on the ground. Many still showed signs of shock from their experiences in the fire, and groans and moans filled the air, as Londoners came to grips with the devastation on the other side of the wall.

In the desolate scene a forlorn figure wandered around the refugees, offering solace and administering what comfort he was able. A kind word here, a helping hand there; he had little more to give than his heart. Every time he paused to give aid, he repeated the same question.

"Have you seen Thomas Farynor?"

Time after time he was greeted with the same blank stare; sometimes the sufferers would verbalise their answers, but the outcome would be the same. Occasionally, as a reward for his kindness, he would be given directions, but these responses always led to a false trail. The figure eventually gave up searching for the day, and headed once more for the city walls.

The Gatleigh household had been the scene of much merriment. The renewing of friendships, and the confirmation of the dying fire, led to a day of feasting and gaiety. Towards evening, Lutel drew Revin and Verde aside.

"We must leave soon; our work is complete."

"What about Rewn?" asked Revin.

"As soon as he returns, we take off."

"He's been rather a long time," observed Verde.

"You know Rewn; he needs space, time to clear his thoughts."

Lutel mused. Back on Mykas he would take himself off on long walks into the violet mountains whenever he felt life was sucking him in.

"He'll be back before dark," she confidently announced.

Lutel was right; as dusk approached, the first time they had seen the setting sun for several days, a tap came on the door. Tom went to answer, and muffled voices could be heard. Lutel strained to catch the utterances; one voice she definitely recognised, the other seemed familiar. "Wait here" was the only muttering that she could make out.

Rewn entered the room alone; Lutel saw at once from the serious look on his face that all was not well.

"May we speak in private?" he asked Rebecca.

Their hostess stood up and, taking Sam's hand, went in search of her husband.

"What is it?" asked Lutel, as soon as Rebecca had left the room.

All eyes fell upon Rewn. He looked hesitantly around the room at his friends, choking on his words.

"I'm not coming back." The words shot out far more brutally than he intended.

"What do you mean?" demanded Verde.

"I'm staying here."

"Why on earth do you want to stay here?"

Rewn smiled nervously at the pun.

"I'm sure you have your reasons," said his sister, recovering from the shock.

"Two reasons," corrected Rewn. "Primarily, I think you know my private guilt over the fire."

"Keep your voice down," Verde urged him, indicating the hallway.

"I can offer these people so much; I can help them rebuild this city. I'm a trained architect – there are many like me back home, but few here. I know I can be of use."

"Back home," echoed Lutel. "You know there will be no second chance if you don't come now?"

Rewn fidgeted with his hands. "The other reason," he said, not knowing quite how to proceed. "I'm going to be married!"

Revin spat out his drink, whilst Verde burst out laughing. Lutel sat back in her chair.

"You're joking," said Verde.

"He's deadly serious."

"Thank you, Lutel."

"Who, where, why… you haven't met anybody," blathered Verde.

"I have," said Rewn. "The baker's daughter."

Lutel nodded knowingly. "Lydia."

"Is that where you have been?" asked Woodman, at last understanding part of the conversation.

"I've been searching for her in the fields all day. I had almost given up hope, and was on my way back, when I literally stumbled over her family."

"Useful things, stumbles," observed Lutel.

"Do I have your blessing?" Rewn asked his sister.

Lutel sighed deeply, collecting her thoughts. "Is this what you really want?"

"I've been thinking about nothing else since I met her."

Lutel stood up and embraced her brother. "I'm not sure how I'll be able to explain to our parents."

Rewn squeezed his sister's hand. The touch was sufficient.

"Then stay, Rewn."

Verde clapped him on the back, whilst Revin took him by the hand.

"Can we meet the lucky lady who is taking you from us?" asked Revin.

Rewn moved towards the passageway. "Come in, Lydia," he called.

The baker's daughter, accompanied by Tom and his family, walked demurely through the door.

"Is everything in order, Christopher?"

Verde looked around the room, with an exaggerated movement of his head. "Christopher?" he mimicked.

Lutel, who recognised the seriousness of the situation, swiftly admonished him with a withering stare.

Rewn held Lydia's hand, and abruptly brushed over the fabrication. "Everything is fine, Lyddy. I'd like you to meet my sister, Lutel."

The girl almost fainted on seeing her maid. She reached out and felt Lutel's arm. "I thought you were…"

"Not quite," said Lutel, placing her hand on her heart and smiling at Rewn. "So you are to be Rew… Christopher's wife?"

"Yes," said the girl coyly. "I've loved him ever since he rescued me, and in all that time I never knew his name. Then when I asked him, and he told me he was called Christopher after the patron saint of travellers – I just knew it couldn't be anything else."

"No," agreed Lutel, drawing out the word. She put her arm around her brother's shoulder. "Well, Christopher, I hope you and Lydia will be very happy."

"I just know we will," said Lydia. "Christopher has told me all about his plans to rebuild the city. He's so clever. I'm really very excited."

"I'm sure you are, and I'm very sorry that we won't be able to stay for the wedding."

Lydia looked hurt, as did Rewn.

"We have very important business, miles from here, and I am afraid we must leave tonight."

Lydia frowned with disappointment and turned to her intended for support.

"Lutel would not miss the wedding unless it was very important," Rewn assured her.

As her future husband did not seem upset at the prospect, Lydia was not prepared to pursue the matter. Nothing was going to spoil her happiness, and she pushed the disappointment to the back of her mind.

Rewn's mind drifted towards more practical matters. "Tom, would it be in order for Lydia's parents to shelter here until something is sorted out?"

"Well, as Mister Revin and his friends are leaving us, I am sure that we can come to some arrangement for you all." Tom glanced at Rebecca for confirmation.

"Would you like me to come with you to fetch them?" suggested Rebecca.

"That would be most kind."

"Come on, Gatleigh," called Rebecca to her husband. "I am sure Mister Rewn would like to say goodbye to his friends."

Lydia was so in love that she noticed nothing suspicious about the naming of her future husband.

"Are you certain that this is what you want?" asked Lutel, when the door had closed and the five of them stood alone.

"Absolutely," responded her brother. "I know she is a little whimsical, but it's mere innocence. I love her deeply."

"Very well, I wish Christopher and Lydia every happiness."

Rewn stared at the floor.

"What is it?"

"When Lydia asked my name I just blurted out Christopher – it seemed applicable. But I thought my break with Mykas ought to be complete, so I'm going to invent a surname."

"Two new names?" said Lutel coolly. "One was always good enough on Mykas."

"On Mykas," intoned Rewn.

"So what is your surname to be?" asked Verde.

"It's an idea I've borrowed from Rathbone," he said. "Remember the Colonel rearranged his name to identify the plotters?"

"Bornhate? Your new name is going to be Christopher Bornhate?" asked Verde incredulously.

"Of course not."

"Well?" drawled Lutel.

"Well, I'm undecided, but from now on my name will be Wern or Wren… Christopher Wren!"

"Well, Christopher Whoever, I wish you well."

Lutel clasped him to her bosom and planted a long loving kiss on his forehead.

The poignancy of the moment was broken by Woodman.

"Where exactly do you come from?"

Lutel pulled away from her brother. Was Woodman ready for Mykas, she wondered, or, more pointedly, was Mykas ready for Woodman? Rewn would have the wits to survive and adapt, she told herself. In the unlikely event, he would know how to evade any charges that would be laid at his feet. But Woodman, you never knew where that mouth might lead him.

"We live many miles from here, John."

Woodman sat silently, and Lutel continued.

"We do not live on your planet; we come from a star in the sky. Would you like to come with us?"

Woodman laughed. "She's been drinking," he said, looking around the room for confirmation.

Stern looks on all of their faces convinced him of Lutel's seriousness.

"How did you get here?"

"In a ship… a flying cart," said Lutel.

"Really?" asked Woodman of Verde.

"It's the truth, John."

"What's it like – where you come from?"

"Beautiful; you would like it."

"And you are willing to take me with you?"

"There's room now, but there will be no coming back for you either, John."

"Bloody good," said Woodman.

EPILOGUE ONE

Final farewells were made before either the Gatleighs or the Farynors returned. It would be for the best, Rewn decided, if he didn't see them off. He didn't want to leave Lydia so soon after finding her, and her presence at the take-off would be out of the question.

Even though Rewn was so radiantly happy, Lutel could not stop a large lump coming to her throat. For a long time now, he had been the most important person in her life, and the final lingering hug lasted several seconds, but for Lutel it seemed a microscopic moment in time.

"Farewell, Revin."

"Goodbye… Christopher."

"Farewell, Verde," said Rewn.

"Good luck, architect."

A lifetime of love and respect was encapsulated in those few fond seconds.

"Take it easy up there," Rewn advised Woodman. "I have the advantage over you of knowing both worlds."

"You're welcome to this one," said Woodman, shaking his friend's hand.

Woodman followed Verde and Revin through the door. Rewn looked at his sister. Lutel opened her mouth to speak; tears welled in her eyes.

"Don't," he said kindly, wiping her cheek. She closed her mouth and instead walked to the door, turned around and blew him a kiss. Rewn rubbed his eyes, and when he opened them, she had gone.

Lutel felt inside her clothing for her key. As she weaved through the refugees towards the open fields, her mind raced confusingly over the events of the last few months. Back to the Wiltshire countryside, Varley's farmhouse, imprisonment in Chippenham, Littlecote House, and finally London with its plague and squalor and cleansing fire.

She looked at Revin and Verde ahead of her; they were busy explaining the workings of a spacecraft to a bemused and disbelieving Woodman. She examined the clothes that she was wearing; what would they make of them back on Mykas? Mykas… what was she going to tell their parents and family? Before she could decide, they had reached the bushes. Verde and Revin were pulling back the branches and deactivating the cloaking system. For the first time Woodman truly believed, as the silver door swivelled open. Verde stepped inside, followed by Revin and a somewhat hesitant Woodman.

As Lutel stood in the hatchway, she gazed back towards the city. Intermittent sparks still rose into the sky. She stared in the direction where she imagined Gatleigh's house to be, trying to picture the scene inside – imagining what Rewn would be saying and doing.

"Come on," called Verde from deep inside.

"Lutel! ...Lutel?" called a voice.

Lutel took one last lingering look, and the hatch closed.

EPILOGUE TWO

Several weeks after the last of the flames had died down, acting on information received, a warrant was issued for the arrest of one John Woodman, bachelor of the parish of Kellaways, Wiltshire. The authorities' plea went unanswered.

EPILOGUE THREE

The eventual arrival in England of King William III and his queen, Mary II, early in 1689, brought a wave of joy and optimism to their subjects. Their coronation resulted in much celebration and festivities, and nowhere more than in a loyal borough in the north-west corner of Wiltshire.

A bronzed man in his later years was busy tidying away the festivities outside his coffee shop.

"It's been a tiring day," he said to his wife.

"It has that," came the reply, "but worth it. I just wish my parents had lived to see the day."

A sign fixed to the wall of their coffee shop and bakery said "London Buildings". They had bought the premises soon after they had retired to the countryside. The husband could never be still, and although he had long hankered for peace and quiet, he longed for a challenge, hence the new business. Two girls, with the black hair and beautiful features of their mother, tidied away tables and chairs from the dusty street. A boy of ten or eleven years scavenged around the table, picking up morsels of food.

"That's enough, Thomas," ordered his father.

The boy gazed at his father with his large green eyes.

"Your Aunt Tulle is over the road."

A mature woman with chestnut hair was rounding the corner of a large black-and-white timbered building. The boy rushed across the street to greet his aunt and bumped into an over-indulgent young reveller.

"Sorry, sorry," said the youth to the son and father.

"That's perfectly all right," said the father, reminiscing. "Perfectly."

Wil Hulbert

Wil was born and educated in Chippenham, Wiltshire. He trained as a teacher at Maria Grey College, Twickenham and spent thirty five years teaching primary children, twenty six of those as a deputy head. He was awarded an MA at Bath College of Education in 1995. He is married to Lin and has two grown-up sons. His hobbies include cycling around the Wiltshire countryside, reading and non-league football. He is a director of Chippenham Town FC. He welcomes visitors to his site, **mpnw.50webs.com** where he can be contacted. There you can also find a selection of photographs and maps relating to *The Murder of Crows*, assisting readers to follow or embark on the actual route taken by the characters from Wiltshire to London using the maps from the book – including a number of impressive inns along the way!

BIBLIOGRAPHY

Avebury Village Trail. Wiltshire Folk Life Society.

A Chippenham Collection. Chippenham Civic Society, 1987

Yelde Hall Museum: Silver Jubilee 1963–1988: Chippenham Official Souvenir Guide. Chippenham Town Council, 1988

West Yatton Down Reserve Guide. Wiltshire Trust for Nature Conservation, 1988

Alton, G, and D Simpkin. *Contemporary Accounts of the Great Plague of London*. Tressell, 1985

Bell, WG. *The Great Fire of London*. Bracken Books, 1994

Bell, WG. *The Great Plague in London in 1665*. The Bodley Head, 1994

Byrde, Penelope. *The Male Image: Men's Fashion in Britain 1300–1970*. Batsford, 1979

Clark, Fiona. *Hats (The Costume Accessories Series)*. Batsford, 1982

Cowie, Leonard. *Plague and Fire: London 1665–66 (Documentary History)*. Wayland, 1986

Cunnington, Willett C, Phillis Cunnington and Charles Beard. *A Dictionary of English Costume*. Adam and Charles Black, 1976

Daniell, JJ. *The History of Chippenham*. Houston & Sons, 1894

Deary, Terry, and Neil Tonge. *Terrible Tudors*. Scholastic, 1993

Defoe, Daniel. *A Journal of Plague Year*. 1772

Driver, Christopher, and Michelle Berriedale-Johnson. *Pepys at Table: Seventeenth Century Recipes for the Modern Cook*. Harper Collins, 1984

Goldney, Frederick Hastings. *Records of Chippenham*. 1889

Goldsburg, Madeline. *The Hat*. Studio Editions, 1990

Hammond, Peter. *Her Majesty's Royal Palace and Fortress of The Tower of London*. Crown Copyright, 1987

Harris, Richard (ed.). *Weald and Downland Open Air Museum Guidebook*.

Hodges, Dr Nathaniel. *Loimologia, or an historical account of the plague in London in 1665*. 1720

Honeywell, Chris, and Gill Spear. *The English Civil War: Recreated in Colour Photographs*. Windrow and Greene, 1993

McKendry, Maxine. *Seven Centuries of English Cooking*. Exeter Books, 1983

Pepys, Samuel. *The Diary of Samuel Pepys*. 1825

Printed in Dunstable, United Kingdom

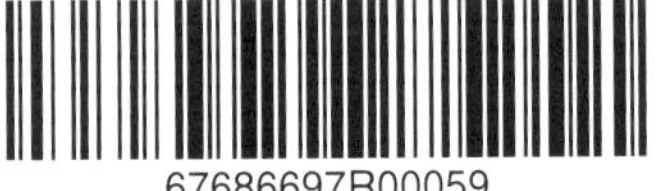

IT'S ALI

...but th

by

Rob Wyborn

Welcome to my philosophy
which I hope will soon be yours too

This book is all about the most important

person in your life

YOU

DEDICATION

Family and friends have a special place in my heart and head and it's those I need to thank publicly for their support, debate, questioning and listening.

To those I express my respect and love:
Marianne, Jeremy, Hans, Britt,
Kris, Seb, Emily, Ben, Jo, Cath, Chris
and lot more that have made this book possible.

Thank you for the influence, inspiration and wine.

ISBN-13: 9781092251150

CONTENTS

ACKNOWLEDGMENT

The stunning cartoon illustrations here are the creation of my incredibly talented nephew Harry Partridge. Thank you, Harry, for putting up with your Uncle's demands and general begging.

You Tube:
HappyHarryToons

Twitter:
@HappyHarryToons

It's All Your Fault

1. THE FIRST BIT

This is the bit about me and how I came to write this book. I think it's interesting, but then, I would think that.

The Short version of this book is:
Man, obese all of adult life. Loses a lot of weight. Discovers he did it by simply changing the way he thinks. Applies the same principles to other areas of his life, influences others around him. Writes book about the process. Sells millions and now lives in Barbados - OK, the last sentence isn't true, yet :)

The even shorter version:
Fat bloke, loses 8 Stone, writes book.

I am not an accomplished writer, as you will no doubt discover as you progress through this book. However, my passion to share the experience of my personal transformation, which I have successfully applied to other areas of my life, has helped me to develop this philosophy and my desire to share it with you.

My intention has been to write this as if you and I were in the same room having a chat over a coffee, or glass of wine, depending on the time of day. My need to laugh may get in the way sometimes, bear with me, there is some good stuff here and I hope that the contents and my style encourage you to use this book and its tools towards achieving what you want for yourself and a happier life.

Pop in and out of it as and when you feel the need. Even though I have written it, I still pick it up and read sections to help me through the odd tough time and to remind myself of how far I have come.

This book started as a journal of my thoughts and experiences. Being a self-employed designer working from home. A single parent for 10 years, then empty nest syndrome when my son left for University, my seven Transient Ischemic Attacks TIAs (mini strokes) in 24 hours, Diabetes, Weight loss and complete transformation into the middle-aged man I am today. It's all good.

Writing my journal evolved to help me think. Thinking is an underused skill and one which is worth learning. We all think we think, but many of us do not think deep enough. I have learned to do this, and it has helped me to provide incredible clarity in every aspect of my life. My journal was, and remains, a cathartic therapy. When we write for and to ourselves, we don't lie. We write our secrets, wishes, dreams, frustrations and all manner of things about our life.

I started writing a journal to record my thoughts and the effects on my life about how I processed through my decision to lose a lot of weight. I thought it would be an interesting practice to record my actions, thoughts and feelings. It was, and still is.

My biggest discovery was learning and accepting that I was entirely responsible for every single aspect of my life. This evolved into discussing my thoughts with friends and learning that I am a skilled listener and able to discuss and debate issues without judgement. This has all resulted in this book, which I hope you find useful, honest, reassuring and spark your desire to think a lot more about everything you hold dear, starting with you.

The inspiration for this book was born from my significant weight loss, so please excuse my references to this

throughout. Since I have learned how to achieve weight loss without any 'wonder' drugs, crazy 'fad' diets, I wondered if I could apply the same thought processes in other areas of my life that I wanted to change and goals I wanted to achieve. I have done that. I can now apply the same formula to help me achieve absolutely anything I want. I have witnessed how, the same determination, focus and general pig-headedness can be applied to absolutely anything in your life. Weight-loss was my 'thing', it was where all of this started. You can substitute my weight-loss for any goal that you desire. You may well already have the perfect body. However, changing my physical appearance is where this philosophy and book started, so it is my experience.

I know and am living proof that this approach and philosophy works. I have seen it manifest itself in my own life. And whilst losing 8 Stone (that's 112b to my American readers, or a small person) to date means that I am physically 2/3rds of the man I was. The effect on my outlook on life has been far greater.

As soon as I had realised that I was and still am, in complete control of my life and responsible for everything I achieve (or not), then I worked on what I had done, how did I do it? What changed in my life? How did I become this person where everything I wanted was possible to achieve?

My friends and family noticed the change in me, the physical change was at best, 20%, the other 80% occurred in my mind. Whilst I have always had a positive outlook on life, people started to notice the positive changes in attitude, confidence as well as the obvious physical changes. They noticed my increased happiness.

My journey started in September 2016. After my annual Diabetes check-up, my excellent Nurse told me that if I didn't do something about my weight and lifestyle, then she would have to increase my medication, this could start to involve injections of Insulin rather than the tablets I had been taking. That was enough for me.

I joined a well-known weight loss group, the reason, well, I wanted to. At that time, I was over 21st, for me it was time, I was ready. The initial few weeks were highly concentrated on planning meals, working out what was good and what was not. How I could get the best from the foods I liked. Losing weight every week changed my mindset. I enjoyed the 'high' of losing weight, more than the short-lived 'high' of a slice of cake.

I wanted to lose weight so much, my meal planning was the first thing I thought of when I woke and keeping notes, a food diary and recording my activity throughout the day, helped me to remain focused. It was the only thing I really cared about. After 5 months I had realised I was on autopilot. I no longer needed the slimming club's handbook or app to work out what I needed to buy in the supermarket each week, I had realised I only ate when I was hungry and that I had taken responsibility for myself.

I started to enjoy exercise, albeit only walking a few miles a week to start with.

Then, along with keeping a journal and spreadsheet of my weekly losses (I love a spreadsheet!), I began to notice changes that were more than just looser fitting clothes. I had noticed that I trained my mind to achieve what I wanted and was convinced I could apply the same strategy to other areas of my life. I wanted a slimmer, healthier body - at the

time of writing this, I have lost over 8 Stone and have started setting other goals, because I know I can achieve anything I want!

What this book isn't

This may seem a negative way to start a publication such as this, but I think it's better to get this out in the open from the start.

This book is not a long, drawn out collection of stories and anecdotes to keep you hooked in until the 'big secret' is revealed. There is nothing that you need to buy or subscribe to in order to get the 'full value' - it's all right here.

This book does not rely on external forces of the Universe or the 'mysterious' laws of attraction, nor is it related to cosmic ordering! Of course, you may have already used Cosmic Ordering and 'ordered' a book to help you - in which case, well done, here it is.

This book does not contain a Secret!

What this book is

This book is my way of explaining an incredibly simple concept. Some of you won't need the whole book, you may well 'get it' within the first few pages.

This book is about you getting what you want. Not what you think you want, not what the media and great advertising tries to tell you what you want, not what your favourite celebrities have and tell you that your life will be better if you buy one. This is about you - there is no-one else involved, you're on your own with this.

It's important to remember that along your journey you're not doing any of this to please others, you are doing it to please you. You're the one we're talking about here - it's all about you.

This is not about being selfish, this is about you focusing on exactly what it is you want.

2. GETTING STARTED

Whilst I have tried to plan this book in a linear/chronological way, it really is up to you how you dive in and out of it. There is no prescribed way to consume it.

As for the 'How to Do It', I have explained the method I have developed and what worked for me. This is not compulsory, the fact that you DO IT, is more important than HOW you do it. Find the way that works for you.

To progress, you will need to 'Get it'. You need to comprehend that you're in total control and have been your entire adult life.

We have all shaped our lives through thousands of small and large decisions, we have made millions of life choices and each one has contributed to bringing you here today.

Of course, not every one of these was clearly thought out and consequences considered; some will have been spur of the moment decisions, the great ones worked out well. There were probably a lot more that didn't.

Every decision you have made in your adult life today has brought you to this moment in time, to this place and to this book.

Look around you, look at your life, few of us are where we thought we would be. Changes happen, people we know, and love can have influence over us, some more so than others, but every element and nuance of your life has equipped you to make the decisions and choices that you have made to date. From now on, you can take total control of those decisions, take total control of your life.

Once you accept that every decision you have made up to now has been your own free choice, consciously or not, then you start to get excited about the future. You can start to design and plan your future achievements.

You already have everything you wanted

Celebrate your incredible ability to have not let anything or anyone get in the way of what you have achieved to date. You have done it all, nothing and nobody has stopped you.

You may be thinking you didn't want to be overweight. You may be thinking you wanted a different or better job, relationship, more money, better stuff. Sorry, but you've got everything that you wanted - otherwise you wouldn't have it.

I should just add, before you start shouting 'Well I didn't want this, or I don't want that…' - we are focusing on the things you DO want, not the things you don't want. Being positive is an incredible super-power - you will develop that.

P
CAPTAIN
POSITIVE

You may be thinking this was not the way you thought things would work out. But of course, it is precisely the way things have happened and you have been in control all the time. Up until now, you hadn't realised or accepted it. So, go on, do it now. Accept it. ...I'm waiting, have you done it yet? Great, then you can carry on reading this, it will make a lot more sense.

This really is the core of concept - once you accept that you're responsible for everything you've done or got in your life, then you can start to take control about what happens in the future. It's as if you could look through your all your decisions to date as an old purchase ledger, all your decisions are there and your signature next to each one authorizing its acquisition. You have been in total control, you have been your own personal buying department, buying decisions and choices throughout your life. You can now start to realise that you're in this job for life, so you can start making decisions and choices about everything you want.

It was never your parent's fault, nor your partner(s), your boss(es), the Council, Government or any other figure in your life. Some or all of them may well have contributed and influenced you along the way, but that is because you have let them - you may have been hoodwinked or seduced into thinking you were not in control of a lot of this stuff - you were. You have been in control of every aspect of your thinking, of every thought you had and every action you have taken. The time is now here for you to own it.

You have made the choices about how hard you have studied, how diligently you have worked, you know how honest you have been, you know how good you really are, you know, deep down, you have got everything you deserved. You know when you've taken the easy option and

you know where, when and with whom you have conducted yourself with integrity - and when you haven't...

If you're sat there thinking some aspect of your life was somebody else's fault, then start to think deeper - maybe you let them make the decisions, [so you could have someone to blame if it went wrong], you gave them the power. To be fair, there is no 'maybe' about it, you did.

You may think I am being a little harsh (just as the title of this book may appear), you're right (kind of). Don't worry, the other side of the coin, the good stuff, is on its way.

Please realise that you have made and are responsible for every decision you have made in your life and the subsequent consequences of such decisions. Once you accept that, then the good stuff really starts.

You may have had wishes and dreams, we all do, but that's all they are. They are rarely well reasoned, considered, thought-out strategies that you have dedicated your life to achieving - if they had been, you wouldn't be reading this. That is not to say that wishes and dreams are not important, they are. They can deliver some relief, and release a few endorphins, mixed with Serotonin, Oxytocin and Dopamine which all go towards lightening our mood and making us feel happy. Maybe some of your wishes and dreams keep recurring, these may well start to become really strong and make their way on to The List. (more about The List later).

You have absolute control over your life. You're responsible for every single aspect of it. Once you accept this, you'll discover that you are the one responsible for where you are today. There is only one thing you have to do to achieve everything you want.

You simply have to change the way you think.

Nothing exists without first, a thought

Thinking is severely underrated and seldom done deeply enough. Your mind is a wonderful, powerful machine. It controls everything you think, do and say. Of course, it does not do this on its own. You have fed it many years of emotions, experiences, feelings, your secrets, in fact you have spoon-fed your mind your entire life and it has rewarded you with making every decision along the way since you became an adult. So, in short, you simply control everything.

Nothing in this world could exist without first having a thought. The chair you're sat on, the clothes you're wearing, every single item you own did not exist before someone had that thought.

This can be tough to realise. Once you've 'got' it - then you can move on.

Let's make it clear. The power of thought is incredible, you can change your mood by thinking. You can make your heart beat faster. You can imagine being followed by a dark shadow on the way home, raise your pulse, make yourself sweat. You can be fearful of stuff that hasn't happened. Fear is only in the future hence it doesn't exist. More of this another book. Once you can truly accept thank you really are in control of your mind and have been your whole life, then you can start taking control and the get the rest of your life sorted on your terms. You really can make yourself - wait for it... HAPPY.

You can’t change the past, but you can change the way you think about it. You can’t change the future, it doesn’t exist. The only thing you can change, is you and the only time you can do it, is now.

Simply accept you have been responsible and in control of everything in your past, then you can be in total control of everything in your future.

3. IT WAS ALL MY FAULT

I had got to 23 stone with little assistance. Nobody stopped me, and nothing got in my way. I did it, I achieved it - Yey! Go Team Robbie.

I didn't let anything stand in my way of that extra portion, that Chinese take away, those beers. I never let time in the gym get in the way of my sedentary lifestyle. I was a success. I was determined. It was all me. No-one else deserved any of the credit. I wasn't 'big-boned', it wasn't 'in my genes', it wasn't my Parents' fault - it was all about me. I chose the extra mouthful. I decided that I need a 'treat' after a good or a bad day. It's easy to convince ourselves we 'deserve' that pint or we have 'earned' that pizza.

When you realise that you are in control of you. You are in control of what you eat, what exercise you do, what job you do, where you go, what you do, how you act. You're even in control of the people and relationships you attract.

You also decide if you are a good person. You also decide how truthful you are to yourself, how much integrity you have, those can be toughies. When you realise this, you can start to replace those rubbish habits and traits that you've nurtured over the years, into great habits and attitudes for the future.

You really can change your life

If you're sat there thinking all the rubbish in your life is down to someone else, then take a look in the mirror and say Hello to person that has been totally responsible - if you

feel the need to give that person a slap, then do it - do it metaphorically - I'm not advocating self-flagellation here.

There is no secret, no method or 12-week course to sign up for. There is only you. You are in total control of your life. You can have the body, job, bank balance, lifestyle you want, the only trick is that you really have to want it.

Nothing has got in your way of achieving everything you have. The body, the job, the money, the lifestyle. You have done it all. Once you can accept this, it follows, that all of us can have or do anything we want.

4. MY PHILOSOPHY

It's All Your Fault. But that's a good thing. Once you can accept responsibility for everything in your life and every decision you have made to date, you can start to change.

You can have everything you want

You can have anything and everything you want. You simply just have to want it. Not dream about, not wish for it, there's no need to 'order' it, you just have to want it and by that, I mean, really want it.

If you 'kinda want it', you'll 'kinda get it'

Wishes and dreams are important, but they should not be confused with what you really want. You may well convert some of those wishes and dreams into achievable goals, so don't give up on them. When you're ready, you'll add them to your list of things that you are determined to achieve.

If you want any evidence to prove this works, simply stop reading and think about yourself for a while. You already have everything you wanted. You have the exact amount of money in the bank you wanted, you have the body you wanted, the relationship you wanted, all the material 'stuff' you wanted. Remember, every decision you have made in your life, right up until now, has brought you to where you are today, doing what you're doing - which is reading this book. Yes, we've been over that bit before, but just in case you got bored and thought you could skip it, I put it in again, just to make sure you really get it.

Yes of course, there will be those of you who don't immediately share this concept. I can hear some of you saying, 'Well, I want more money in the bank', 'I want a better car', 'A bigger house', 'a slimmer body'... - you get the idea.

I pay respect to those who may feel they can't have what they want, for many reasons, illness, disability and circumstances beyond their control. In my experience such people are accepting of their conditions and limitations and remain positive. We have all seen the people who have lost limbs, but their passion is to paint, play competitive sports and plainly, just do amazing things that leave us able-bodied numpties really quite ashamed. This demonstrates one thing.

You need to be Able-Minded, not able-bodied!

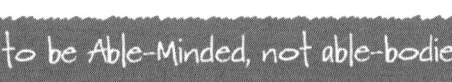

People with disabilities have adapted to their own personal circumstances, some use their mouth to paint, some their feet to write, this can be a good example to us all. How many more inspiring documentaries do you have to watch to 'get it'. If you want it, really want it, you'll get it. Determination is all you need.

This is all about what you DO want - not what you don't want. It's about what you want, not what you've got. It's about being positive and dealing with the present not the past. All we can do with the past is change our opinion of it, that's it.

The past does not have a post code, we can't live there. There is only one day that matters. We can't change what

happened yesterday and we can’t change tomorrow, we can only have an effect on today.

5. IT'S SIMPLE

Understand this, because something is Simple, does not automatically make it easy. Saying something is easy implies that no effort is required. Referring to it as Simple purely indicates that this is all really straight forward.

The language we use, not just to others but with ourselves is important. We grow up using certain phrases and unless someone picks up on the negative connotation, then we continue, unchecked.

Our language is powerful, no more so than the daily dialogue we have with ourselves. Changing your negative terminology to positive is a simple concept. To start with it may not be easy, but just because something is not easy, doesn't mean it's not worth the effort - after all, we're talking about you achieving what you want and to do this, all you have to do is change the way you think.

Let me simplify this further. This all works by simply prioritising our thoughts. If we truly want something, then we will do everything we need to do to achieve it.

Of course, it sounds simple and fundamentally, it is. I have met many people during my research who have questioned my philosophy, this has been a great benefit as it has forced me to consider all aspects of wanting to achieve something. In the end, my doubters have realised, appreciated and implemented my philosophy.

Here it is. We can all have everything we want. In fact, we already have everything we wanted up to today. Now of course, some of you will say something like, 'well I don't want this size/shape body/job/income'. Well sorry, it may

seem harsh, but yes you do (or did), until now…

As responsible adults we should enjoy the process of taking responsibility for ourselves. We can't blame anyone else, our friends, family, our exes our Councils or Government. We either accept the way things are or we take action to make an effort and affect change. Accept the things you cannot change, change the things you can.

Are you ready to accept the status quo? If you want the next months and years to be the same as the last months and years, then do nothing. Put this book down and continue on with your life.

I'm guessing you're not prepared to accept the way things are - your body, your job, your lifestyle your bank balance. So, you need to do something about it. It's all down to you, no-one else is going to do it for you and you don't need to do it for anyone else - this is all about you.

As soon as I realised that I was in control and could lose weight and reverse my Diabetes, I realised it was down to me, no-one else. I did it for the most important person. ME.

I have lost weight before, for nagging girlfriends, wife, sister's wedding… and was happy to do it, but as soon as the event or relationship finished, I simply put it all back on again.

When you accept that you're in total control, then it's simple to lose weight - in fact, it's simple to do anything.

If you really want to write a self-help book and you truly want to do it, then you will. You're currently reading one of the wants I had - I wanted to write this book and now you're

reading it. See, it does work! you just have to bloody want it enough and make it important enough to put time, effort and energy into it.

6. THE TOOLS

These tools are in no particular order. you may well need every one of them (I know I do), or just a few. You may already have some of them in your toolbox and some you may have but have not used for a long time. Some you may already have but didn't know you could use them to achieve your own desires.

Here they are:

(I) BE POSITIVE

This really could be the most important tool of them all. Being positive needs to spread through every vein of your life, you need to embrace a positive approach to everything.

Set out on a task thinking you will not succeed, then there is a high probability that you'll be proved right - you will fail.

Take a positive attitude with you wherever you go. When you wake up, check your positive attitude is by your side and that is stays with you all day, every day. Establish a constant positive attitude to everything you say and do, and you'll soon learn how it becomes an incredibly powerful benefit to your life, you can't afford to get complacent, you need to keep on top of this.

Log-in each morning and make sure all your switches are all flicked to positive. Some days will be harder than others, but over time, it will become natural. A positive outlook is an important relationship, it's probably the most important relationship you can have. Like everything worth having, it's worth looking after, working at and not taking for granted

- do this and it will repay you dividends for the rest of your life.

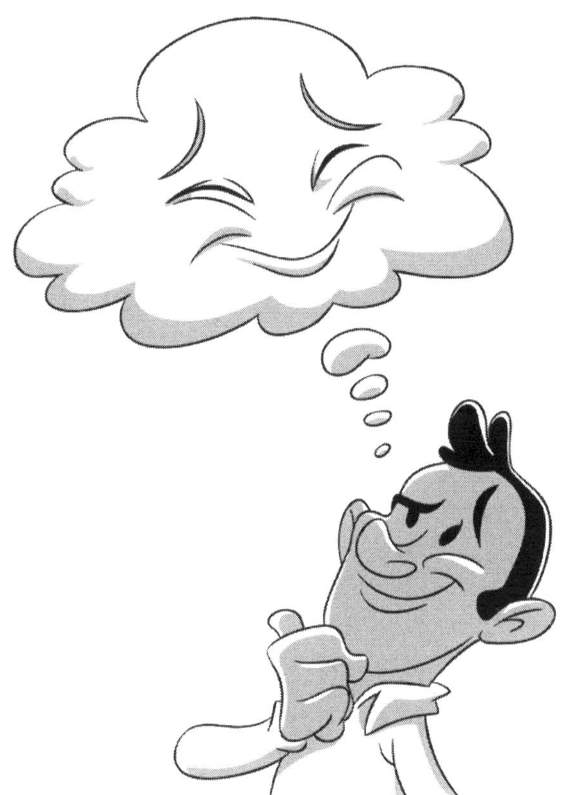

BE POSITIVE

Working at creating and maintaining a positive mindset takes effort, it takes effort every day. It can't just be for the duration of reading this book. [It's no good just nodding and making approving noises here], you need to work hard at keeping your positive attitude front and centre and give it top billing. This may be the toughest section. It could be the simplest thing you can do to change your world, but it can also be the toughest. This is not something you can do part-time; it needs total commitment. That said, there are still times for me when the positive vibe alludes me, as soon as I realise this is happening I have to work/think hard to change things back again. I start to recognise the symptoms and do something about stopping it getting any worse. Sometimes this means doing something different or taking a break.

Now go forth and spread this positivity though your whole being, as well as thinking positive thoughts, listen to the language you use, notice when the narrative and vocabulary is negative and start to change the way you speak, the words you use. Replace anything you can't do with something you can do.

Really try to listen to yourself ann even ask family or friends to tell you the words and phrases that you constantly use.

We get quite lazy with our vocabulary, we rarely utilise different words, tending to stick with what we know. This can be dangerous. Once we start to think about our language, we can start to recognize words, phrases and patterns. Check yourself. Check to hear how negative your lexicon may be (see what I did there?). Lexicon: the vocabulary of a person, language or branch of knowledge.

Once we start using new words, we start to think a lot more about how we communicate. Just like learning a new language, our minds have to work a little harder. This is a good thing. So, from now on, try to Mind Your Language.

For reasons I personally can't compute, be it nature or nurture, we appear to be naturally programmed to be negative. 'Don't touch that, it's hot!', 'Be careful that dog may bite!', maybe our parents (and if you have kids, then you too) did this to us. Through protection and wanting to secure our safety, they have fired so many negative arrows at us that we became armed with them so we could go on protecting ourselves.

So, we need to change our minds, or at least start with our language and approach to it. When did we last ask our children, 'what was the best part of your day?', instead of 'how was school today?' – the first question elicits a positive response, the latter requires no more than a 'fine', or an 'all right', only when our child says 'it was horrible' do we ask them to elaborate, then we're back in the negative thinking tank.

Take 10 minutes and listen to a TED Talk by Alison Ledgerwood – A simple trick to improve positive thinking. This is about how we are not only programmed to be negative, but how much harder it is to shift our negative thoughts to positive ones.

Listen to how other people talk, how negative they can come across. The language they use, the tone of their voice, even the melody of their sentences, when they're being negative, their sentences tend to go down at the end, like a sad song, all of this starts to influence their opinions. It can

also have an effect on their audience.

Now listen in to people who are being positive or talking about good news. Their faces tend to smile, and the tone of their voice is generally higher, the melody of sentences tend to raise at the end.

Make notes about your vocabulary - can you spot your negative dialogue, thoughts and tone? Think about how you could re-write those conversations with a positive twist.

Be Positive Bullet Points

- Switch it on as soon as you wake up
- Listen - to others and yourself
- Change your vocabulary and swap negative words and phrases for positive ones
- Stop thinking/talking about all the things you can't do and concentrate on all the things you can do.
- Be grateful. For everything and everyone in your life.

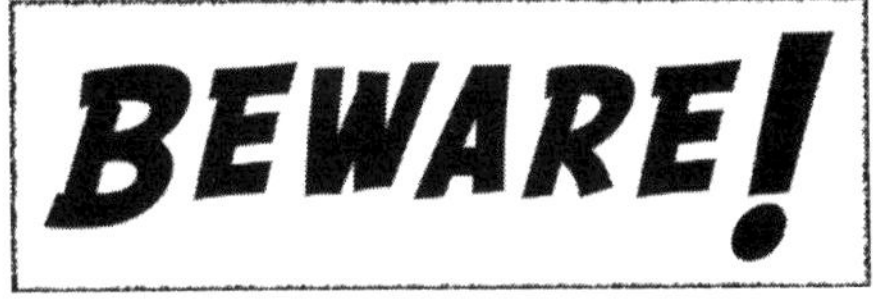

Establishing a full-time positive attitude is hard work. It's tough when you wake up and stays tough. During your day there are hundreds of obstacles that appear from nowhere - a late bus, a stressed email, an unwelcome comment. Your immediate reaction can be negative, but you can work through it and turn that negative switch to positive.

Looking Forward

Keep at it and it will become natural, you will find yourself taking the positive approach to conversations and discussions.

Having a positive attitude gives you an unfair advantage and something to look forward to. It's so important to get excited. I figure I have 25-30 years left on this planet and I am excited about every single moment ahead of me.

Now Spread it around

It's a good thing. If you ever think you seem to be surrounded by negative people, you're probably right, there are a lot of them about. Guess what? You can do something about that.

Of course, the easy option is to stop mixing with those types - you know who they are. However, taking the easy option is not always the right option - more of that later.

The tougher option is to influence those negative people around you. When we are in conversation with family and friends it's quite easy to nod and accept a lot of what is being said - it makes life easier and less opportunities for disagreements. If you're serious about being positive, then start listening properly to those around you and try to help those with negative opinions and thoughts and highlight the positive aspect of what they are saying.

Living with a positive attitude not only benefits you, when you demonstrate it and genuinely live it, then others will start to 'want a bit of that'.

Time for exercise.

Try a little experiment - If you like people watching,

then try and take it to a new level - People Listening.

Find a busy cafe and settle down with a coffee and a book or magazine, it doesn't matter what, you're not going to read it.

Relax and tune in to a conversation or two.

you'll be surprised by what you hear

When I was writing this, I was within ear-shot of a lady on her phone to a friend who was obviously going through a rough time. This lady appeared to turn everything around and told her friend that nothing was that bad, that to think about all the good things in her life and how great it was to have such awesome friends, family, a warm house (it was winter) and healthy, happy kids.

Of course, for the purposes of this book it would have been great to add an experience of someone being really negative, but hey - we have to be truthful, so here it is :)

It can be a little easier to be supportive and positive for others as you may only need to be positive for a short while whilst with them. Remaining positive for yourself 24hours, every day, is a much tougher ask - and there will be times when you let your guard down - but with practice, you'll recognise these times and work out your own way of coping and get back on track.

This is useful. It helps to listen to the language and tone of others, you may just recognise a few traits that are similar to yours - when you realise how you sound, you can start to learn a great deal.

Shaking All Over

These days I have learned to spot the waves of negativity. If I can't rearrange my thoughts and make the negative/positive switch immediately, then I need to do something completely different to 'shake myself up a bit'.

For me, switching from the project I am working on to doing something completely different like picking up my guitar or going for a long walk. Even doing the laundry or washing up can really help. This helps me to let my mind refocus on something else for a while.

Taking time-out to do nothing is really valuable. It's amazing how many people have no idea how to do nothing. The importance of doing nothing should not be under-estimated.

Doing nothing isn't not really doing nothing. It's as difficult as not having your next thought. Whether it's learning the ability to completely switch off, meditating, or just being silent, it allows your subconscious to evolve and develop your thoughts on their own, with your interference.

Remaining positive is tough to start with, it takes a lot of effort and quite frankly, hard work. There is no let up, you can't ease-off. If you find yourself moaning about the 30% failure rate, what can be so difficult about celebrating the 70% Success?

In the face of bad news, it can be tough to draw on your positive reserves, but they are there, and they can really help you and others around you to see the wonderful affect your positivity can have. Try it. You can help others through tough times by helping them see a positive outlook from what may initially appear to be dark days.

The Father of a friend of mine died whilst I was writing this, he was 97 and had a 'good innings' His son was understandably upset when he told me. He is about the same age as me, I mentioned what a fabulously rich vault of memories, stories and experiences he had with his dad - over 50 years of laughs, learning and love. My friend soon cheered up and started to retell of the many close shaves his Dad had got into - we laughed. It was Positive.

Negativity

I think it's important to mention our nemesis here. Negativity. Being negative is easy, it's for lazy people. This may seem a negative idea but stick with me. Have you noticed just how easy it is for people to be negative and put a negative spin on almost every situation? This is because it takes absolutely no effort at all, it's the easiest thing in the world. It's the prerogative of the lazy. Lazy people with little work ethic love negativity. Why?

They never have to do anything

Negativity is where Jealousy and Envy are born and breed. Negative people love being around other negative people, they compete with their tales of misery and sorrow. This is often so they can attract sympathy and attention. This is a well-worn method of communication and connecting with people. When a positive person gets in on their show, you'll witness the disruption of the group. The negative hard-liners will go deeper into their negative pit and wonder who that Weirdo is.

Others may just see that positive attitude as an attractive

personality trait and want some of that for themselves. These people are catching the disease of positivity, the perfect antidote to the virus of negativity.

(II) STOP COMPARING

It's important to reiterate this - getting what you want, is all about you, no-one else. So, stop comparing yourself to others. Comparing yourself to others is a futile exercise that no good can come from. At best you can only compare yourself to your own, personal perception of others. You may think they're happy, wealthy, have a big house, a flash car, the perfect relationship etc., the list can go on and we can become obsessed with it. In truth, you just do not know the truth.

How much debt are they in? Do they struggle with addiction, Depression, Anxiety or other illness? Do they have some or all of these because of social or family pressure, there are a myriad of other reasons and of course, are they happy?

The answer could be yes, but the truth will never be known, so until then, do not covet thy neighbour's Ox, simply look after your own.

(III) COMMIT TO THE LONG GAME

All the good things don't happen immediately.

Weight-loss is a great example. Tell someone they can lose a pound in a week, a typical response is, 'Really, is that all? I won't bother thanks. Now tell them that this time next year they could be 4st lighter, then they get excited. All they need to do is commit to it. Next year, they can look back and see how far they've come.

Even the stuff that appears to happen quickly, is mostly the result of a lot of planning, hard work, determination and concentrated positive decision making.

Don't try to force things in an attempt to make them happen sooner. As long as you're doing the right things, then the right things will happen.

This means you can stop micro-thinking. Keep your focus on the bigger goal and let the small stuff take care of itself. Don't get obsessed, get on with what you know you should be doing and let everything develop at its own pace. Be confident, you are focusing on what you want, all the small things will happen for a reason, just accept that you will react and cope with those situations accordingly. You really need to Go with The Flow.

GO CELEBRATE

(IV) CELEBRATE

Celebrate goals and targets along the way, what gets celebrated, gets repeated. As well as focusing on what you want to achieve and your targets along the way, take a little time out to decide how you want to celebrate those successes. For me and my weight-loss journey it was about buying smaller clothes or taking the time to go out on a special date. It was not about a slap-up meal.

Celebrate in a way that works for you and your new thinking. If weight loss is your goal, then find something other than food to celebrate with. If making or saving money is what you want, then do something that isn't going to set you back, financially or in terms of what you want.

Get creative and remember your Sprinkles.

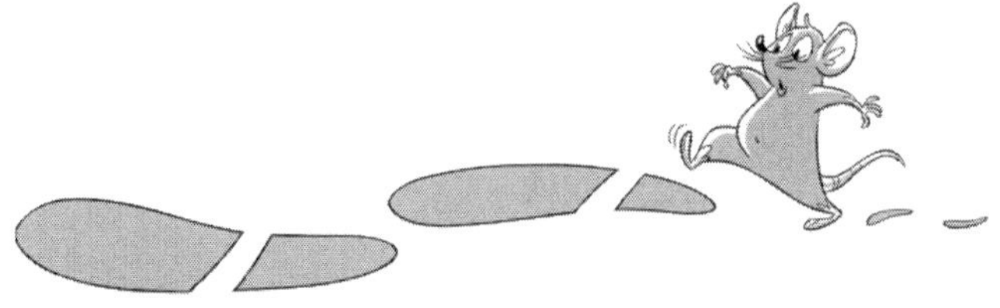

TINY STEPS

(V) TINY STEPS

This goes hand-in-hand with the Long Game, it's important to ensure you have a good understanding of what this really means. We are highly unlikely to achieve our goal within a few days, even weeks or months. Depending what you want to achieve then you could be on a long journey, at times, that long road can also get a bit steep and slippery to say the least.

Tiny steps are really important, they're important to recognise and appreciate. They are also really helpful for when things appear to not be going as planned - you can look back at what you have already achieved and prove to yourself that you have done it before, you can do it again.

A useful metaphor is of the Mountaineer wanting to get to the summit simply has to start with a single step. After that, it's a series of single steps, each one is simple, but added together they amount to a huge achievement.

Appreciate what you are doing and realise that by using every ounce of your determination, you will achieve your goal - keep going.

(VI) PREPARE FOR CHANGE

This may be interpreted as a bit of a cop-out but persevere. On your journey towards what you want, there may well be a change of direction or two. On the surface, this change may appear to be unwelcome, certainly not planned and really come out of left field.

Let me explain, back to the Mountaineer. Standing at the foot of the mountain there are a lot of single steps ahead. These are not necessarily going to be in a straight line, on the way up you may need to go sideways, or even back down a few steps to find a firmer foothold to get back on the path ahead. Be realistic, there will be obstacles that we could not have envisaged, you will need to navigate around these and take time to enjoy the challenge.

Don't fight it. As long as you've been totally focused on what it is you want to achieve, then you just need to accept the change. You have established your primary goal and that you need to have faith in yourself that every decision you make will be the right one because you seriously want this more than anything else.

When you have faith in yourself, then have faith in what may appear to be a change of direction. No-one has claimed this journey will be a straight, direct road. There are likely to be a few diversions and odd little routes and paths you are guided down - embrace them.

(VII) BE IN THE ROOM

Nigel Risner is a well-known and incredibly talented, effective, motivational speaker. I once saw him 'perform' his stuff and felt privileged to have done so. Watch his videos, buy his books. One of his favourite philosophies is to 'BE IN THE ROOM'. This means concentrate 100% on the task in hand.

Whether you're in a meeting with someone, or a challenge has been set and you need to get it done. Be IN THE ROOM.

We've all been guilty of letting our mind wander, even at critically important times in our lives. This is detrimental to the effort we are putting in.

Even the smallest task, chance liaison or what may feel like an unimportant meeting. Be in The Room - give that occasion your full, undivided attention. Think about the other people in that meeting, be interested, get involved, stop thinking about what you can get out of it and think about what you can put into it.

(VIII) 21 DAY RULE

Probably the best thing about the 21 Day Rule is that there isn't a 21-day rule. It takes time to form a new habit and the often mis-quoted Maxwell Maltz is credited with the 21-day rule that it takes about 3 weeks for any new habit to develop and become a normal part of our life. In truth, it takes a minimum of three weeks for a new habit to take hold, for some it takes considerably longer. But here, we are working on a faster method, one that can help take Maltz's view and super-charge it. A new diet, a get-fit plan, a change of career, after about 3 weeks you stop telling people you have a 'new' plan or regime. It just becomes part of you. It's who you are. After about 3 weeks you stop telling people that you have started going to gym, running, stopped smoking, drinking etc., it is not big news anymore, it's just who you are.

Of course, you want immediate results, after all you are prioritising the one thing that right now, is the most important goal in your life. You're going to be establishing new habits, discarding the way you used to do things and take on new possibilities and attitudes.

Think about any project/interest/hobby you may have started, the chances are, if you didn't stick with it for more than 3 weeks, then it's probably not a big part of your life anymore. I still have some 'only used once' fishing tackle. This is nothing. Think about it. If you can't last 21 days, then the goal you are working towards is not the goal you seriously wanted, and you were just playing at it.

If this should be the case and things change, then it may well be for the right reason. Don't be afraid of change. You may just need to think seriously about what it is you want.

(IX) CONFIDENCE

As in so many areas of life, confidence plays an enormous role, as you start to see even the smallest improvements or results in your progress, these start to build confidence in you, in your faith and in your fantastic ability. These have a cumulative effect, the more you do, the more cells of confidence you build and these multiply as soon as you recognise even the smallest, yet fantastic progress you are making. As your cells of confidence grow, they bind and lock together, become stronger and less likely to be beaten down.

With confidence comes belief. You are now building an incredible fortress that not only protects you but provides a strong base from which to generate and achieve whatever you choose, to have anything you want and do anything you want. Your belief becomes your strength, and this becomes your confidence - it's awesome.

ADD A LITTLE REASONING

(X) ADD REASONING TO TASTE

Focusing and prioritising on what it is you want to achieve is incredibly personal. It's all about you and no-one else. There will be times when you'll feel alone, well sorry, this may be harsh, you are.

Talking about it all in great detail with friends, family, or anyone that will listen is great and helps you to hear your thoughts which only goes to reinforce them, at worse, when you hear them, they become more real and this can also help you make slight adjustments along the way.

Not everyone is going to want to listen to you bang on about what you want and how you're planning to get it. That's fine. Here is where you need to develop an internal dialogue and discuss your concerns with yourself. After all, you already know the answer to all your life's questions, we only talk about them with other people, so we can get endorsement, validation or have someone agree with us whether they share our opinion or not.

I recommend that you keep a journal, whether it's just notes and scribblings on scraps of paper, or an online/mobile app. Keep writing your thoughts and ideas. This helps in so many ways. Firstly, you're decanting them from your mind, leaving valuable space for more thoughts. Secondly, you can read back through them and see your progress and how your thinking and attitudes have developed. I started writing a Journal for my weight-loss. This has now manifested itself into the book you're reading now.

(XI) YOU GOTTA HAVE FAITH

I say there is no faith or religion that will give you what you want, and I believe this to be true. But having faith is not the same as having A faith.

Faith - noun: complete trust or confidence in someone or something

Whilst I do not have a religious bone in my body, I respect those that do. This is all about having a real faith in yourself, as you alone are responsible for what you do. No-one else.

By now you're accepting that you have been responsible for the decisions you have made in your adult life up to today. Whatever the outcome, good or bad, you made them no-one else. Own this. Own them. Be proud of it.

By accepting responsibility for all the rubbish stuff in your life, then you automatically get to grab the rewards for all of the good stuff. Yes, It's All Your Fault.

A good friend of mine is Muslim, he explains his faith to me that, everything that has gone wrong in his life has been his fault. Whereas, everything that has gone right, he credits his god. Virtually every religion is designed upon similar principles. Do something bad, it's your fault, but if you pray and follow the instructions and guidance of a mythical creature and a book of fairy tales, then this 'being' will reward you at his or her discretion. If they don't get around it before your death (they have a large workload), then don't worry, they'll be wonderful place waiting for you…

When people question your beliefs, it can easily throw you off track, you start to wonder if they're right and you're wrong, self-doubt starts to smother you and you start to question everything. Here you need to stop.

Yes, family, friends and loved ones who care deeply about you of course, want the best for you and don't want to see you get hurt. When we take full responsibility for our choices, actions and thoughts, then we can become bullet-proof. We plan our lives, we plan our days, we take control. Having faith in ourselves means exactly that, you have faith in you, it's an unshakable faith and one that only you can shape as life goes on and you evolve.

This is not to say that you should not listen to others, it's important. Not only to hear what people say, but it's also important for them to be able to say it. But this is where, when you have consumed their comments and advice, and anecdotes dressed up, so they sound like real-life stories that amazingly reflect your situation, you need to make clearly considered and analysed judgement as to their value.

Your goal is just that, it's yours. You started on this journey for you and the biggest tool in your toolbox is your absolute faith in yourself to achieve it. It will get questioned and challenged, but you have the strength to muster your faith and use it when you need to.

Remind yourself every day that you have limitless reserves of faith in your own ability to overcome anything and everything.

REMEMBER YOUR SPRINKLES

(XII) REMEMBER YOUR SPRINKLES

This section is credited to a special person who taught me about Sprinkles. She is a wise, caring, intelligent, incredibly funny and a gorgeous human being.

Happiness is not a destination, it's a journey. If we're considerate, observant, caring and respectful to others as well as ourselves, then we can recognise and appreciate the Sprinkles of Happiness in every day.

People do not smile all day every day, mostly, we just get on with life. However, Sprinkles of Happiness do touch us every day. Maybe a kind word, a funny story, a silly thought. Maybe something better, a random act of kindness, a sincere compliment, maybe just a conversation with friend, when you start to observe them, there are a lot more Sprinkles in your day than you might imagine.

I started to make a note of them on my calendar. Some days it was simply a nice text, or a nice comment from someone, others may have been spending time or just sharing a little silliness and fun with a special person (see above). Sometimes it can be a piece of music, a walk, fresh air, nature… the list is endless.

After a while, on the low days, you can look back and see the enormous amounts of Sprinkles that have touched you and you can justifiably feel blessed.

Don't expect a downpour. If you're waiting for happiness to happen, or you think you're working towards to it. Then stop. You're not going to suddenly walk into a Tsunami of happiness. You just need to be mindful that you receive quite a few Sprinkles every day. It's down to you to

recognise them, make a note of them, and appreciate every single one of them. If you can look back and see how many Sprinkles have fallen on you, you be truly amazed. It may be that perfectly deserved cup of tea, or a hug from someone you care about. They're all Sprinkles. Be thankful for every single drop of them.

IS STUFF TOO SLOW?

(XIII) WHEN YOUR TIMELINE IS TOO SLOW

Personally, this was, and still can be, a big issue for me. You set out your plan for what you want to achieve. Even if you accept it may take a year or more to achieve it and you can clearly see the 'bigger picture', it can be hard when you don't observe noticeable changes. In respect of weight loss, then losing 1lb a week, means that you can lose over 4 stone in a year - this of course, is brilliant. We would all like to fast-forward 12 months and be there now. That isn't going to happen. Next week, you would have lost 1lb. Yes, it appears slow and frustrating, but it's important to remain focused, know that you're doing the right things. Sometimes a change of attitude can work wonders. Instead of being hung up on only losing a pound, think about celebrating your loss (not with cake!)

So, step back and see the whole picture. You're on a new path, you're clearly focused and prioritising on exactly what you want. You WILL achieve it. Not by wishing and dreaming, but by not letting anything get in your way of what it is you truly want.

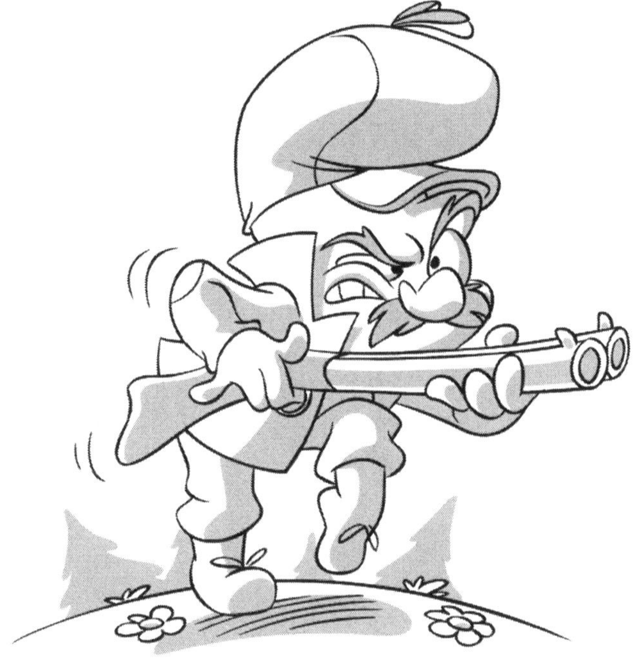

HUNT THE SABOTEURS

(XIV) HUNTING THE SABOTEURS

Saboteurs come in many guises. Look in the mirror, the most familiar face is of course, Self-Sabotage. This is a real nasty piece of work, it can be waiting just around the corner, or can creep up behind you, it can just be waiting for the perfect opportunity to pounce on your unguarded soul - and bang - it will be there, doing its evil work.

Then there are the outside Saboteurs, the people you meet who may be jealous of your determination, which is often drawn from frustrations of their own. If they can't succeed, they don't want anyone else to. They can start to try and undermine your confidence and your purpose.

You probably know who these people quite well, they support the Negative Party, they have their own negative tendencies and views. Take a breath - these are people that you may be able to help. When you have demonstrated how successful you have been with your new level of determination, they may just sit up and take notice. They'll want what you've got. Buy them a copy of this book!

There may be times when you let your guard down, take your 'eye off the ball', or just relax when you probably know you shouldn't. This is where you can do some real damage. You really need to guard against it at all times. The longer you can remain focussed and prioritising what you want, then the harder self-sabotage will find a way to attack, you can defeat it.

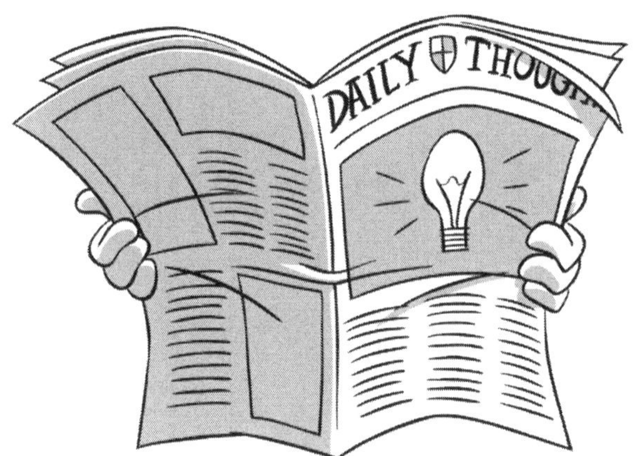

DAILY THOUGHTS

(XV) DAILY THOUGHTS

So, you have identified what it is you want to achieve, this is the one thing you want more than anything else, it is your primary focus, it's right up at the top of the tree.

Now switch on. This is now the first thing you think about when you wake up, it is constantly in your thoughts throughout the day and the last thing you think about before you go to sleep.

As long as this truly is the most important goal, then there are no problems. There will be obstacles - life does that. These obstacles are good. These obstacles test you and reinforce your desire. These obstacles will tempt you, distract you and try to throw you off course. Realise that you're strong, resourceful and as you're not going to let anything, or anyone stand in your way, then you'll naturally navigate these bumps in the road.

This is not a hobby. This is not something you spend a bit of time on in the evening and weekends - it ain't fishing. This is it. This is totally it; this is what you are obsessed with - this is your total thought processes - until you have it 'locked-in' and on autopilot, this is your 'Thing'.

Of course, life goes on and all the normal stuff needs to be done. But now everything is being done with your own soundtrack. Remember we are responsible for everything in our lives. Some of us have far more responsibilities than others and of course, may also have the responsibilities of others on our shoulders. Children, elderly relatives, there are many. However, because what you're doing here, is focusing on what you want, you are taking responsibility for you and your needs. After all, you have already worked out all the

benefits that your achievement will bring, this will only help you deal with your additional responsibilities better - you may also have decided the goal you are working towards is going to help you with your responsibilities.

An often quoted saying… 'you can achieve anything if you put your mind to it' we've heard a thousand times, but how seriously have we taken that advice. To 'Put your Mind To It' is purely to focus and prioritise exactly what you Want.

Focus, Prioritise and just... Get it done

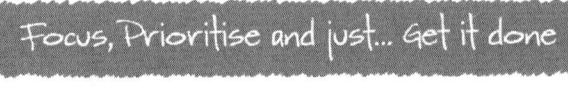

You'll soon get to know how well you're doing with regards to your goal. We see what we want - this is a popular observation. Have you noticed that once you start thinking about something, then those thoughts start to take over? How many times have you thought about an old friend, and then you bump into them, or they call you? Of course, coincidences happen, or do they?

Personally, I think everything happens for a reason. I needed to buy a car a few years ago and really quite fancied buying another SAAB. I had got so focussed on that brand, that I started to notice so many of them on the road. Of course, there were no more than normal, but I had started to notice them, it was as if I was 'attracting' or 'drawing' them towards me. I wasn't, it was just that they started to become more prominent in my consciousness.

When you're focussed on what it is you want, then you'll start seeing the changes and opportunities in your life. Maybe not immediately, it may take a few days, a week or

more, but if you're self-aware of your daily actions, then you'll easily start to notice small changes in your life.

So maybe you want more money, one way of achieving that is to get more work. If this is your true focus, then you'll start to notice the small changes in your life. Maybe you will accept invitations that you have previously shunned. Maybe you'll take that extra risk, jump at the chance to do something out of your 'comfort zone'. You may become more work organised, procrastinate a little less and slowly start to become more efficient and effective in your work.

Opportunities to earn extra income will not magically appear at your door, but you'll start noticing them around you. You may overhear a neighbour or colleague talking about a new project they need some help with. Before, you may have apologised for not knowing someone who could help them out, maybe now you stop apologising and either offer your assistance or offer to find someone who can help.

It's so incredibly important to stay true to yourself. Be a good person, do good things, help other people without asking what's in it for you. Your rewards will come. We will all get what we want.

7. THE PROCESS

This process worked for me and for others I have worked with. You just need to understand the concept, if you want to design your own way of working, then do it. It's more important to just DO IT.

So, what do you want?

During my research for this book, I have asked many people what they want, and it's been surprising just how vague people are, the reason being is that they really have not given it any serious thought.

When I start to push them (*gently*), to start thinking about what they want, what they want to achieve – it starts to get tough. At times, quite emotional (*for us both*).

Can you answer that question? What is it that you want so badly, so passionately, that you're not going to let anything stand in your way? What is it that will allow you summon up unlimited reserves of dedication and determination? What is it that means you're not going to let anyone talk you out of it, discourage you?

It's really easy just to spout out the 'normal' stuff about what people want, but this philosophy is not about writing an easy list. This is about serious thinking.

Thinking is a terribly underrated practice. Most people do not think about a subject or situation in any depth. They may read the bullet points and consider they 'get it'. This is simply not good enough. To prevent us from just regurgitating other people's, or the media's opinion (that's easy) - we need to truly think and consider how that subject or situation impacts on us or the people we love and how do

we understand it. Do we need to ask more questions, do we need to question the well-publicised responses - well, yes, we do.

The same should be said of our goals. Don't just say, 'hey, I wanna lose some weight' - that's easy.

Give yourself time to seriously consider that losing weight is the one thing, above all else, that you want.

Give serious thought as to the consequences of your actions, how it will impact your life and the people around you. How may it impact your work and every other aspect of your life? Once you have considered all of these and agreed that your goal aligns with your values.

So, this is where it starts. There are a million self-help books that will coerce and encourage you to use a myriad of methods to change the way you think in order for you to get what you want in life, to be honest, so far this book is not so different. There are 3 main areas to consider.

1. You need to truly get the concept that you can achieve anything if you want it so bad that you are willing to dedicate all of your determination to achieving it.

   That bit is pretty simple and has been spouted out millions of times – 'Hey! You can achieve anything if you put your mind to it' – maybe every parent, relative and friend have spouted such wise old sayings through the years. You've heard it so many times.
2. This book delivers the tools that I used to get what I wanted and these tools are universal, they fit everyone and anyone can use them – you may not need all of them, but once you learn them, they are

yours for life.

So, there you are: You now have the understanding of how this stuff works and you're being given the tools to achieve everything what you want.

OK, so there is just the one element missing. If you already know what it is that you want, then great, off you go, use the tools here and go get it.

However, for most people, there is a burning question, one that will hamper your progress if you can't answer it.

This is where this book is different. It's all very well telling you how to get what you want, but how do know what it is you want? Now we start to get down to the real gritty stuff – this is the big number 3.

WHAT DO YOU WANT?

WRITE THE BLOODY LIST

Now! Write the Bloody List

What do you want? On the surface, this is a harmless question. To start with, most people will just reel off a superficial shopping list of 'things'. But this is tougher than you think, it's going to take a bit more thought. After all, we're serious about this stuff, it's not a board game.

When you really get down to it and think about what you really want, what you really, really, want (sorry Spice Girls) - then it gets a bit more challenging.

Most people could draw up a list of wishes, dreams, one-days, only ifs and I'd love to... Which is great, but go deeper, go really deep. Give it serious thought. When you start thinking, you'll start to realise you can't decide on this stuff in just one session, this stuff may take hours or days.

What are the recurring things you have thought about, the stuff that keeps nagging at you, the stuff you have probably put off until you have enough time/money/space etc.?

Well, start to really think about this stuff. This list is serious, it deserves your concentration, after all this is all to do with you.

Remember this is not what you think others may think you should have or do, forget them - this is about you.

If, like me you have a graphic memory and like to see things written down or sketched out, then go ahead and do whichever way works for you.

You'll probably write a long list, that's fine. When you're

done, check back on it in a few days and edit it if need be - maybe you thought of something else you want, maybe you want to scrub a few initial ideas, that's all good.

Take it seriously, careful consideration is required. This will be a major step in your life, and you need to be realistic. I am 58 and not going to score the winner at Wembley for Swindon Town. So that goes on my fantasy list and not my goals.

Now, organise your list - can you scrub the fantasy items and get serious with what you have left. Start to drill down into your list so you can prioritise it. Prioritising is something we are going to discuss a great deal more as we work through this.

This is really quite a fluid approach, you can find the way that works for you. Whether you need to scribble on scraps of paper, commit it all to a luxury journal or work it all out on spreadsheet - work whichever way suits you best. It's more important that you DO IT.

Step 1

Write down all the goals you want to achieve. Large or small, it doesn't matter. This will not be as easy as you think - most people do not have a considered list of goals; most have a lot of generic wishes and dreams and 'one days' and 'only ifs'.

So, get writing, let it all out. This list is going to change, scrubbed out, scribbled on and rewritten many times.

Writing this list will start an important process in your thinking. You will start to think - about you.

Once you are committed to thinking about it, everything will become clear. It may be important to keep a small notebook on you at all times, as your thoughts will help you and these thoughts may come to you at any time and sometimes when you're not expecting them. Get out for a walk or some activity that will start to release those powerful little endorphins, these help to clear your head of all the rubbish going on and allows the stuff you're really thinking about rise to the top of your conscience - then you can clearly identify what's important to you.

Some people can achieve this through meditation. Meditation techniques vary with as many people that practice it. The standard teaching process is to think about your breathing and only your breathing - every breath in and every breath exhaled. When your mind wanders off to something else, you bring it back to your breathing.

Well, this can be an incredibly powerful method to think about what you want to achieve. Go to a peaceful place, take

your list and think about every item on it, you'll start to recognise where your thinking is going and what is important.

Give some thought to the consequences of what you want. Every action we take has a relative consequence. Remember, we are the authors of our life's story. We could quite easily write our biography of our life to date, but this is about composing our life from this moment on.

Once you get this concept, that you are designing your future, then things can get a little bit crazy and a whole lot of fun. When your focused on what you want, then nothing will stand in your way.

Take a quick look at all the 'successful' people in the world, from businesspeople to sports stars, artists, authors and just about anyone that could be conceived as successful. This is purely a concept, and everyone has a different understanding of the word, but bear with me.

If you have read about these people, the Richard Bransons, the Helen McCarthys, the J.K.Rowlings or Sir James Dysons, there is no doubt they all share a common trait. No, it's not that have become successful, famous or wealthy (these are not the same things by the way). It's that none of them have ever given up. They have all been determined to succeed in their given field, their passion.

Now try and name all the successful people you know that have given up, not been focused on their passion and turned around and gone home at the first sign of difficulty.

Step 2

So now you have your list, you have studied it, crossed out lots of things and then added a those and few more back in. Your list maybe quite short or be considerably long and not even finished, that's fine.

Your list is important, it may well have taken you a few days, weeks or more to compile, consider and reconsider - this is good, it means you have started to seriously think about what it is you want.

Now, write each goal on a separate piece of paper. When I have done this with people, most of them realise that more than 20-25 items on the list, can become a bit of a burden, but nonetheless, whilst it takes a little longer to go through the next part of the process, it's a good exercise. You can start to realise the futility of what you first thought was important.

The examples shown here are purely that, examples. Make sure you write your own list.

Here is just an illustration, yours will certainly look different to this.

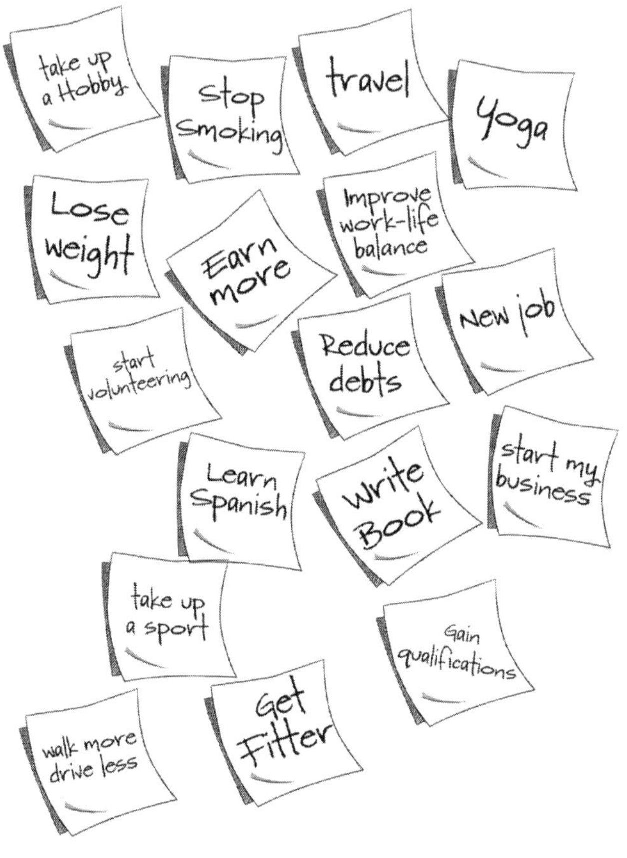

You're now going to set your goals up against each other, one at a time. This is how you're going find out which one is the top banana.

Now take these goals, turn them over and shuffle them.

Pick out two random pieces, turn them over and decide which one is more important to you than the other. If you think you can't decide, get tough. From the examples shown, would you rather spend a day doing Yoga or a day learning Spanish?

How about a day having lost weight, or a day with a new qualification?

You will probably start to play with these conundrums and try to keep picking them to get some nice 'easy' choices.

That's fine, but you're just delaying the truth. After your first round of selections, then you need to do the same again with the 'winners'.

Be totally honest with yourself (who else are you kidding here?), put the ‘winners in one pile and the ‘losers in another - we’ll come back to those later.

Once you have been through the pile. Do the same again with the ‘Winner’. Keep doing this and keeping the ‘Winners’ piles separate, until you get down to the final ‘winner’.

Once you have them neatly organised, you can now create your Positive Pyramid.

Put your ‘Winner’ at the top of your Positive Pyramid and then your next round of ‘Winners’ in a row beneath that. So now your Positive Pyramid may start to look a little like this.

Take the ‘losers’ and add those to the bottom of your

Positive Pyramid.

Now you have the first look of your Positive Pyramid. Study it. You now have all the time you need to rearrange anything you like. However, you can only change one for one. So, in the example shown, if you really want to give up smoking more than you want to volunteer, then swap those two goals.

Carry on like this until you are completely satisfied with your Positive Pyramid. Remember, everything on your list is important, you're not ignoring anything, you are simply prioritising your goals and achievements.

Now you can really see them, they are just starting to become a little more real.

You may have something really important to you on your bottom row. Great, where do you want to place it? Which other want do you want to swap it with? Be careful, you can ONLY swap them with each other, it's no good putting everything on the same line. Keep doing this, it can be tough - it's meant to be - these are your choices and you're now choosing what you want to happen in your life.

Once you have worked through this process, your Positive Pyramid will have evolved into a Positive vertical list. At the top, the single, most important target in your life right now. All your other goals will be carefully considered and placed in order of importance.

All of your goals are important, when we start talking about being on Autopilot, then it's time for those other wants to step up.

Happy? I really can't emphasise enough just how important it is to give this process serious consideration. You have already given a lot of thought to what you want and now you have to get them in order - this way you'll see which one is most important to you.

Rearranging this list may have taken you a few days or weeks. You may keep coming back to it after considering your choices. That's all good. You'll know when the time is right.

By undertaking this process you'll see that your mind will start thinking about these things during your day, whilst driving, walking or just going about your day. They will become part of your consciousness.

You will start to naturally rearrange your list, there may well be one item that keeps coming up, the one you can't let go of. I wonder where that one may go?

So now you can start Step 3 - or can you?

Step 3

To be honest, because you have got this far by giving careful consideration to your goals and spent time prioritising your list, the chances are you have already started this step.

This step is just doing it - you are already thinking about your priority want, morning, noon and night - after all it is the most important thing you think about. It's just that now you have realised what is really important to you and are setting your mind to achieving exactly that. OK, you have identified your No.1 goal - that's the top banana. You'll know it's the one. You'll think about it when you wake up and when you go to sleep, and at all the other times throughout the day. Once it's ingrained into your daily process, you'll start to realise the decisions you make, the work you do, the ideas that have, are all working towards your desire.

Your list of goals is no different. Whatever you have identified to be most important at this time of your life, will still be there in 3 weeks, it's the one you have dedicating your determination to achieving.

You need to retain focus on your goal. You can't decide you want something, then do nothing about it, that just gets filed under wishes, dreams and one-days.

It can sound obvious, if you want to achieve something then you are going to have to do something about it. What do you need to do?

If during this time your goal has changed, then that goal

was not the one that was most important. It was obviously not worthy of your effort, thoughts, concentration and determination. Look at your list again and identify what it is you have been working towards, the chances are it has been nothing obvious, that is fine. This just means the goal that you identified was not your primary one. Don't beat yourself up - adjust and move on. After all it has not been what you have been thinking of morning, noon and night. It means you have not given this process serious thought. You thought that once you had written a list, that was it.

Sorry, that's not how this works - now you're thinking about a list of wishes and dreams and you're not prepared to put in the concentration and dedication to your goal. You don't want it enough and you're perfectly happy with the status quo.

There is an answer to this.

Go back and read this book again.

Answer these questions honestly and then you'll know what is most important to you at this moment in time. It does not mean you're giving up on your other goals, but they have to go to one side for the time being.

OK - so you're happy with the 'winner', then you have to accept, that you are going to focus on that one want, nothing else, just that.

Prioritise

Of course, your list may have been exhaustive, your excitement may have got the better of you and you have a list of a hundred goals. That's fine. But you should by now have identified which single goal is top of the list and trumps all the others. Don't worry, you're not ignoring the rest of the list, but you're prioritising just one.

When you start to concentrate on your priority, you'll start to recognise a few changes. It will take two to three weeks for your new priority to fully align with you. So, keep at it, persevere. Of course, you may find yourself wandering off target, and not doing the things that you think you need to be doing. It may be that you have identified weight-loss to be your primary goal. Then you find that the piece of cake in the cafe is just too damn irresistible.

This may happen once in a while, but if you recognise this type of thing happening on a regular basis, guess what? Losing weight was not your priority. Shock, Horror? How much of a surprise was that for you? Probably not at all. So, come on, think about what it is you truly want.

TARGETS AND GOALS

8. TARGETS AND GOALS

This can be the fun part. You’ll go through what may be quite a long process. With regards to weight loss, this can certainly be true. However, it’s so important to set realistically achievable targets and goals.

As part of my journey I marked dates in my diary when I wanted to be a certain weight or fit into a particular item of clothing. I had a holiday booked with three other guys to Barbados, it was five months away. I didn't want to be the heaviest one there. I admit, the other big guy was 6’4”, so, proportionally heavy, nonetheless, it was a target for me. I achieved it and it felt soooo good.

After that, it was the smaller things, being able to buy ‘normal’ clothes, from ‘normal’ high street retailers. Every 6 weeks or so I had to go shopping again - hated the expense but loved the necessity.

So, your end goal is what you absolutely want. A definitive. It’s an amount of money, the amount you weigh, the job you want.

However, your targets are the smaller milestones along the way. With respect to the new job or career, maybe you’ve had to gain more experience, or get more qualifications, these are your targets. Getting that job is your goal. Getting that mortgage maybe your goal, but saving or earning more money, reducing your debts, getting better at fiscal management, switching brands, changing habits are all your targets along the way.

9. QUESTION TIME

These are my questions, the ones I asked myself during my journey, the ones I had to figure out on my own, a process that helped me enormously. We all know our own answers, we talk to others, mystics, clairvoyants, and mostly anybody that will listen, though we can never be sure of how genuine their listening powers are, how much they truly care about our questions. We can never be quite sure that they are 'In the Room'.

We like to 'air' our questions and it's good for us to hear them out loud and not just our own internal mumblings.

When you've got an audience (of one or many), take more notice of their non-verbal reactions - the eyes say a lot. Words can be carefully designed to deliver a subtle undertone of a message, but the eyes and body language rarely lie.

What if things go off-plan?

In the early days, it can be easy to slip off-plan, after all, you're getting used to a new routine. Do not let this concern you, just take a breath and remind yourself what you're doing and why you're doing it. Refocus your efforts and you'll be back on your plan in no time. Of course, if you find yourself slipping off-plan on a regular basis, then you'll need to revisit your list. You're letting obstacles get in your way and stopping you from achieving what you want.

If this is the case, this is probably not the goal you truly wanted. If working towards it is too hard, then you're finding it easy to give up and need to either re-focus your efforts or move on to what it is you truly want.

How do I know it's working?

You will start to notice changes in your daily habits and routines. After all, you are rewiring the way your mind thinks and works. As you push your primary goal to the front of the queue, then some of the other stuff will get pushed out of the way. This is all perfect. There is good reason why your days are changing.

You're re-training your mind and with any new routine, it takes time to become natural. Once you are happy with the progress and new pattern, you'll start to see the positive changes in your life which come about because you are focusing on what you truly want. You'll also start to recognise the change in tone and subject matter of your conversations.

Can I jump-start my changes?

At any time, if you feel that things aren't changing, then you grab those jump leads, wire yourself up and jump start your own changes (please do not connect yourself to any source of electricity).

There are many things you can do in your normal day to add a twist, a different perspective or a new way of doing things.

Can you start your day a few minutes earlier, meditate, take a short walk or a little exercise before your normal day begins? Maybe read a chapter of that book you keep meaning to.

Going to work? How about a different route, how about getting off the bus a stop earlier? - Break time - Can you visit a different cafe, try a different sandwich?

You just need to shake things up a little bit. If you do things a little differently, you'll start to see the world from a slightly different perspective, you'll notice people, places and experiences - all exciting stuff.

Will there be a new Me?

That's what you're working towards. We are focusing on change here. In some cases, these changes can be significant, both physically and mentally. These are brought about as a consequence of the new you aligning your life to achieve your primary goal and your new thinking.

A simple explanation is weight loss. If your goal is to lose weight, then you can expect, with a degree of certainty the more obvious changes. The size and shape of your body, the difference in your physical abilities. In my experience, these changes equated to about 20% of my transformation. The other 80% is in my mind. Your mind controls everything you do, so when your mind puts your body through significant change, then it too can start to behave in new ways. You will need to embrace those changes...

How strong is my desire?

Quite simply, it has to be absolute. Remember, this is something you want - you want it above all else, you are determined to overcome any obstacle because nothing is going to stand in your way. You're in control and you are going to get what you want.

Even the slowest hurdler achieves their goal - getting to the finish line as quickly as possible - they may be slow and not win any medals - but they are focussed and determined to succeed on their terms. They will still get to the finish line. The hurdler who gives up at the first or tenth hurdle simply did not want it enough.

You will achieve your priority. You always do. The want that you have identified is the most important thing to you - you will simply not give up; you will find the ways to overcome any obstacles that get in your way. Your focus and determination mean you will get what you want.

Can you test your desire? Yes, you can, but don't. During your journey you will be challenged on a regular basis, sometimes from the least expected sources. So please do not make any more problems than you're already going to meet along the way.

Do not assume anything. Do not assume that everyone is on your side or that all your friends and relatives share your new approach and vision. There is a really good chance that they don't. It's not because they don't care. They have their own issues and lives to cope with. This really is all about you. Not in a selfish way, but how you manage your self-determination and single mindedness.

So, don't test your desire. Be confident that you have got this far, and your desire is true and absolute. The goal you have identified is so important to you that you will not let anyone question your desire to succeed. Not even yourself.

Is there anything in your way?

This can be a loaded question. You can take a look at the new path ahead of you and easily map out any potential problems. You can do this carefully and diligently. Some of you will do this and take a practical view and start to plan how you will overcome those obstacles. That bit is easy.

Take the Hurdler for example - the desire is to get to the finish line in the shortest time possible. Clearly there are

obstacles ahead and these need to be overcome. Whilst each of the hurdles will create their own challenge, the latter ones may be harder than the earlier ones when fatigue has set in. But at least the hurdler knows it all in advance and can train for it and practice over and over again.

The great thing about being a hurdler, is that no-one is going to put another hurdle in their way midway through their race. Alas, if only our lives were as simple as hurdling. If we could see all of our potential problems ahead of us, we could all work out what we need to conquer them, and we could even practice at weekends - bring in an experienced coach to help us. So, with all the great planning and forecasting of the potential pitfalls along the way of our new path, life will definitely put an extra hurdle or two in your way. I am sure most of you have experienced something like this.

It's these times when you will need those never-ending reserves of emotional strength and your absolute faith in yourself. You're the only one who can find the solution to your hurdles, this is all about you, your immense faith in your own abilities that means you can conquer everything that is put in your way. OK, you may not be able to fight it, knock it to the ground or utterly destroy the hurdle, but you can work it out, using your own skills and abilities how to get around it/over it and leave it in its wake.

Having belief in your own abilities is crucial, you're a strong, capable individual that can achieve anything that you set your mind to. That is exactly what you're doing here. Setting your Mind to It.

So, Is there anything in your way. Well, yes, of course there is. Life can be like that, it can try to screw you over, it

can be an unforgiving beast. Let it, and it will win. Fight it with the faith in yourself, you'll see that life will soon start to concede to your demands. You really are in control.

What is stopping you?

There may not be anything stopping you. You may be well on your way to achieving your goal.

But of course, if you have any doubts whatsoever, then the answer is, You.

Is this just fantasy?

We can be terribly hard on ourselves. We get frustrated when things don't go as planned, or they just don't go fast enough. Most of us just want it NOW!

Managing your own expectations can free you up and keep focussed on your desire. The mountaineer won't get to the top without taking the first step, in the early days, it may seem slow with little obvious progress, but with determination, patience and genuine self-belief, there will be fantastic dividends. Looking back and seeing how far you've come is an incredible way to recharge your positive energy.

With weight loss, we would love to have a few stone removed overnight, but reality tells us that a pound or two a week is actually brilliant progress. So, after 4 weeks you can't fit into those 'incentive' jeans, but don't give in.

Remember what you're doing and why you're doing it. Be happy with Tiny Steps. Stop being disappointed at your self-perceived slow progress and celebrate your fantastic development.

This is where you really need to employ that positive mindset. You have chosen a goal that you are going to achieve, it may take a while and there maybe a few hiccups along the way, but you're making progress and you will achieve our goal. Unsure? Go back and read the Be Positive chapter - you just can't get enough of the positive stuff!

When can I engage Autopilot?

We all want to switch to Autopilot status as quickly as possible, but once again, you have to be patient. I thought I was ready for my Autopilot, so I switched from doing all the good things I had planned and just let stuff happen naturally. For me, this meant having an extra drink once or twice a week, just snacking and not preparing meals properly.

After a week I noticed that I had not lost any weight, three days later my scales told me I had put the 2lb back on that I had lost the week before. I really hadn't made that many changes, but I was more relaxed, thinking that my autopilot had taken over. I was wrong. I had to go back to manual controls for a few weeks. This was a valuable experience and one worth being aware of.

A week later and I saw the results of taking back control, for me this happened after only 2 or 3 days. I just had a quiet word with myself, remembered why I was doing this, what a great success I have had so far and how exciting today and tomorrow will be.

Keep on Trucking

You're awake in the morning and for some reason, you'll not 'on it' you don't feel focussed or positive - maybe you don't feel anything, you're thinking that taking a Duvet Day

may just be the perfect solution, or you just want the World to go away for 24 hours. These are days where your thoughts and actions appear not to be under your control, you can almost see yourself going off-plan and don't feel like you have the resources to cope with counteracting your actions and thoughts.

There is a chance that you may just be right! This IS one of those days - but stop. Maybe one of these days have arrived just to ground you, help you take notice of where you are, how far you've come.

However, whilst that is a perfectly valid explanation, the determined you, the 'won't take no for an answer' you, the 'positive' you can harness these days. These days are really important. These are the days you need to dig deep, muster all the positive energy you possible can and power through. Yes, that's easier to type here than do, I know. But this can be a good trick.

When you feel like you may sabotage your plan - do something else. For me, whenever I have those days, I shake things up a bit. Change my plans and do something different. As I am writing this section, I am having one of those days. Currently, my priority is more work (I'm a designer by trade, website, graphics…). This plan has been good and effective, and I have started to notice small and big changes in my routine and life. But today, it's like someone (me) has shaken up my snow-globe of a brain and everything appears a mess. Yes, I have work and deadlines to meet, but when your mind is telling you to 'throw the homework on the fire and take the car downtown', then listen. For me, I had some interesting notes for this book. I started to make a few more detailed scribblings and decided to start writing these and do more work for this book.

This is giving me a pleasant distraction. I remain on my main path of my goal, but I am just taking a breather on the roadside, taking a look around, seeing the bigger picture. I am able to congratulate myself and take a positive attitude towards my actions. I am not ignoring my work, I am taking time for me. When this happens, it can have an incredibly positive effect on you and everything you're thinking about. It really can energise and reinforce your faith in yourself.

It quite literally demonstrates that you are putting yourself first.

10 THE FUTURE

The next goal

Be careful. Your next goal is all about timing. Once we witness our fantastic progress, we can be justifiably keen to switch on our autopilot and take all our experiences, new knowledge and skills on to the next goal on our list.

This will happen, it will be incredible, exciting and further boost your confidence in knowing that you can achieve absolutely anything. But this comes with a warning, in my experience, we would all like to switch on our autopilots as soon as possible after take-off, if we're not ready and we've not had to overcome some adverse conditions, then it's nearly certain that we'll need to revert to manual mode for a while. Worry not, the time will come, but there is no certain way to decide when this will be or how far along your journey you have travelled.

When you've set your autopilot, but things start to go off-plan, then it's time to switch back to manual for a while, recalibrate your settings and go again. Remember, there is only forward momentum. We can veer off our chosen path from time to time, but as with age, we're going forward, and nothing can stop us.

So be prepared to put your next goal on pause whilst you work on the odd crosswind. Then when you're steady, you can engage your autopilot and off you go again. This will all add valuable experience and help you to recognise similar feelings and actions in the future.

They will be there, but you're learning how to cope with obstacles, and that's all these are.

So where now?

You've been responsible for everything you have, the decisions you have made along the way have brought you to where you are. This has all been controlled by your thoughts, your mind, your determination.

Now it's time to take control. Design your future. Achieve what you want.

Your mind is a wonderful thing and controls everything you achieve, your mood, your happiness, your outlook on life and the way you live your life.

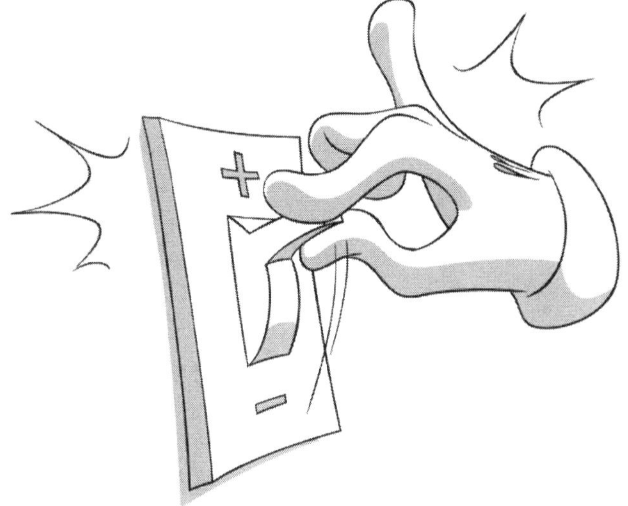

MAKE THE SWITCH
FROM NEGATIVE TO POSITIVE

Now take control

Imagine your mind is an awesome machine that NASA would be proud of. A million switches and controls - these have all been set to guide you through your life. You now realise that it has been you that has influenced all those settings. Now you can climb into the cockpit and take control of that machine. Take a seat at the controls and start making adjustments and navigate the route of where you want to go. Flick all those switches from negative to positive, sit back and enjoy taking control of your Universe. Now, you can control your mind, your thoughts and the processes that work towards achieving everything you want, you just have to take control

... but you knew that already.

ABOUT THE AUTHOR

From Sign writer to Graphic Designer, Songwriter to Web Monger, Rob's journey to being a published writer has been an interesting and eventful path. His experiences and research have evolved into a passion to write and explain how we can all benefit from positive therapy and achieve everything we desire.

Rob lives in Wiltshire, on the southwestern edge of the Cotswolds.

Learn more about future publications from Rob
https://www.robwyborn.com